CITY of ILLUSION

Victoria Ying

colorist Lynelle Wong

VIKING

VIKING
An imprint of Penguin Random House LLC New York

First published in the United States of America by Viking,
an imprint of Penguin Random House LLC, 2021.

Copyright © 2021 by Eight9Eighty9Productions LLC

Visit us online at penguinrandomhouse.com.

Library of Congress Cataloging-in-Publication Data is available.

Manufactured in China

ISBN 9780593114520 (PB) / 9780593114513 (HC)

10 9 8 7 6 5 4 3 2 1

The art for this book was created with Comic Draw App, Procreate, and Photoshop.

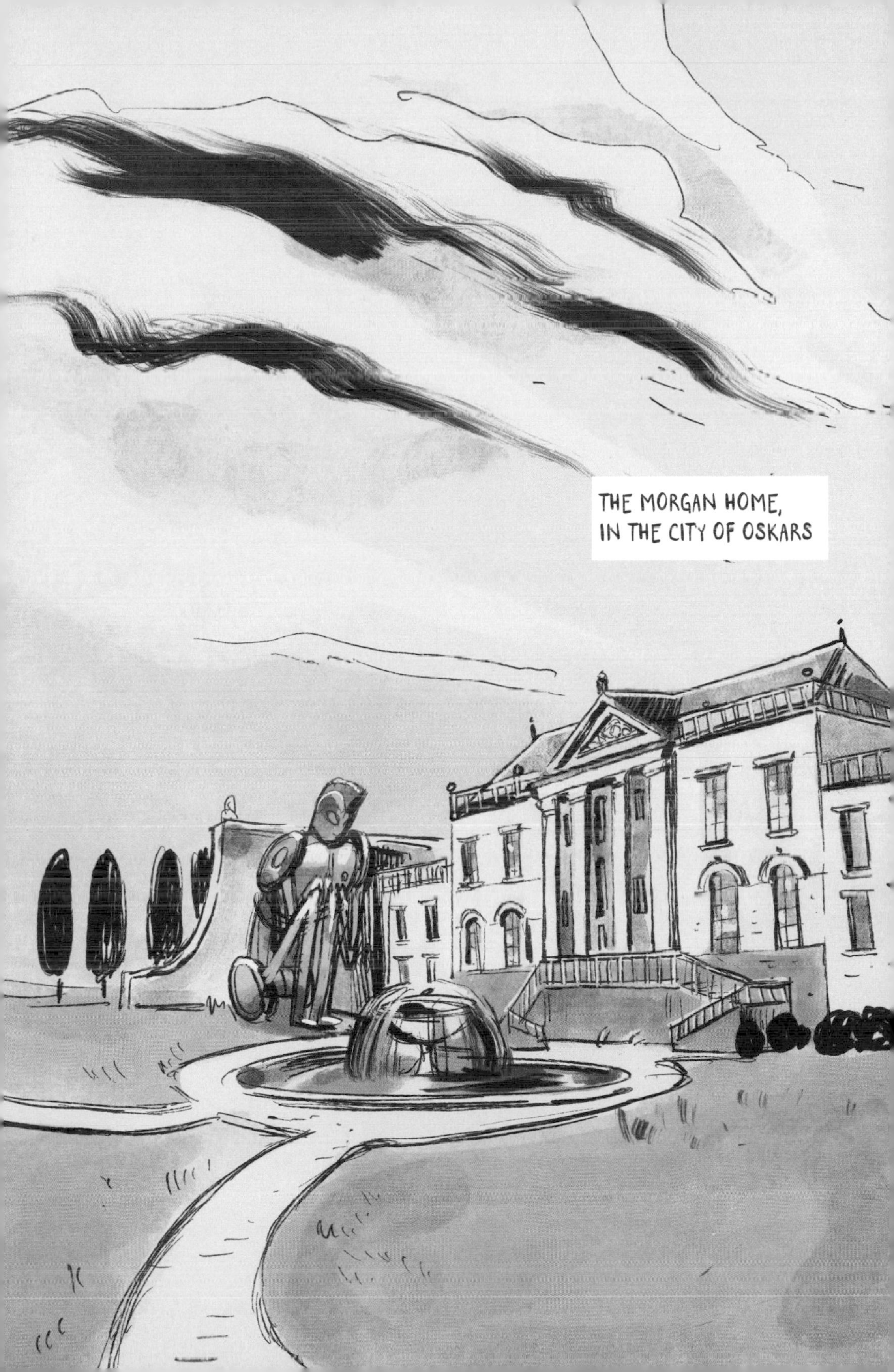
THE MORGAN HOME,
IN THE CITY OF OSKARS

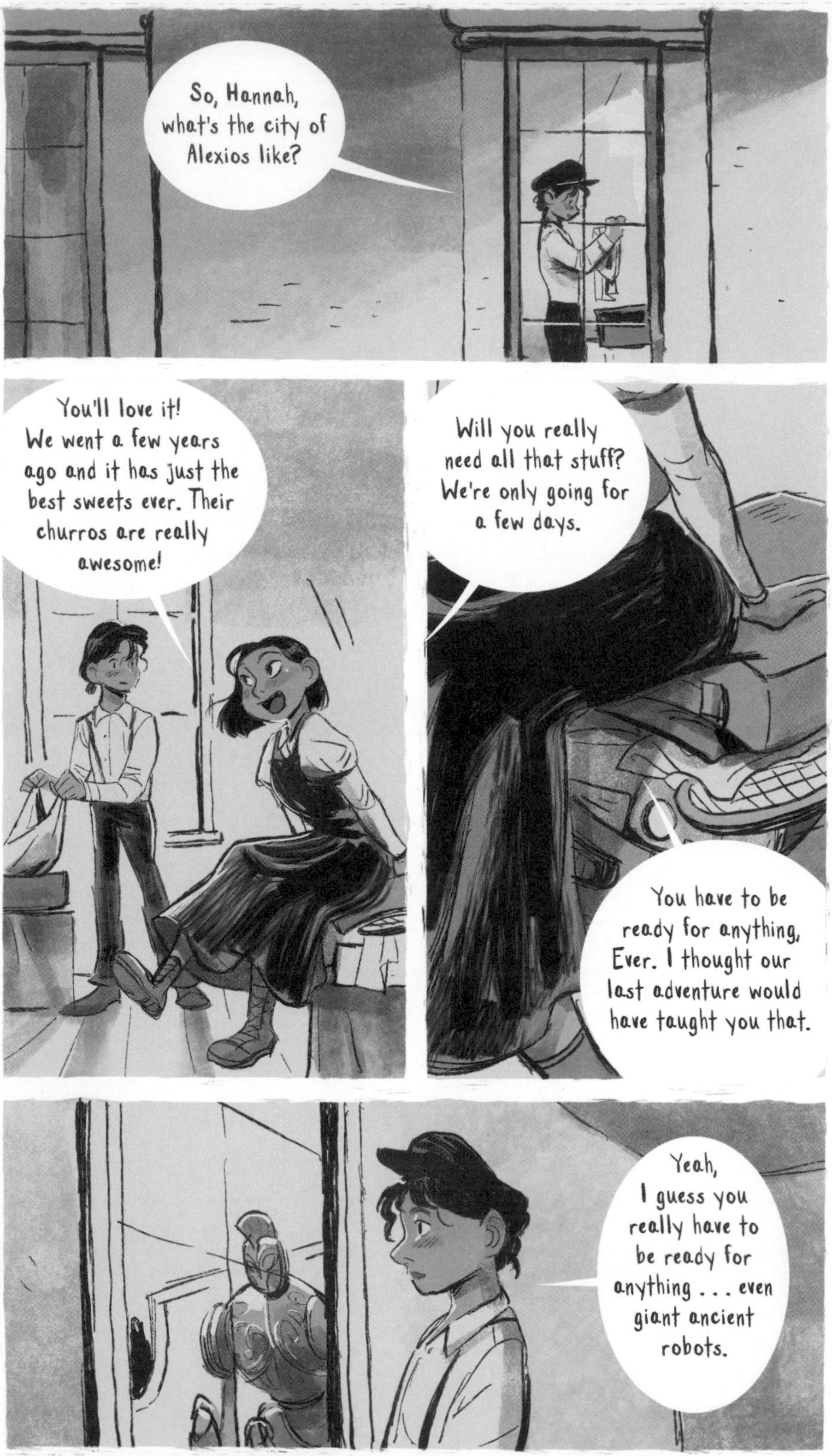
So, Hannah, what's the city of Alexios like?
You'll love it! We went a few years ago and it has just the best sweets ever. Their churros are really awesome!
Will you really need all that stuff? We're only going for a few days.
You have to be ready for anything, Ever. I thought our last adventure would have taught you that.
Yeah, I guess you really have to be ready for anything . . . even giant ancient robots.

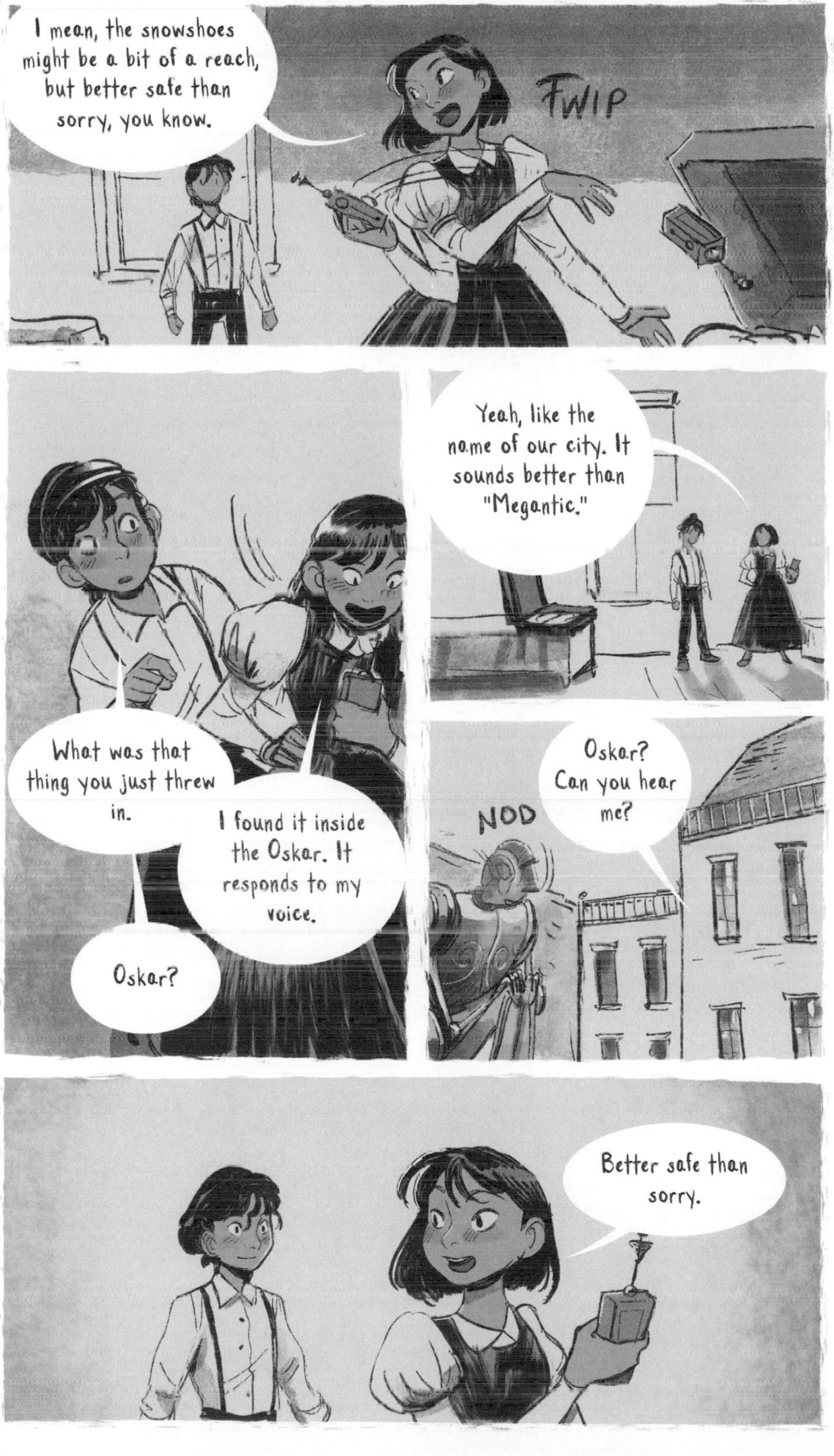
I mean, the snowshoes might be a bit of a reach, but better safe than sorry, you know.
FWIP
What was that thing you just threw in.
I found it inside the Oskar. It responds to my voice.
Oskar?
Yeah, like the name of our city. It sounds better than "Megantic."
Oskar? Can you hear me?
NOD
Better safe than sorry.

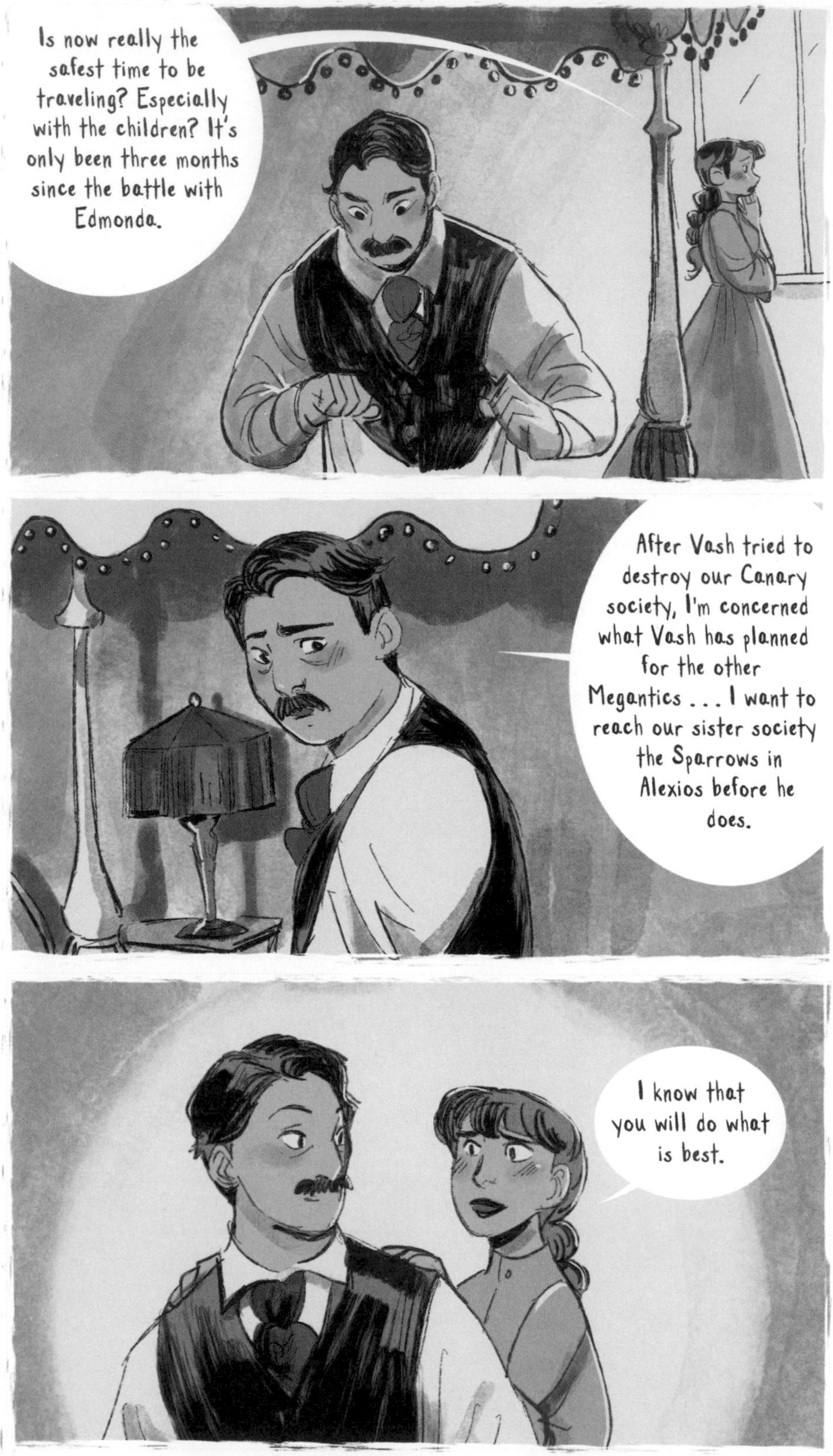
Is now really the safest time to be traveling? Especially with the children? It's only been three months since the battle with Edmonda.
After Vash tried to destroy our Canary society, I'm concerned what Vash has planned for the other Megantics . . . I want to reach our sister society the Sparrows in Alexios before he does.
I know that you will do what is best.

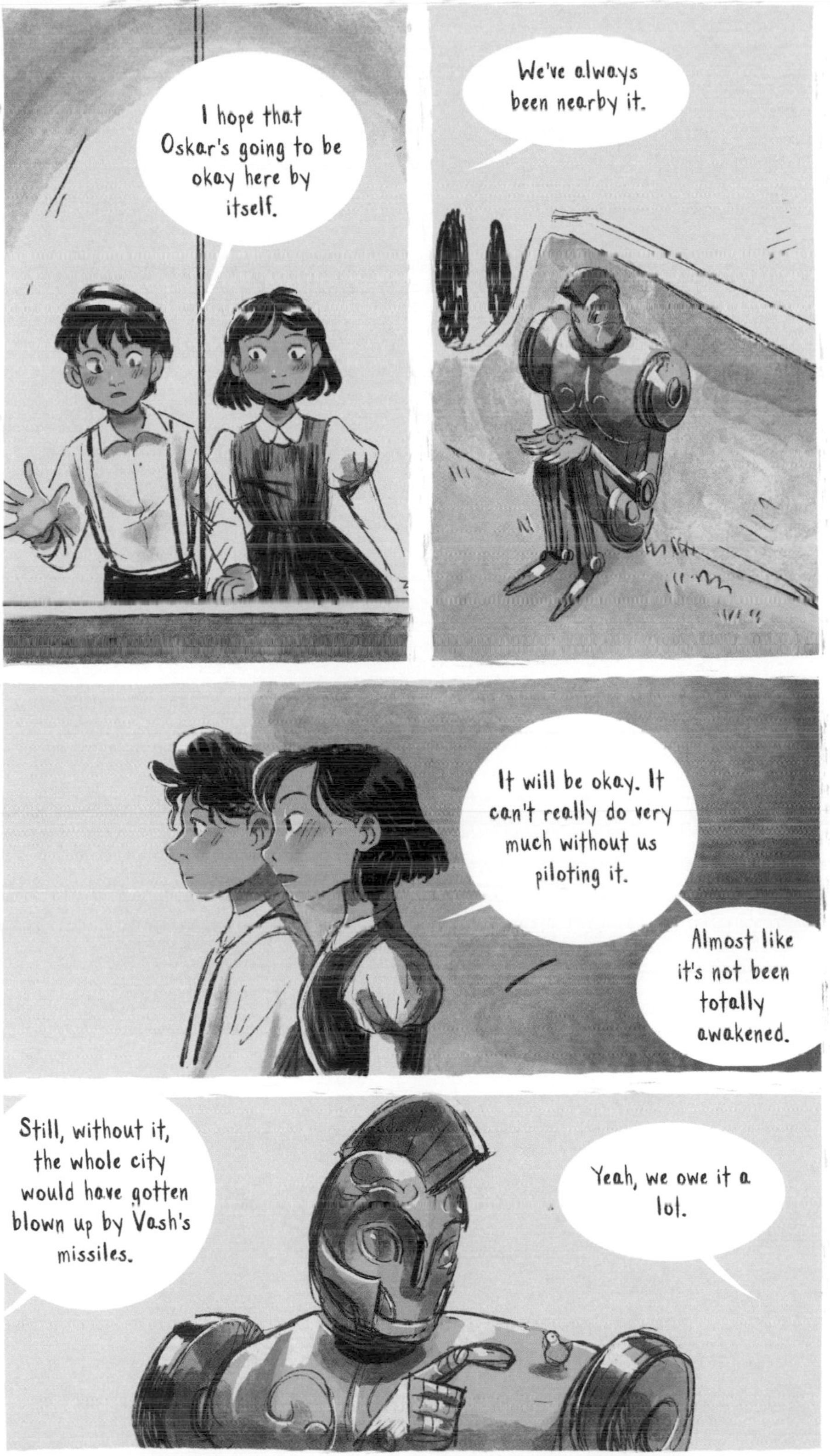
I hope that Oskar's going to be okay here by itself.
We've always been nearby it.
It will be okay. It can't really do very much without us piloting it.
Almost like it's not been totally awakened.
Still, without it, the whole city would have gotten blown up by Vash's missiles.
Yeah, we owe it a lot.

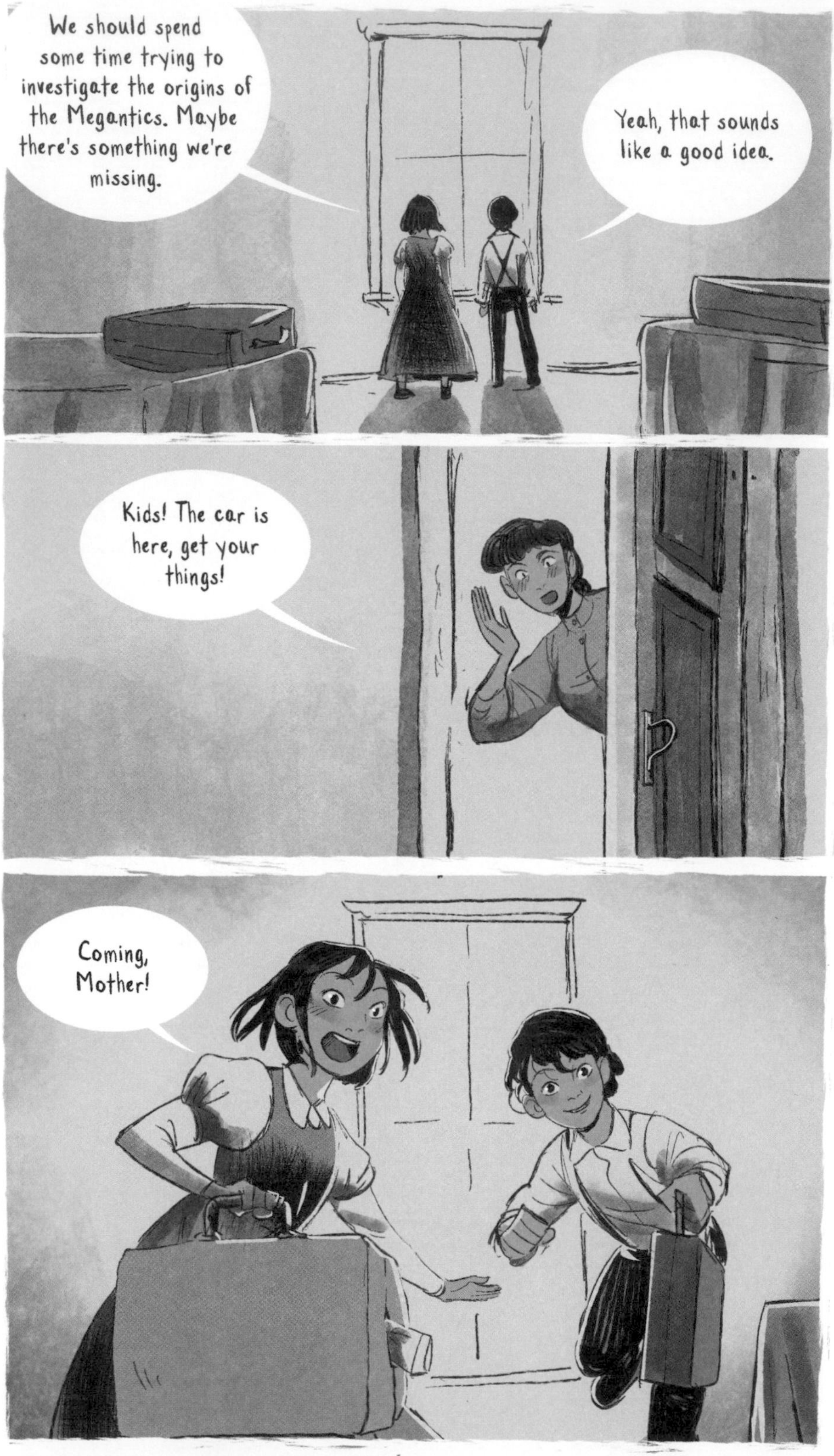
We should spend some time trying to investigate the origins of the Megantics. Maybe there's something we're missing.
Yeah, that sounds like a good idea.
Kids! The car is here, get your things!
Coming, Mother!

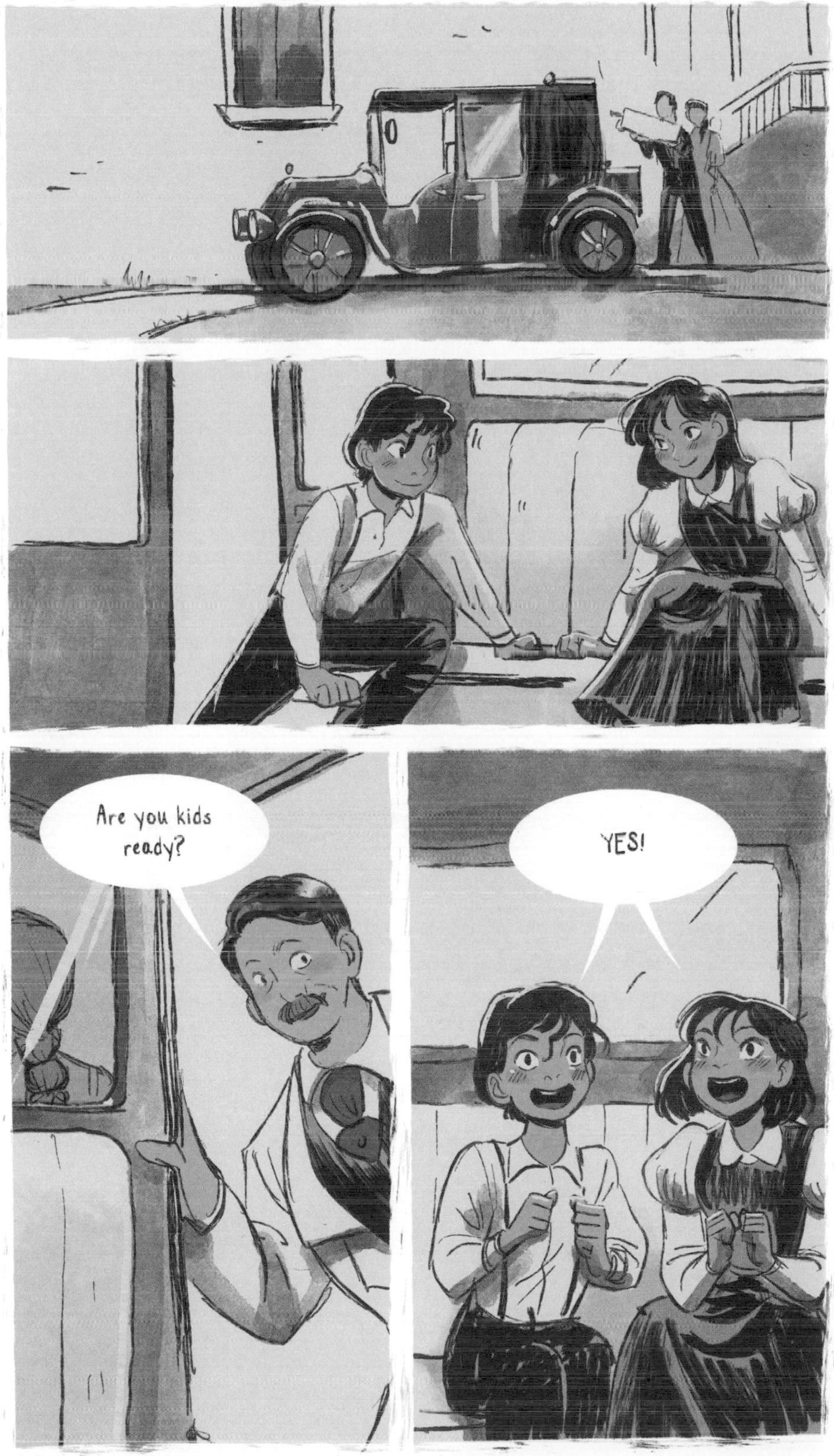
Are you kids ready?
YES!

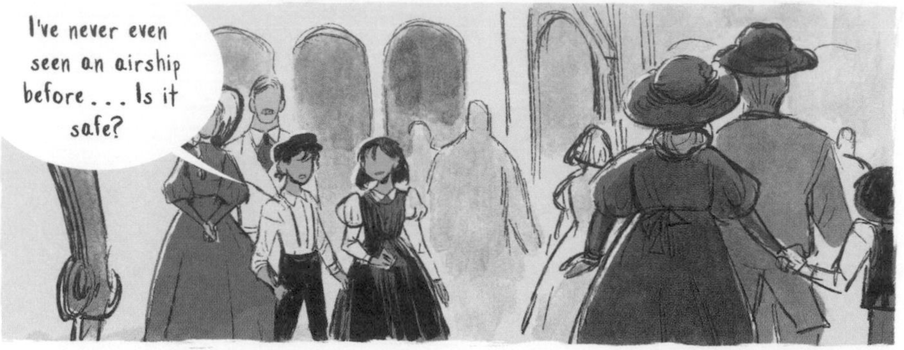
I've never even seen an airship before . . . Is it safe?

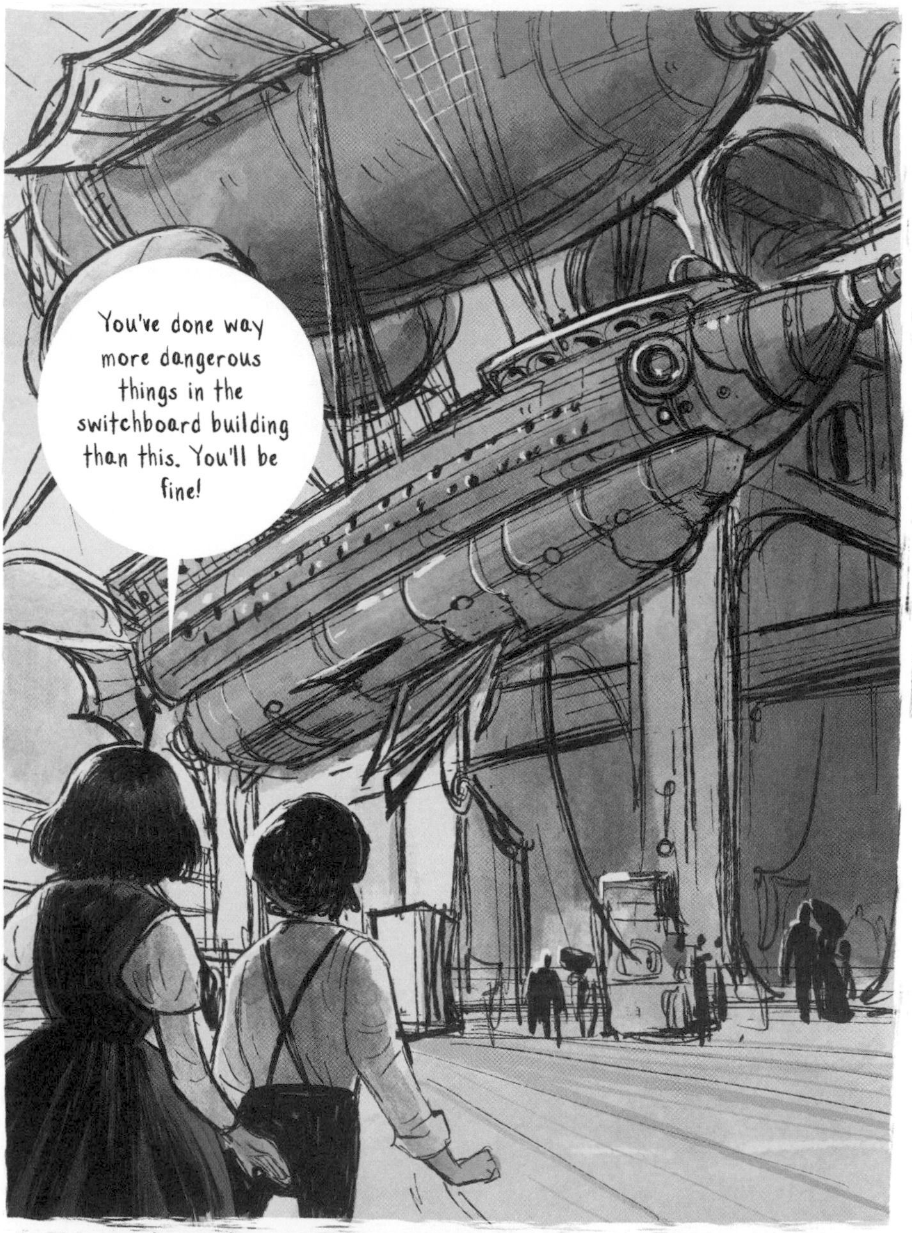
You've done way more dangerous things in the switchboard building than this. You'll be fine!

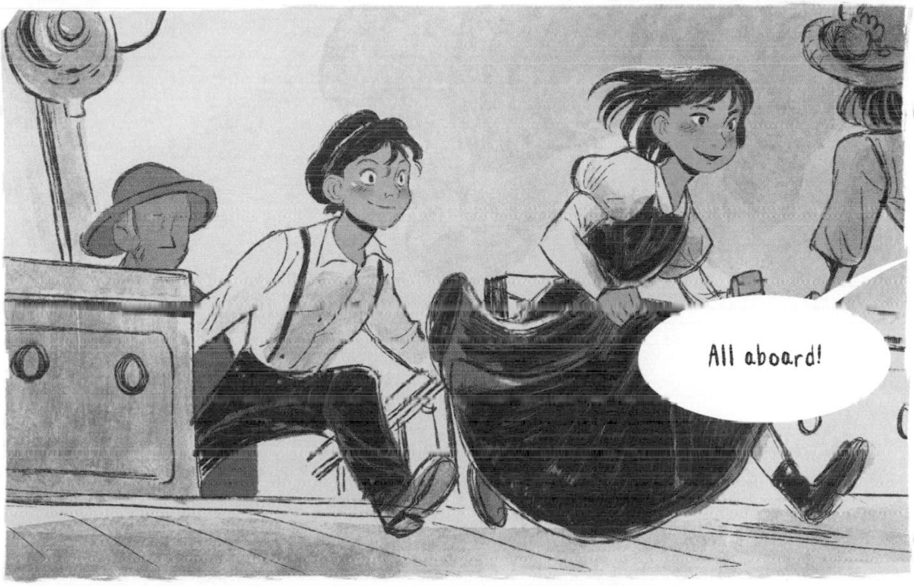
All aboard!

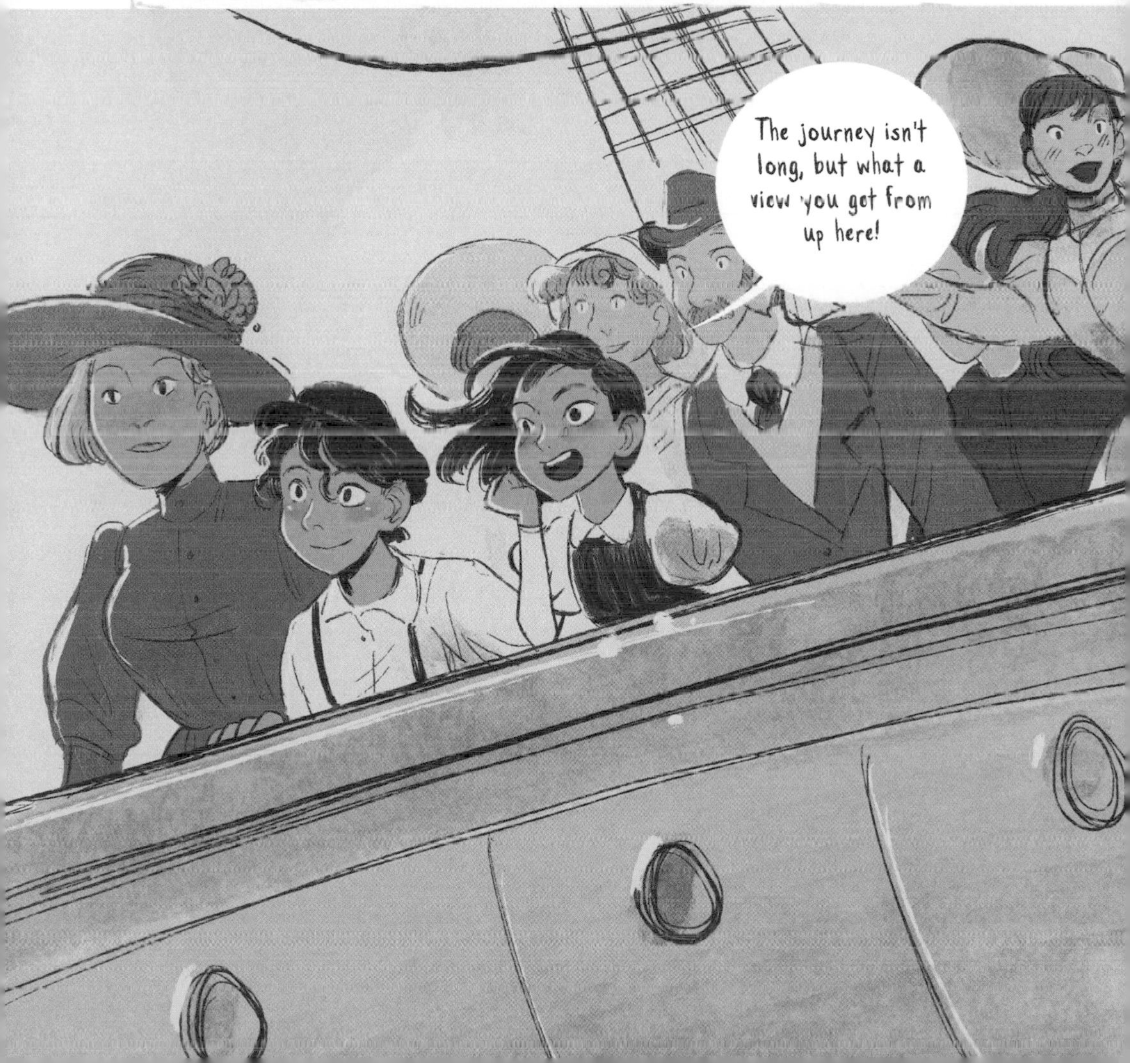
The journey isn't long, but what a view you get from up here!

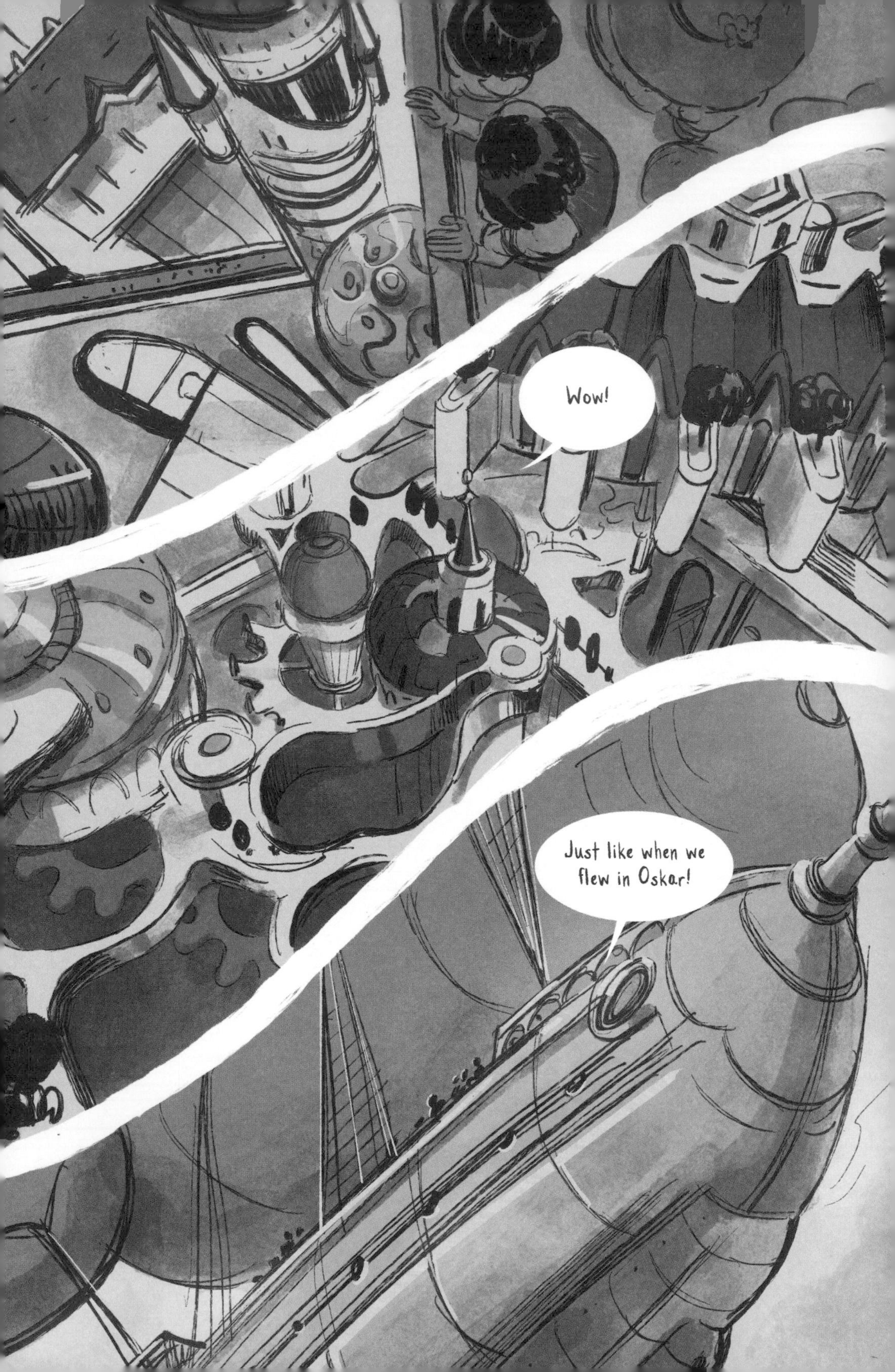
Wow!
Just like when we flew in Oskar!

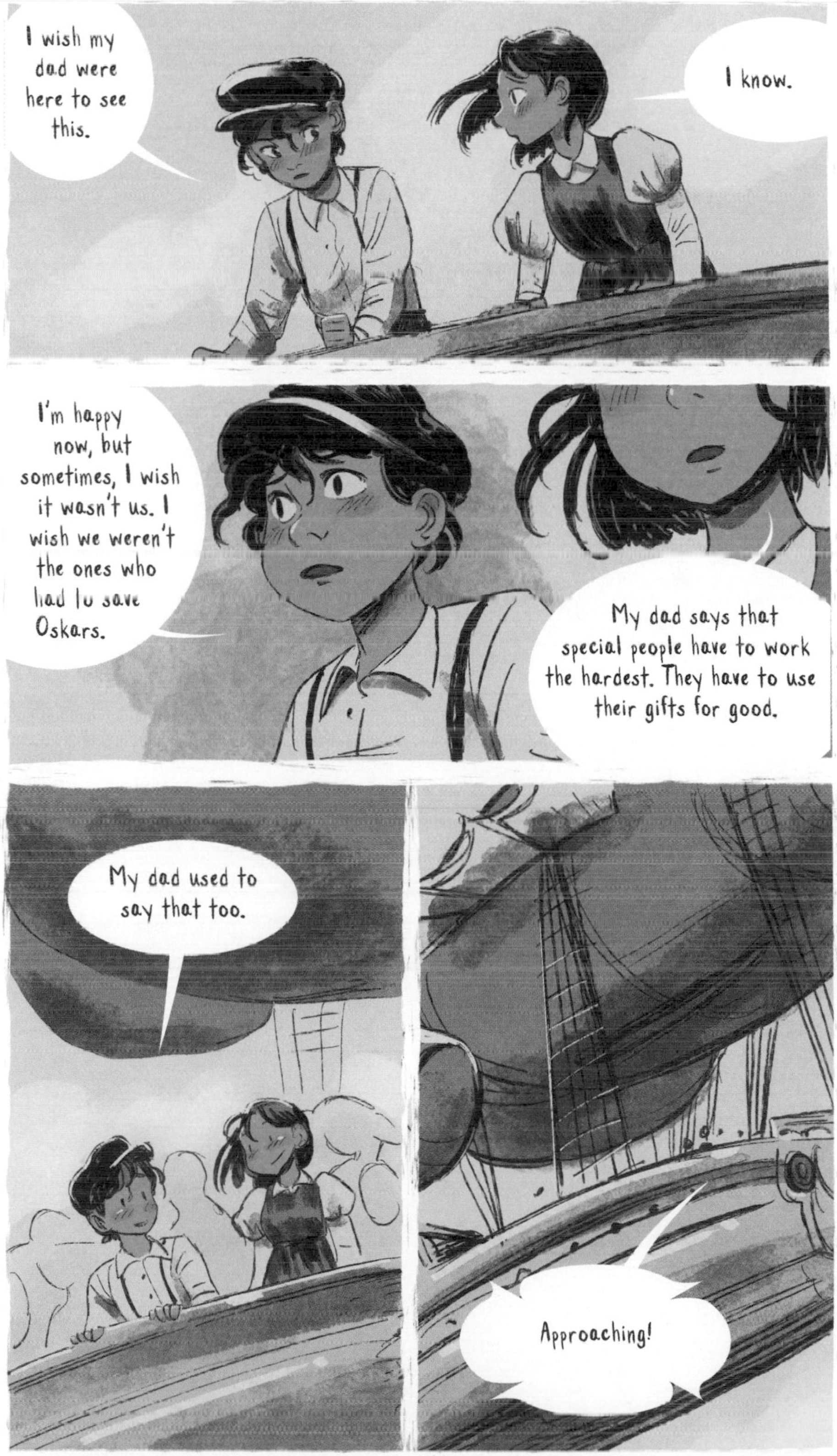
I wish my dad were here to see this.
I know.
I'm happy now, but sometimes, I wish it wasn't us. I wish we weren't the ones who had to save Oskars.
My dad says that special people have to work the hardest. They have to use their gifts for good.
My dad used to say that too.
Approaching!

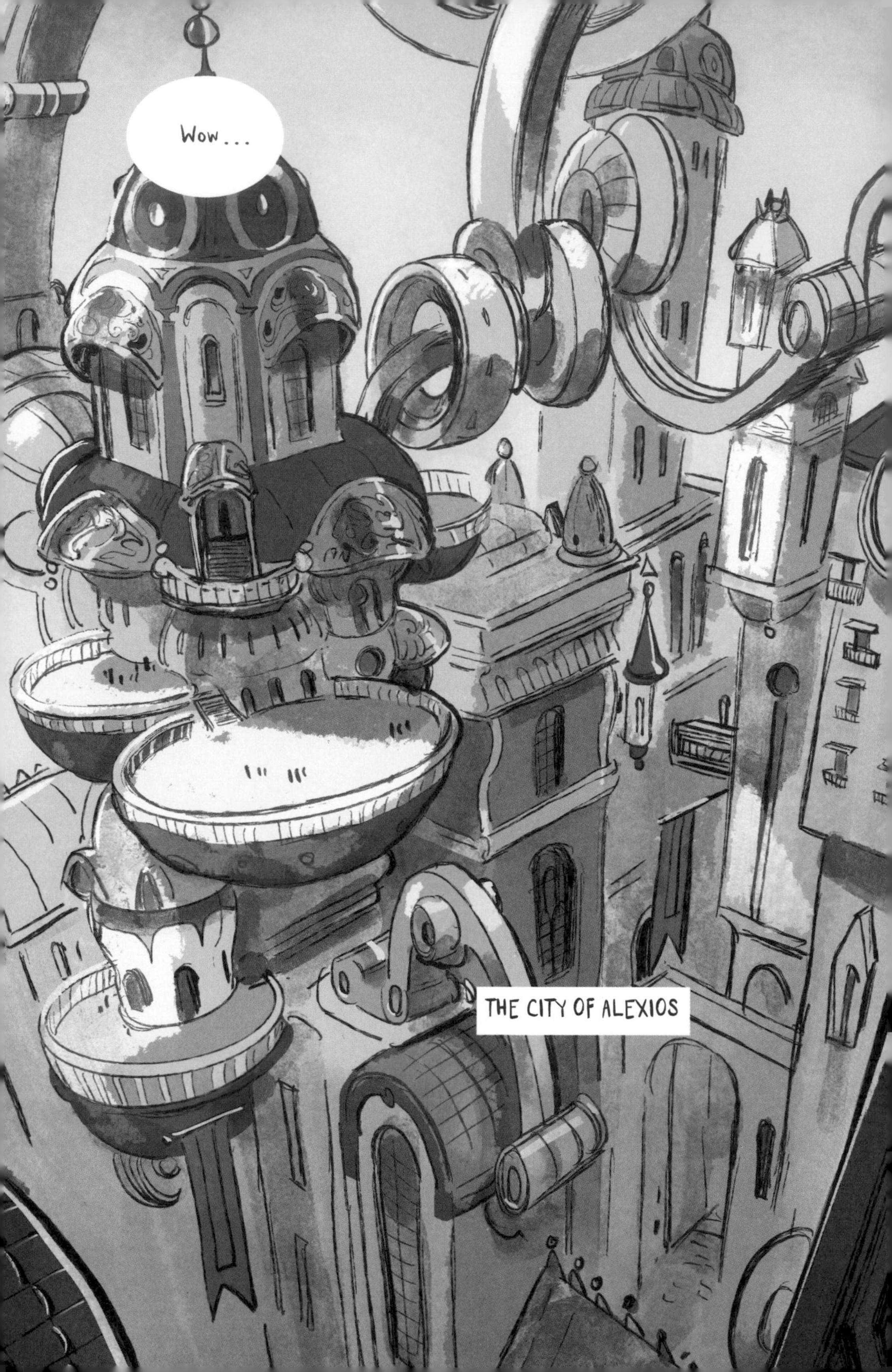
Wow...
THE CITY OF ALEXIOS

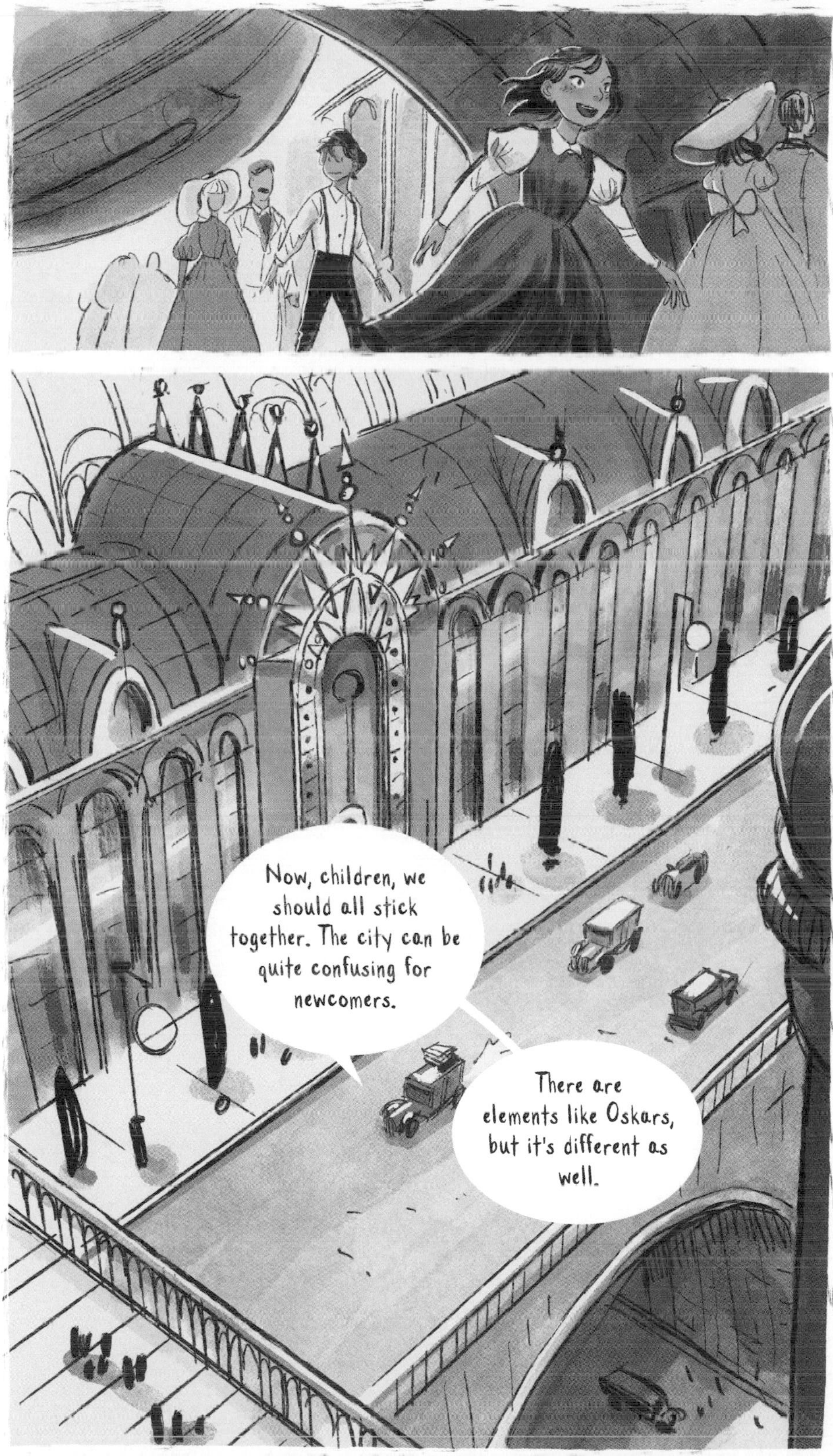
Now, children, we should all stick together. The city can be quite confusing for newcomers.
There are elements like Oskars, but it's different as well.

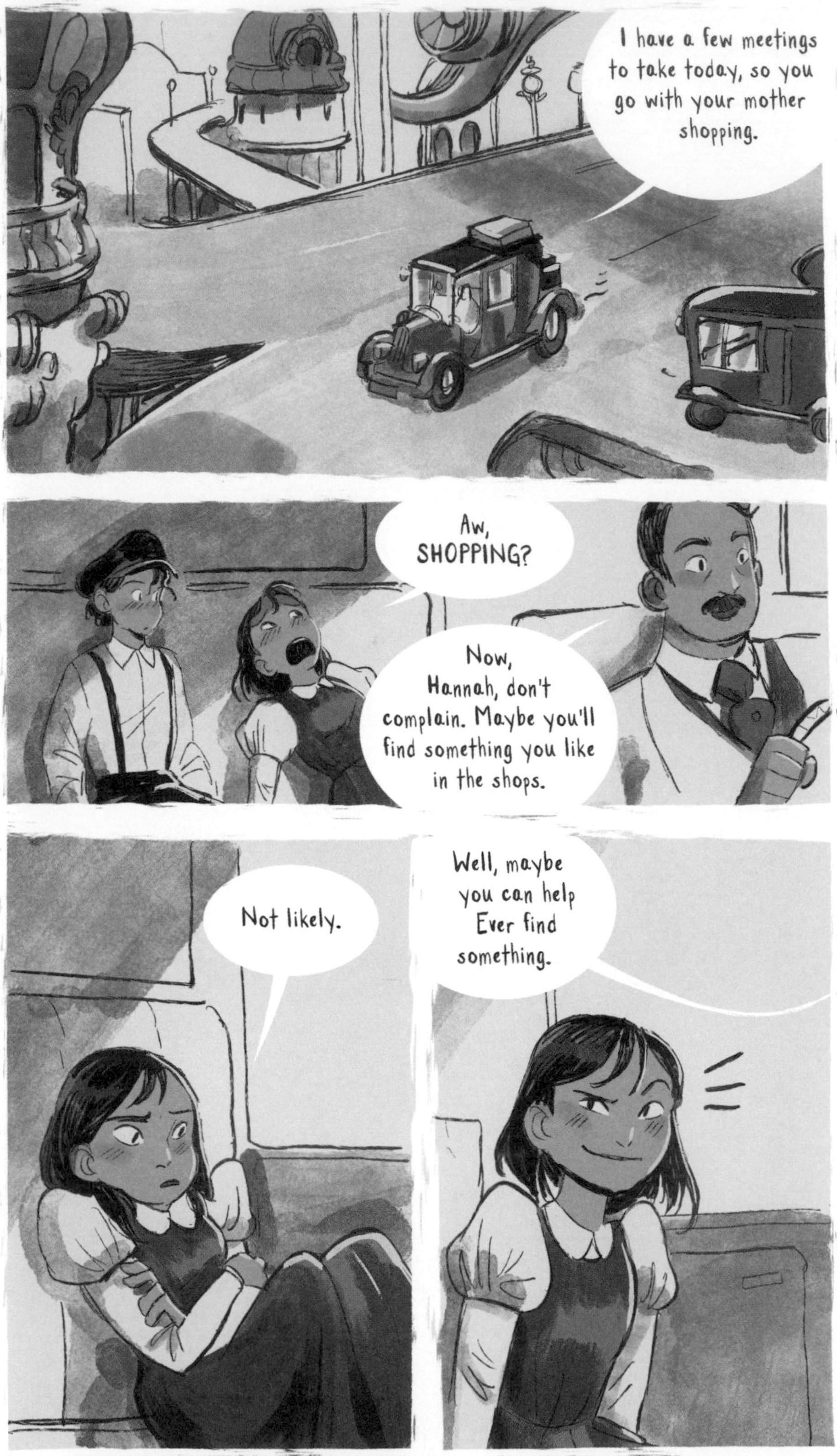
I have a few meetings to take today, so you go with your mother shopping.
Aw, SHOPPING?
Now, Hannah, don't complain. Maybe you'll find something you like in the shops.
Not likely.
Well, maybe you can help Ever find something.

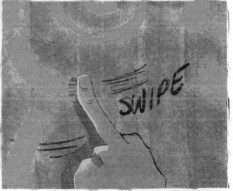

SWIPE

TTHRUMMM

TTHRUMM

WHOOOOM

HSOOSHHHH

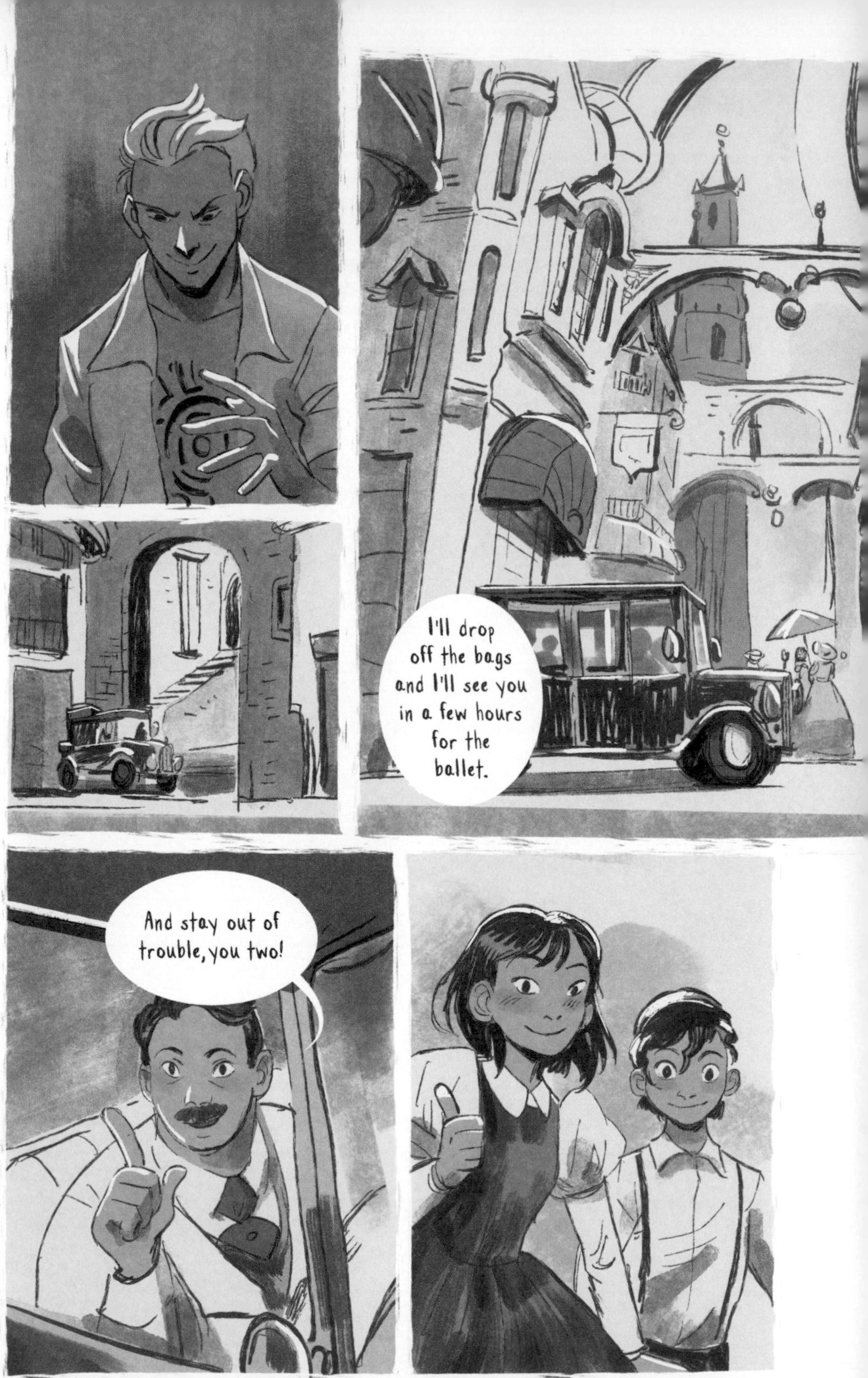
I'll drop off the bags and I'll see you in a few hours for the ballet.
And stay out of trouble, you two!

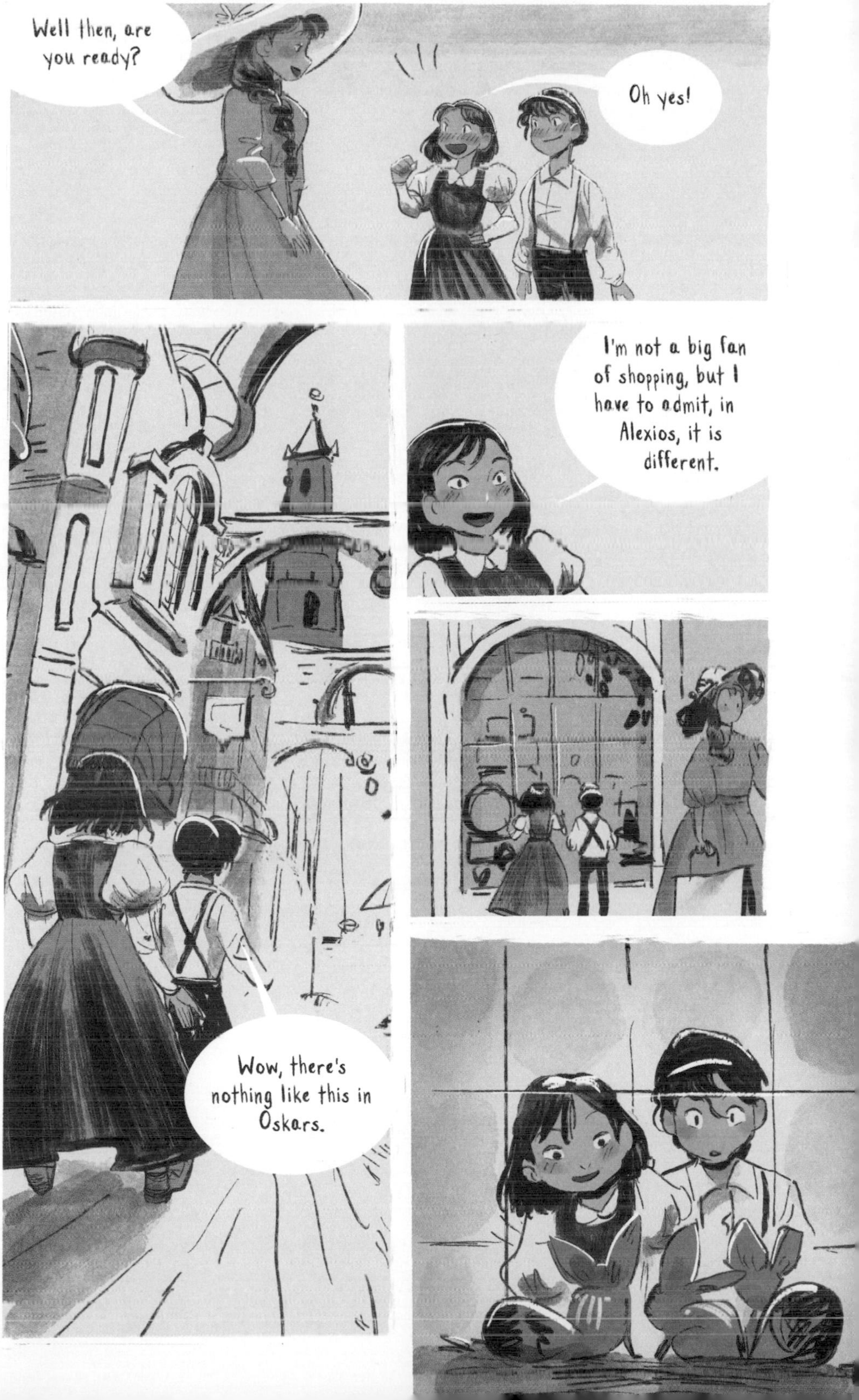
Well then, are you ready?
Oh yes!
I'm not a big fan of shopping, but I have to admit, in Alexios, it is different.
Wow, there's nothing like this in Oskars.

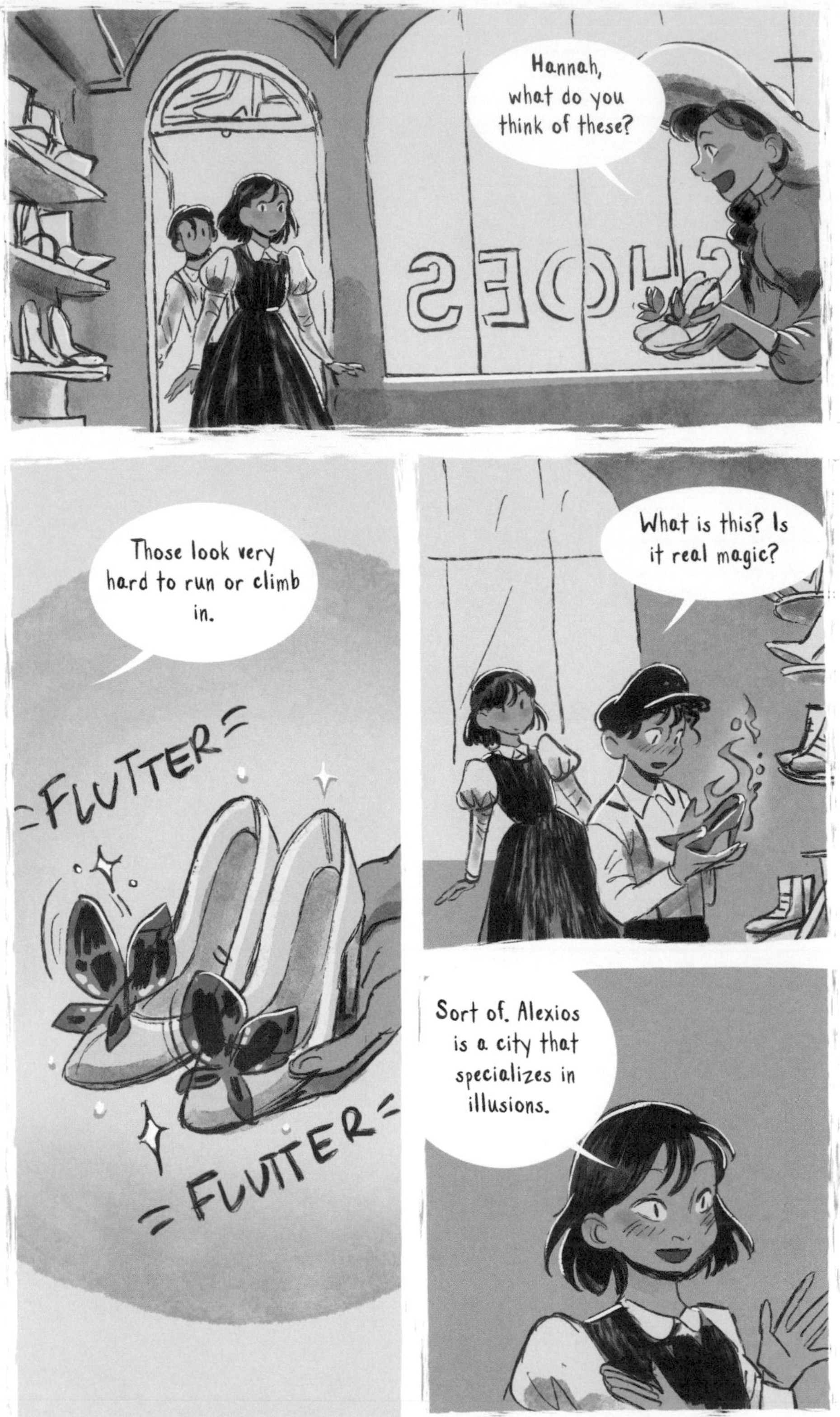
SHOES
Hannah, what do you think of these?
Those look very hard to run or climb in.
FLUTTER
FLUTTER
What is this? Is it real magic?
Sort of. Alexios is a city that specializes in illusions.

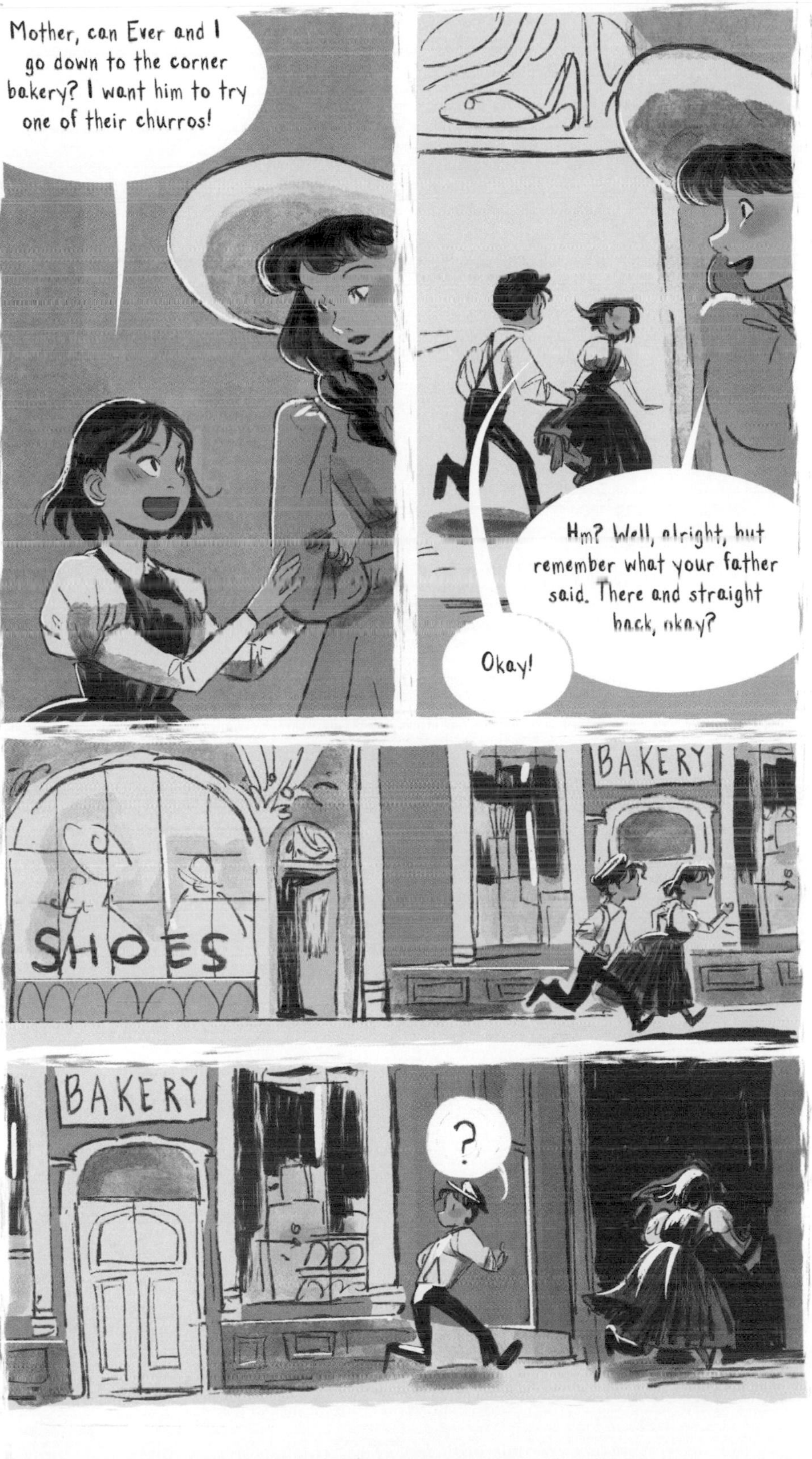
Mother, can Ever and I go down to the corner bakery? I want him to try one of their churros!
Hm? Well, alright, but remember what your father said. There and straight back, okay?
Okay!
SHOES
BAKERY
BAKERY
?

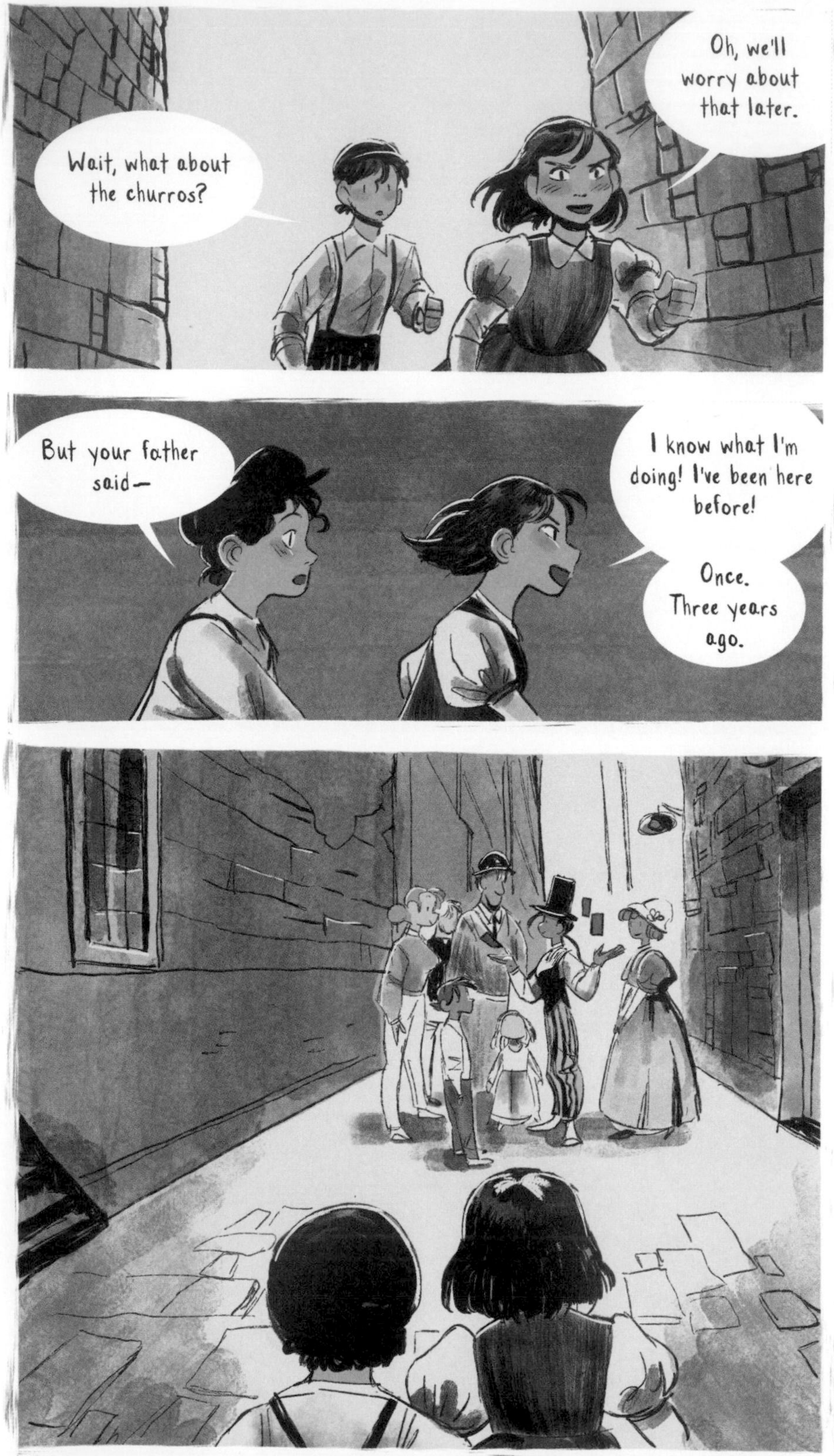
Wait, what about the churros?
Oh, we'll worry about that later.
But your father said—
I know what I'm doing! I've been here before!
Once. Three years ago.

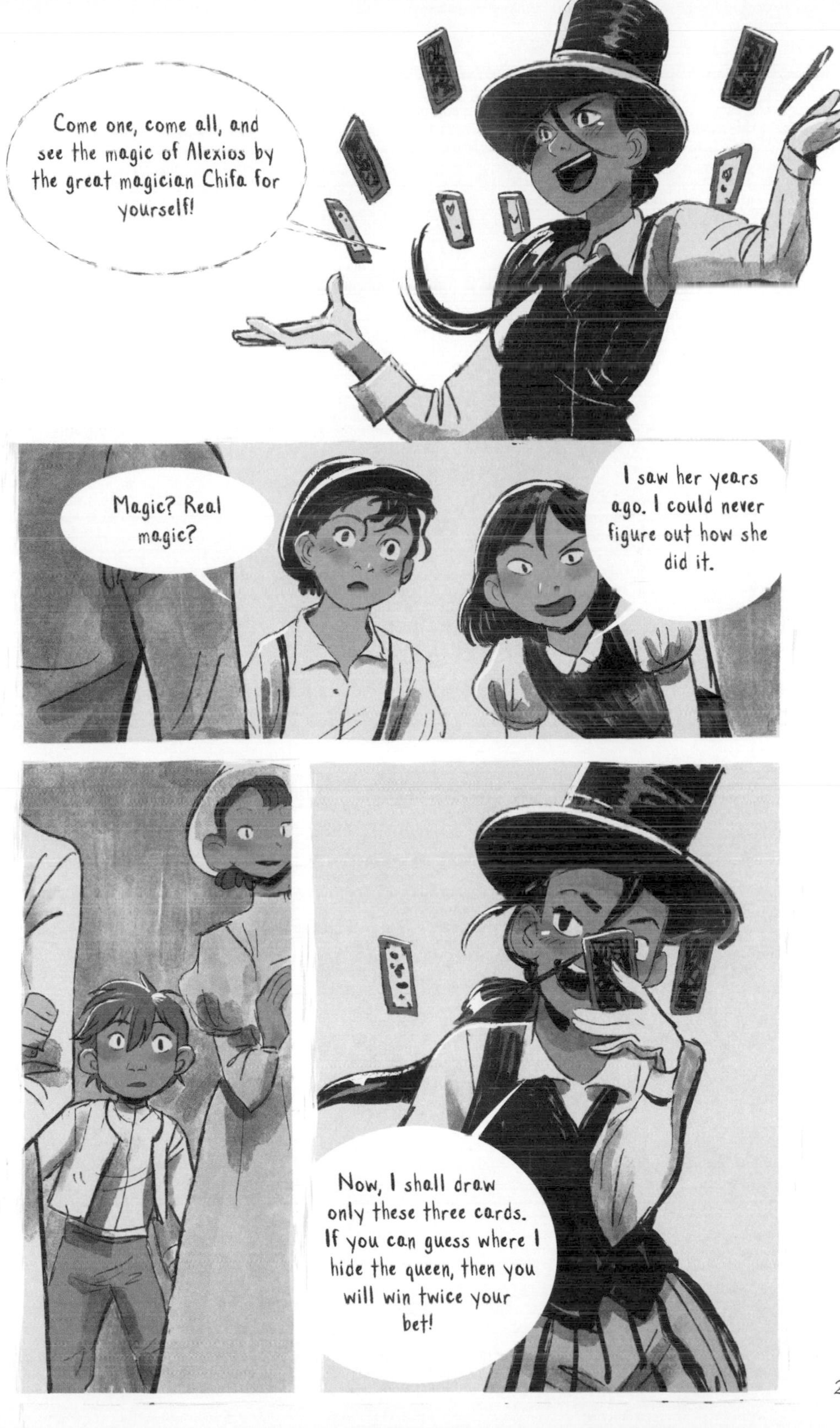
Come one, come all, and see the magic of Alexios by the great magician Chifa for yourself!
Magic? Real magic?
I saw her years ago. I could never figure out how she did it.
Now, I shall draw only these three cards. If you can guess where I hide the queen, then you will win twice your bet!

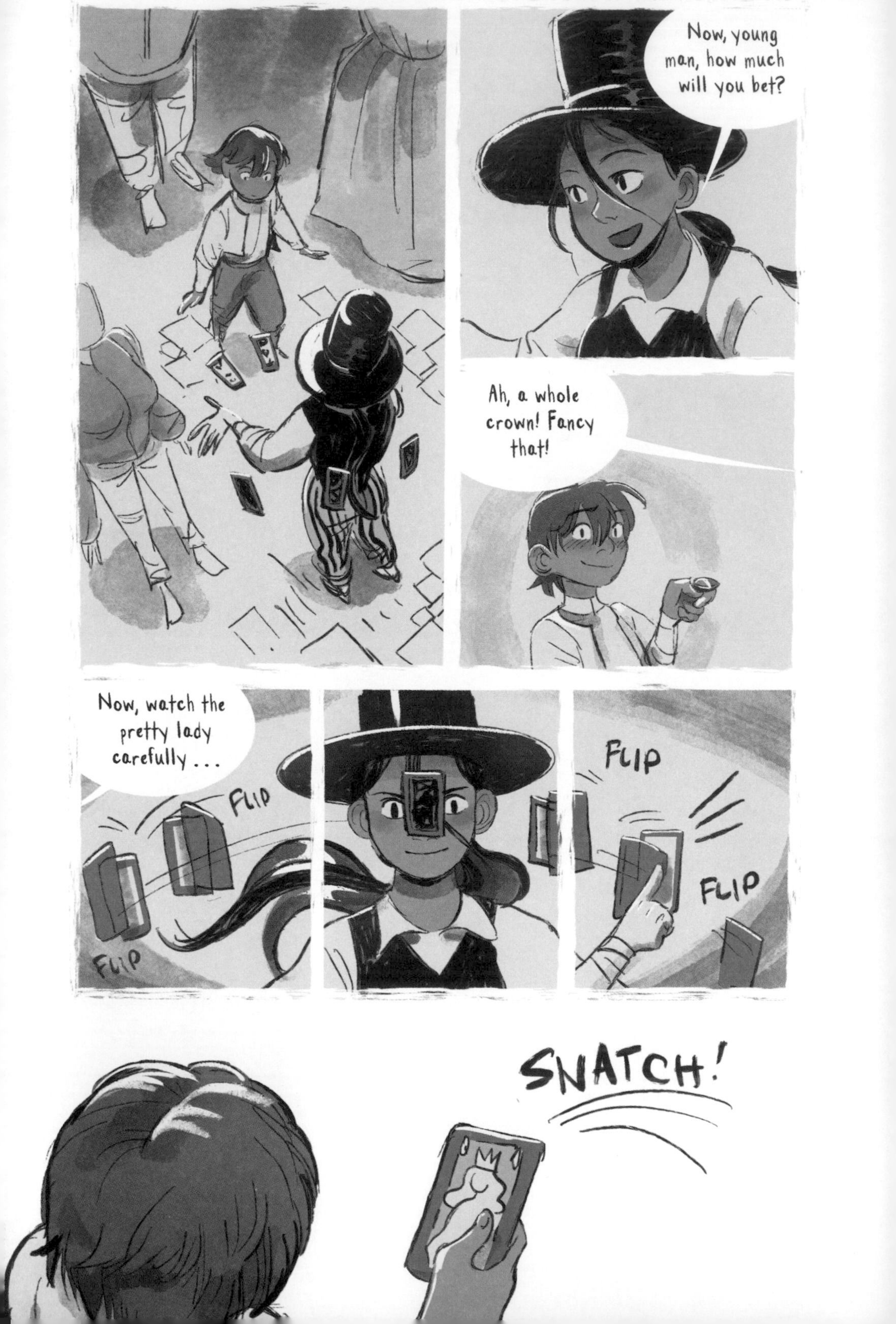
Now, young man, how much will you bet?
Ah, a whole crown! Fancy that!
Now, watch the pretty lady carefully . . .
FLIP
FLIP
FLIP
FLIP
SNATCH!

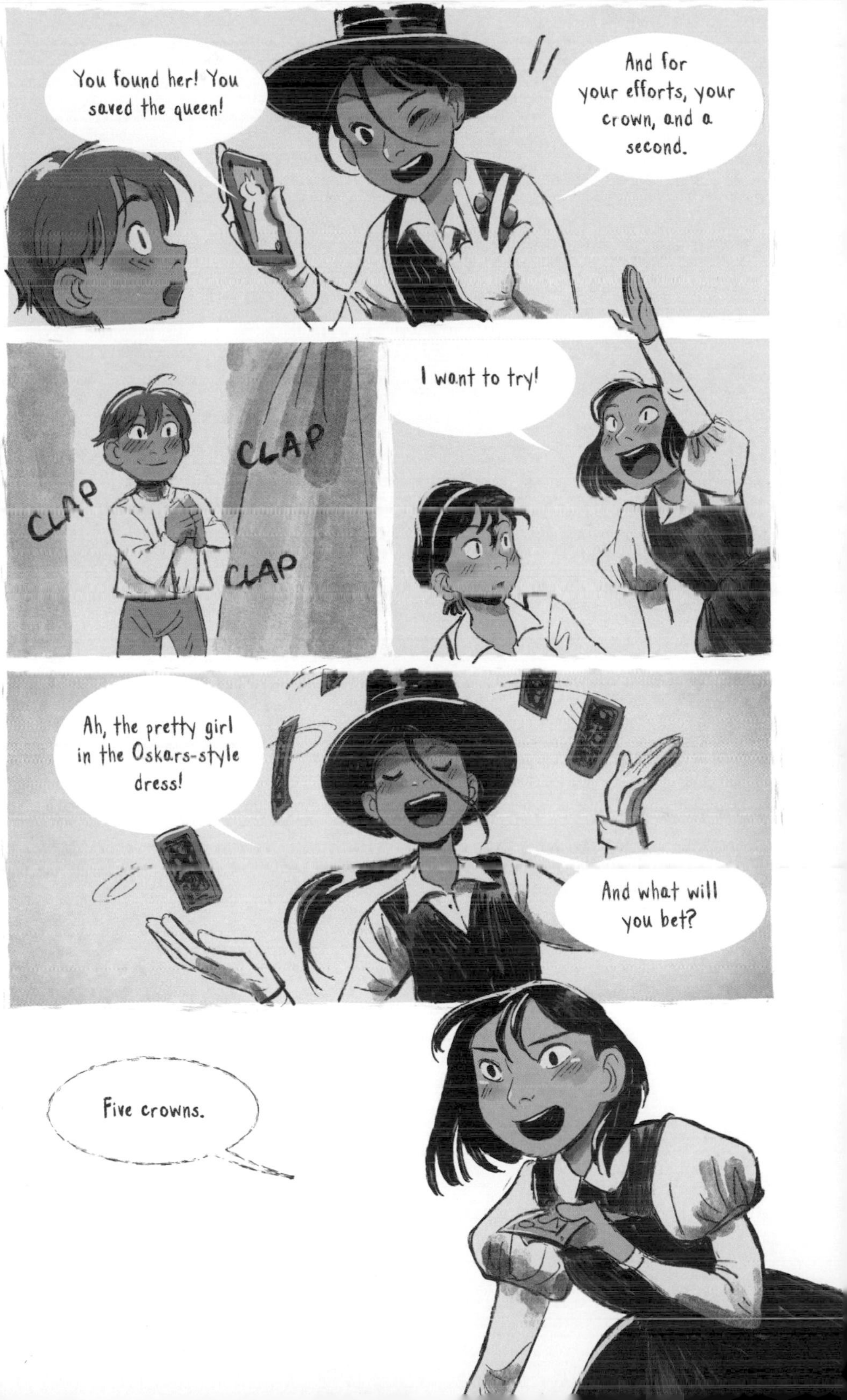
You found her! You saved the queen!
And for your efforts, your crown, and a second.
CLAP
CLAP
CLAP
I want to try!
Ah, the pretty girl in the Oskars-style dress!
And what will you bet?
Five crowns.

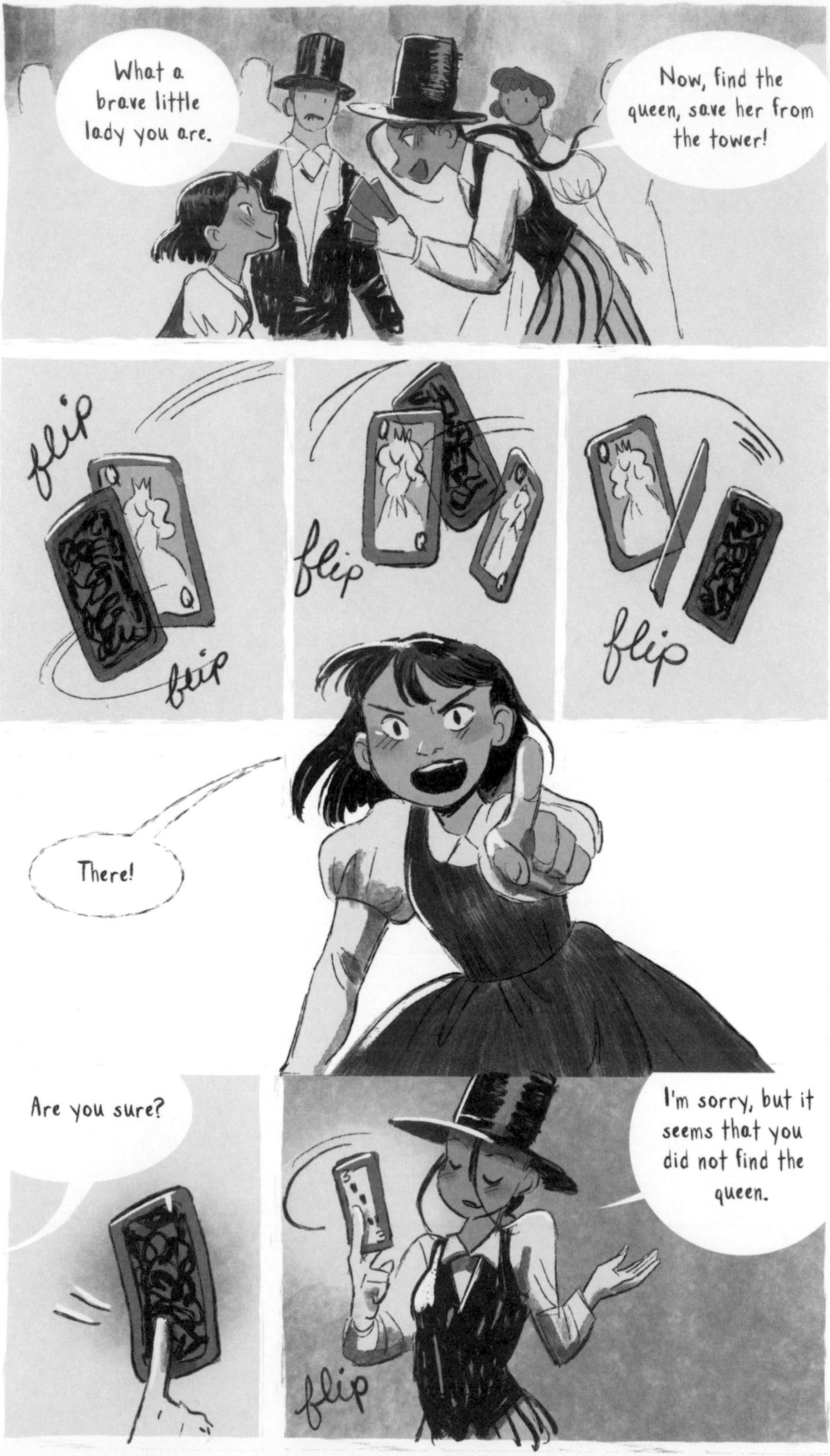
What a brave little lady you are.
Now, find the queen, save her from the tower!
flip
flip
flip
flip
There!
Are you sure?
I'm sorry, but it seems that you did not find the queen.
flip

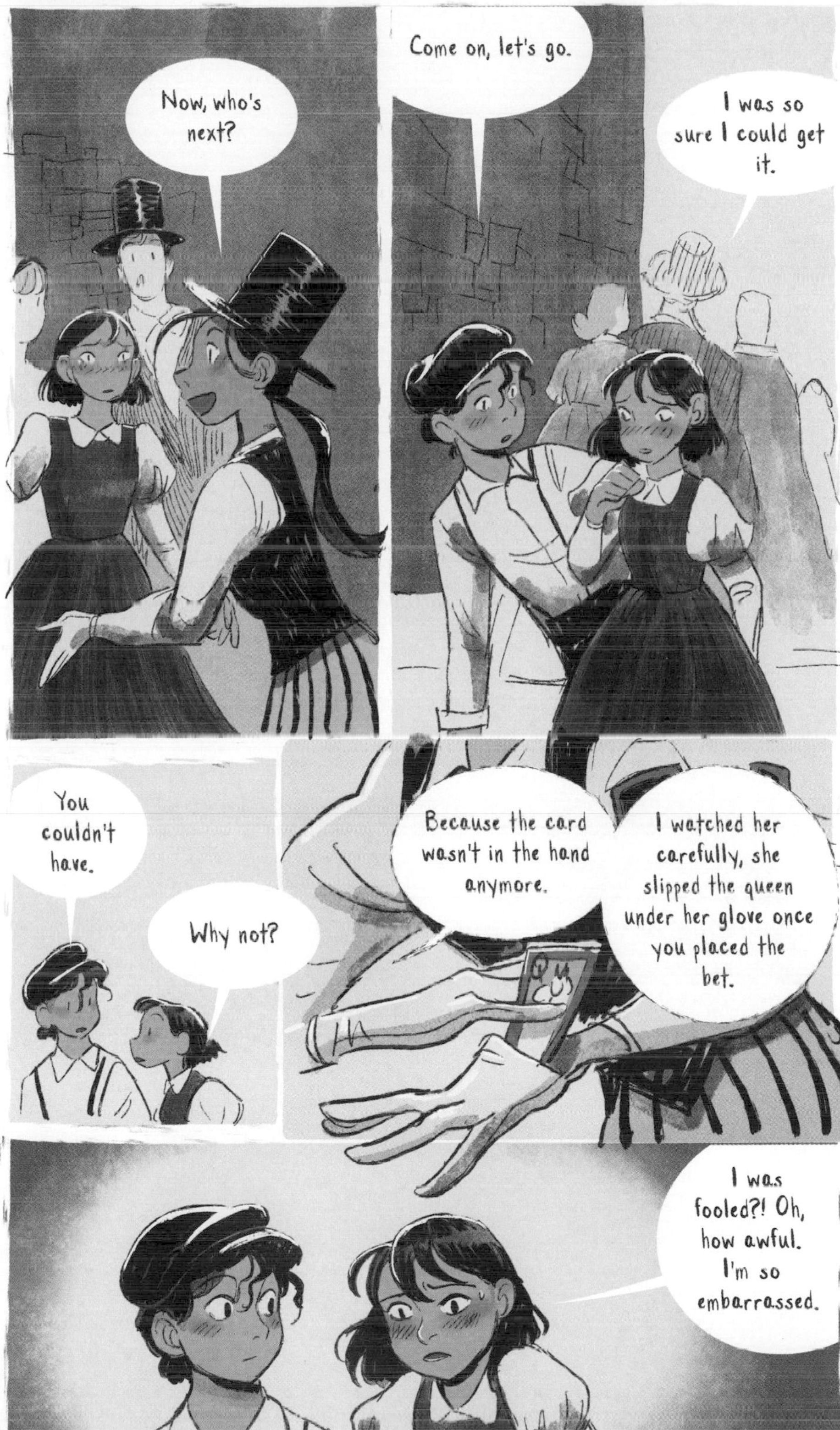

Now, who's next?
Come on, let's go.
I was so sure I could get it.
You couldn't have.
Why not?
Because the card wasn't in the hand anymore.
I watched her carefully, she slipped the queen under her glove once you placed the bet.
I was fooled?! Oh, how awful. I'm so embarrassed.

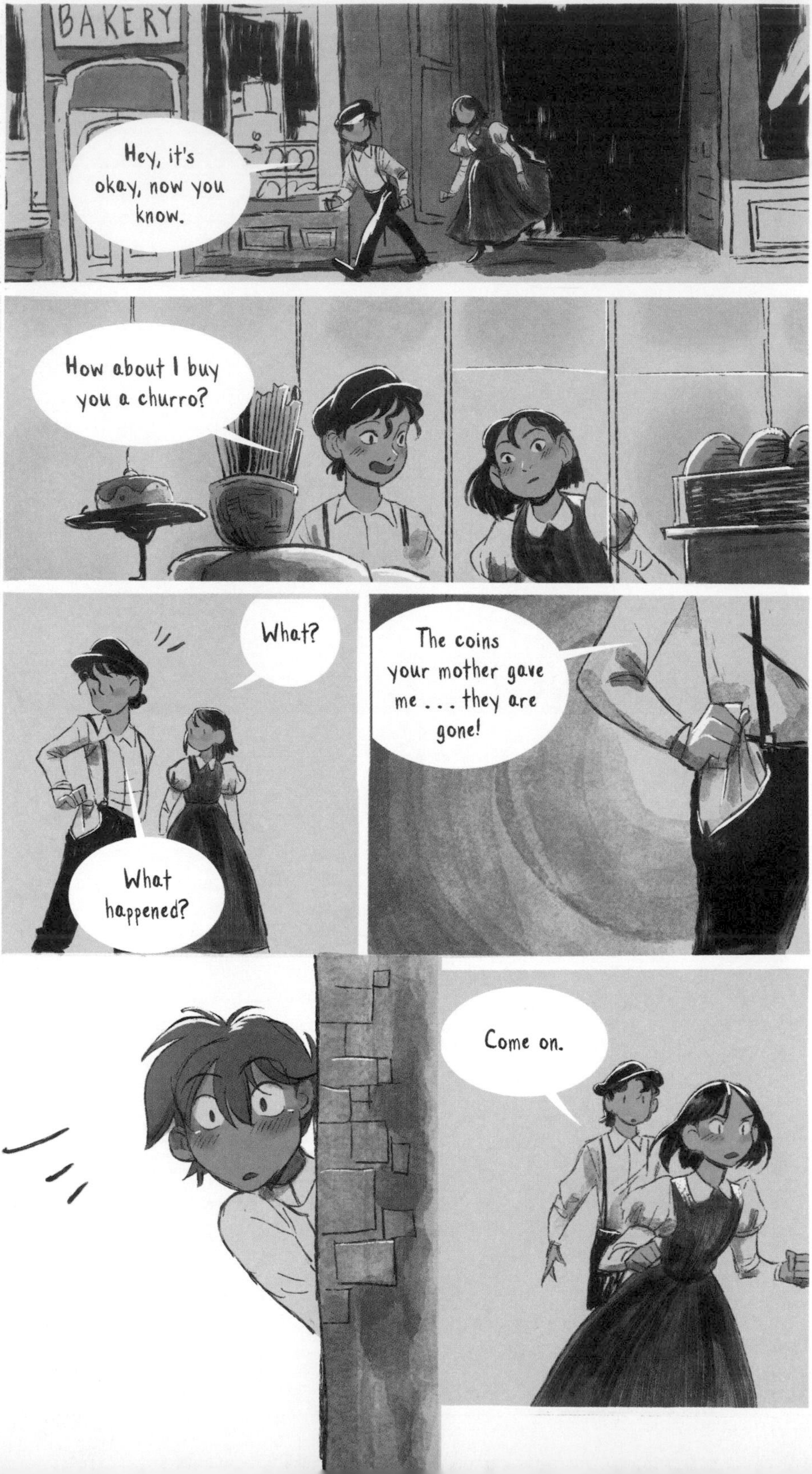
BAKERY
Hey, it's okay, now you know.
How about I buy you a churro?
What?
What happened?
The coins your mother gave me . . . they are gone!
Come on.

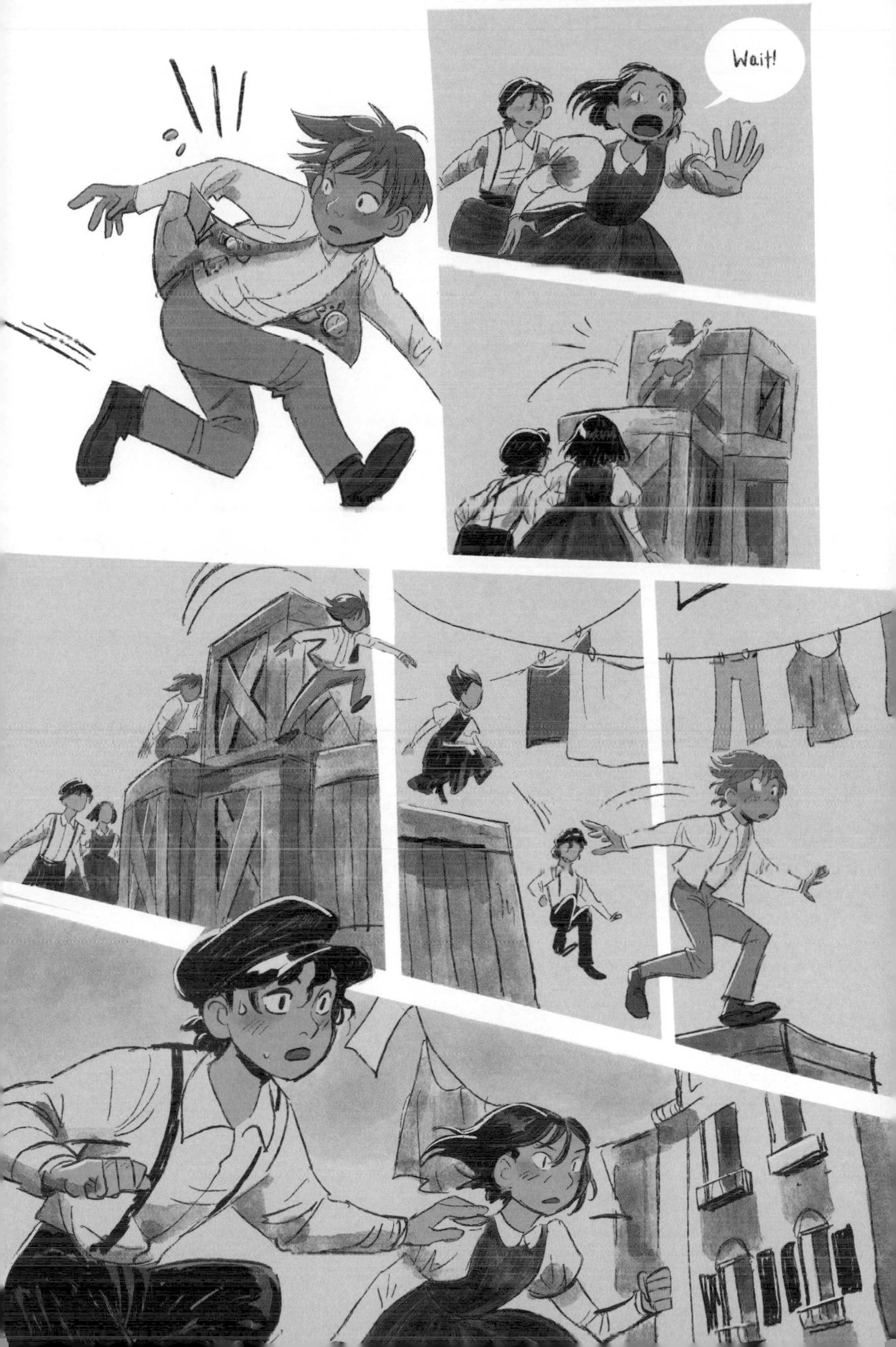
Wait!

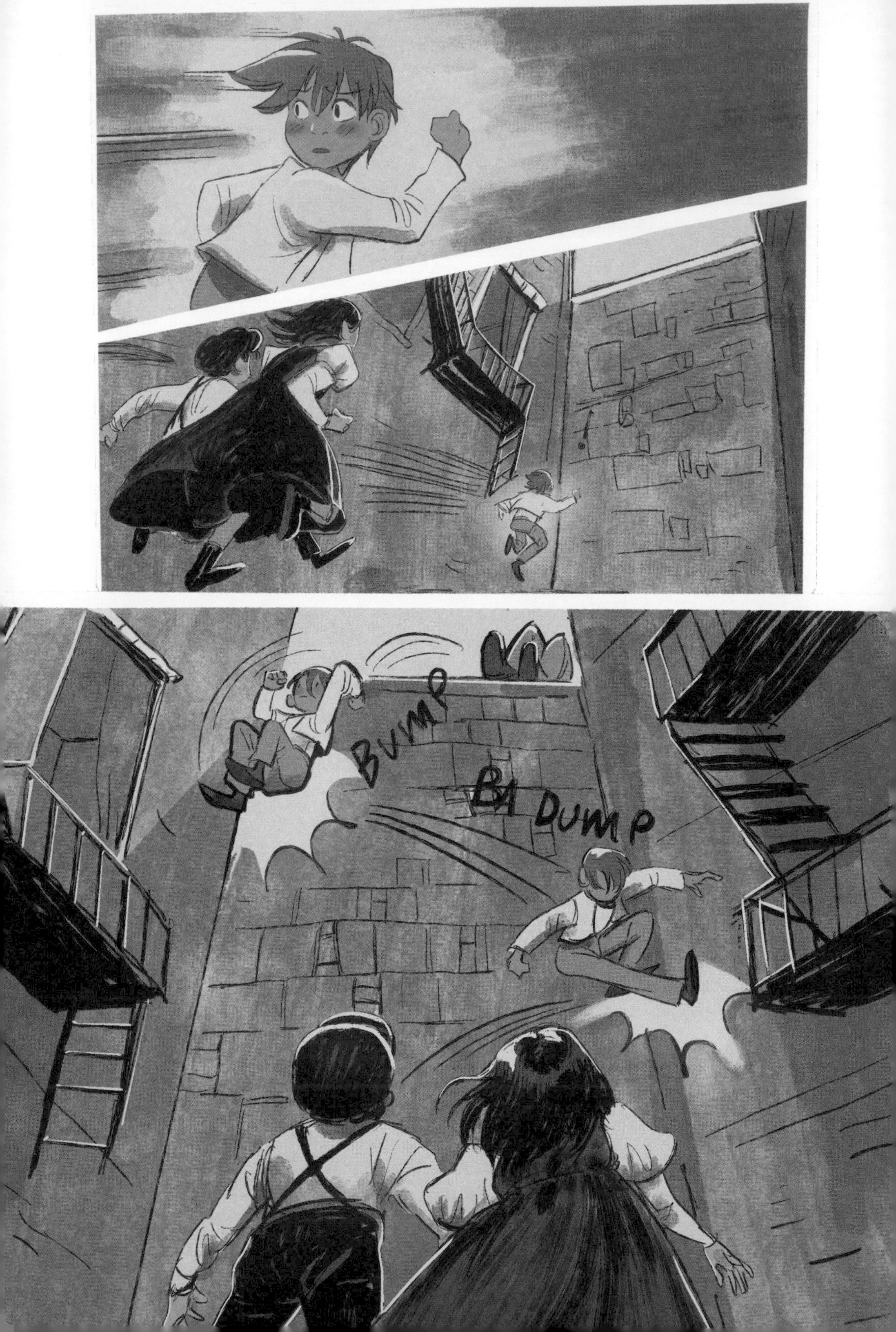
BUMP
BA DUMP

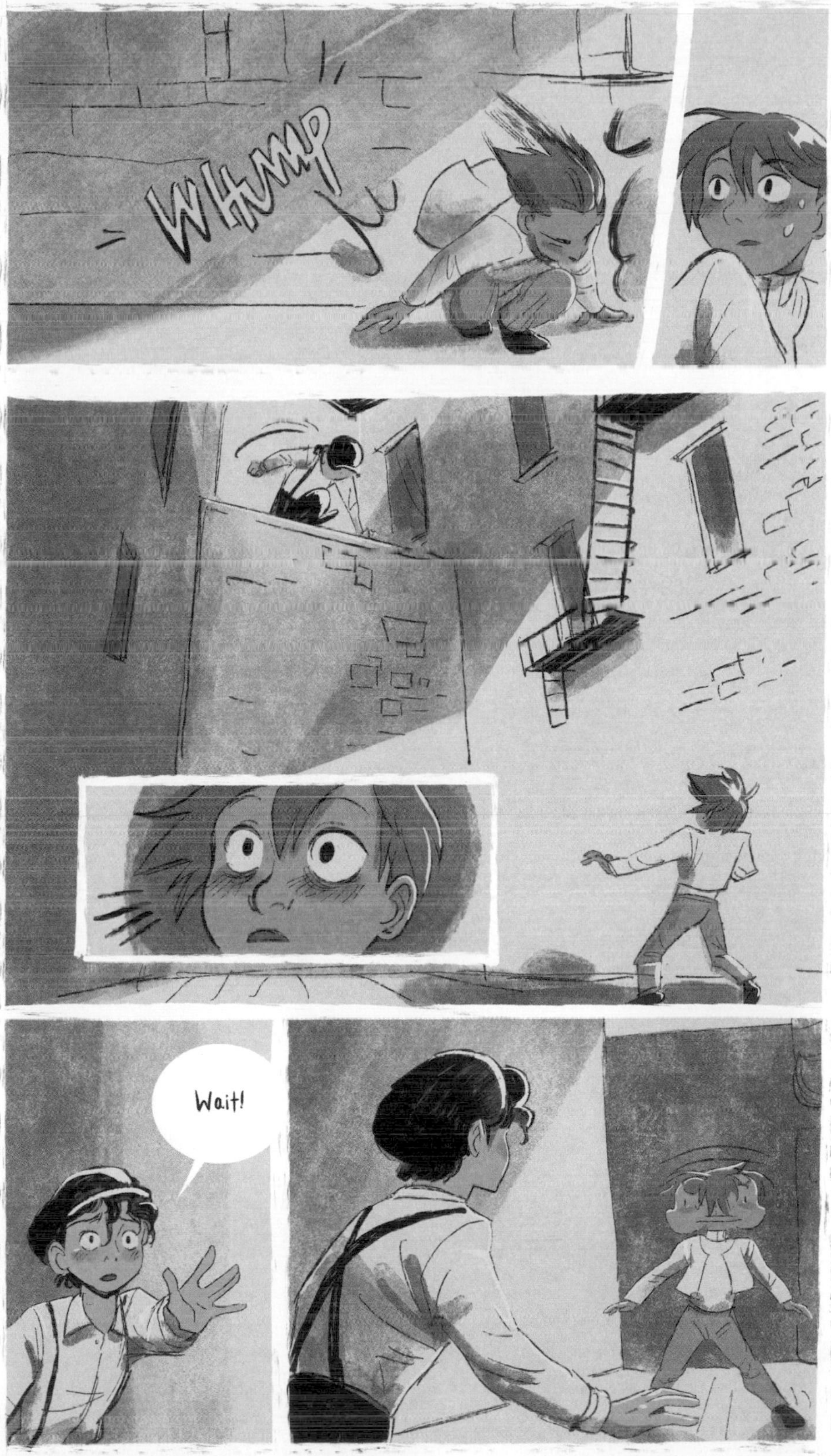
WHUMP
Wait!

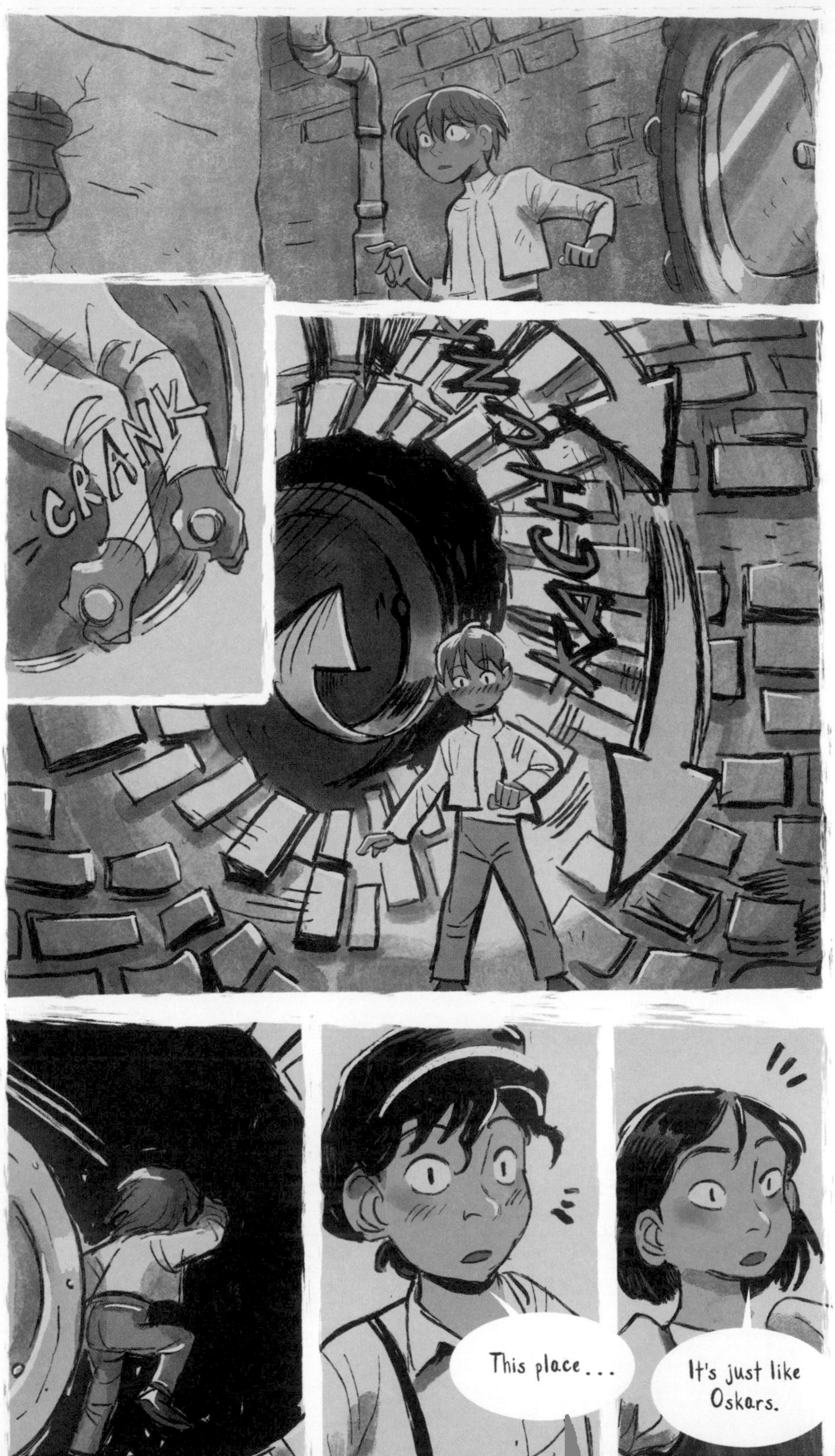
CRANK
KACHUNK
This place...
It's just like Oskars.

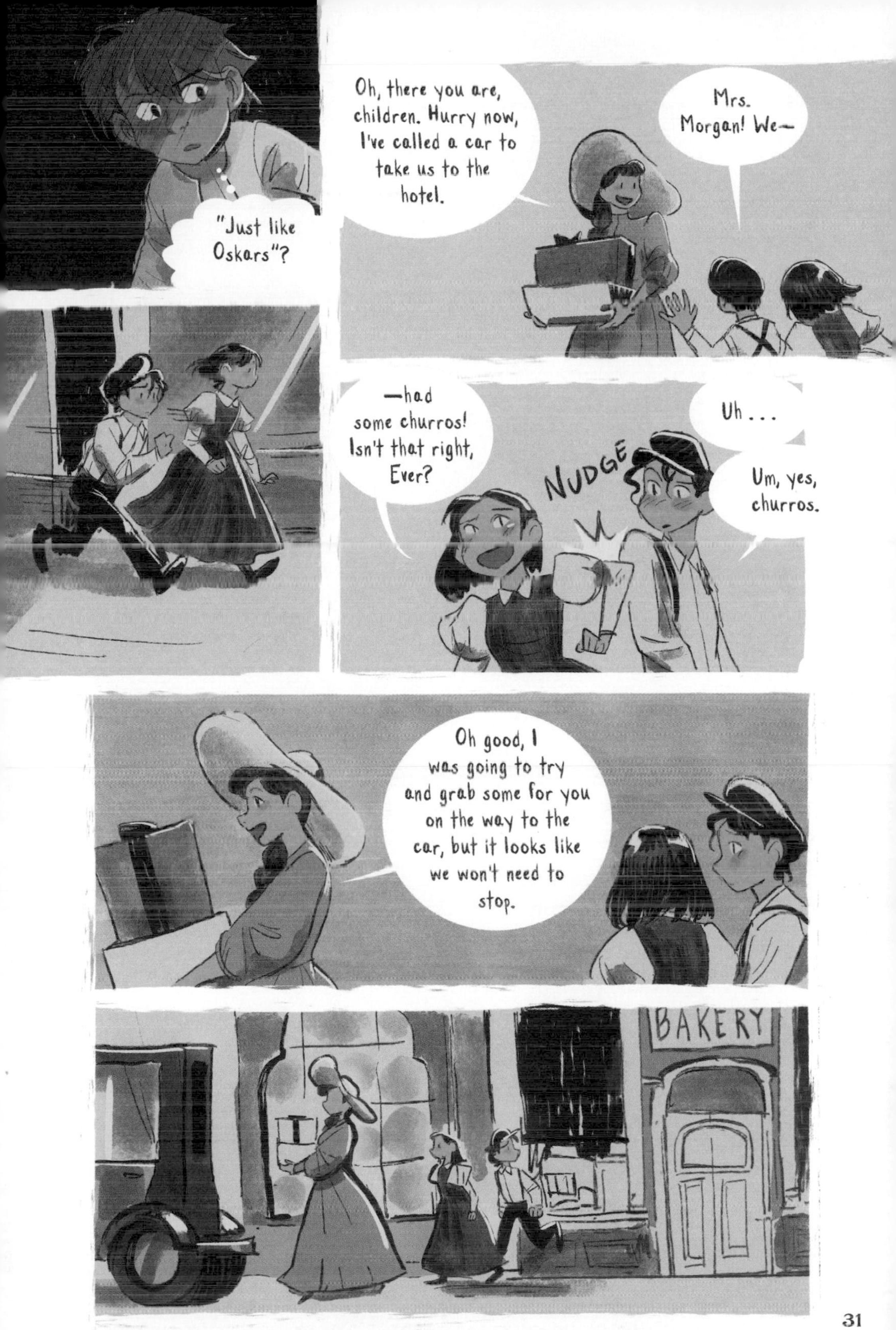
"Just like Oskars"?
Oh, there you are, children. Hurry now, I've called a car to take us to the hotel.
Mrs. Morgan! We—
—had some churros! Isn't that right, Ever?
Uh . . .
NUDGE
Um, yes, churros.
Oh good, I was going to try and grab some for you on the way to the car, but it looks like we won't need to stop.
BAKERY

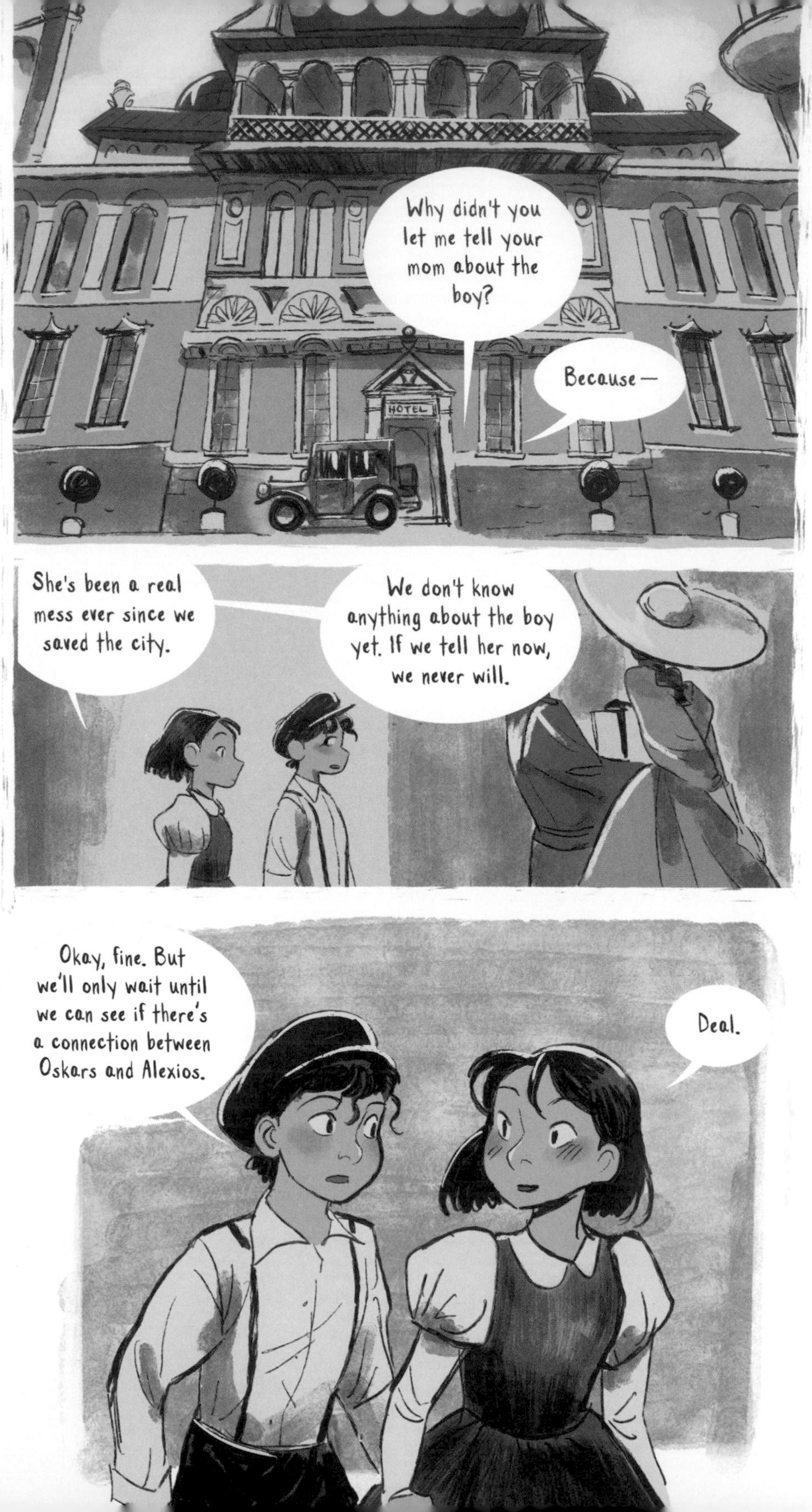
HOTEL
Why didn't you let me tell your mom about the boy?
Because—
She's been a real mess ever since we saved the city.
We don't know anything about the boy yet. If we tell her now, we never will.
Okay, fine. But we'll only wait until we can see if there's a connection between Oskars and Alexios.
Deal.

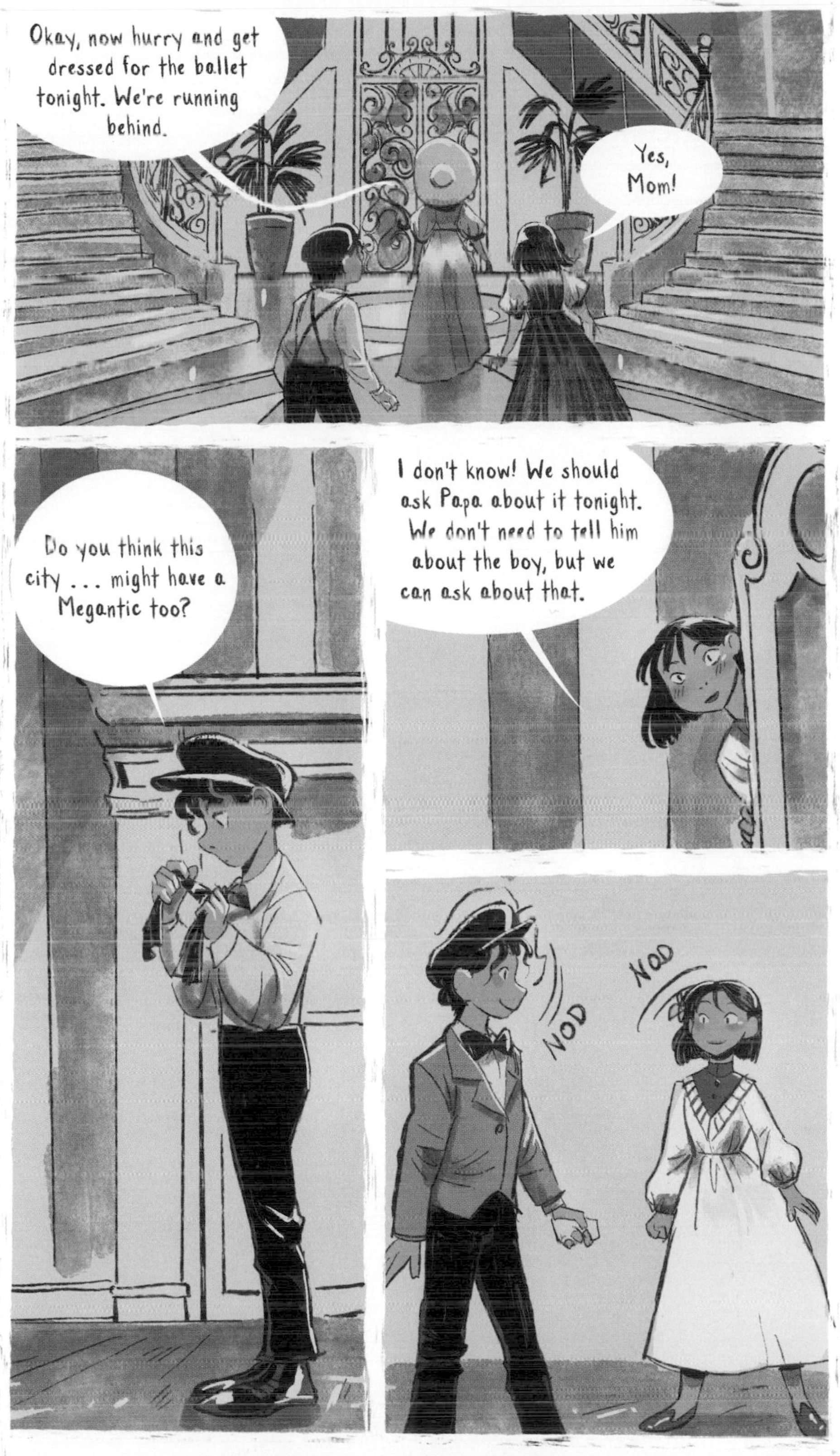

Okay, now hurry and get dressed for the ballet tonight. We're running behind.
Yes, Mom!
Do you think this city . . . might have a Megantic too?
I don't know! We should ask Papa about it tonight. We don't need to tell him about the boy, but we can ask about that.
NOD
NOD

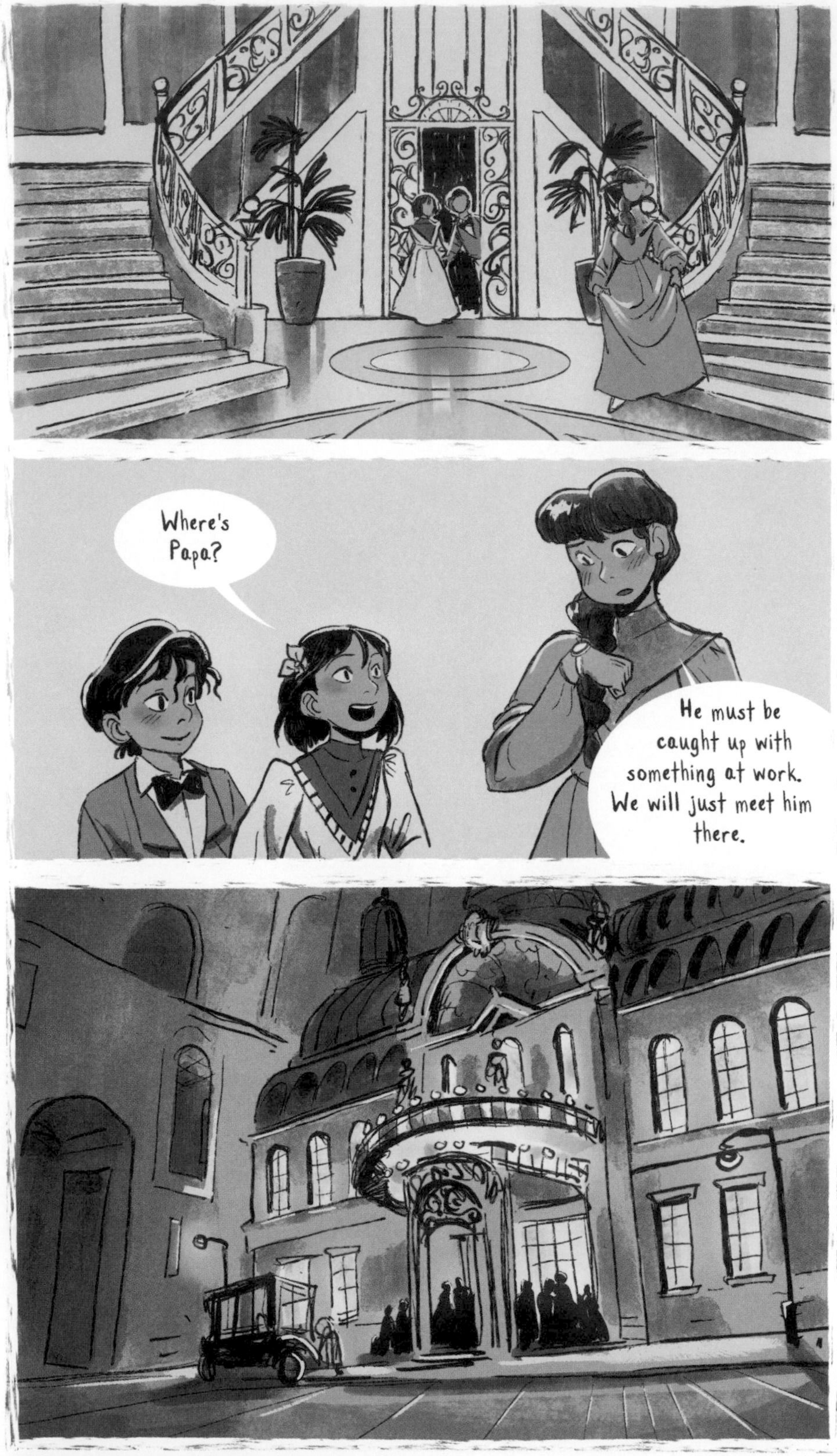
Where's Papa?
He must be caught up with something at work. We will just meet him there.

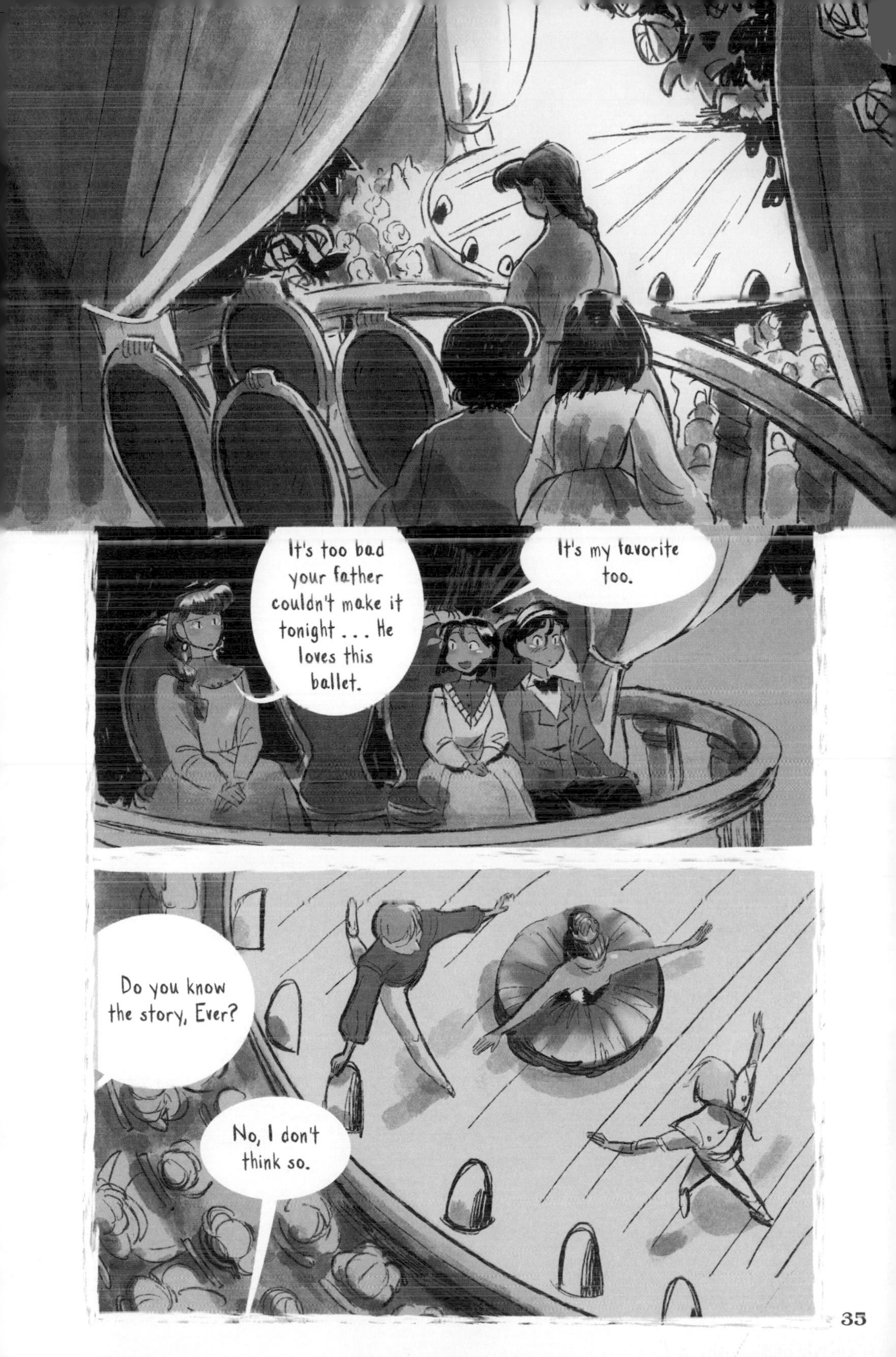
It's too bad your father couldn't make it tonight . . . He loves this ballet.
It's my favorite too.
Do you know the story, Ever?
No, I don't think so.

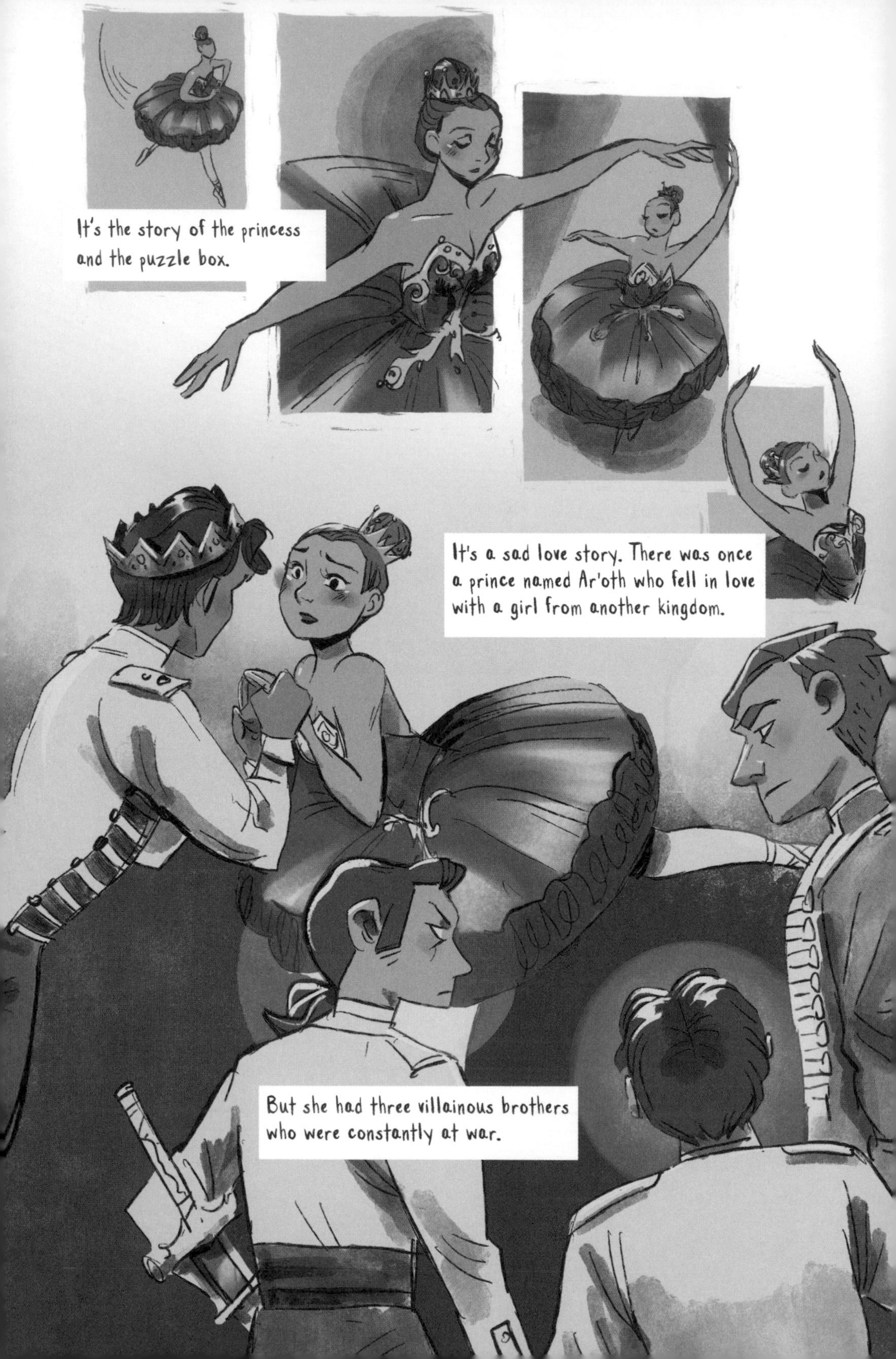
It's the story of the princess and the puzzle box.
It's a sad love story. There was once a prince named Ar'oth who fell in love with a girl from another kingdom.
But she had three villainous brothers who were constantly at war.

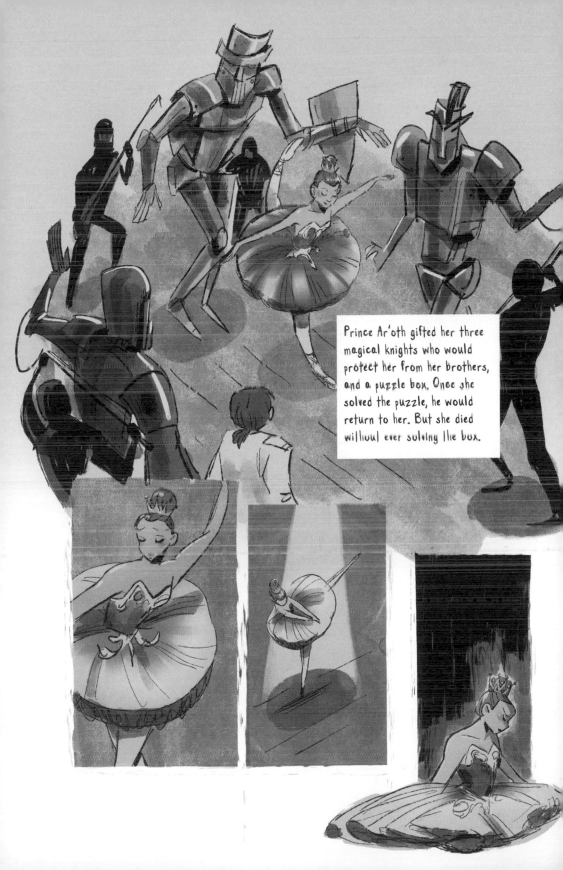

Prince Ar'oth gifted her three magical knights who would protect her from her brothers, and a puzzle box. Once she solved the puzzle, he would return to her. But she died without ever solving the box.

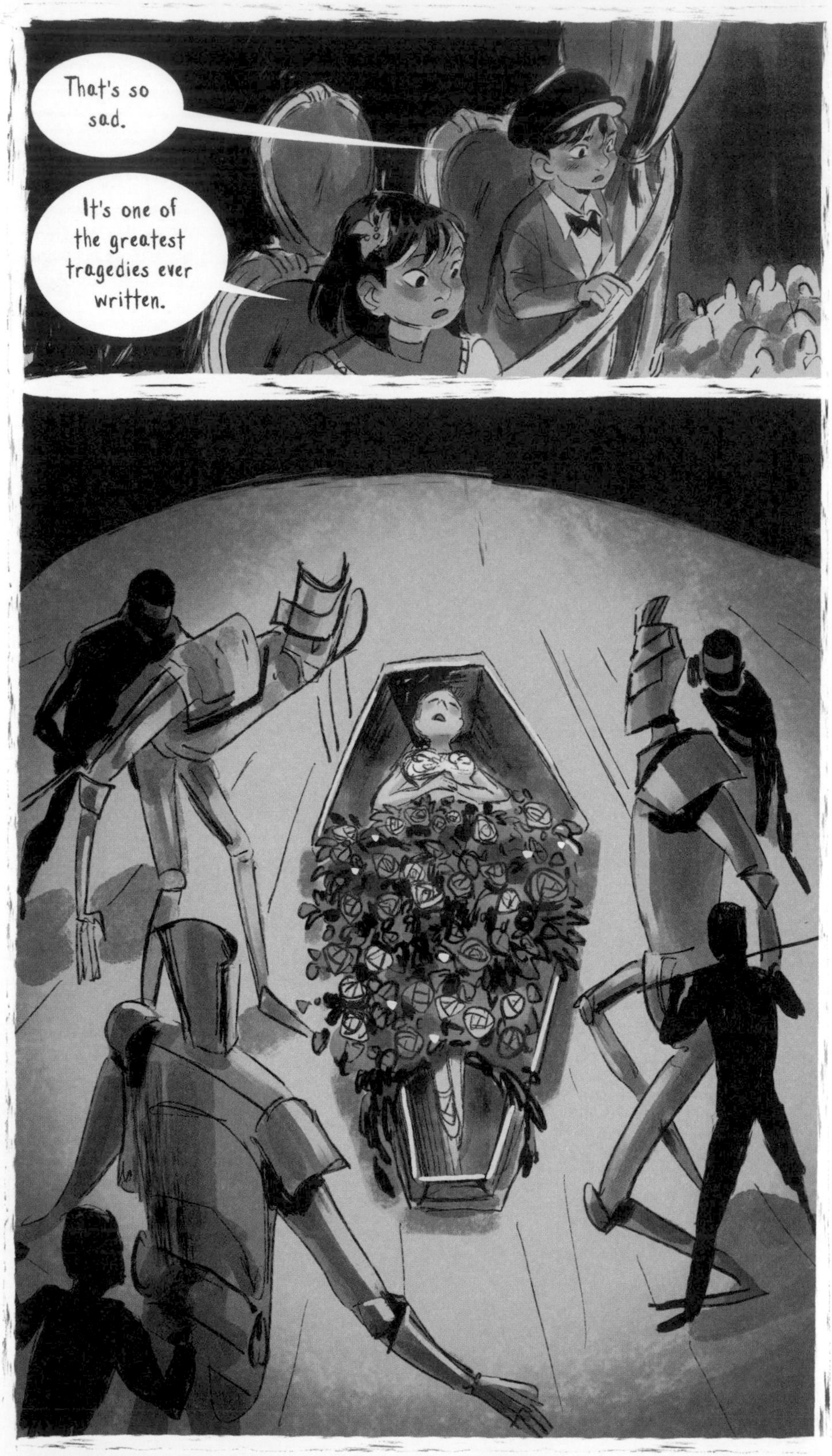
That's so sad.
It's one of the greatest tragedies ever written.

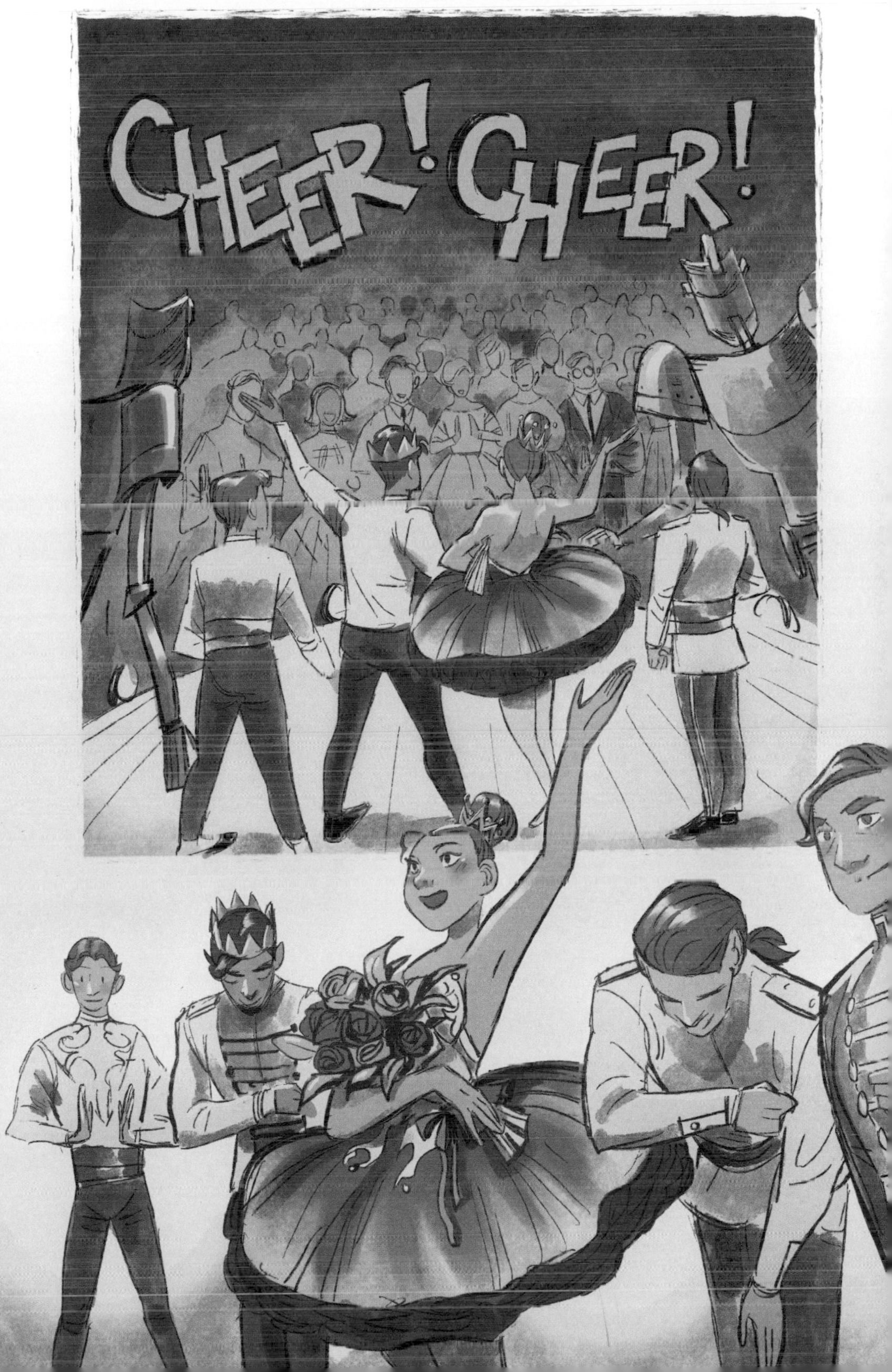
CHEER! CHEER!

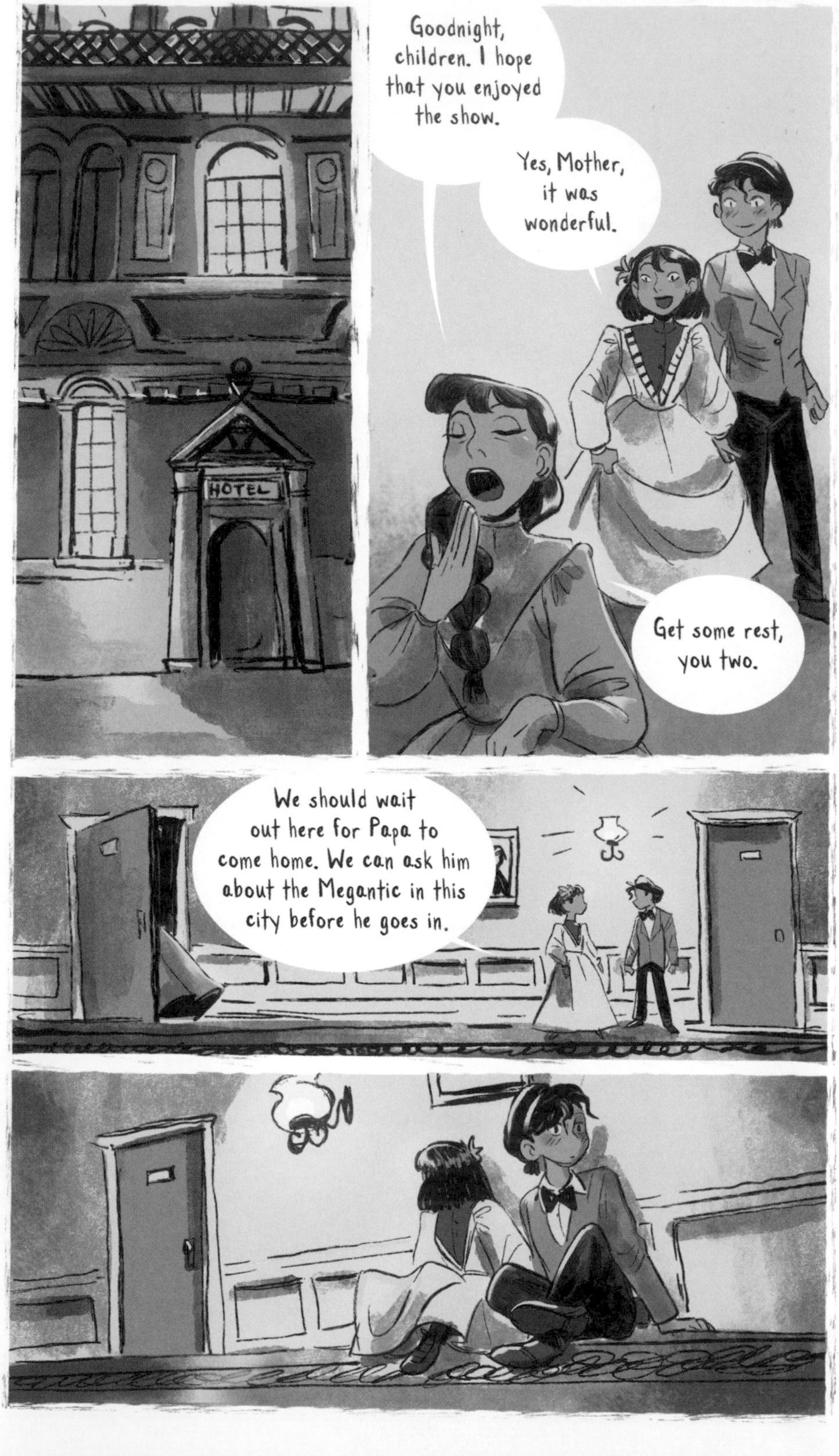

HOTEL
Goodnight, children. I hope that you enjoyed the show.
Yes, Mother, it was wonderful.
Get some rest, you two.
We should wait out here for Papa to come home. We can ask him about the Megantic in this city before he goes in.

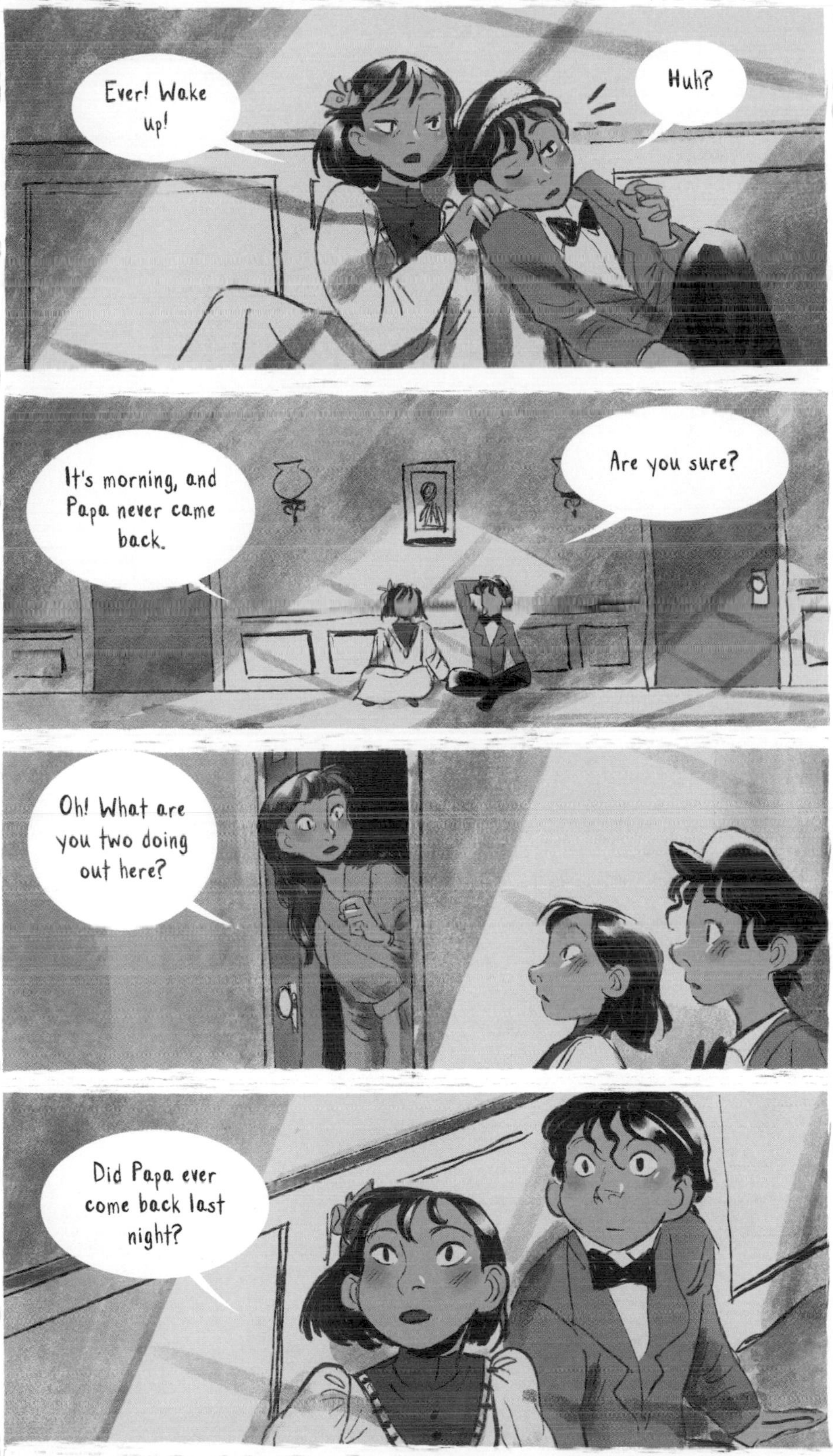
Ever! Wake up!
Huh?
It's morning, and Papa never came back.
Are you sure?
Oh! What are you two doing out here?
Did Papa ever come back last night?

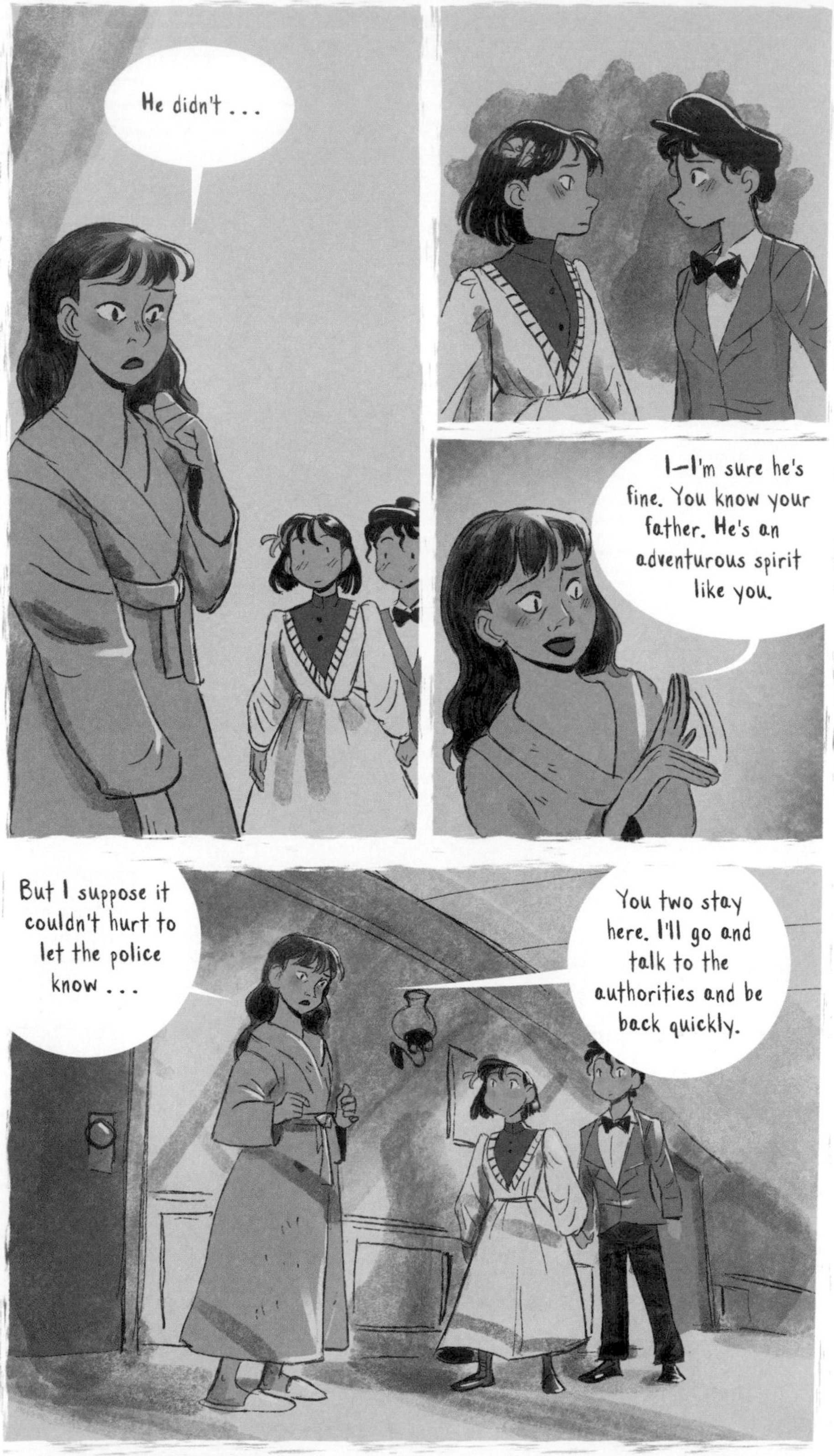
He didn't . . .
I—I'm sure he's fine. You know your father. He's an adventurous spirit like you.
But I suppose it couldn't hurt to let the police know . . .
You two stay here. I'll go and talk to the authorities and be back quickly.

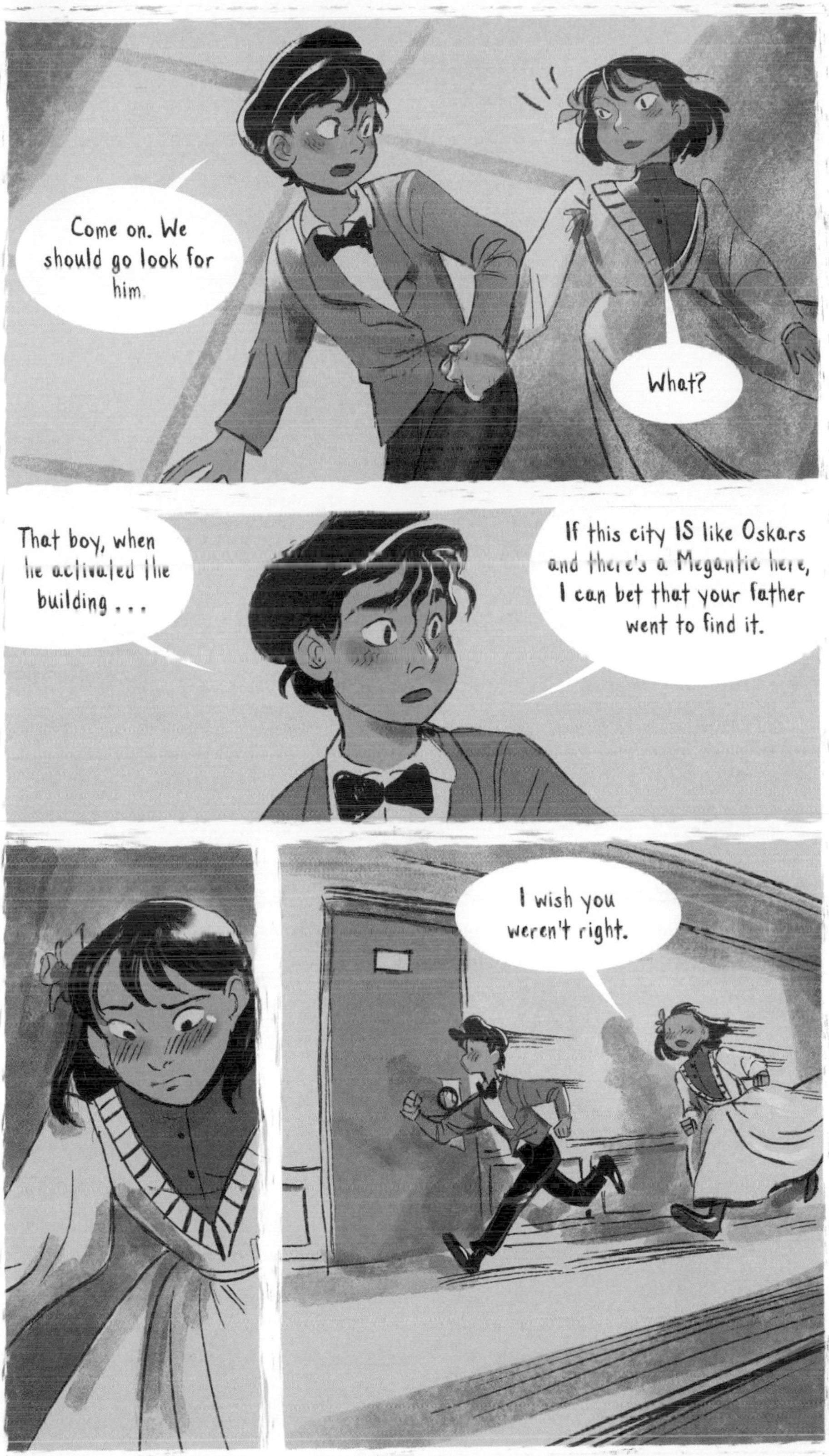
Come on. We should go look for him.
What?
That boy, when he activated the building . . .
If this city IS like Oskars and there's a Megantic here, I can bet that your father went to find it.
I wish you weren't right.

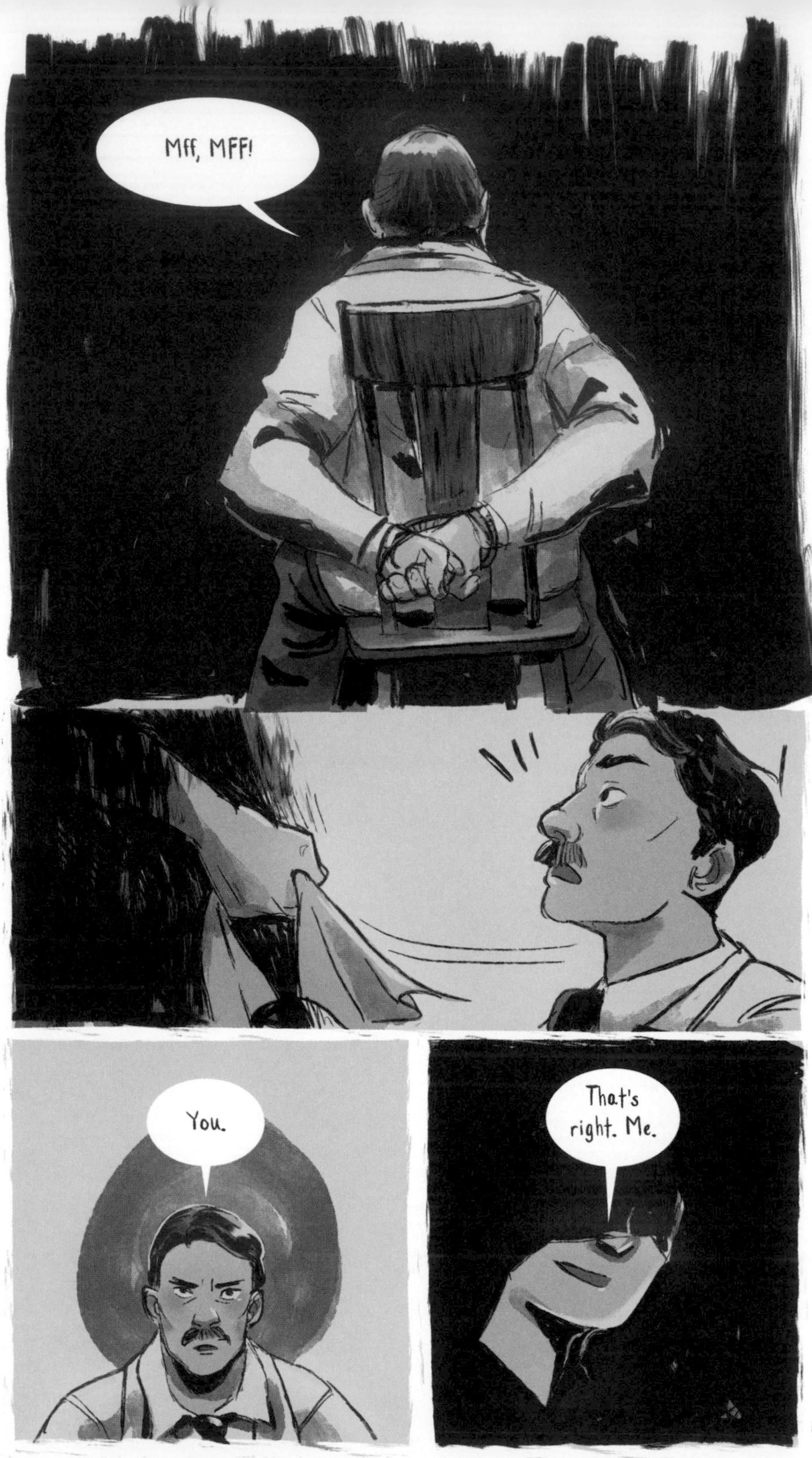
Mff, MFF!
You.
That's right. Me.

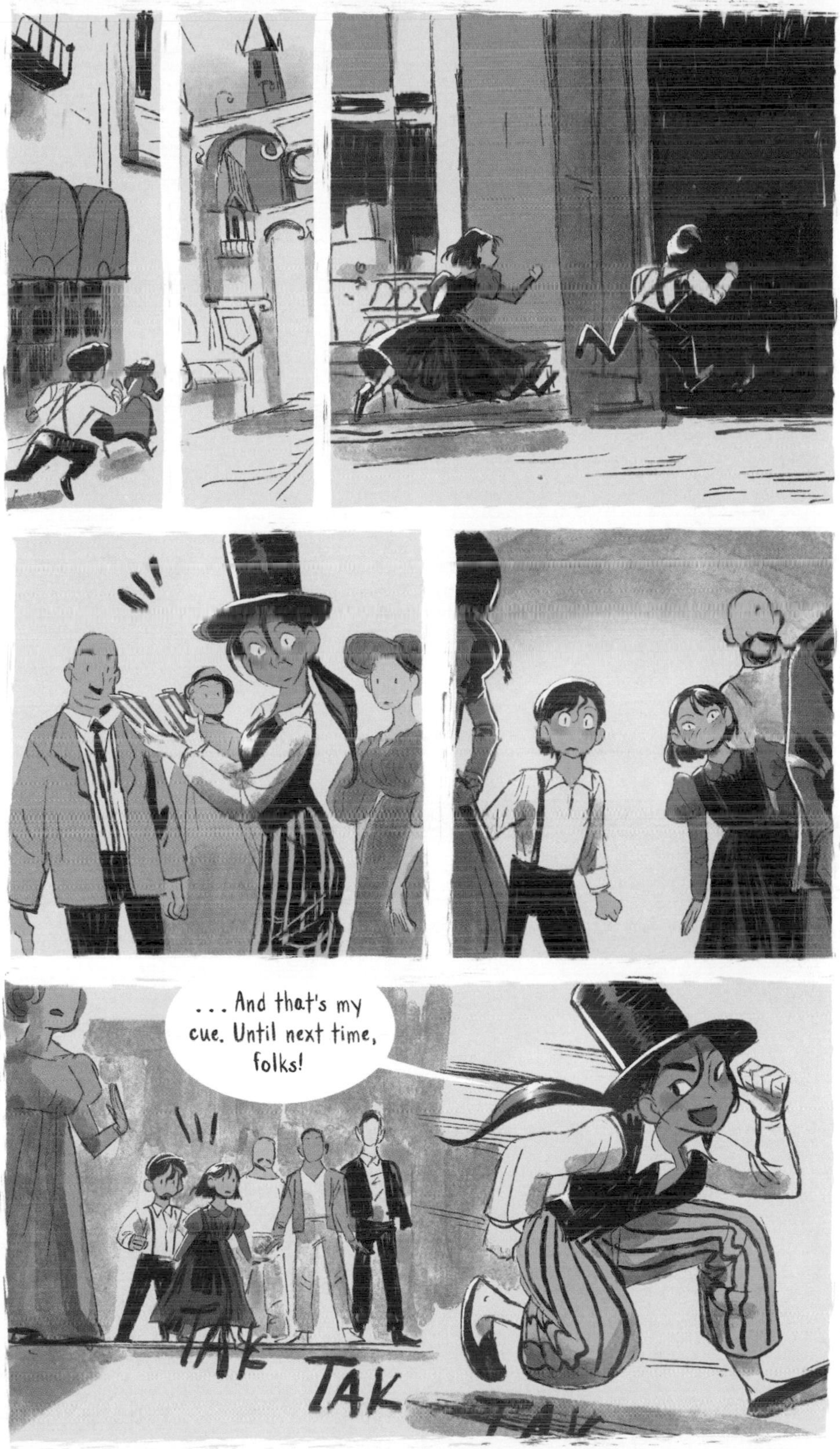

. . . And that's my cue. Until next time, folks!
TAK
TAK

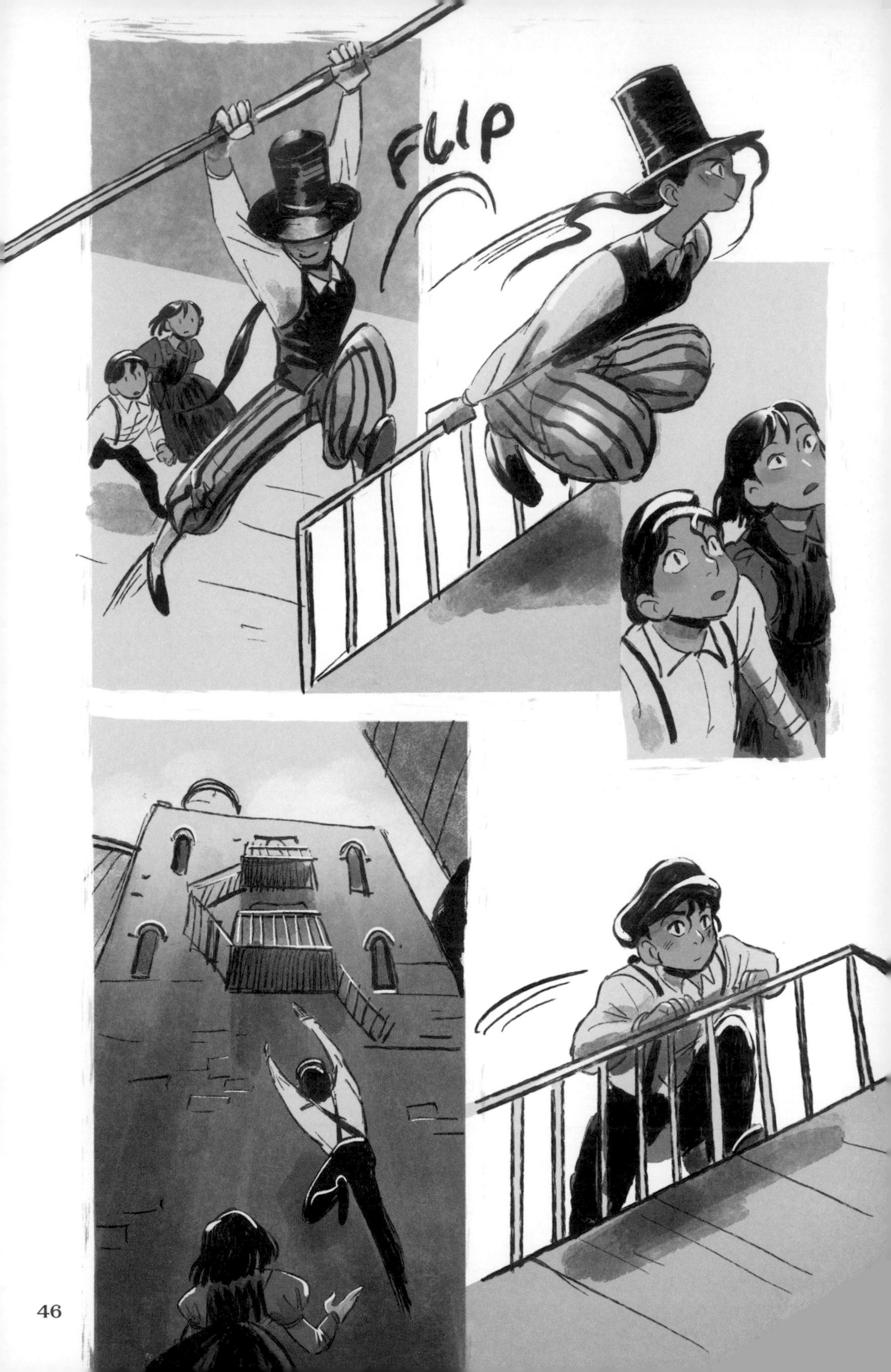
FLIP

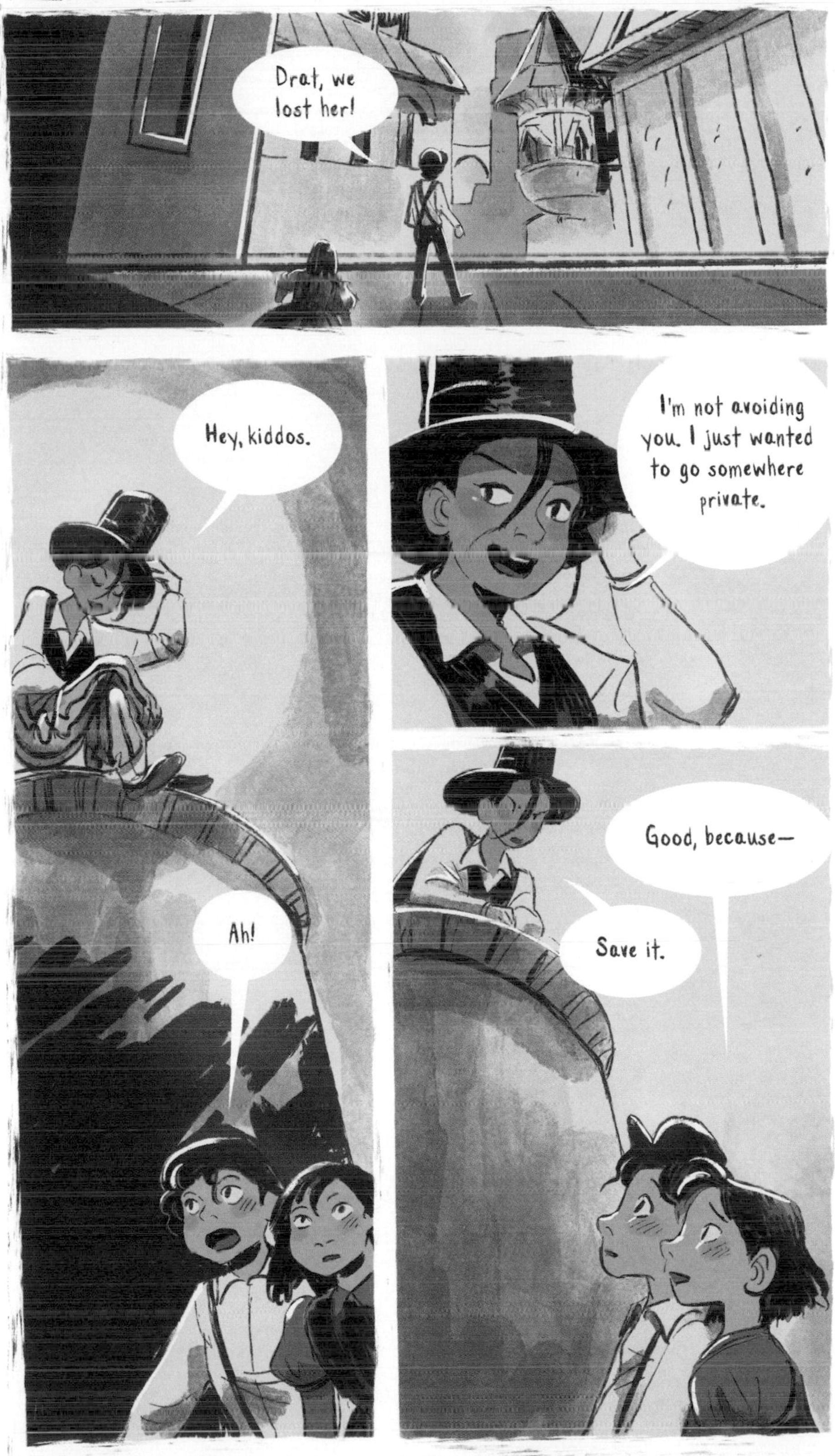
Drat, we lost her!
Hey, kiddos.
Ah!
I'm not avoiding you. I just wanted to go somewhere private.
Good, because—
Save it.

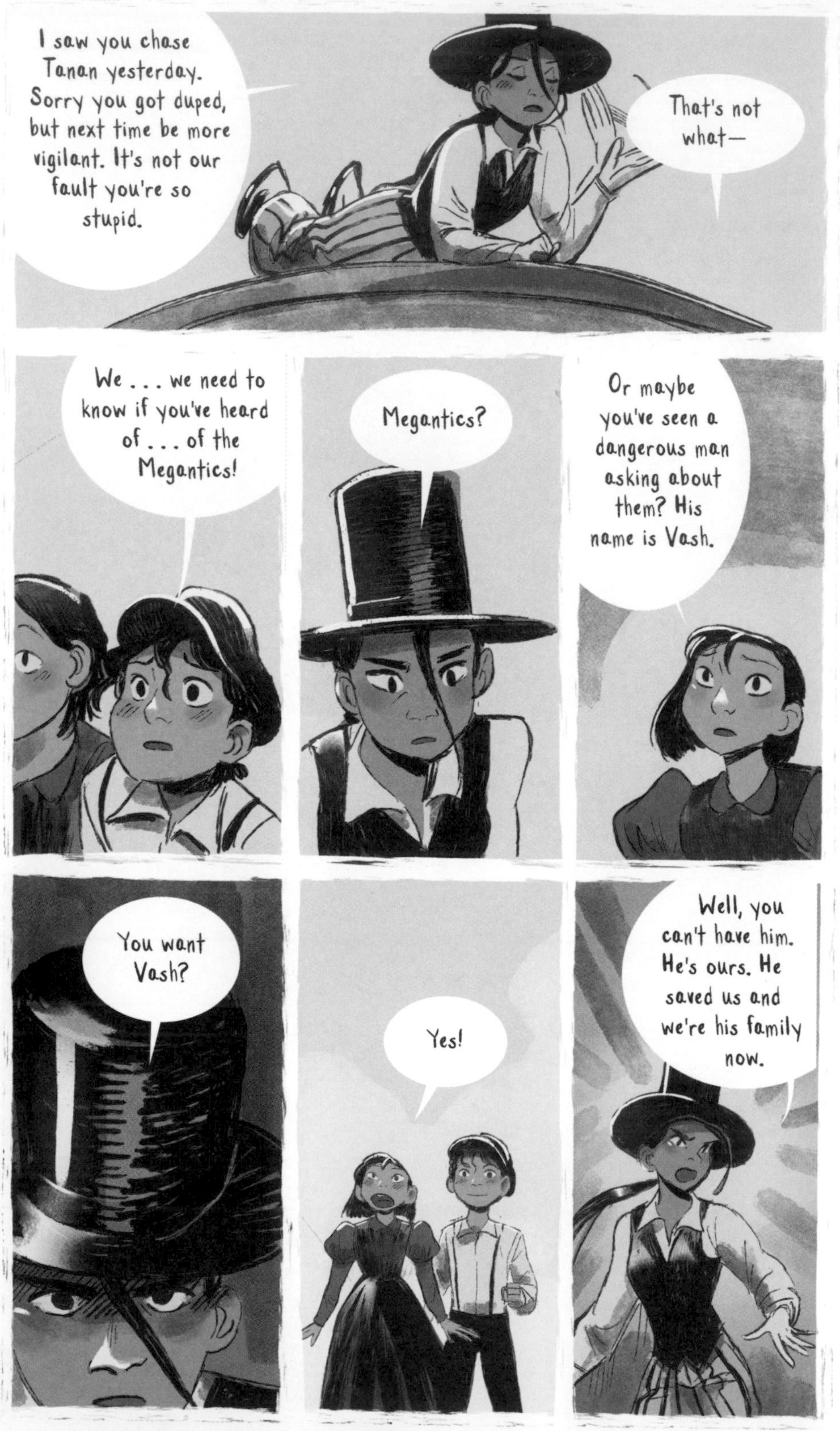
I saw you chase Tanan yesterday. Sorry you got duped, but next time be more vigilant. It's not our fault you're so stupid.
That's not what—
We . . . we need to know if you've heard of . . . of the Megantics!
Megantics?
Or maybe you've seen a dangerous man asking about them? His name is Vash.
You want Vash?
Yes!
Well, you can't have him. He's ours. He saved us and we're his family now.

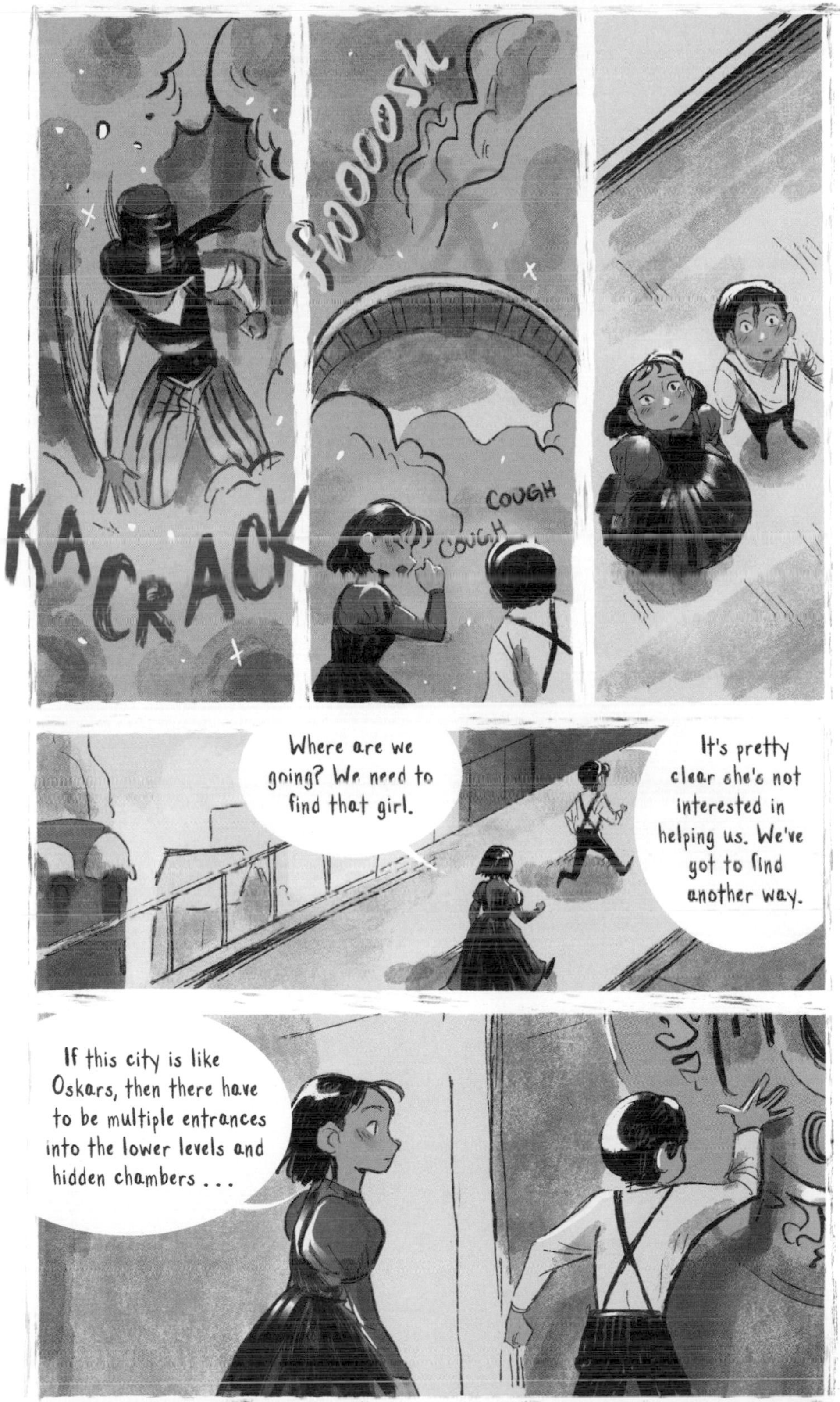
KA CRACK
FWOOOSH
COUGH
COUGH
Where are we going? We need to find that girl.
It's pretty clear she's not interested in helping us. We've got to find another way.
If this city is like Oskars, then there have to be multiple entrances into the lower levels and hidden chambers . . .

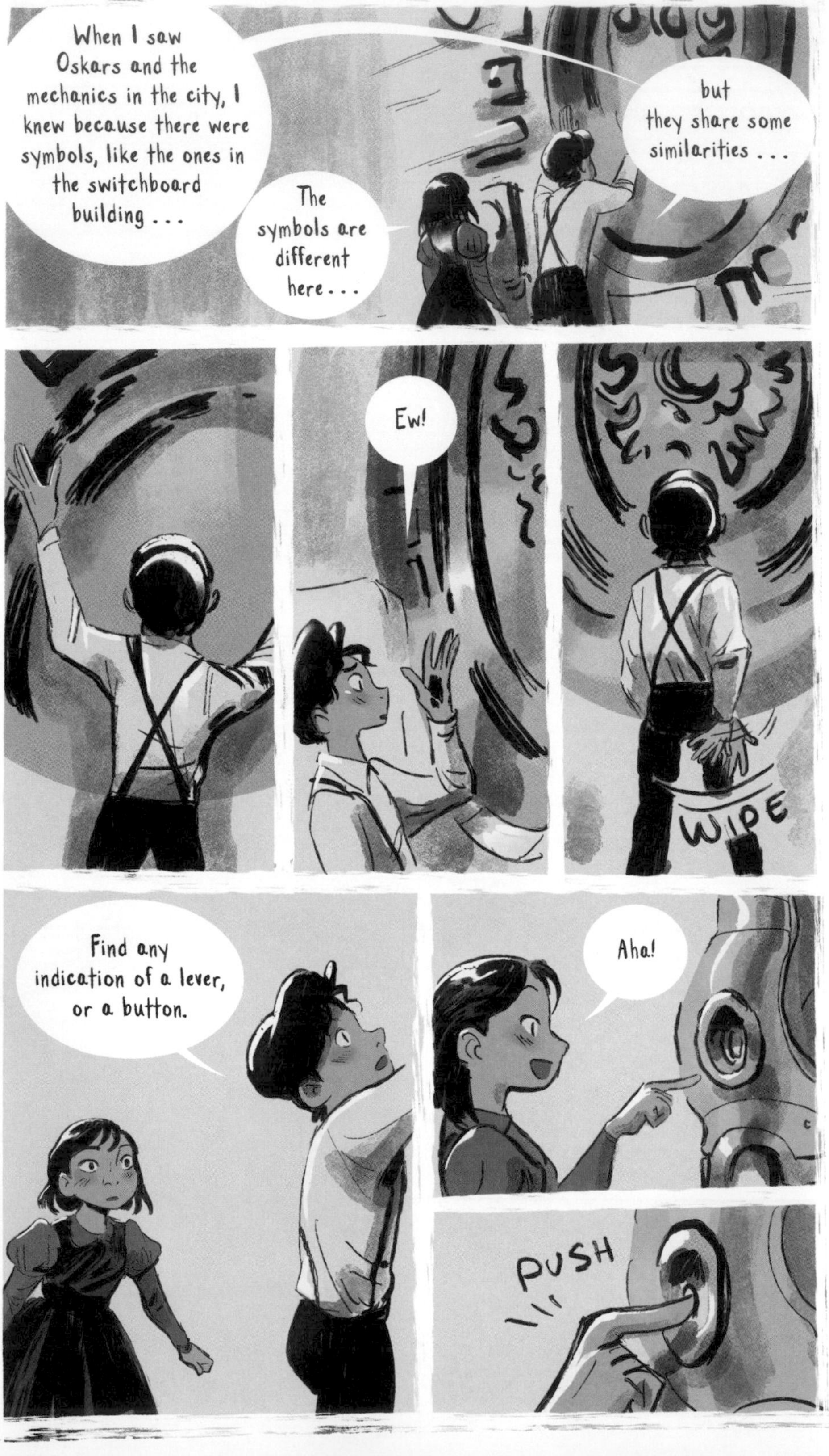
When I saw Oskars and the mechanics in the city, I knew because there were symbols, like the ones in the switchboard building . . .
The symbols are different here . . .
but they share some similarities . . .
Ew!
WIPE
Find any indication of a lever, or a button.
Aha!
PUSH

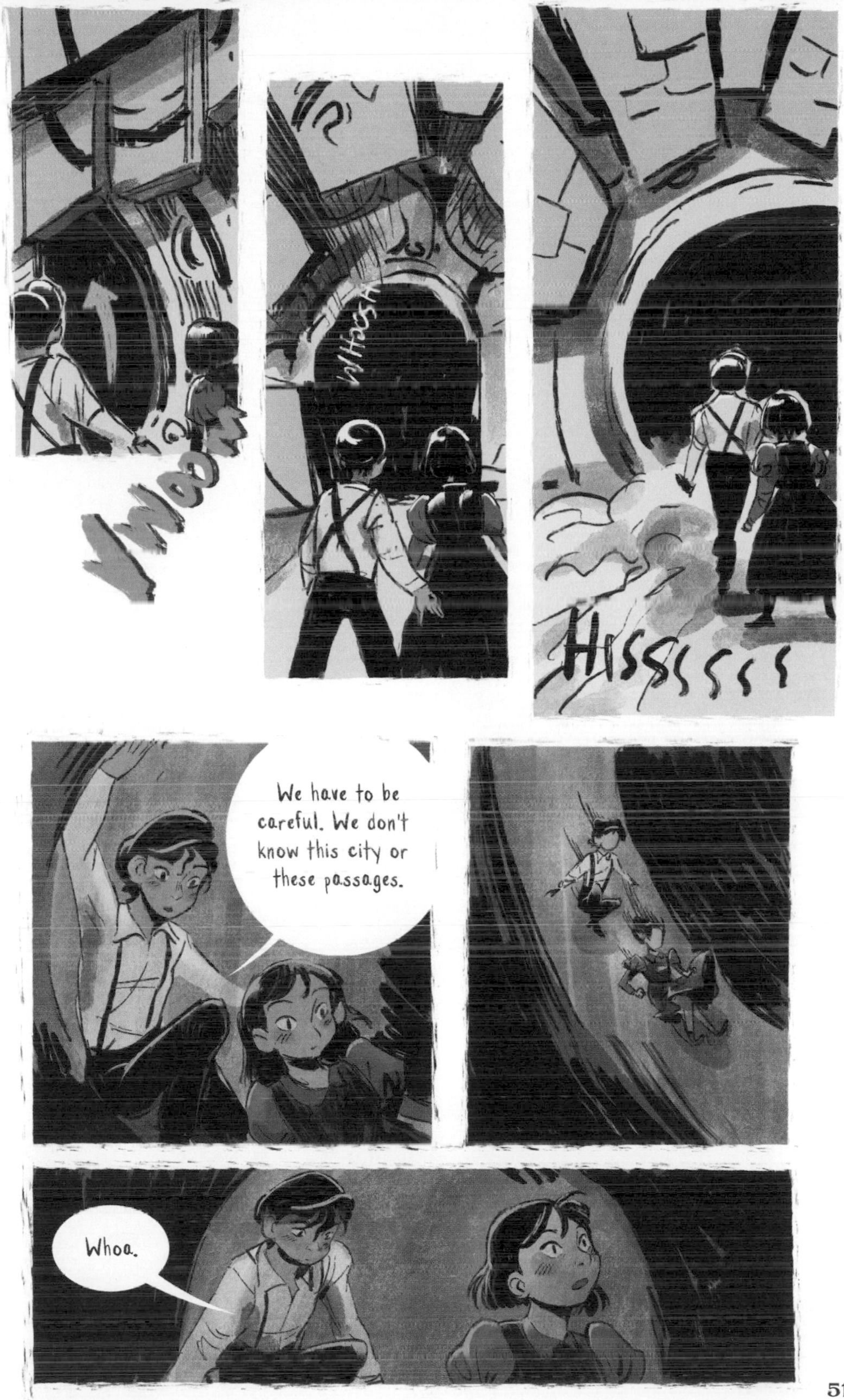
WHOOM
WHOOSH
HISSSSSS
We have to be careful. We don't know this city or these passages.
Whoa.

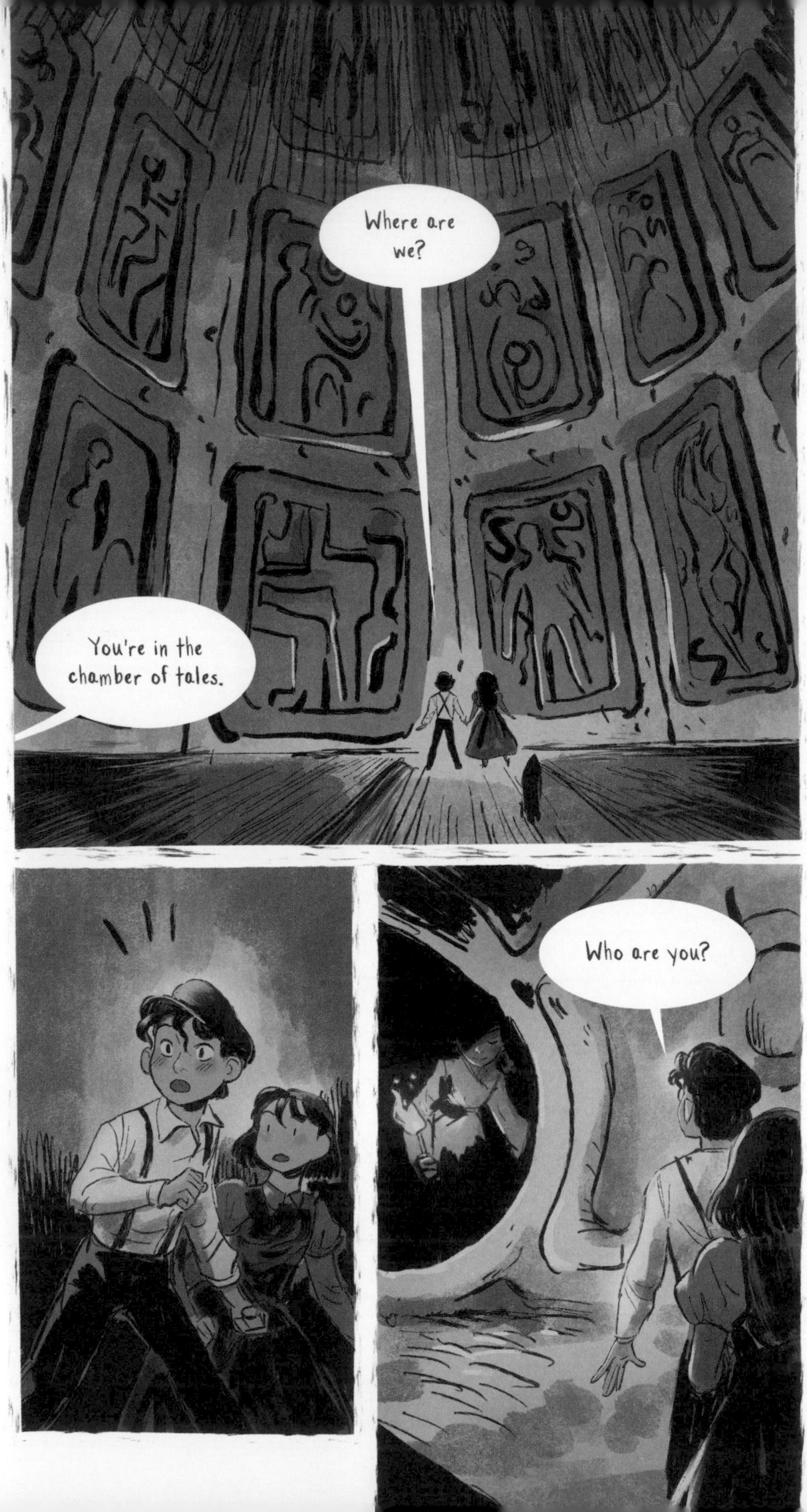
Where are we?
You're in the chamber of tales.
Who are you?

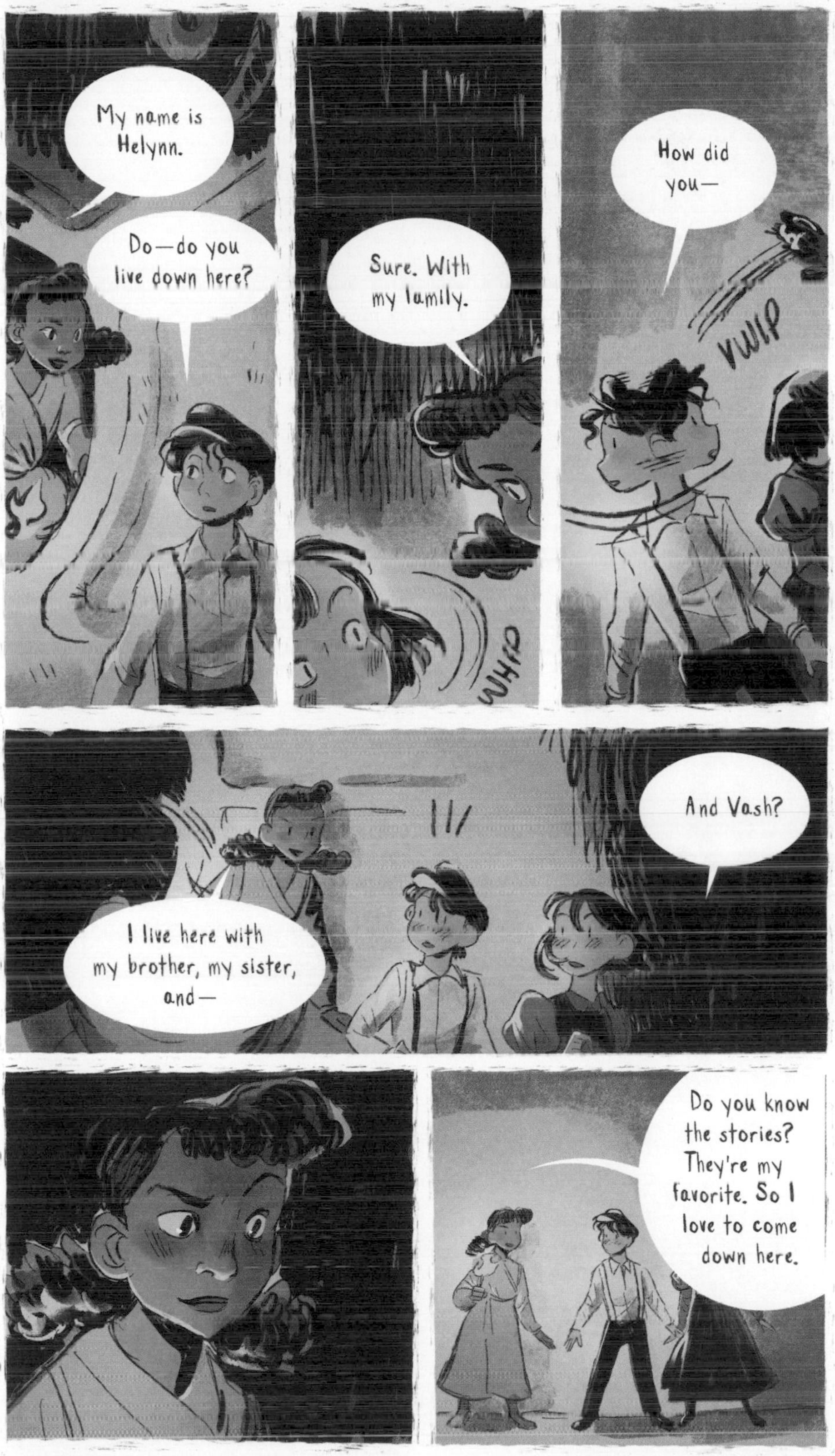
My name is Helynn.
Do—do you live down here?
Sure. With my family.
WHIP
How did you—
VWIP
And Vash?
I live here with my brother, my sister, and—
Do you know the stories? They're my favorite. So I love to come down here.

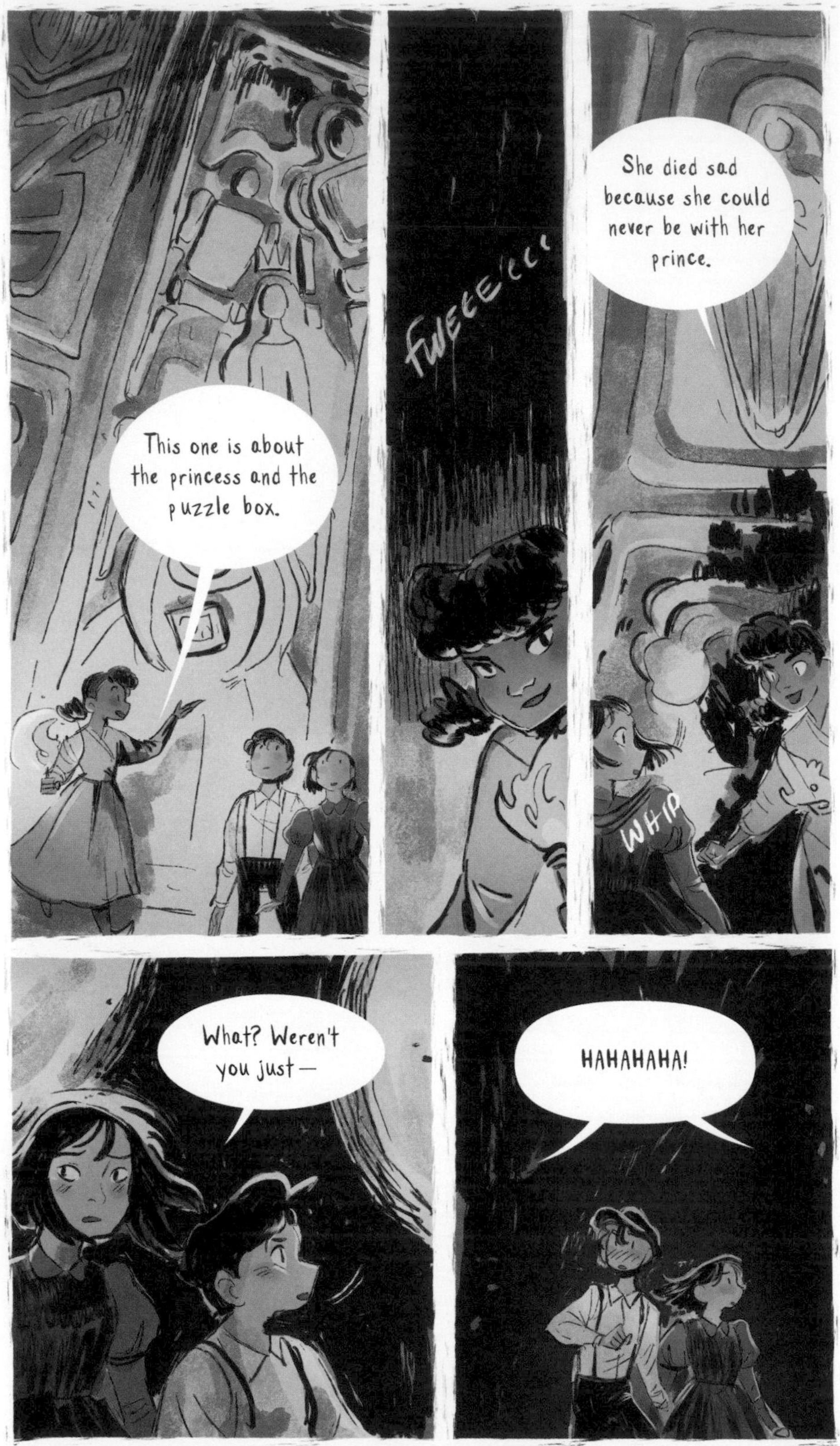
This one is about the princess and the puzzle box.
FWEEE'''
She died sad because she could never be with her prince.
WHIP
What? Weren't you just—
HAHAHAHA!

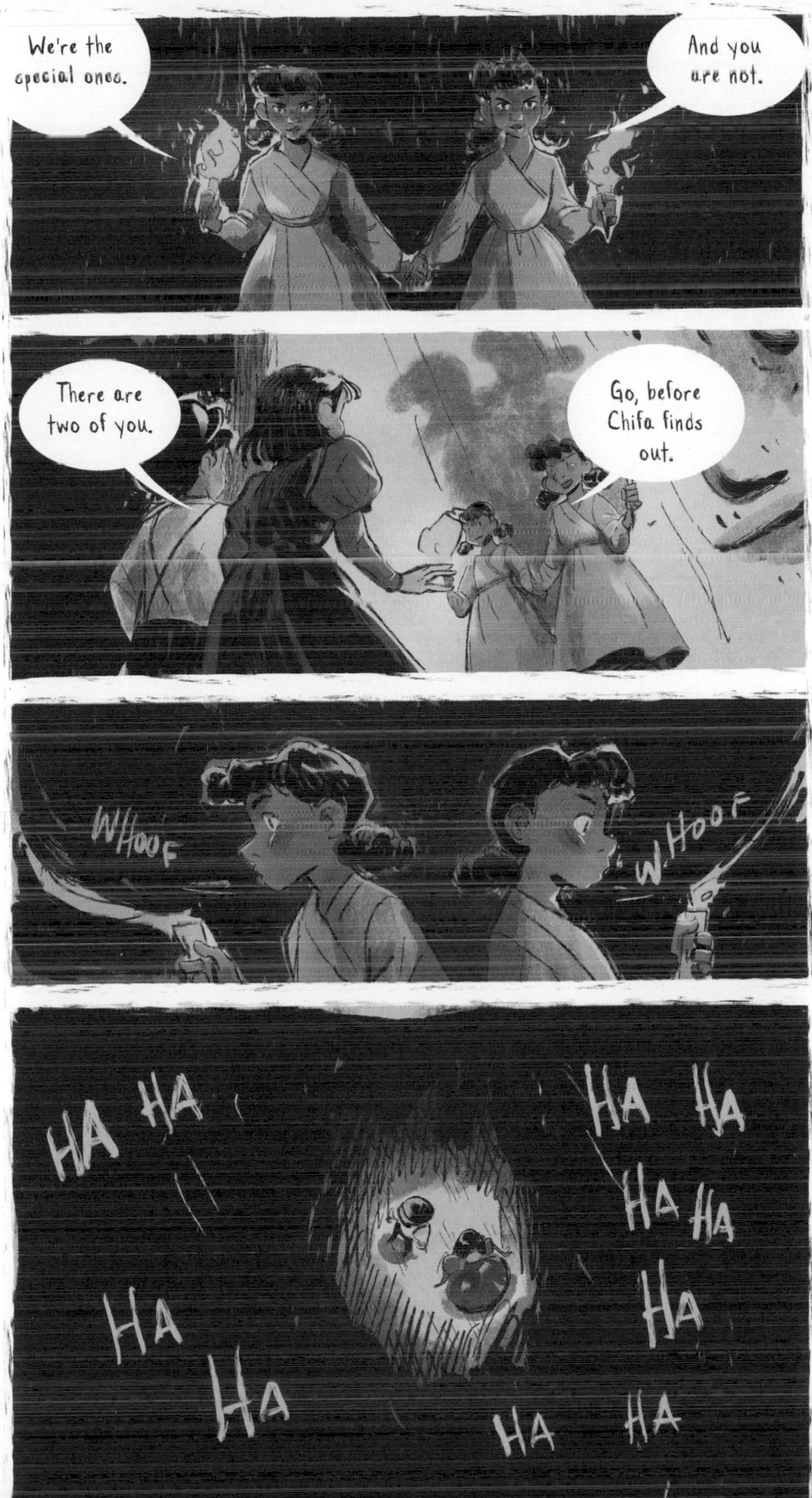
We're the special ones.
And you are not.
There are two of you.
Go, before Chifa finds out.
WHOOF
WHOOF
HA HA
HA HA
HA HA
HA
HA
HA
HA
HA HA

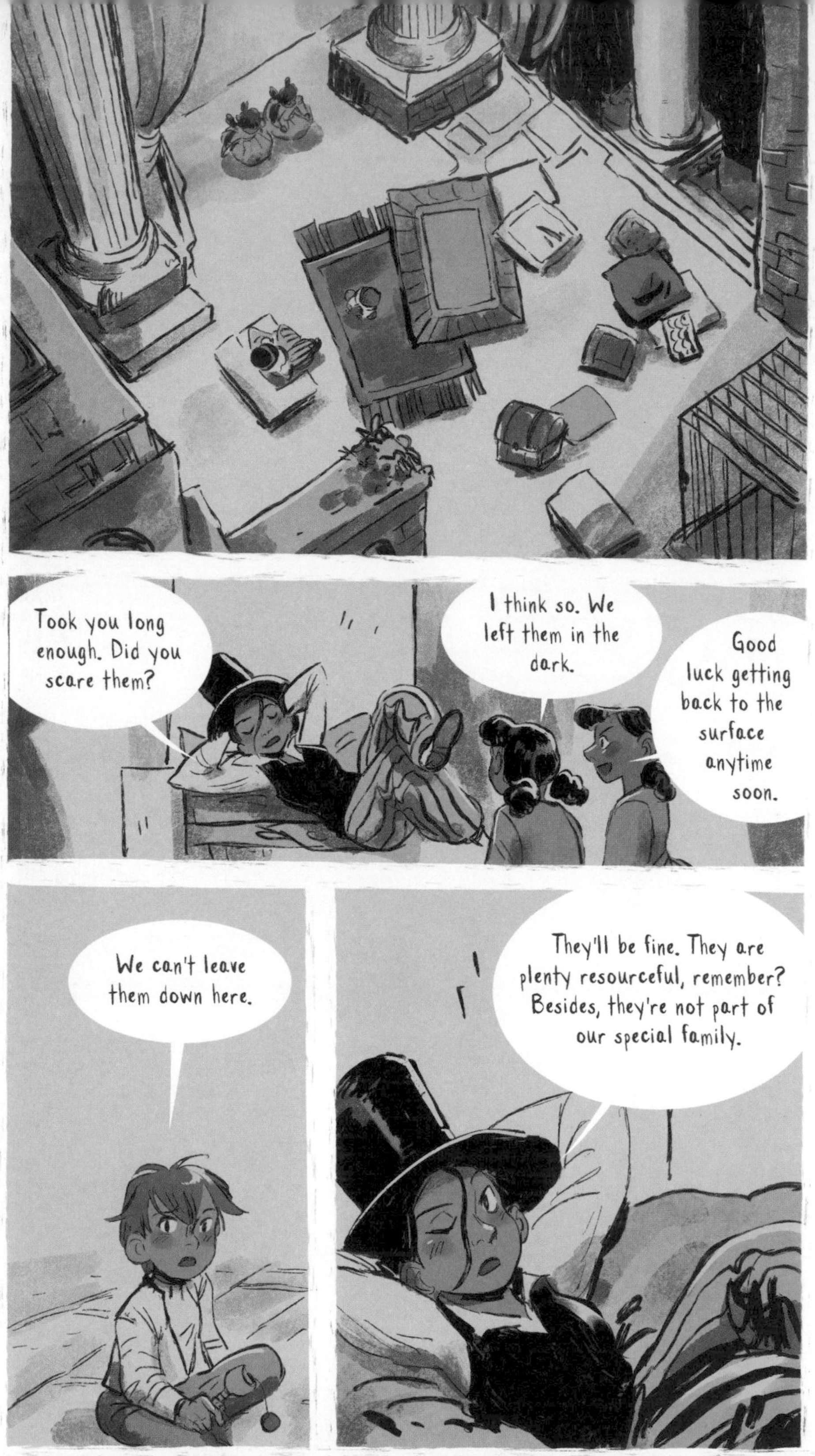

Took you long enough. Did you scare them?
I think so. We left them in the dark.
Good luck getting back to the surface anytime soon.
We can't leave them down here.
They'll be fine. They are plenty resourceful, remember? Besides, they're not part of our special family.

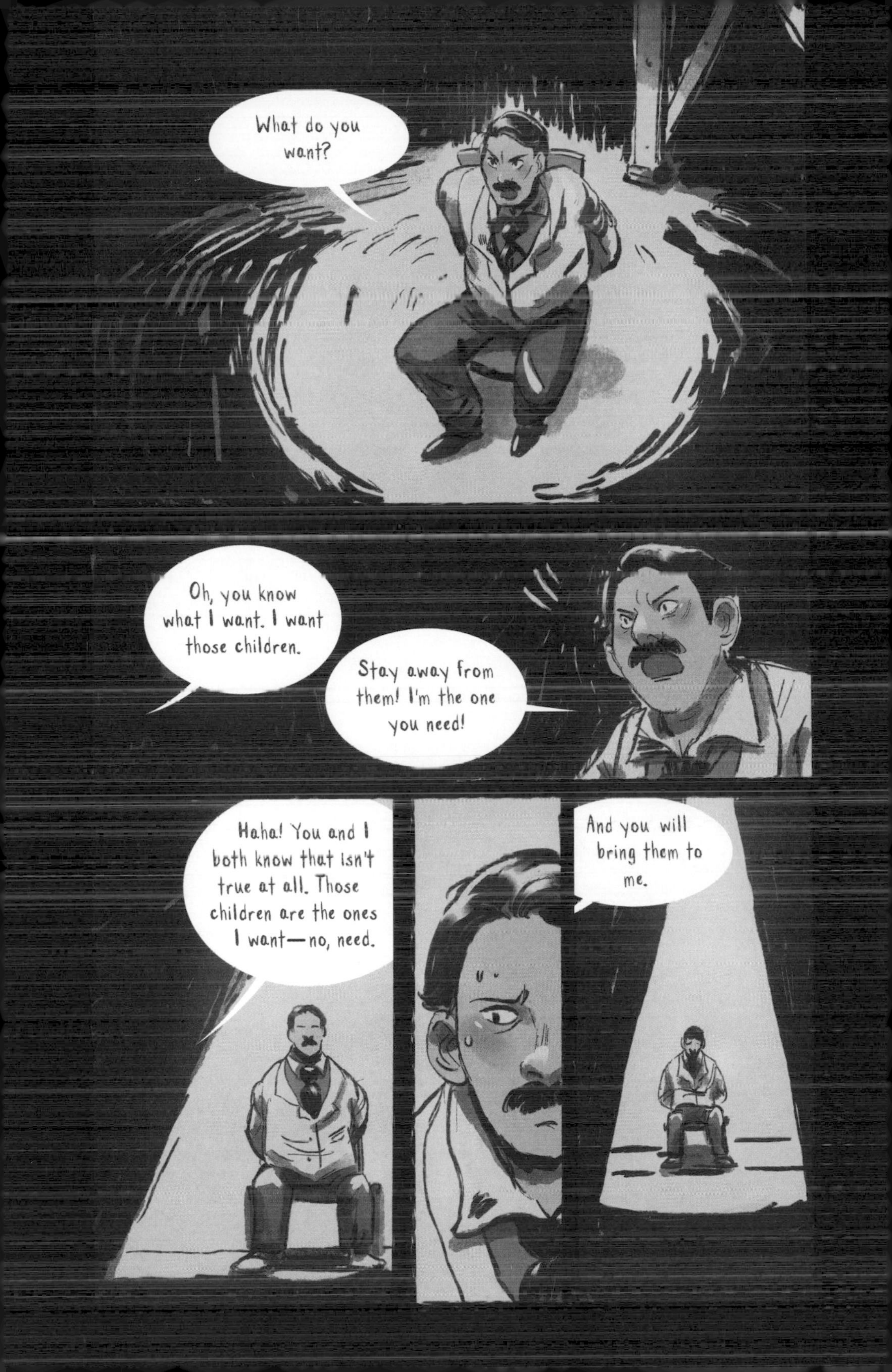
What do you want?
Oh, you know what I want. I want those children.
Stay away from them! I'm the one you need!
Haha! You and I both know that isn't true at all. Those children are the ones I want—no, need.
And you will bring them to me.

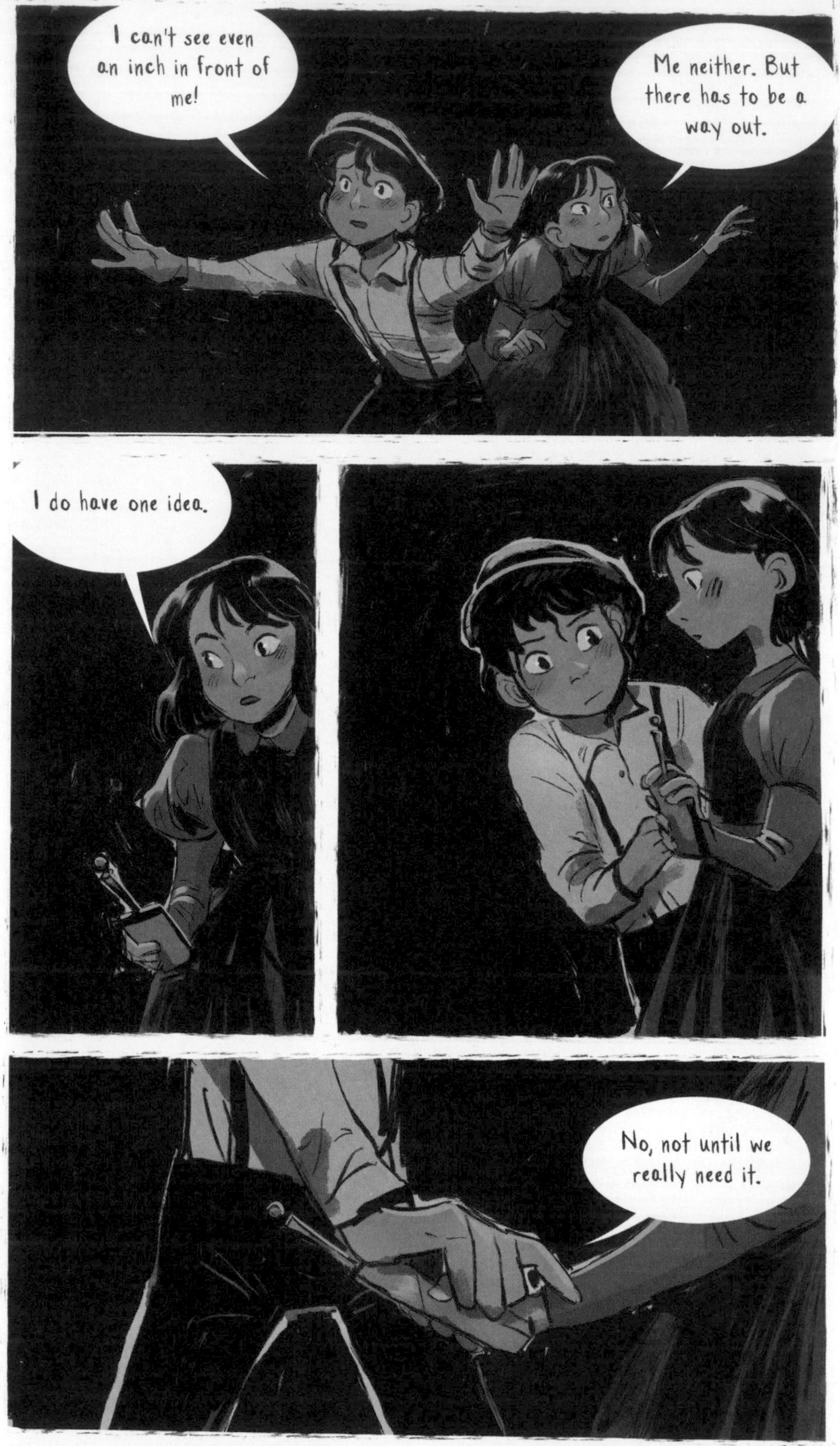
I can't see even an inch in front of me!
Me neither. But there has to be a way out.
I do have one idea.
No, not until we really need it.

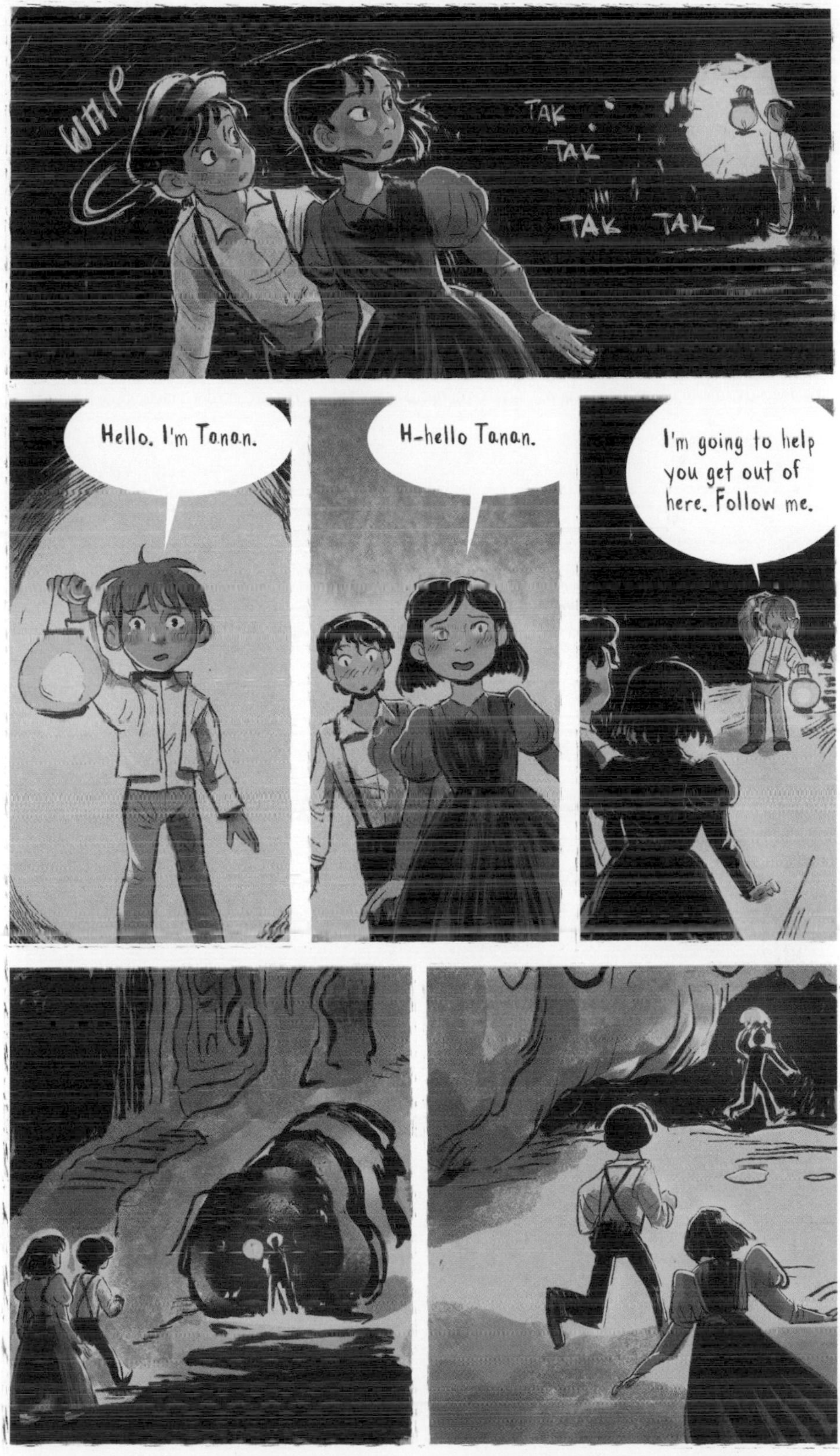
WHIP
TAK
TAK
TAK
TAK
Hello. I'm Tanan.
H-hello Tanan.
I'm going to help you get out of here. Follow me.

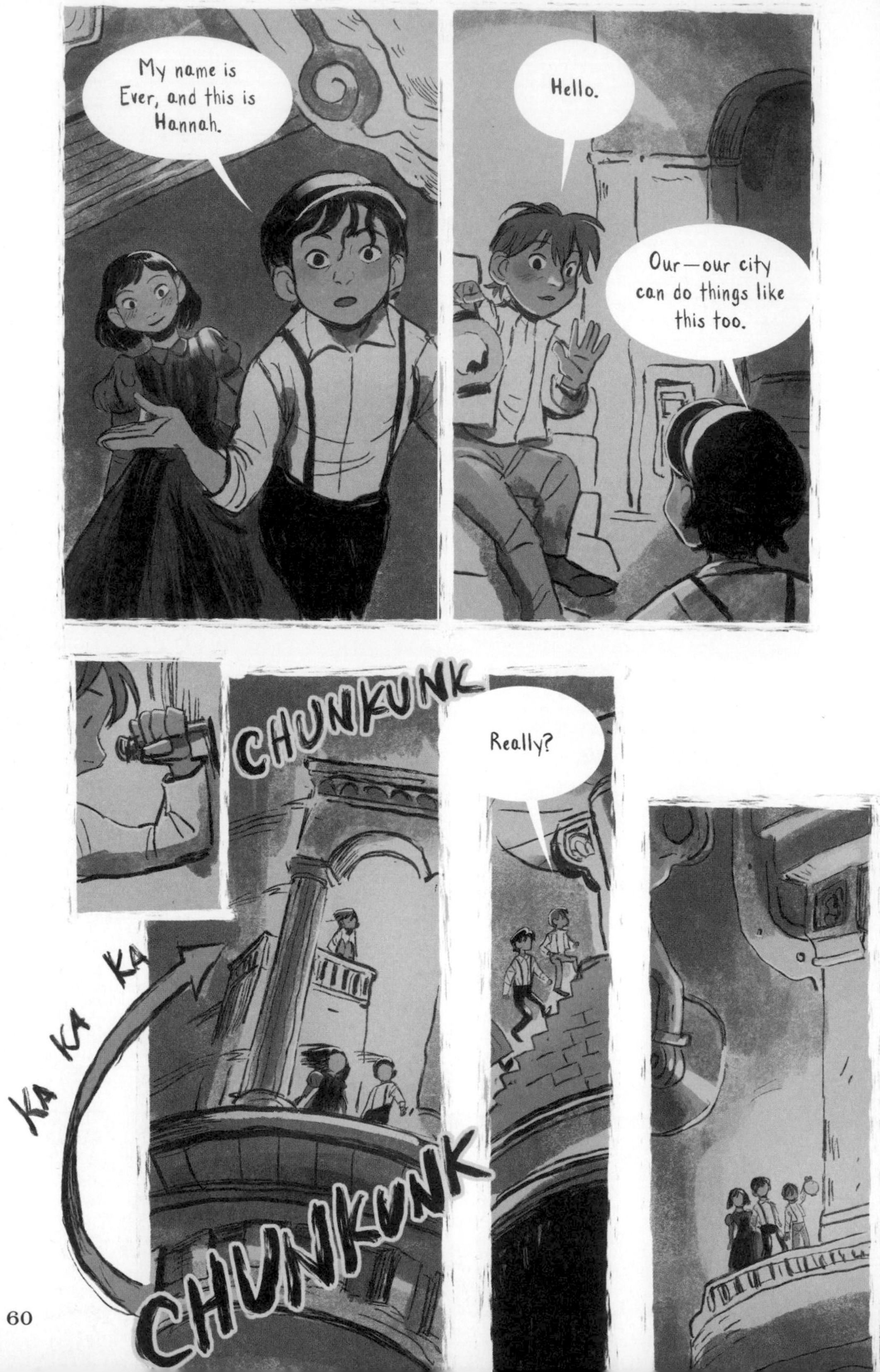
My name is Ever, and this is Hannah.
Hello.
Our—our city can do things like this too.
CHUNKUNK
Really?
KA KA KA
CHUNKUNK

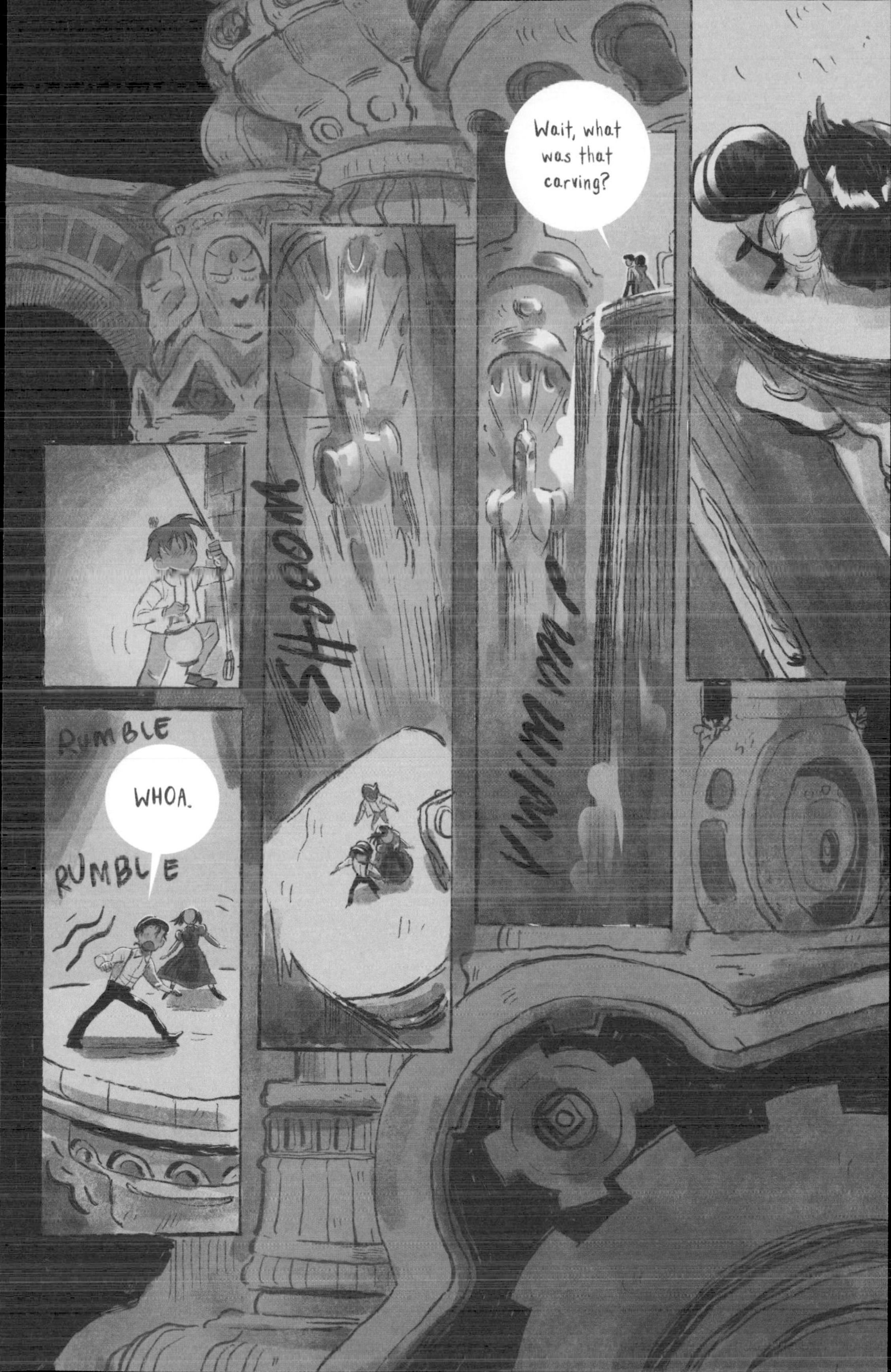
RUMBLE
WHOA.
RUMBLE
SHOOOM
Wait, what was that carving?

KA CHUNK

SHOOOP!

Don't come back, okay? Chifa won't like it.

Wait.

I'm sorry. I can't stay and talk.

No, let him go.

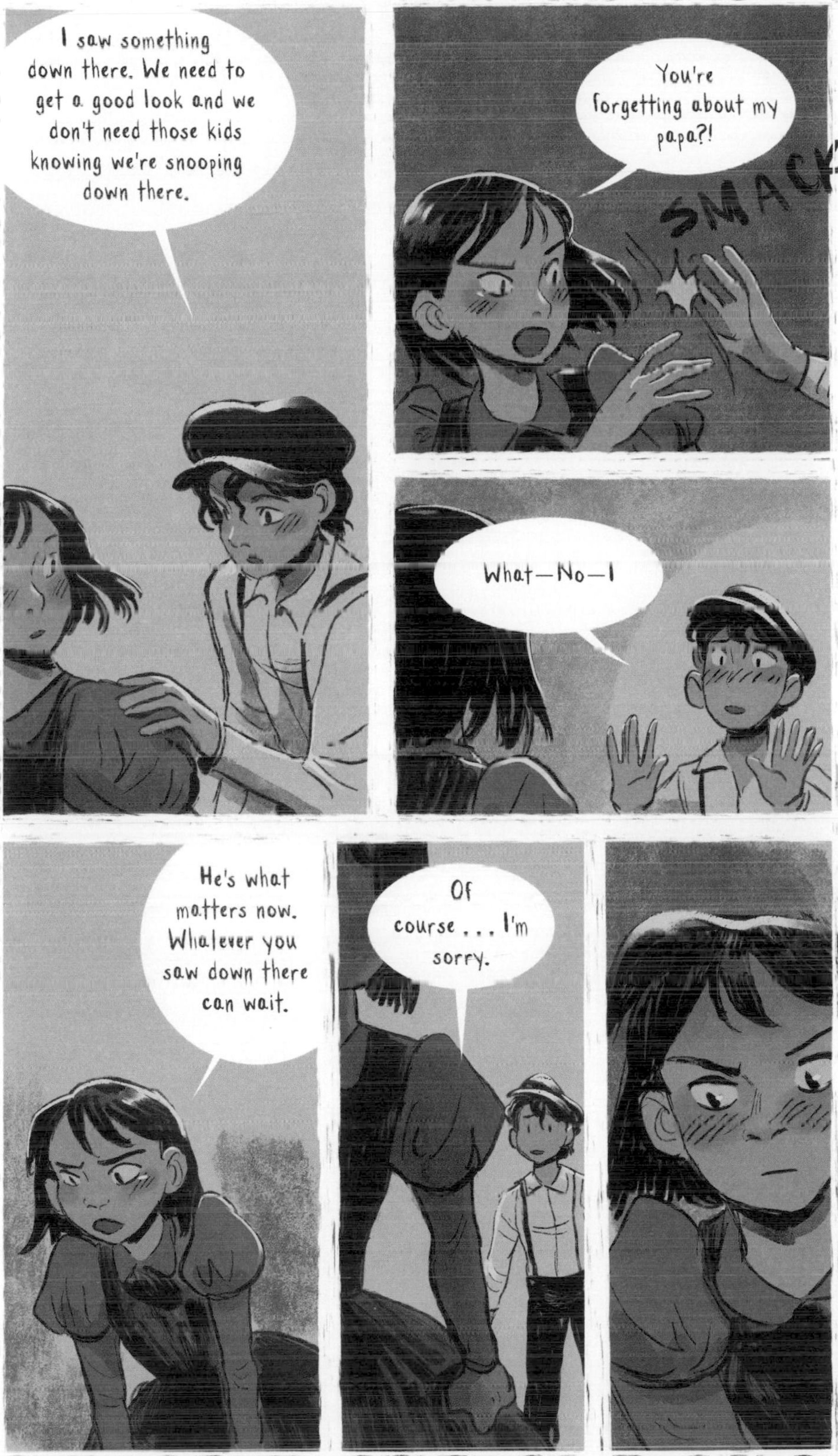
I saw something down there. We need to get a good look and we don't need those kids knowing we're snooping down there.
You're forgetting about my papa?!
SMACK
What—No—I
He's what matters now. Whatever you saw down there can wait.
Of course . . . I'm sorry.

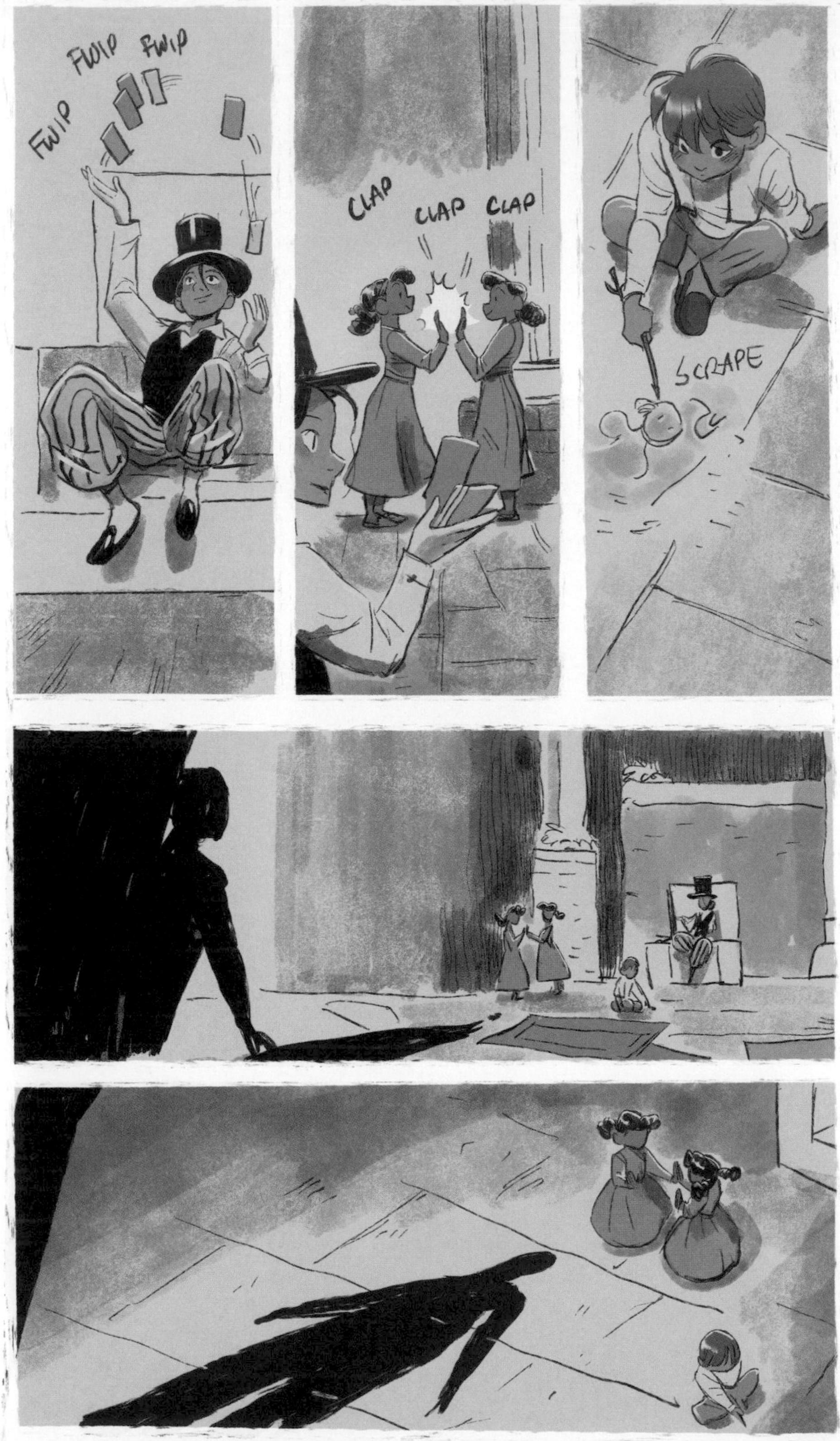

FWIP
FWIP
FWIP
CLAP
CLAP
CLAP
SCRAPE

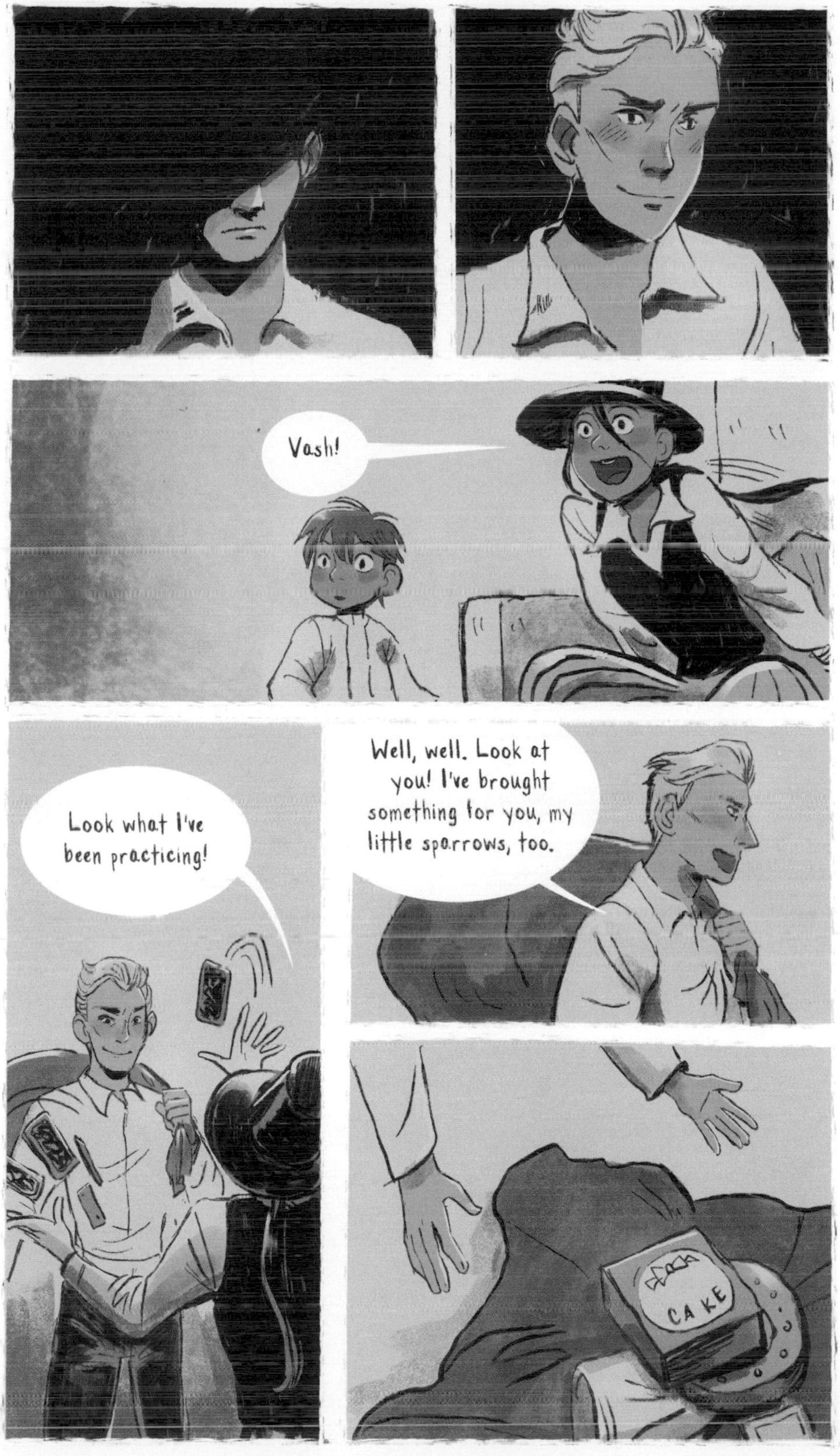
Vash!
Look what I've been practicing!
Well, well. Look at you! I've brought something for you, my little sparrows, too.
CAKE

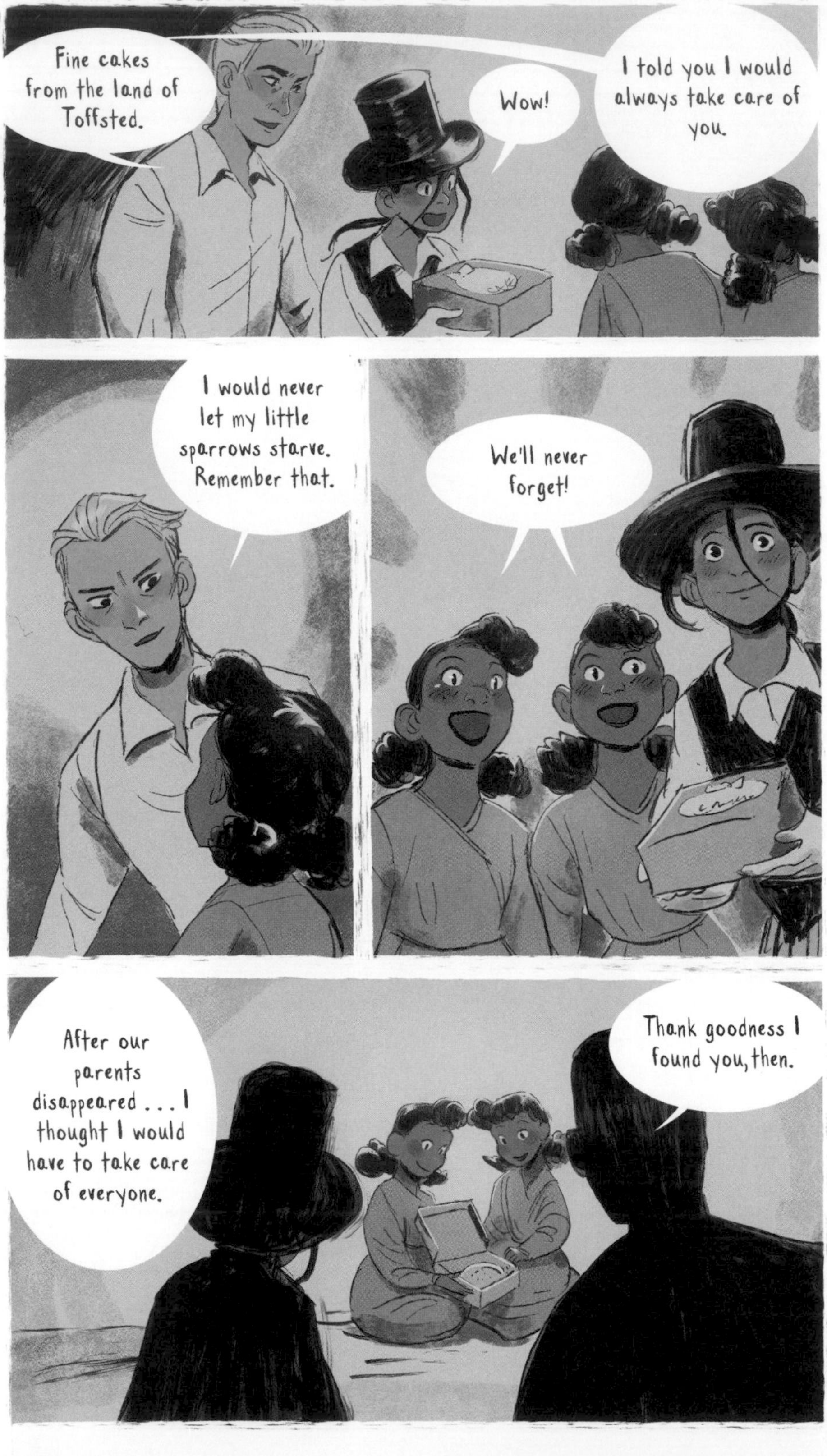
Fine cakes from the land of Toffsted.
Wow!
I told you I would always take care of you.
I would never let my little sparrows starve. Remember that.
We'll never forget!
After our parents disappeared . . . I thought I would have to take care of everyone.
Thank goodness I found you, then.

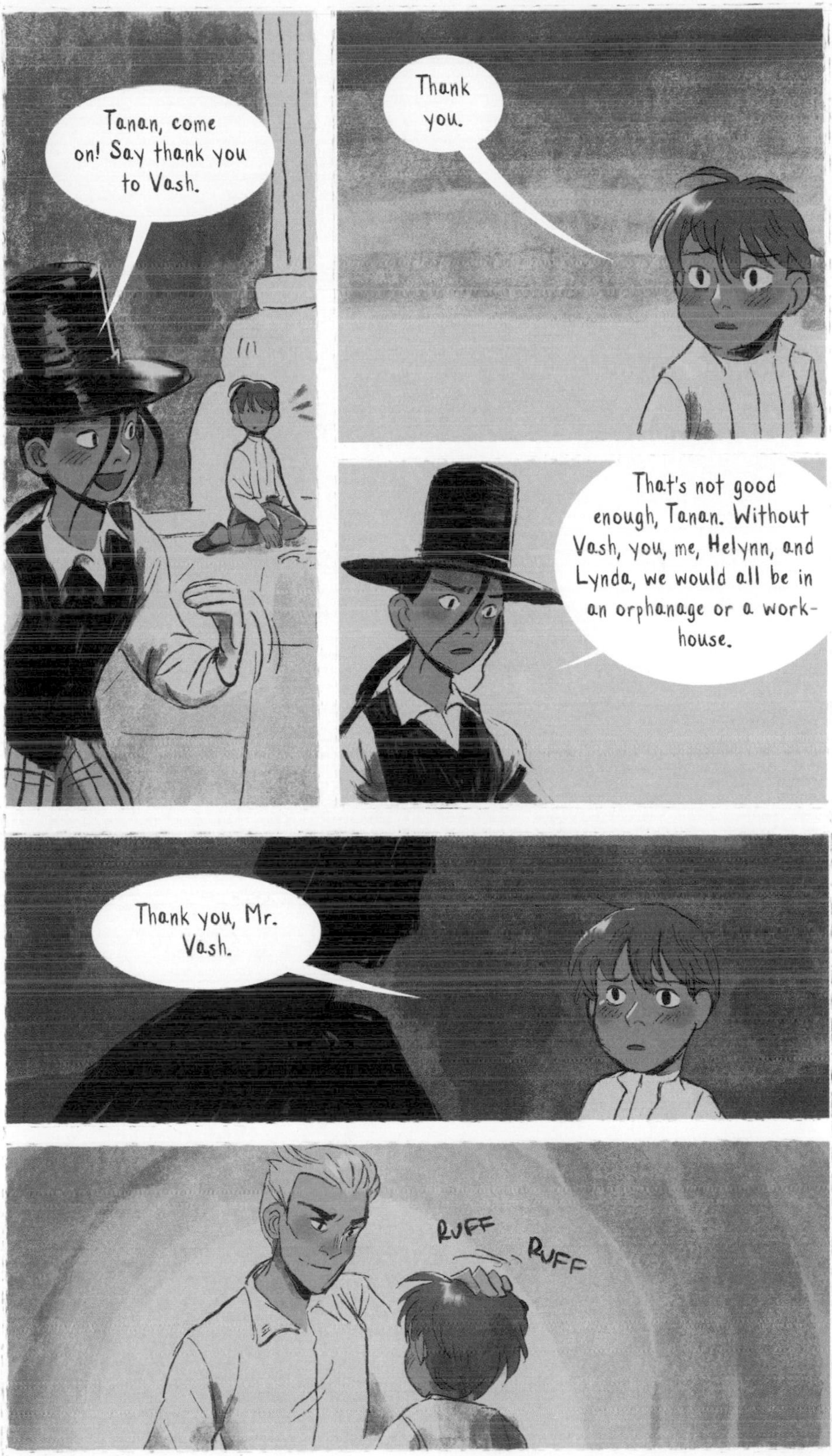
Tanan, come on! Say thank you to Vash.
Thank you.
That's not good enough, Tanan. Without Vash, you, me, Helynn, and Lynda, we would all be in an orphanage or a work-house.
Thank you, Mr. Vash.
RUFF
RUFF

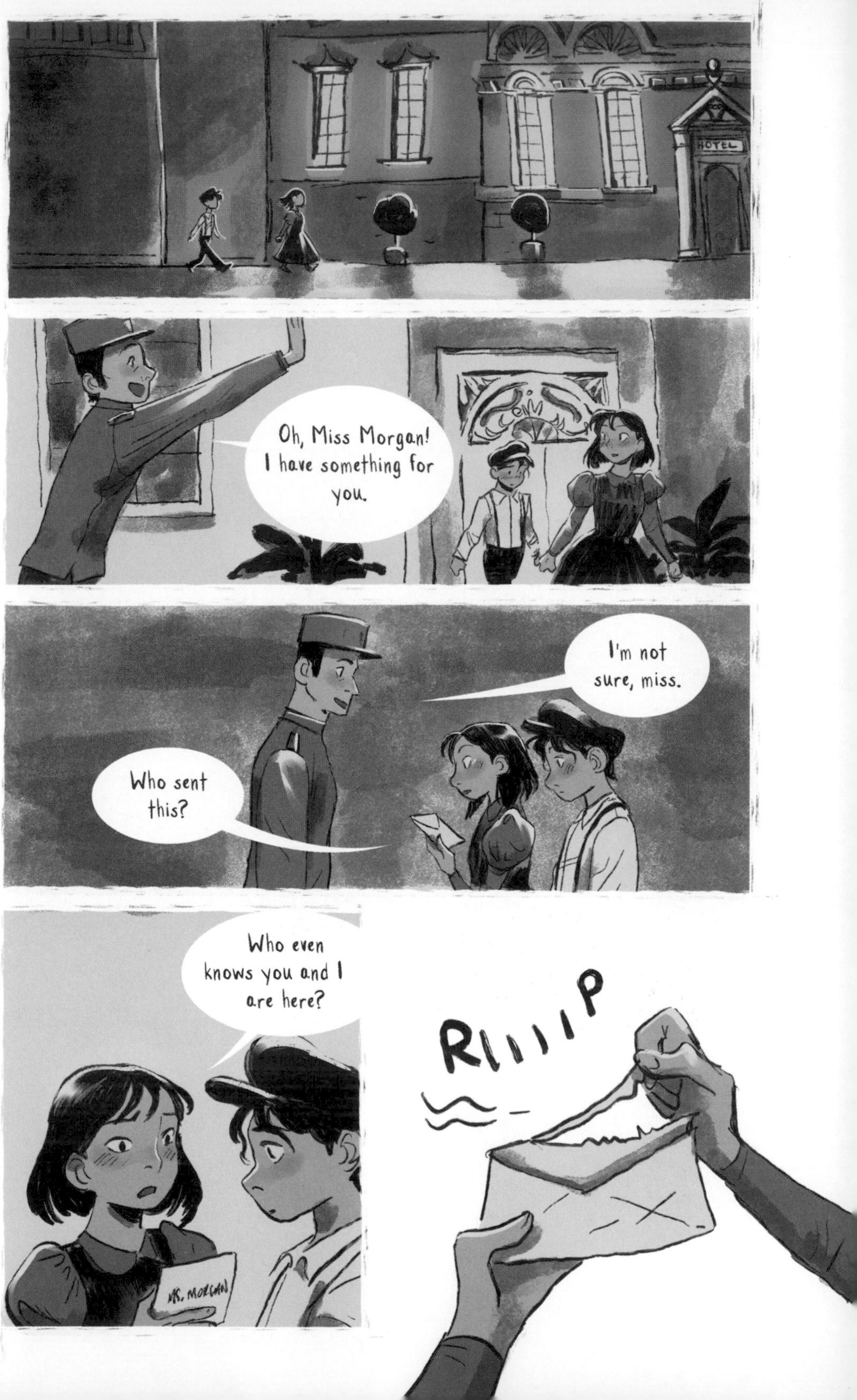
HOTEL
Oh, Miss Morgan! I have something for you.
I'm not sure, miss.
Who sent this?
Who even knows you and I are here?
MS. MORGAN
RIIIIP

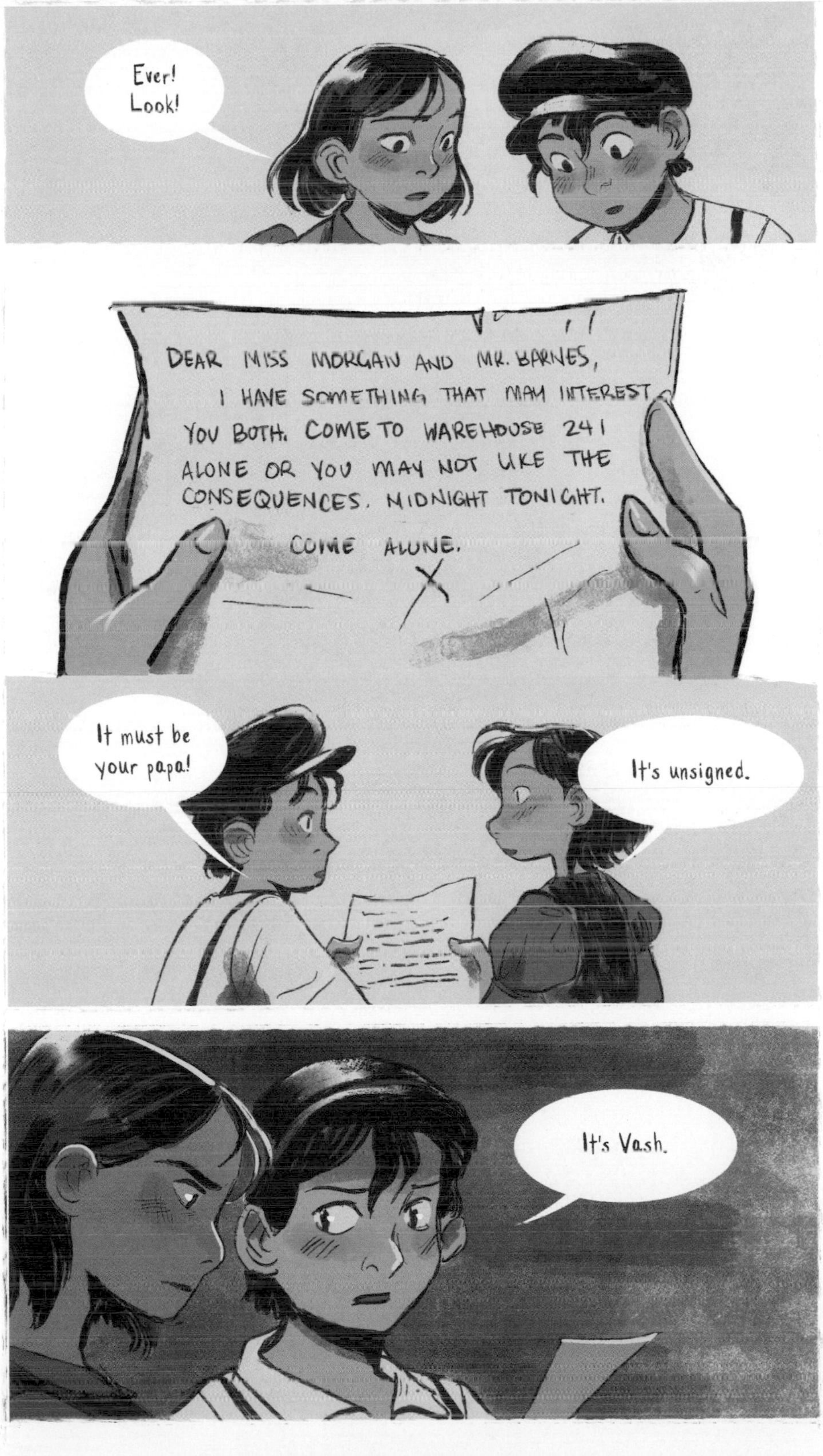
Ever! Look!
DEAR MISS MORGAN AND MR. BARNES,
I HAVE SOMETHING THAT MAY INTEREST YOU BOTH. COME TO WAREHOUSE 241 ALONE OR YOU MAY NOT LIKE THE CONSEQUENCES. MIDNIGHT TONIGHT.
COME ALONE.
X
It must be your papa!
It's unsigned.
It's Vash.

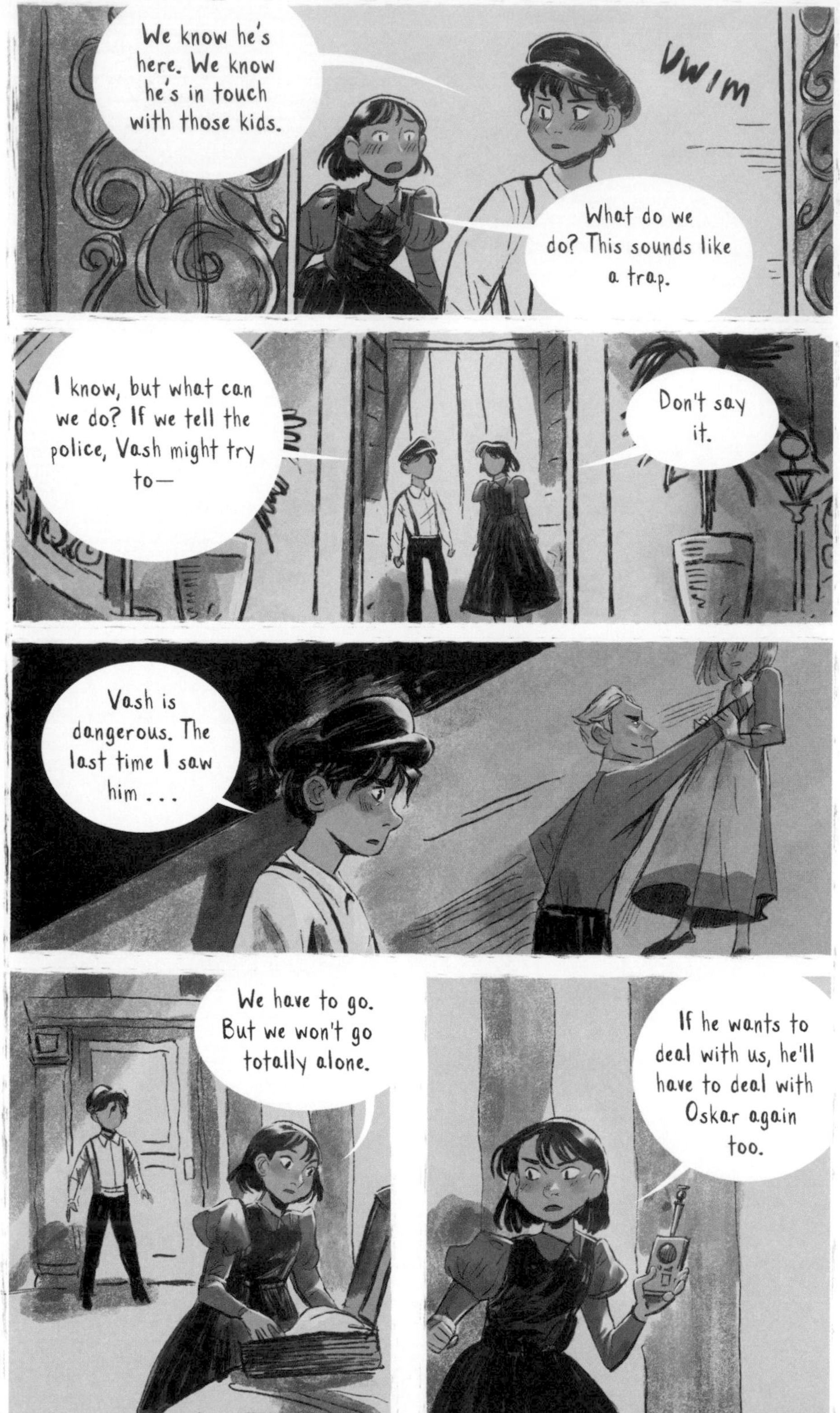
We know he's here. We know he's in touch with those kids.
UWIM
What do we do? This sounds like a trap.
I know, but what can we do? If we tell the police, Vash might try to—
Don't say it.
Vash is dangerous. The last time I saw him . . .
We have to go. But we won't go totally alone.
If he wants to deal with us, he'll have to deal with Oskar again too.

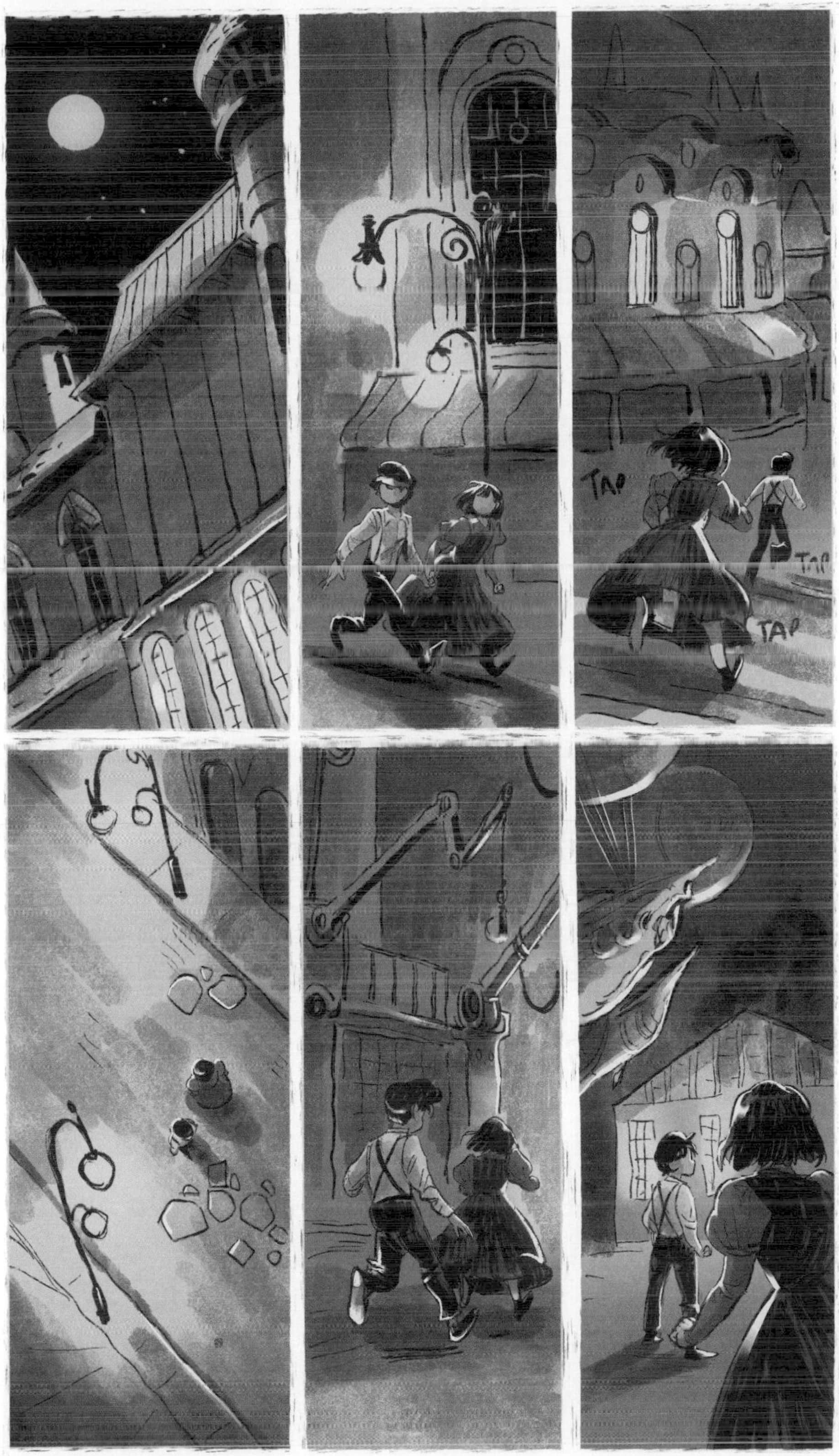
TAP
TAP
TAP

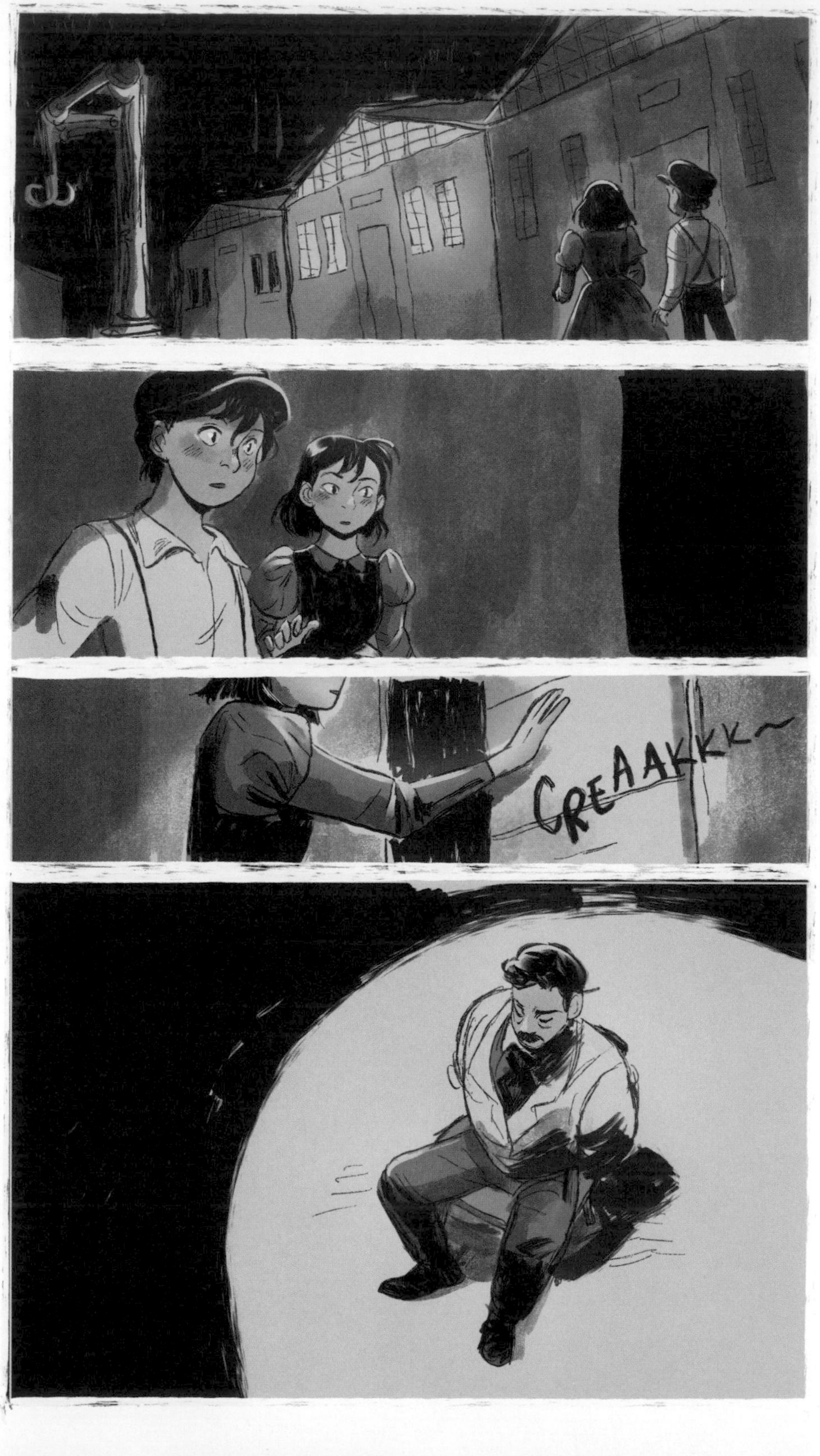
CREAAKKK~

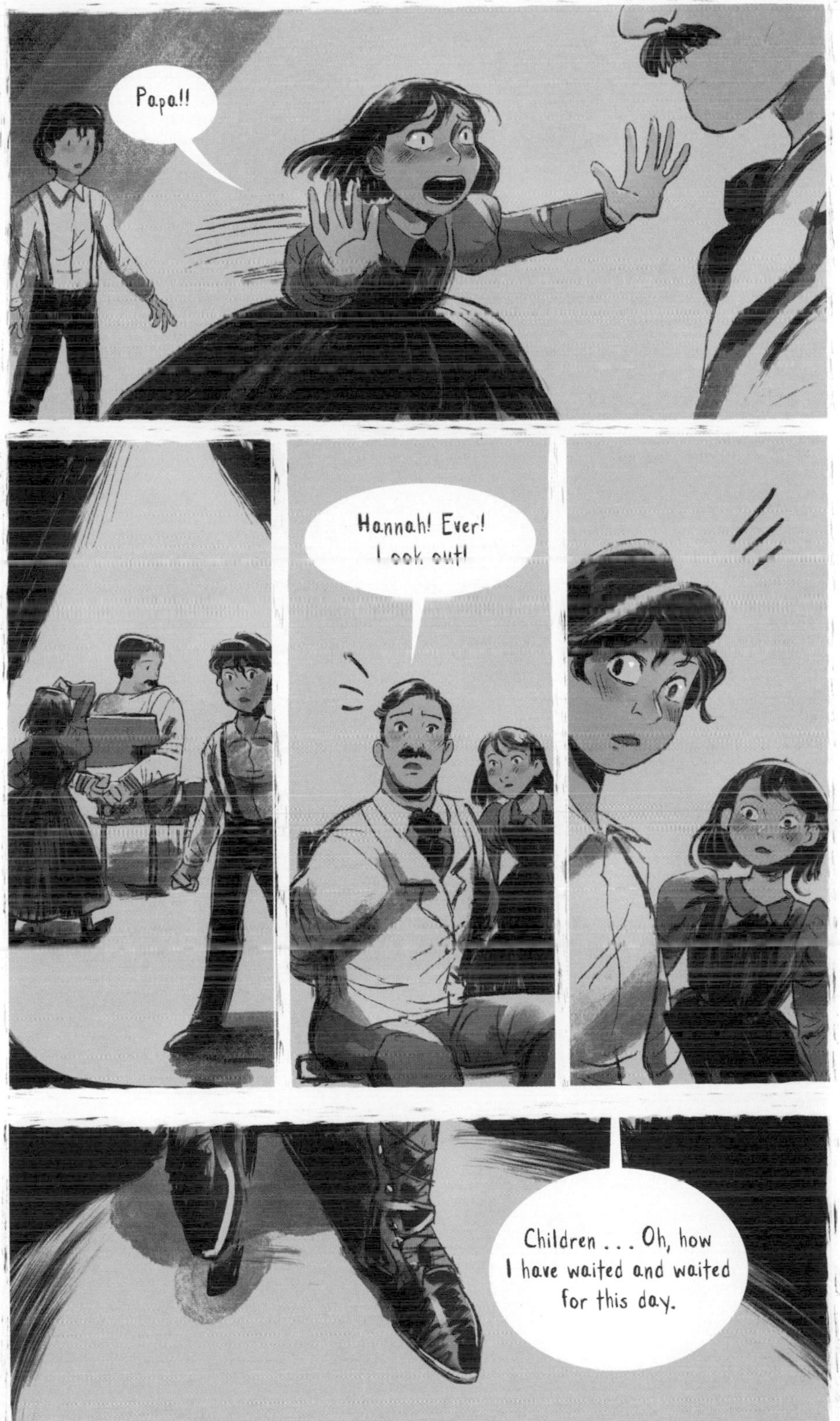
Papa!!
Hannah! Ever! Look out!
Children . . . Oh, how I have waited and waited for this day.

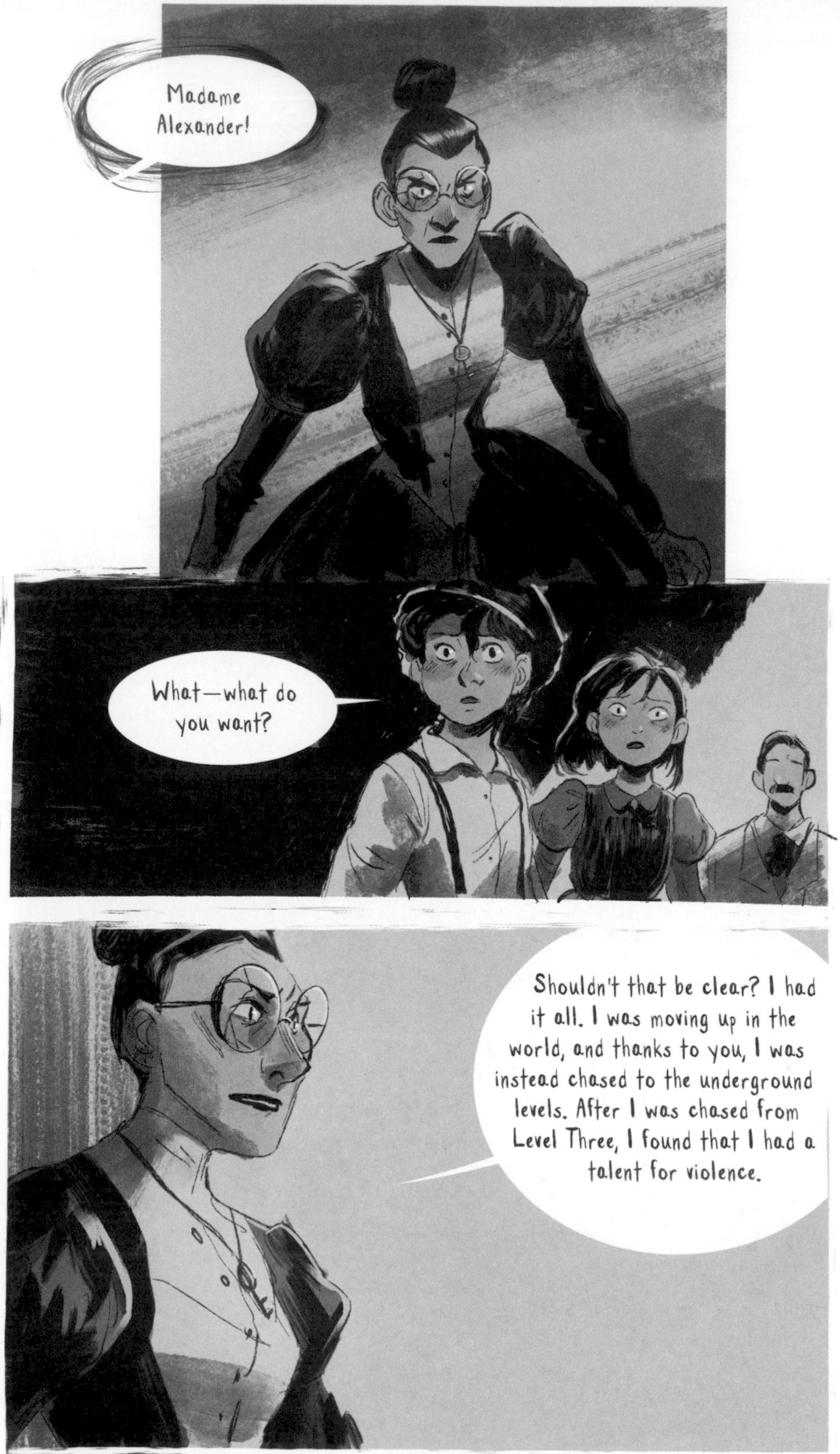
Madame Alexander!
What—what do you want?
Shouldn't that be clear? I had it all. I was moving up in the world, and thanks to you, I was instead chased to the underground levels. After I was chased from Level Three, I found that I had a talent for violence.

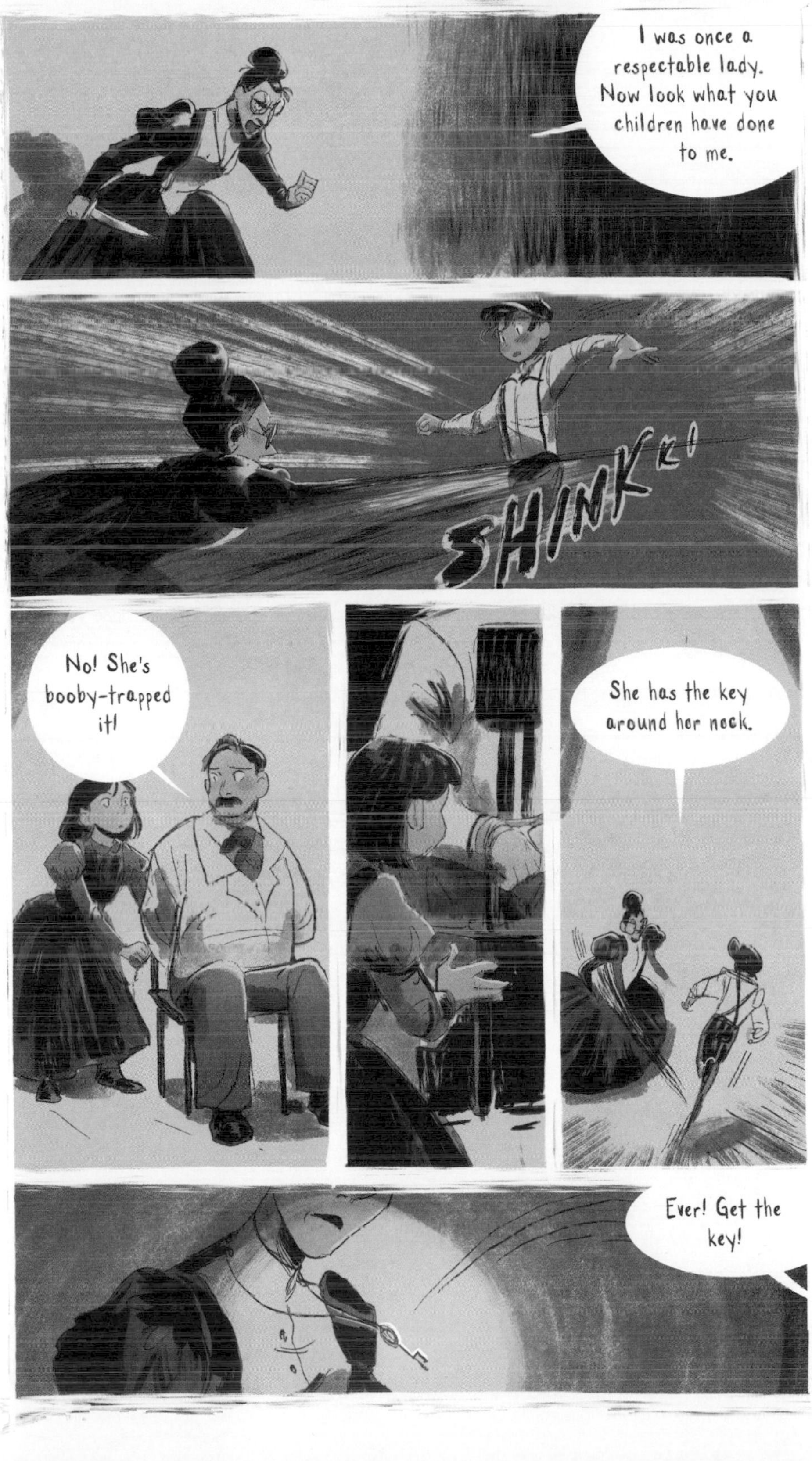
I was once a respectable lady. Now look what you children have done to me.
SHINKK!
No! She's booby-trapped it!
She has the key around her neck.
Ever! Get the key!

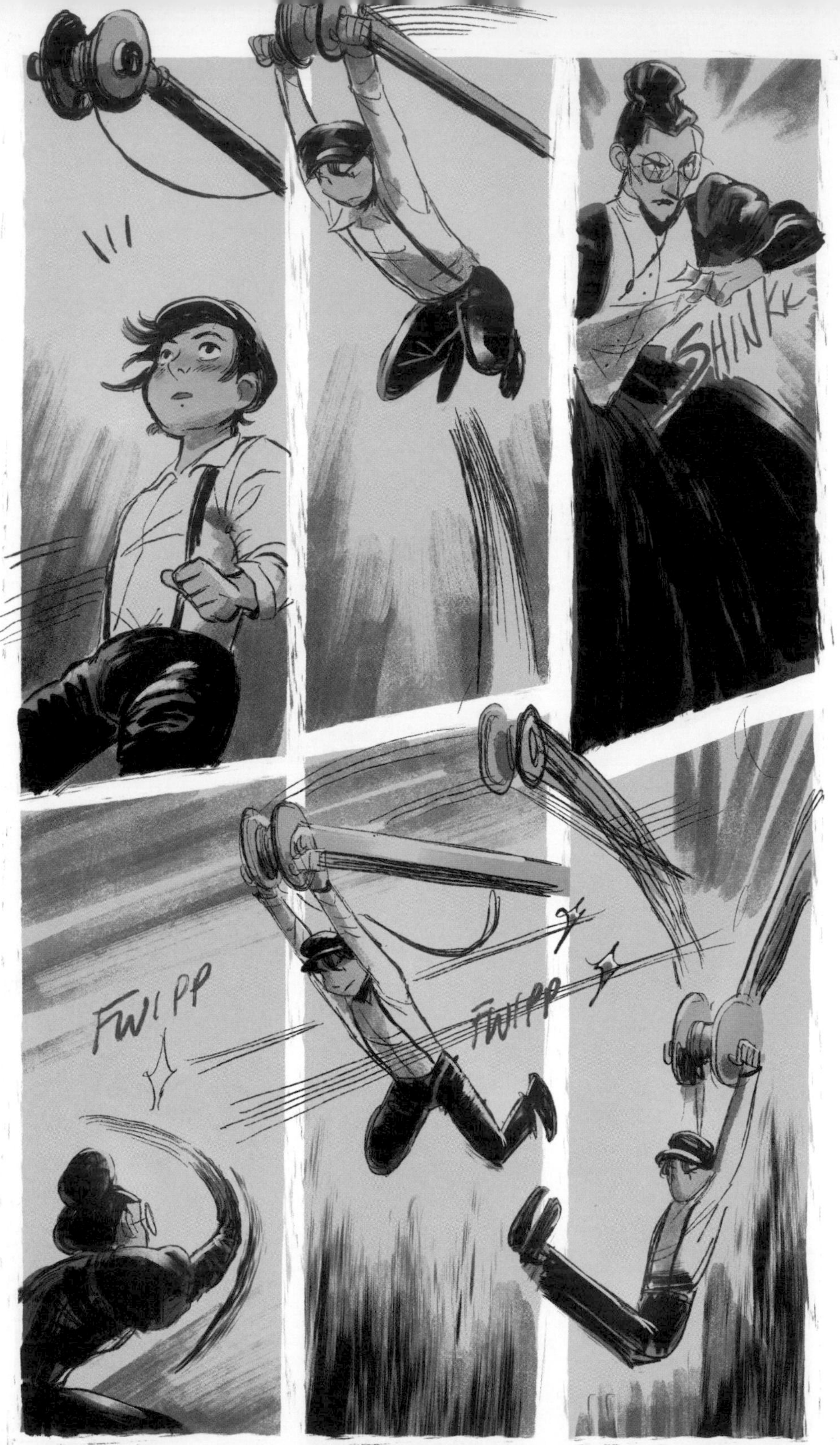
SHINKK
FWIPP
FWIPP

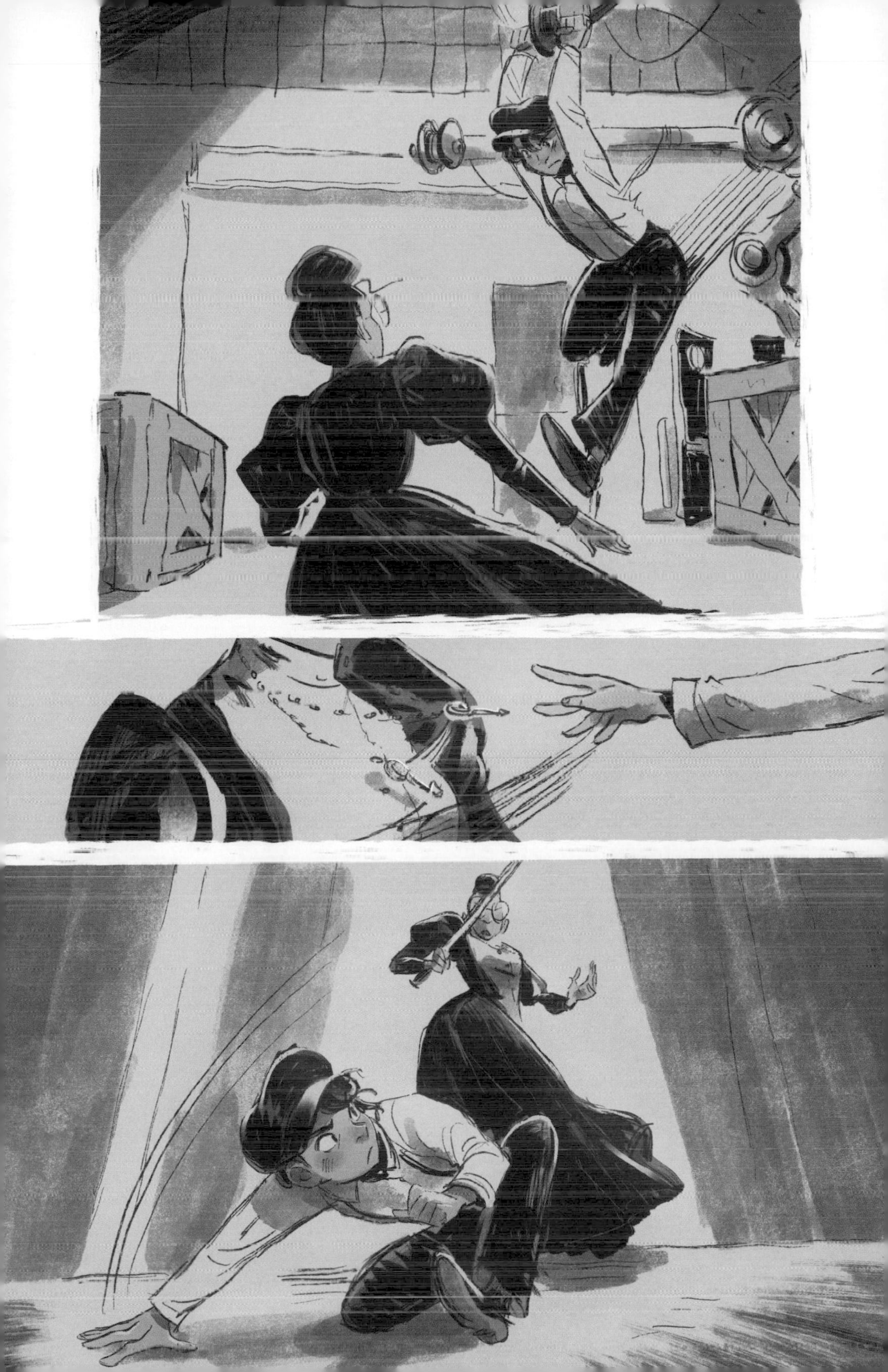

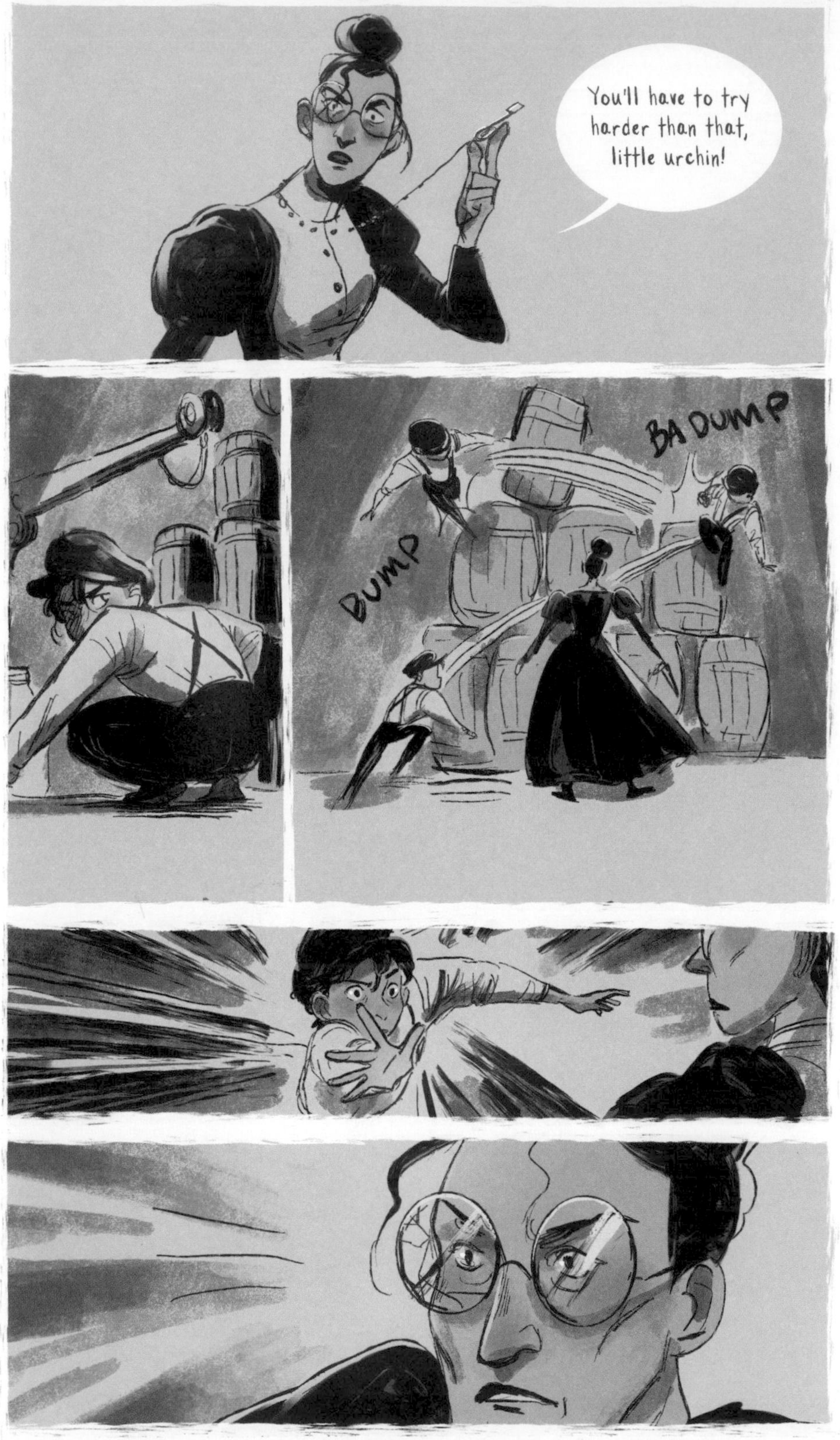
You'll have to try harder than that, little urchin!
BA DUMP
BUMP

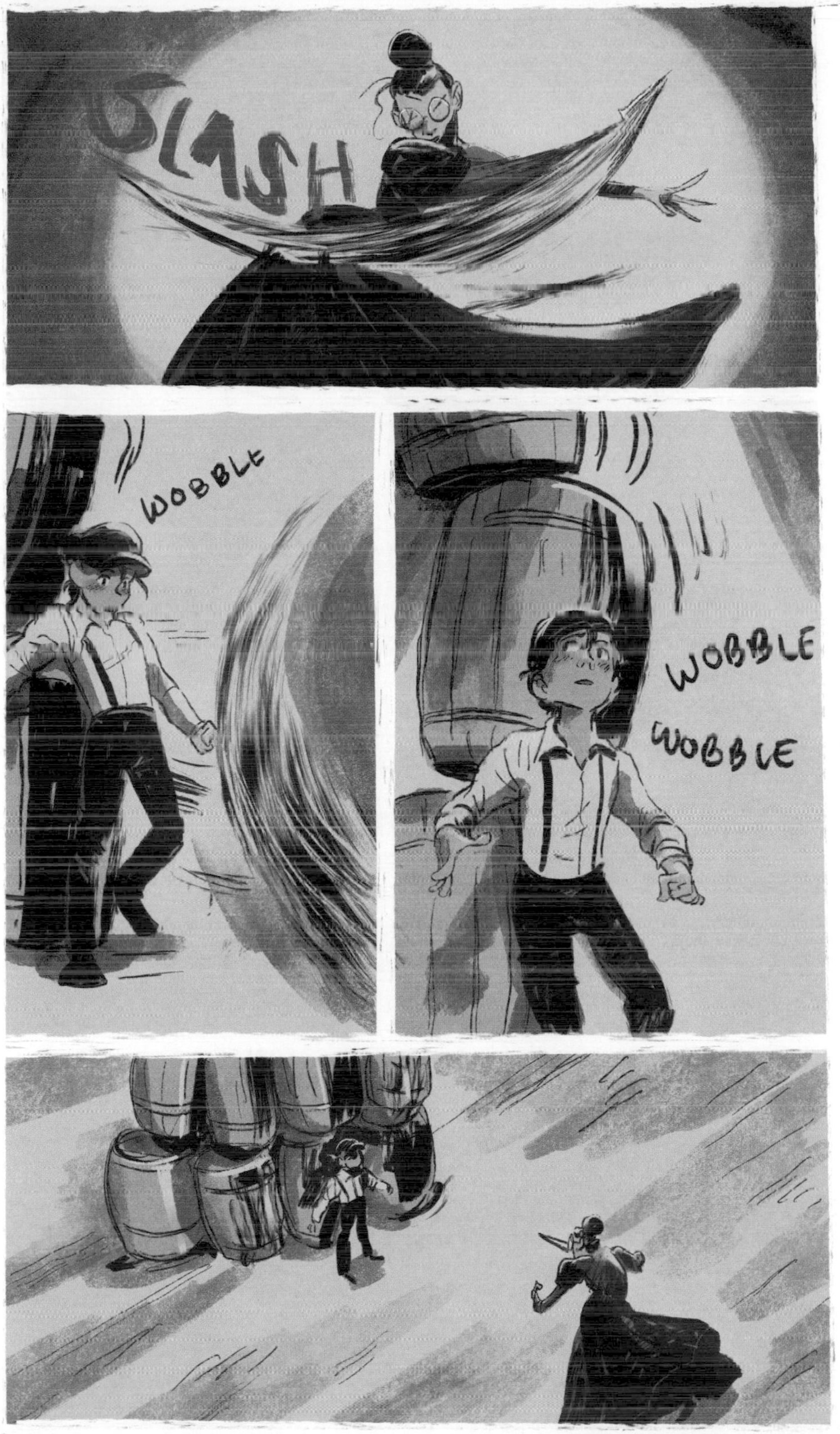
SLASH
WOBBLE
WOBBLE
WOBBLE

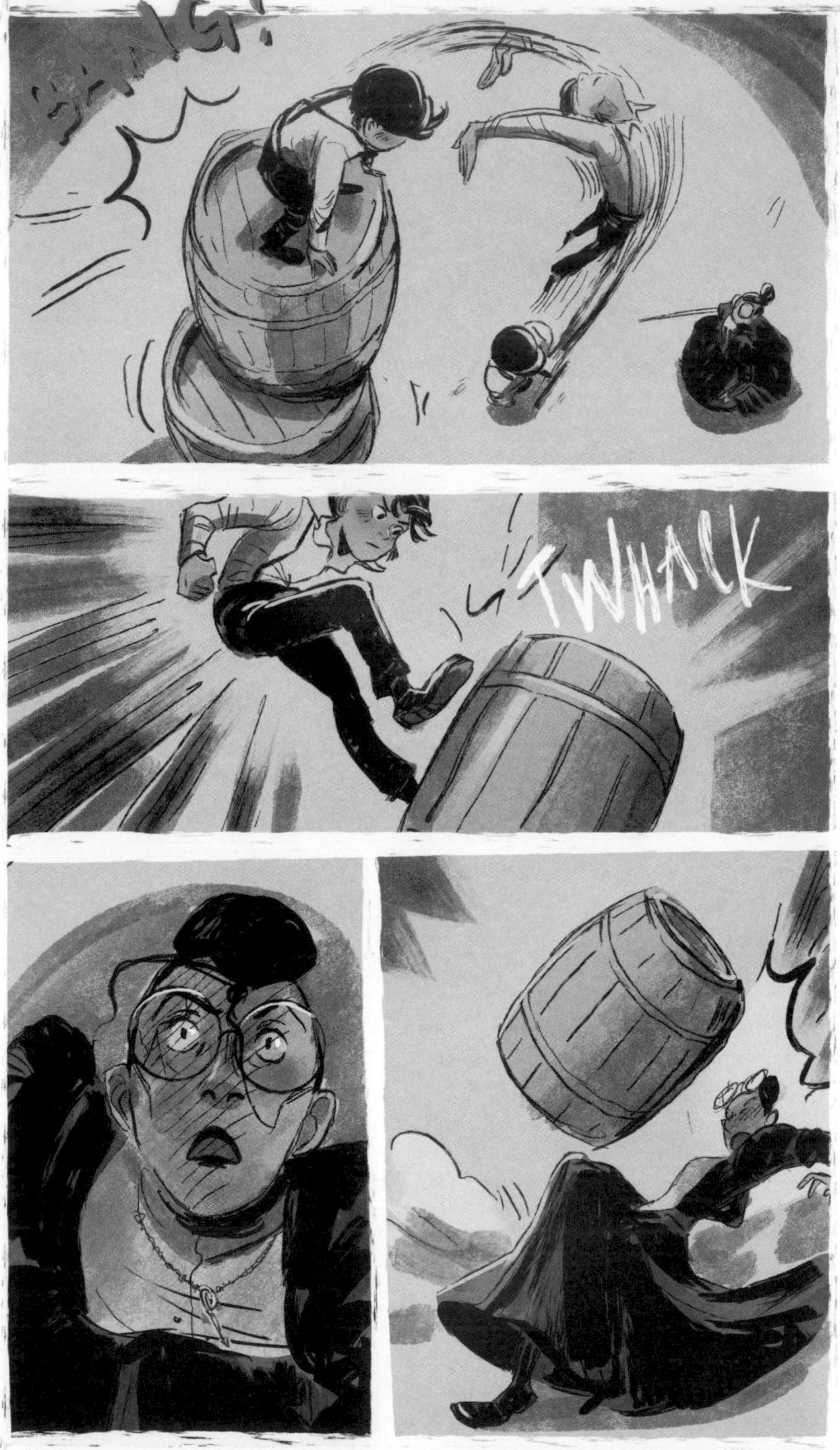
BANG!
TWHACK

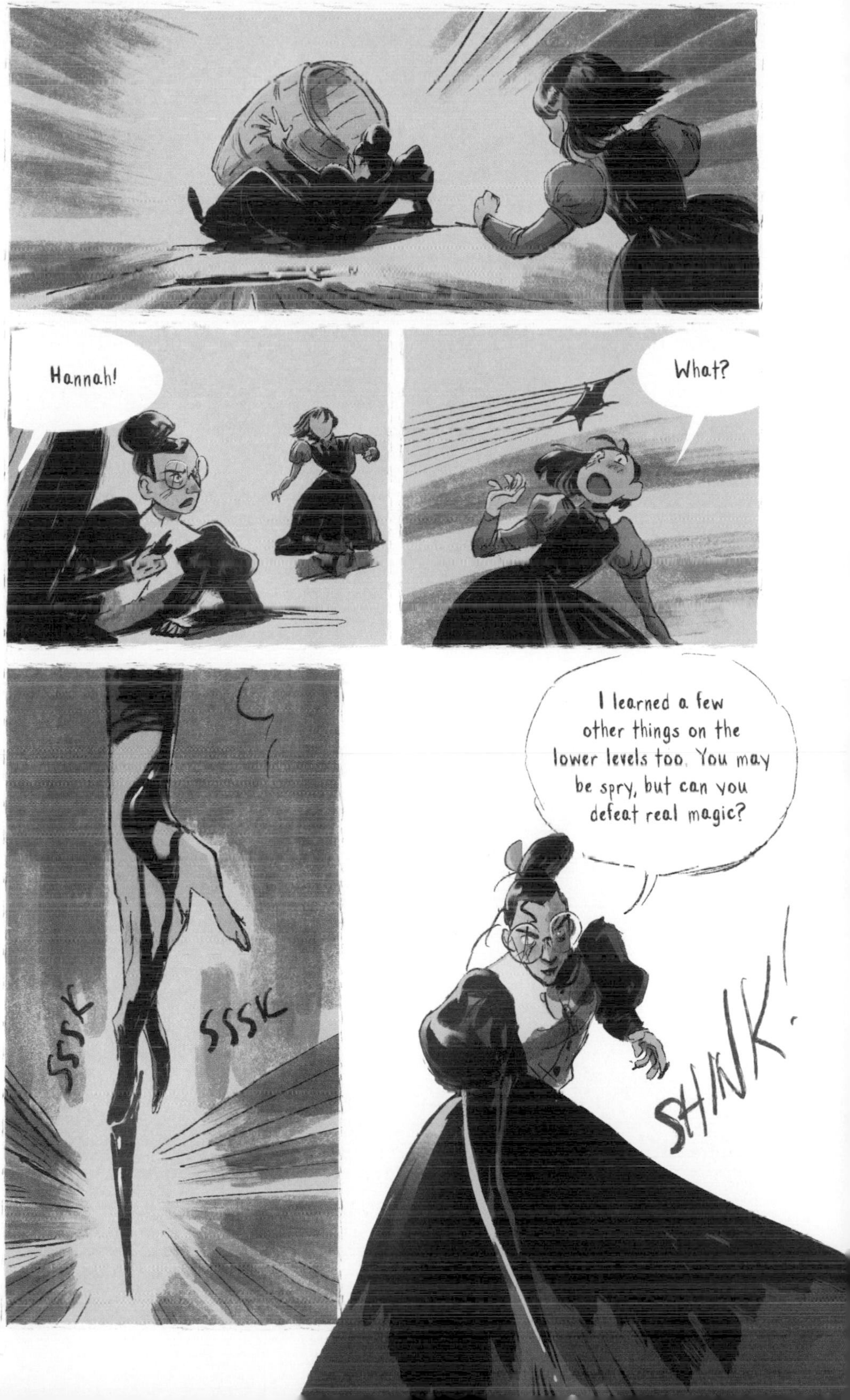
Hannah!
What?
SSSK
SSSK
I learned a few other things on the lower levels too. You may be spry, but can you defeat real magic?
SHINK!

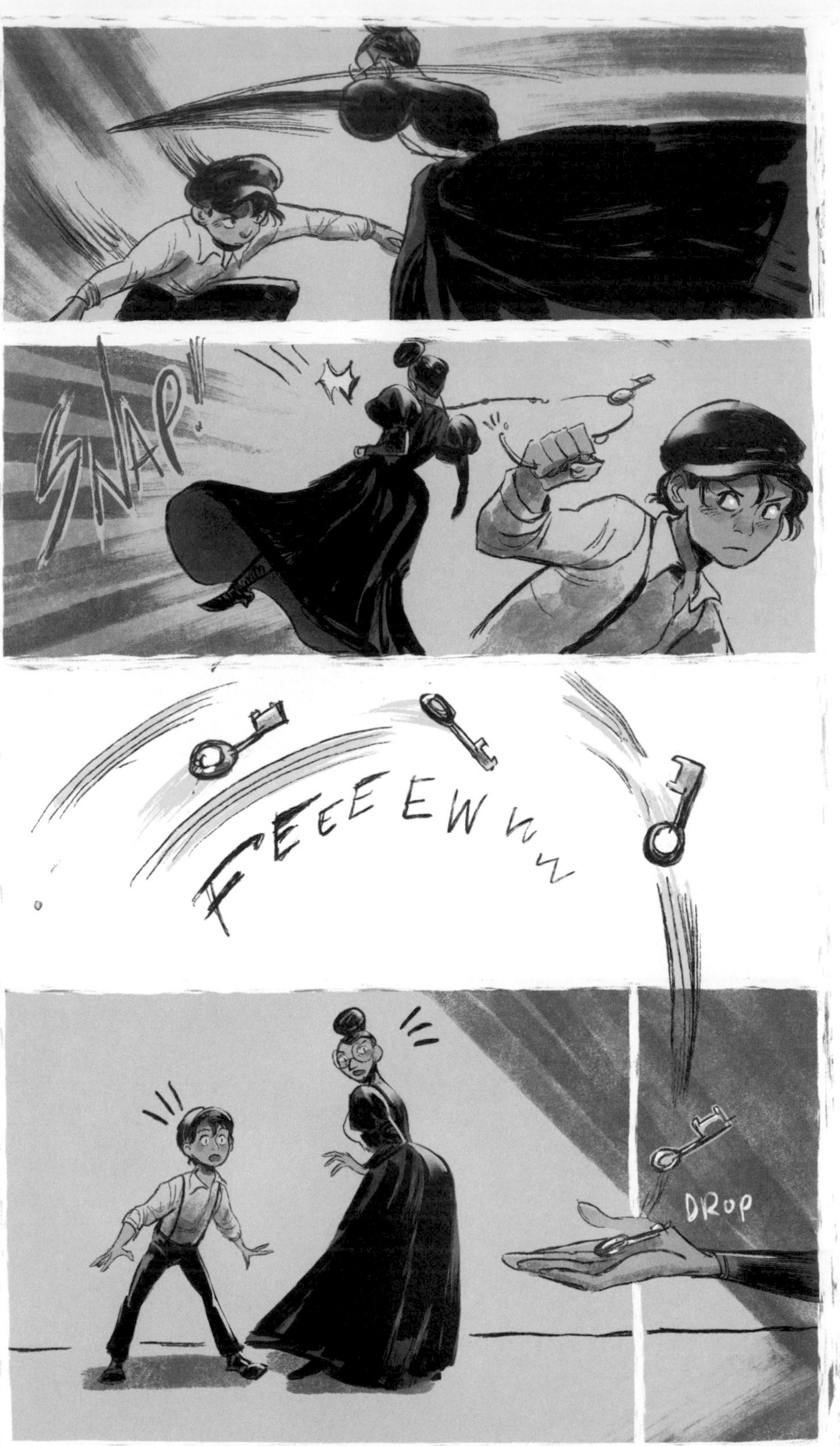
SNAP!!
FEEEEEWWW
DROP

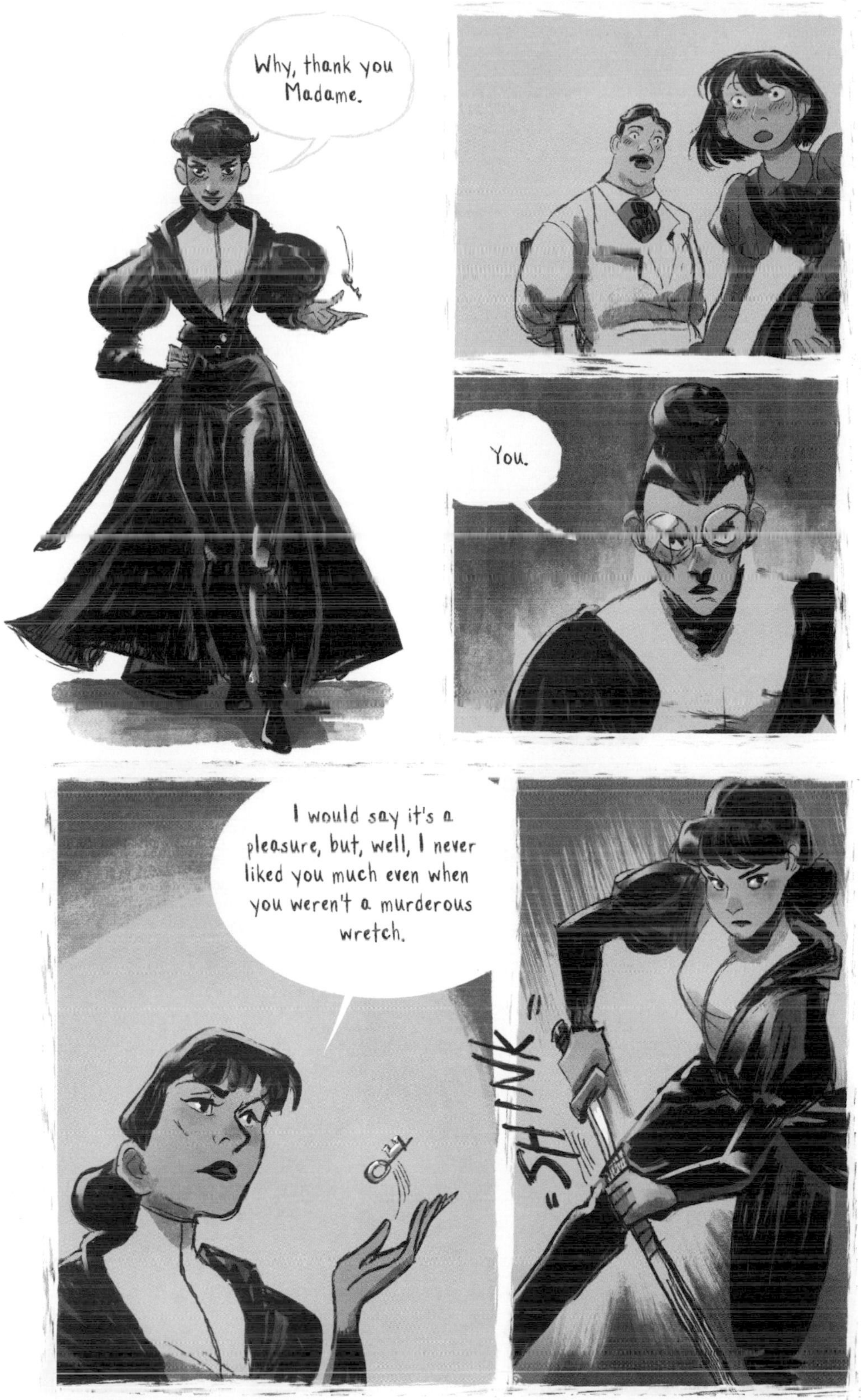
Why, thank you Madame.
You.
I would say it's a pleasure, but, well, I never liked you much even when you weren't a murderous wretch.
"SHINK"

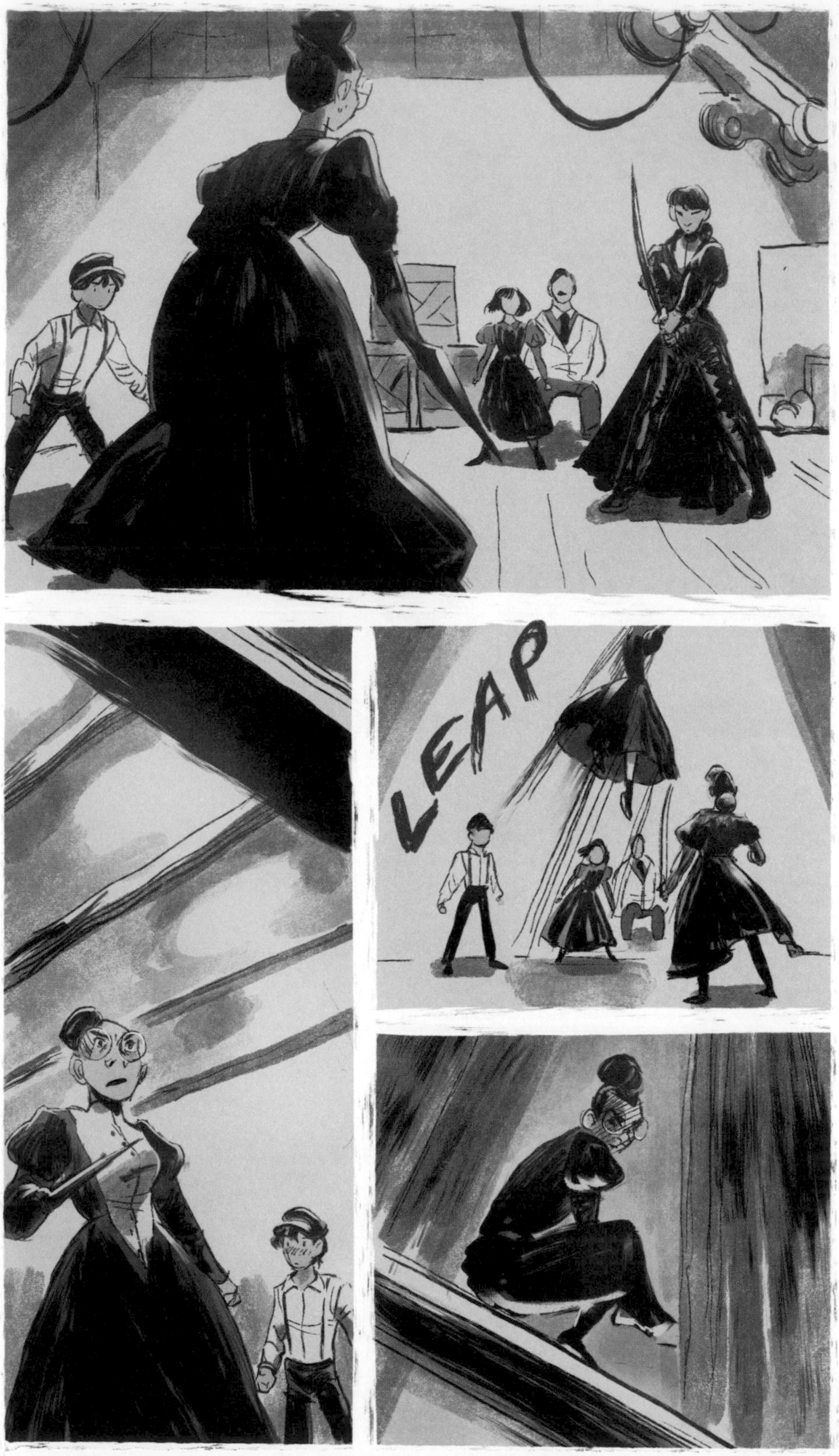
LEAP

Lisa! How did you know we were here?

I was tracking Vash. We got a tip.

Let's get you out of these.

Does Madame Alexander have something to do with Vash?

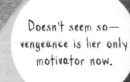

Doesn't seem so— vengeance is her only motivator now.

What was that ancient magic she used?

...I don't know. The lower levels of the city are full of mysteries. I don't like it at all.

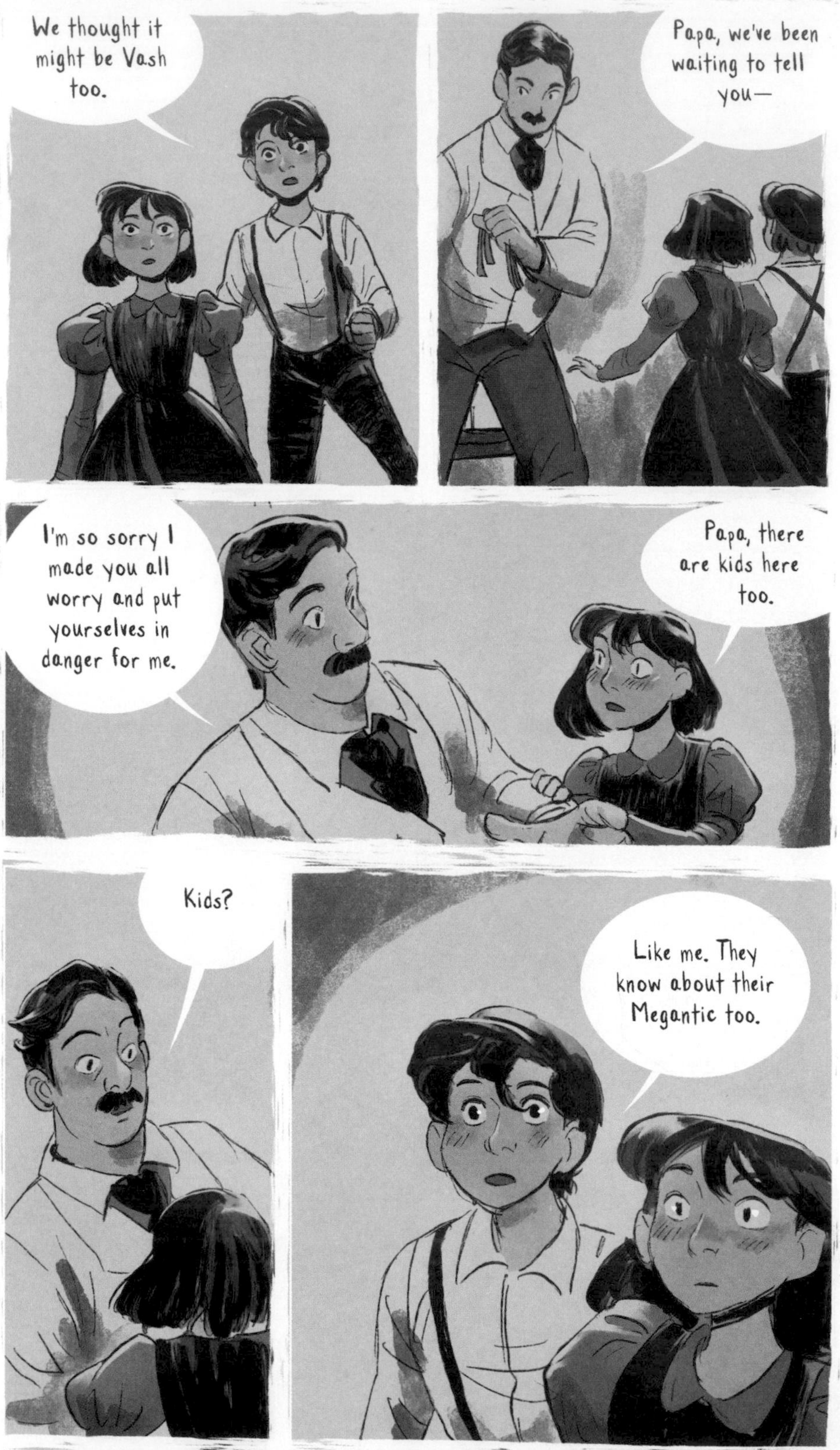
We thought it might be Vash too.
Papa, we've been waiting to tell you—
I'm so sorry I made you all worry and put yourselves in danger for me.
Papa, there are kids here too.
Kids?
Like me. They know about their Megantic too.

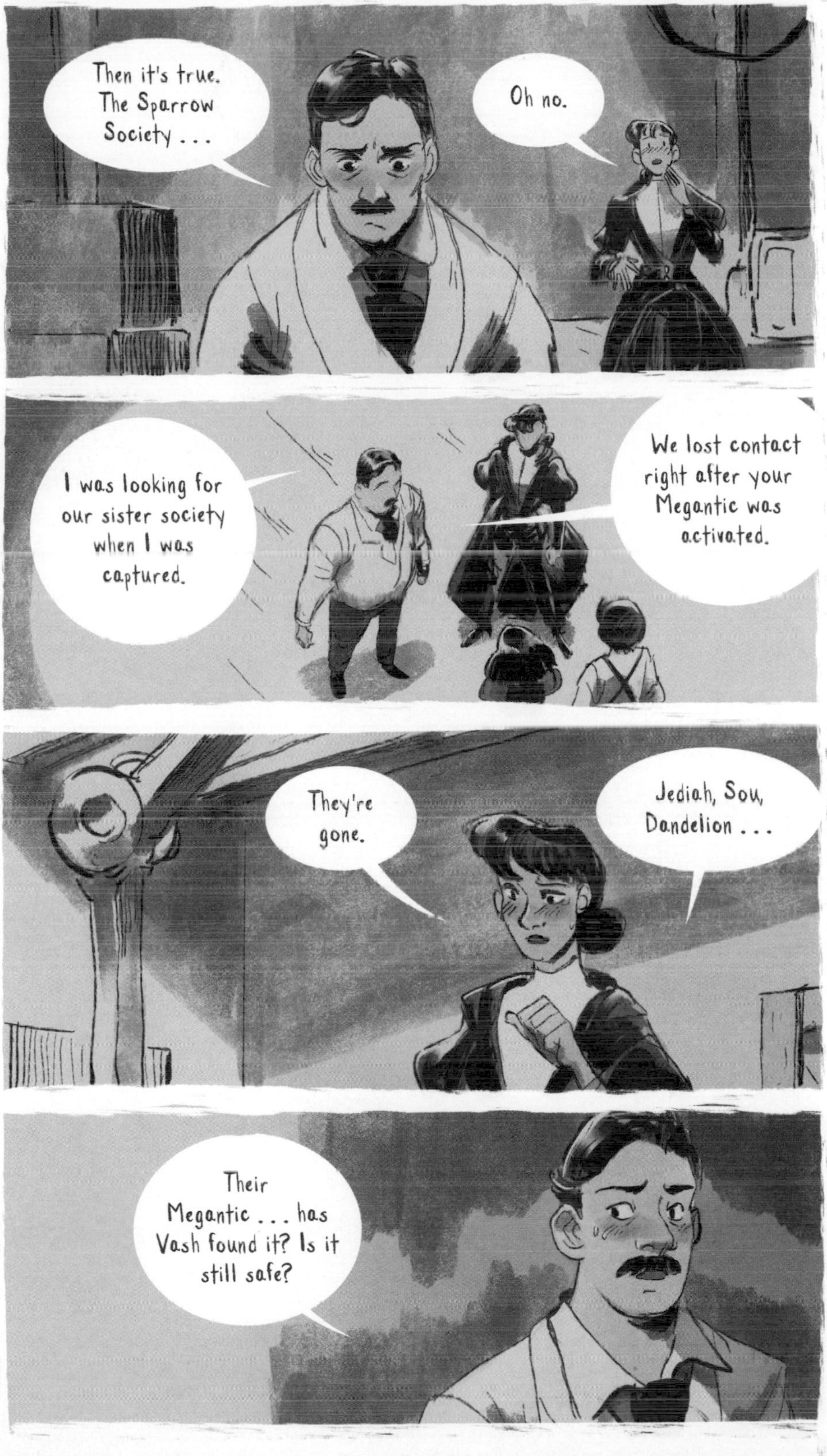
Then it's true. The Sparrow Society . . .
Oh no.
I was looking for our sister society when I was captured.
We lost contact right after your Megantic was activated.
They're gone.
Jediah, Sou, Dandelion . . .
Their Megantic . . . has Vash found it? Is it still safe?

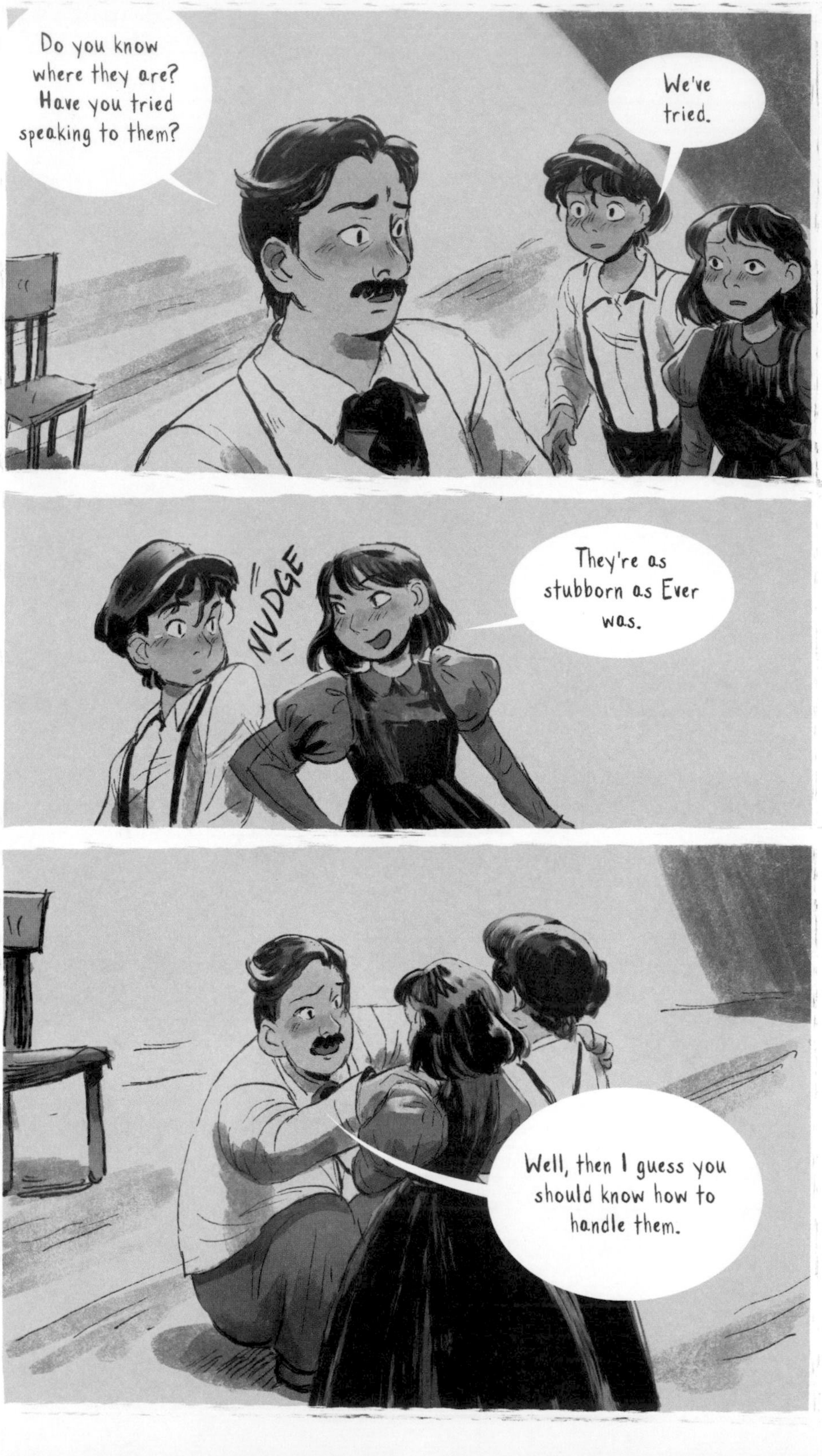
Do you know where they are? Have you tried speaking to them?
We've tried.
NUDGE
They're as stubborn as Ever was.
Well, then I guess you should know how to handle them.

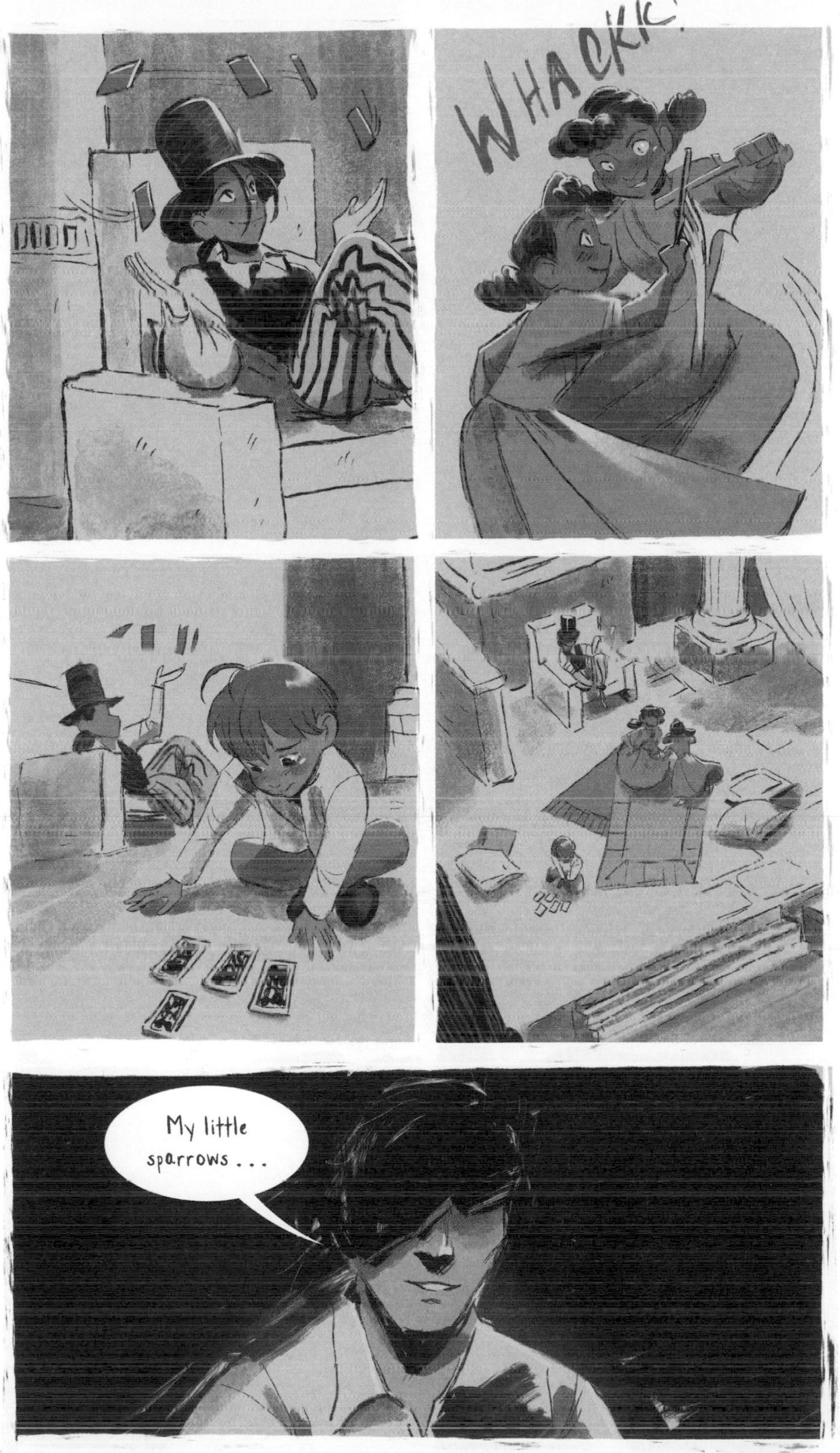
WHACKK!
My little sparrows . . .

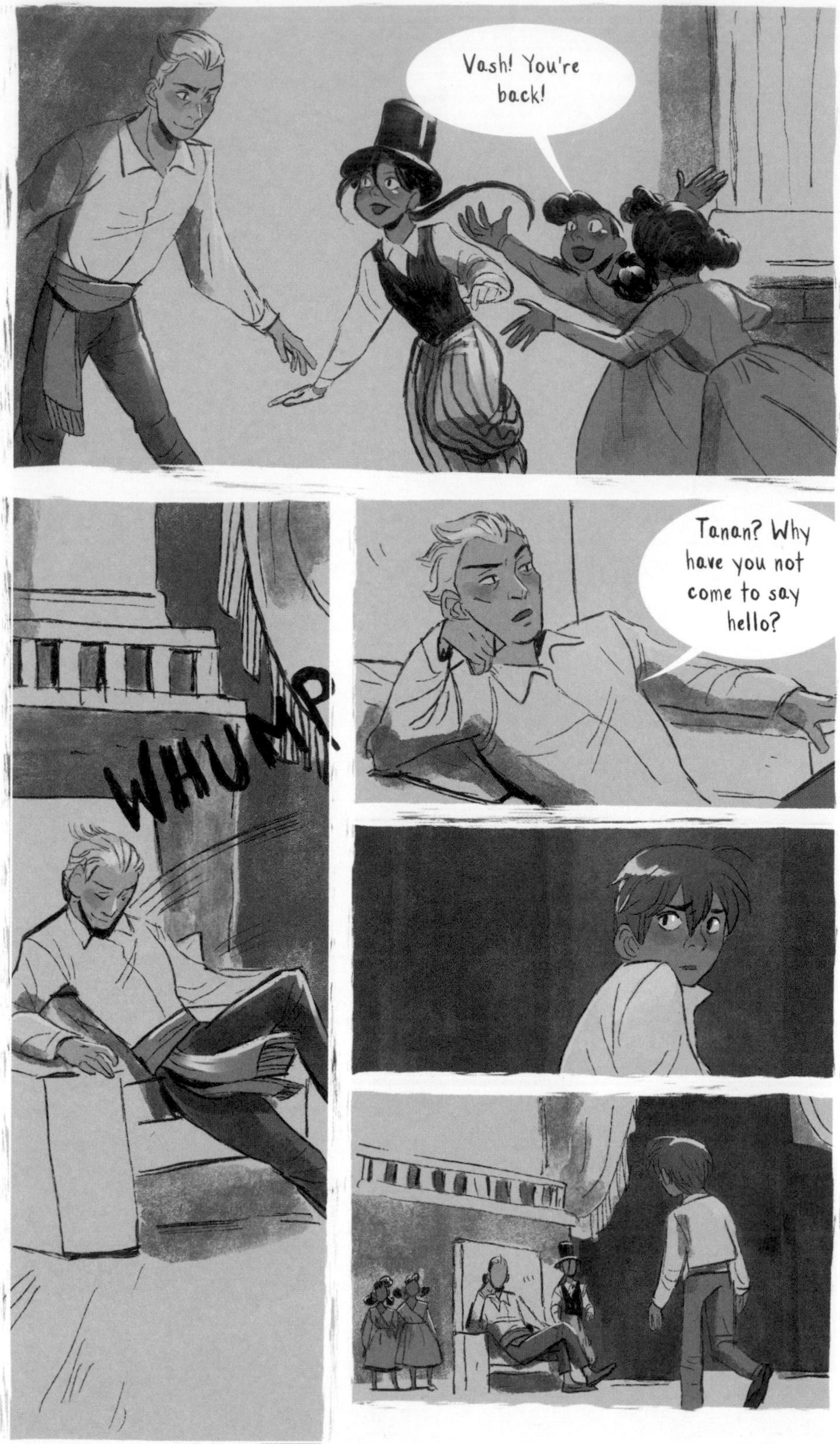
Vash! You're back!
WHUMP!
Tanan? Why have you not come to say hello?

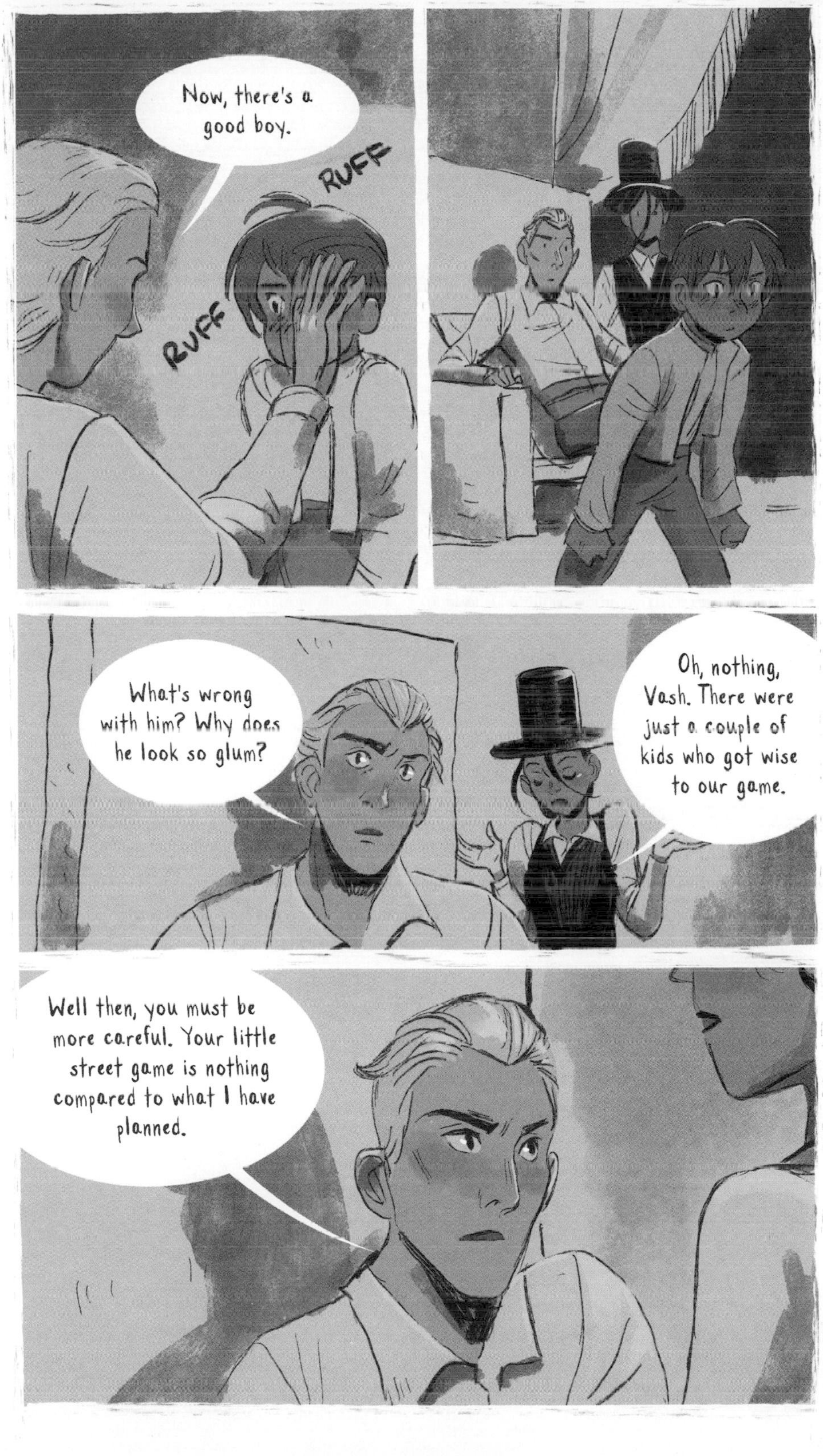

Now, there's a good boy.
RUFF
RUFF
What's wrong with him? Why does he look so glum?
Oh, nothing, Vash. There were just a couple of kids who got wise to our game.
Well then, you must be more careful. Your little street game is nothing compared to what I have planned.

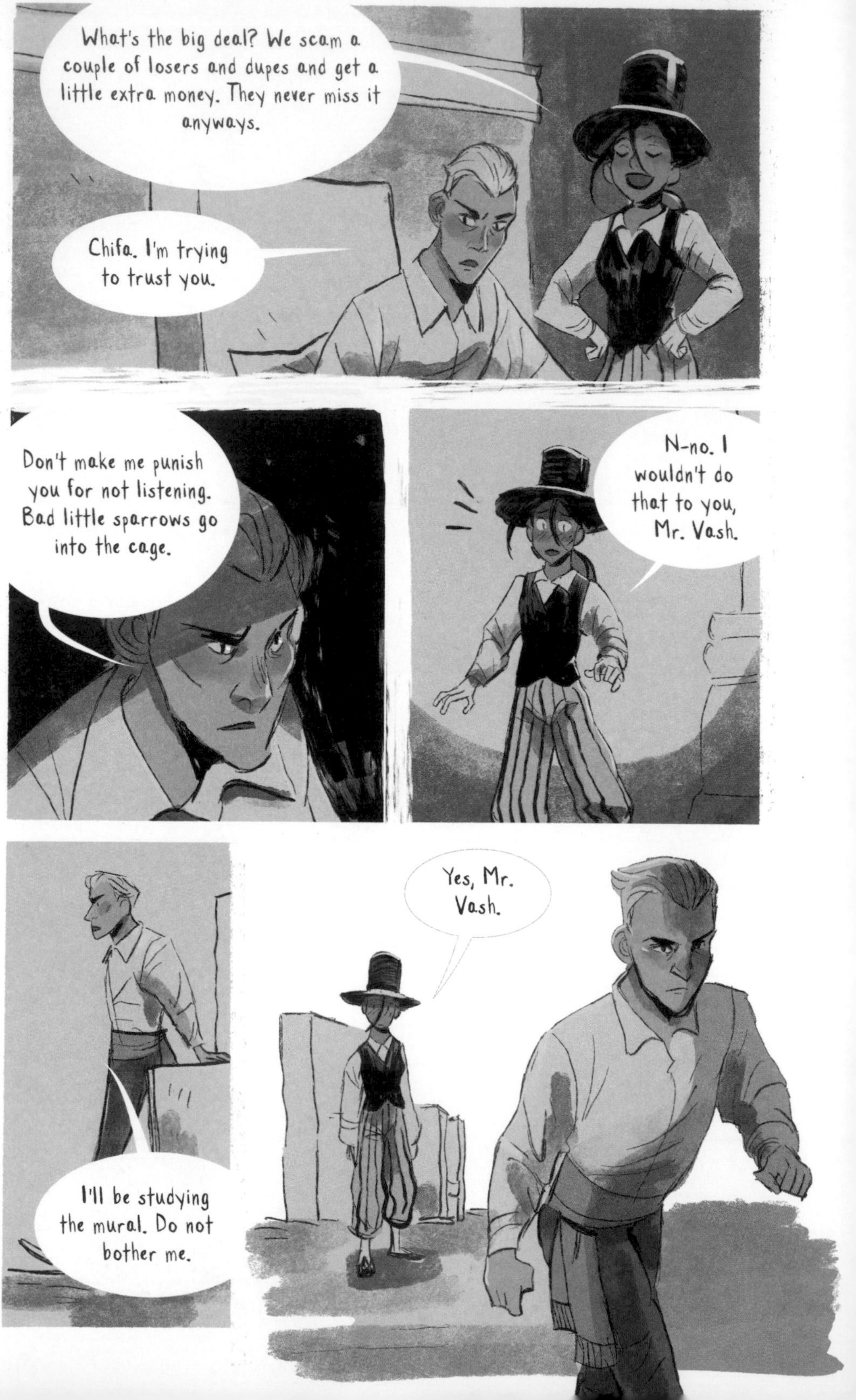

What's the big deal? We scam a couple of losers and dupes and get a little extra money. They never miss it anyways.
Chifa. I'm trying to trust you.
Don't make me punish you for not listening. Bad little sparrows go into the cage.
N-no. I wouldn't do that to you, Mr. Vash.
I'll be studying the mural. Do not bother me.
Yes, Mr. Vash.

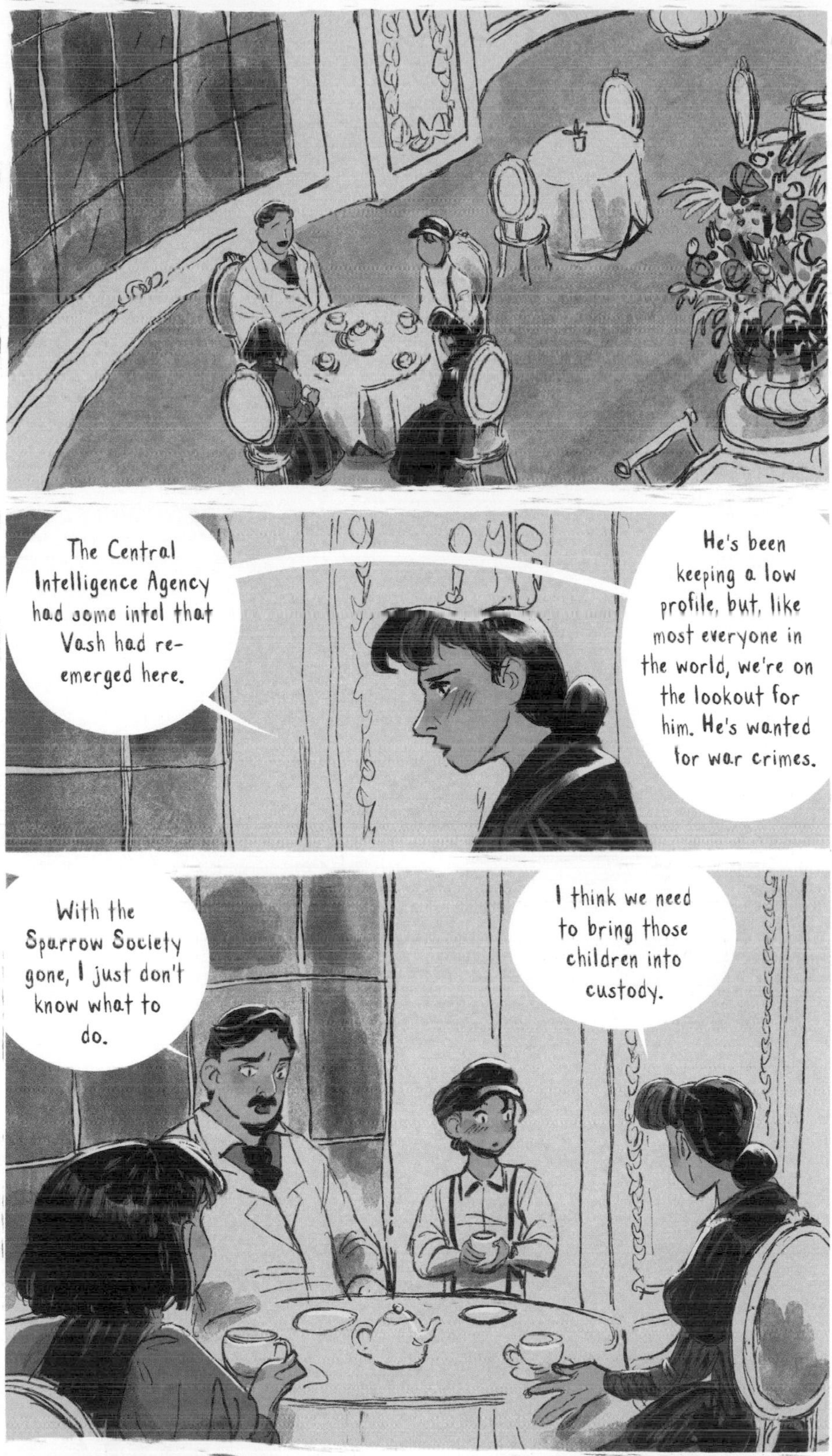
The Central Intelligence Agency had some intel that Vash had re-emerged here.
He's been keeping a low profile, but, like most everyone in the world, we're on the lookout for him. He's wanted for war crimes.
With the Sparrow Society gone, I just don't know what to do.
I think we need to bring those children into custody.

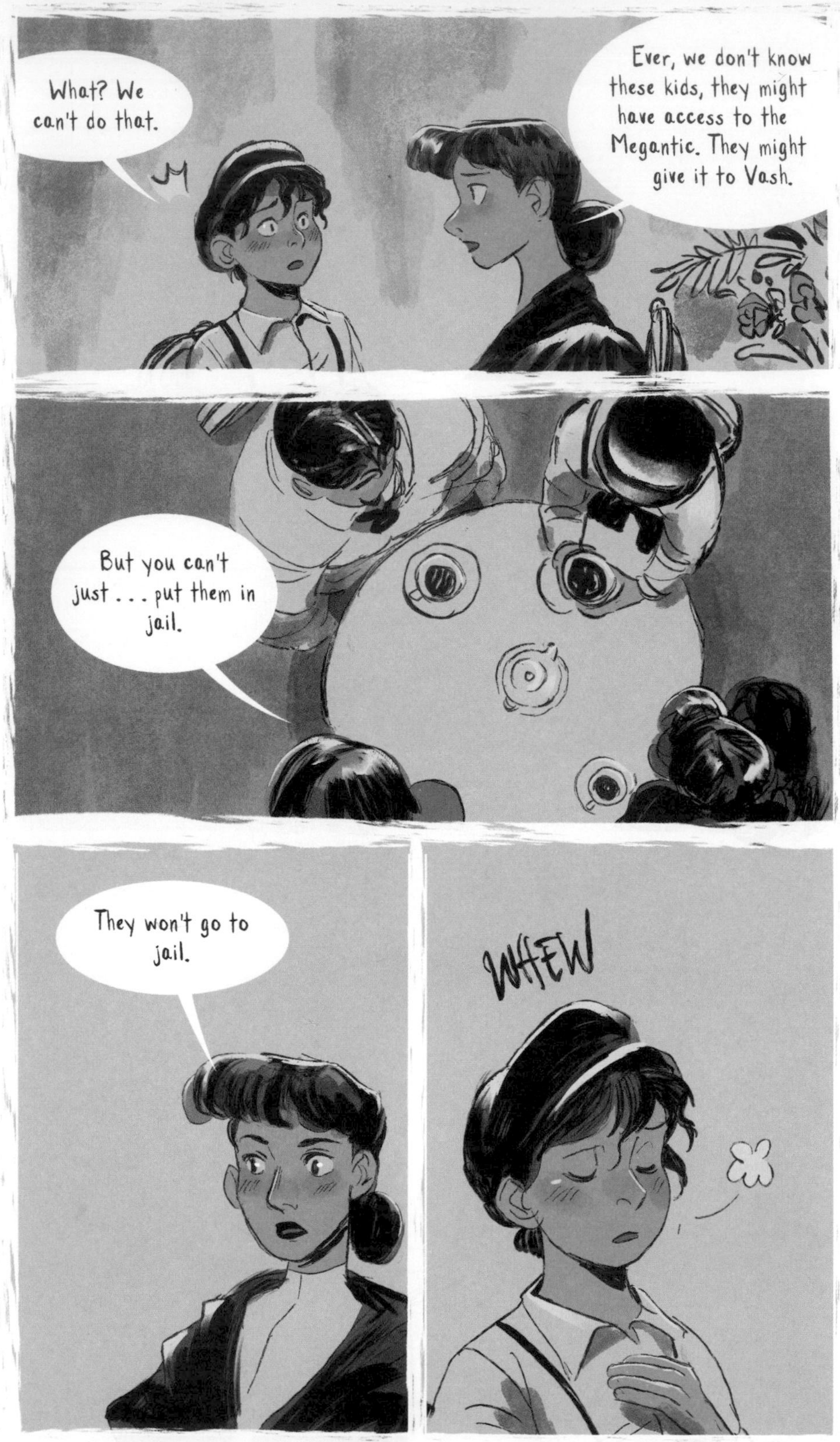

What? We can't do that.
Ever, we don't know these kids, they might have access to the Megantic. They might give it to Vash.
But you can't just . . . put them in jail.
They won't go to jail.
WHEW

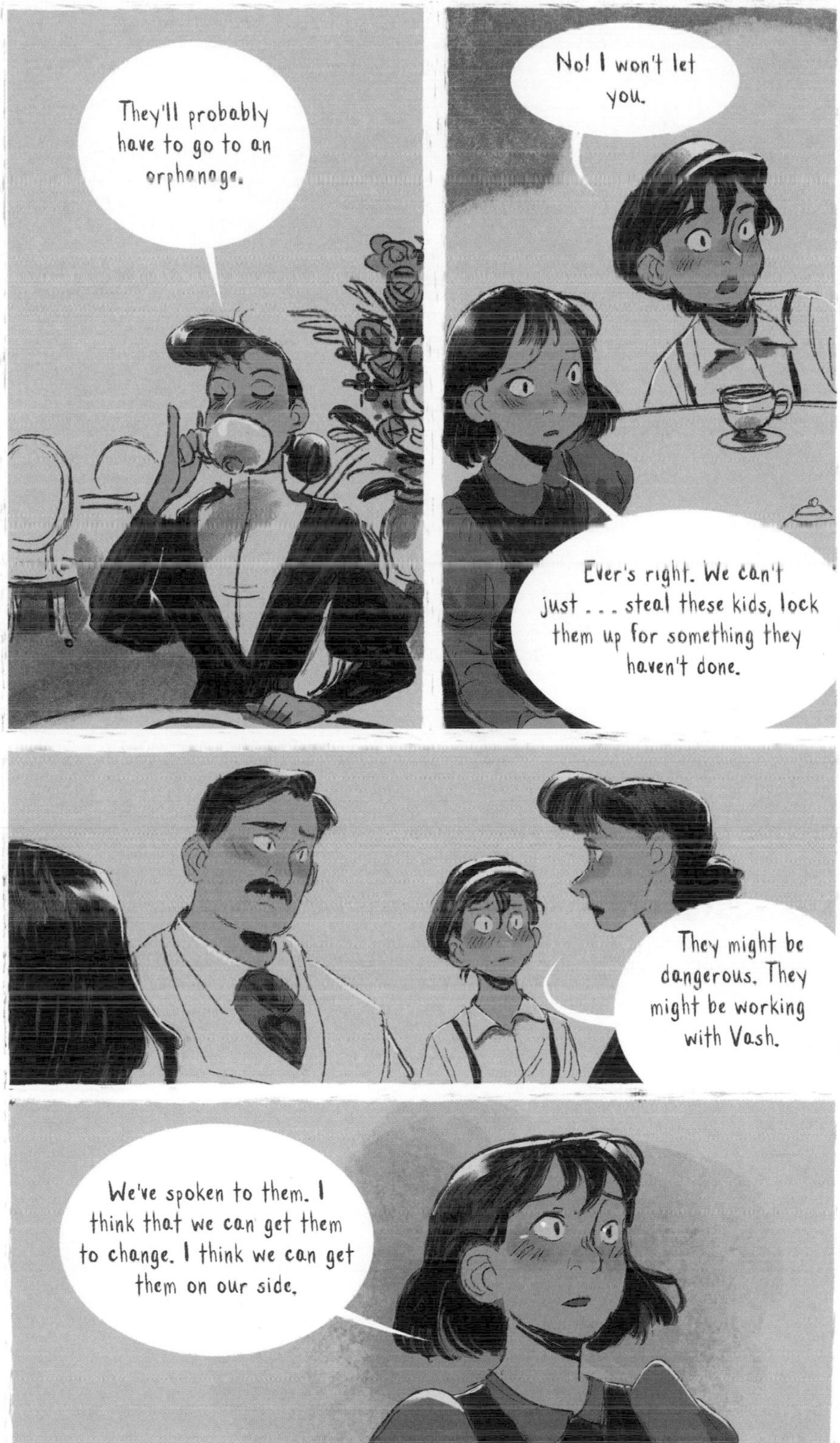
They'll probably have to go to an orphanage.
No! I won't let you.
Ever's right. We can't just . . . steal these kids, lock them up for something they haven't done.
They might be dangerous. They might be working with Vash.
We've spoken to them. I think that we can get them to change. I think we can get them on our side.

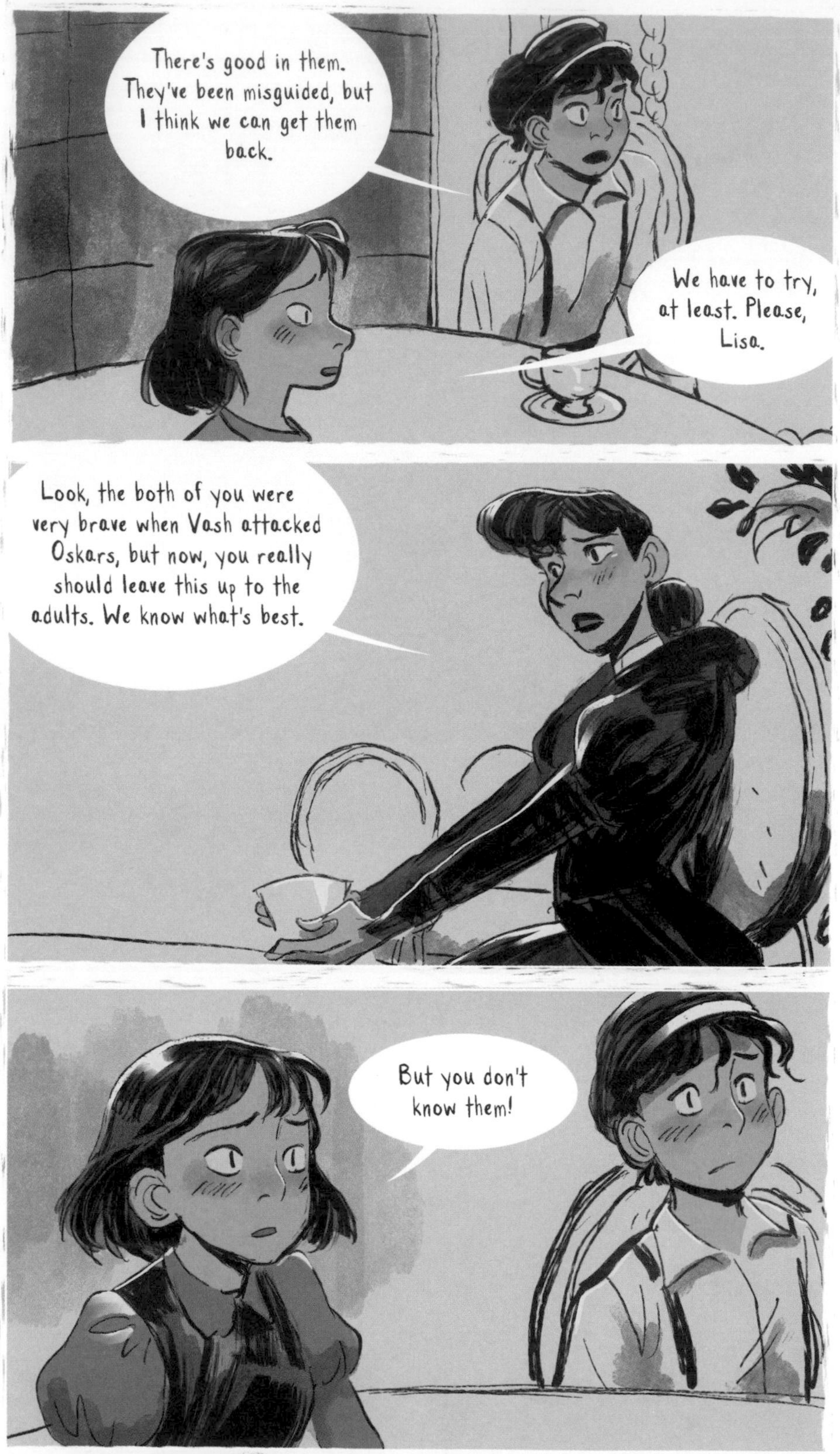
There's good in them. They've been misguided, but I think we can get them back.
We have to try, at least. Please, Lisa.
Look, the both of you were very brave when Vash attacked Oskars, but now, you really should leave this up to the adults. We know what's best.
But you don't know them!

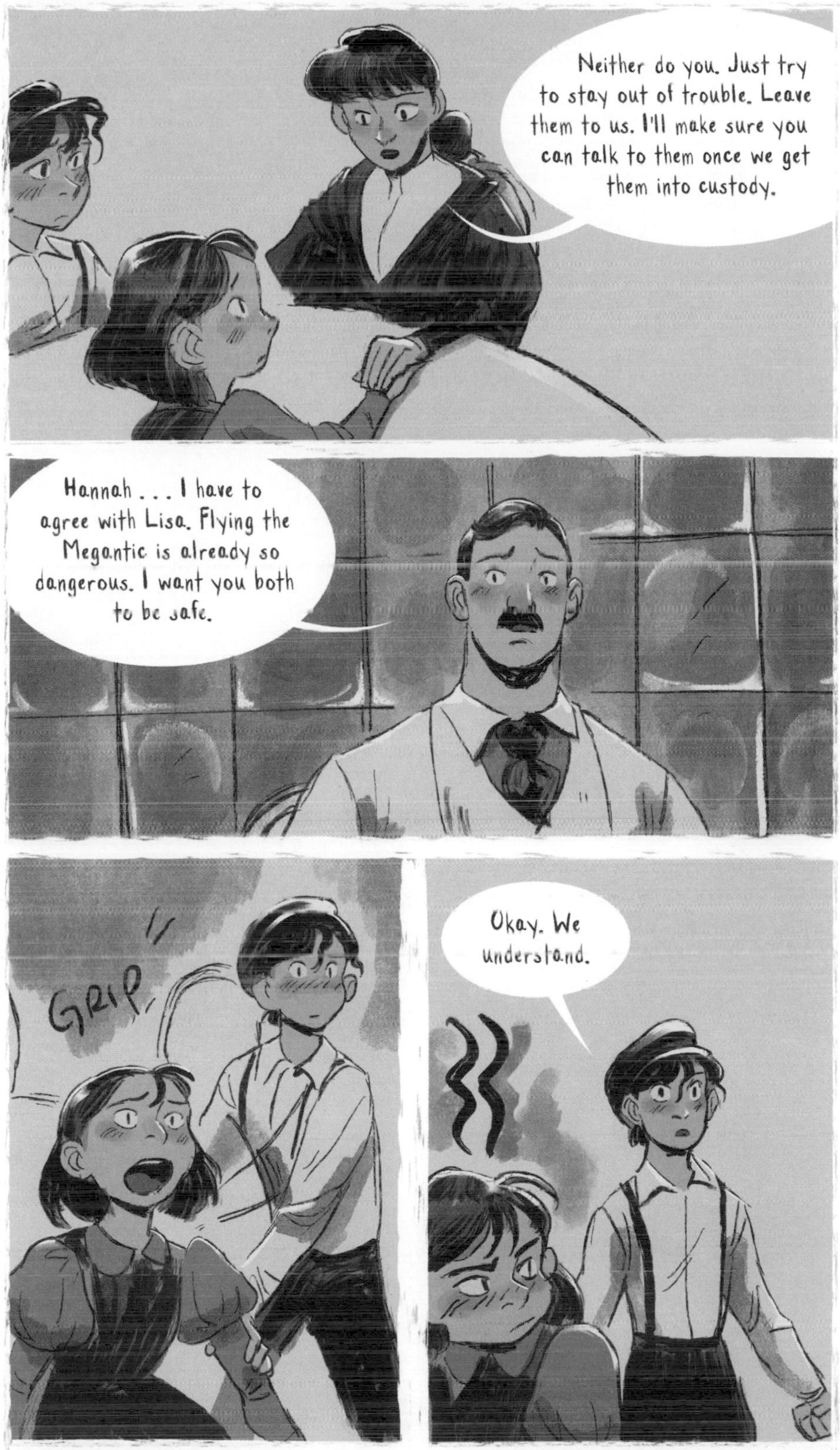
Neither do you. Just try to stay out of trouble. Leave them to us. I'll make sure you can talk to them once we get them into custody.
Hannah . . . I have to agree with Lisa. Flying the Megantic is already so dangerous. I want you both to be safe.
GRIP
Okay. We understand.

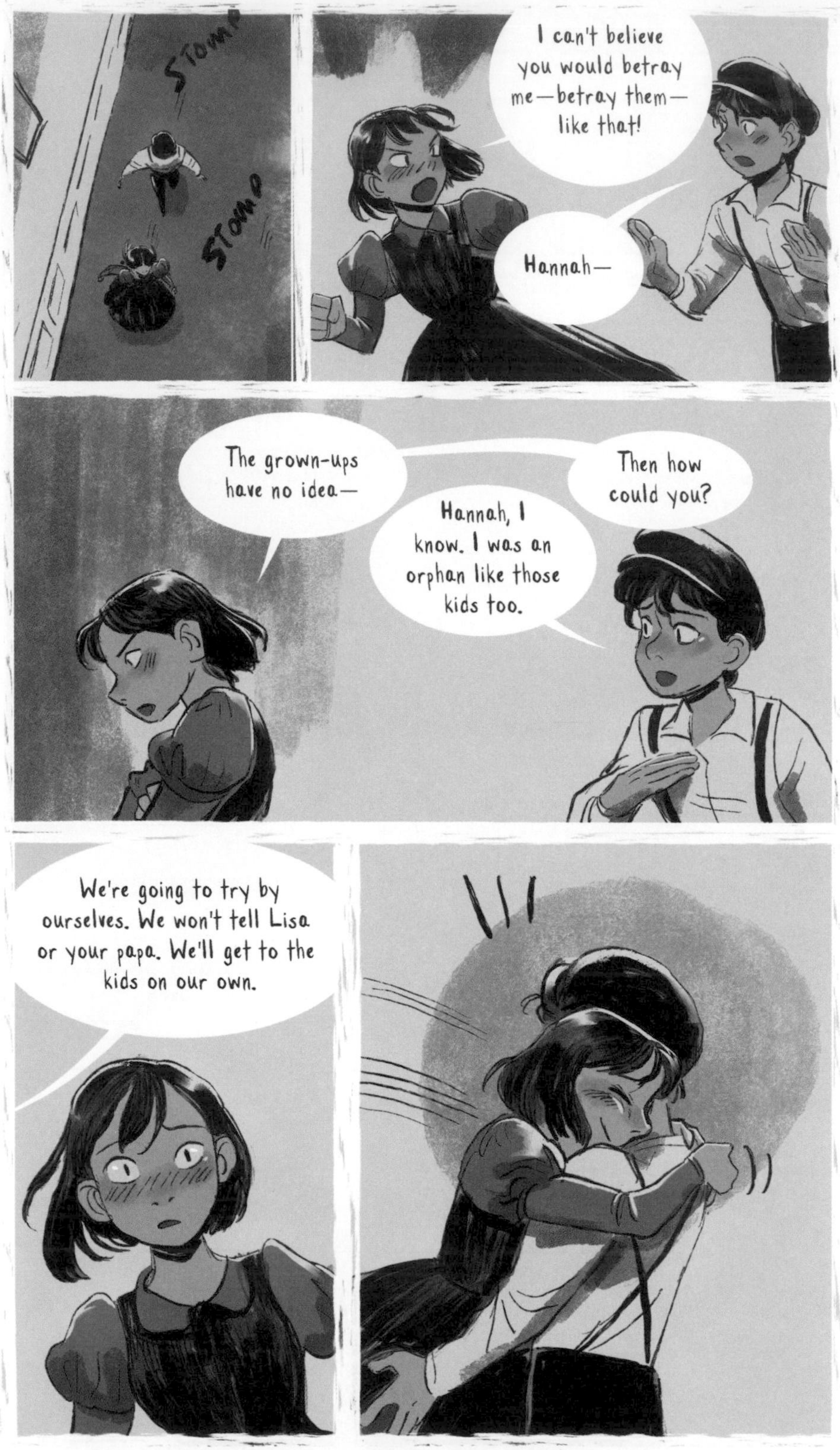
STOMP
STOMP
I can't believe you would betray me—betray them—like that!
Hannah—
The grown-ups have no idea—
Then how could you?
Hannah, I know. I was an orphan like those kids too.
We're going to try by ourselves. We won't tell Lisa or your papa. We'll get to the kids on our own.

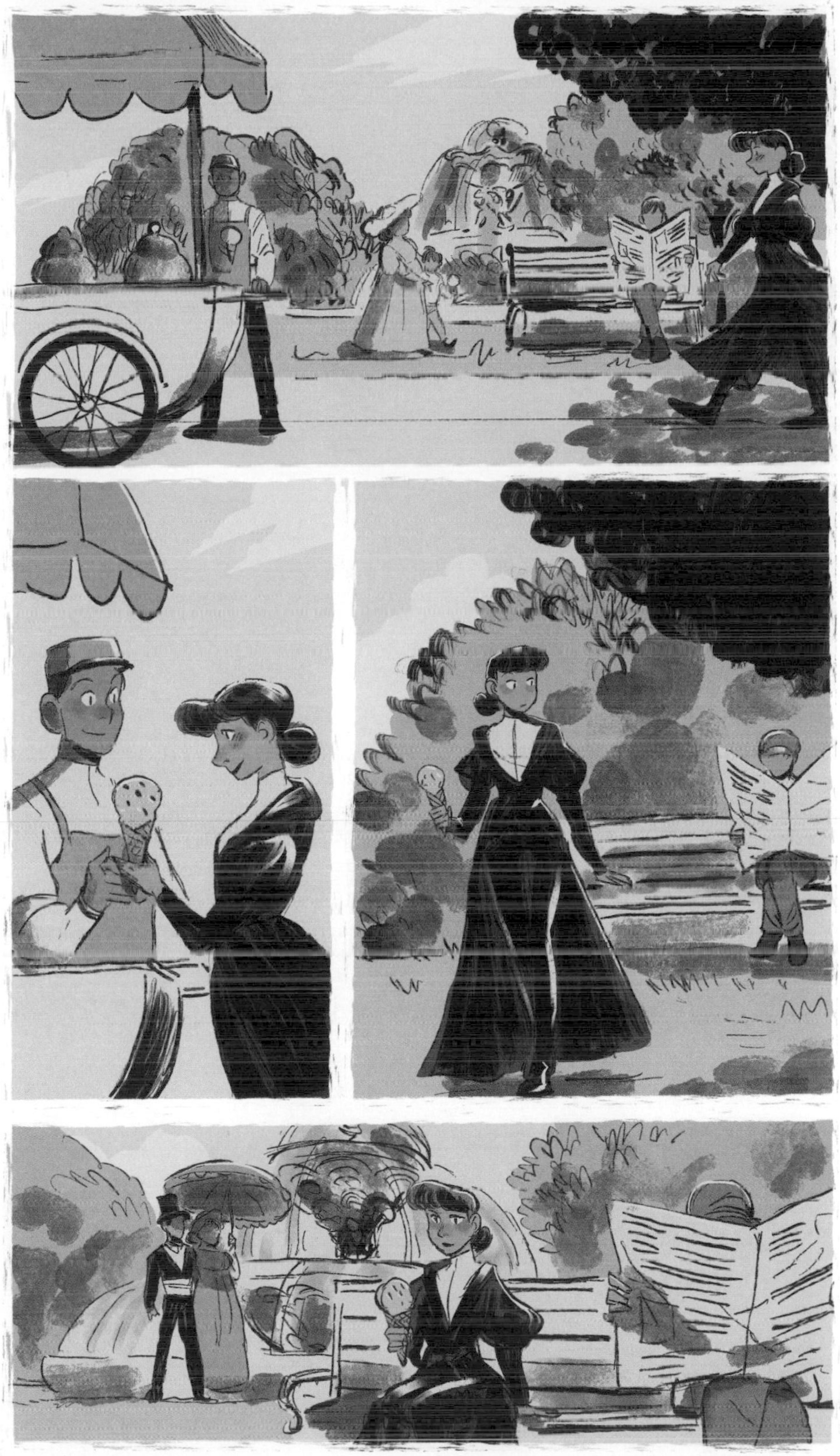

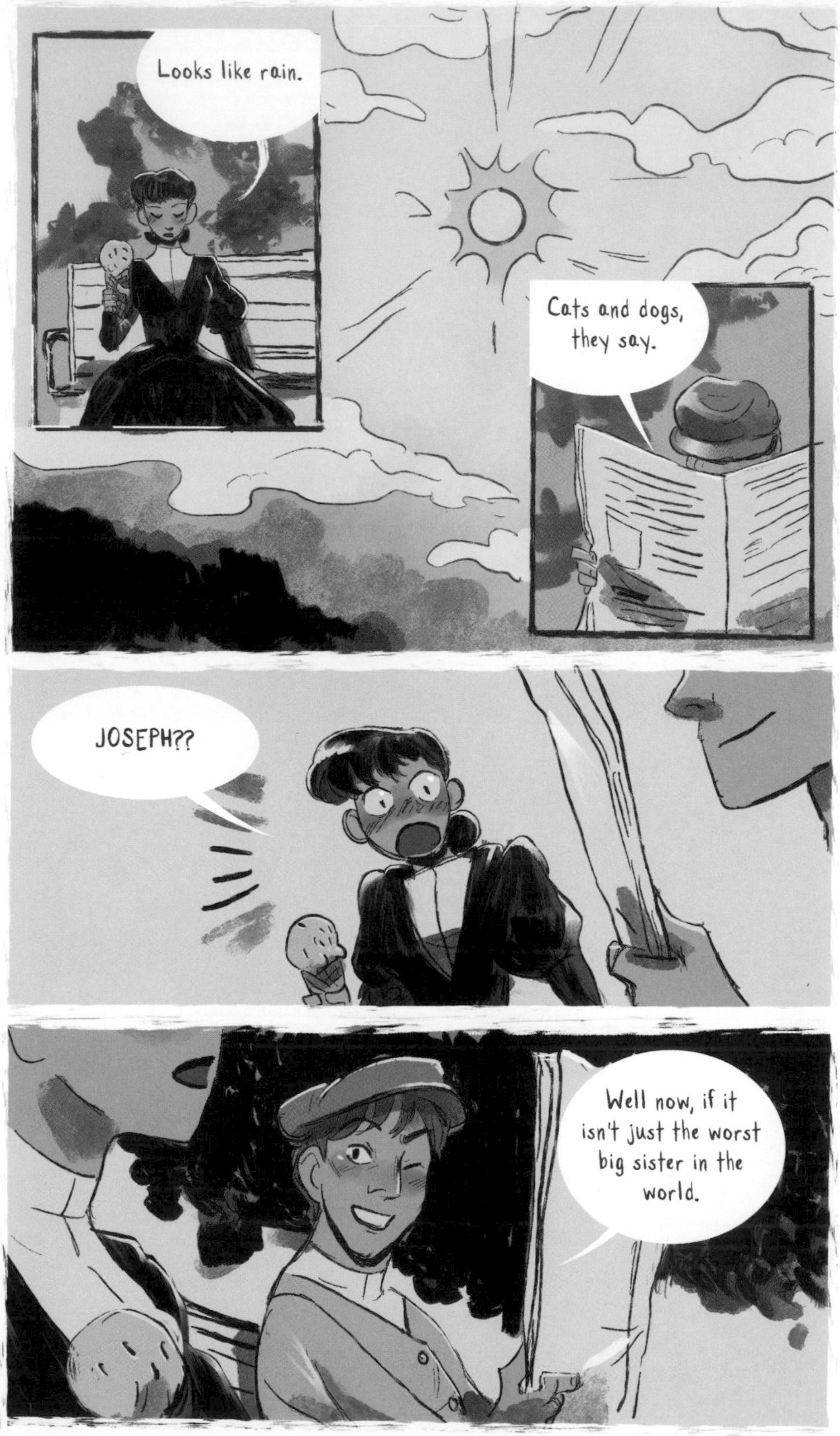
Looks like rain.
Cats and dogs, they say.
JOSEPH??
Well now, if it isn't just the worst big sister in the world.

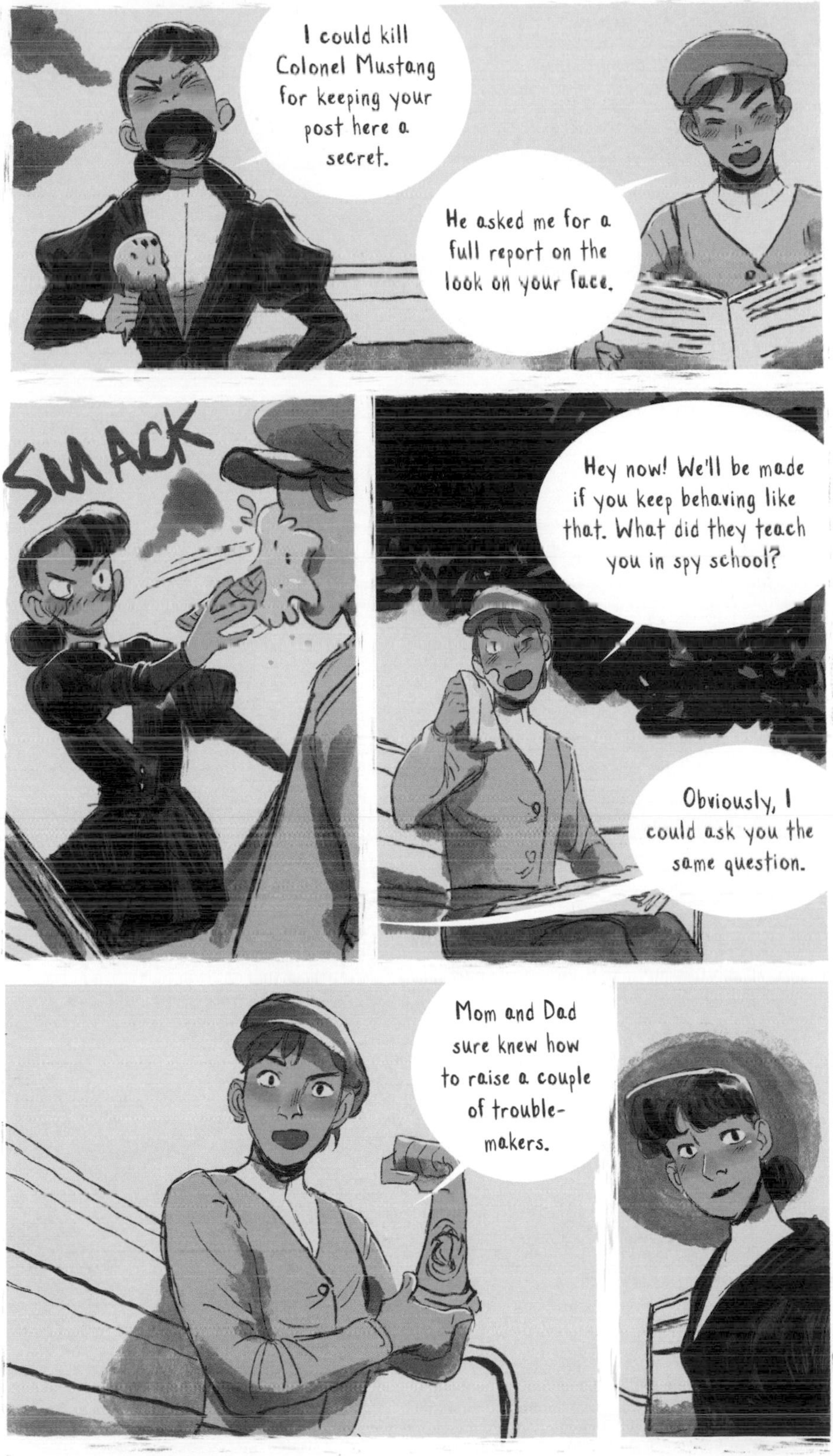
I could kill Colonel Mustang for keeping your post here a secret.
He asked me for a full report on the look on your face.
SMACK
Hey now! We'll be made if you keep behaving like that. What did they teach you in spy school?
Obviously, I could ask you the same question.
Mom and Dad sure knew how to raise a couple of trouble-makers.

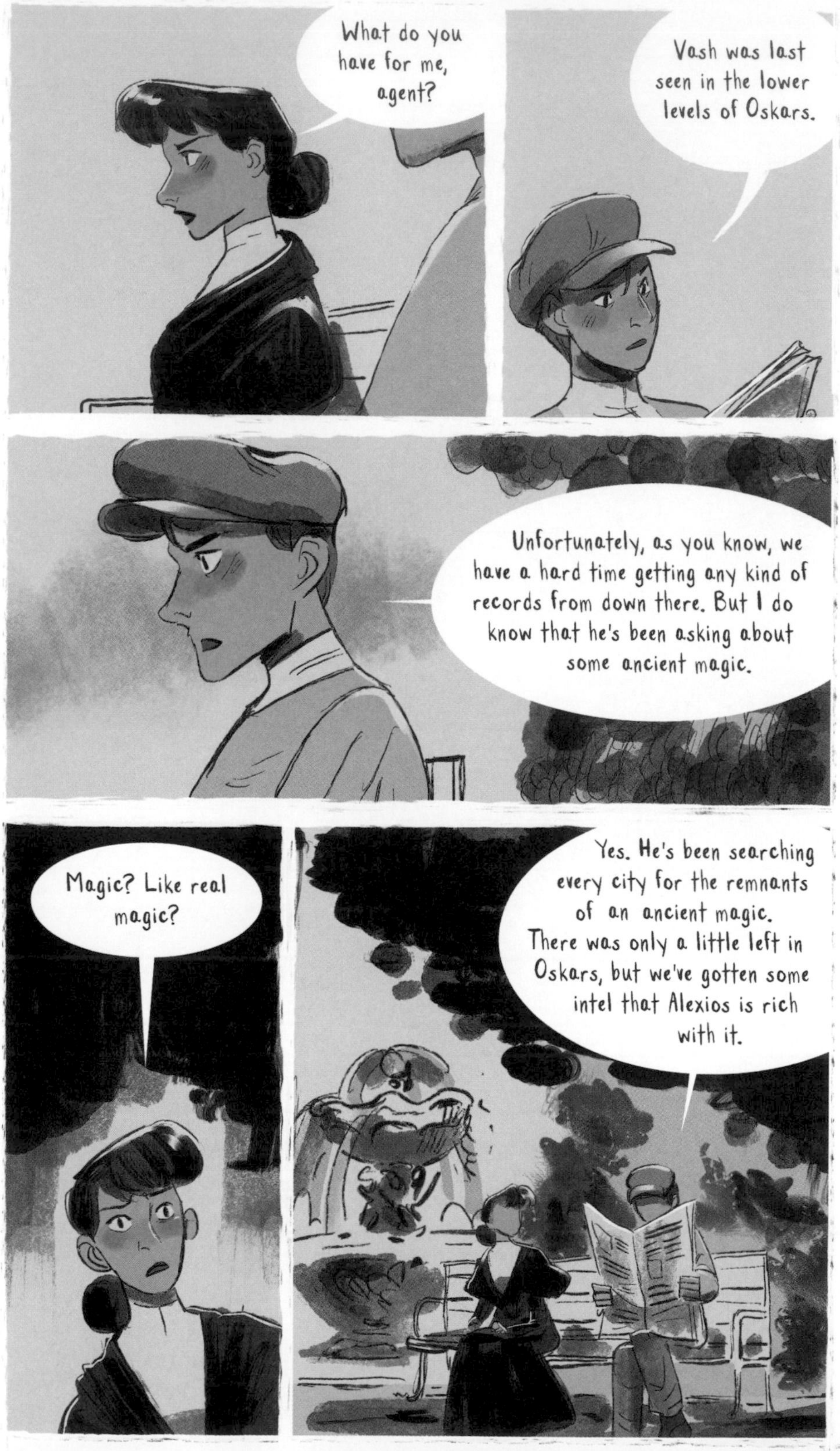
What do you have for me, agent?
Vash was last seen in the lower levels of Oskars.
Unfortunately, as you know, we have a hard time getting any kind of records from down there. But I do know that he's been asking about some ancient magic.
Magic? Like real magic?
Yes. He's been searching every city for the remnants of an ancient magic. There was only a little left in Oskars, but we've gotten some intel that Alexios is rich with it.

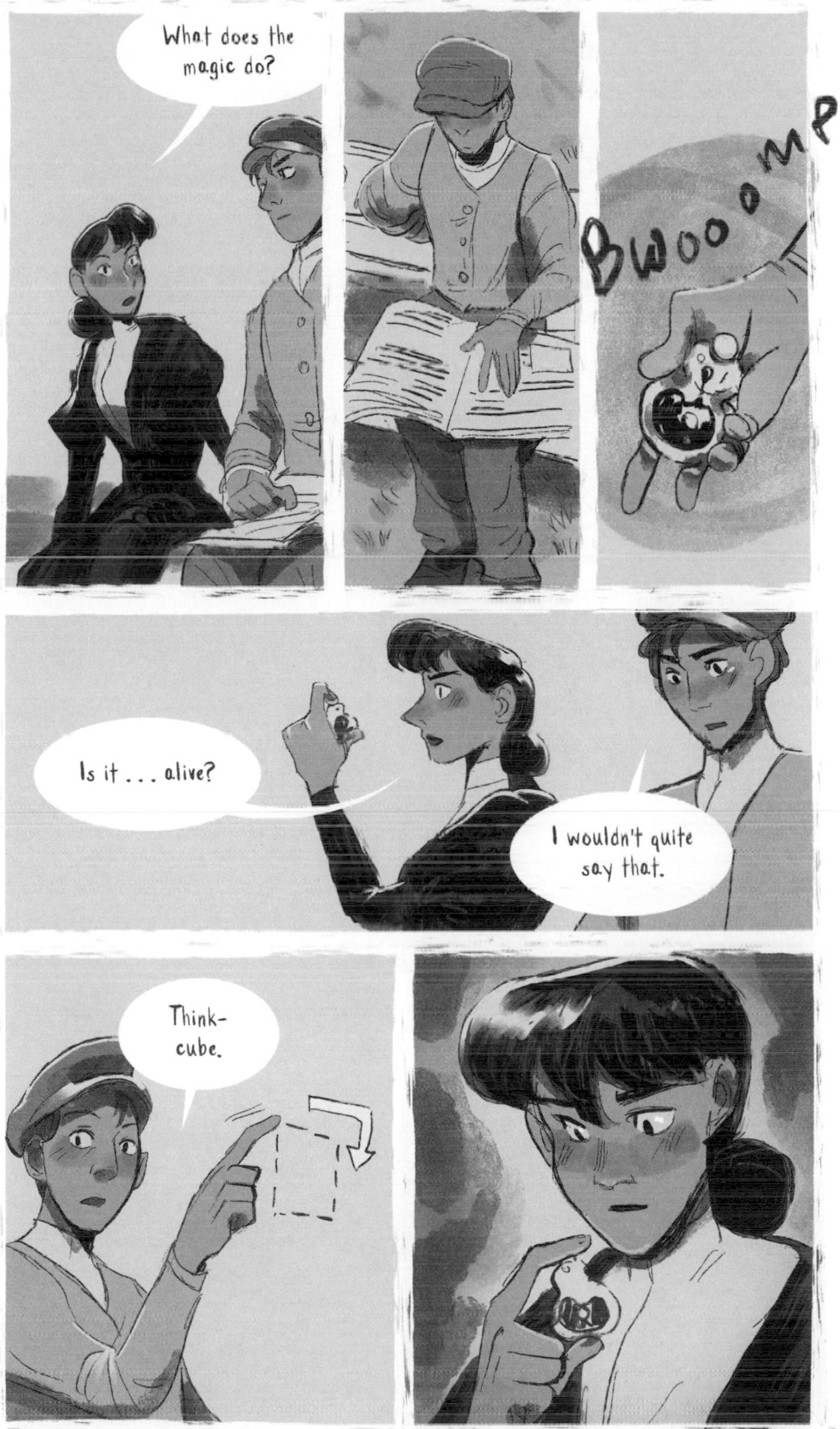
What does the magic do?
BWOOOOMP
Is it . . . alive?
I wouldn't quite say that.
Think-cube.

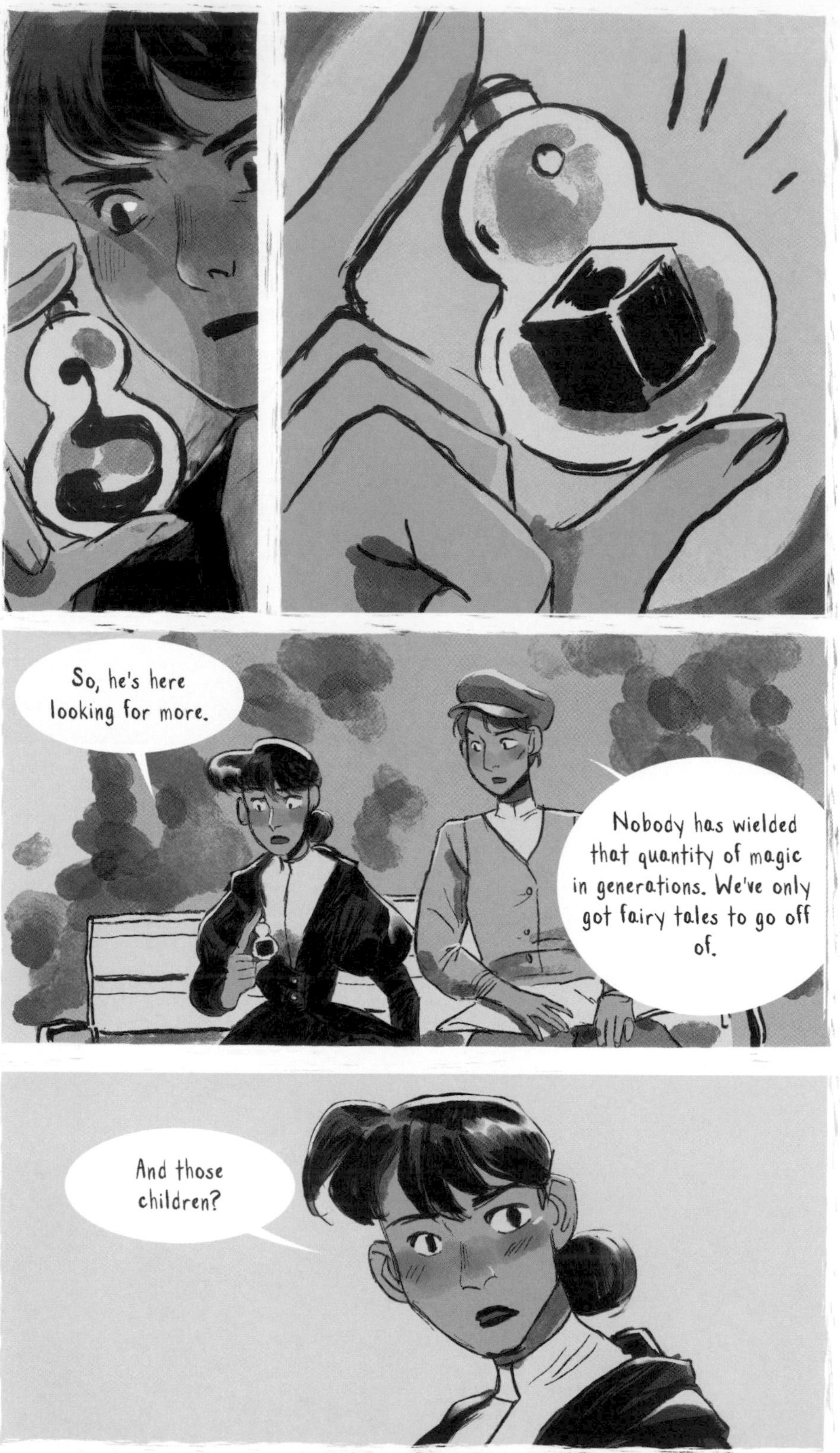
So, he's here looking for more.
Nobody has wielded that quantity of magic in generations. We've only got fairy tales to go off of.
And those children?

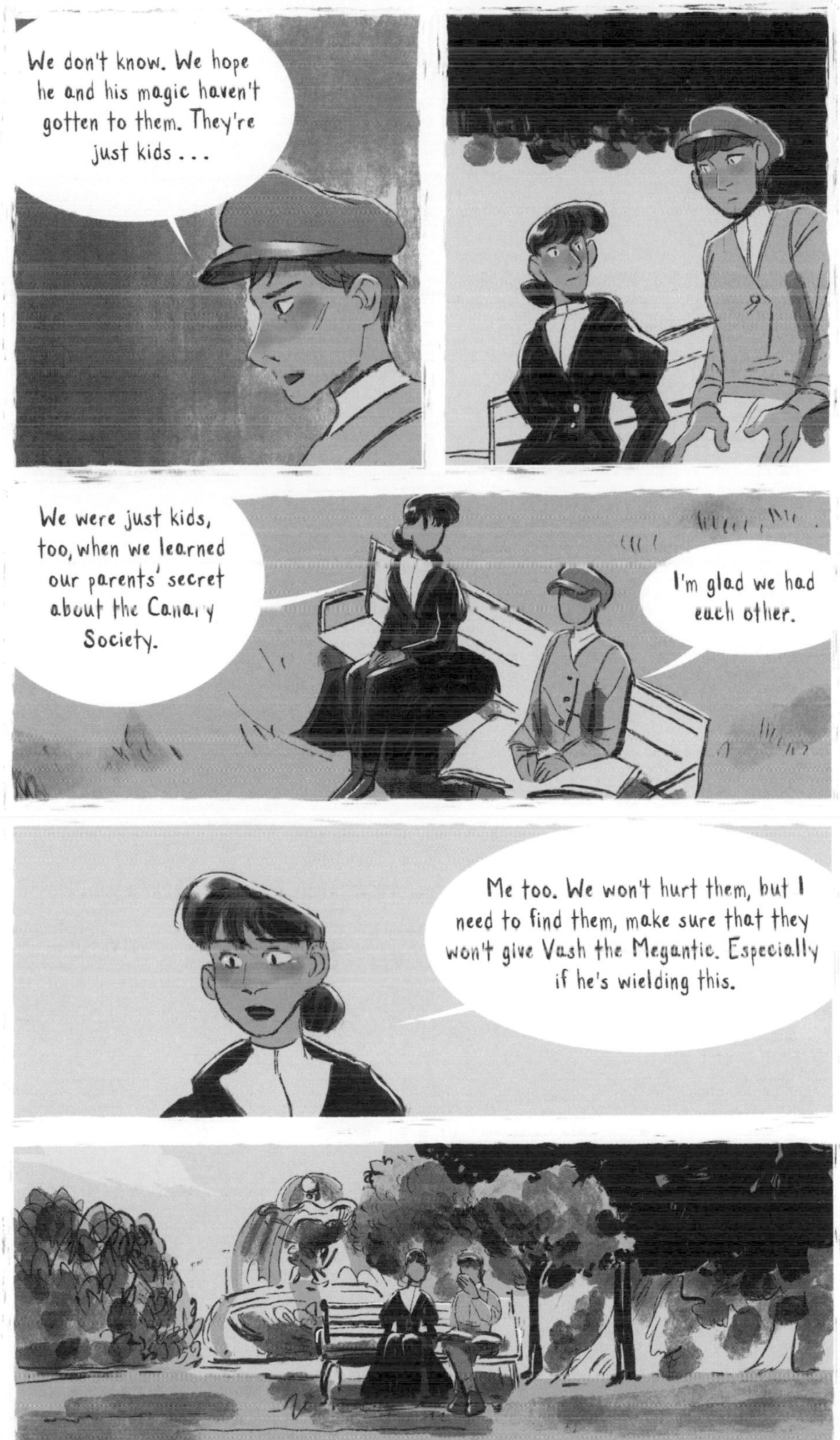
We don't know. We hope he and his magic haven't gotten to them. They're just kids . . .
We were just kids, too, when we learned our parents' secret about the Canary Society.
I'm glad we had each other.
Me too. We won't hurt them, but I need to find them, make sure that they won't give Vash the Megantic. Especially if he's wielding this.

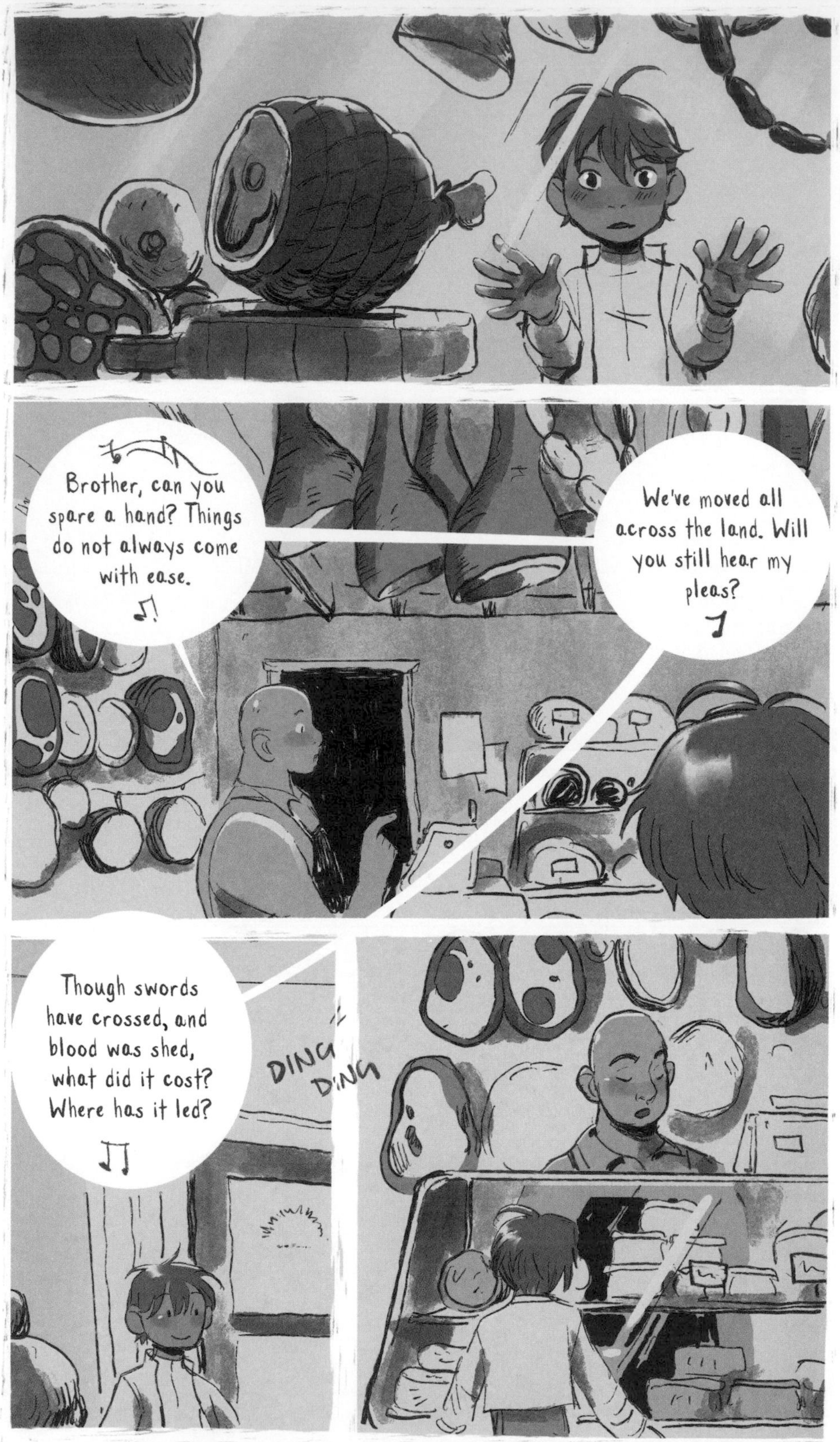
Brother, can you spare a hand? Things do not always come with ease.
We've moved all across the land. Will you still hear my pleas?
Though swords have crossed, and blood was shed, what did it cost? Where has it led?
DING DING

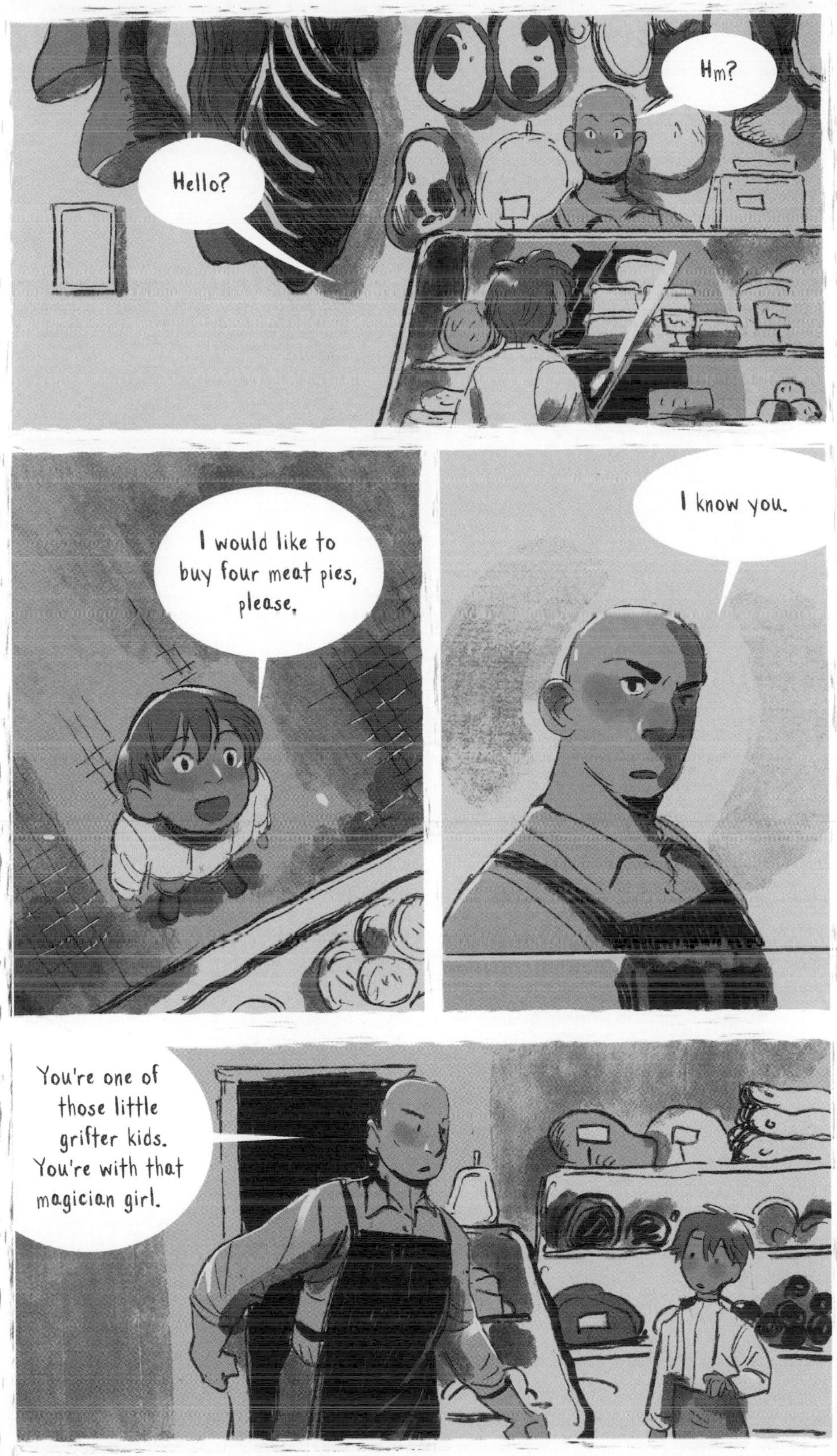
Hm?
Hello?
I would like to buy four meat pies, please.
I know you.
You're one of those little grifter kids. You're with that magician girl.

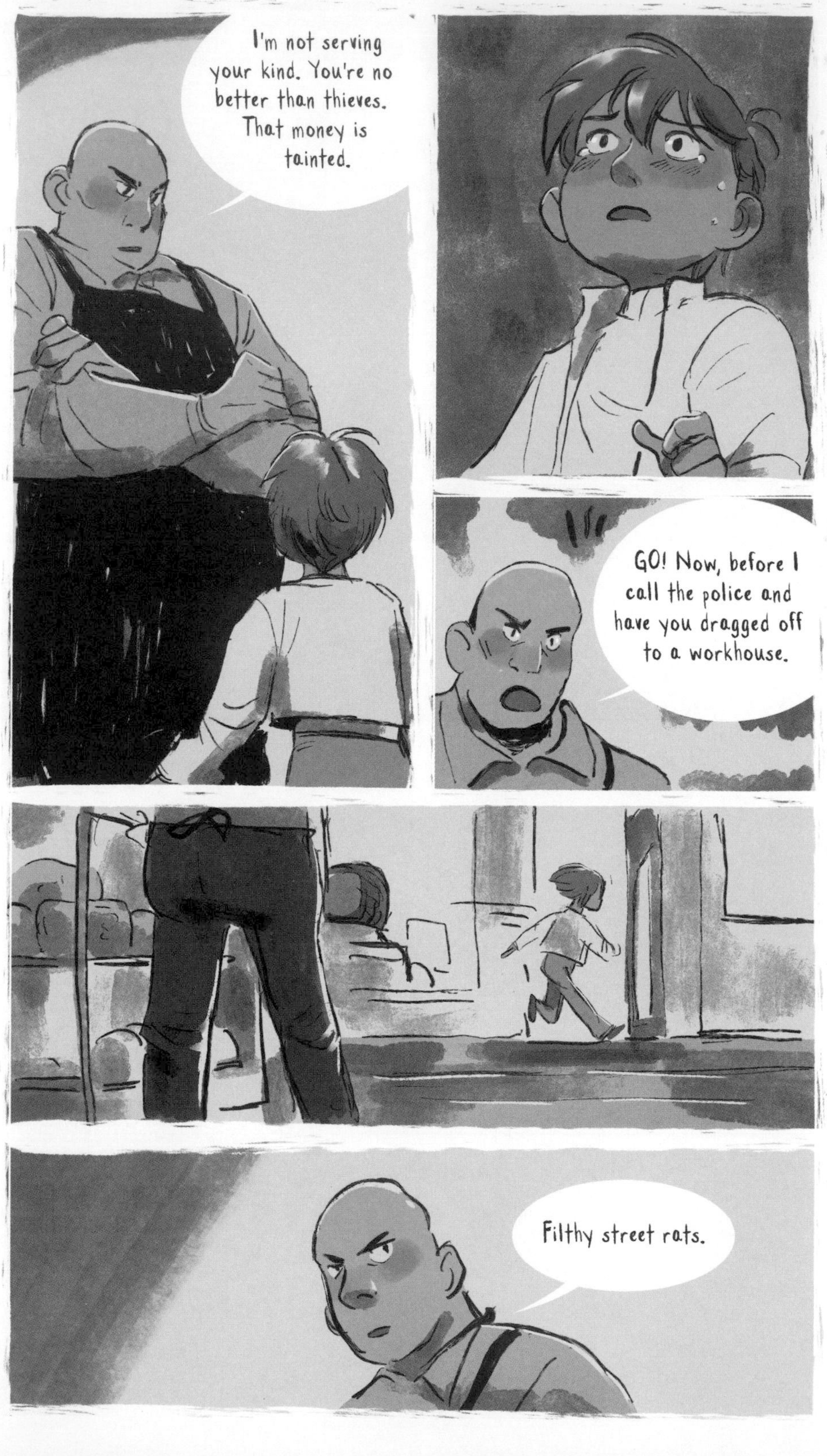
I'm not serving your kind. You're no better than thieves. That money is tainted.
GO! Now, before I call the police and have you dragged off to a workhouse.
Filthy street rats.

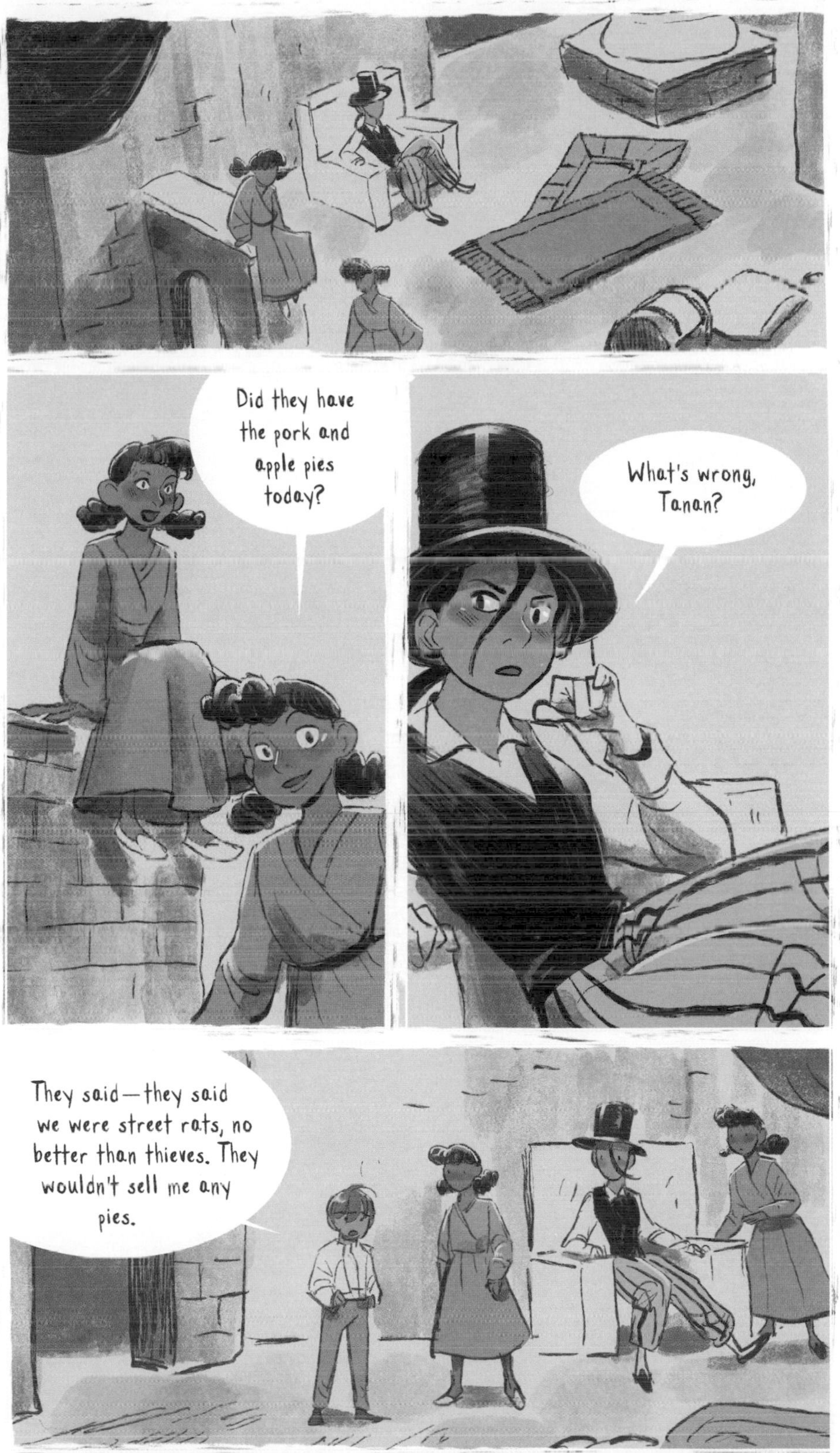
Did they have the pork and apple pies today?
What's wrong, Tanan?
They said—they said we were street rats, no better than thieves. They wouldn't sell me any pies.

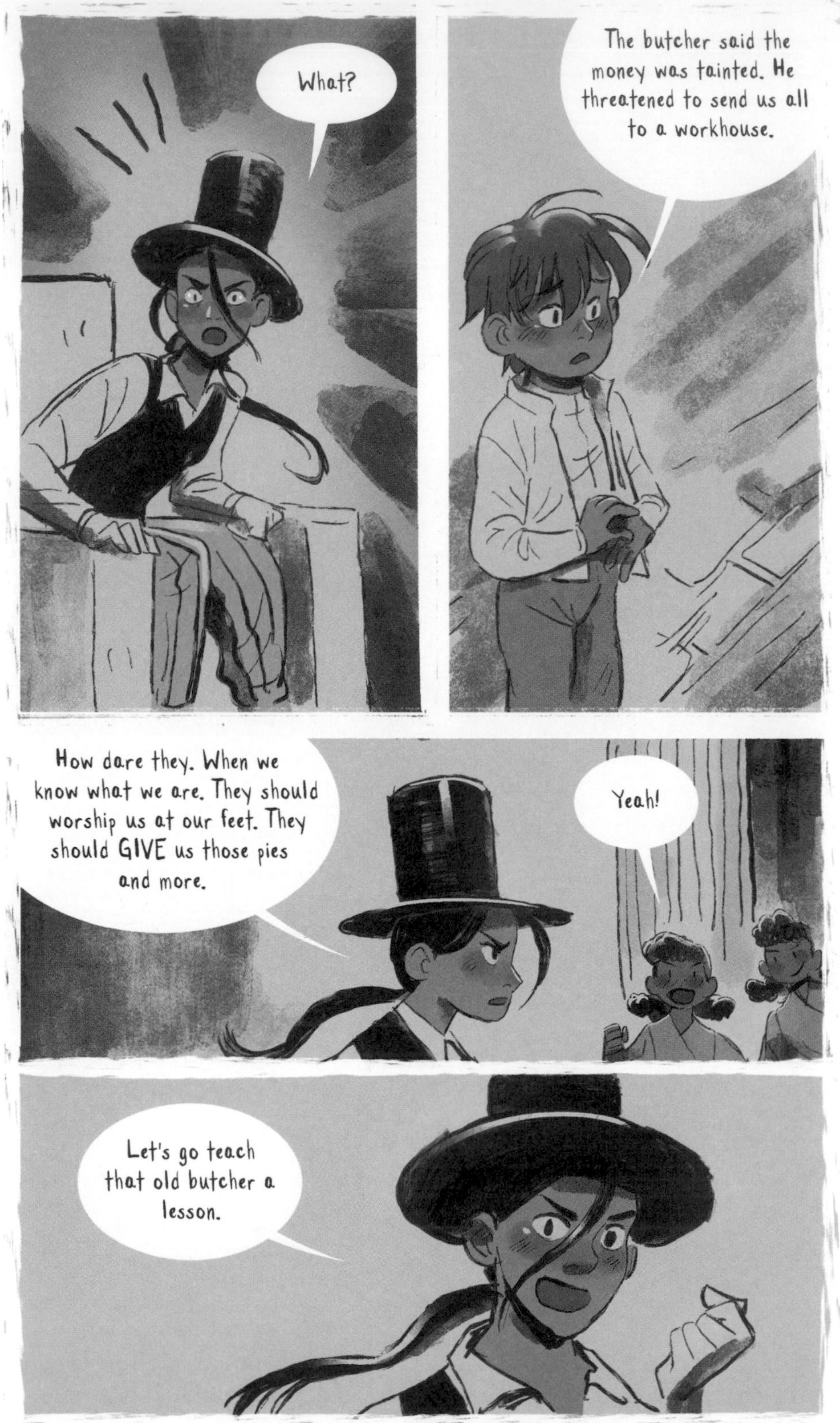
What?
The butcher said the money was tainted. He threatened to send us all to a workhouse.
How dare they. When we know what we are. They should worship us at our feet. They should GIVE us those pies and more.
Yeah!
Let's go teach that old butcher a lesson.

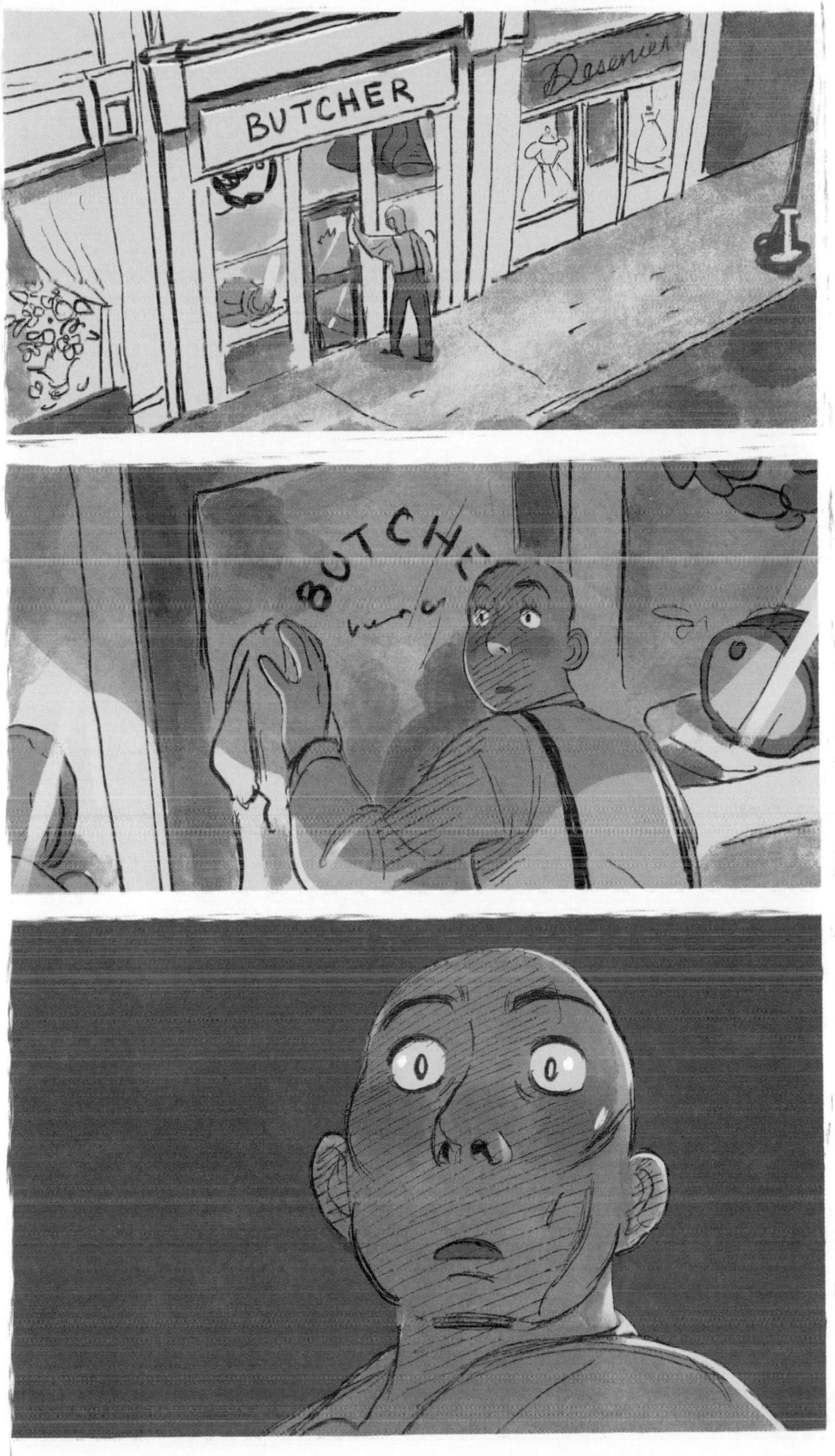
BUTCHER
BUTCHE

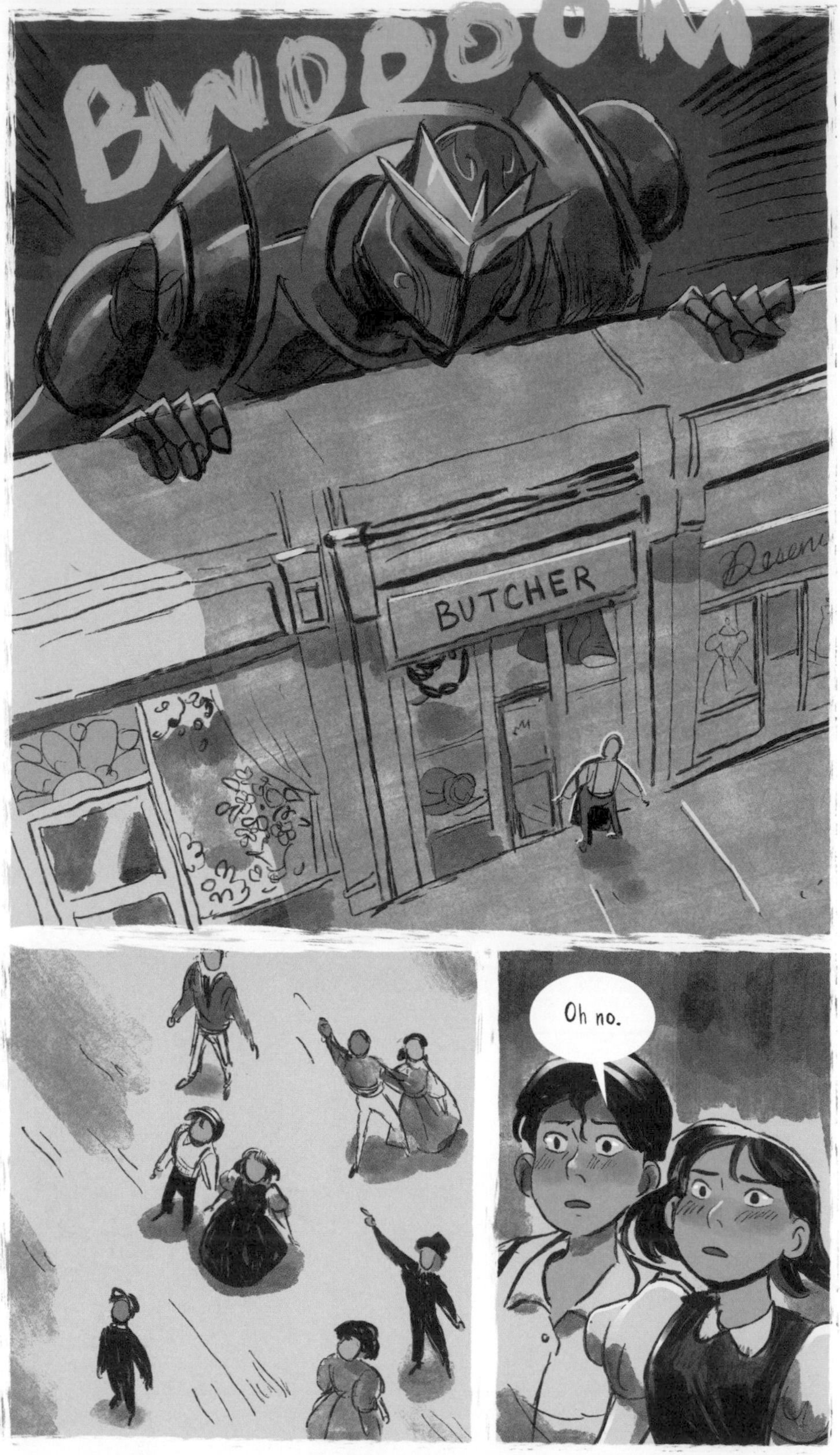
BWOOOOM
BUTCHER
Oh no.

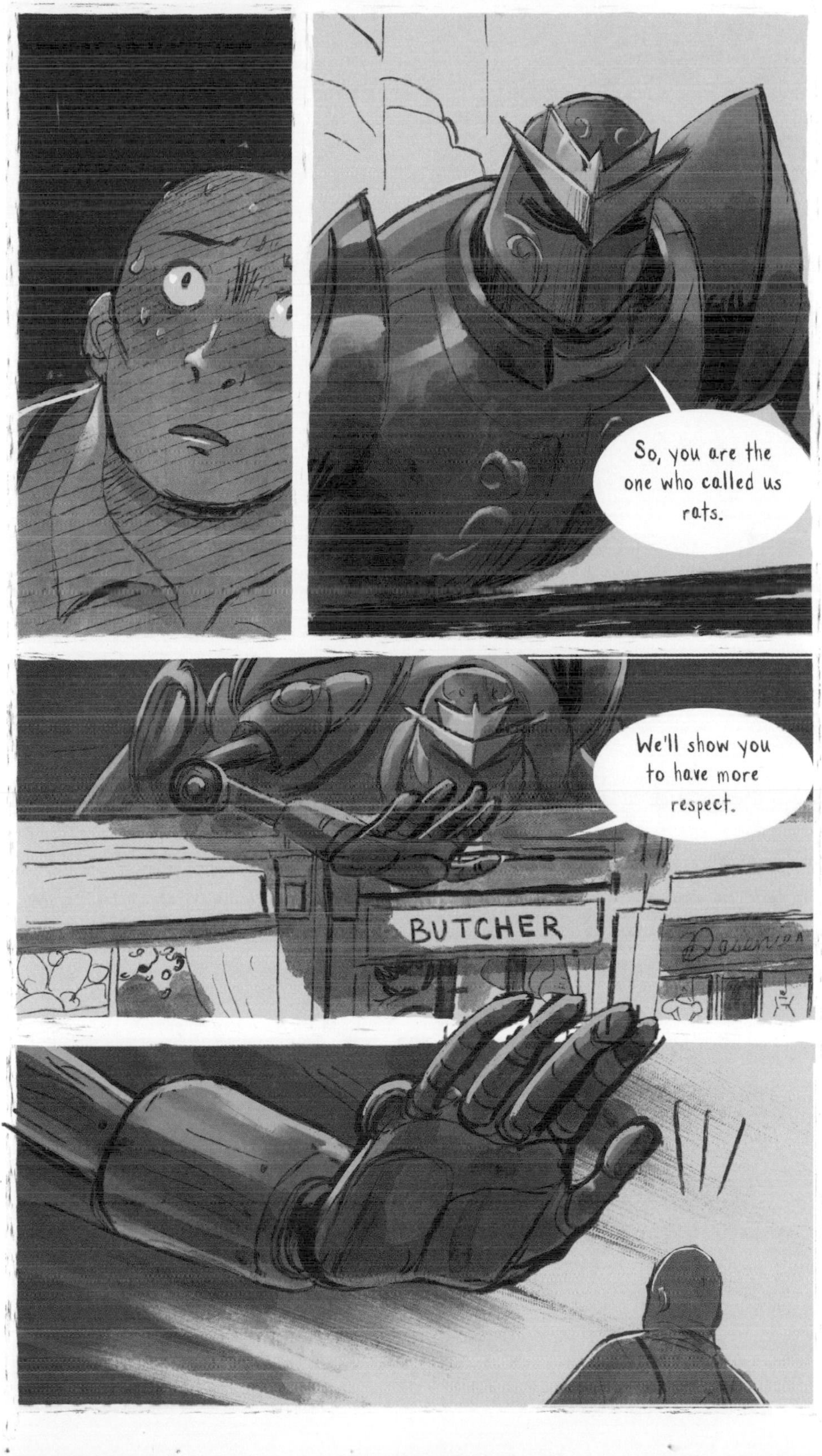
So, you are the one who called us rats.
We'll show you to have more respect.
BUTCHER

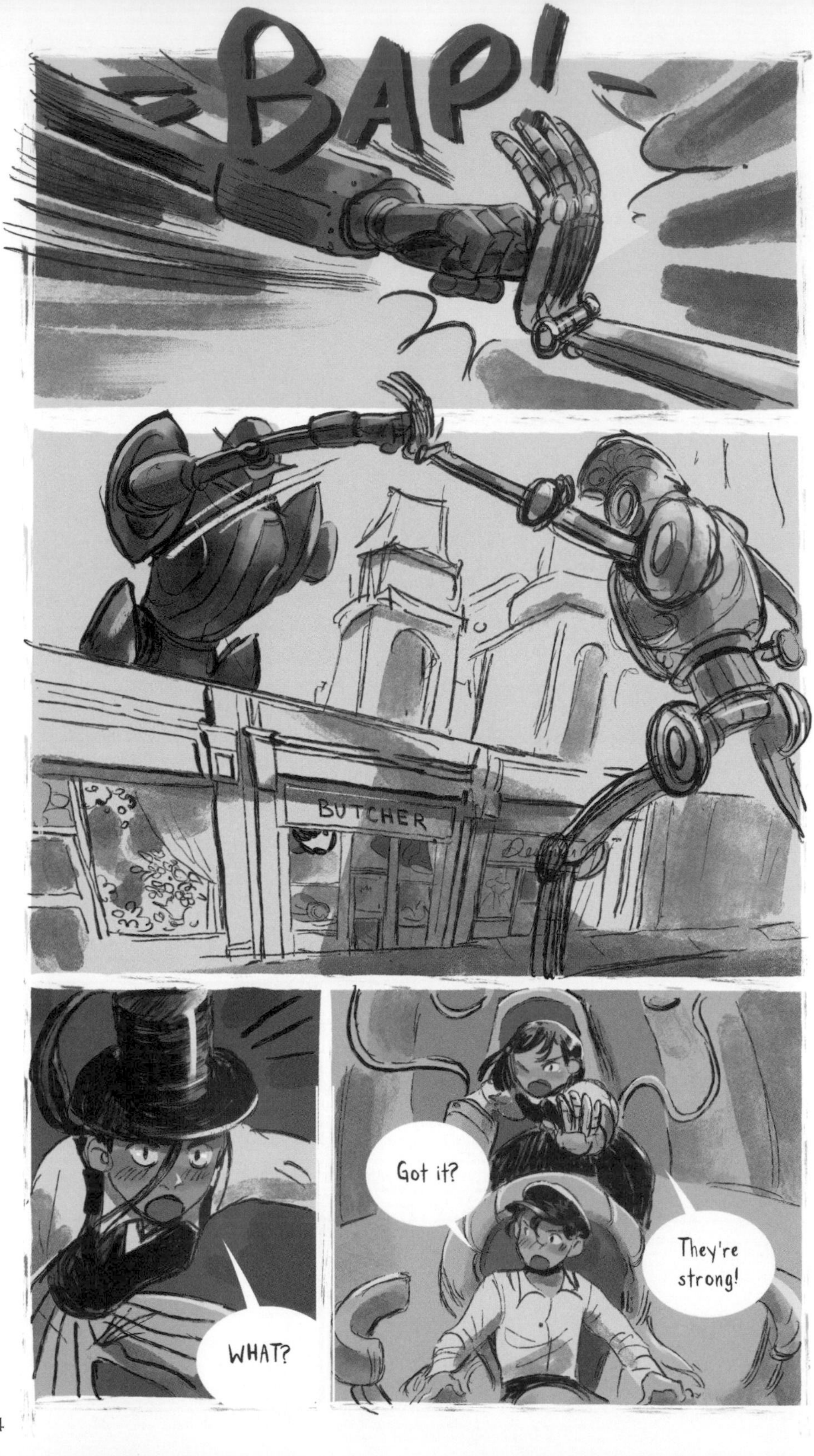
BAP!
BUTCHER
WHAT?
Got it?
They're strong!

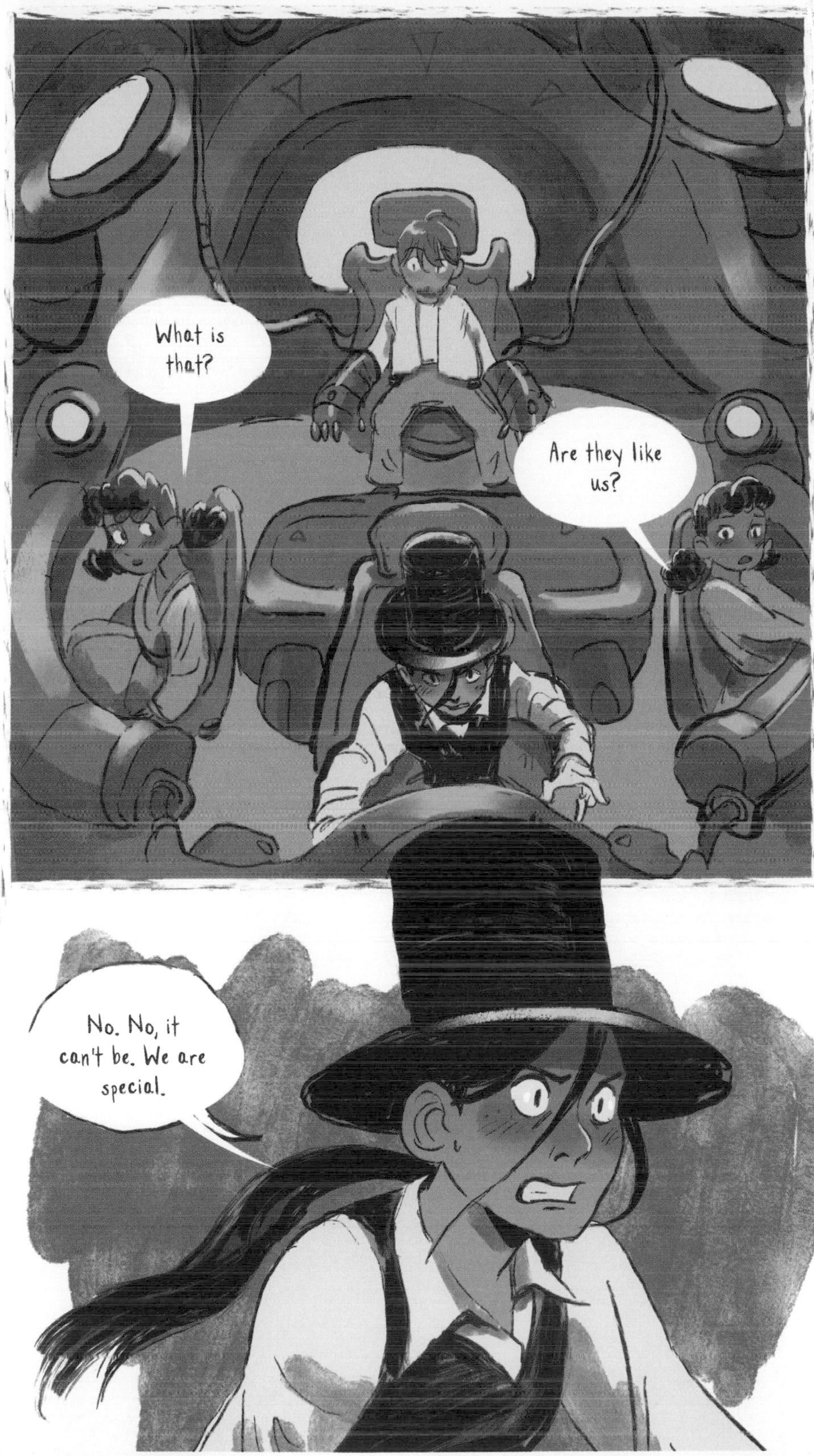
What is that?
Are they like us?
No. No, it can't be. We are special.

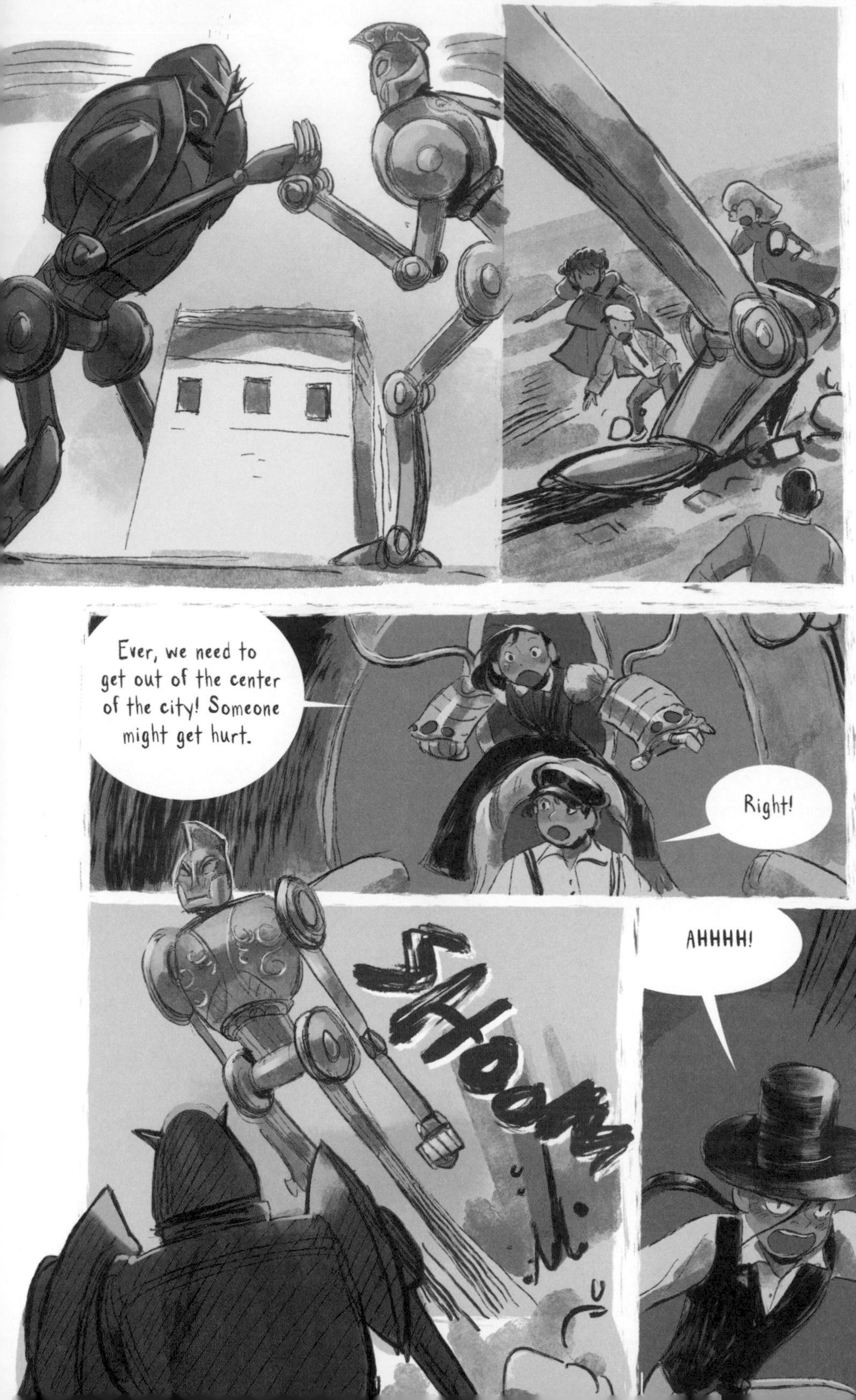
Ever, we need to get out of the center of the city! Someone might get hurt.
Right!
SHOOM
AHHHH!

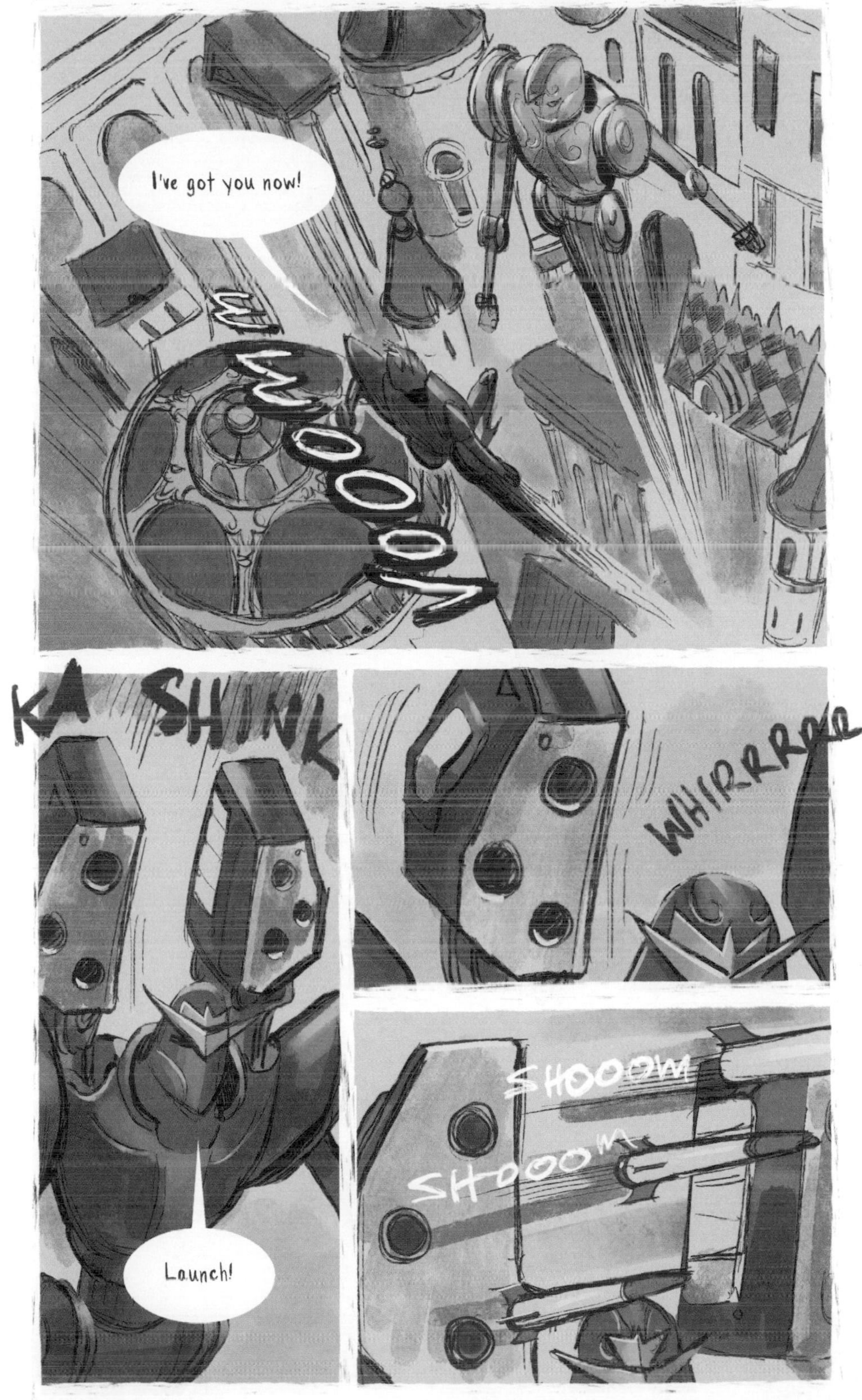
I've got you now!
KA SHINK
WHIRRRRR
Launch!
SHOOOM
SHOOOM

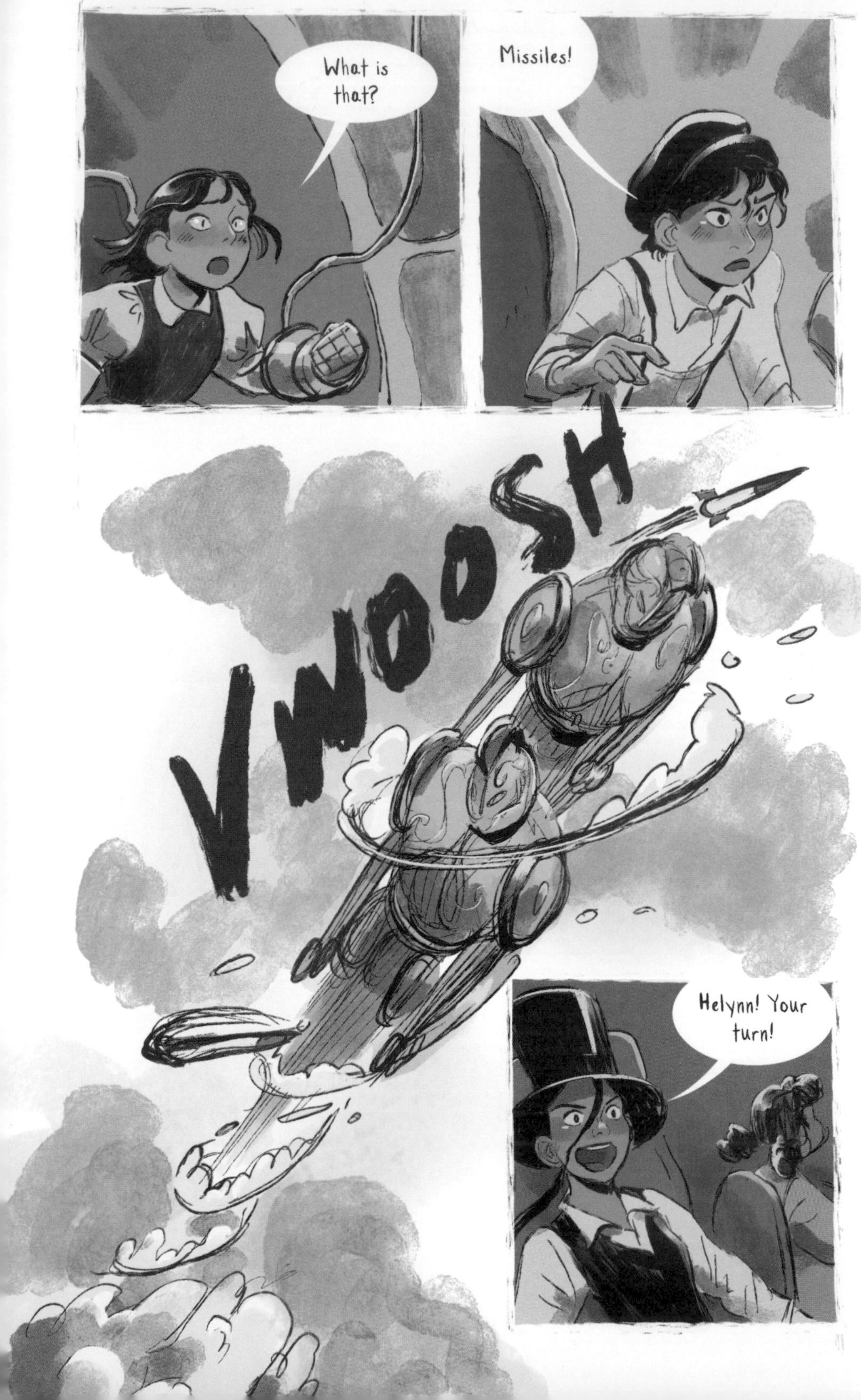
What is that?
Missiles!
VWOOSH
Helynn! Your turn!

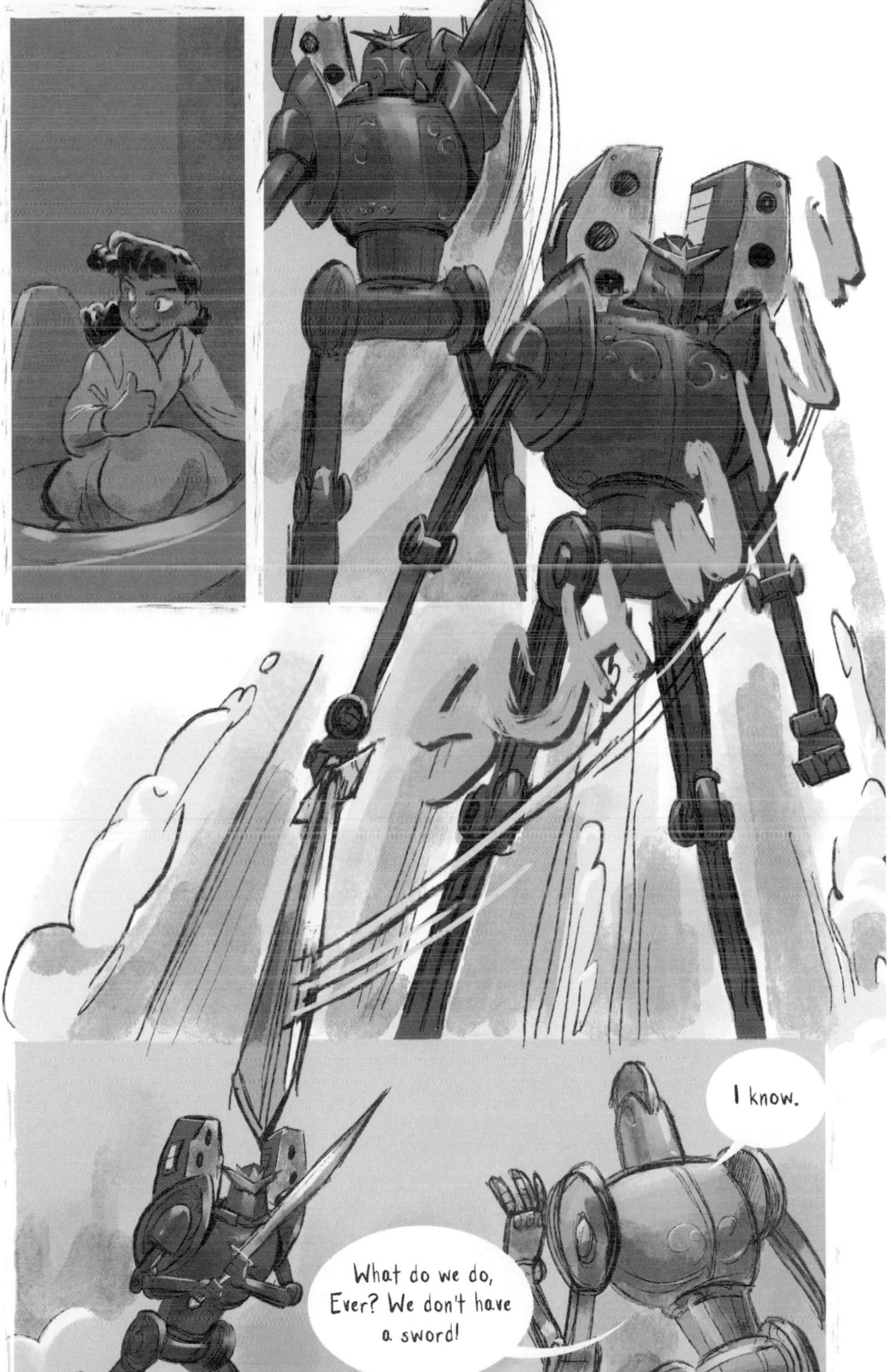
What do we do, Ever? We don't have a sword!
I know.

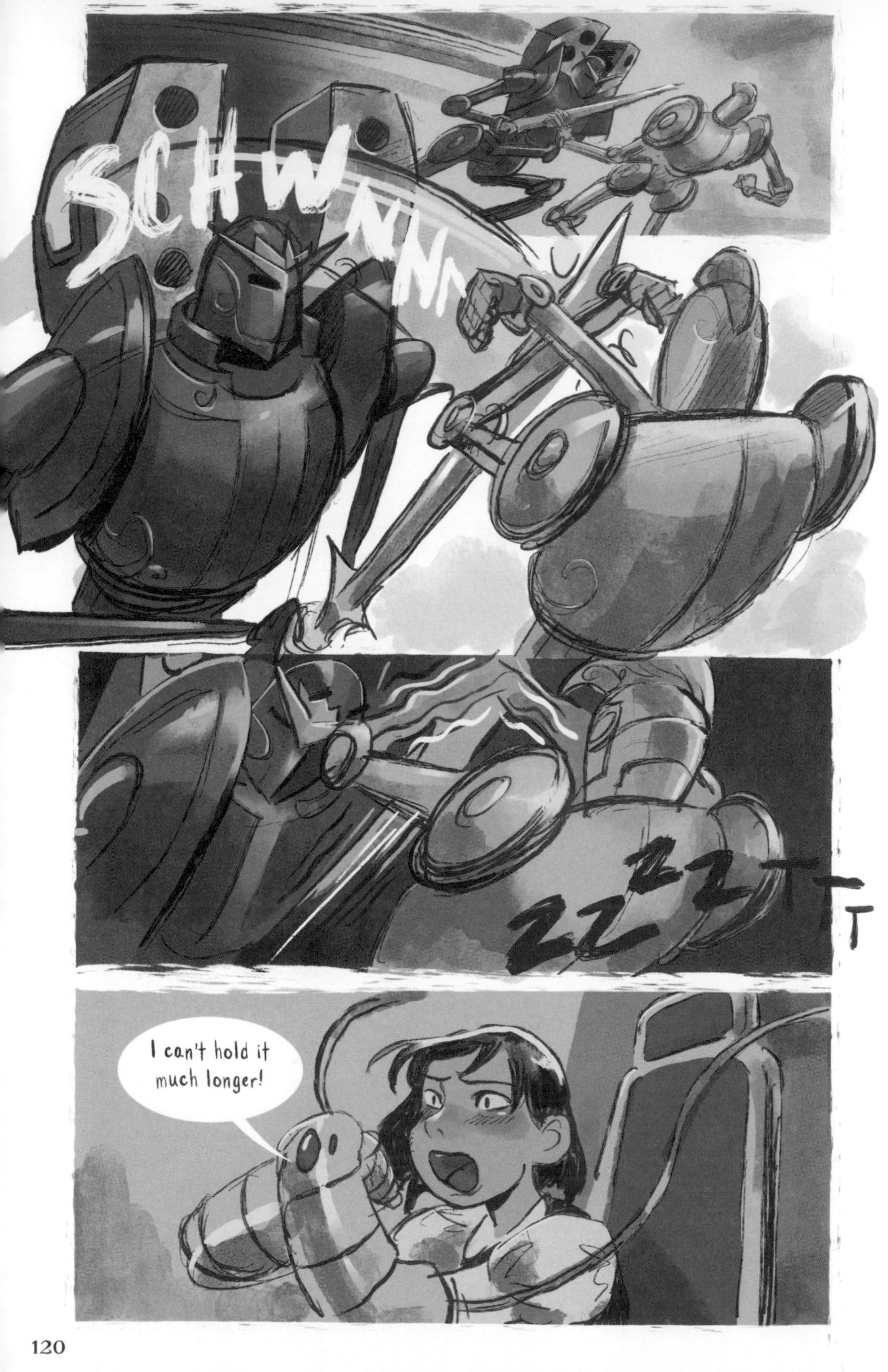
SCHWNNN
ZZZZZTTT
I can't hold it much longer!

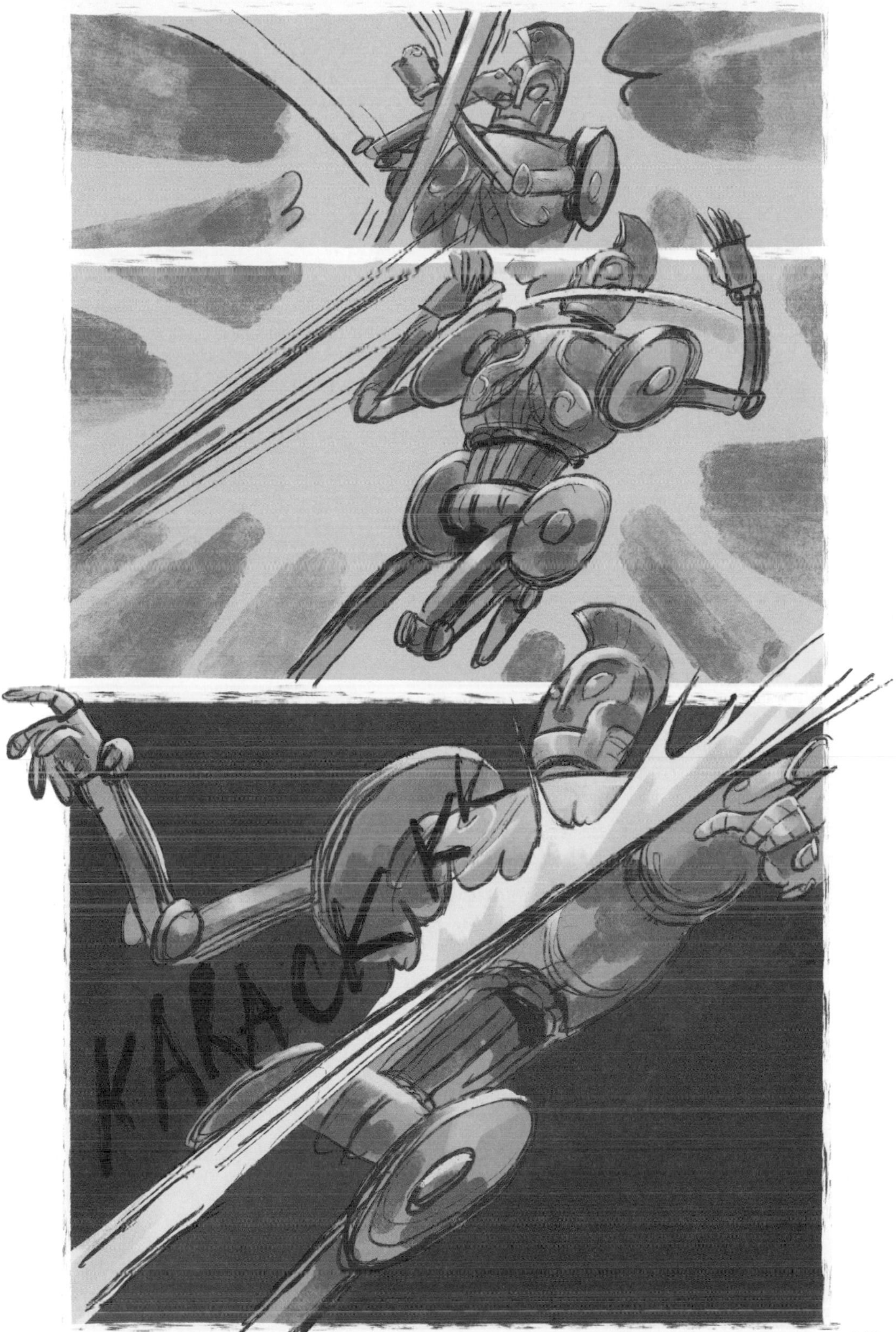
KARACKKK

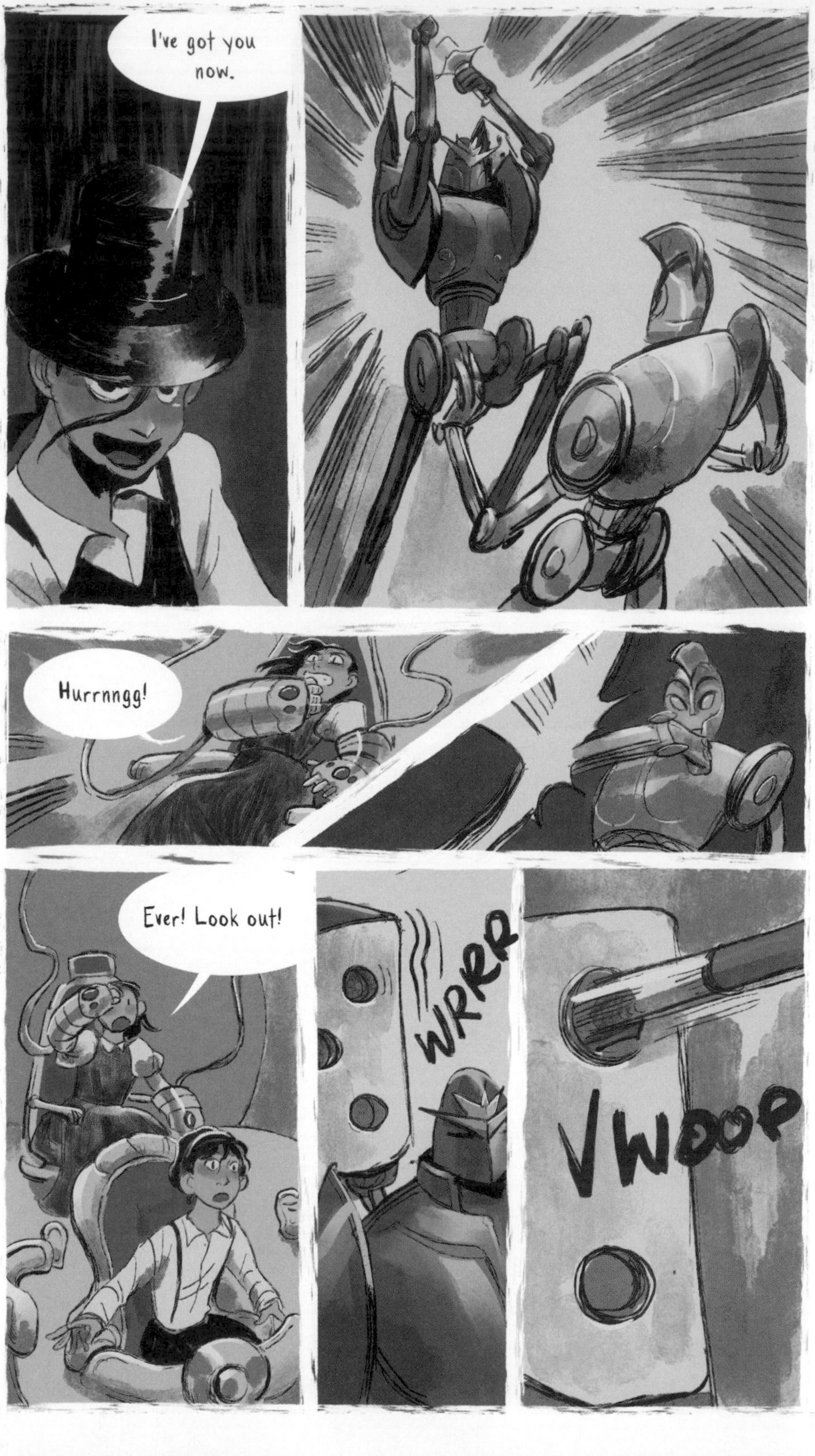
I've got you now.
Hurrnngg!
Ever! Look out!
WRRR
VWOOP

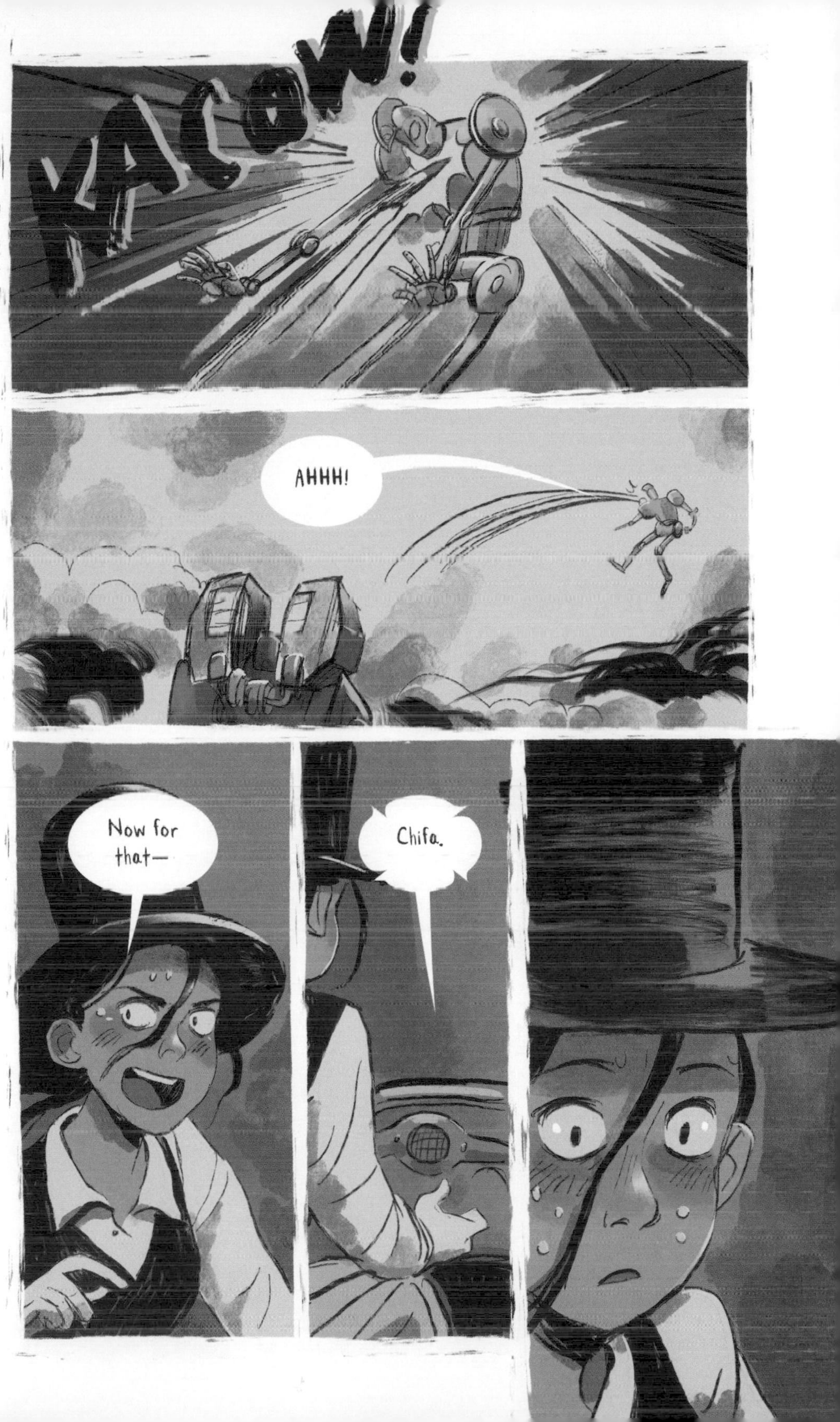
KACOW!!
AHHH!
Now for that—
Chifa.

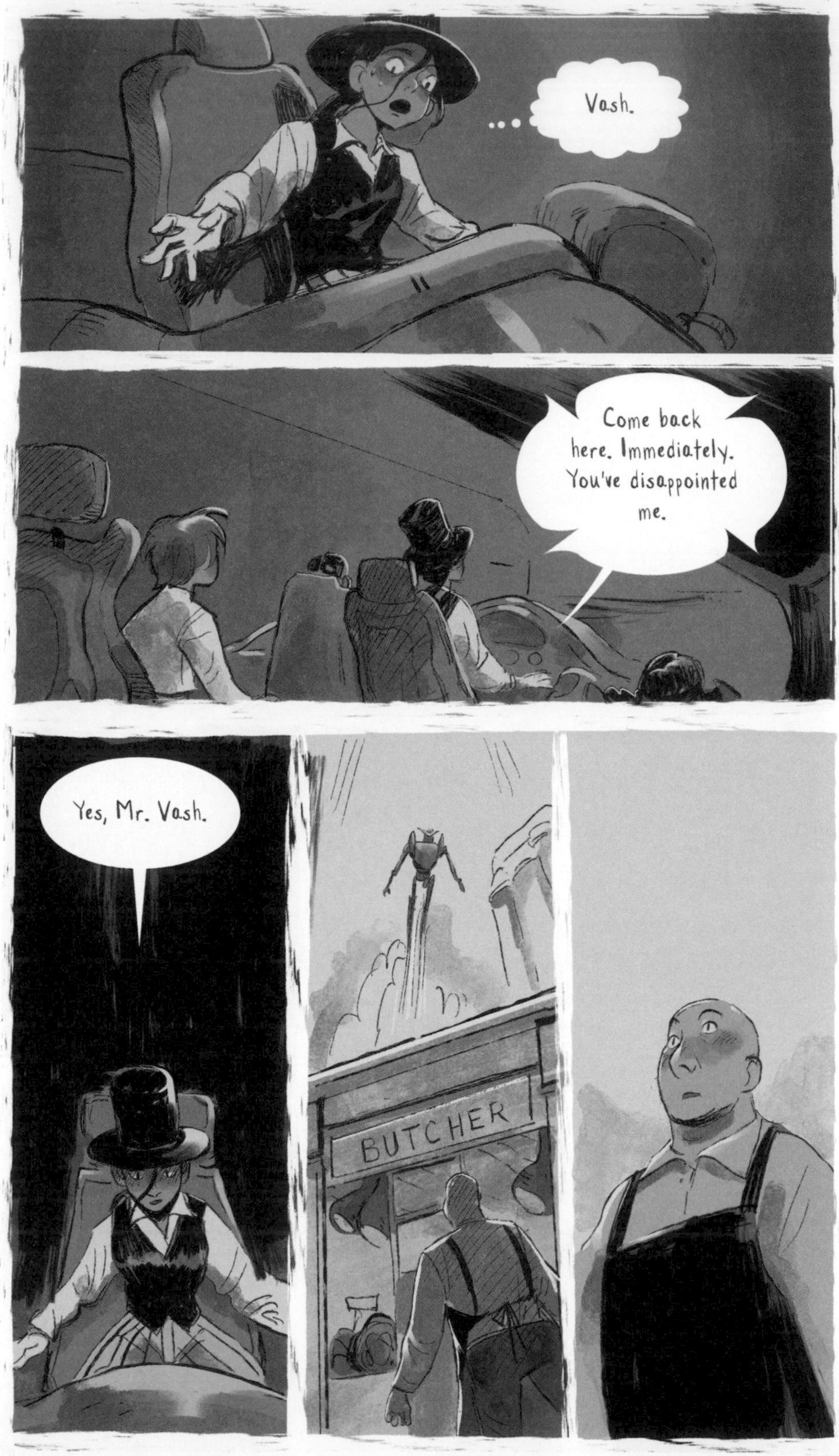
...
Vash.
Come back here. Immediately. You've disappointed me.
Yes, Mr. Vash.
BUTCHER

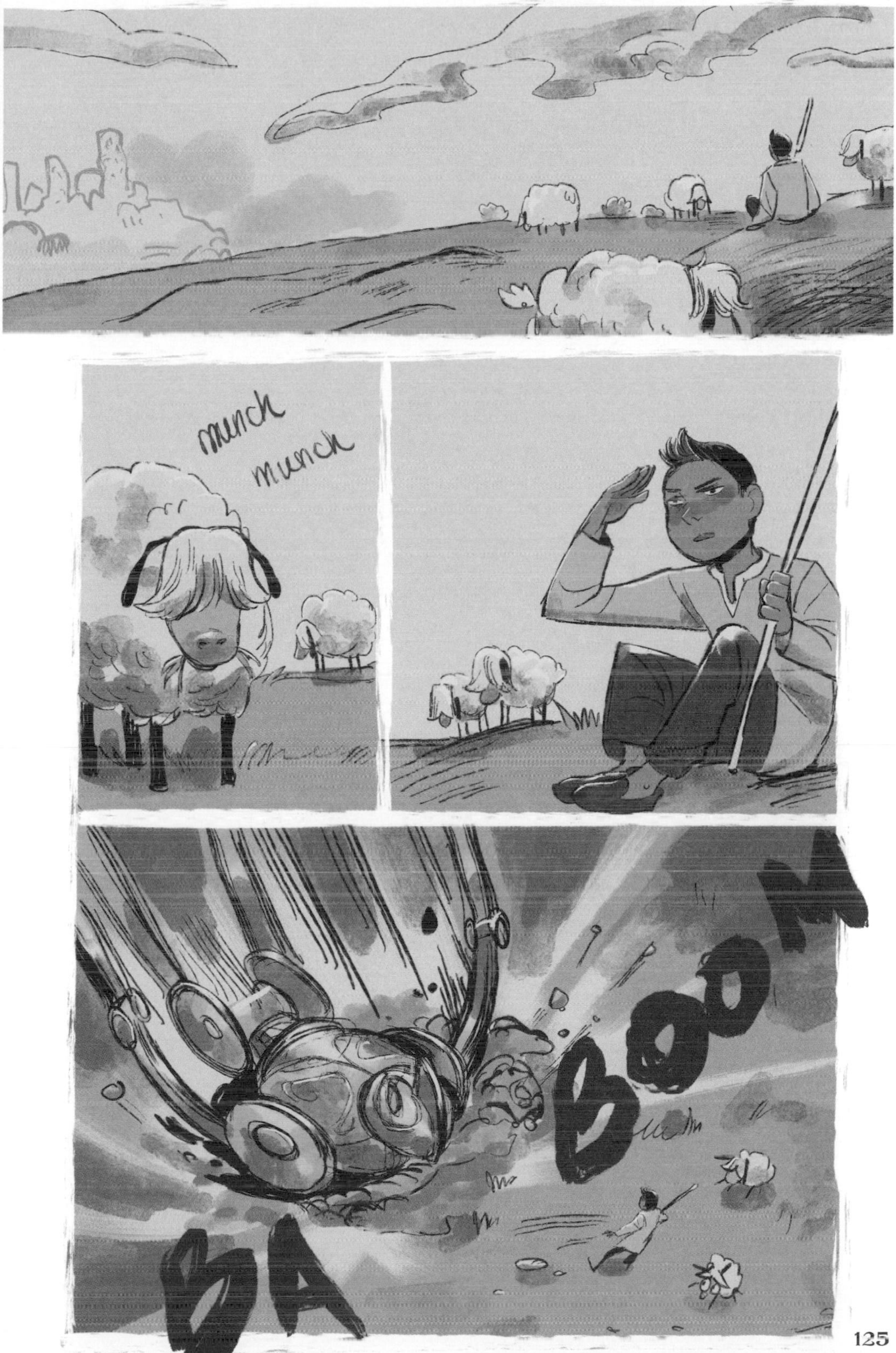
munch
munch
BA
BOOM

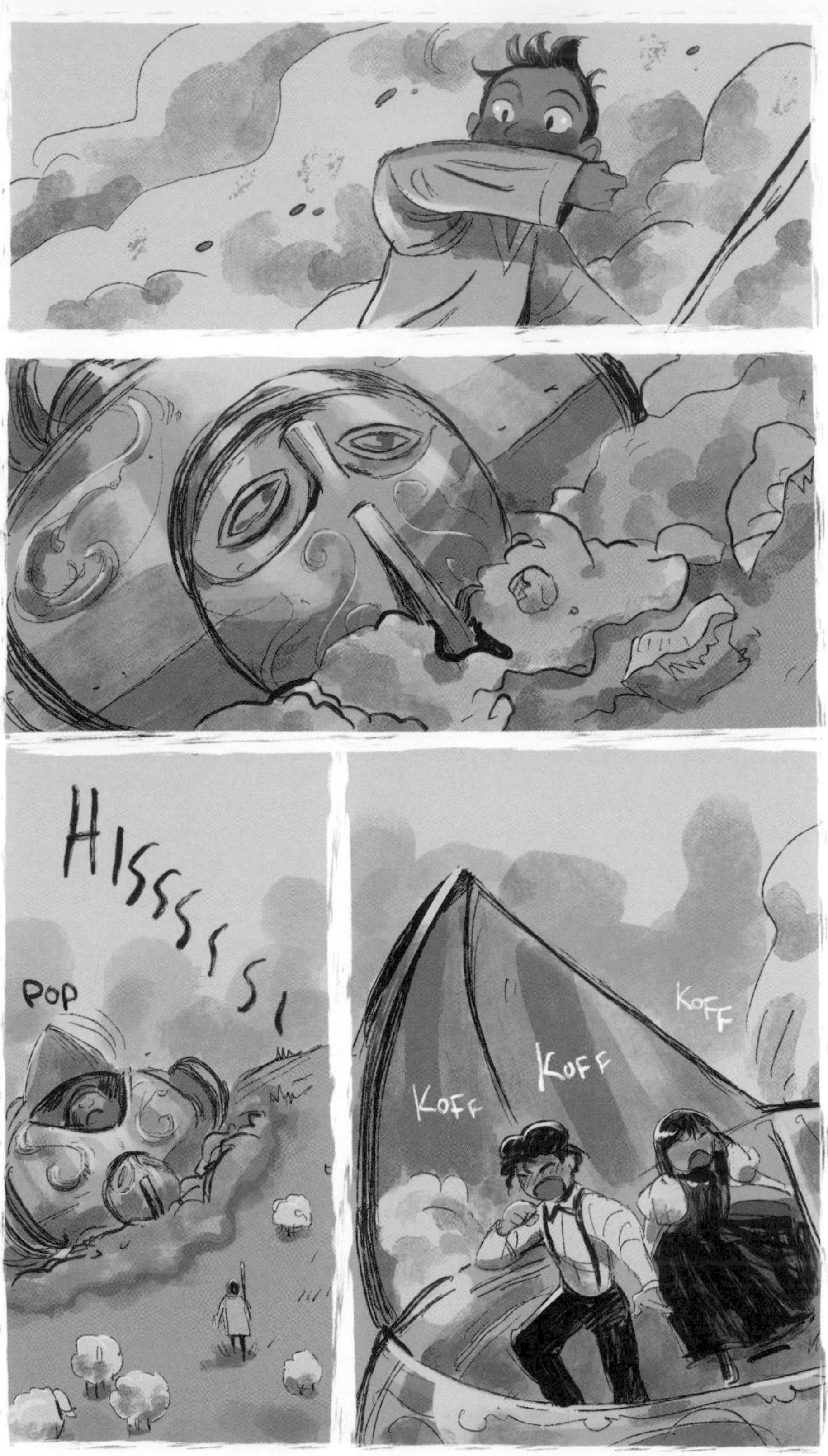
HISSSSSSI
POP
KOFF
KOFF
KOFF

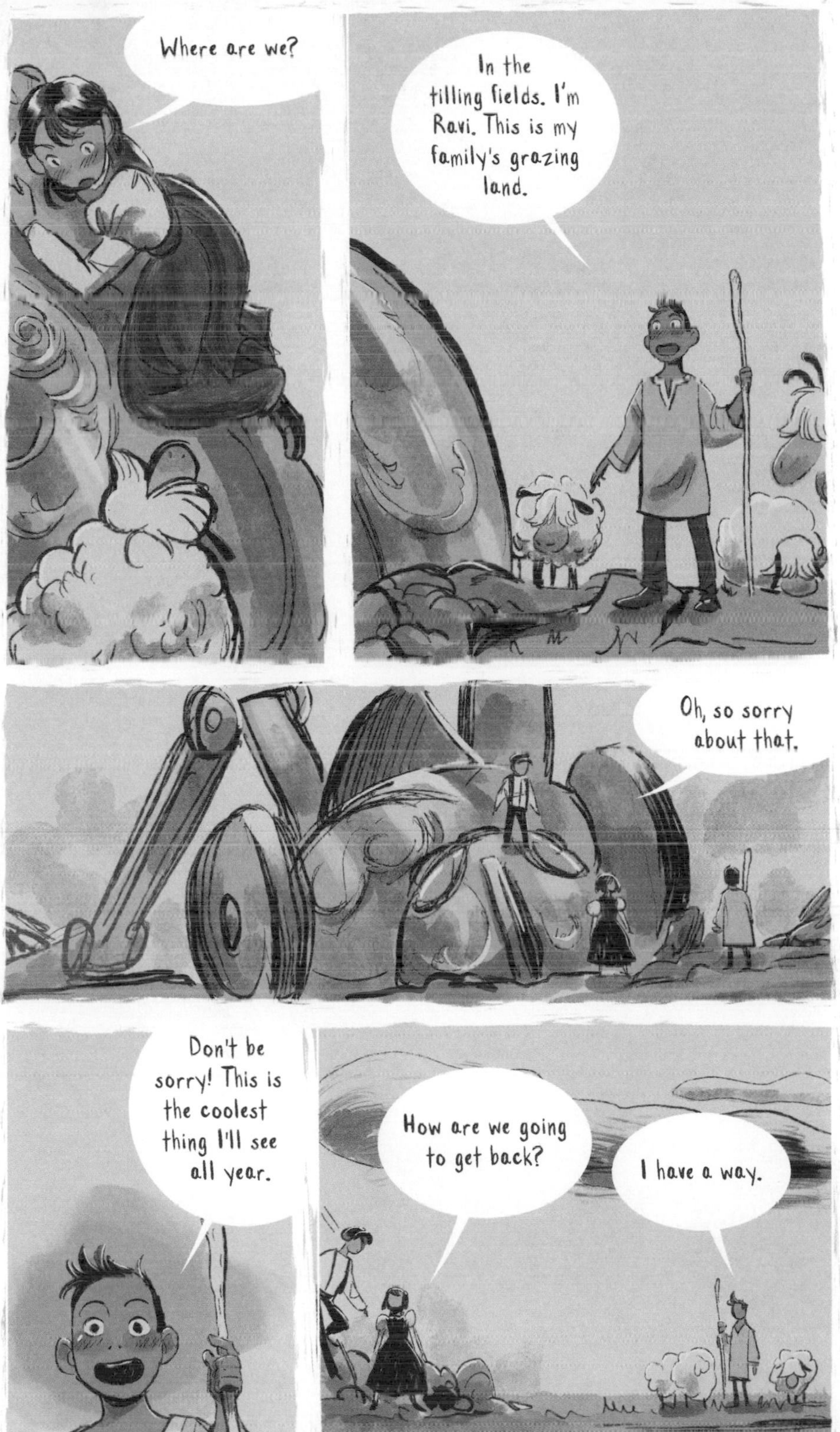
Where are we?
In the tilling fields. I'm Ravi. This is my family's grazing land.
Oh, so sorry about that.
Don't be sorry! This is the coolest thing I'll see all year.
How are we going to get back?
I have a way.

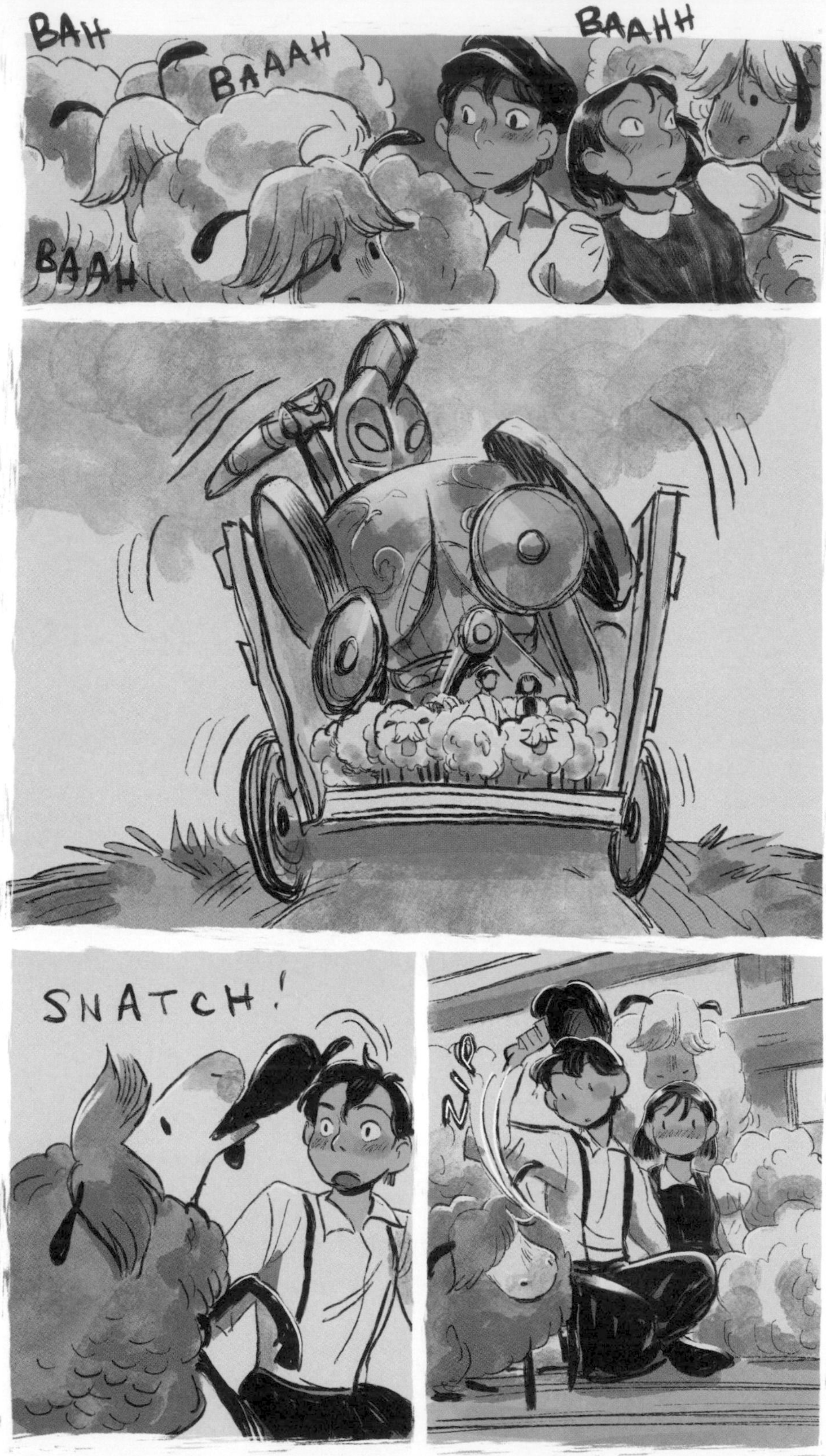
BAH
BAAAH
BAAHH
BAAH
SNATCH!

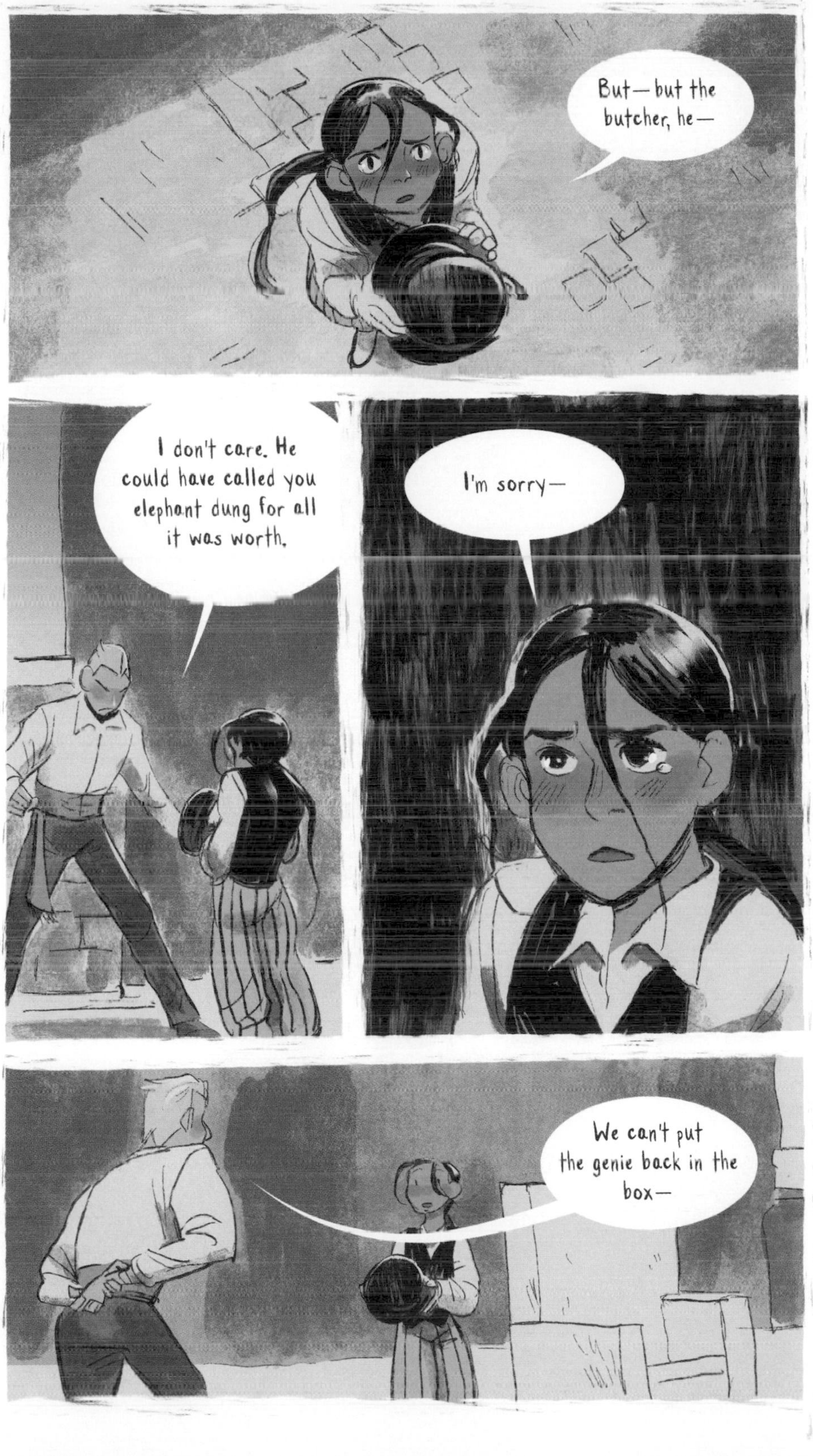
But—but the butcher, he—
I don't care. He could have called you elephant dung for all it was worth.
I'm sorry—
We can't put the genie back in the box—

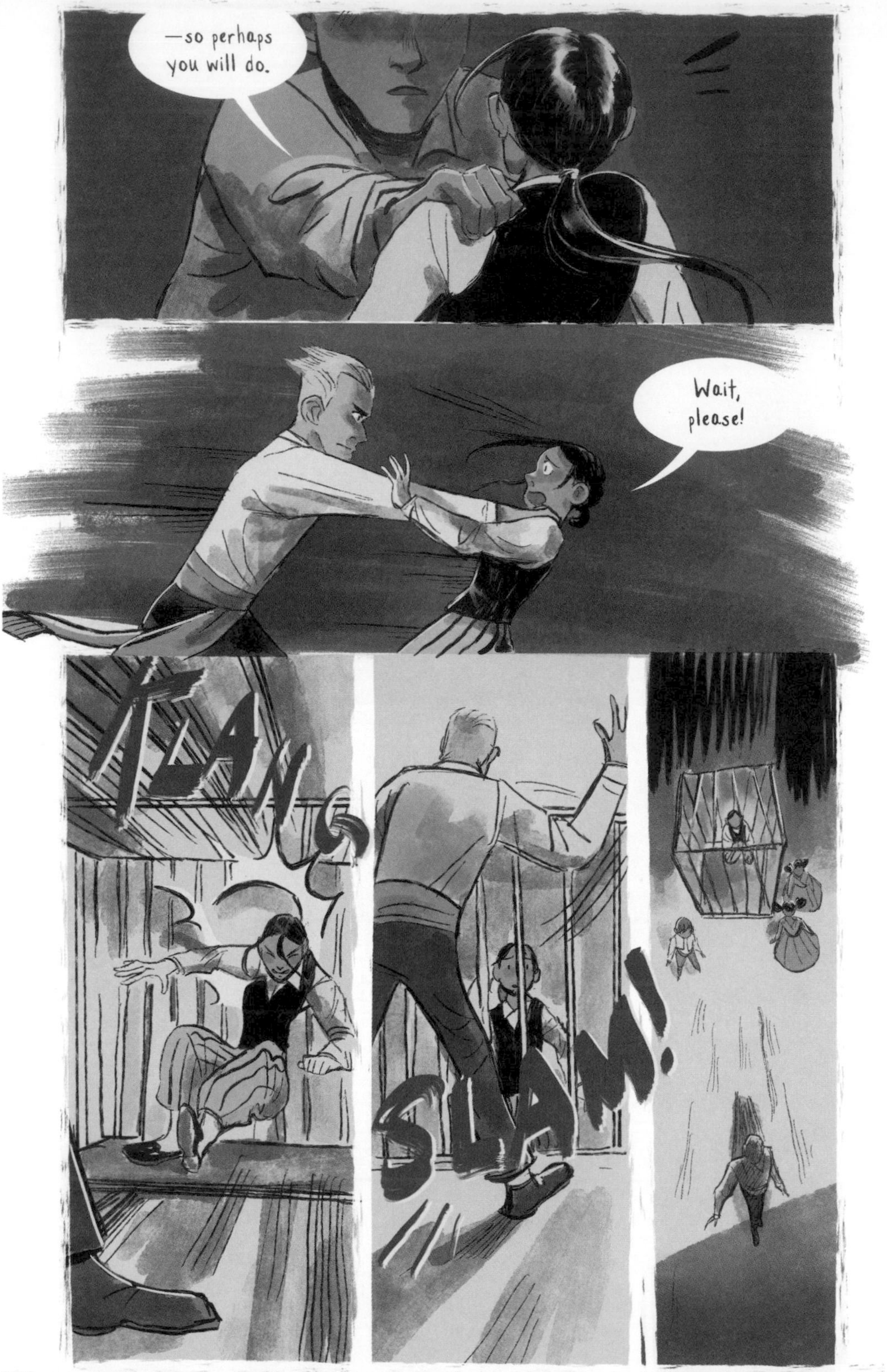
—so perhaps you will do.
Wait, please!
KLANG
SLAM!

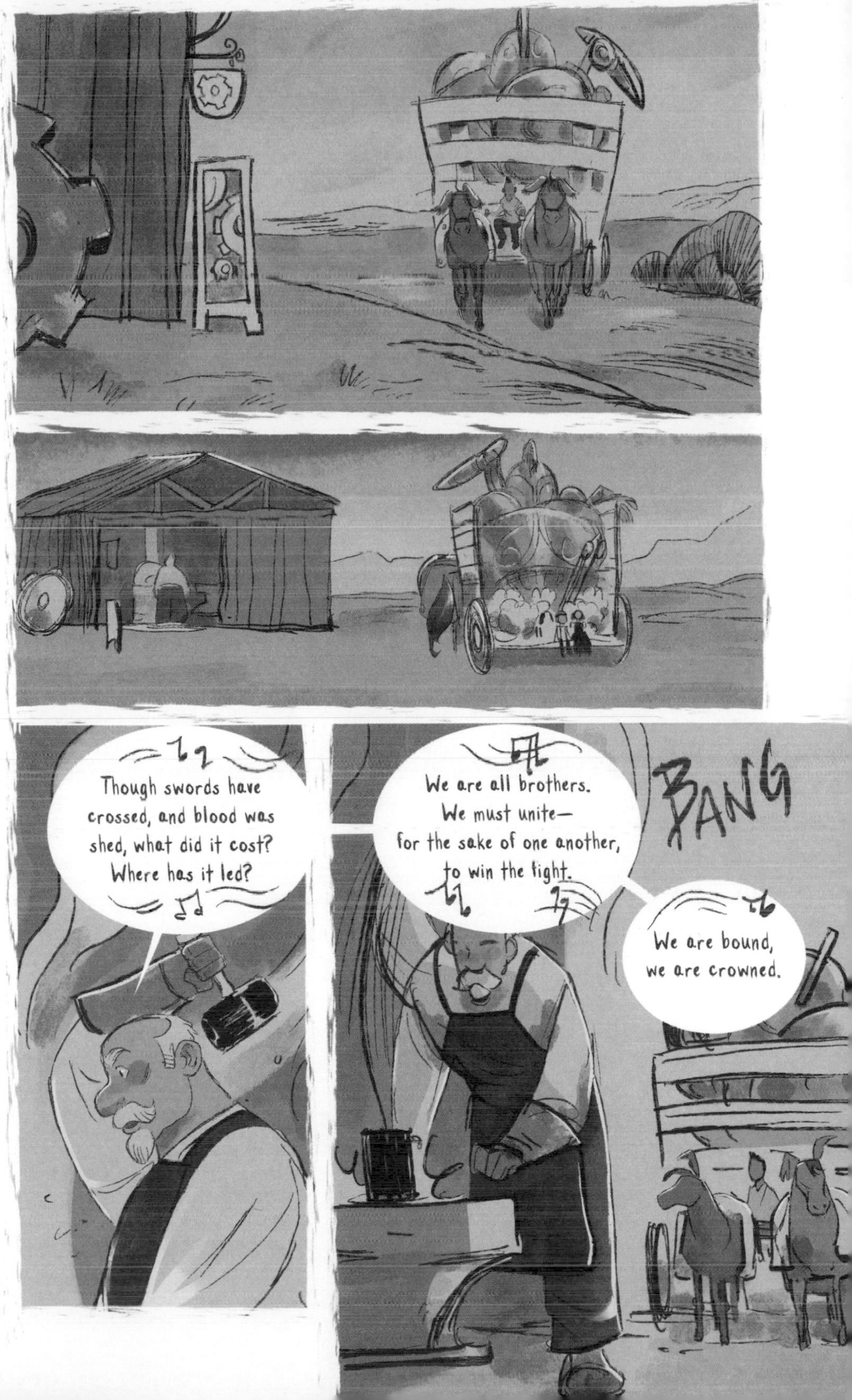
Though swords have crossed, and blood was shed, what did it cost? Where has it led?
We are all brothers. We must unite— for the sake of one another, to win the fight.
BANG
We are bound, we are crowned.

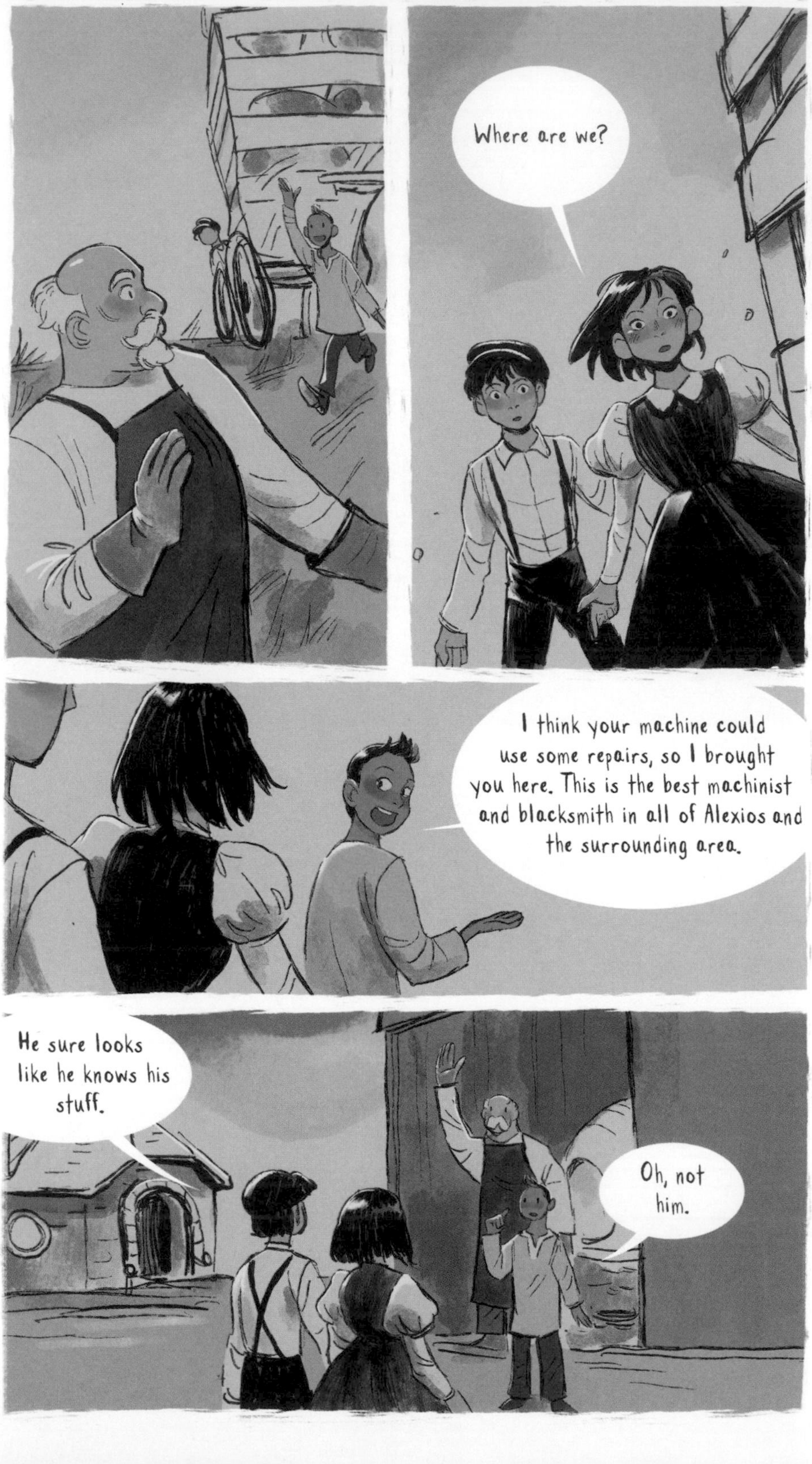

Where are we?
I think your machine could use some repairs, so I brought you here. This is the best machinist and blacksmith in all of Alexios and the surrounding area.
He sure looks like he knows his stuff.
Oh, not him.

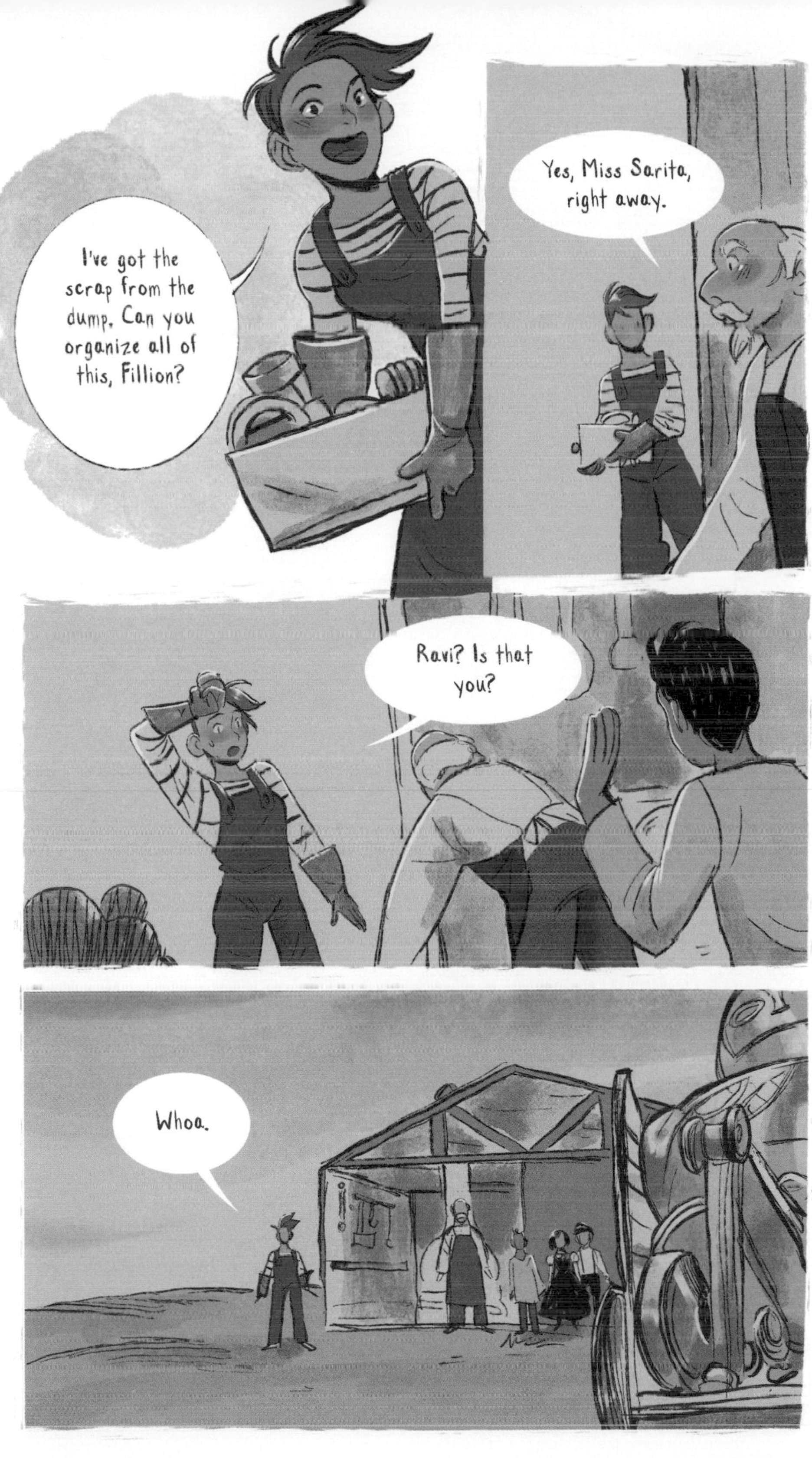
I've got the scrap from the dump. Can you organize all of this, Fillion?
Yes, Miss Sarita, right away.
Ravi? Is that you?
Whoa.

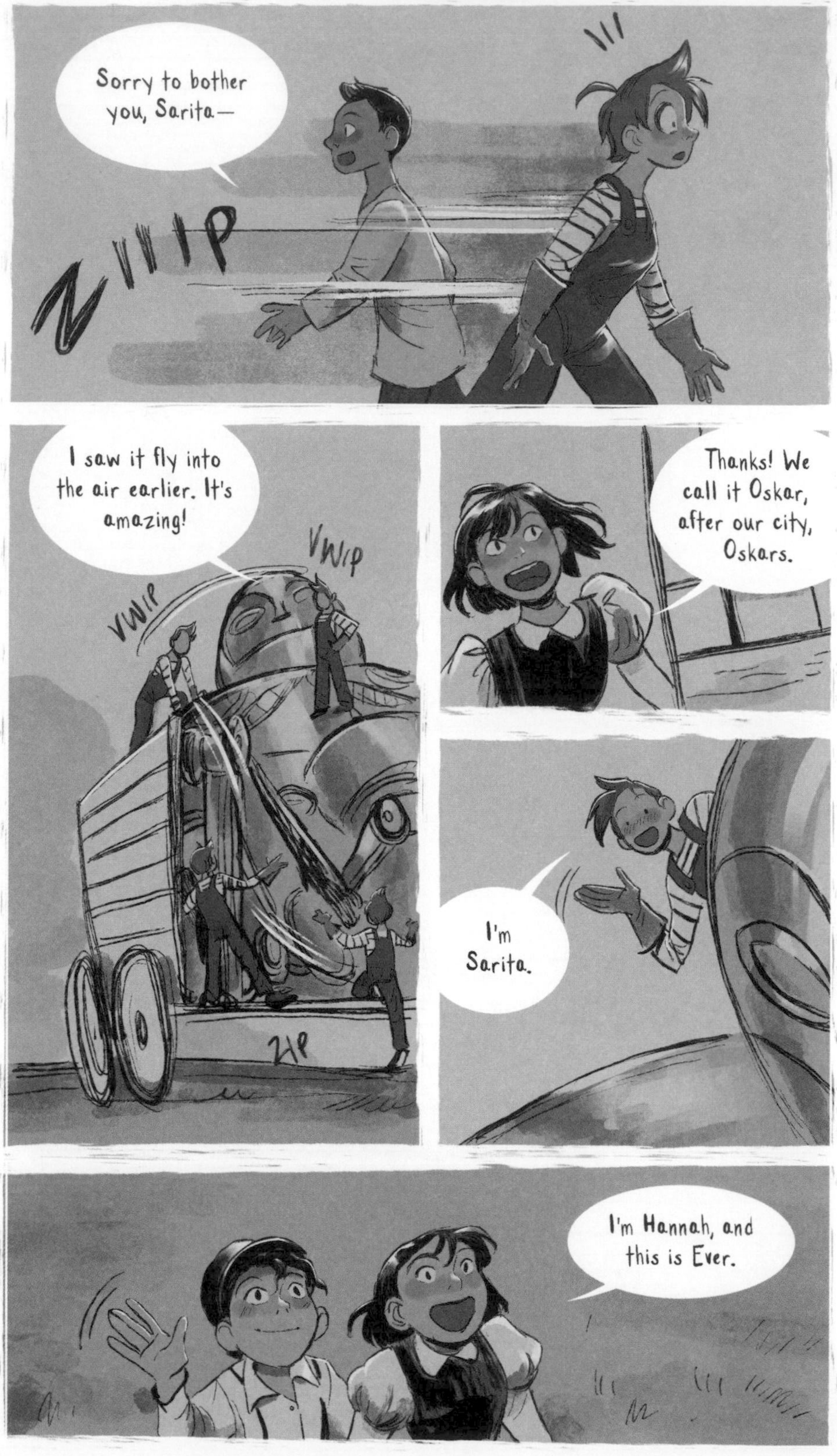
Sorry to bother you, Sarita—
ZIIIIP
I saw it fly into the air earlier. It's amazing!
VWIP
VWIP
ZIP
Thanks! We call it Oskar, after our city, Oskars.
I'm Sarita.
I'm Hannah, and this is Ever.

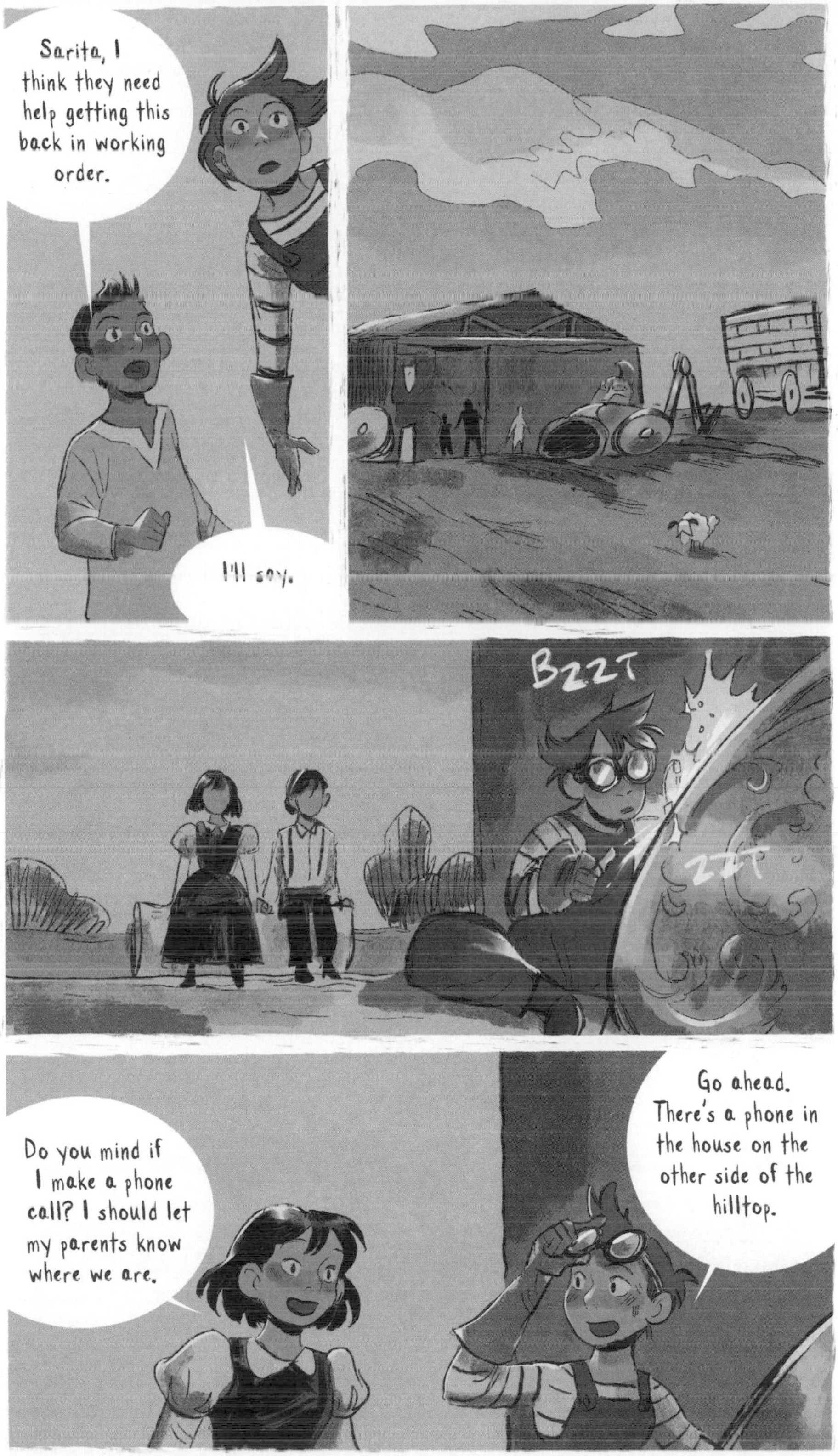
Sarita, I think they need help getting this back in working order.
I'll say.
BZZT
ZZT
Do you mind if I make a phone call? I should let my parents know where we are.
Go ahead. There's a phone in the house on the other side of the hilltop.

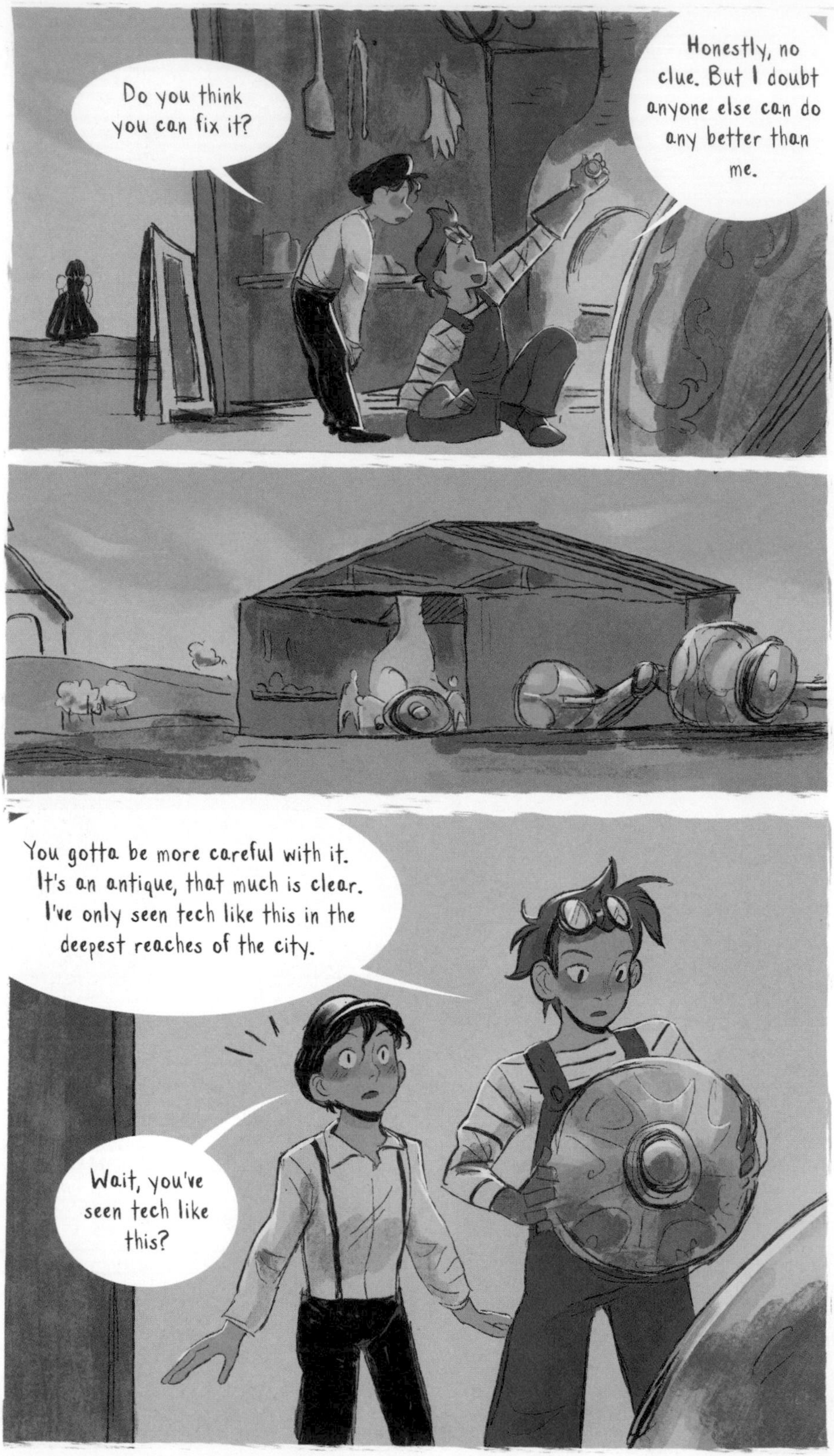
Do you think you can fix it?
Honestly, no clue. But I doubt anyone else can do any better than me.
You gotta be more careful with it. It's an antique, that much is clear. I've only seen tech like this in the deepest reaches of the city.
Wait, you've seen tech like this?

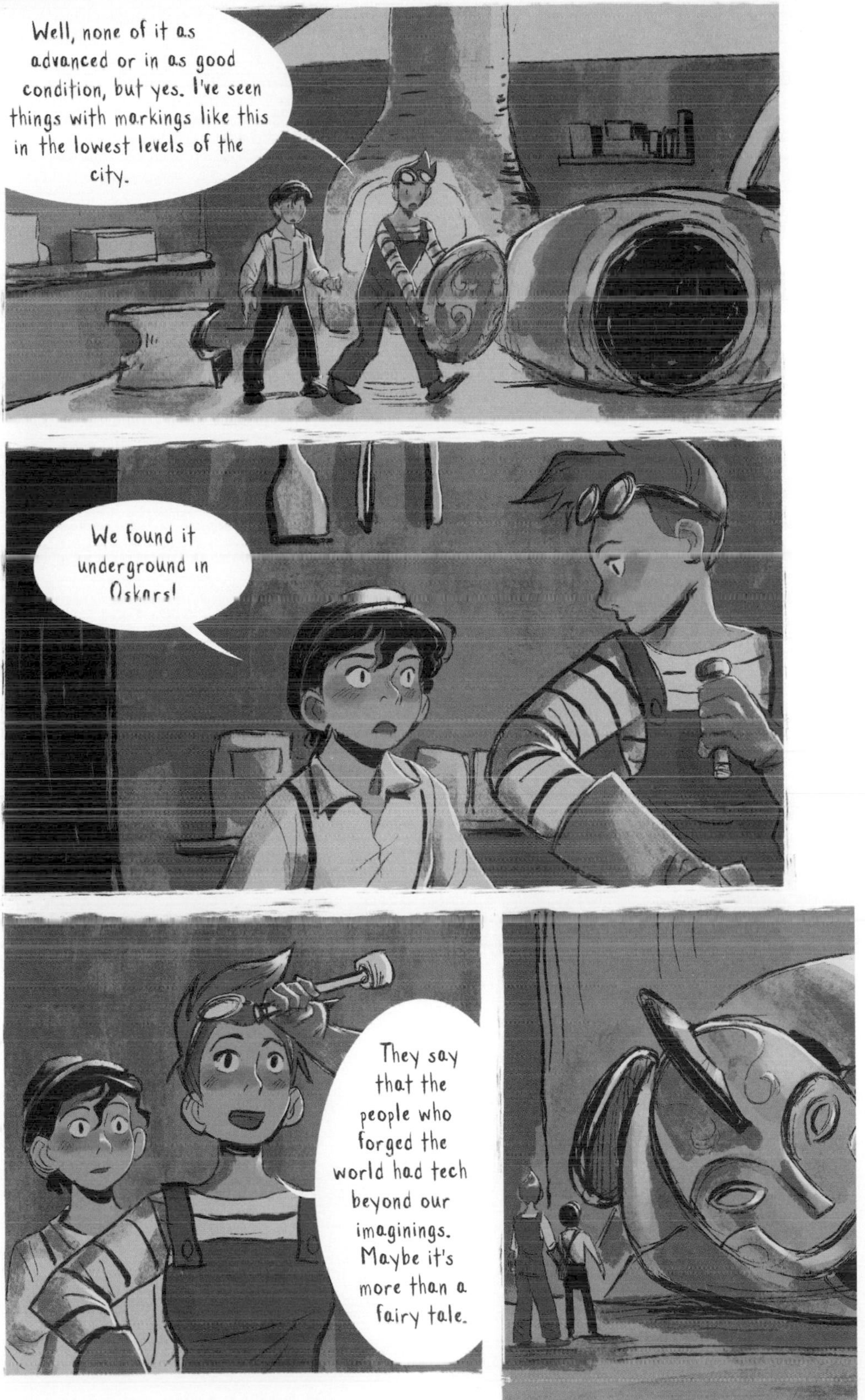
Well, none of it as advanced or in as good condition, but yes. I've seen things with markings like this in the lowest levels of the city.
We found it underground in Oskars!
They say that the people who forged the world had tech beyond our imaginings. Maybe it's more than a fairy tale.

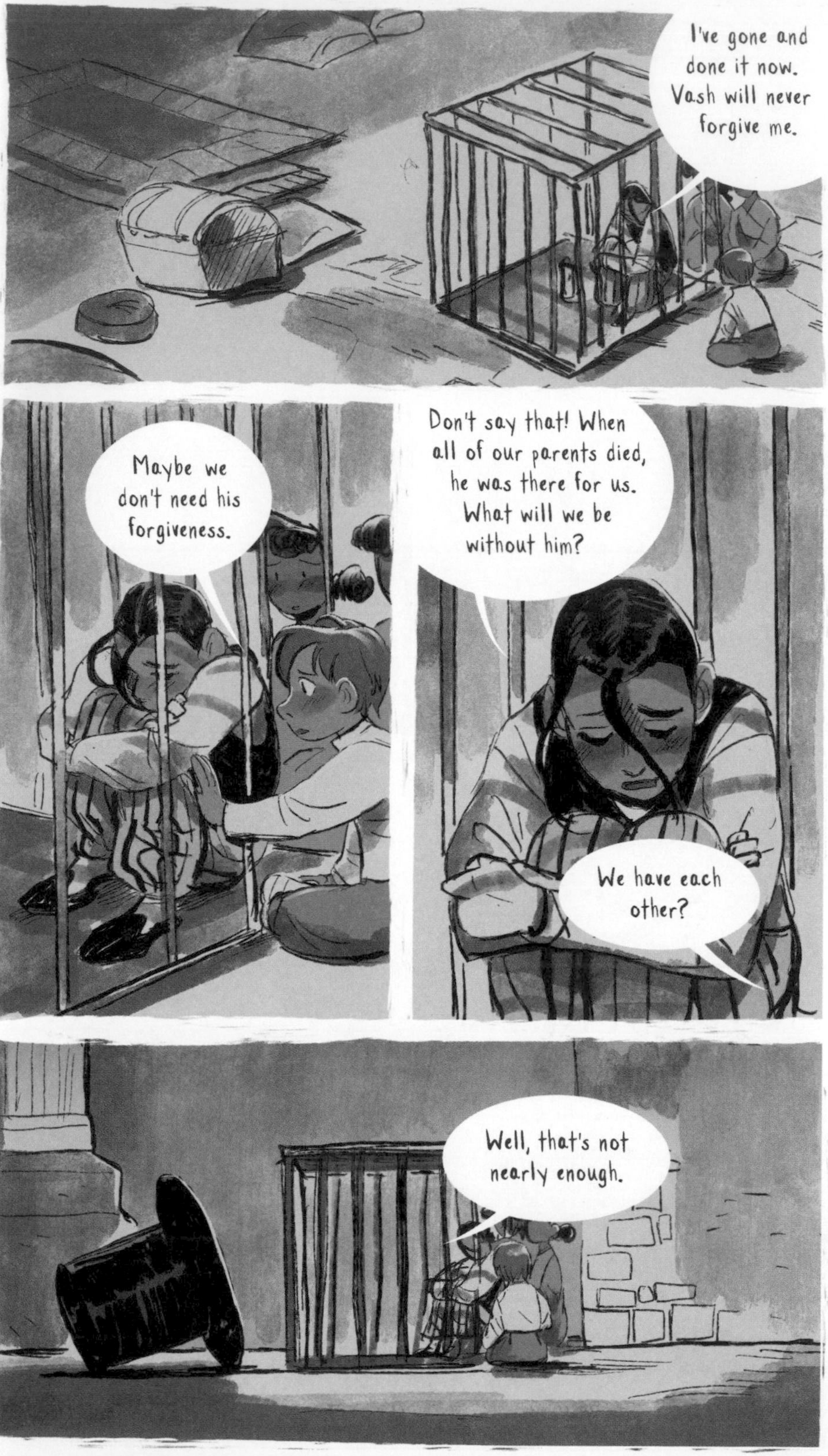
I've gone and done it now. Vash will never forgive me.
Maybe we don't need his forgiveness.
Don't say that! When all of our parents died, he was there for us. What will we be without him?
We have each other?
Well, that's not nearly enough.

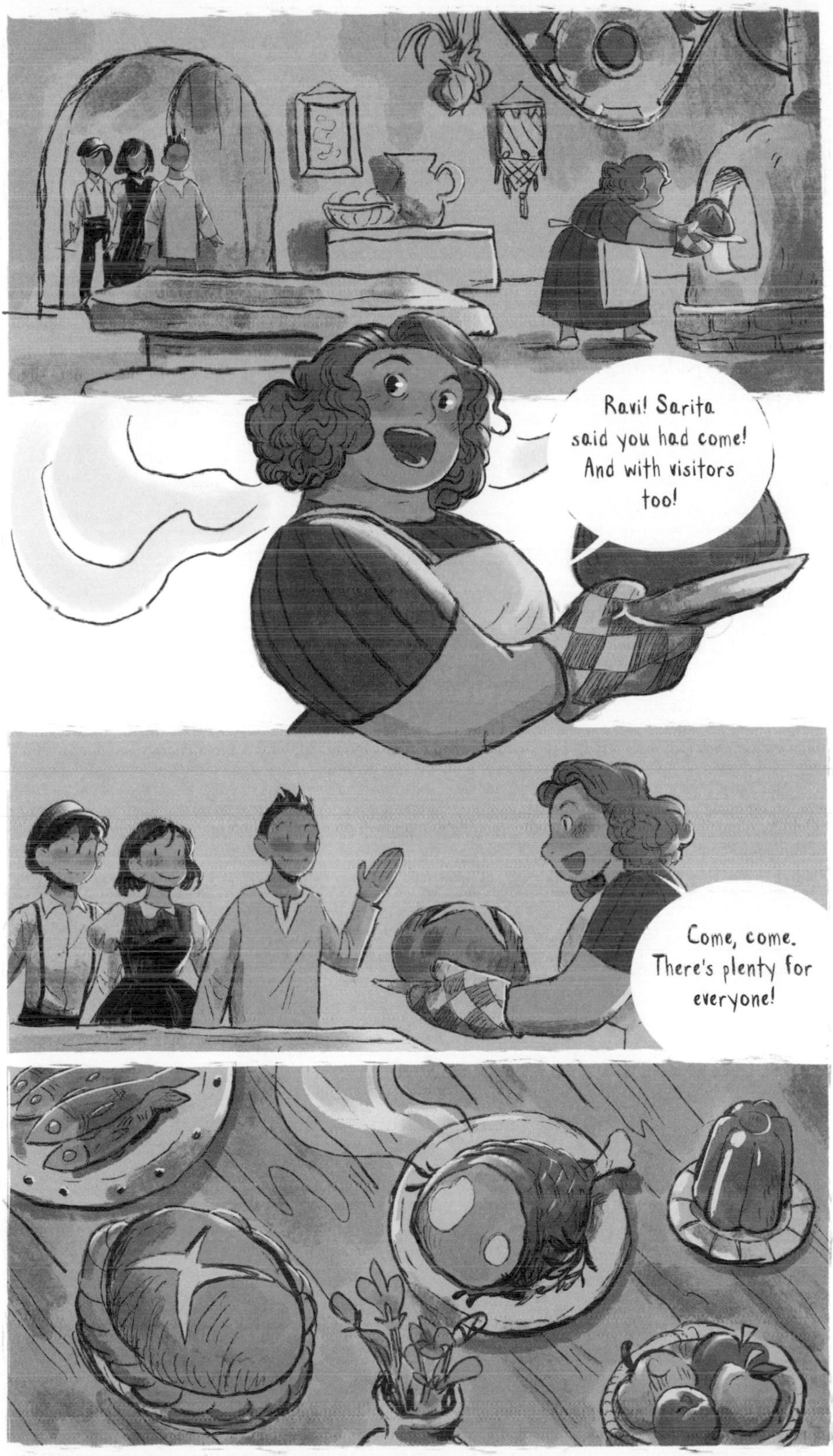
Ravi! Sarita said you had come! And with visitors too!
Come, come. There's plenty for everyone!

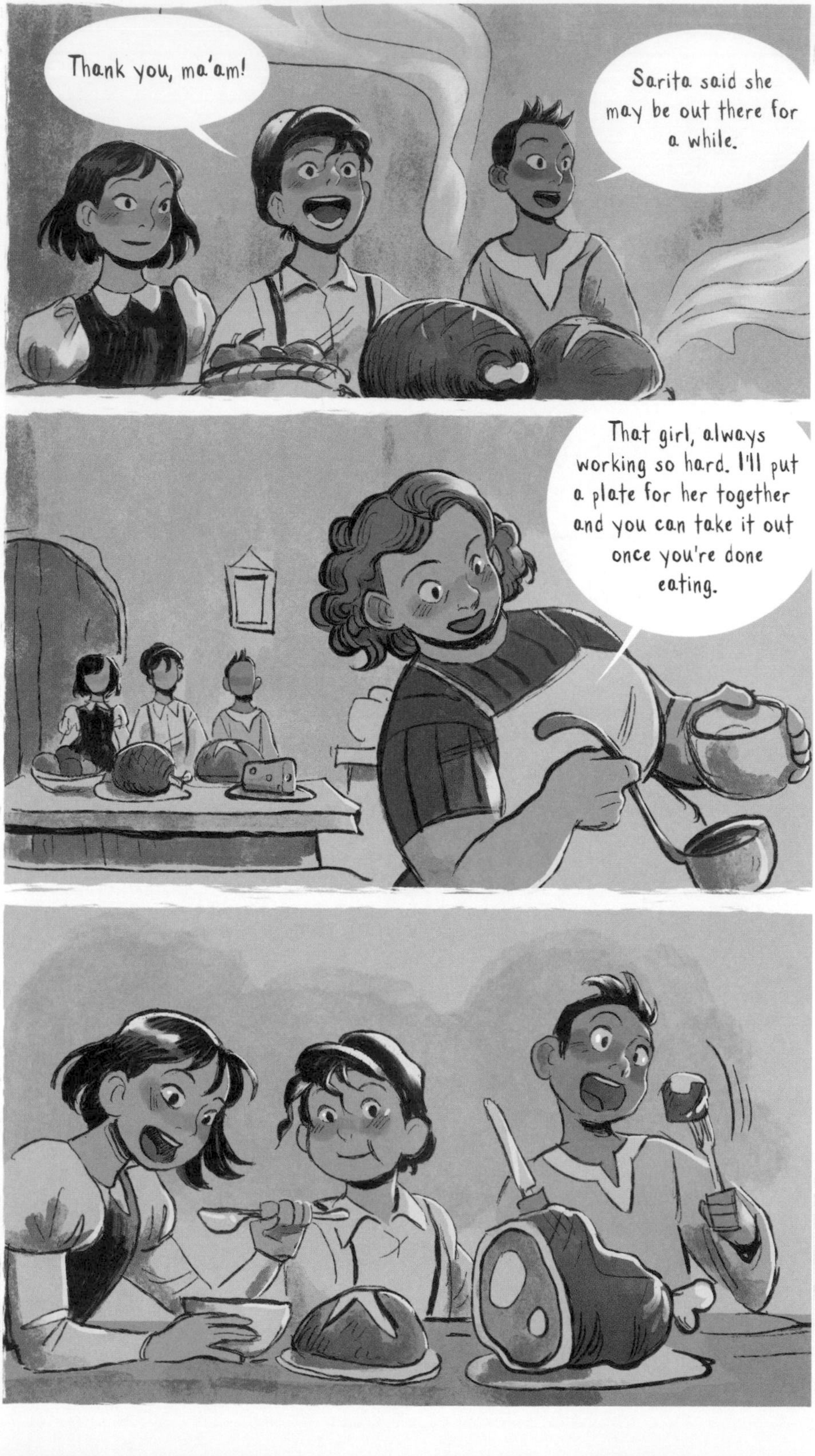
Thank you, ma'am!
Sarita said she may be out there for a while.
That girl, always working so hard. I'll put a plate for her together and you can take it out once you're done eating.

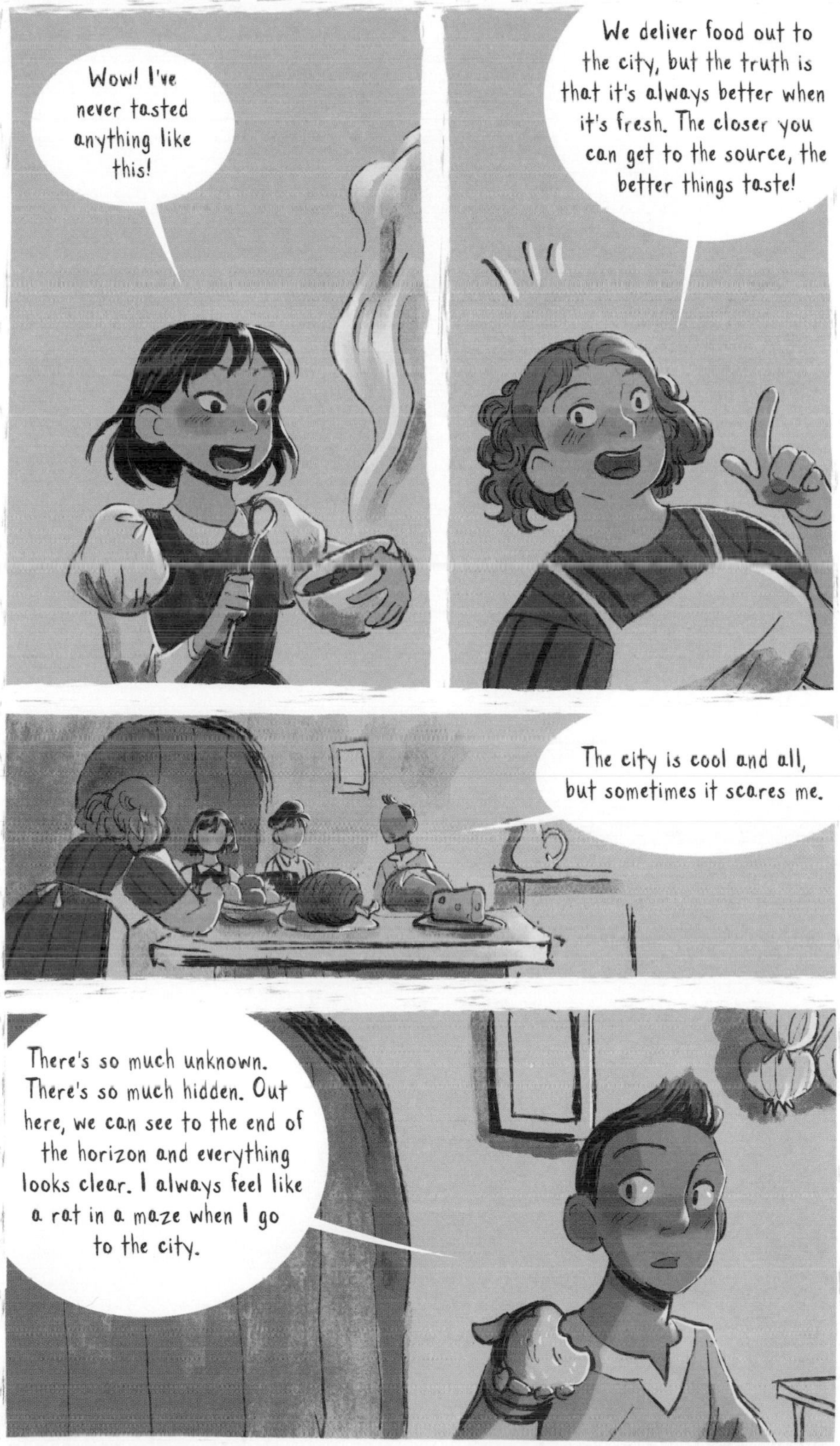
Wow! I've never tasted anything like this!
We deliver food out to the city, but the truth is that it's always better when it's fresh. The closer you can get to the source, the better things taste!
The city is cool and all, but sometimes it scares me.
There's so much unknown. There's so much hidden. Out here, we can see to the end of the horizon and everything looks clear. I always feel like a rat in a maze when I go to the city.

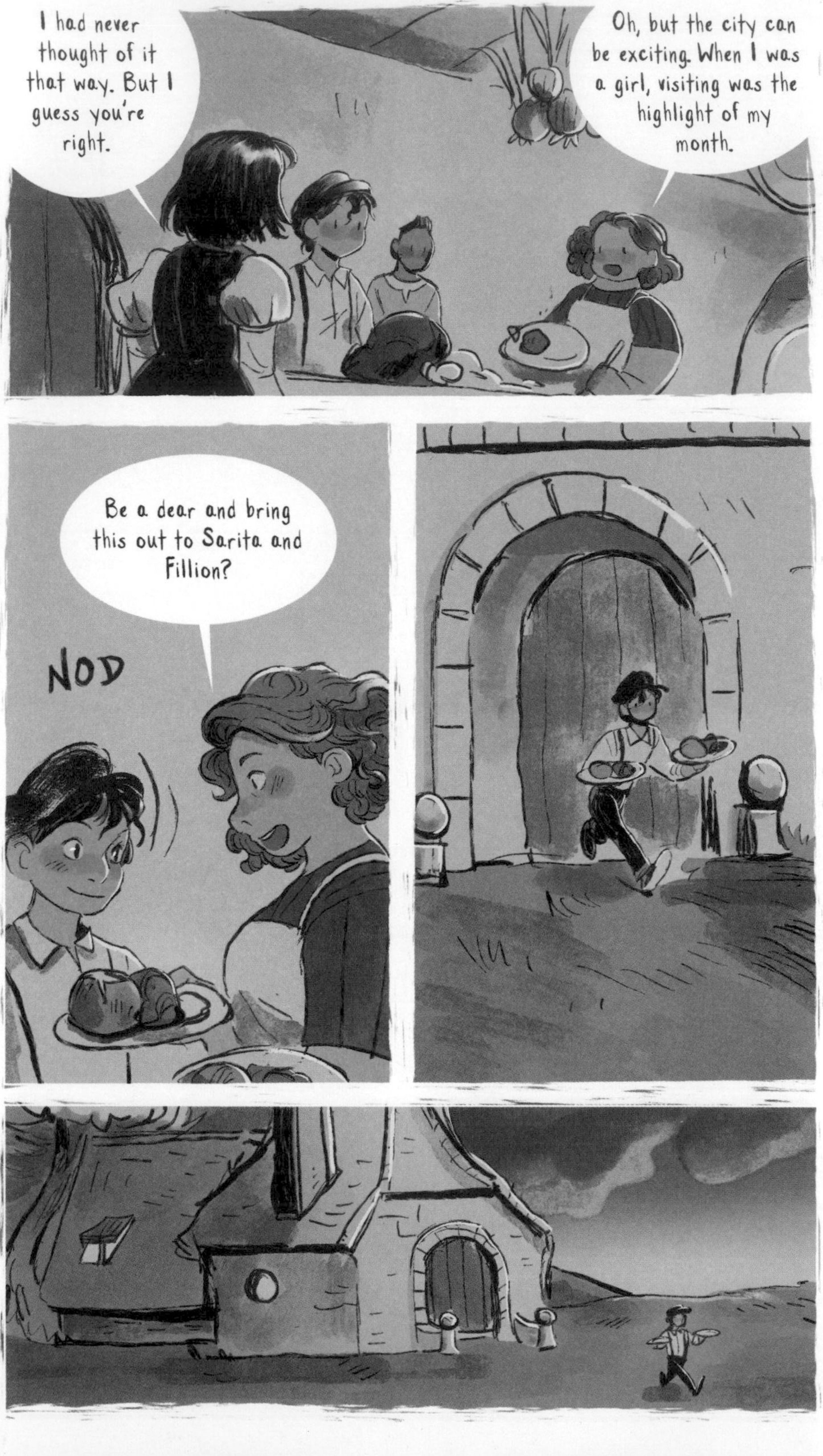
I had never thought of it that way. But I guess you're right.
Oh, but the city can be exciting. When I was a girl, visiting was the highlight of my month.
Be a dear and bring this out to Sarita and Fillion?
NOD

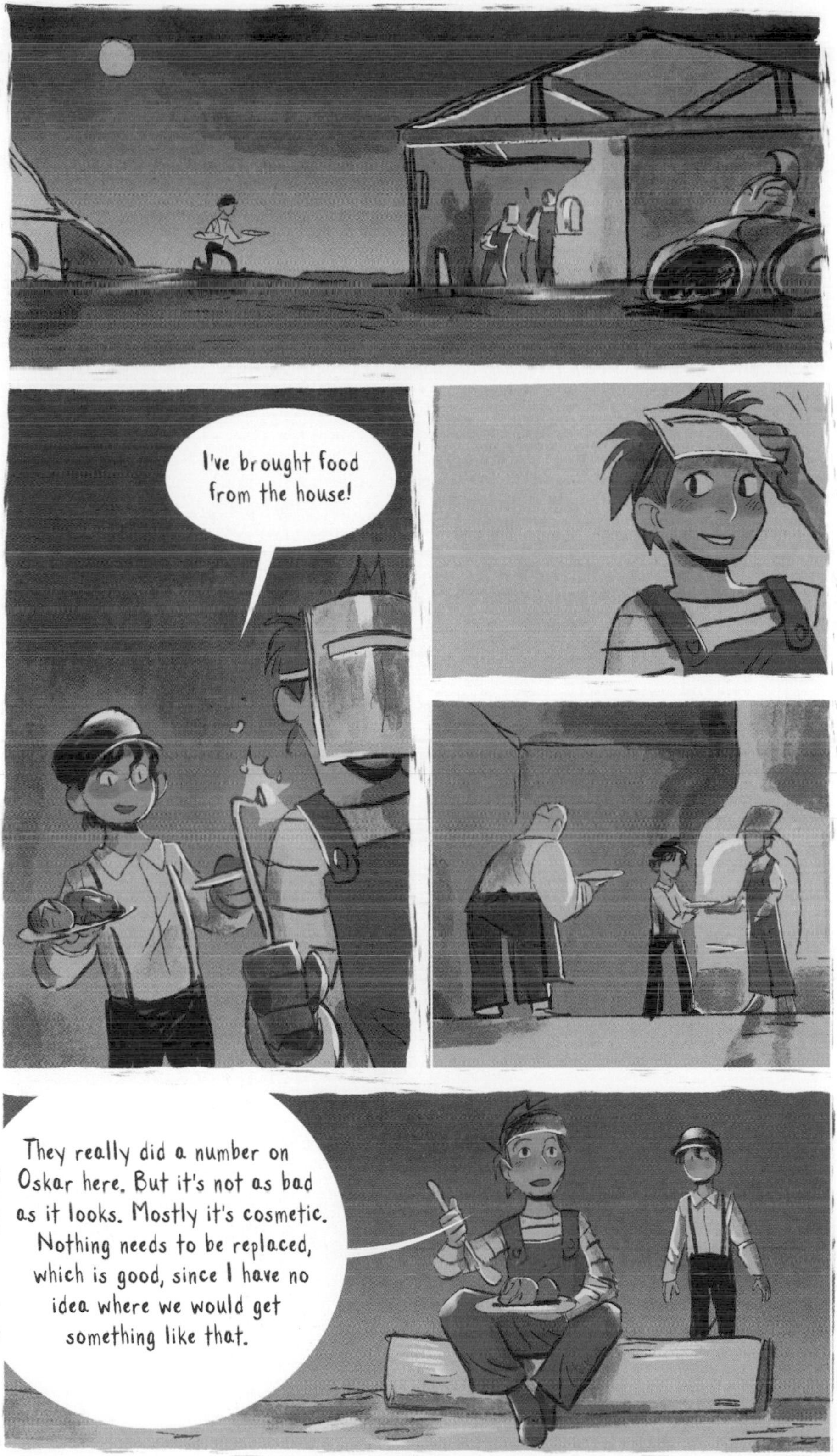
I've brought food from the house!
They really did a number on Oskar here. But it's not as bad as it looks. Mostly it's cosmetic. Nothing needs to be replaced, which is good, since I have no idea where we would get something like that.

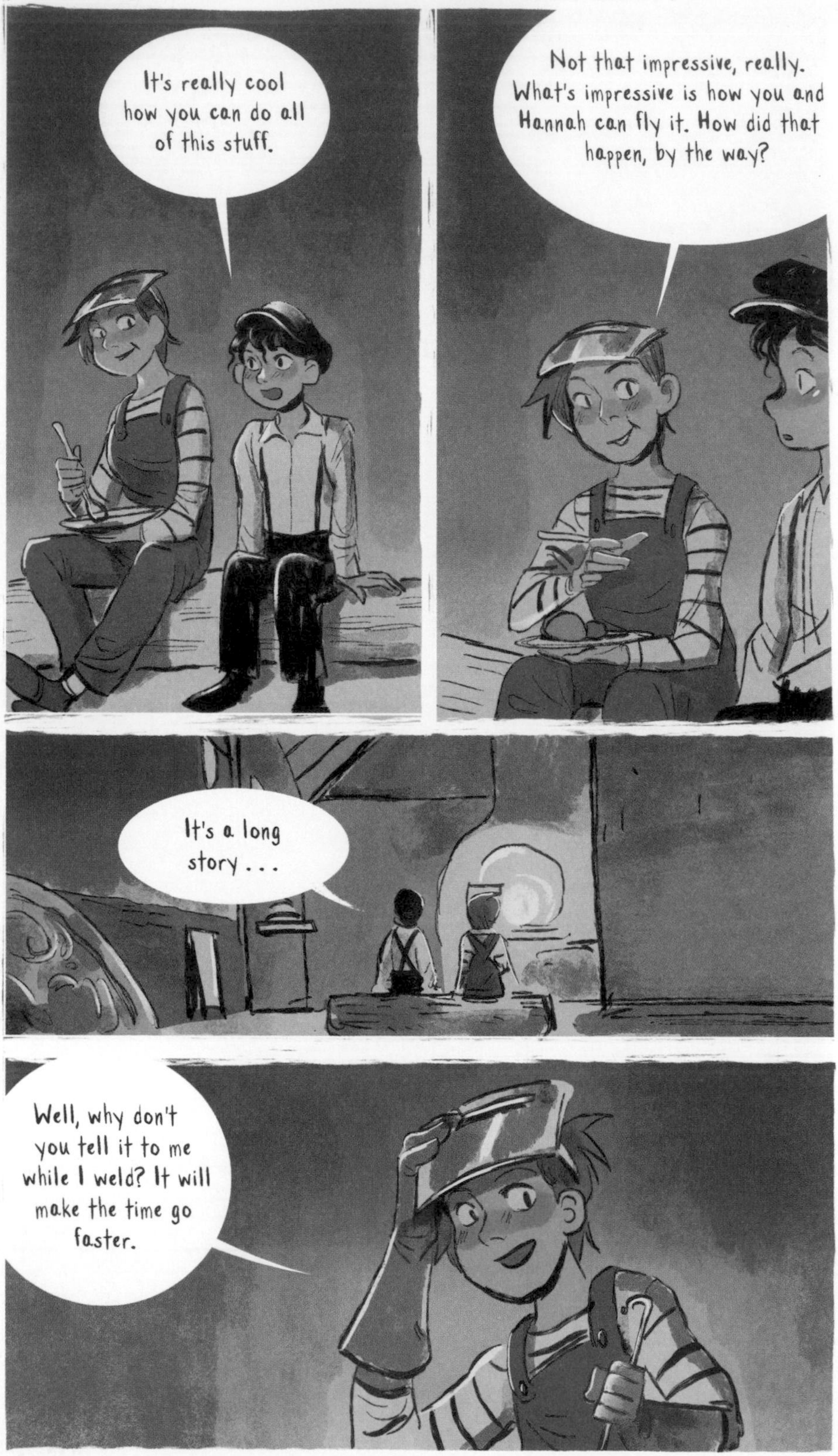
It's really cool how you can do all of this stuff.
Not that impressive, really. What's impressive is how you and Hannah can fly it. How did that happen, by the way?
It's a long story . . .
Well, why don't you tell it to me while I weld? It will make the time go faster.

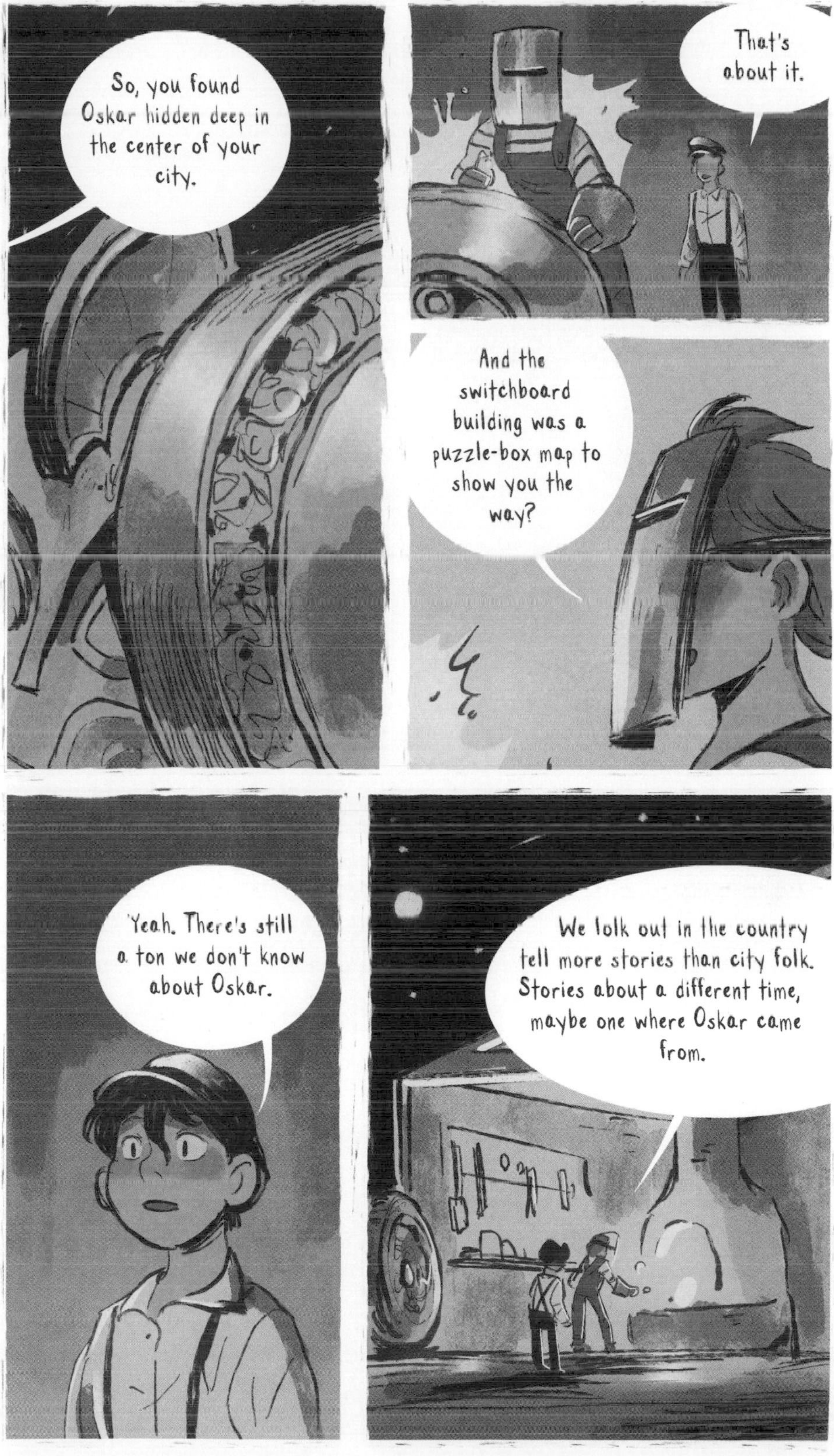
So, you found Oskar hidden deep in the center of your city.
That's about it.
And the switchboard building was a puzzle-box map to show you the way?
Yeah. There's still a ton we don't know about Oskar.
We folk out in the country tell more stories than city folk. Stories about a different time, maybe one where Oskar came from.

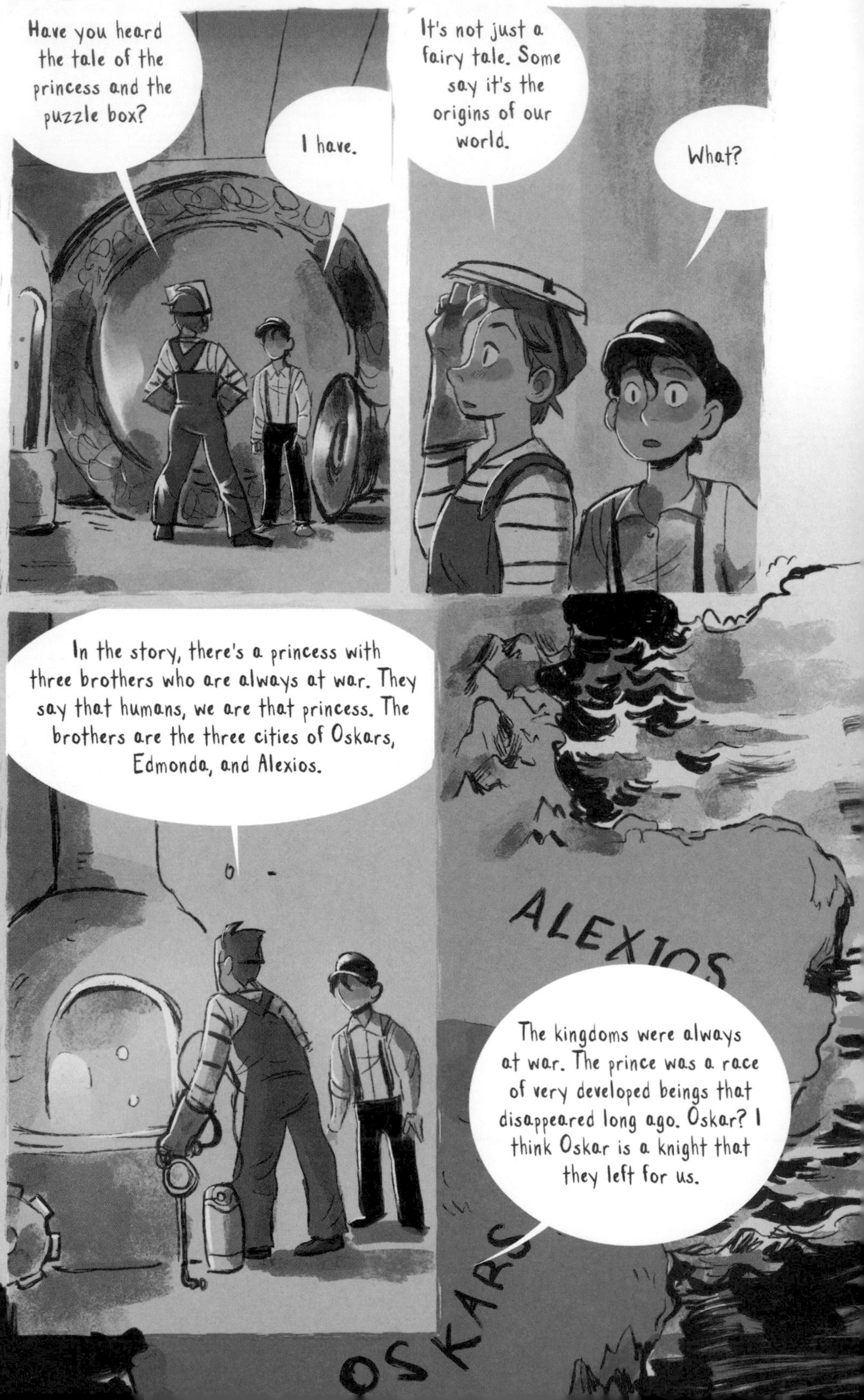
Have you heard the tale of the princess and the puzzle box?
I have.
It's not just a fairy tale. Some say it's the origins of our world.
What?
In the story, there's a princess with three brothers who are always at war. They say that humans, we are that princess. The brothers are the three cities of Oskars, Edmonda, and Alexios.
ALEXIOS
The kingdoms were always at war. The prince was a race of very developed beings that disappeared long ago. Oskar? I think Oskar is a knight that they left for us.
OSKARS

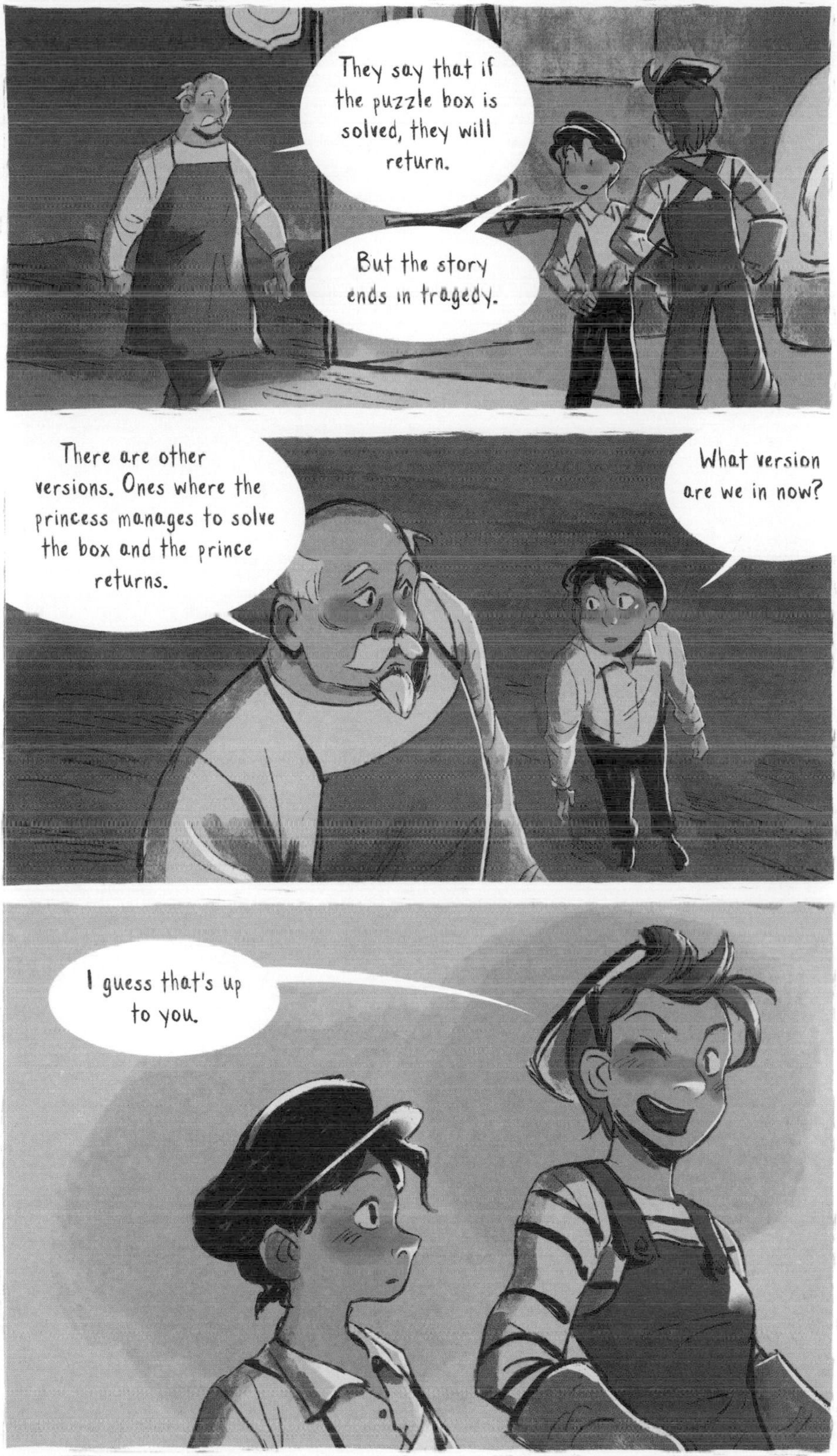
They say that if the puzzle box is solved, they will return.
But the story ends in tragedy.
There are other versions. Ones where the princess manages to solve the box and the prince returns.
What version are we in now?
I guess that's up to you.

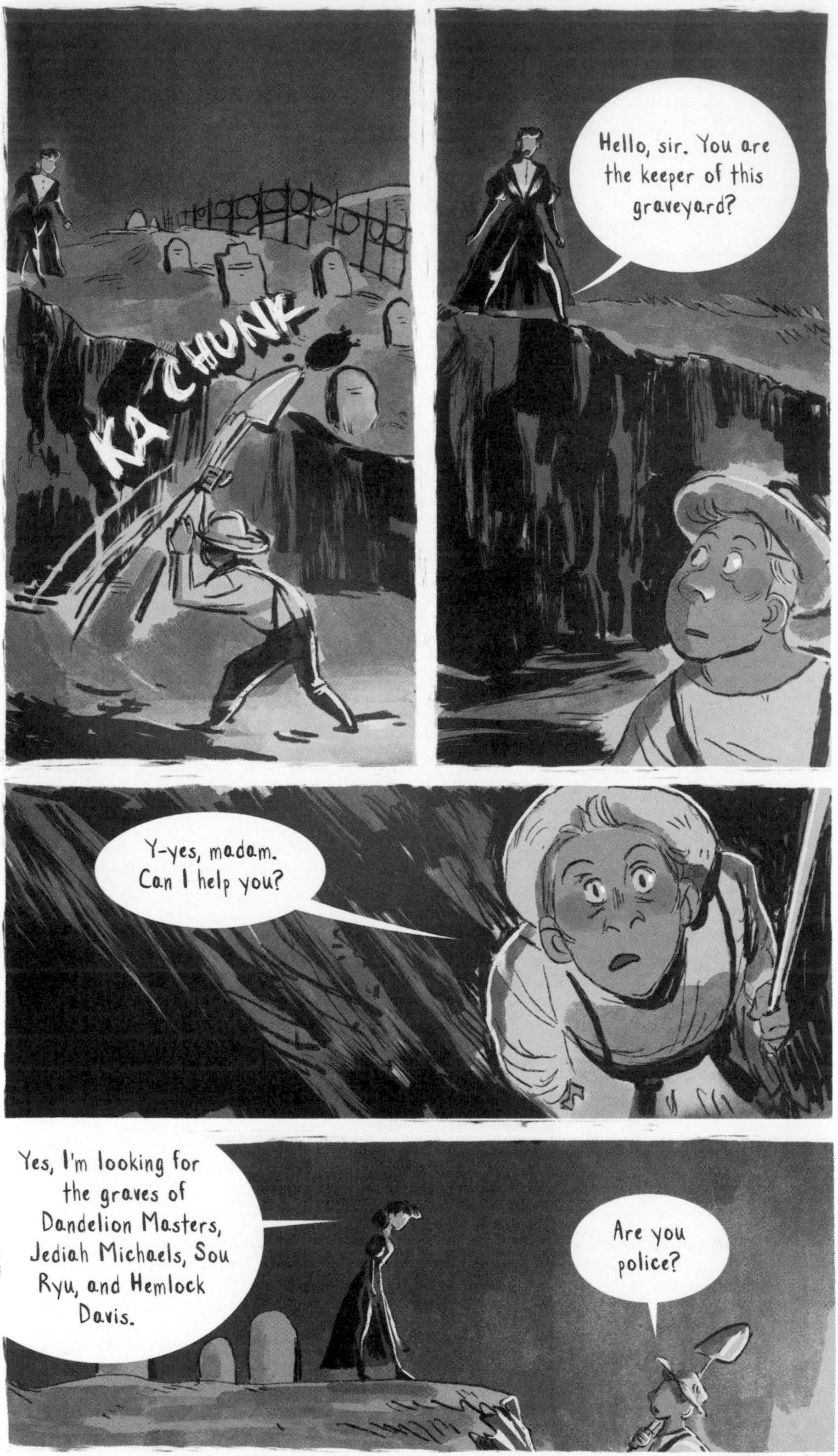
KA CHUNK
Hello, sir. You are the keeper of this graveyard?
Y-yes, madam. Can I help you?
Yes, I'm looking for the graves of Dandelion Masters, Jediah Michaels, Sou Ryu, and Hemlock Davis.
Are you police?

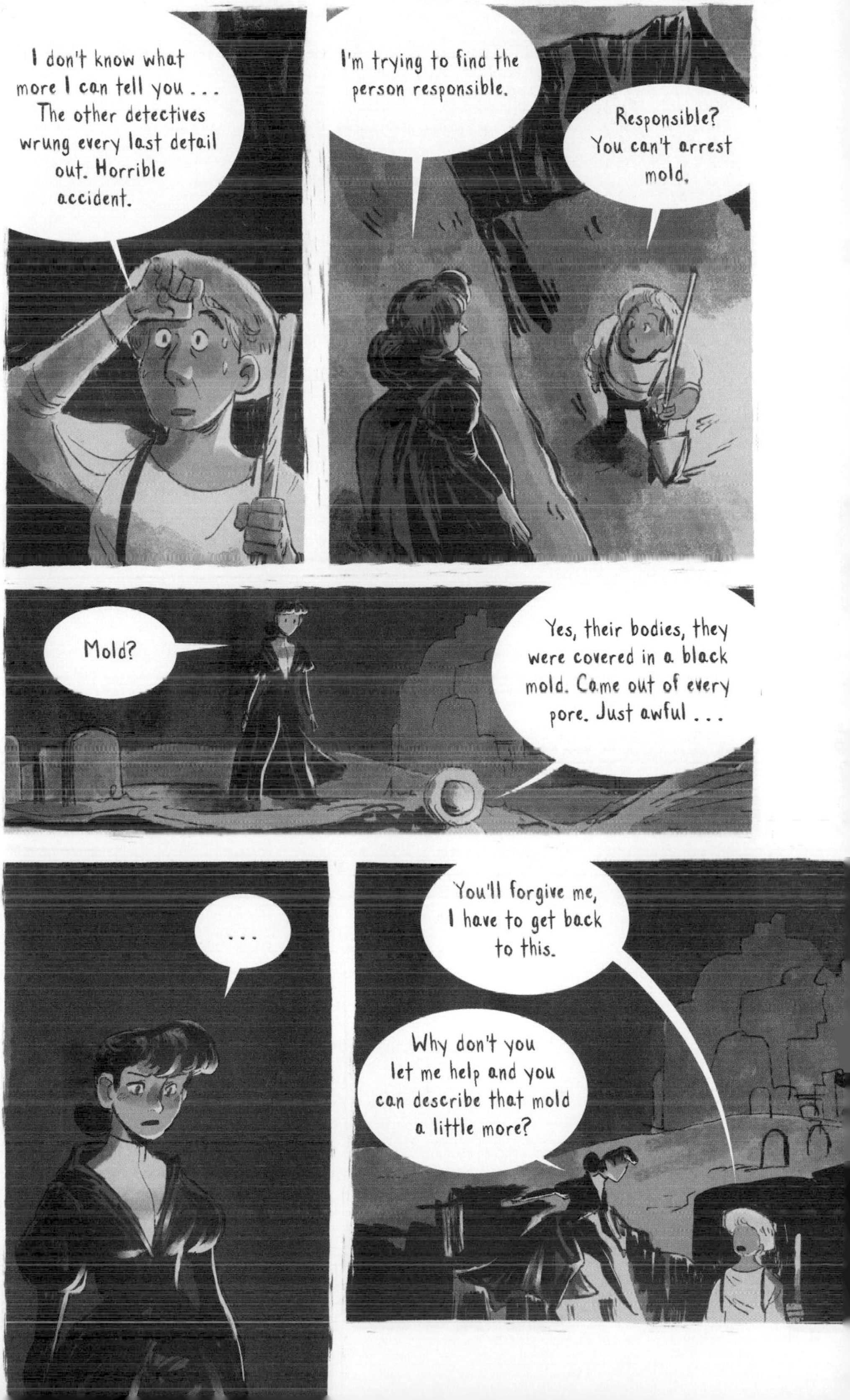
I don't know what more I can tell you . . . The other detectives wrung every last detail out. Horrible accident.
I'm trying to find the person responsible.
Responsible? You can't arrest mold.
Mold?
Yes, their bodies, they were covered in a black mold. Came out of every pore. Just awful . . .
. . .
You'll forgive me, I have to get back to this.
Why don't you let me help and you can describe that mold a little more?

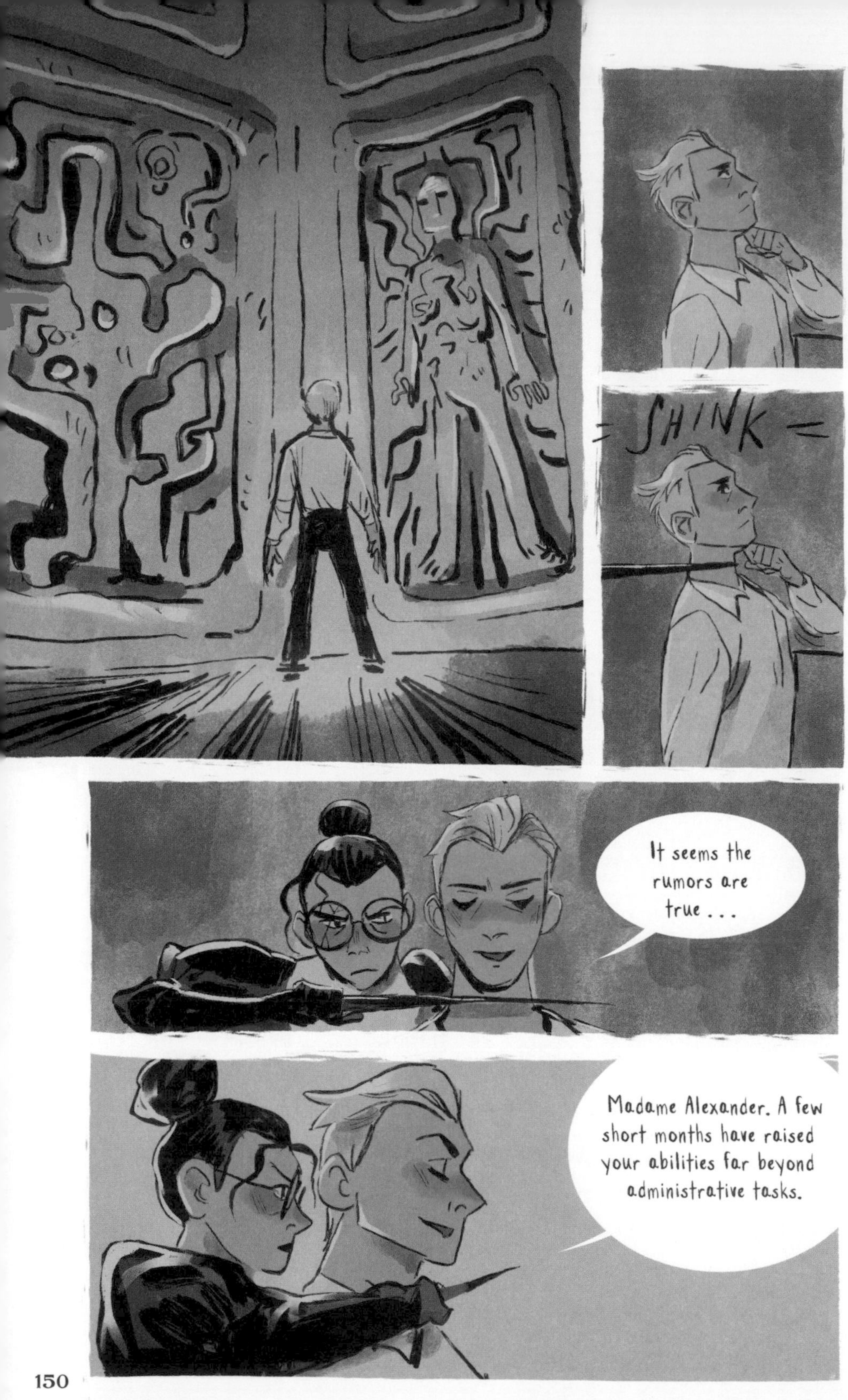
SHINK
It seems the rumors are true . . .
Madame Alexander. A few short months have raised your abilities far beyond administrative tasks.

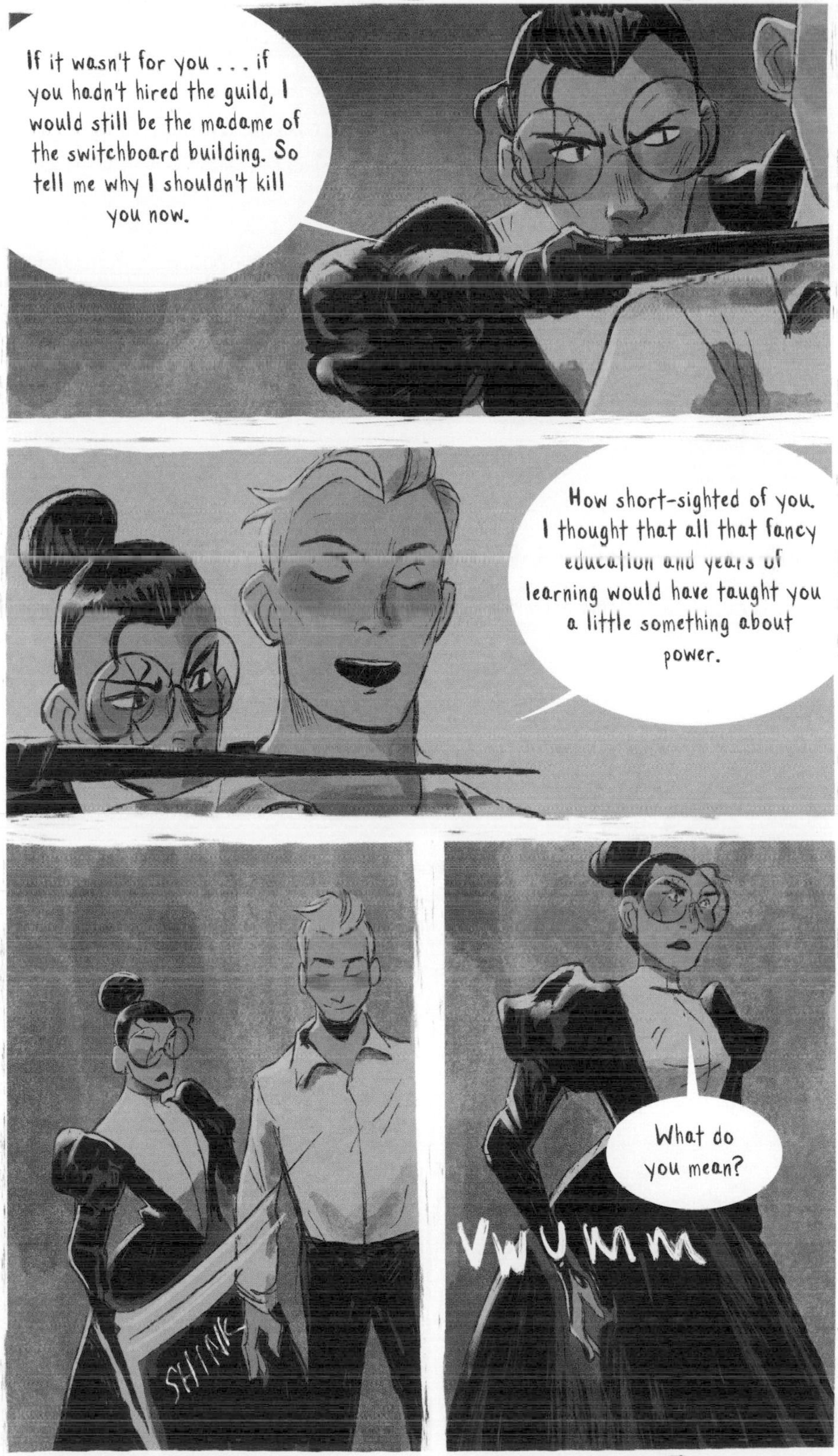
If it wasn't for you . . . if you hadn't hired the guild, I would still be the madame of the switchboard building. So tell me why I shouldn't kill you now.
How short-sighted of you. I thought that all that fancy education and years of learning would have taught you a little something about power.
SHINK
What do you mean?
VWUMM

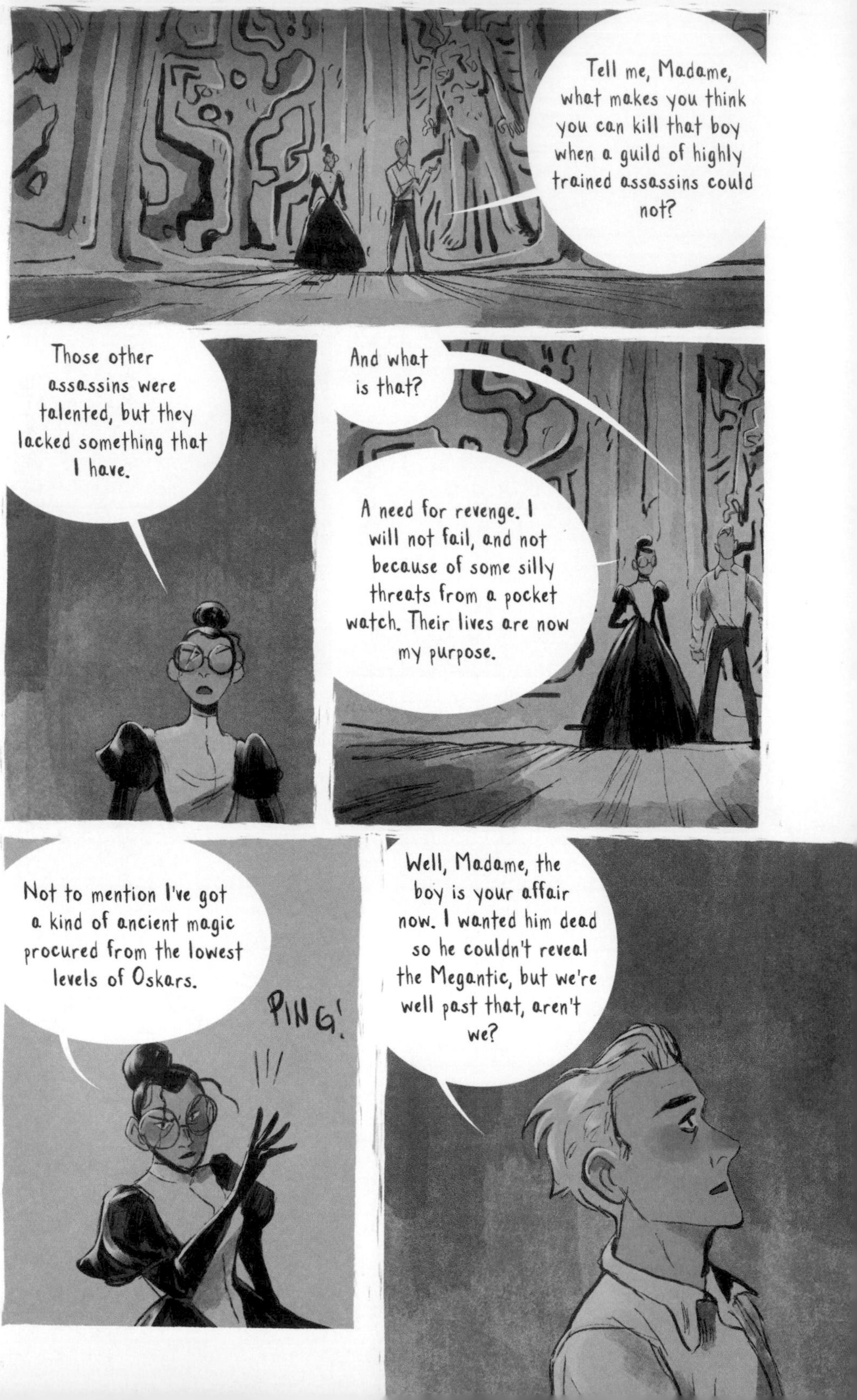
Tell me, Madame, what makes you think you can kill that boy when a guild of highly trained assassins could not?
Those other assassins were talented, but they lacked something that I have.
And what is that?
A need for revenge. I will not fail, and not because of some silly threats from a pocket watch. Their lives are now my purpose.
Not to mention I've got a kind of ancient magic procured from the lowest levels of Oskars.
PING!
Well, Madame, the boy is your affair now. I wanted him dead so he couldn't reveal the Megantic, but we're well past that, aren't we?

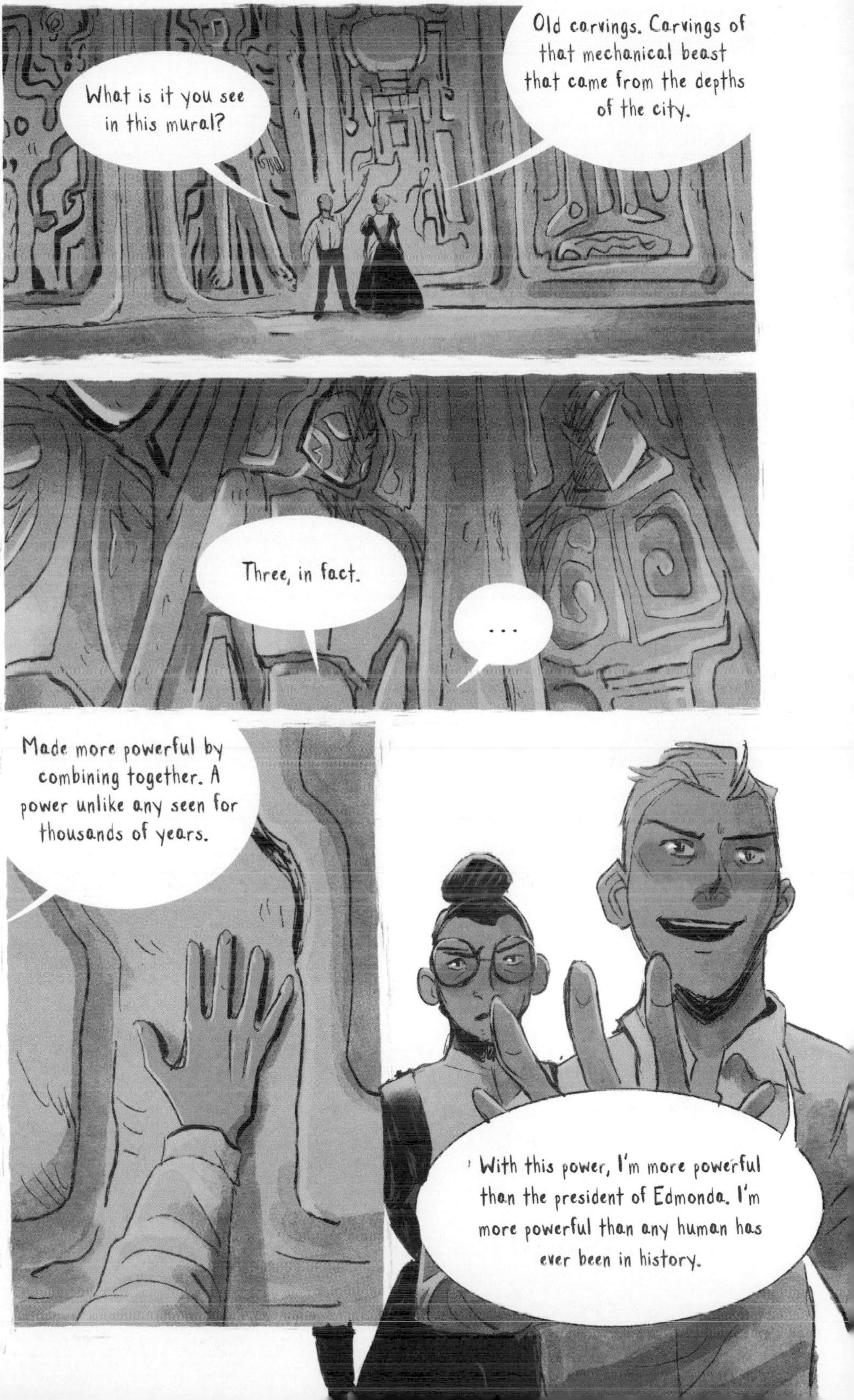
What is it you see in this mural?
Old carvings. Carvings of that mechanical beast that came from the depths of the city.
Three, in fact.
...
Made more powerful by combining together. A power unlike any seen for thousands of years.
With this power, I'm more powerful than the president of Edmonda. I'm more powerful than any human has ever been in history.

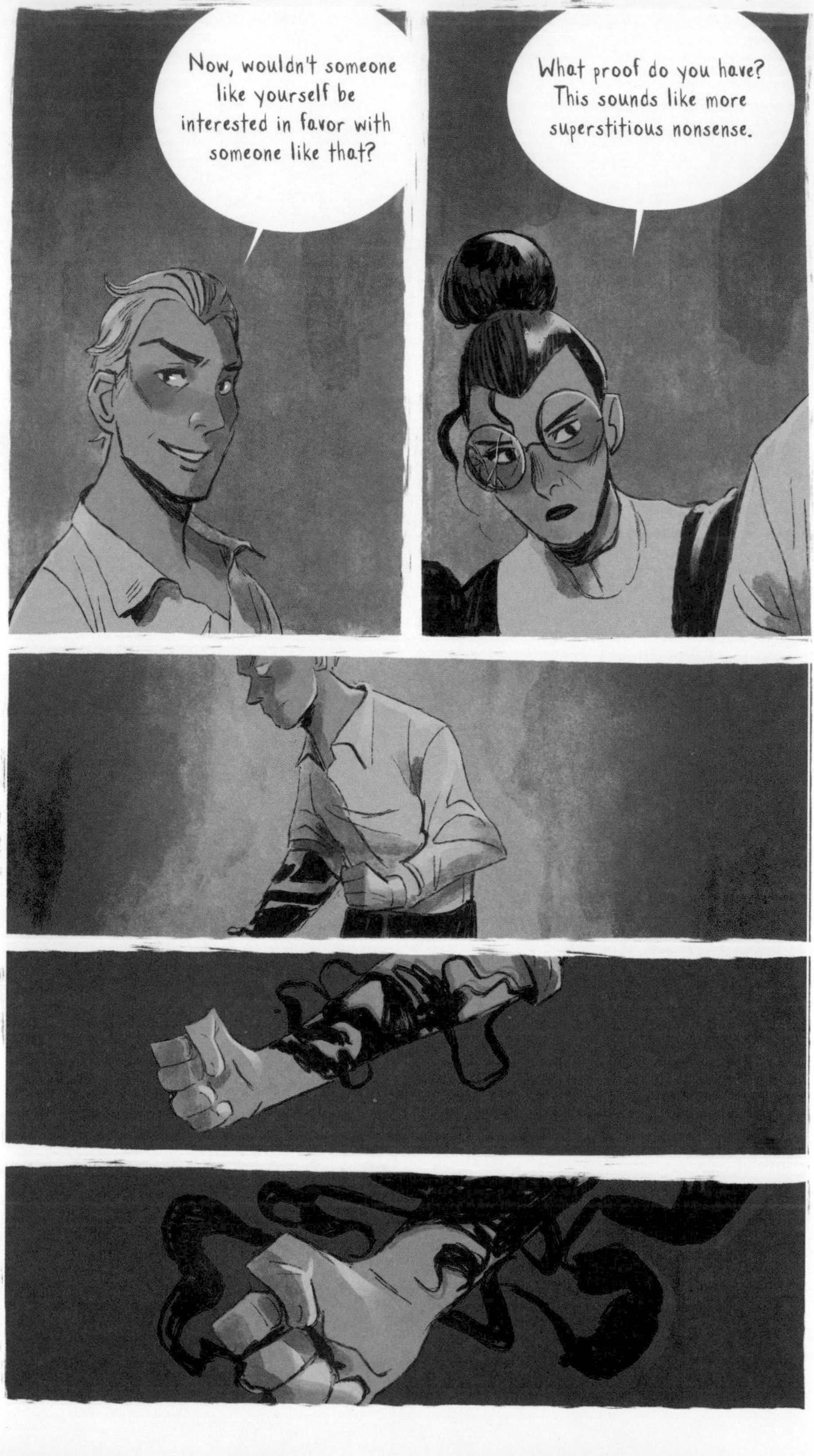
Now, wouldn't someone like yourself be interested in favor with someone like that?
What proof do you have? This sounds like more superstitious nonsense.

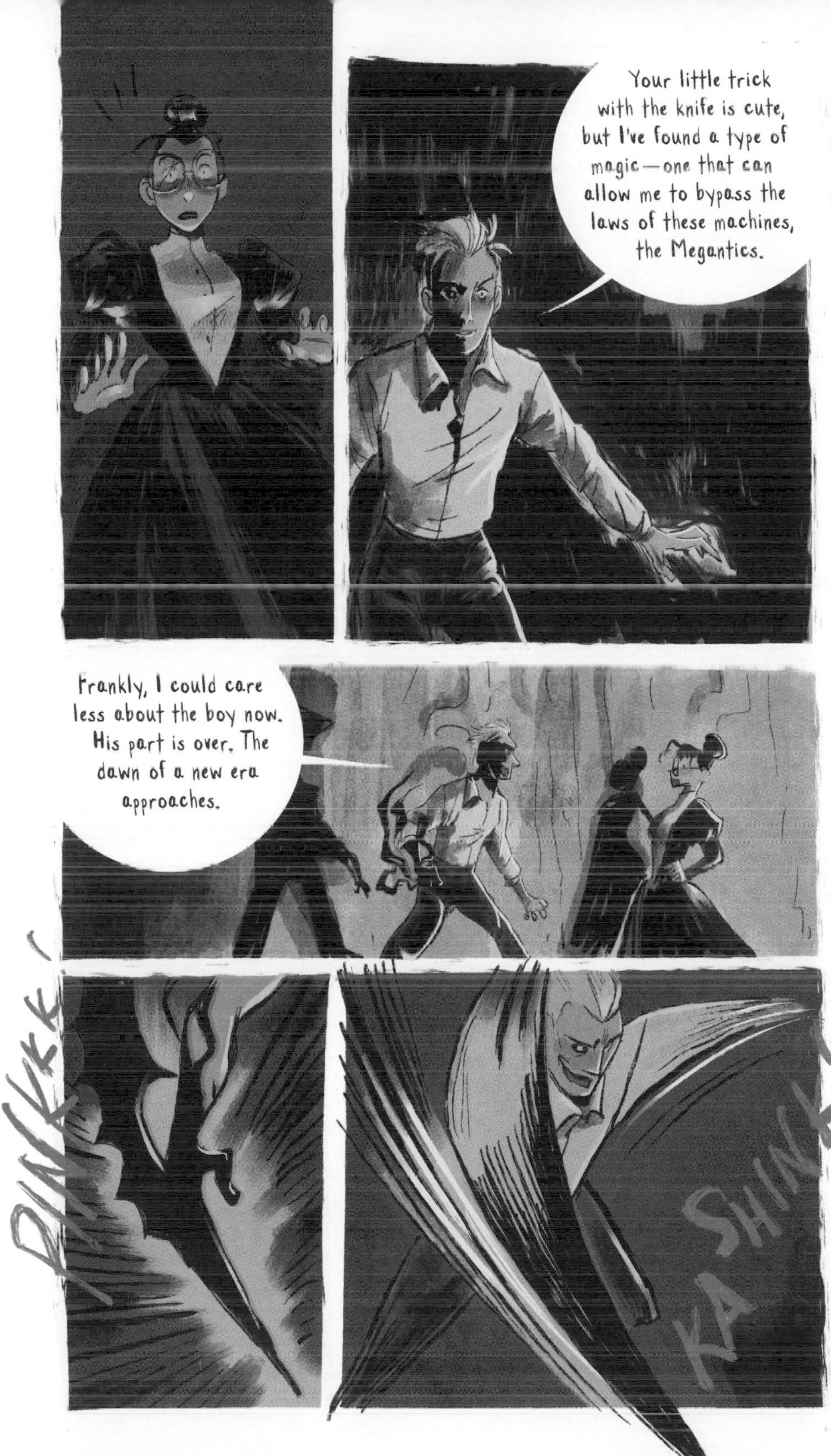
Your little trick with the knife is cute, but I've found a type of magic—one that can allow me to bypass the laws of these machines, the Megantics.
Frankly, I could care less about the boy now. His part is over. The dawn of a new era approaches.
RINKKEEK
KA SHINK

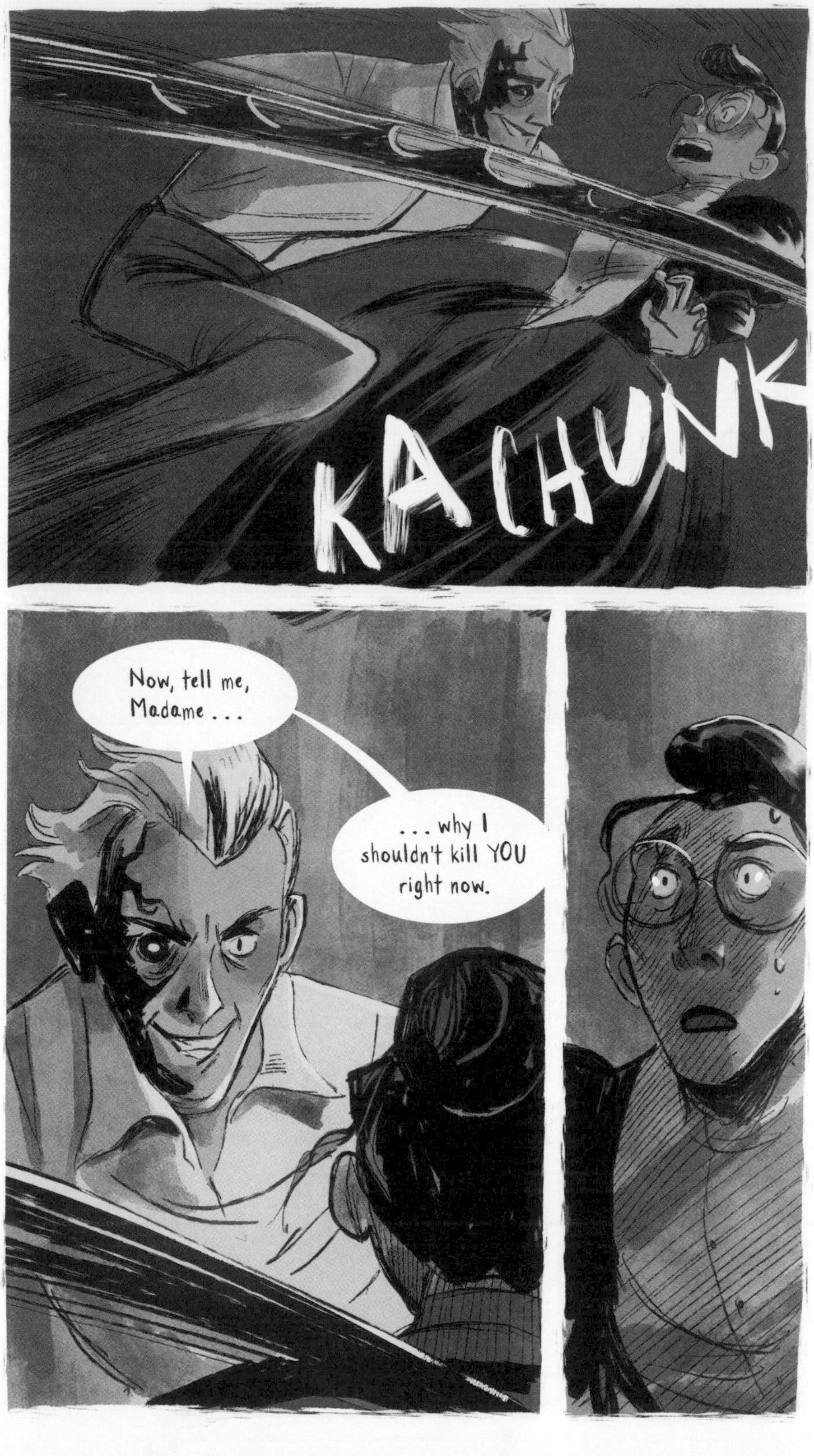
KACHUNK
Now, tell me, Madame . . .
. . . why I shouldn't kill YOU right now.

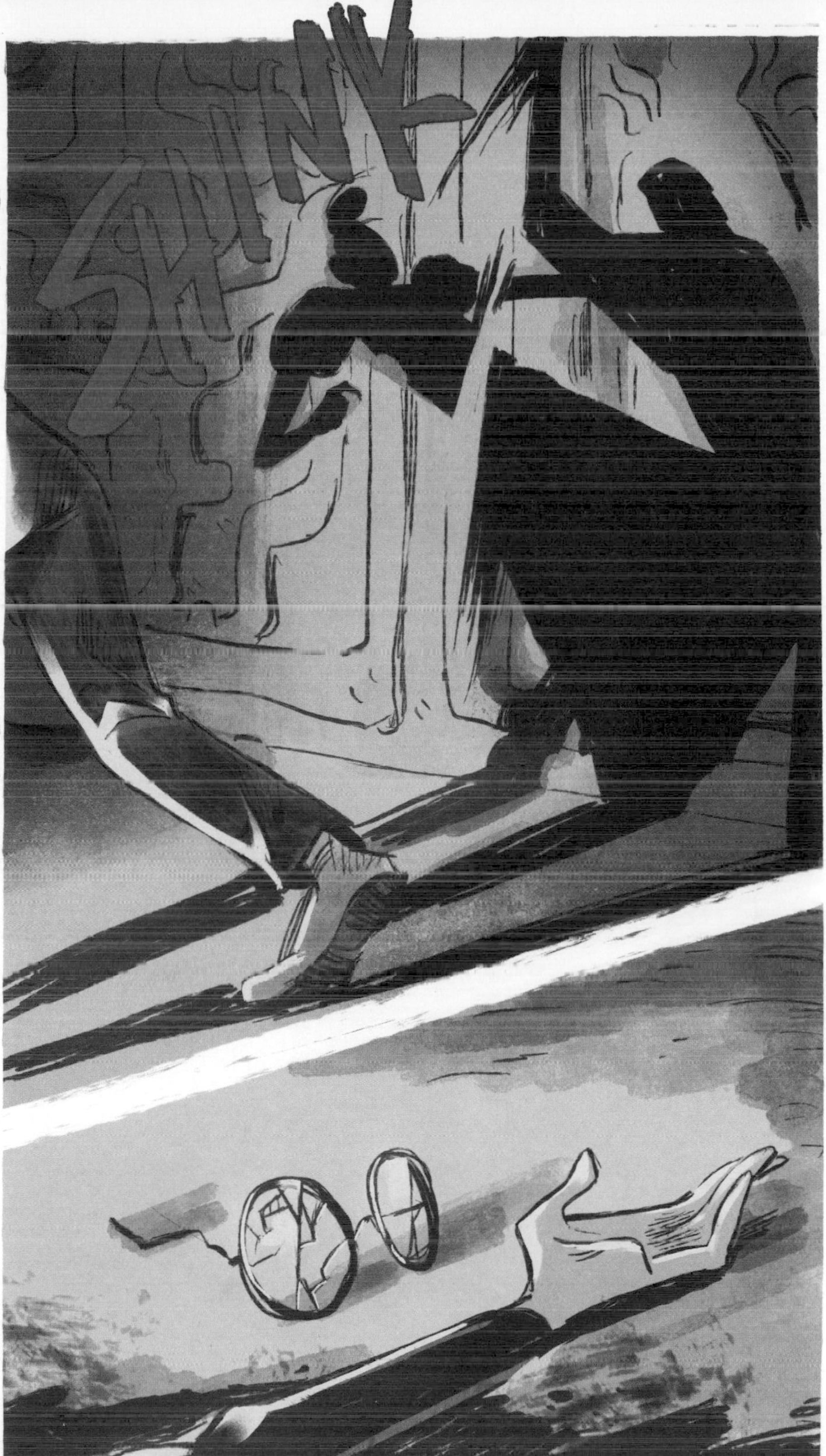
SHIINK

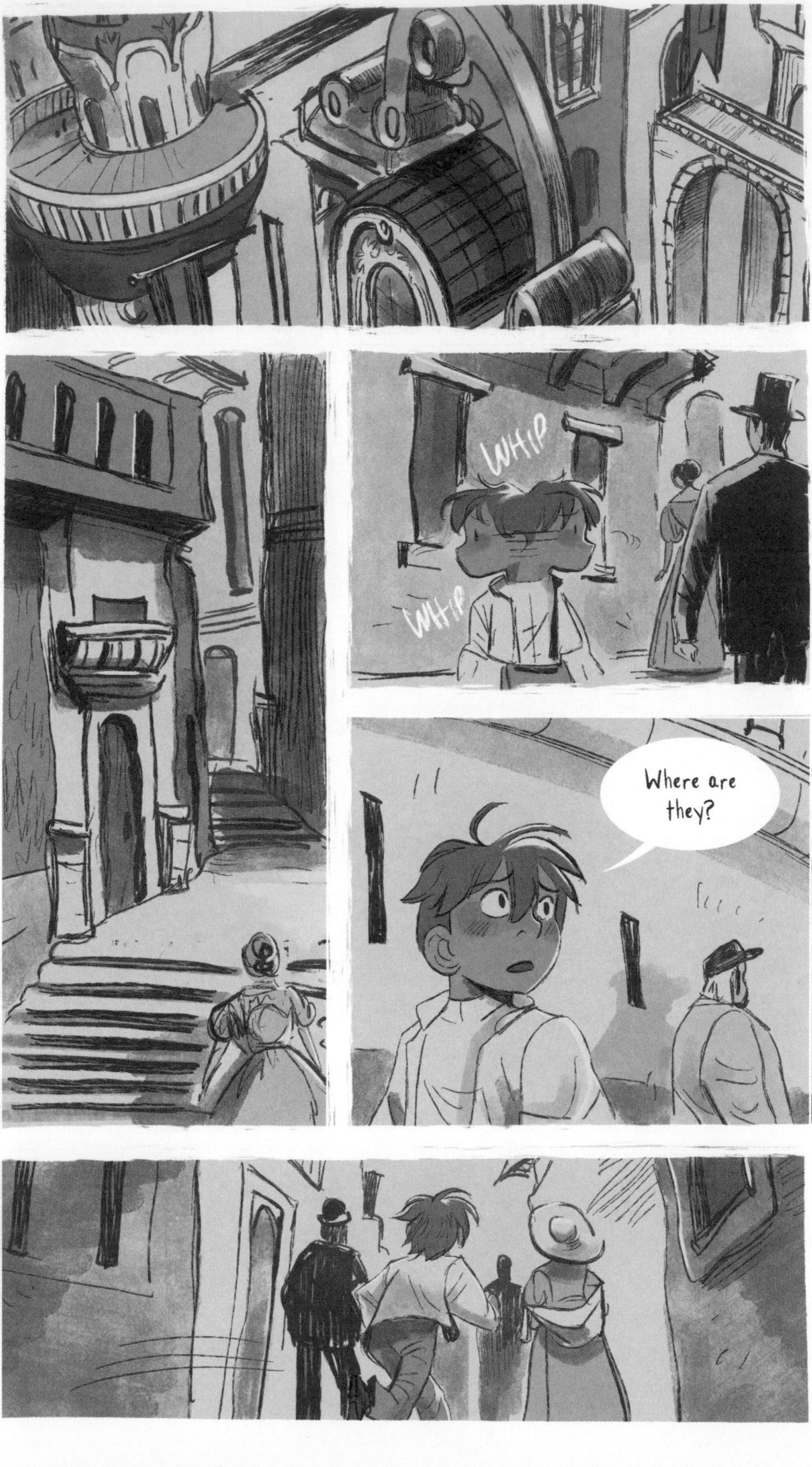
WHIP
WHIP
Where are they?

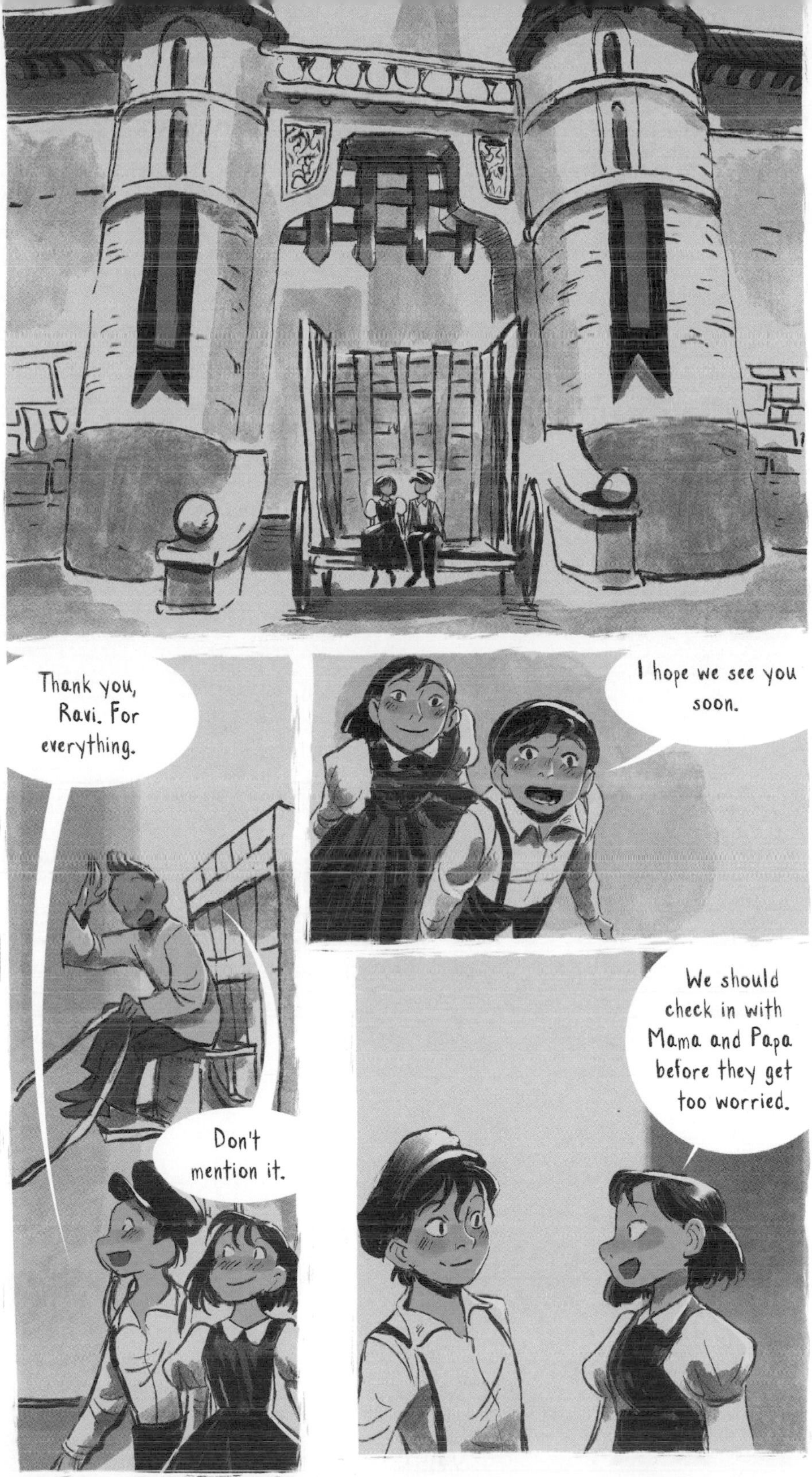
Thank you, Ravi. For everything.
I hope we see you soon.
Don't mention it.
We should check in with Mama and Papa before they get too worried.

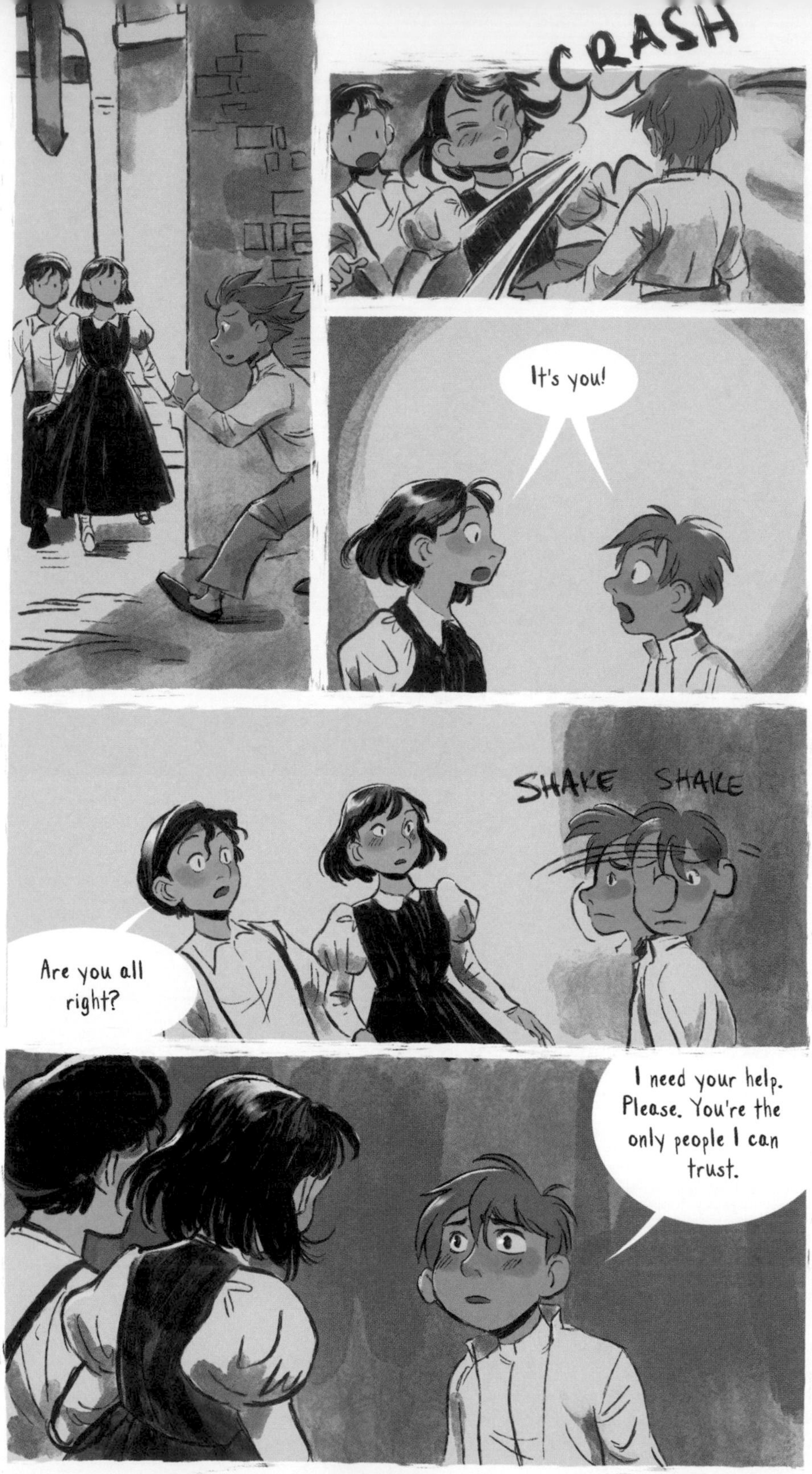
CRASH
It's you!
SHAKE SHAKE
Are you all right?
I need your help. Please. You're the only people I can trust.

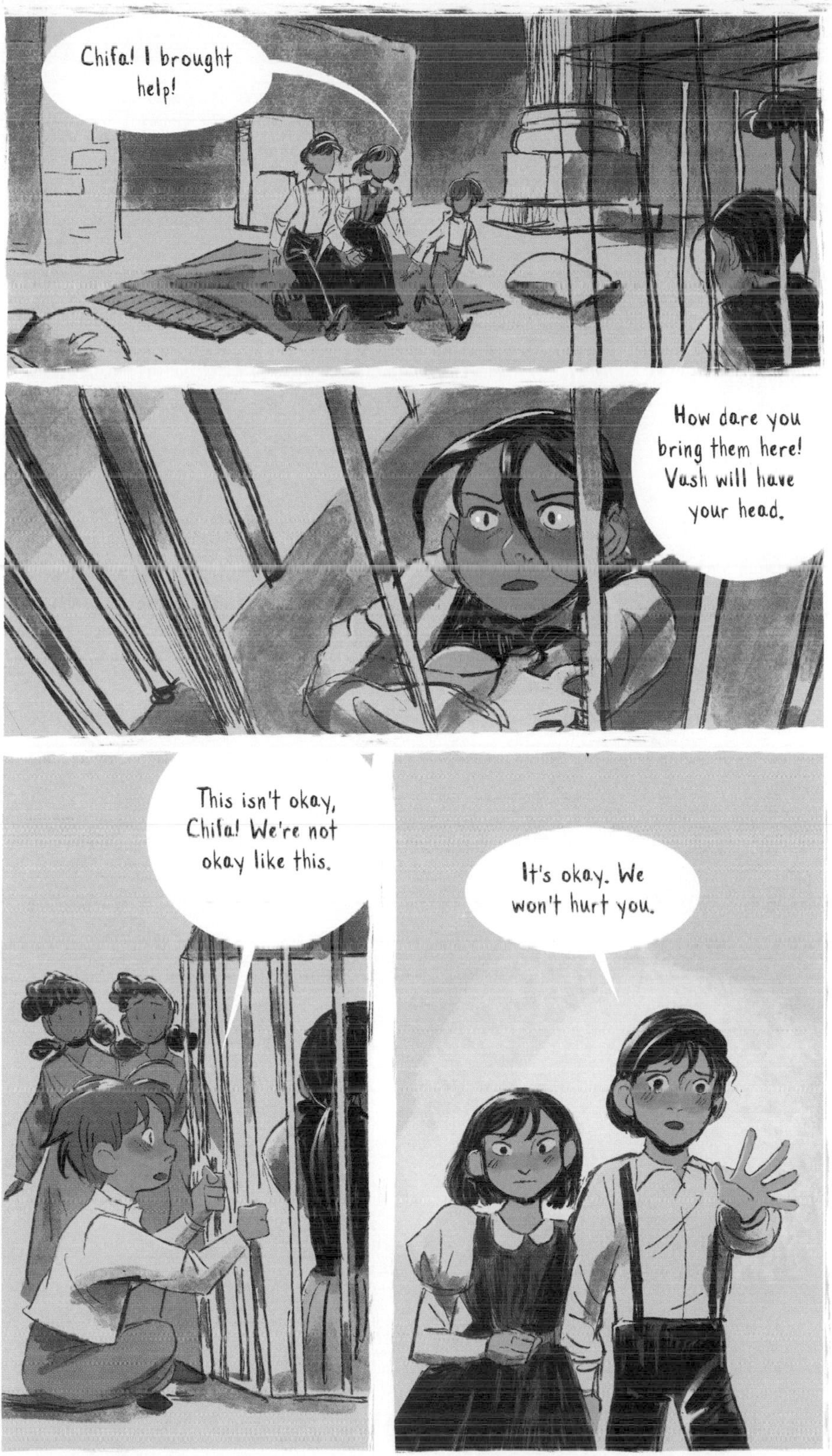
Chifa! I brought help!
How dare you bring them here! Vash will have your head.
This isn't okay, Chifa! We're not okay like this.
It's okay. We won't hurt you.

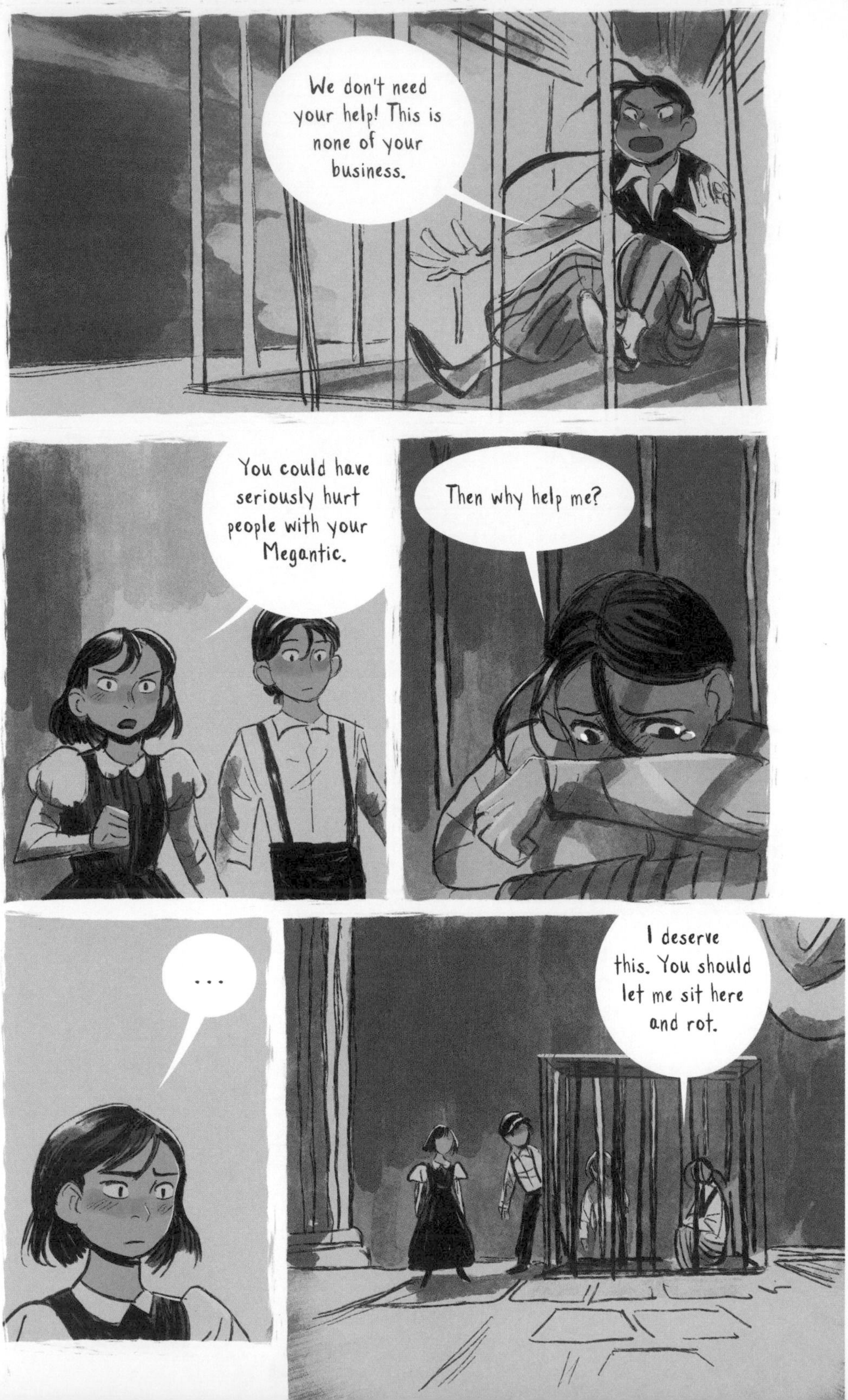
We don't need your help! This is none of your business.
You could have seriously hurt people with your Megantic.
Then why help me?
. . .
I deserve this. You should let me sit here and rot.

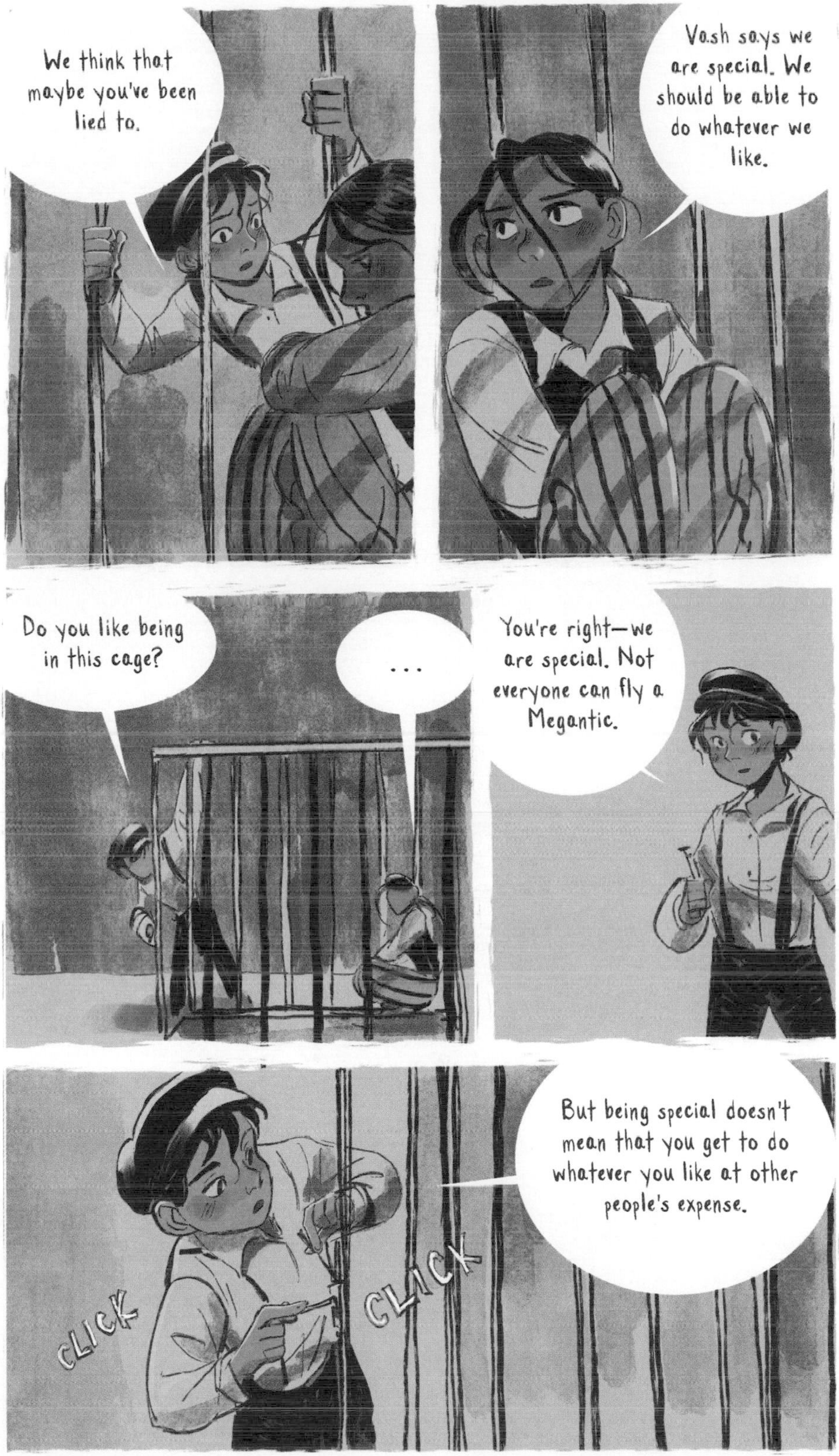
We think that maybe you've been lied to.
Vash says we are special. We should be able to do whatever we like.
Do you like being in this cage?
...
You're right—we are special. Not everyone can fly a Megantic.
But being special doesn't mean that you get to do whatever you like at other people's expense.
CLICK
CLICK

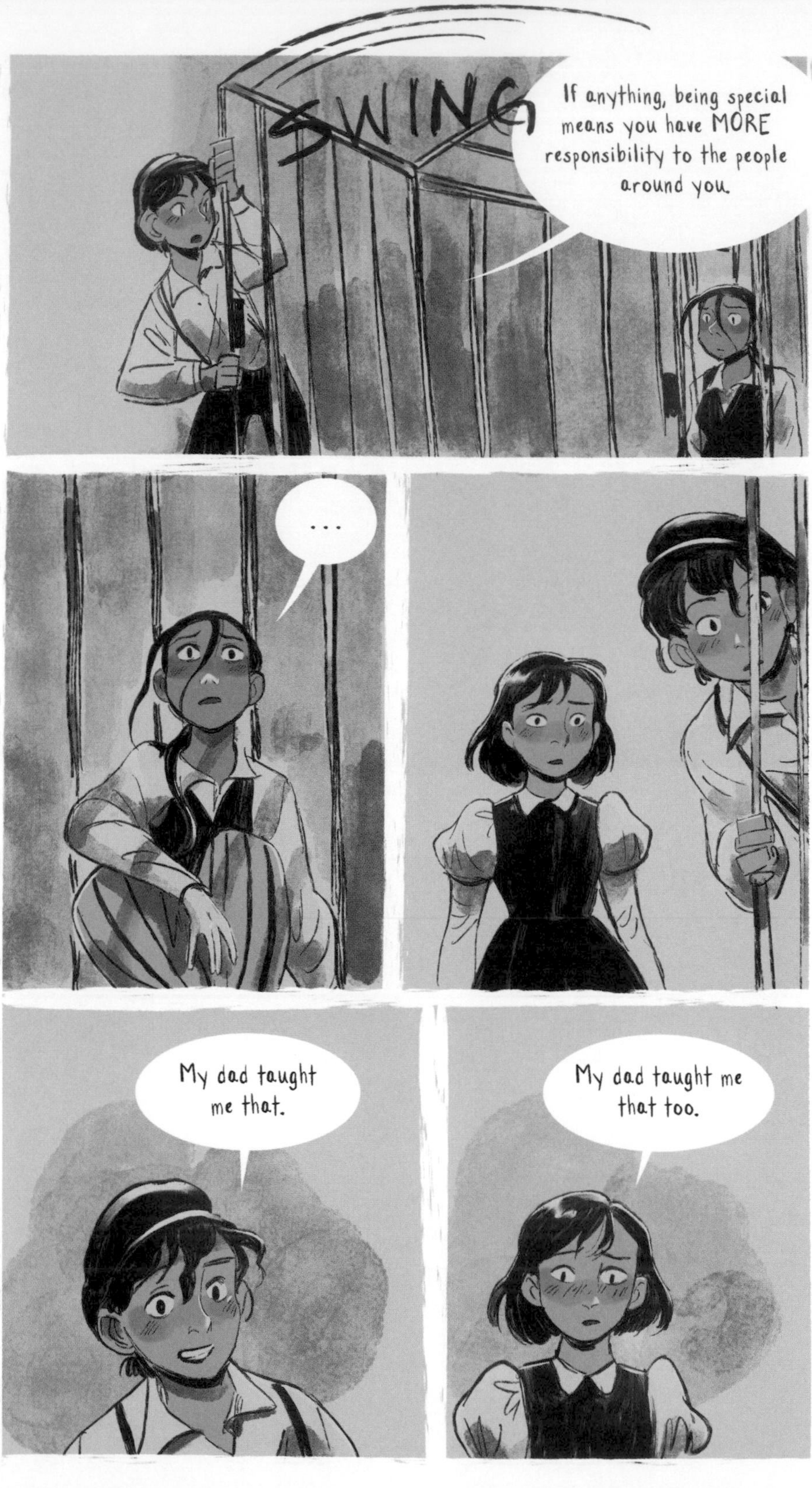
SWING
If anything, being special means you have MORE responsibility to the people around you.
...
My dad taught me that.
My dad taught me that too.

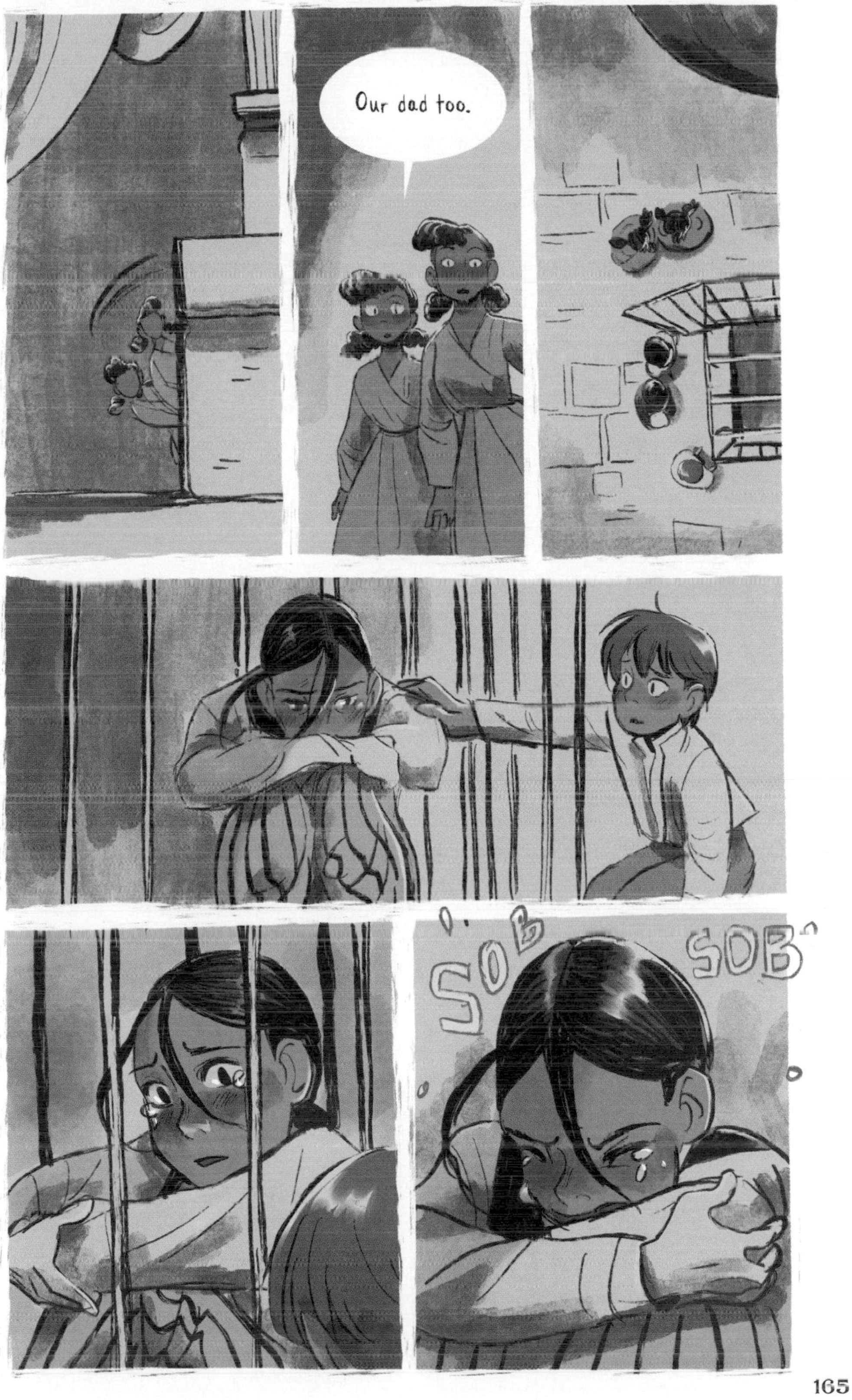
Our dad too.
SOB
SOB

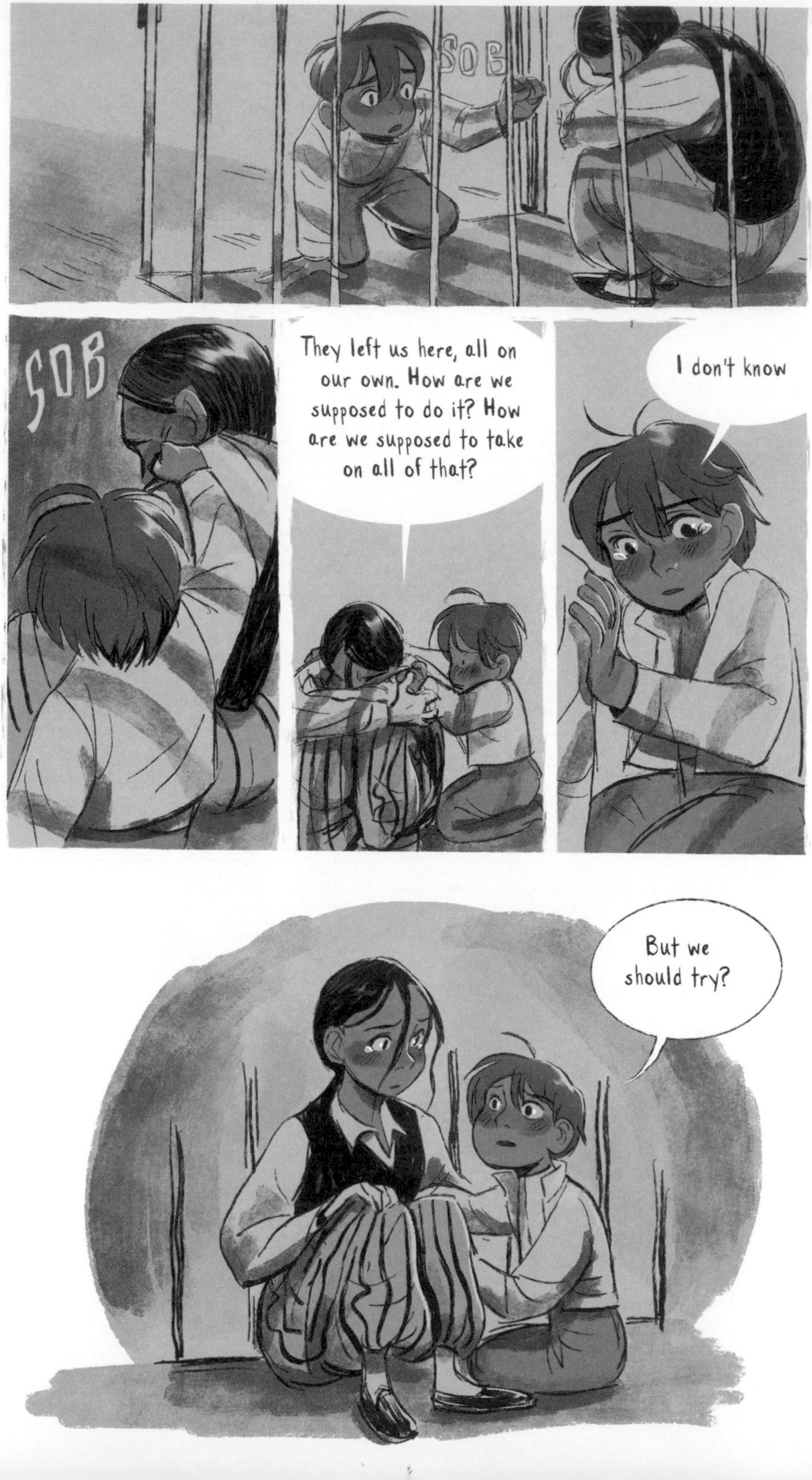
SOB
SOB
They left us here, all on our own. How are we supposed to do it? How are we supposed to take on all of that?
I don't know
But we should try?

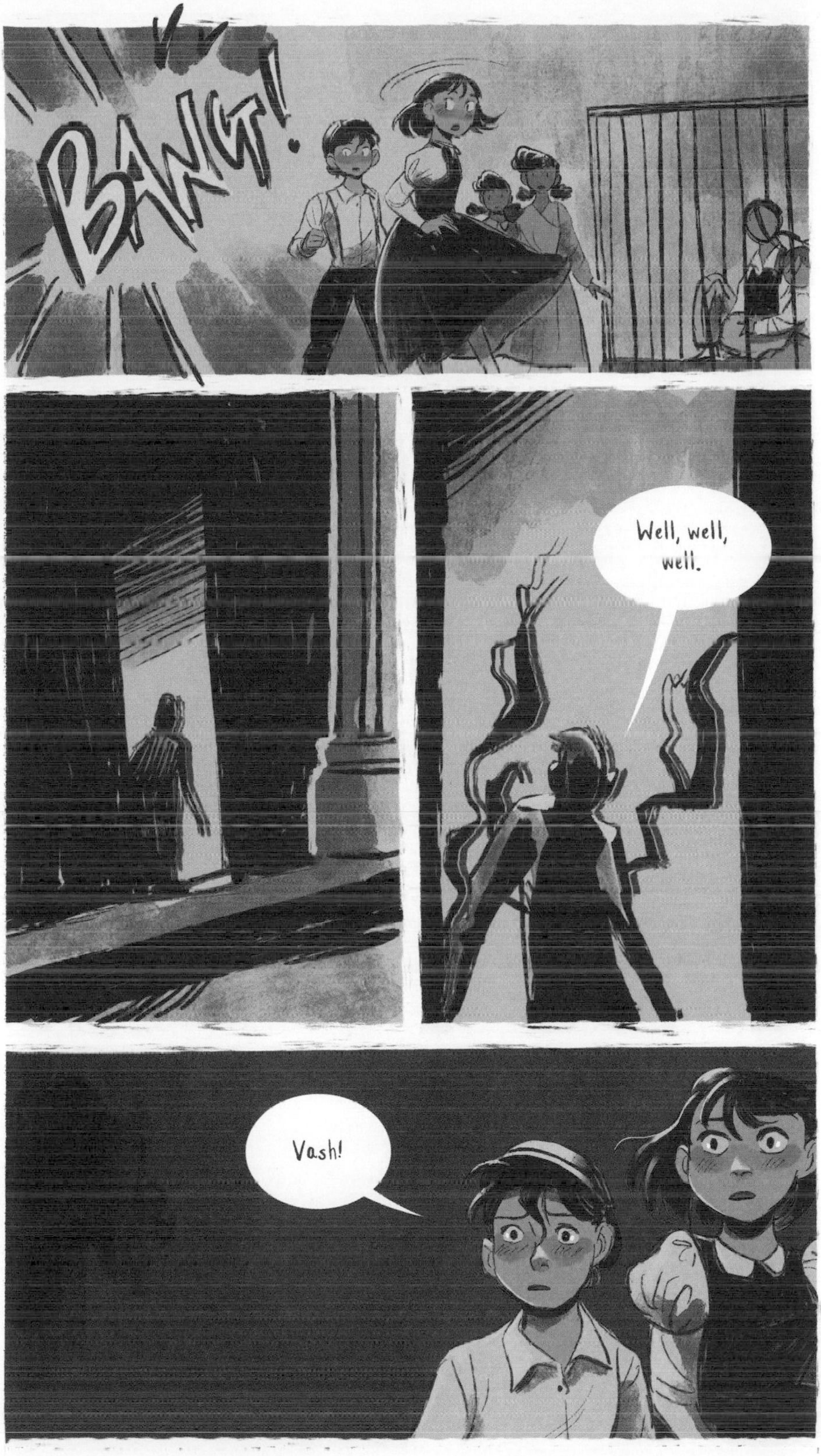
BANG!
Well, well, well.
Vash!

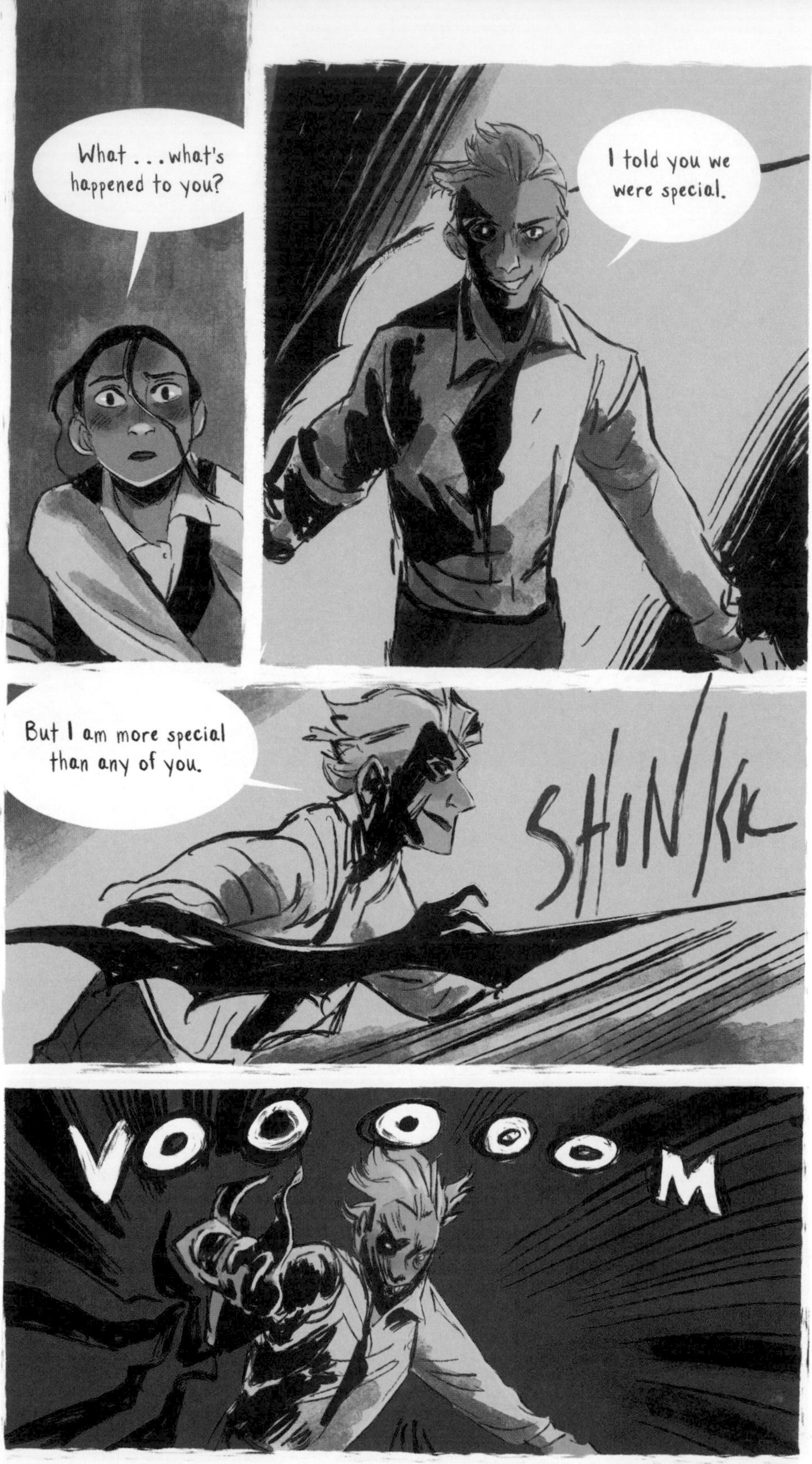
What . . . what's happened to you?
I told you we were special.
But I am more special than any of you.
SHINKK
VOOOOOOM

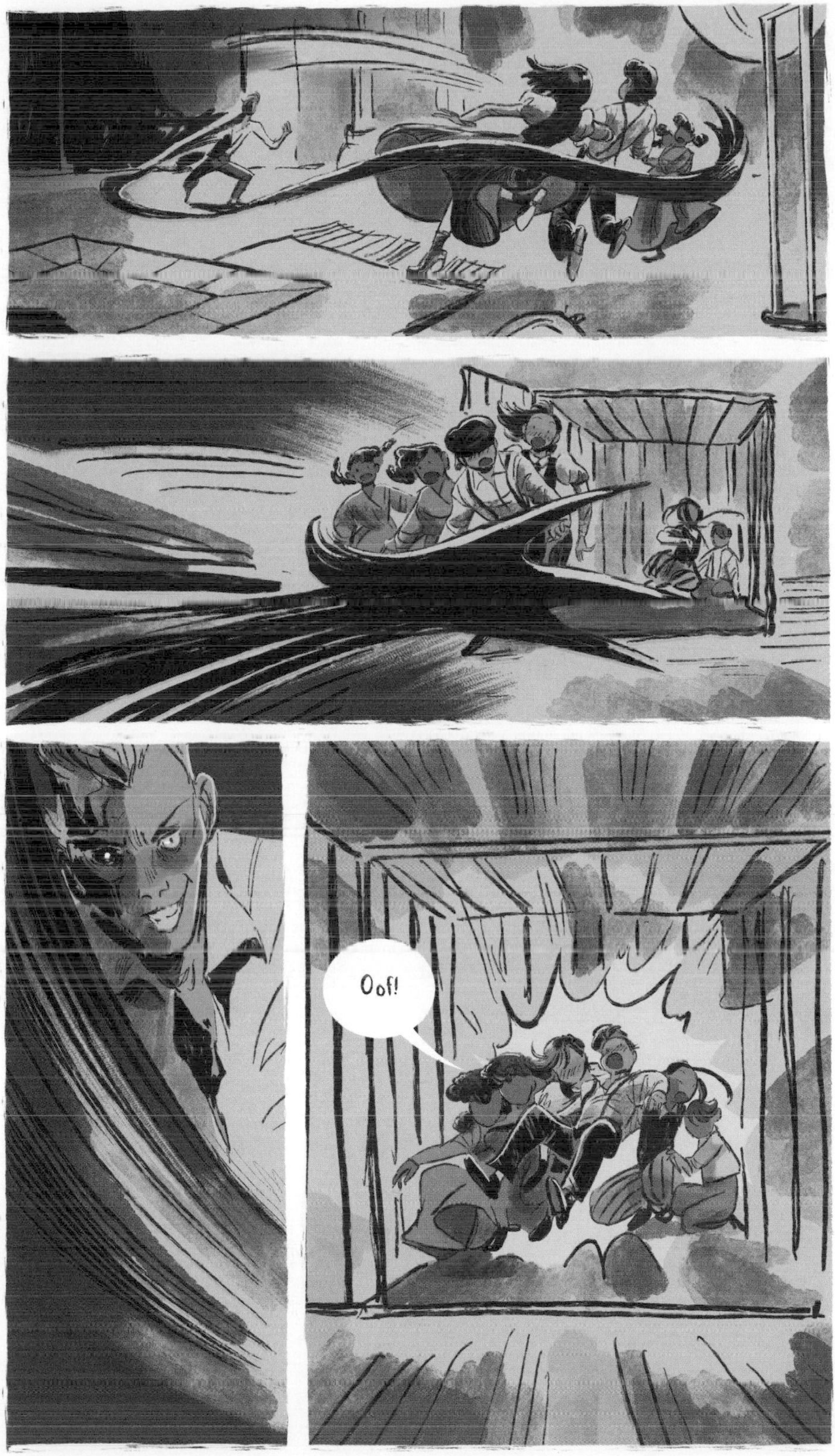
Oof!

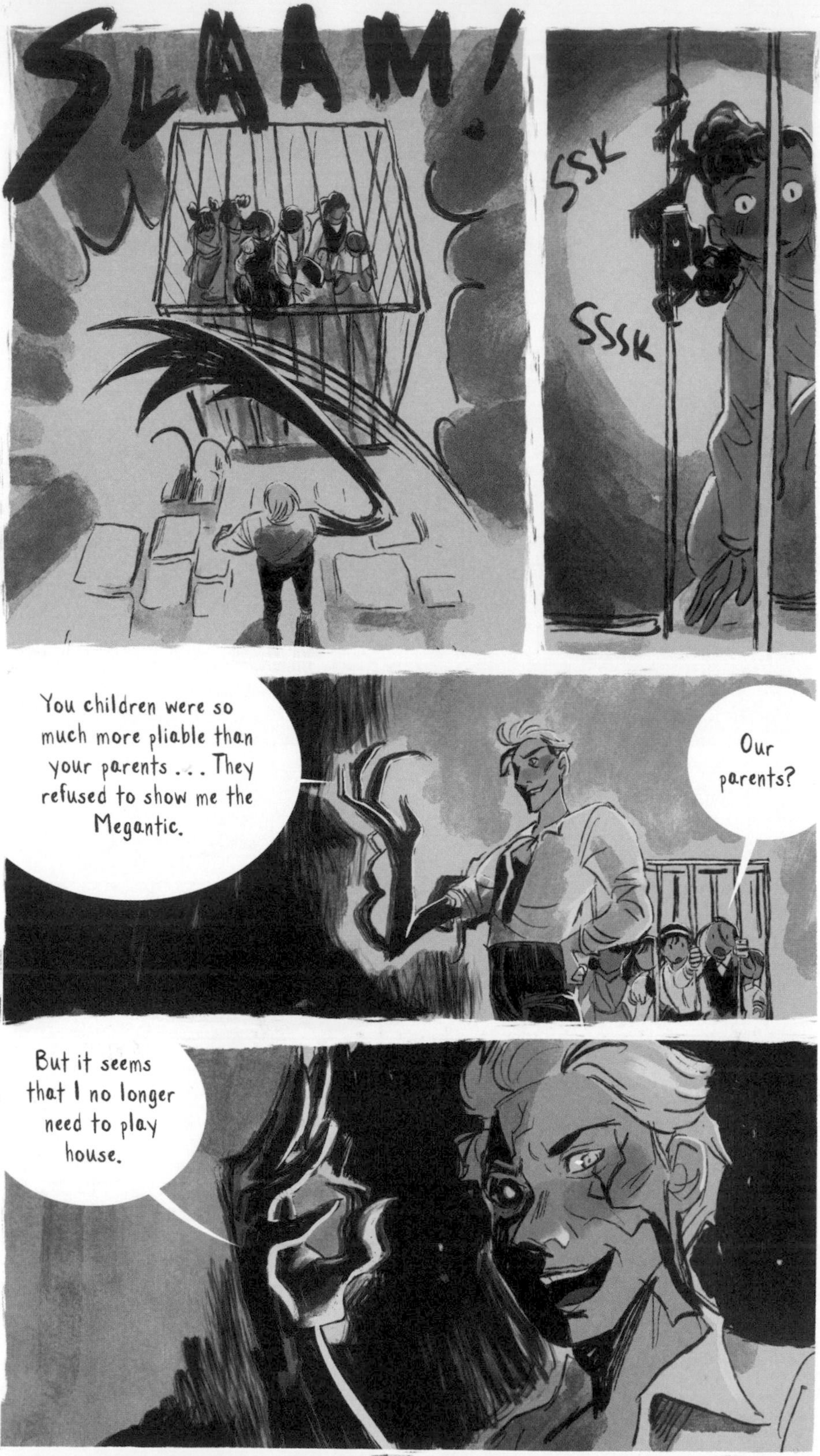
SLAAM!
SSK
SSSK
You children were so much more pliable than your parents . . . They refused to show me the Megantic.
Our parents?
But it seems that I no longer need to play house.

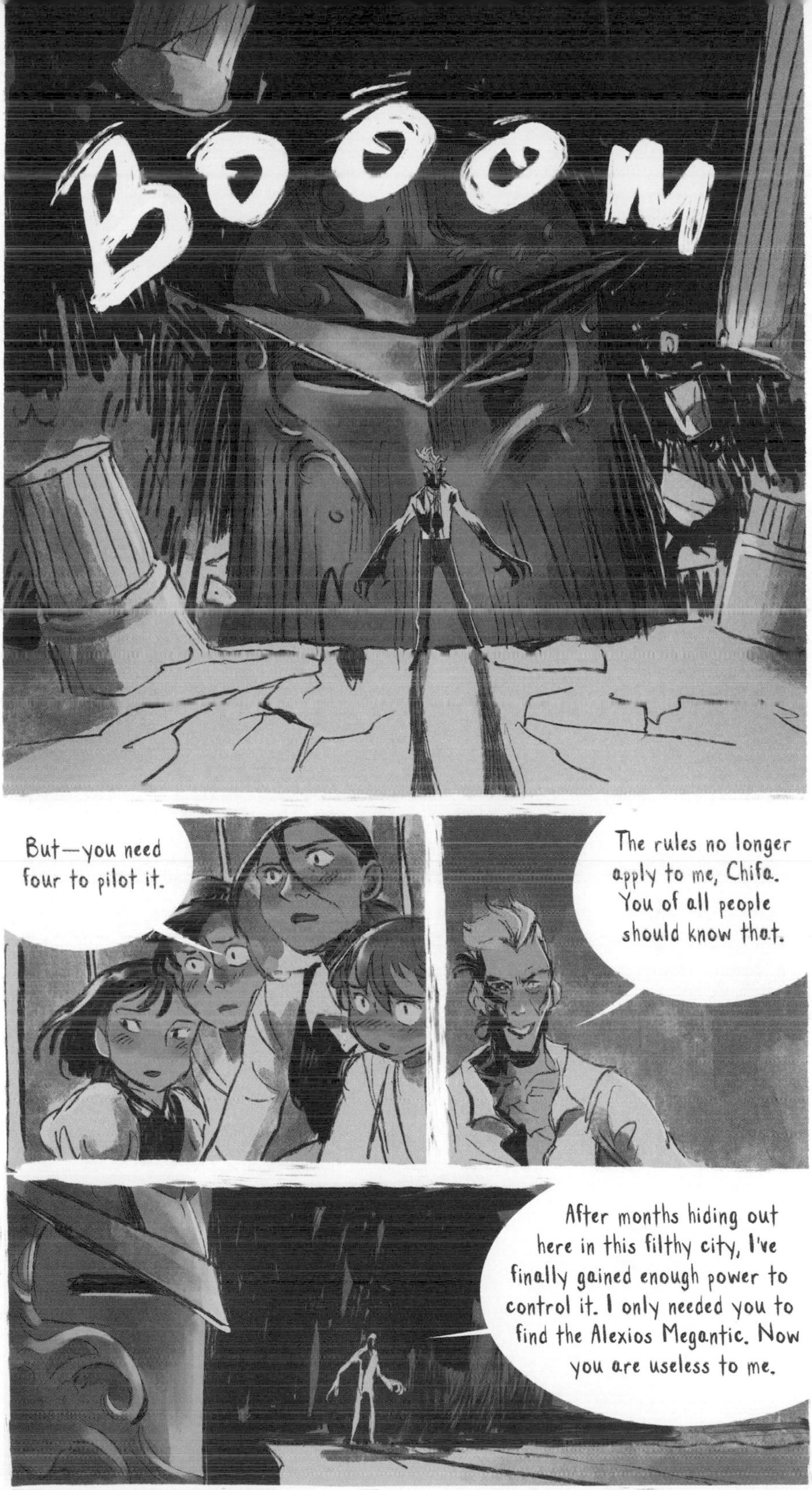
BOOOOM
But—you need four to pilot it.
The rules no longer apply to me, Chifa. You of all people should know that.
After months hiding out here in this filthy city, I've finally gained enough power to control it. I only needed you to find the Alexios Megantic. Now you are useless to me.

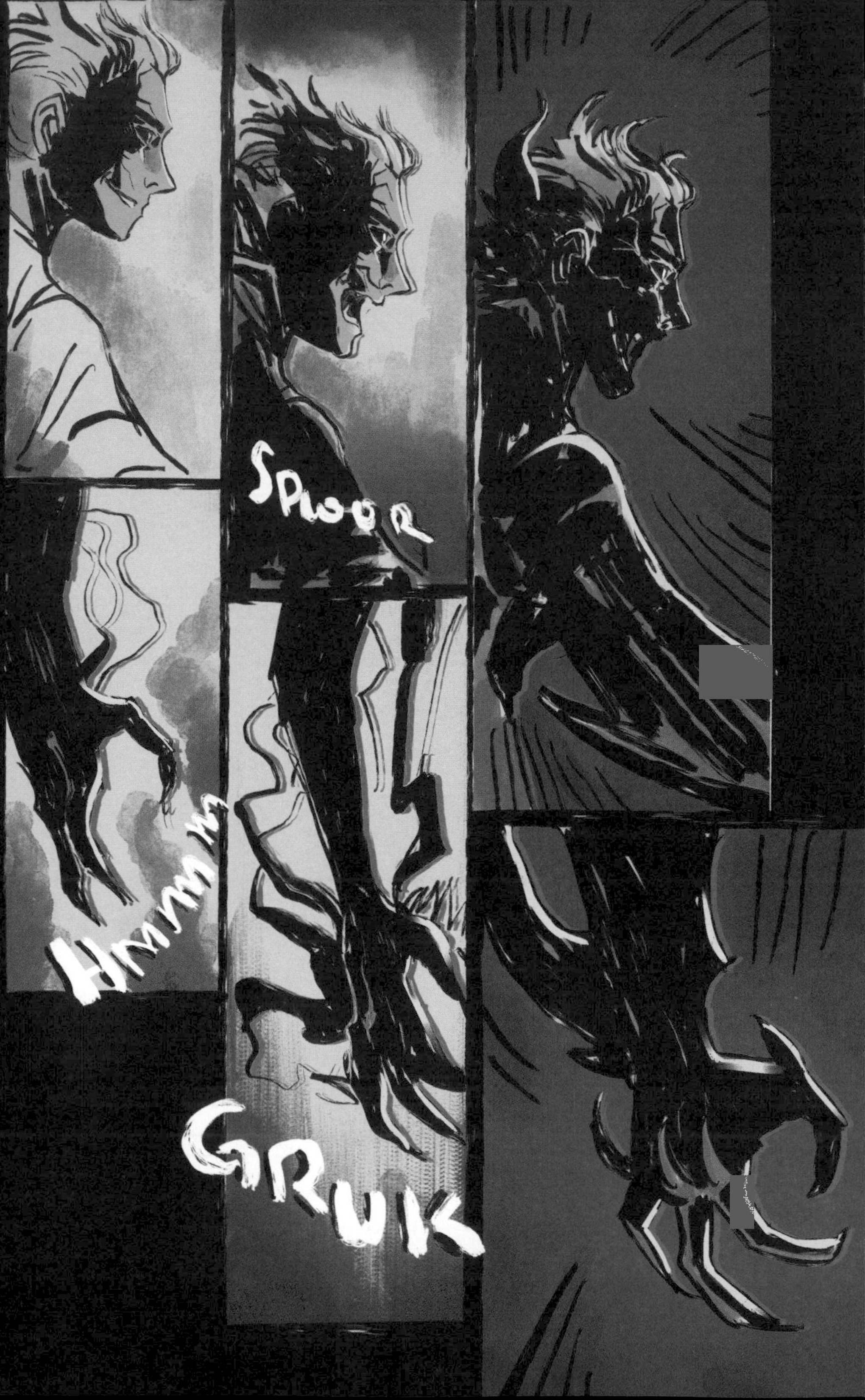
SPLOOR
HMMMM
GRUK

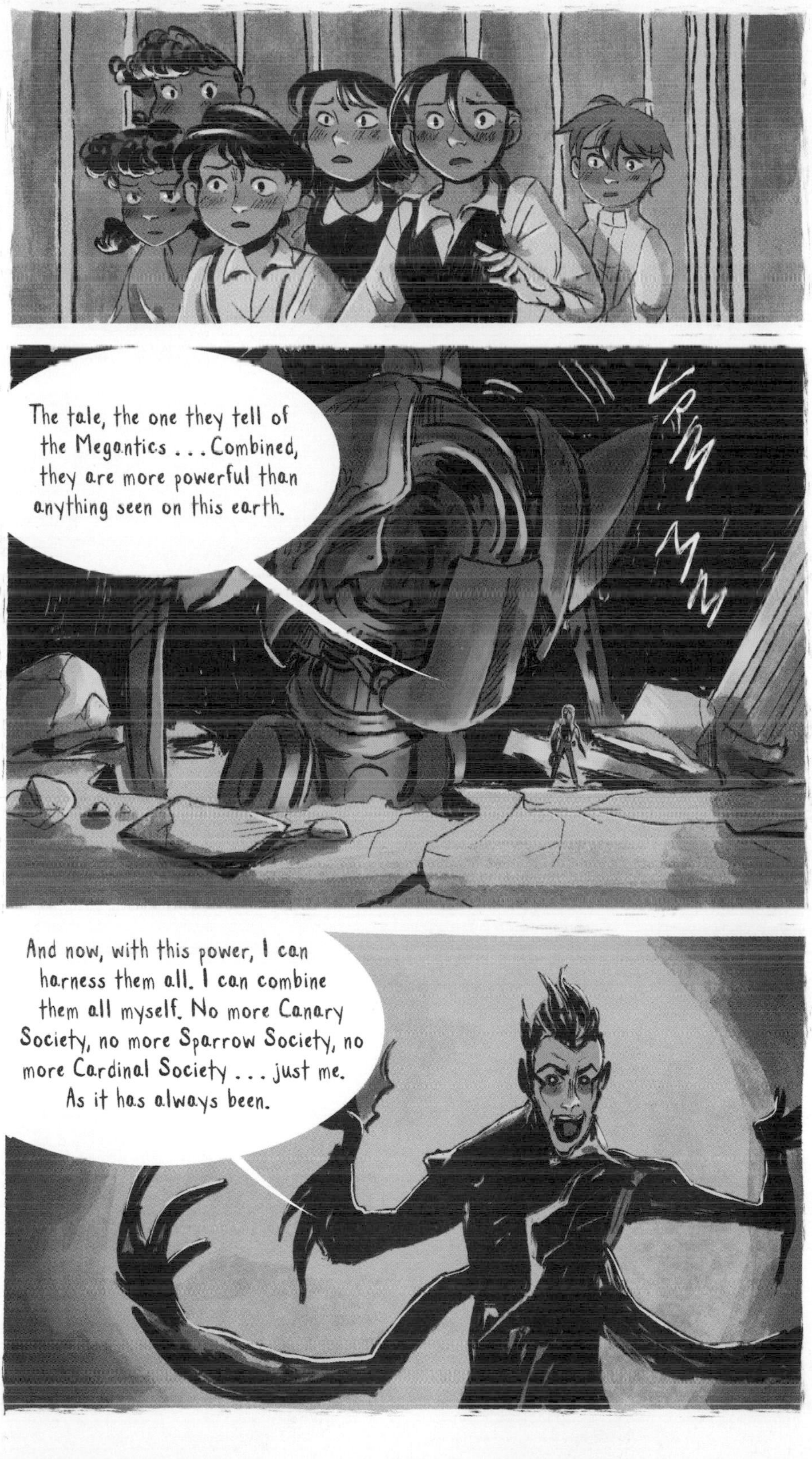
The tale, the one they tell of the Megantics . . . Combined, they are more powerful than anything seen on this earth.
VRMMMM
And now, with this power, I can harness them all. I can combine them all myself. No more Canary Society, no more Sparrow Society, no more Cardinal Society . . . just me. As it has always been.

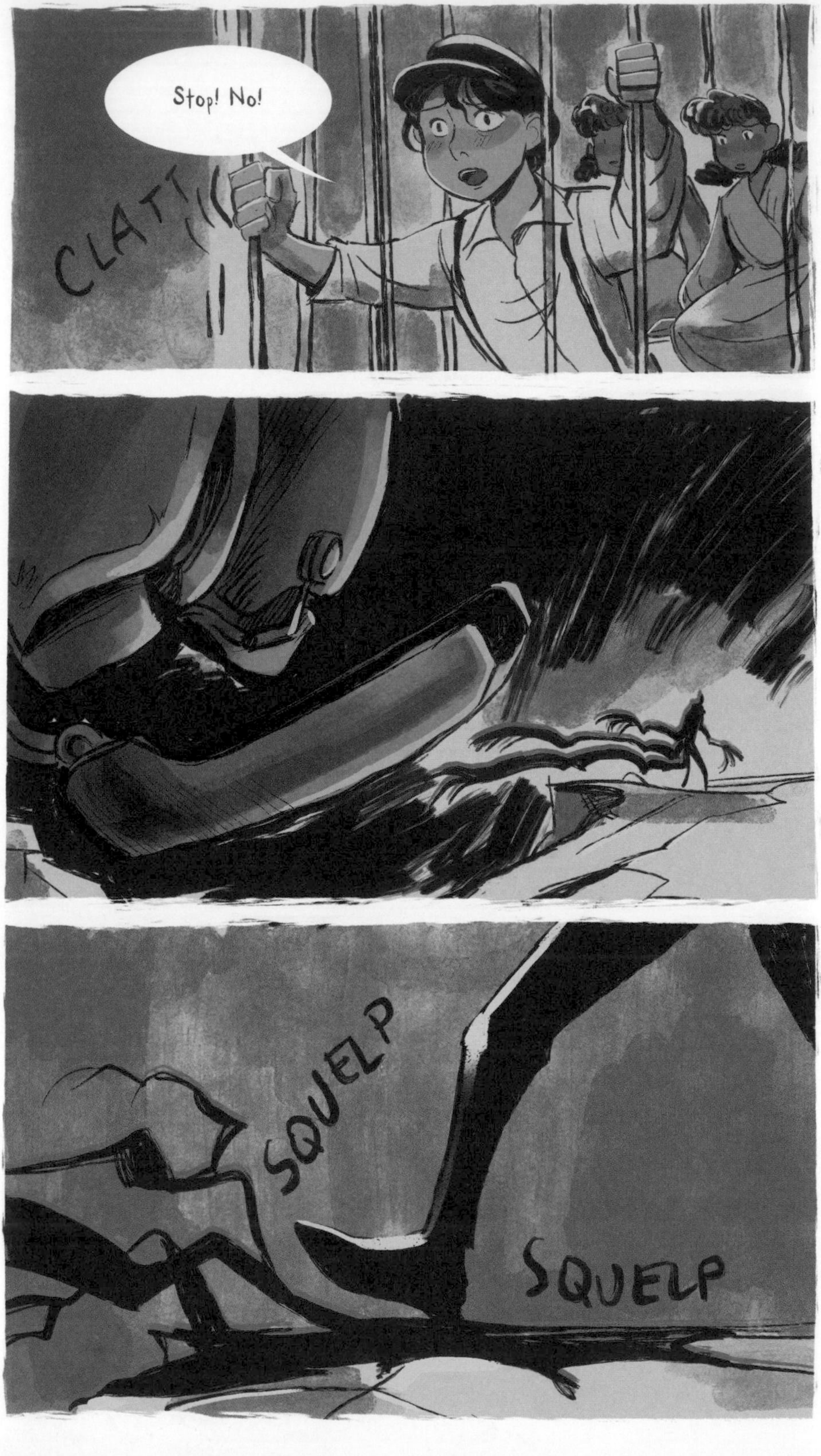
Stop! No!
CLATT
SQUELP
SQUELP

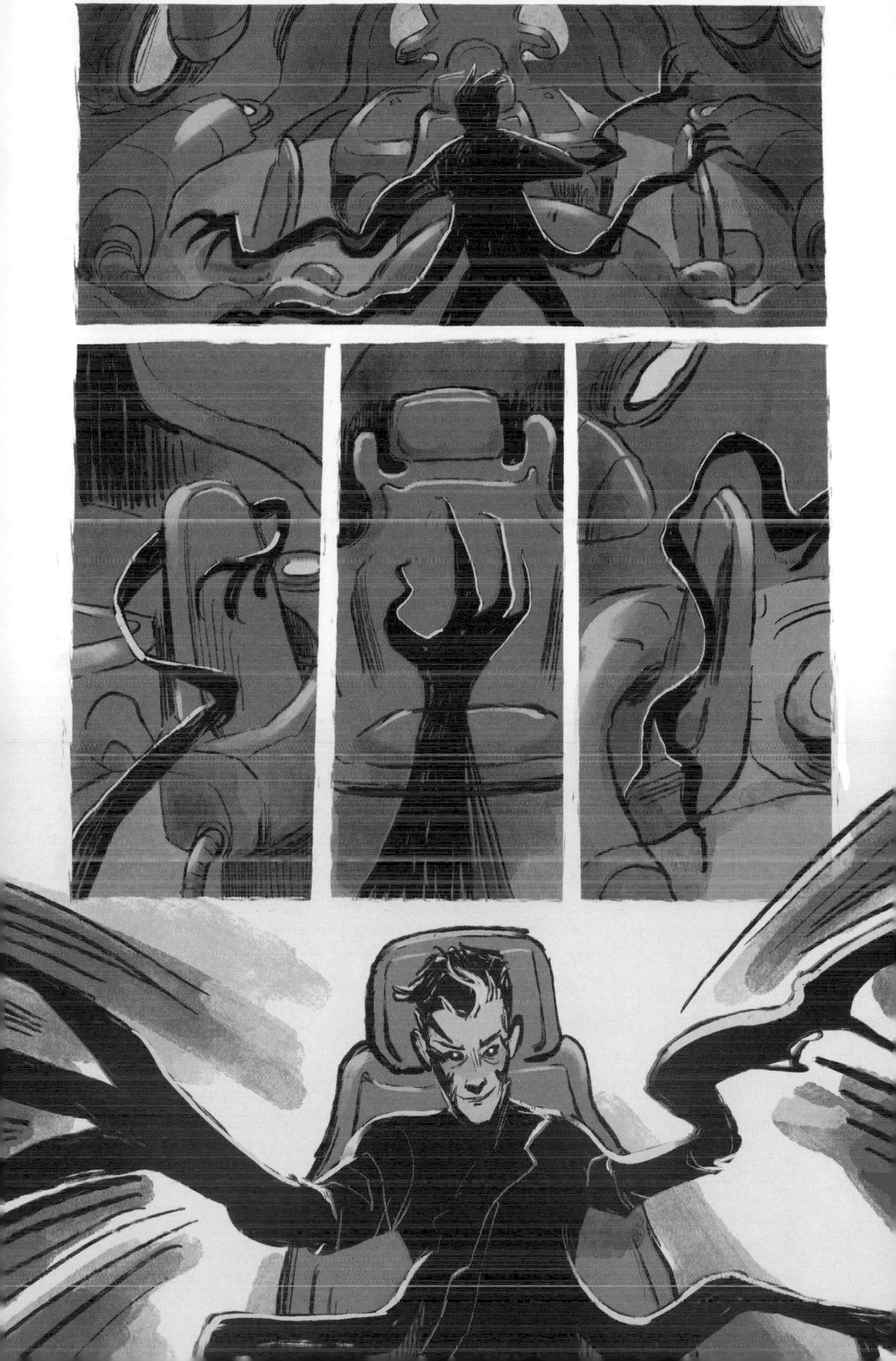

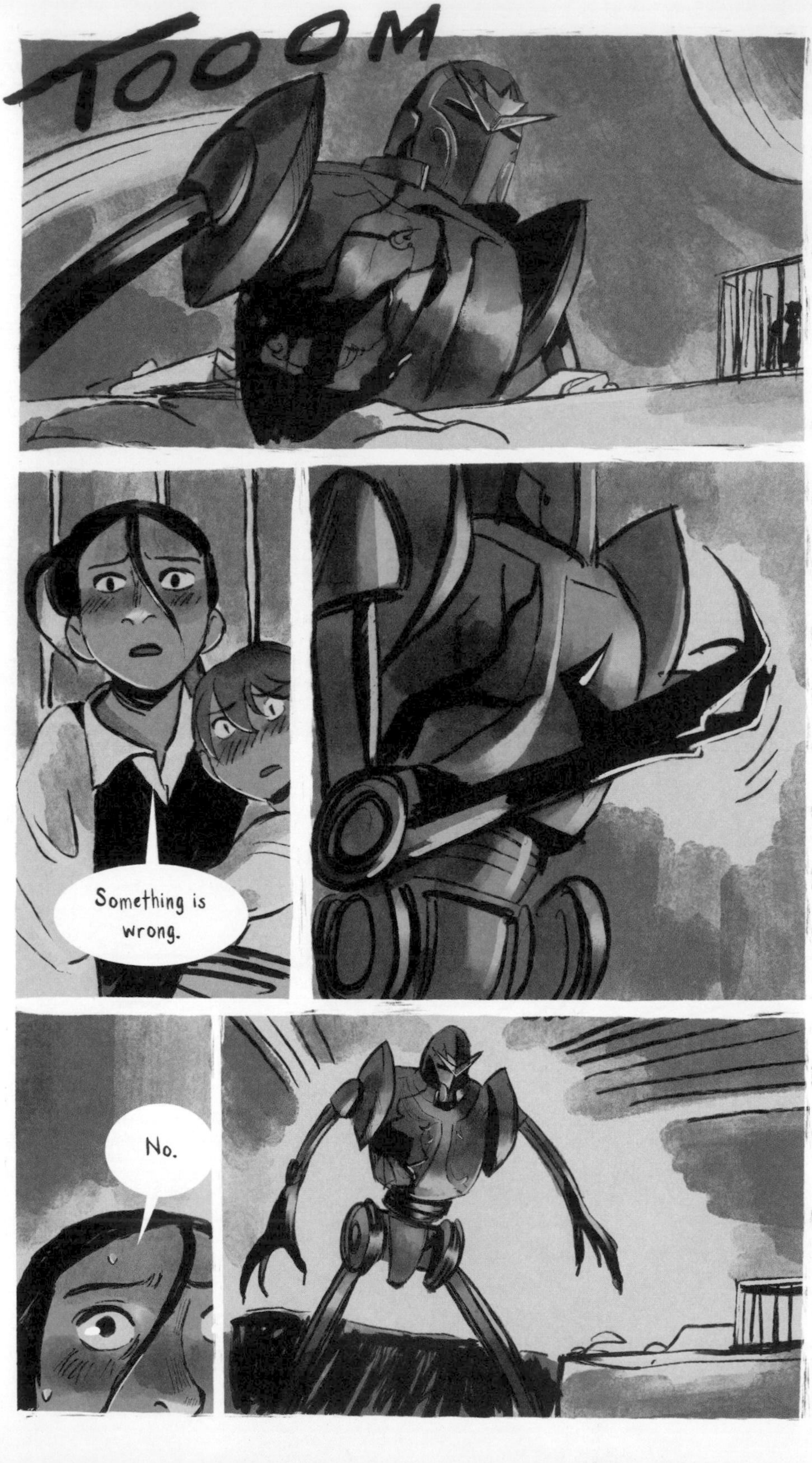
TOOOM
Something is wrong.
No.

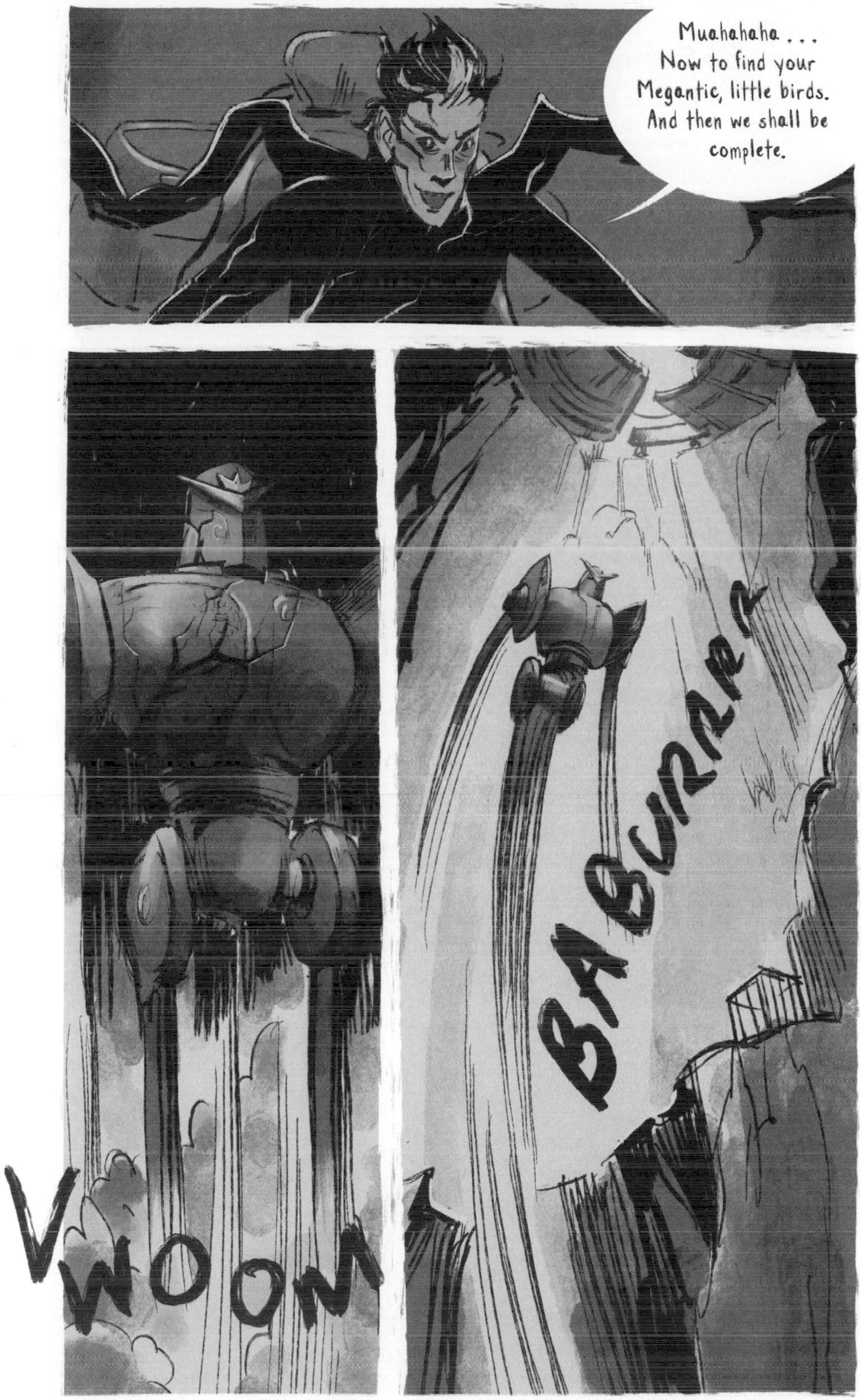
Muahahaha . . . Now to find your Megantic, little birds. And then we shall be complete.
VWOOM
BABURRRR

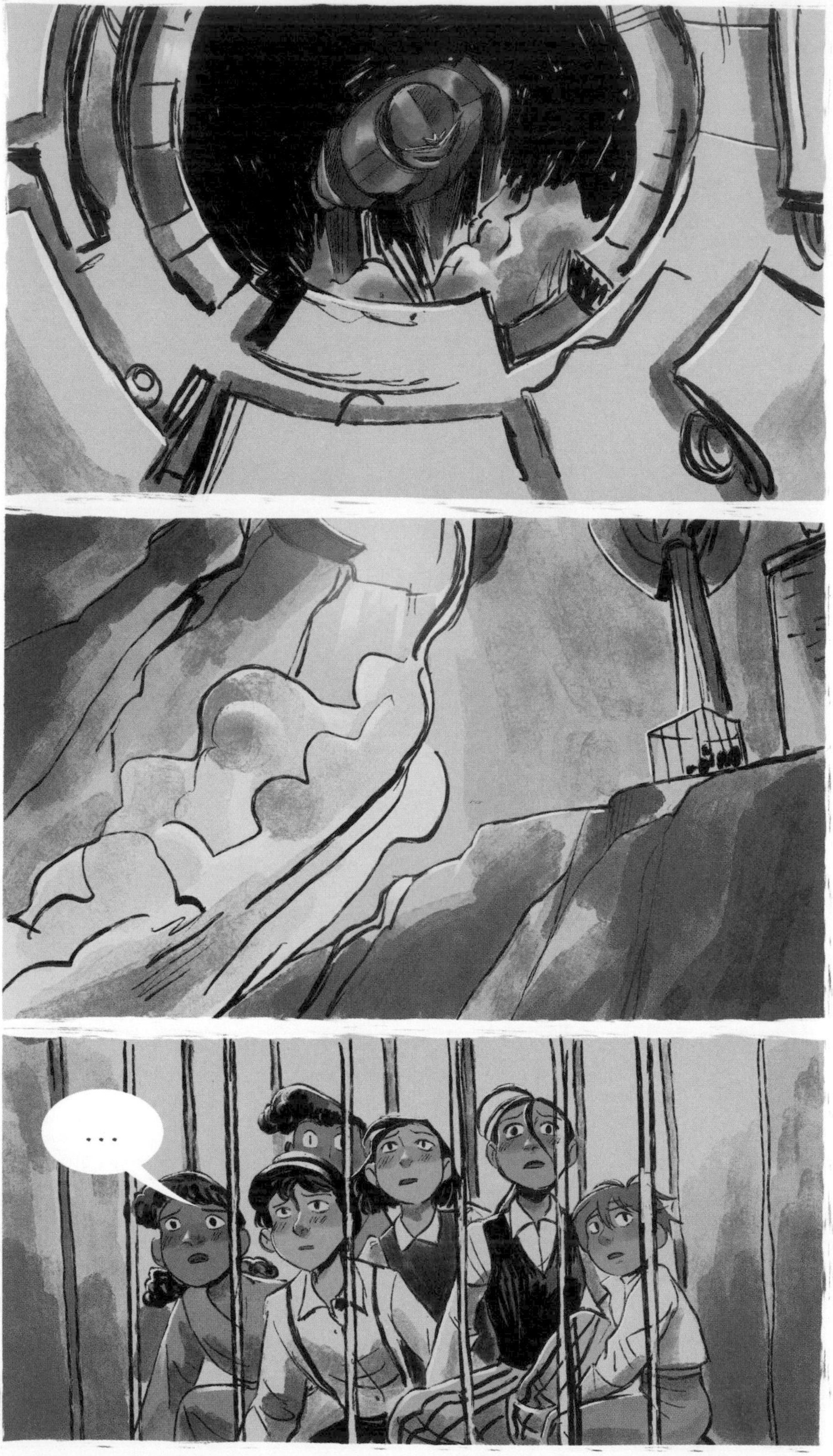
...

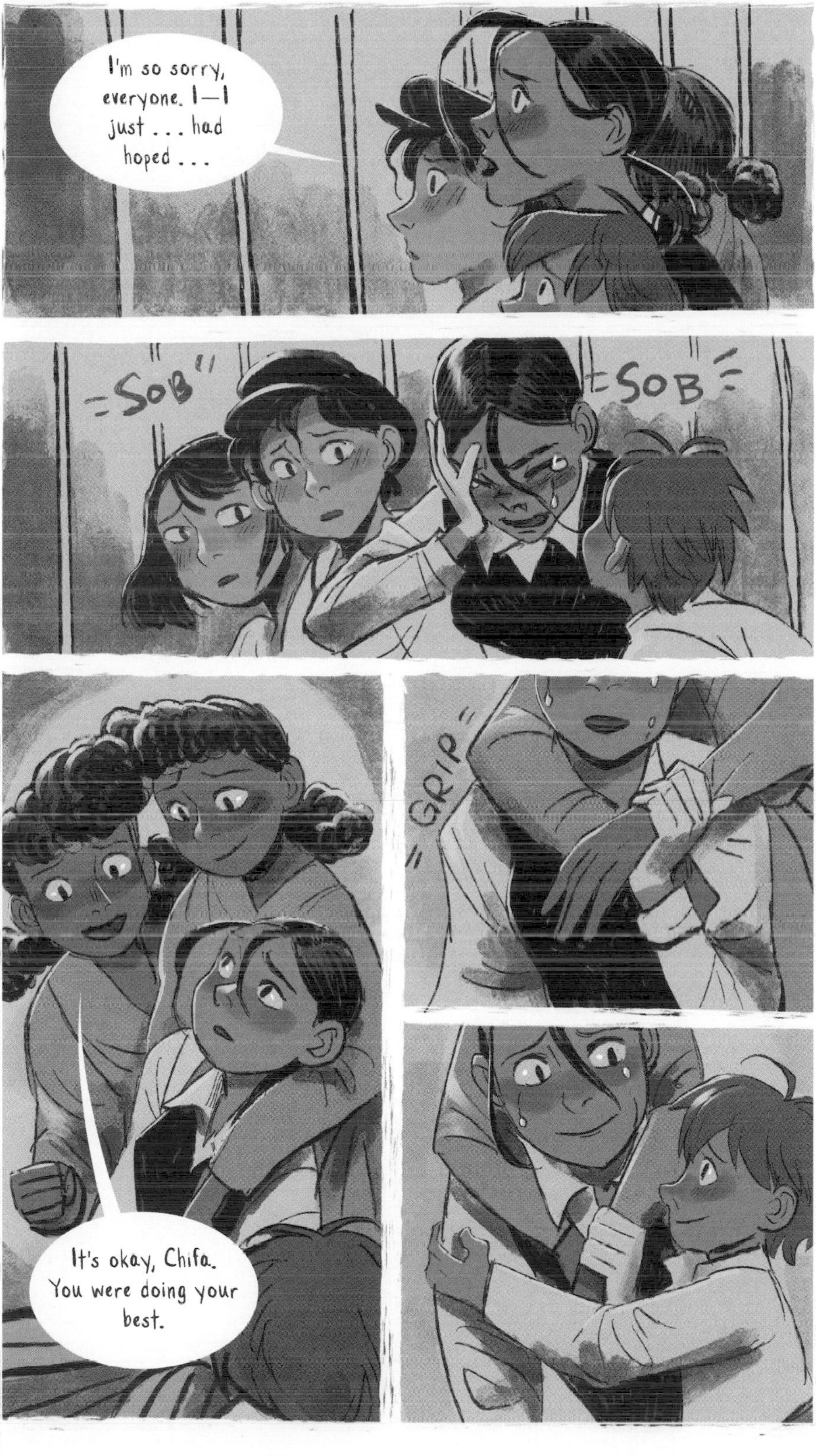
I'm so sorry, everyone. I—I just . . . had hoped . . .
SOB
SOB
GRIP
It's okay, Chifa. You were doing your best.

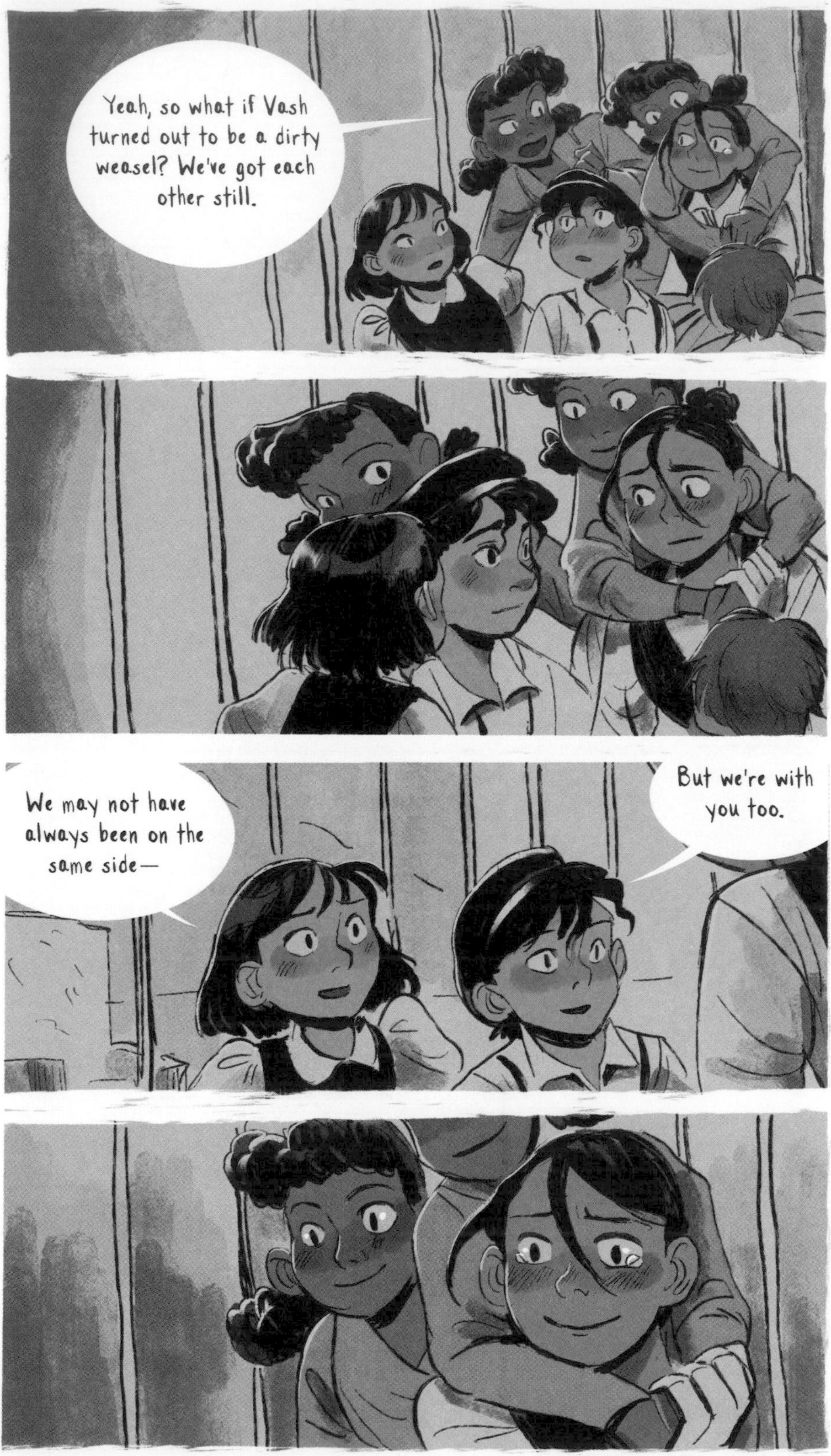
Yeah, so what if Vash turned out to be a dirty weasel? We've got each other still.
We may not have always been on the same side—
But we're with you too.

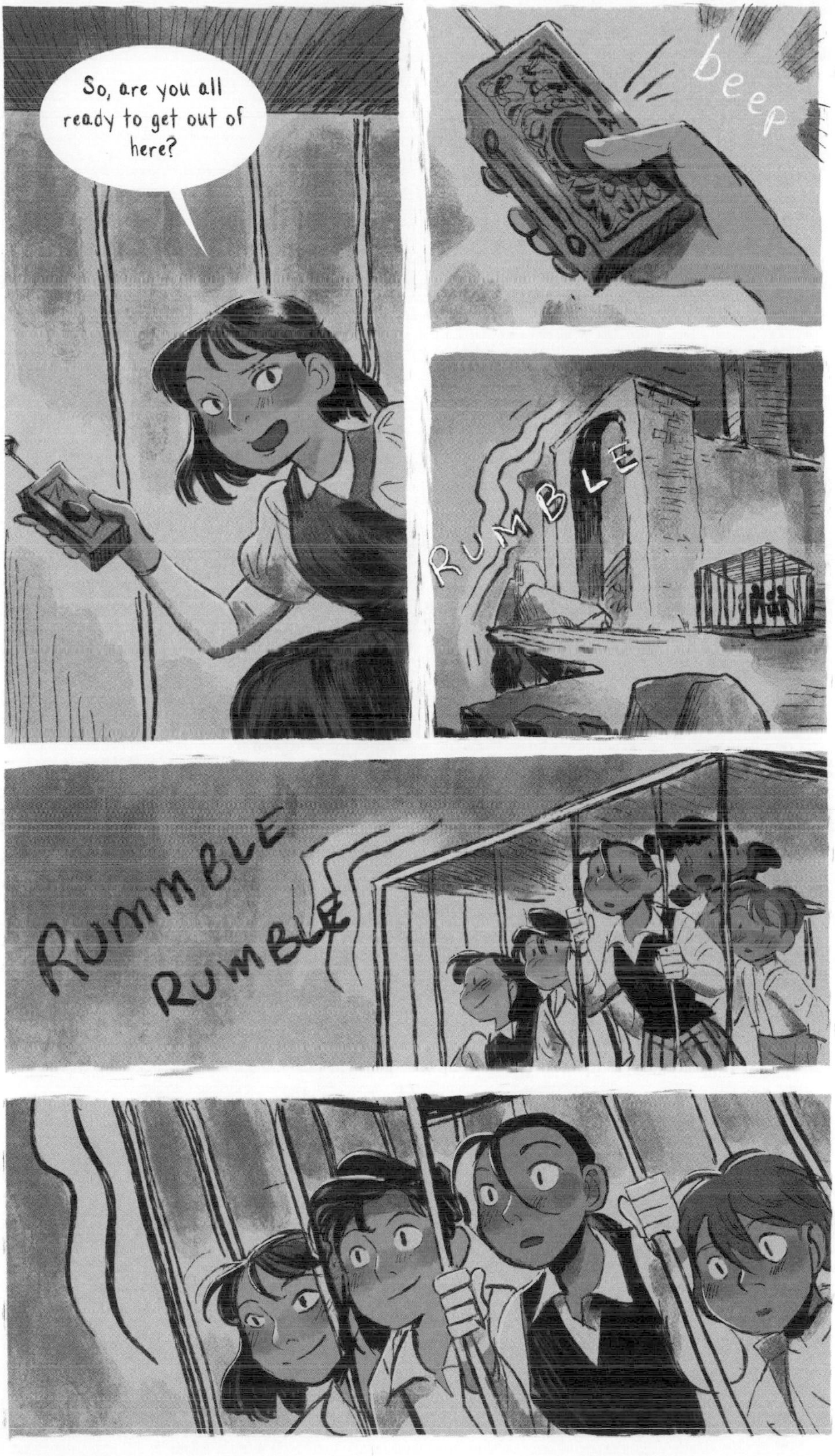
So, are you all ready to get out of here?
beep
RUMBLE
RUMMBLE
RUMBLE

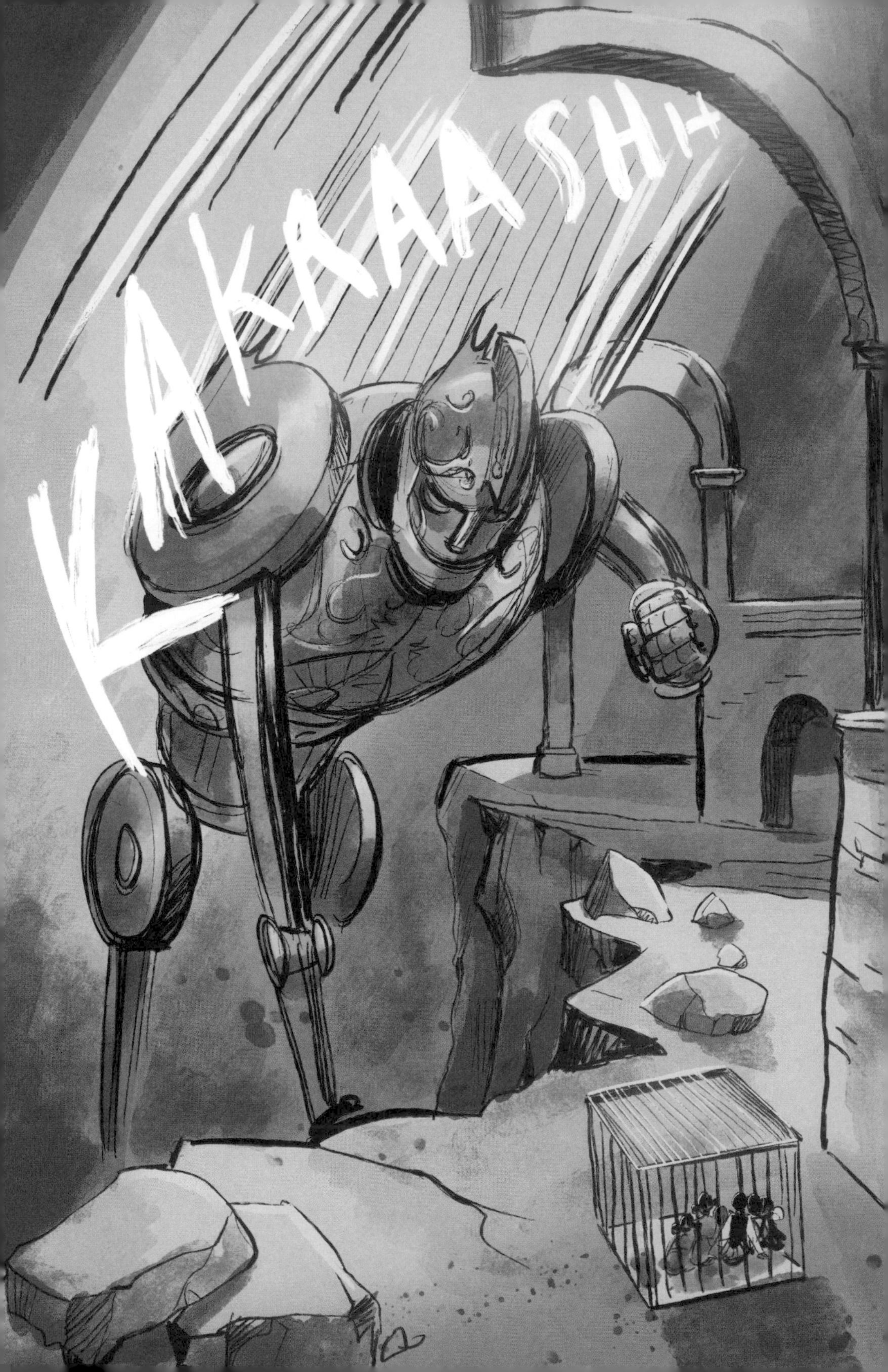
KAKRAASH

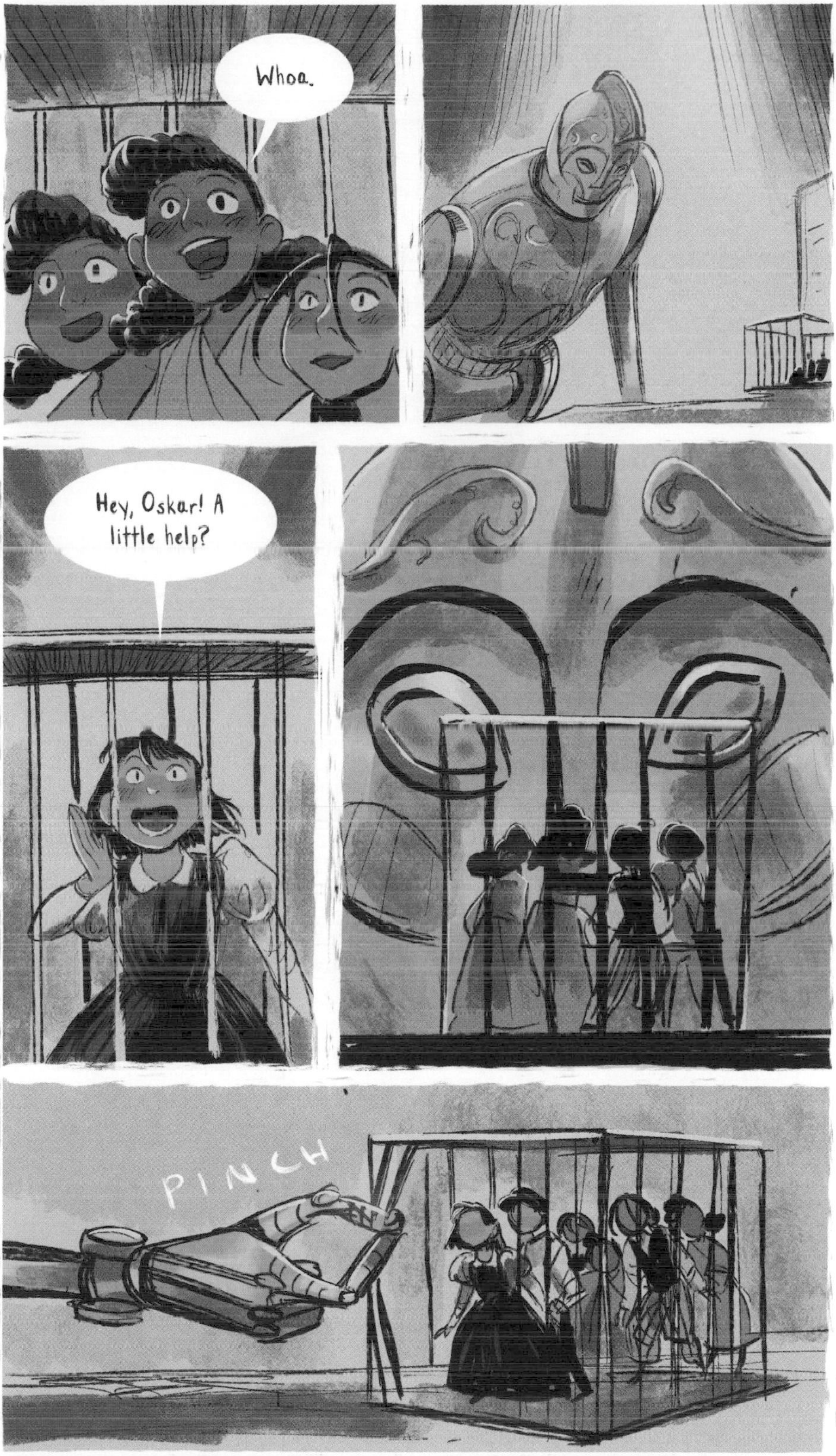
Whoa.
Hey, Oskar! A little help?
PINCH

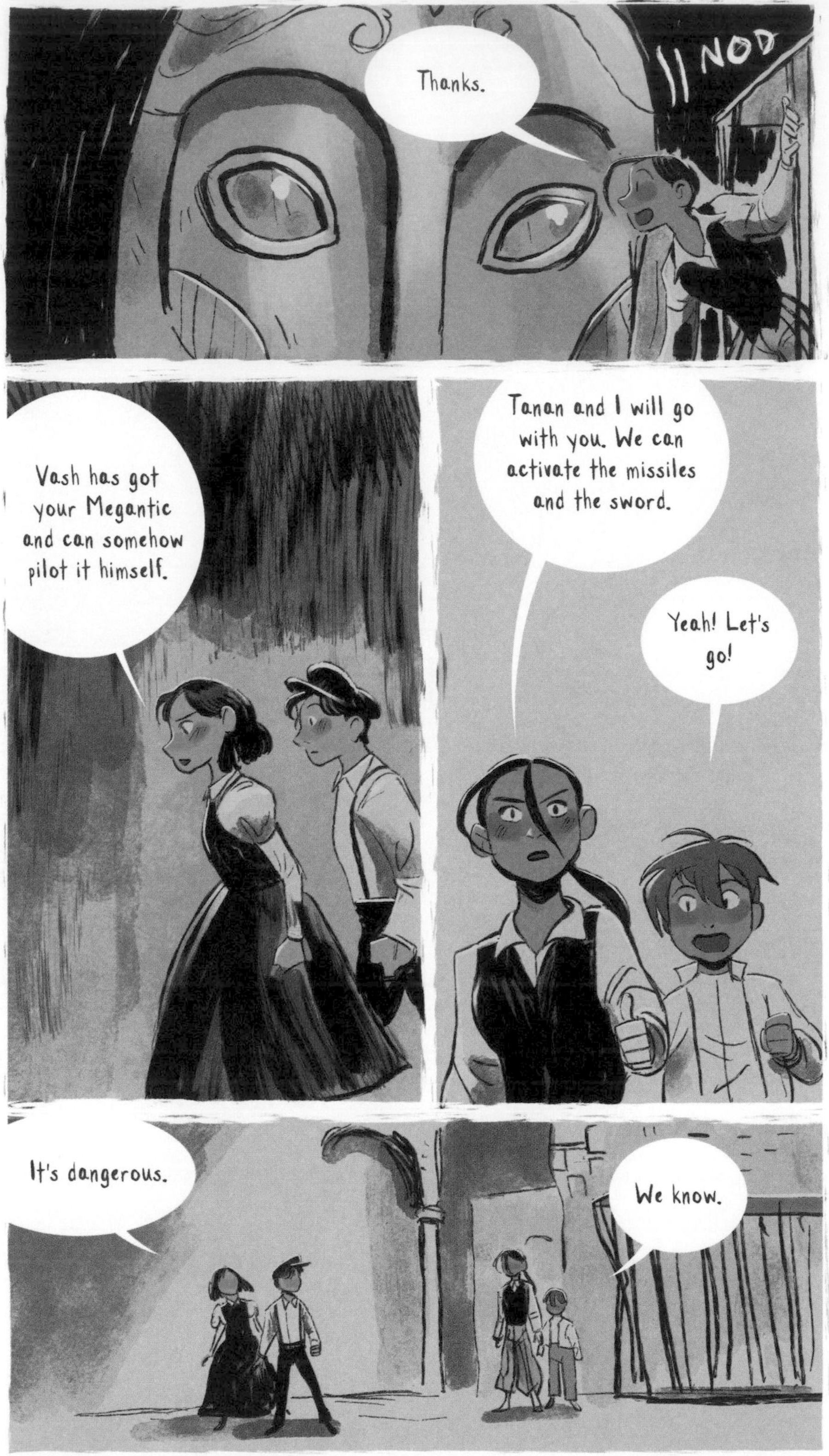
Thanks.
NOD
Vash has got your Megantic and can somehow pilot it himself.
Tanan and I will go with you. We can activate the missiles and the sword.
Yeah! Let's go!
It's dangerous.
We know.

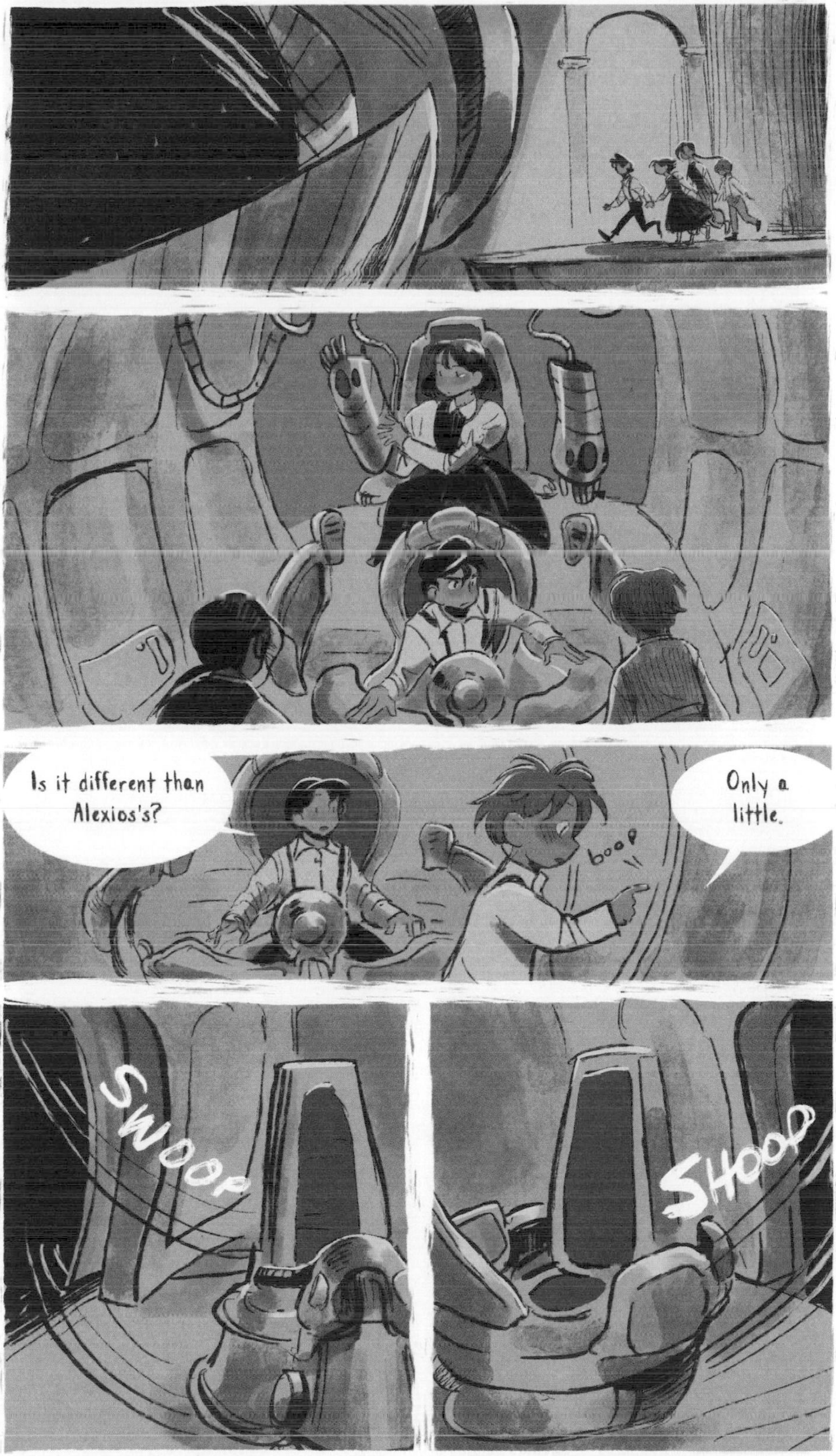
Is it different than Alexios's?
Only a little.
boop
SWOOP
SHOOP

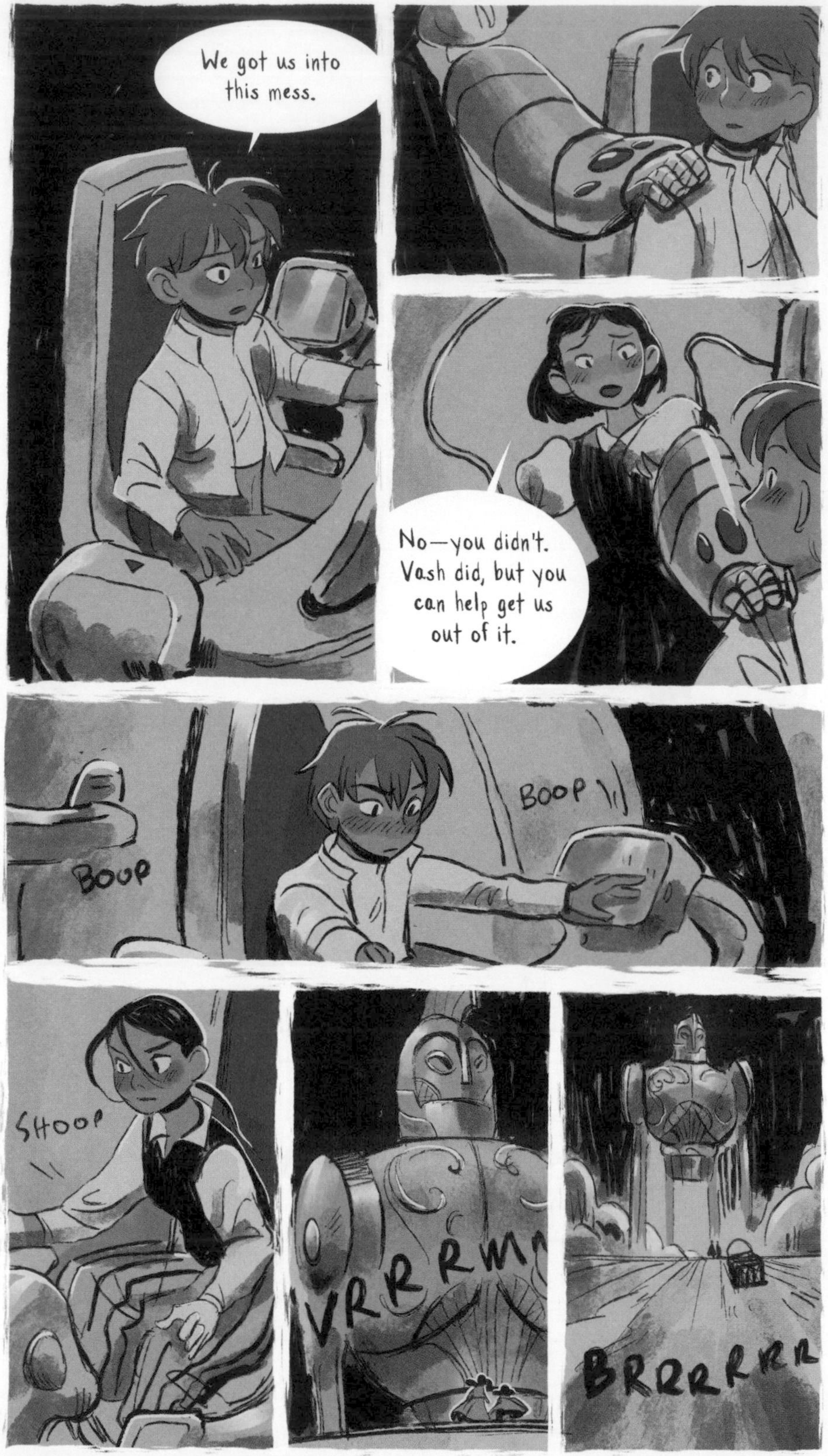
We got us into this mess.
No—you didn't. Vash did, but you can help get us out of it.
BOOP
BOOP
SHOOP
VRRRWM
BRRRRRR

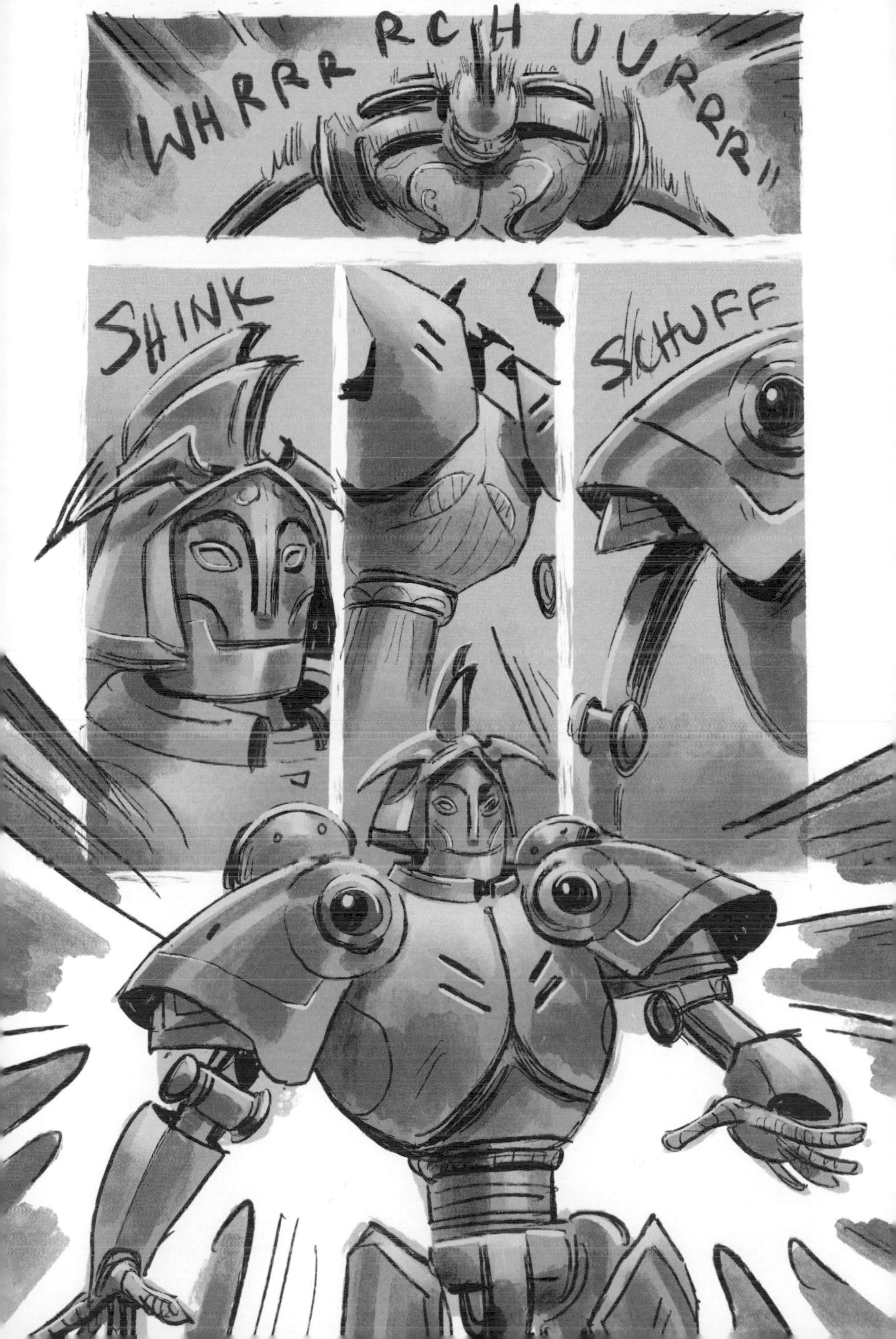
WHRRR RCH UURRR
SHINK
SCHUFF

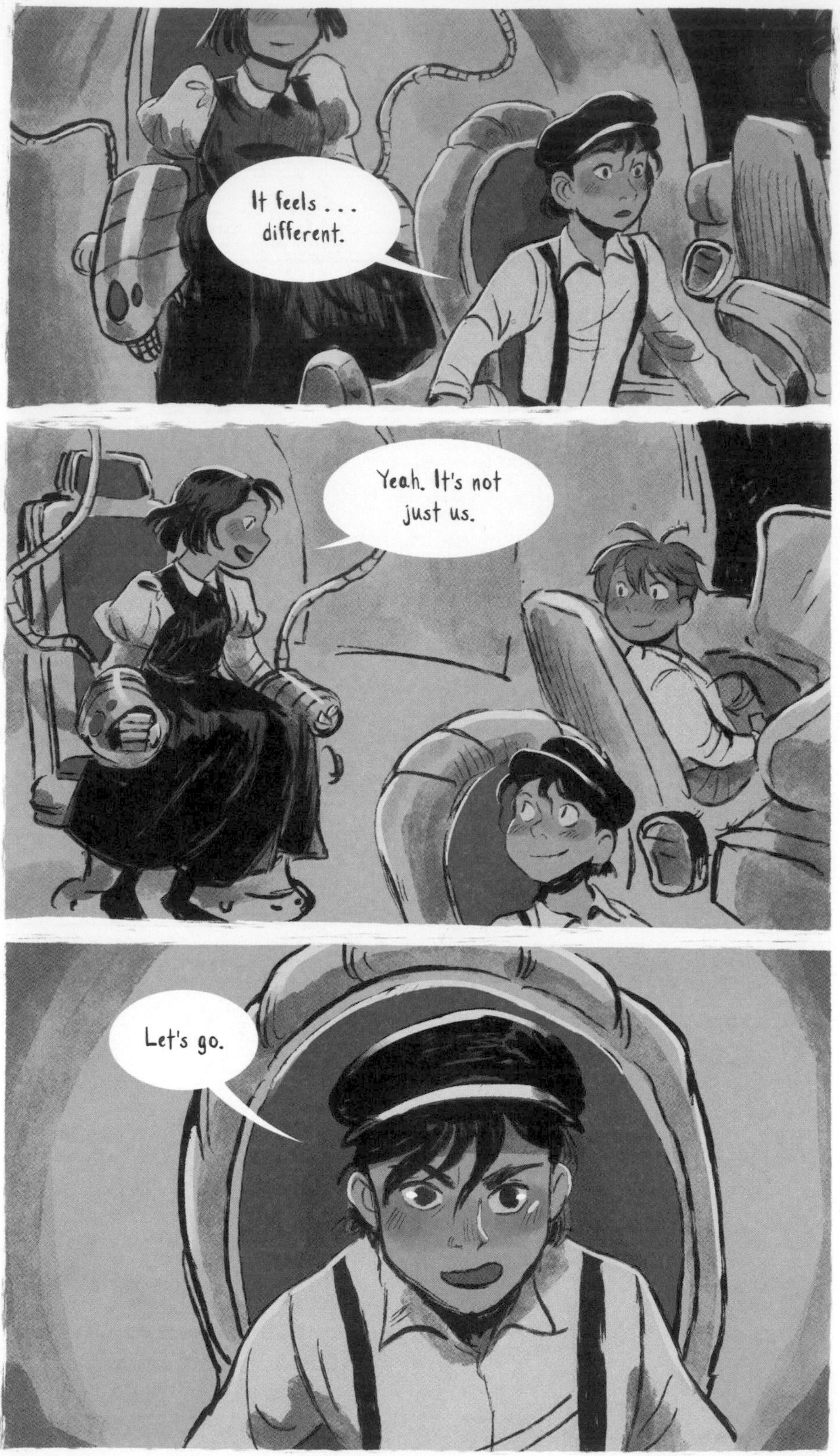
It feels . . .
different.
Yeah. It's not
just us.
Let's go.

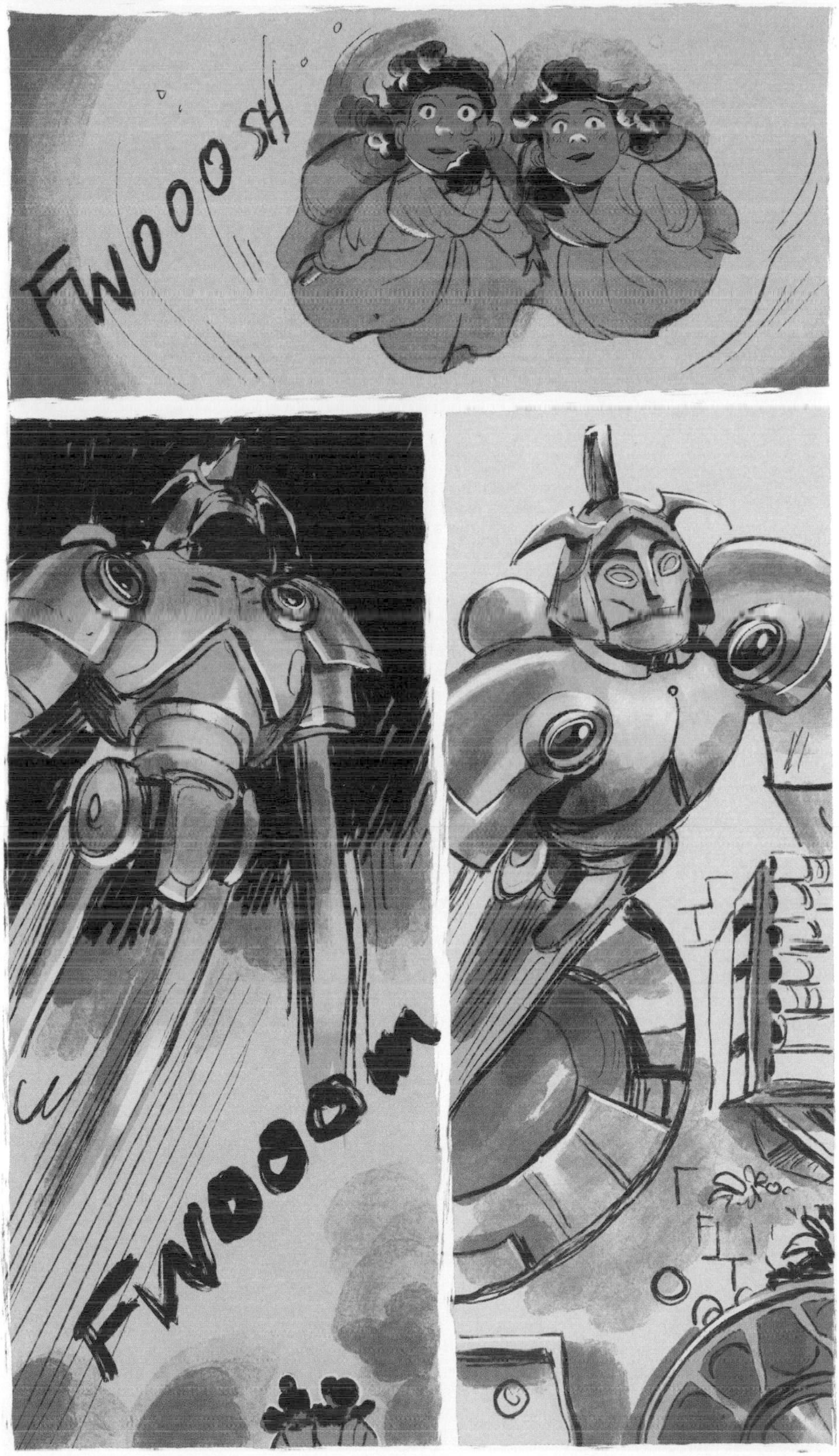
FWOOOSH
FWOOOM

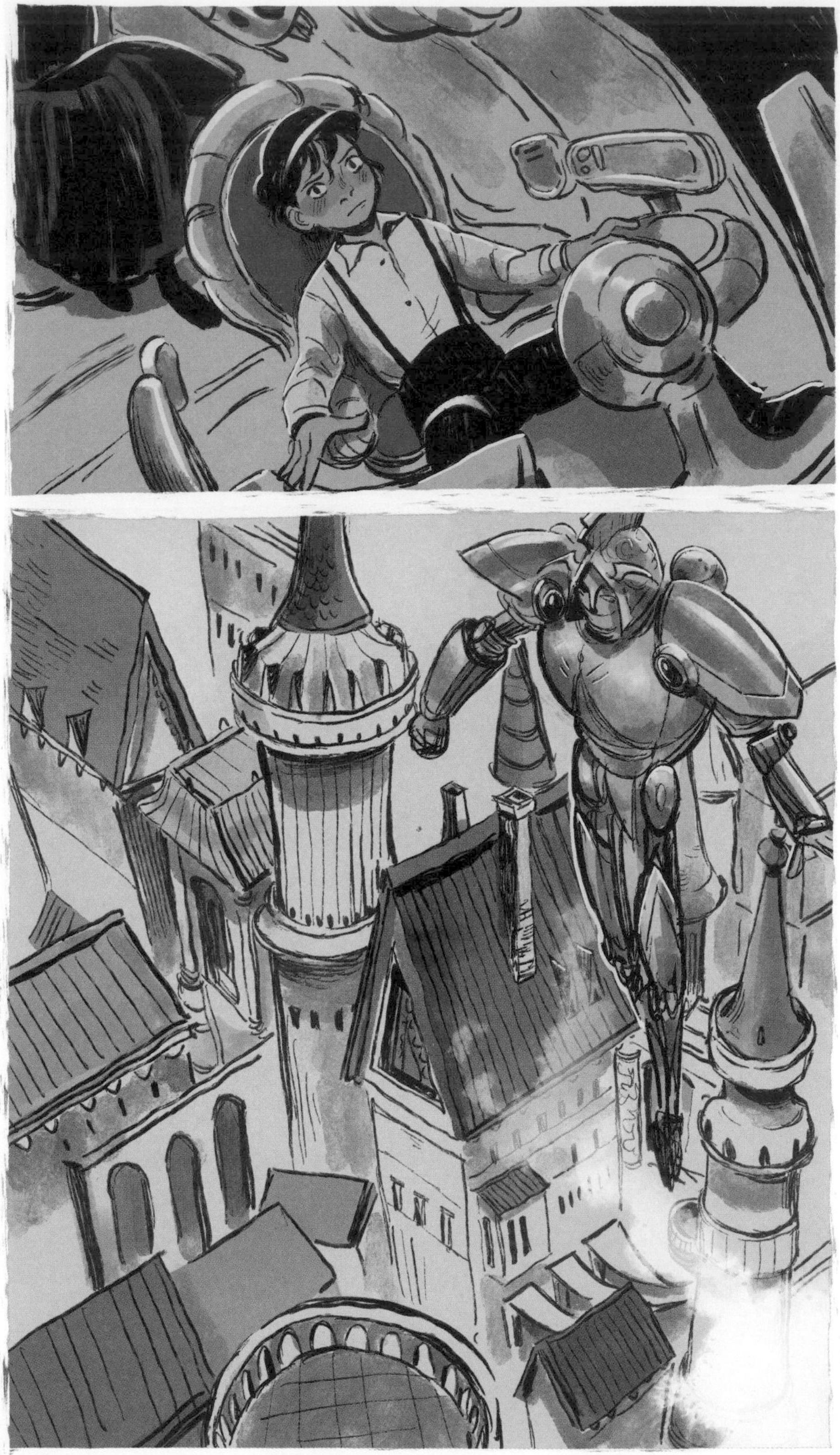

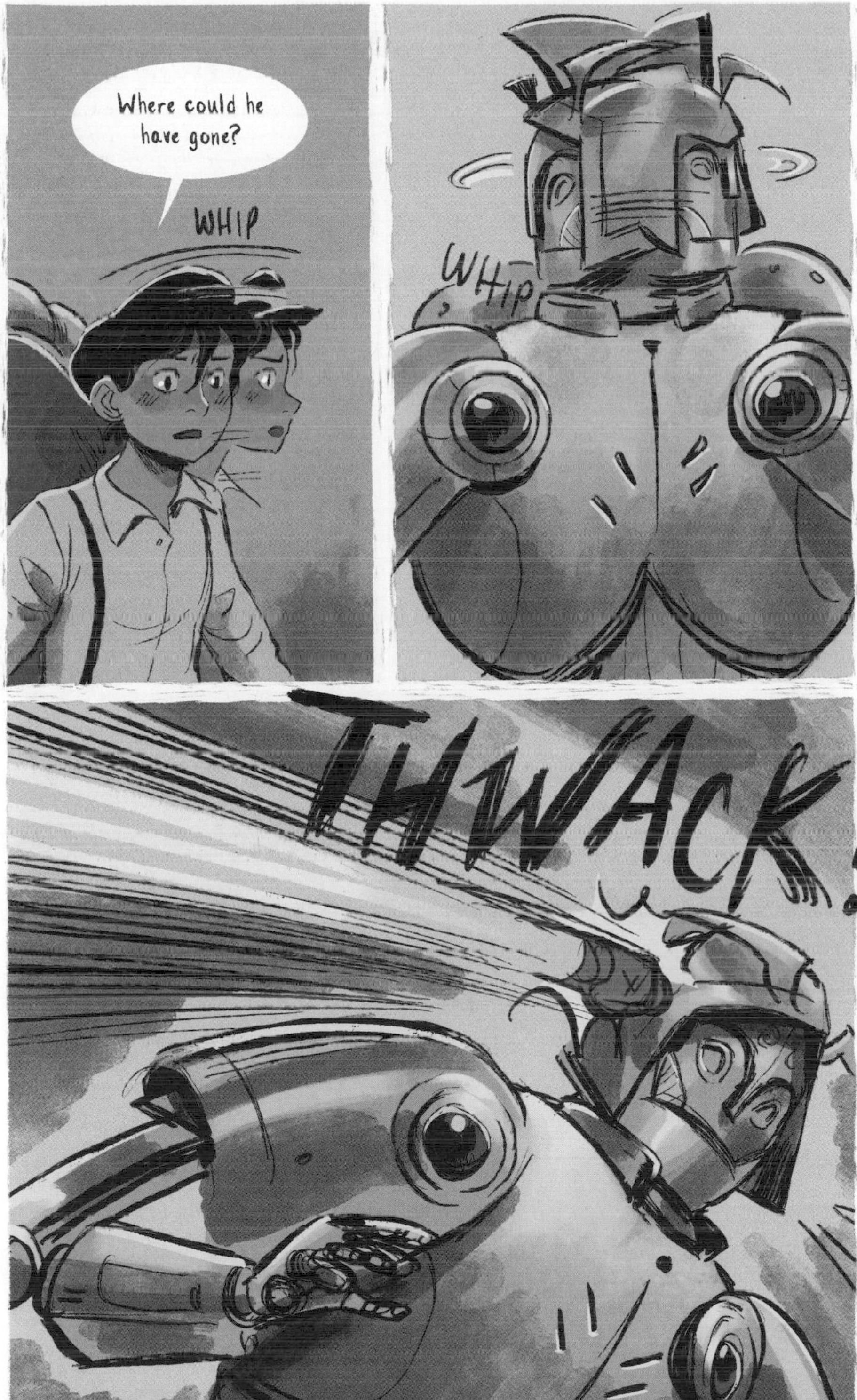
Where could he have gone?
WHIP
WHIP
THWACK!

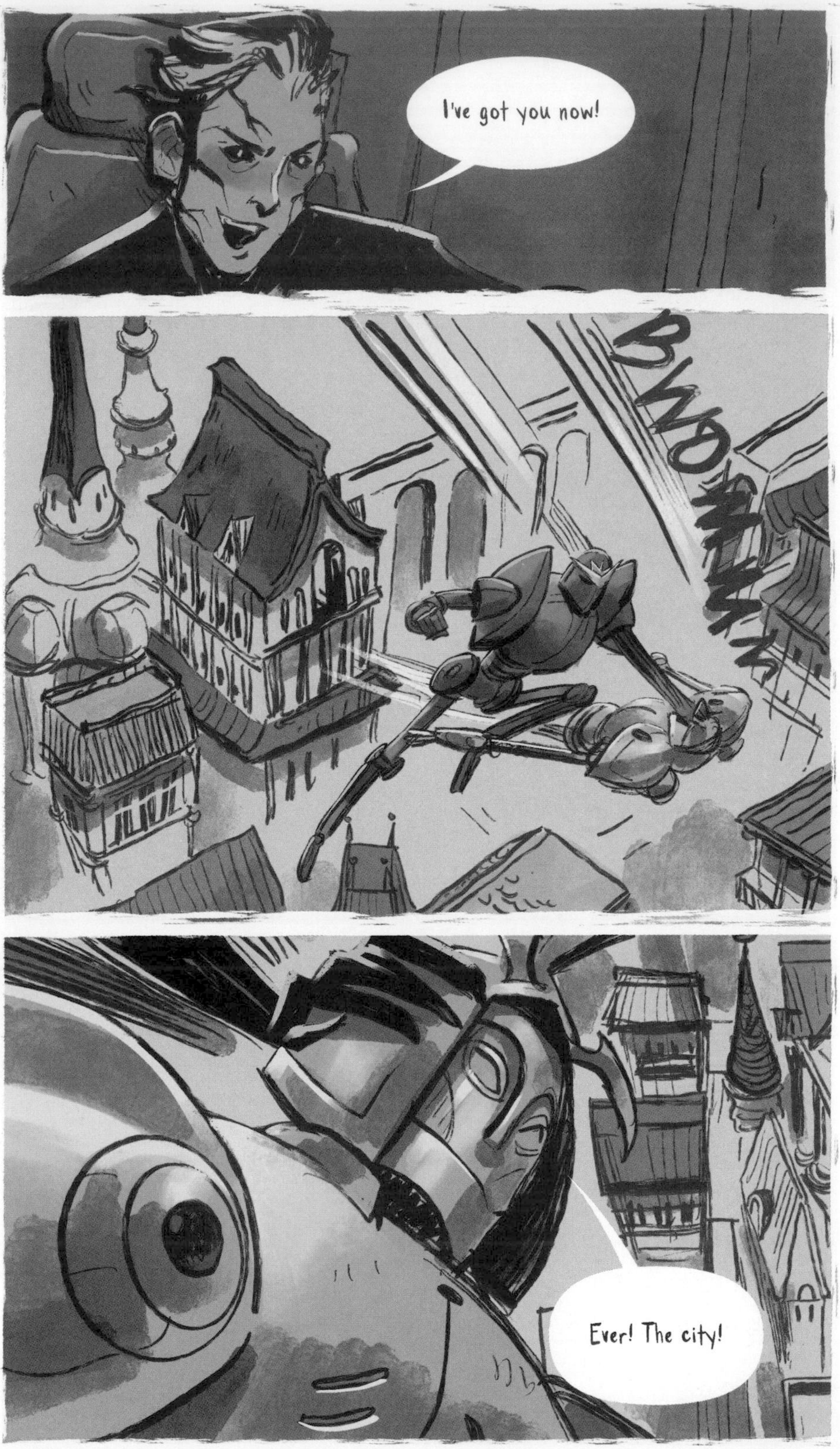
I've got you now!
BWOMMMM
Ever! The city!

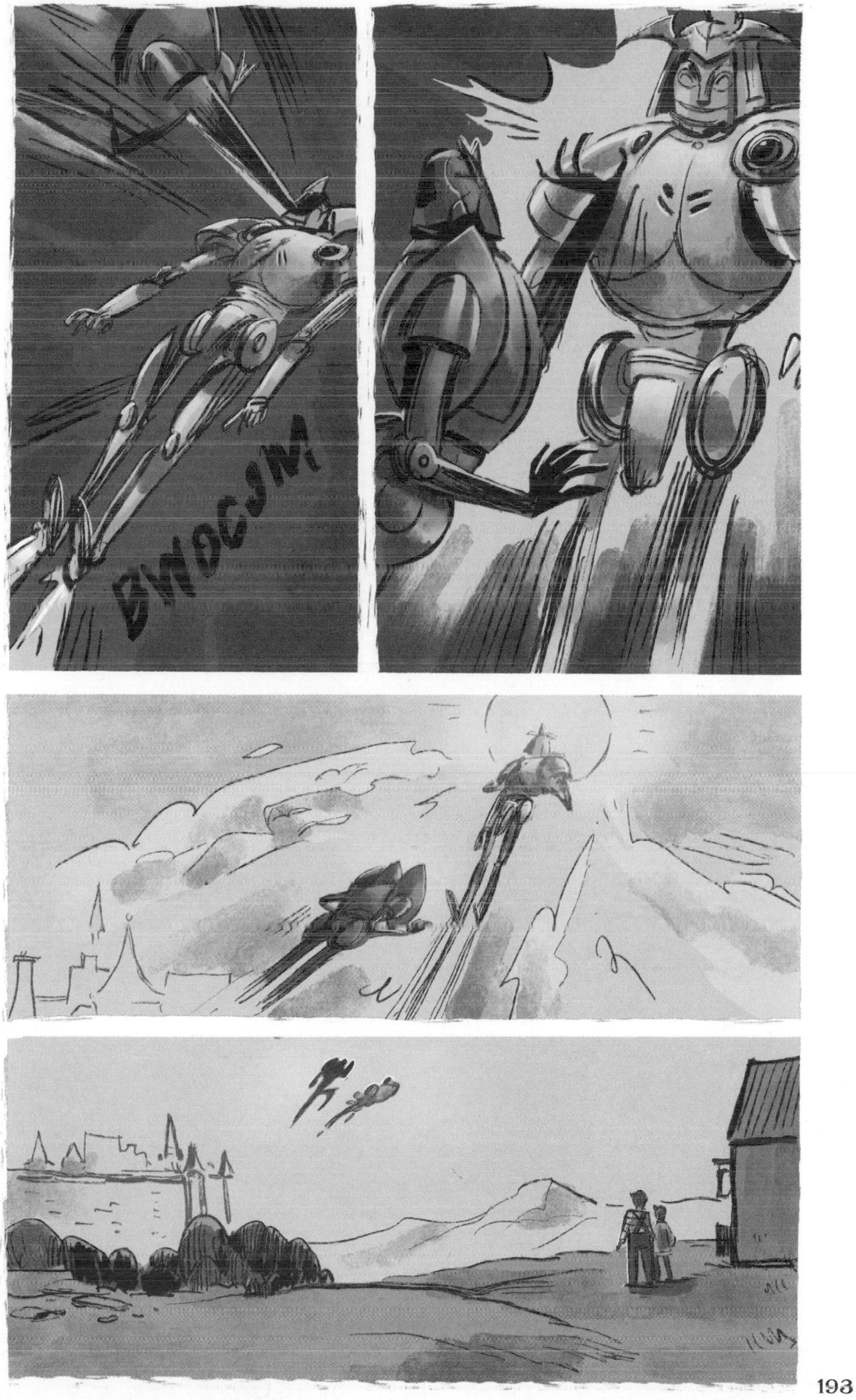
BWOOSH

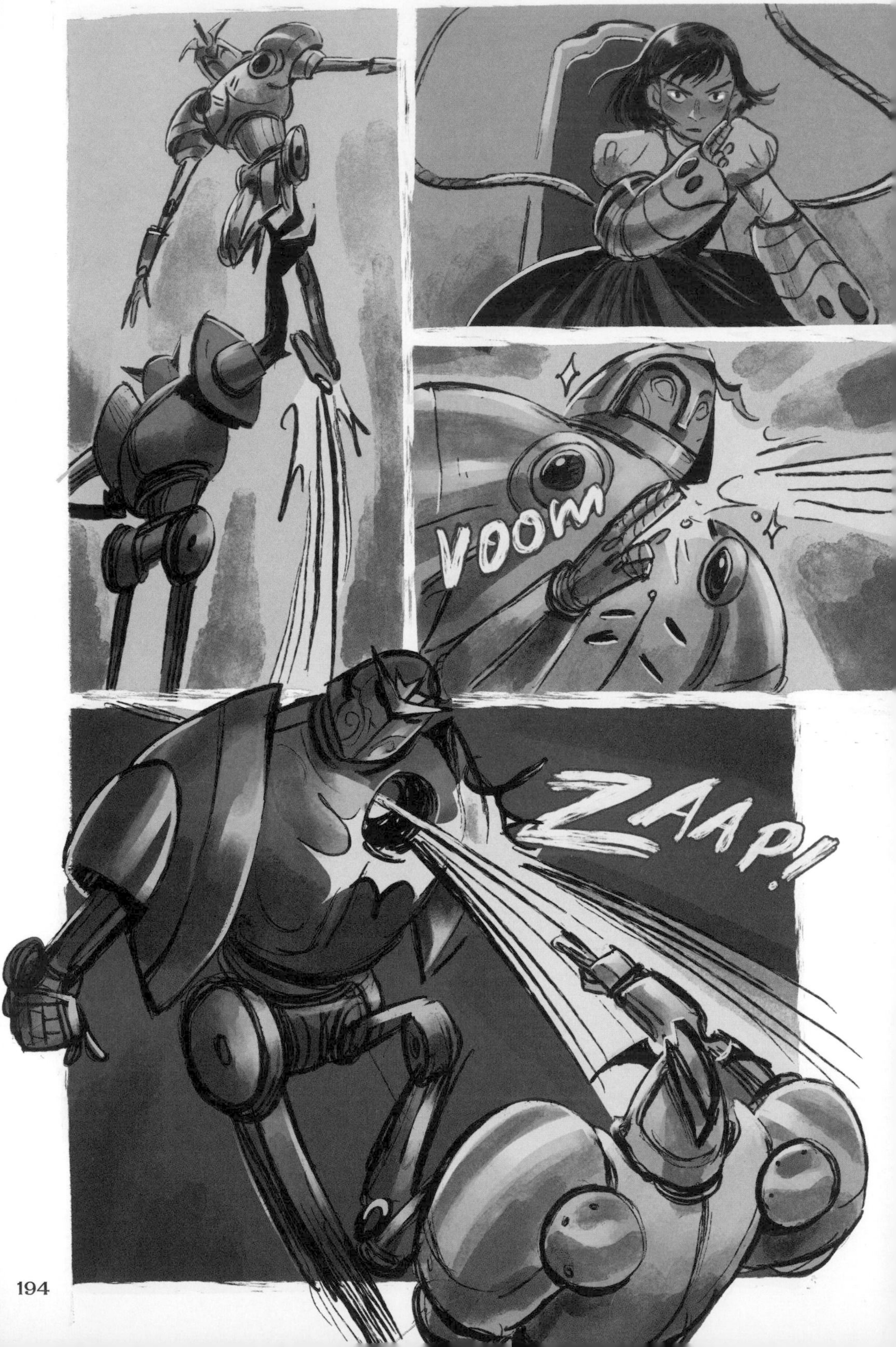
VOOM
ZAAP!

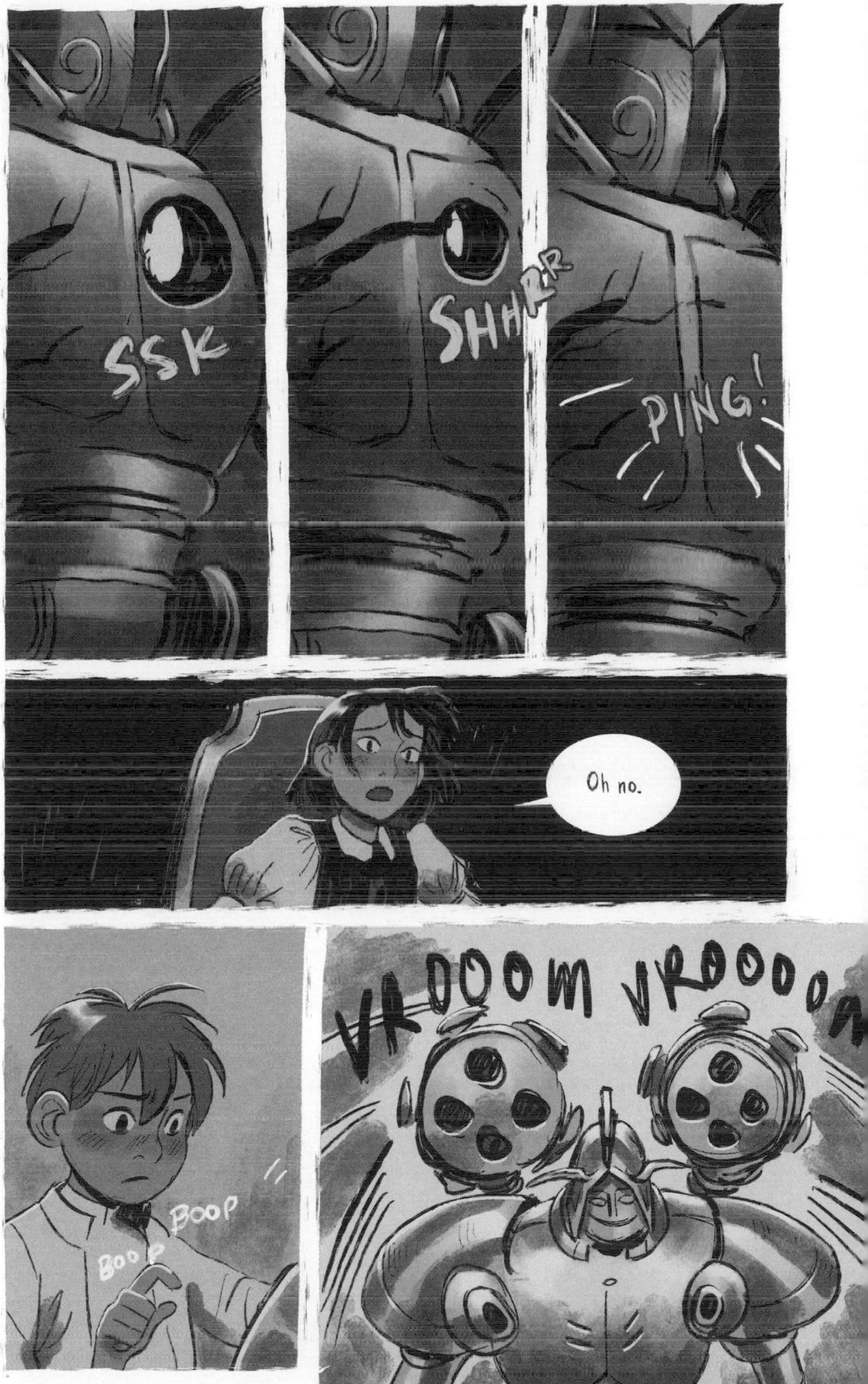
SSK
SHHRR
PING!
Oh no.
BOOP
BOOP
VROOOM VROOOOM

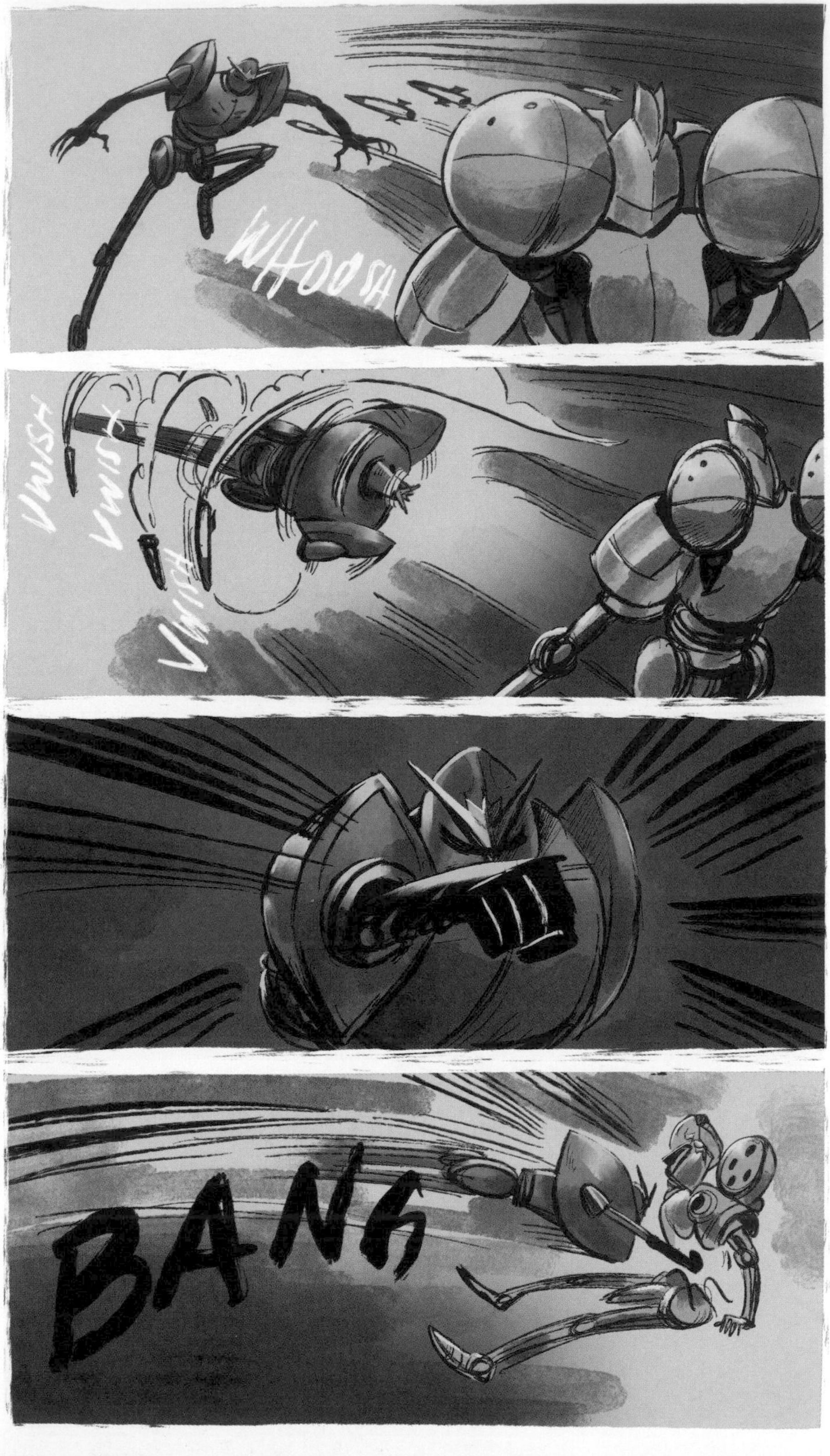
WHOOSH
VWISH
VWISH
VWISH
BANG

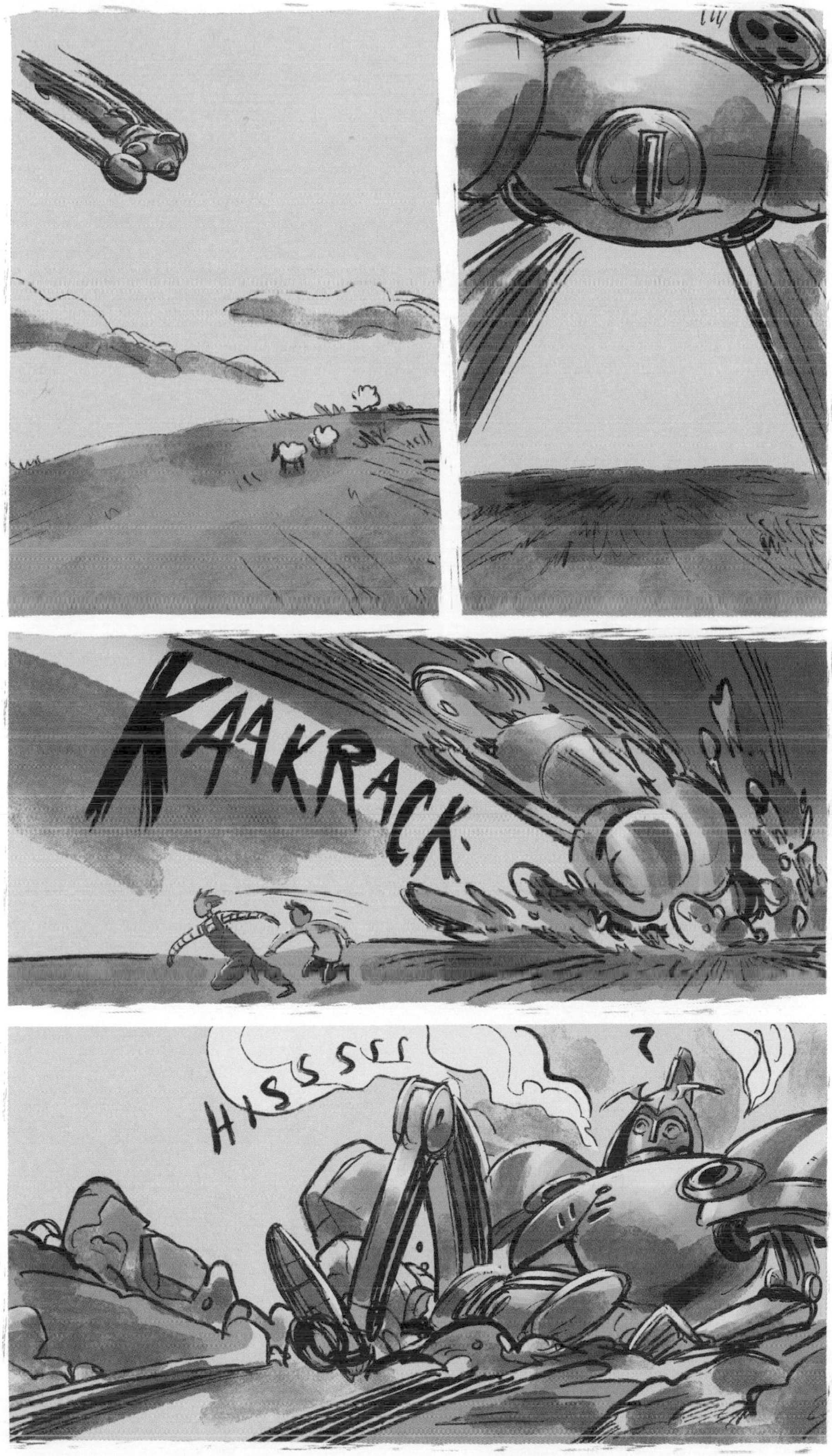
KAAKRACK
HISSSSSS

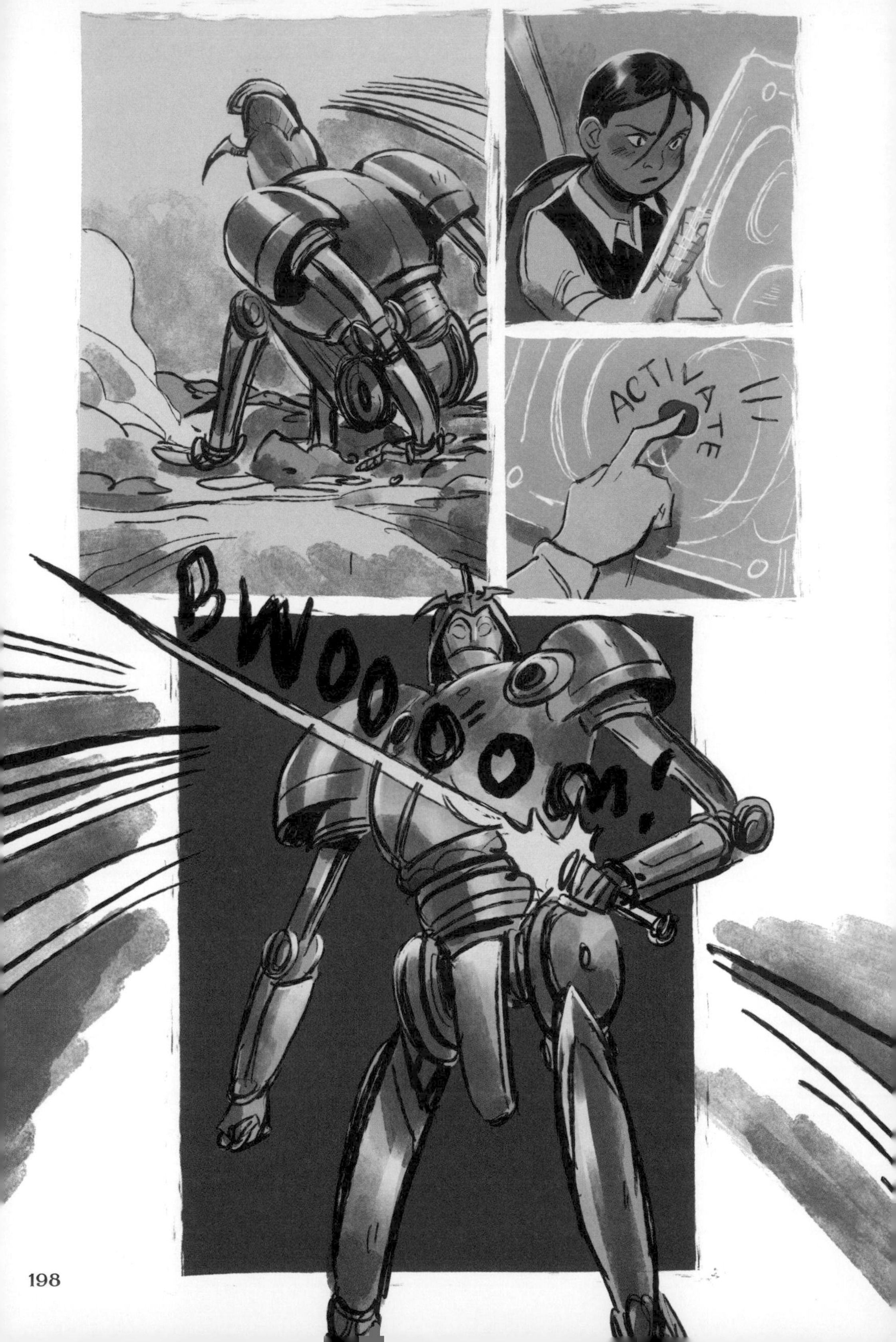
ACTIVATE
BWOOOOOM!

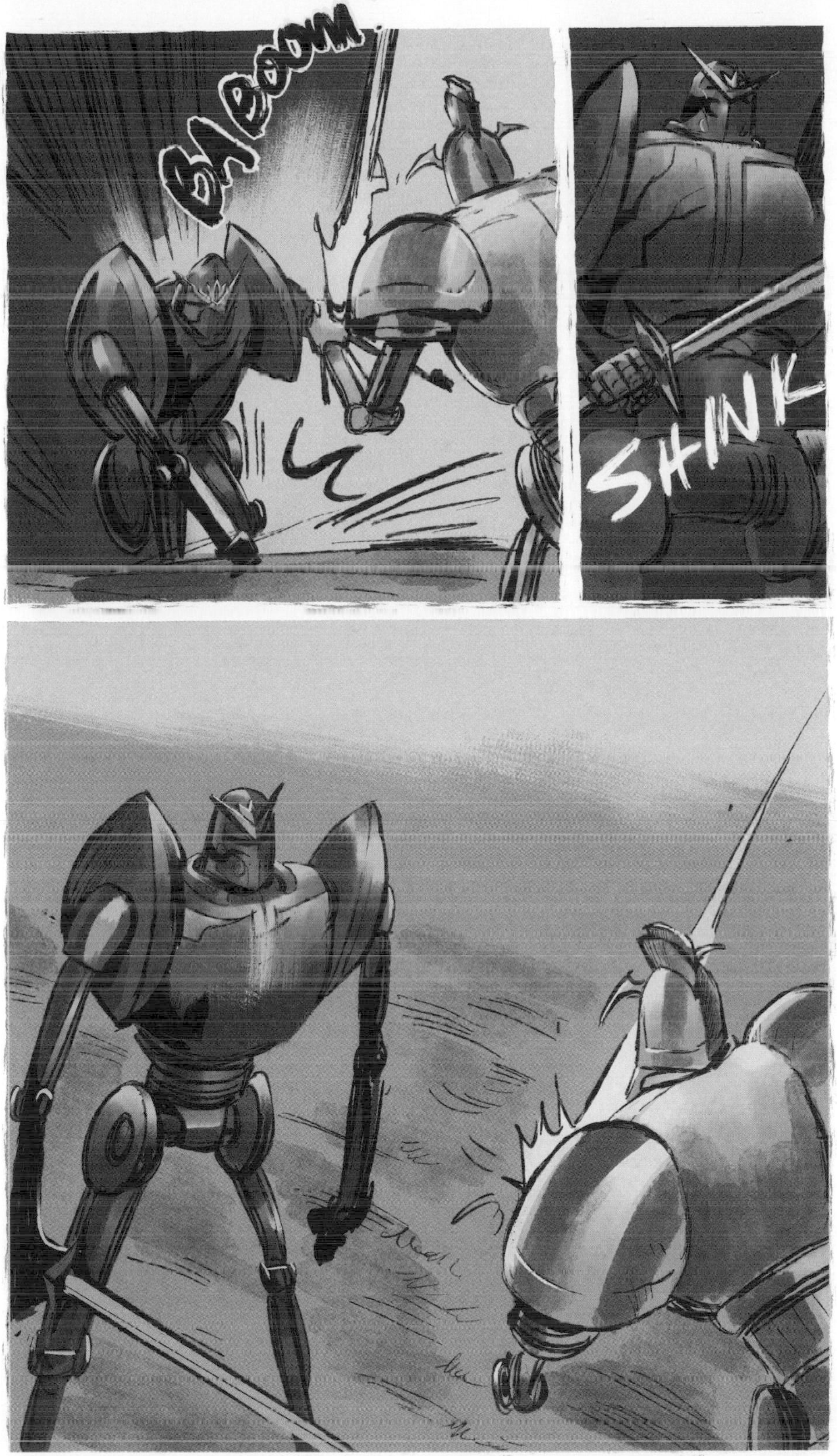
BABOOM!
SHINK

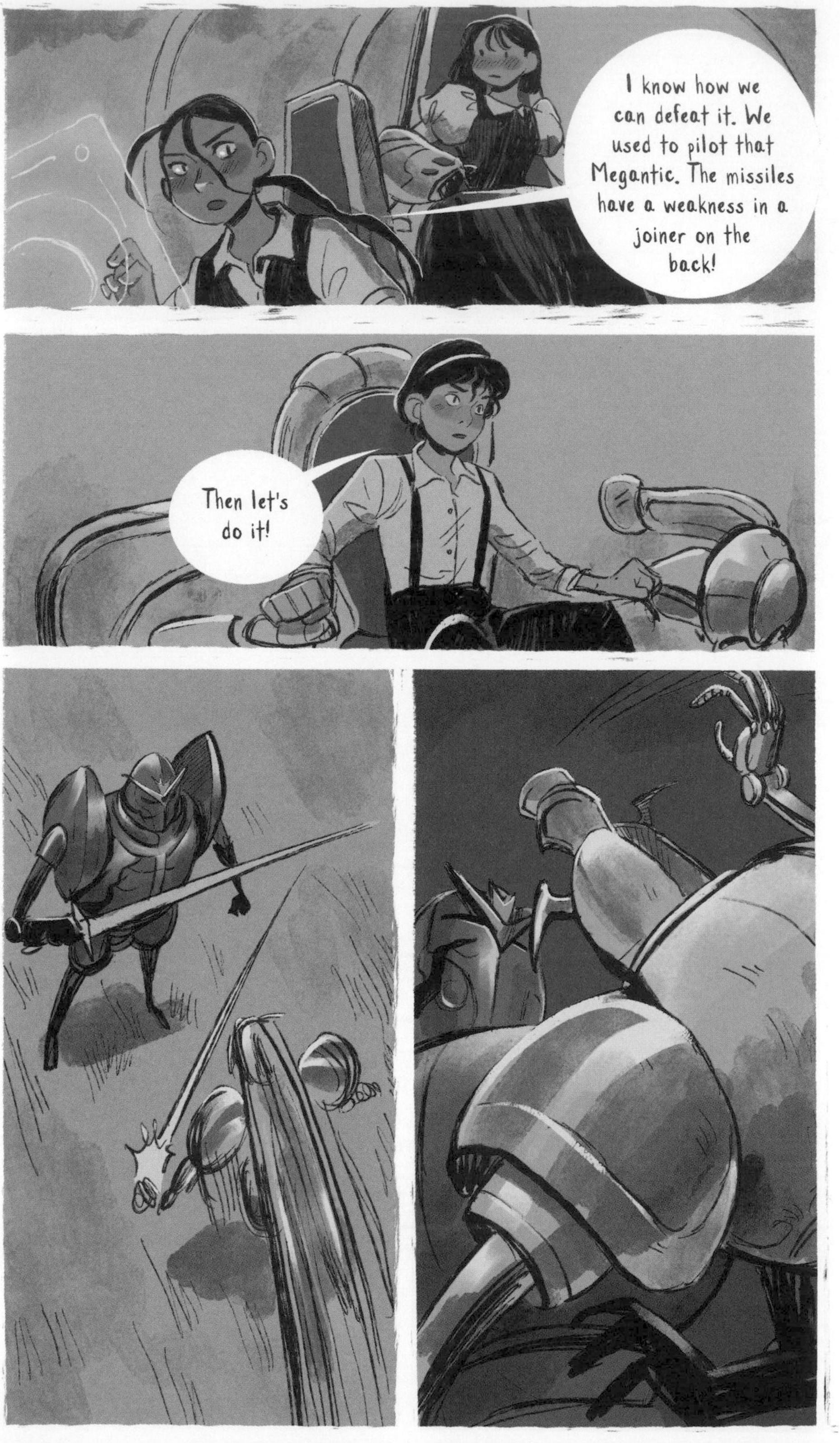
I know how we can defeat it. We used to pilot that Megantic. The missiles have a weakness in a joiner on the back!
Then let's do it!

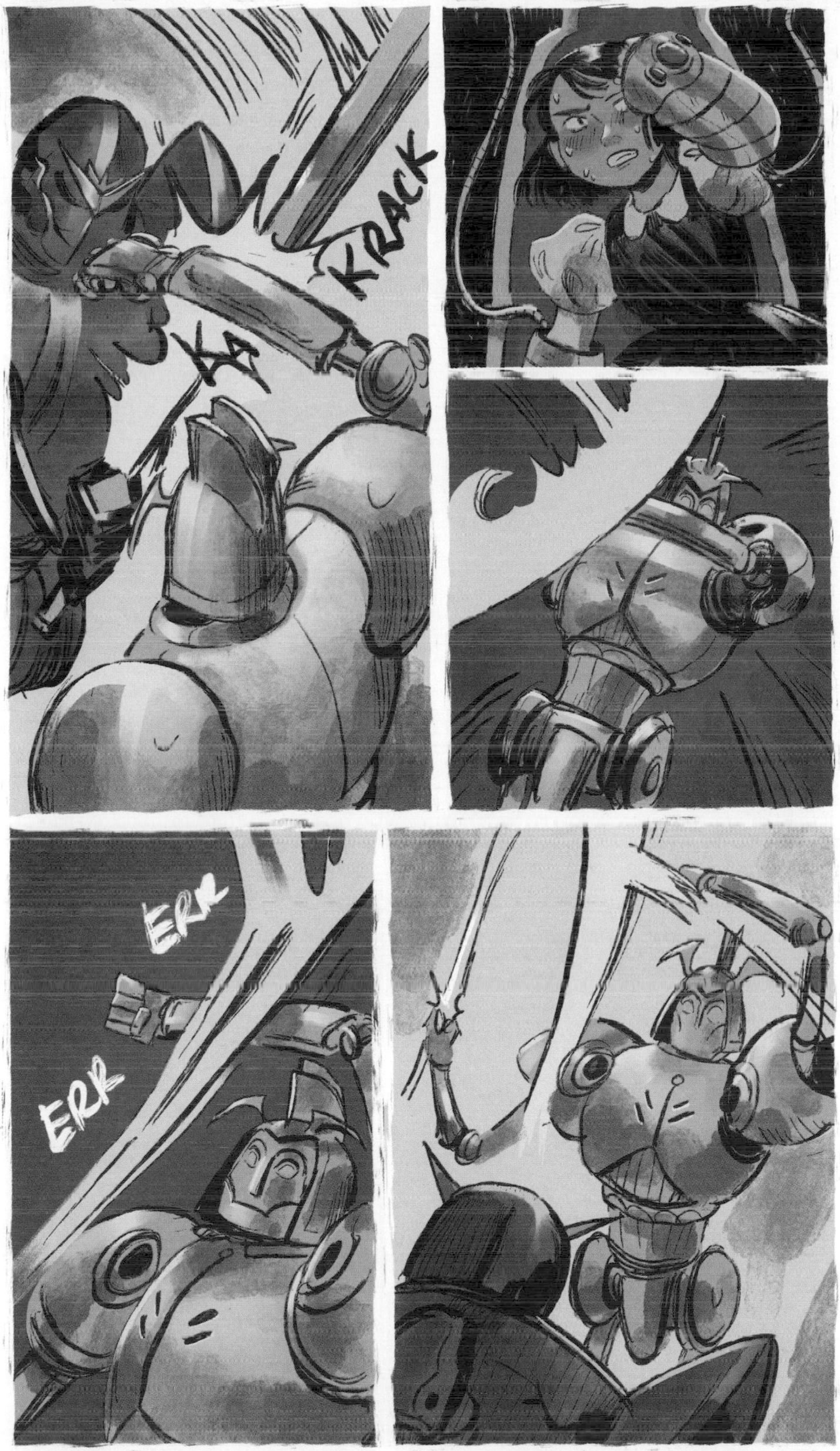
KA
KRACK
ERR
ERR

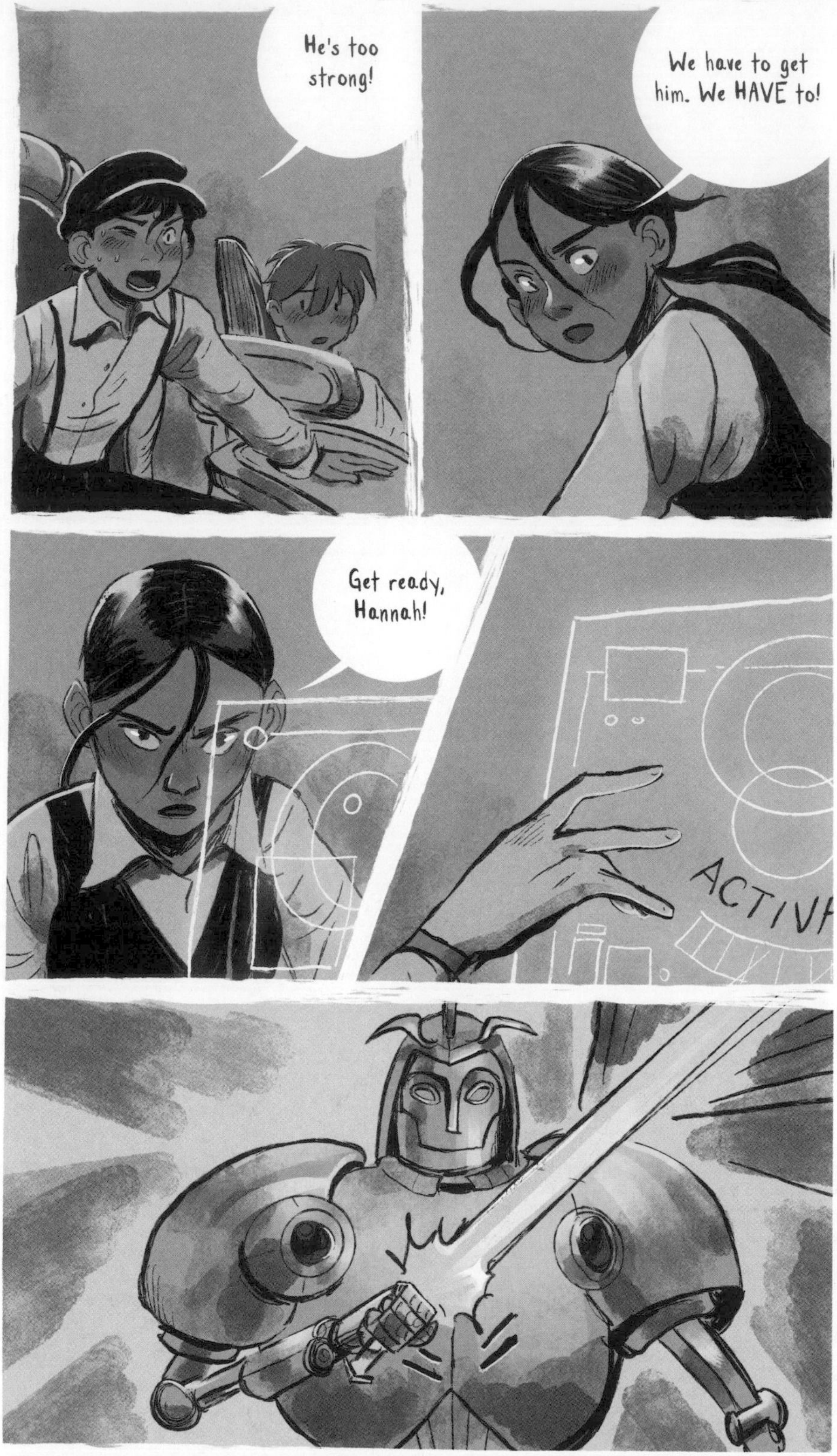
He's too strong!
We have to get him. We HAVE to!
Get ready, Hannah!
ACTIVA

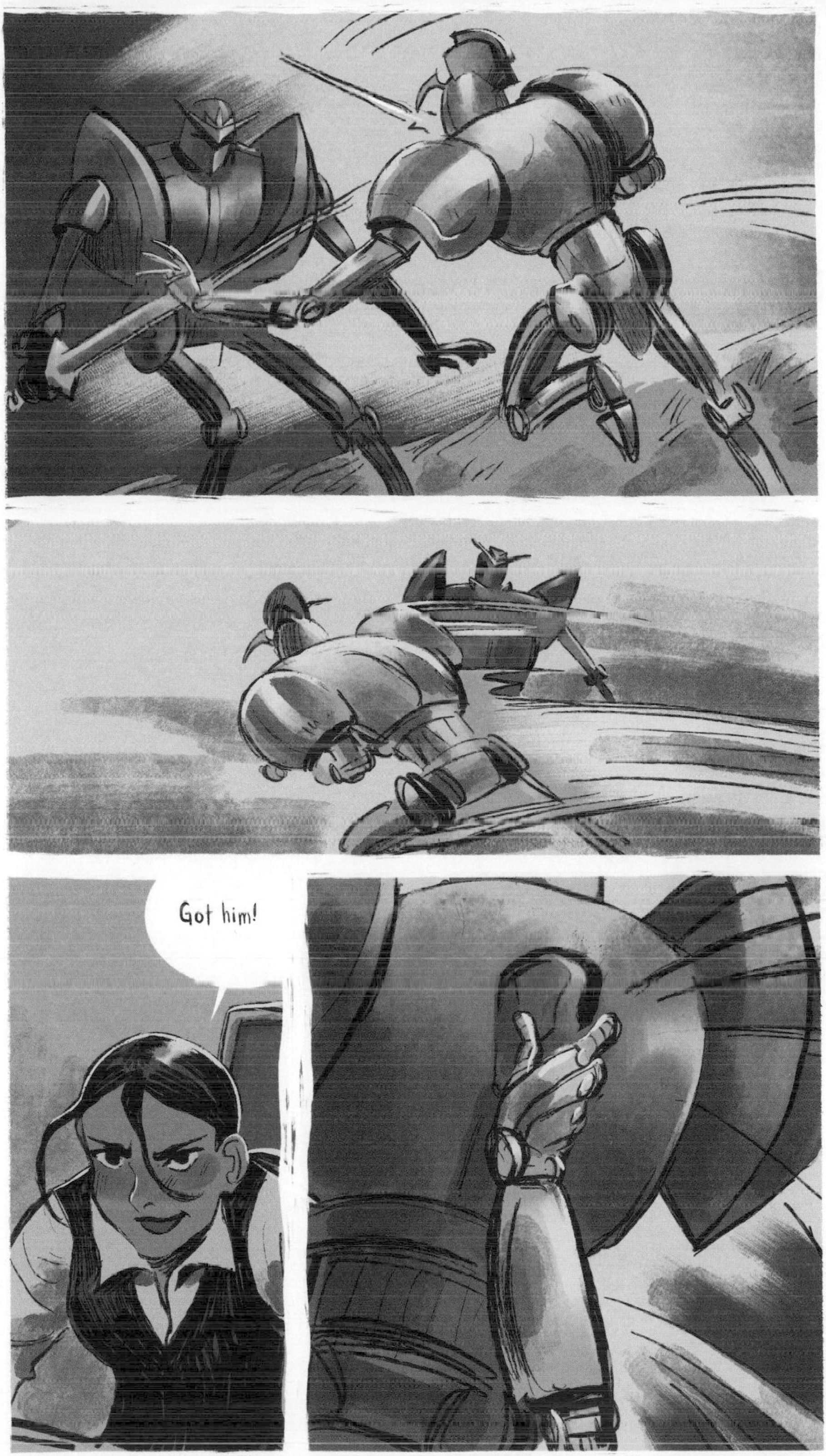
Got him!

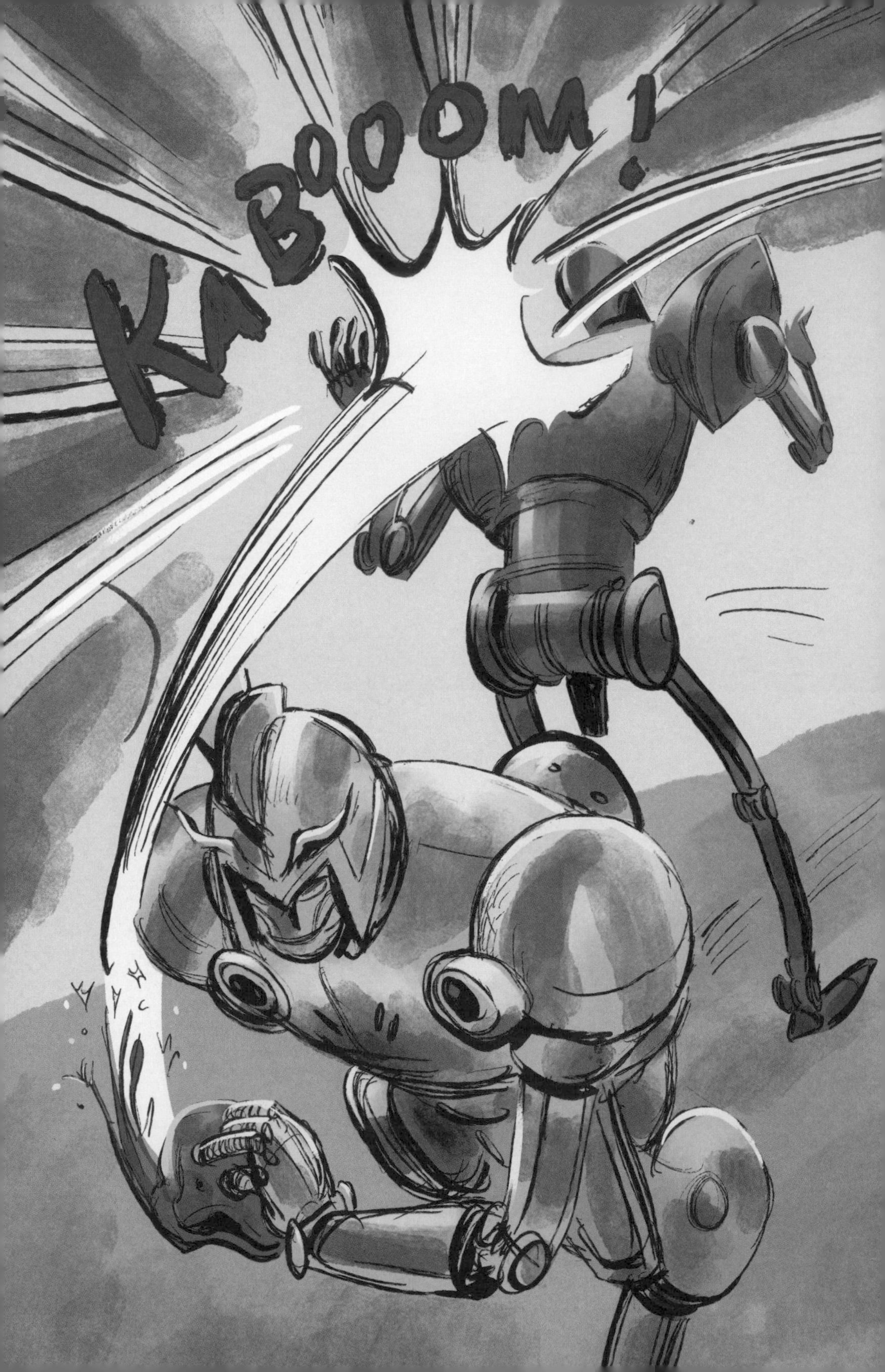
KABOOOM!

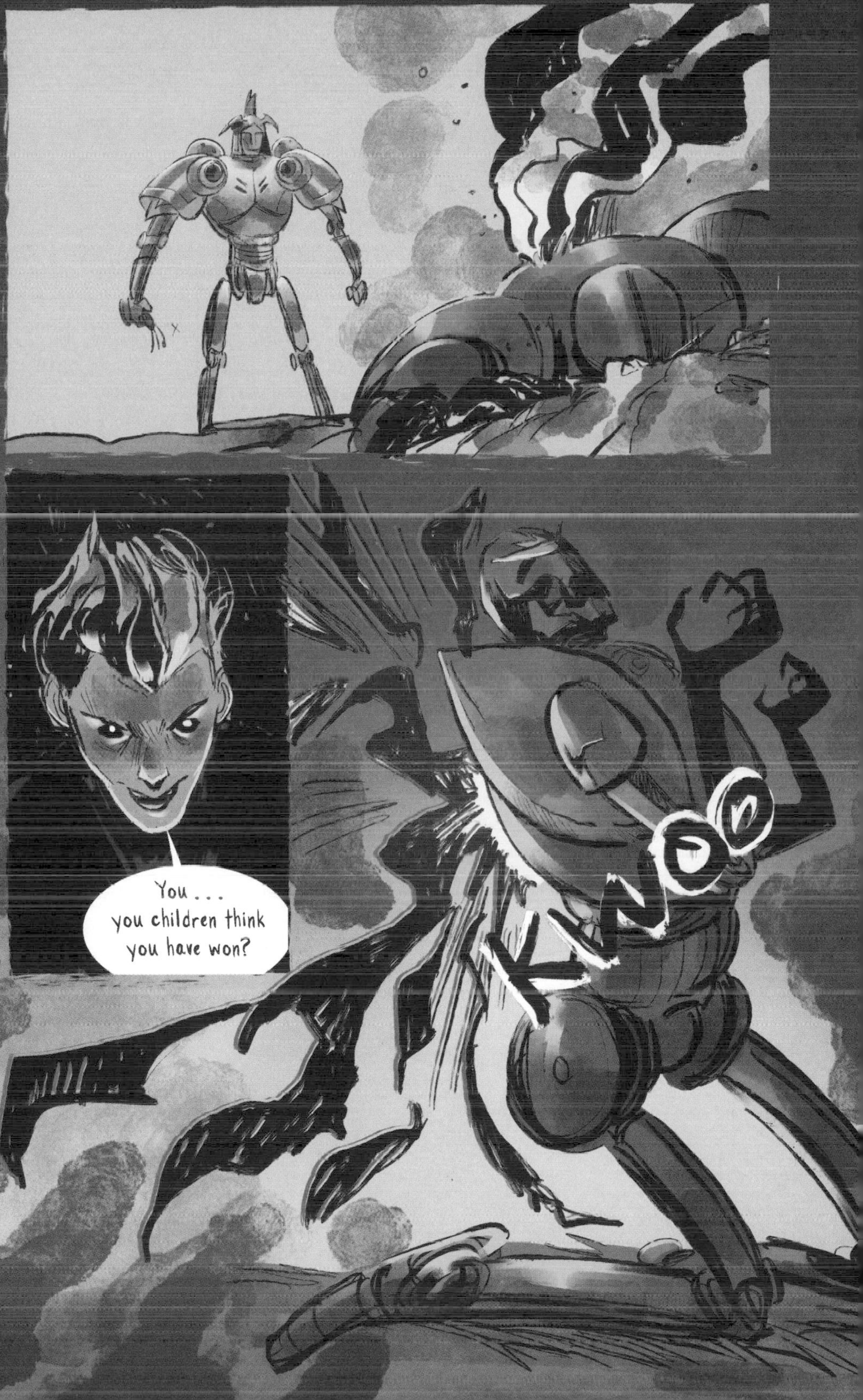
You . . . you children think you have won?

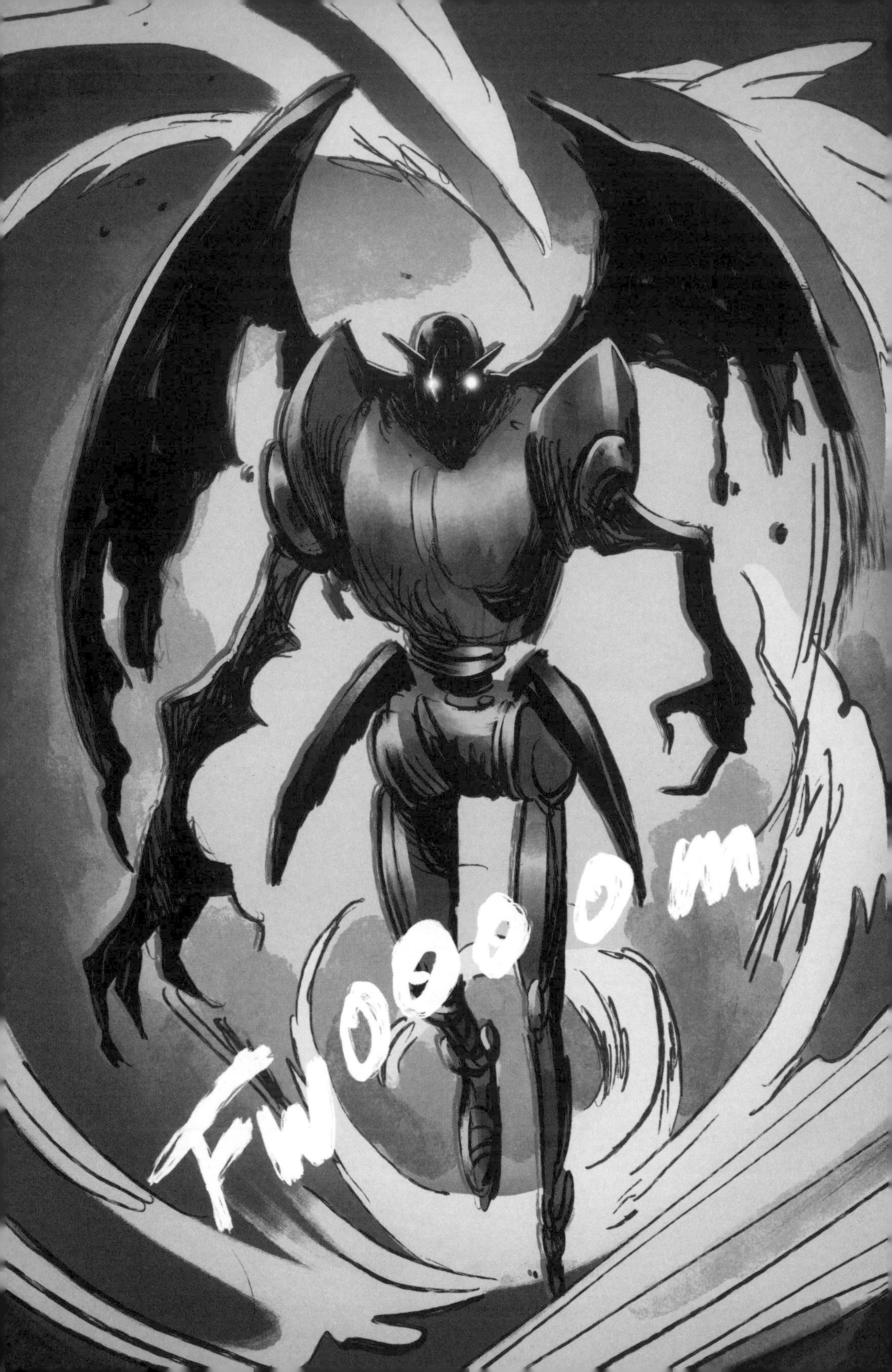
FWOOOOOM

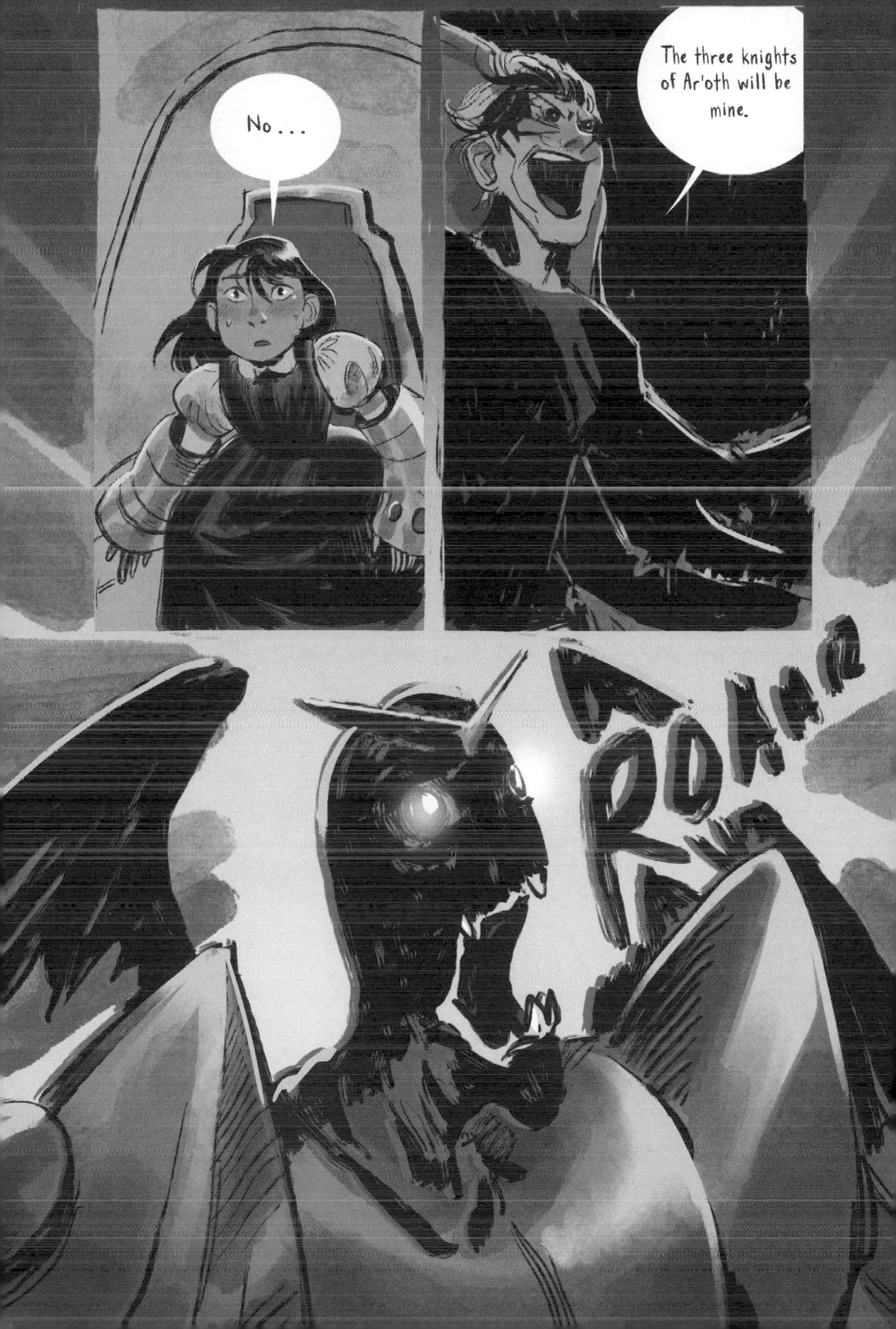
No . . .
The three knights of Ar'oth will be mine.

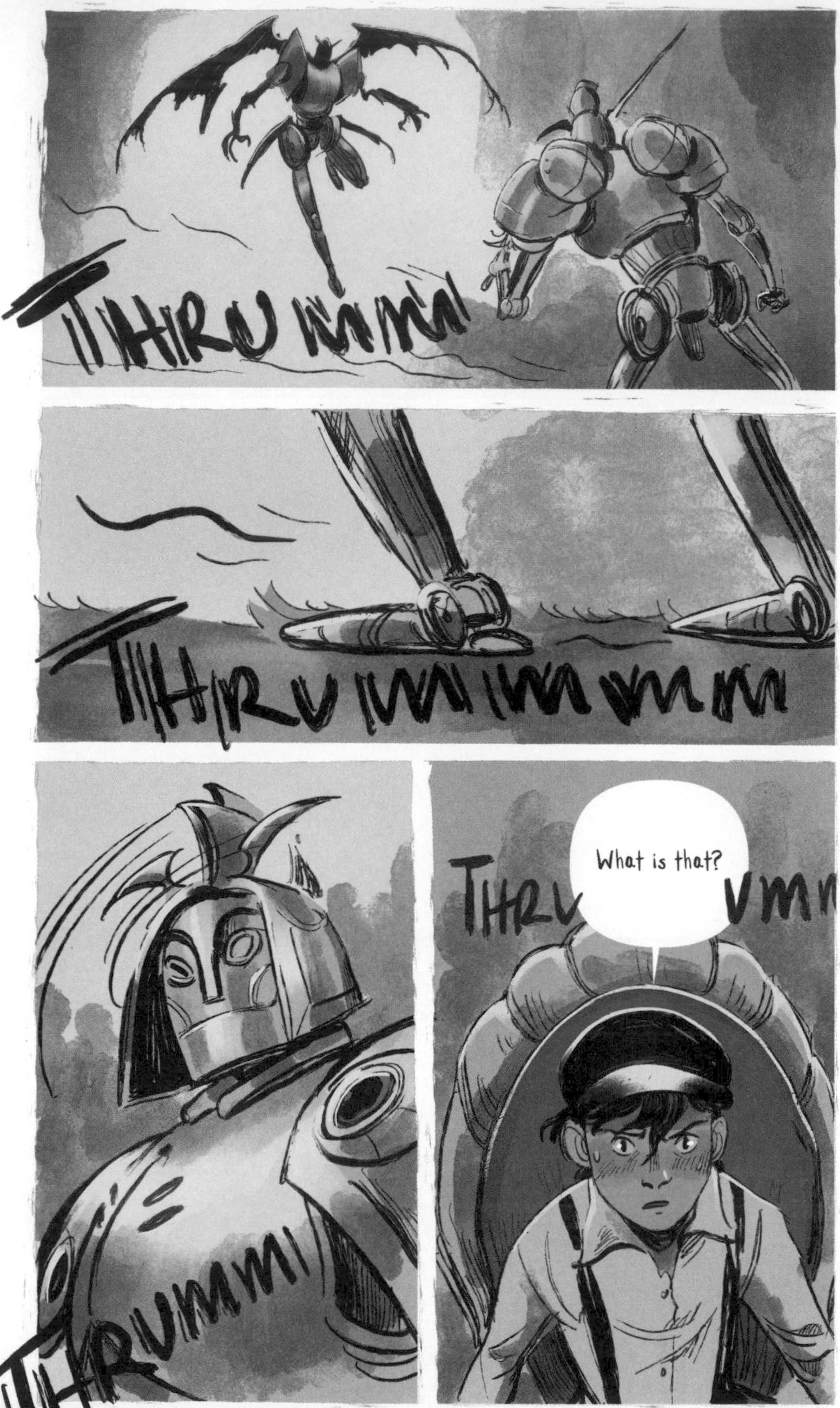
THRUMMM
THRUMMMMMM
THRUMM
THRU
What is that?
UMM

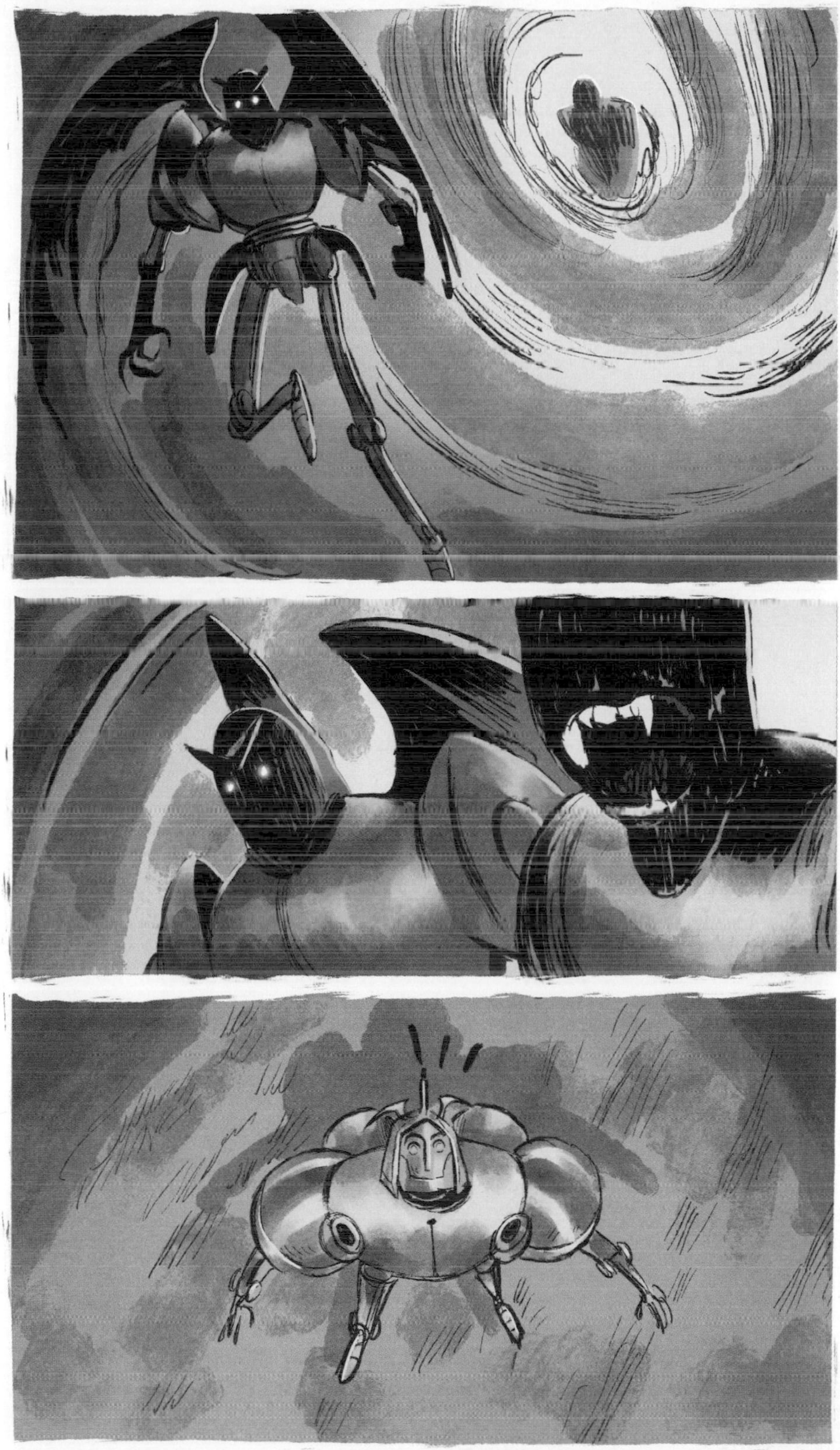

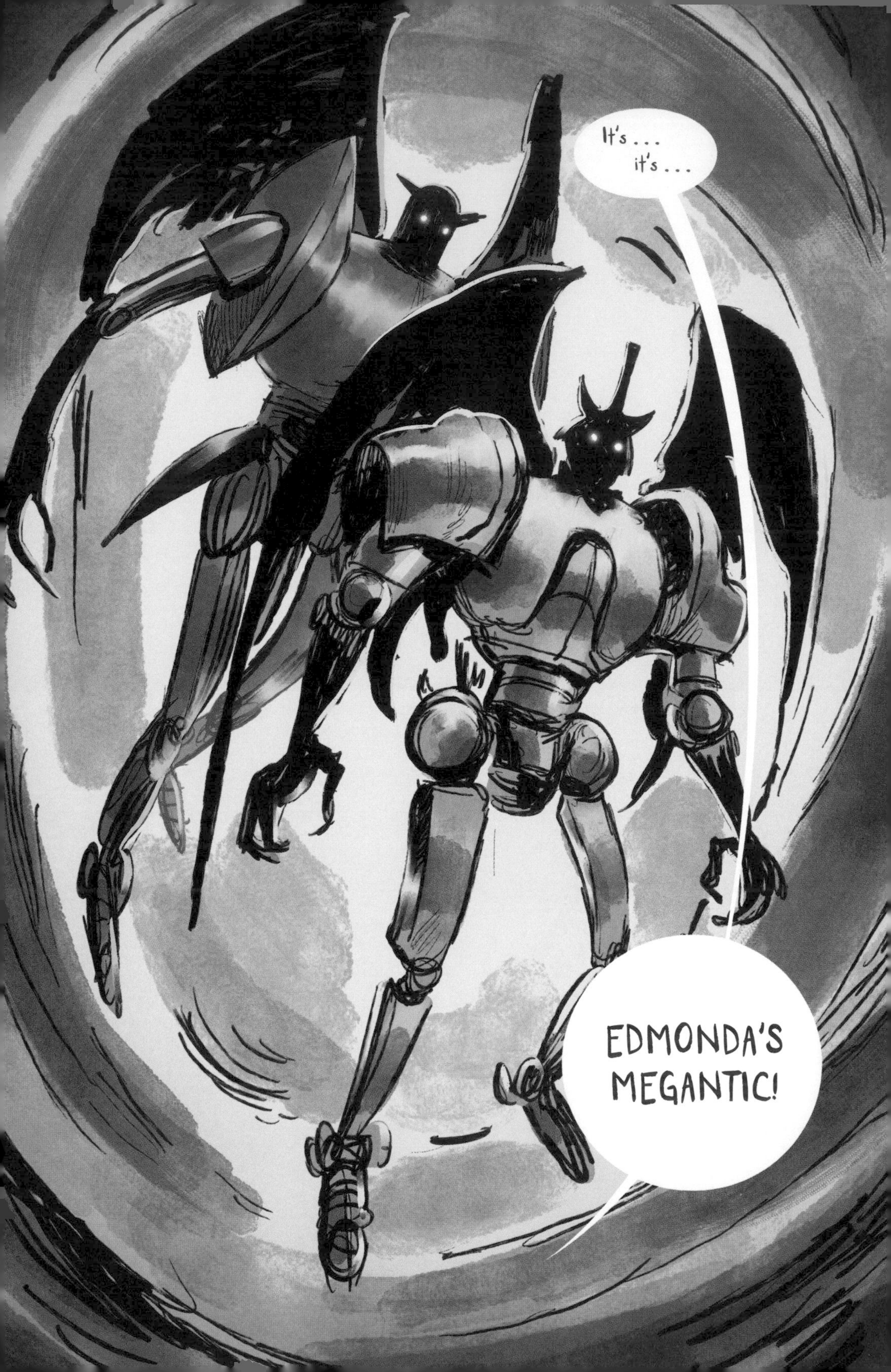
It's . . . it's . . .
EDMONDA'S MEGANTIC!

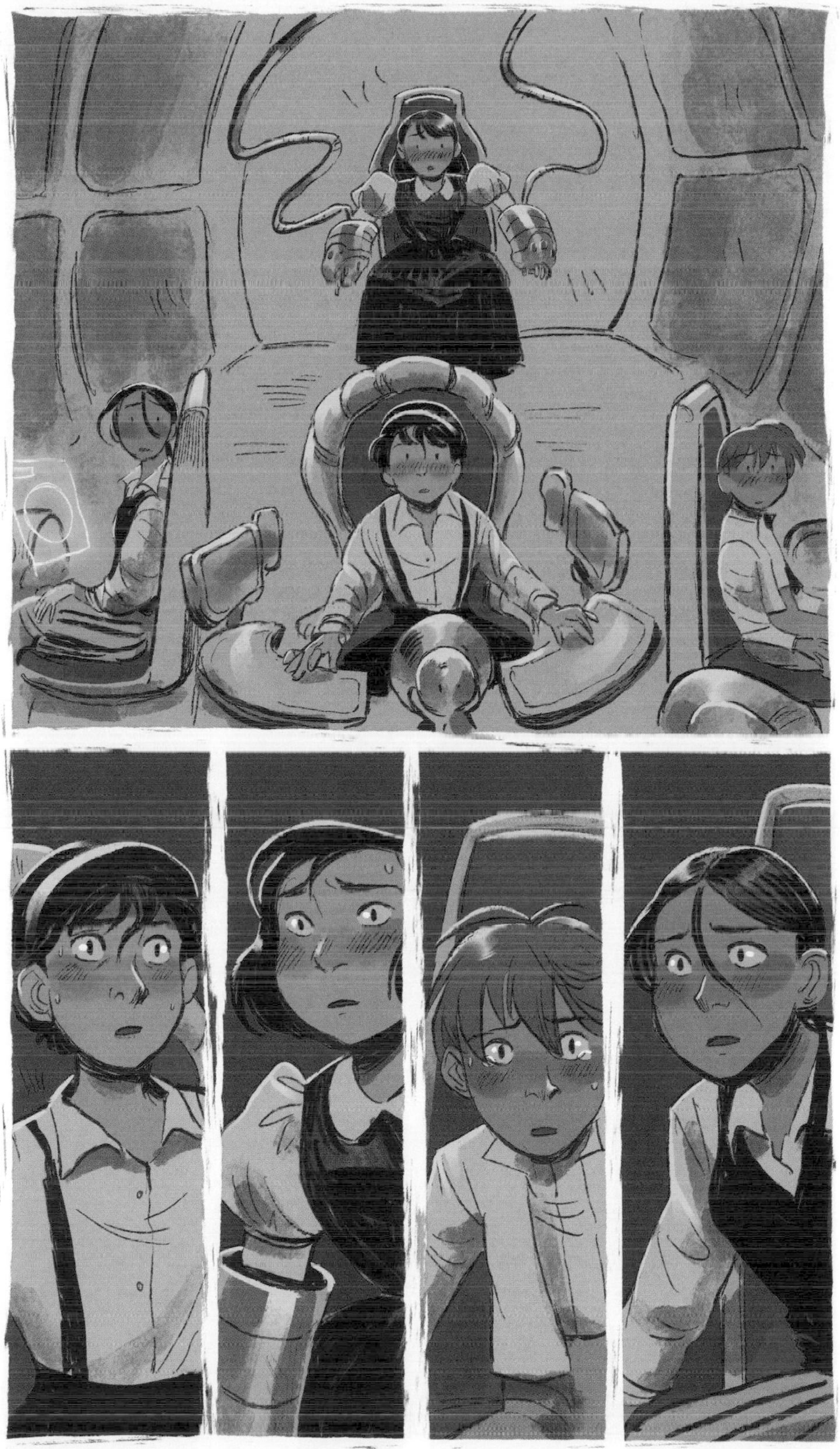

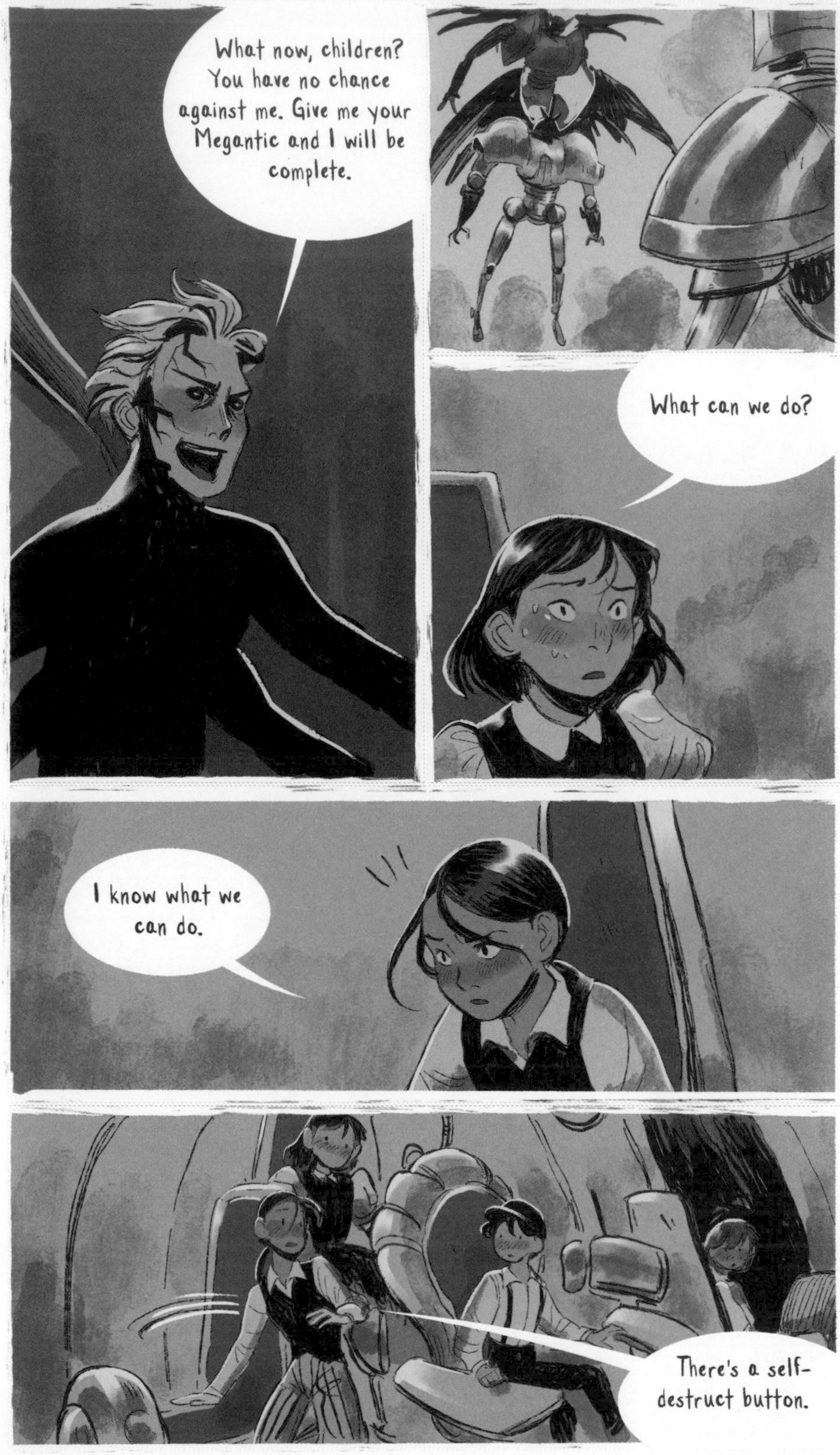
What now, children? You have no chance against me. Give me your Megantic and I will be complete.
What can we do?
I know what we can do.
There's a self-destruct button.

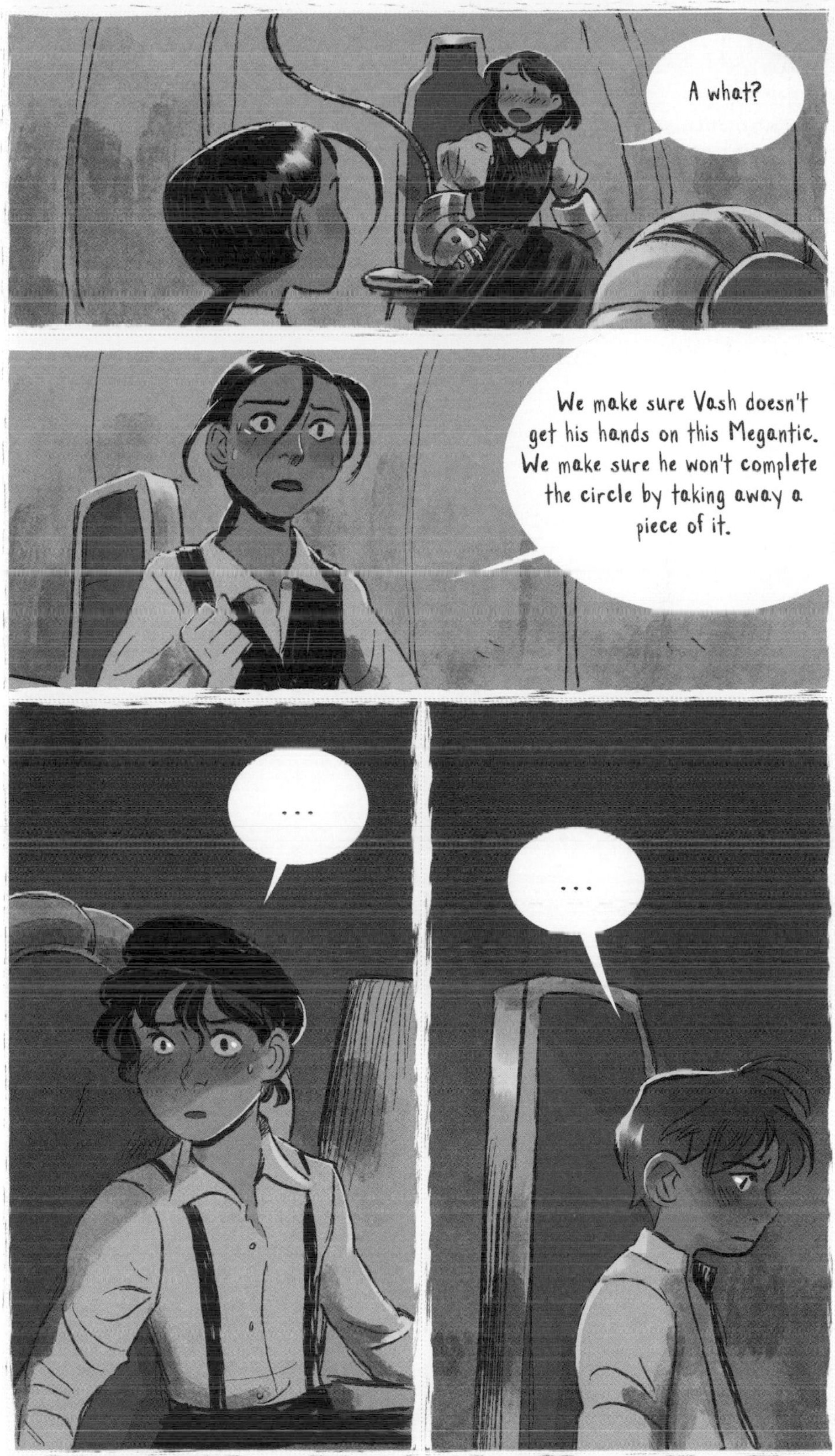
A what?
We make sure Vash doesn't get his hands on this Megantic. We make sure he won't complete the circle by taking away a piece of it.
...
...

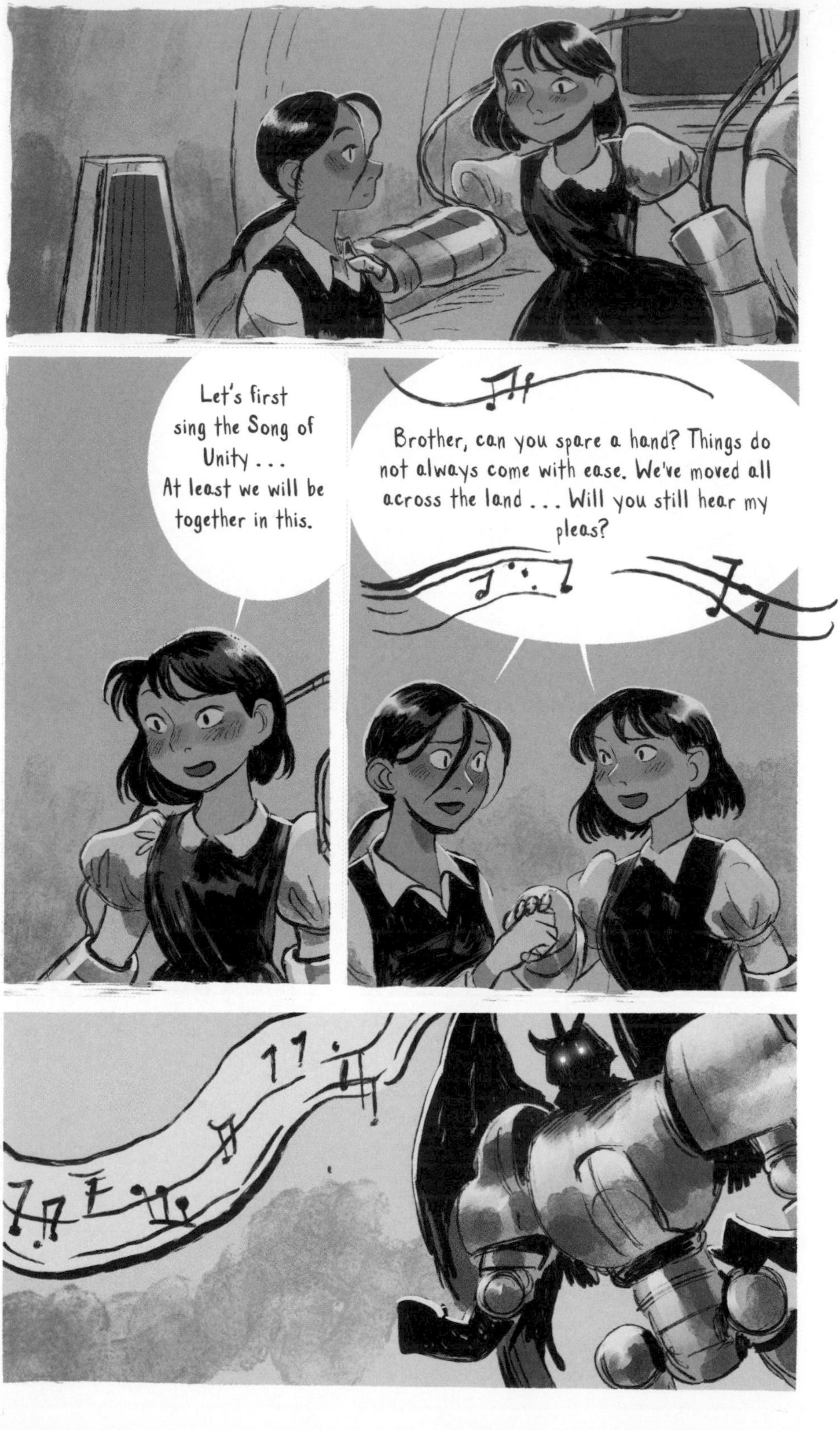

Let's first sing the Song of Unity . . . At least we will be together in this.
Brother, can you spare a hand? Things do not always come with ease. We've moved all across the land . . . Will you still hear my pleas?

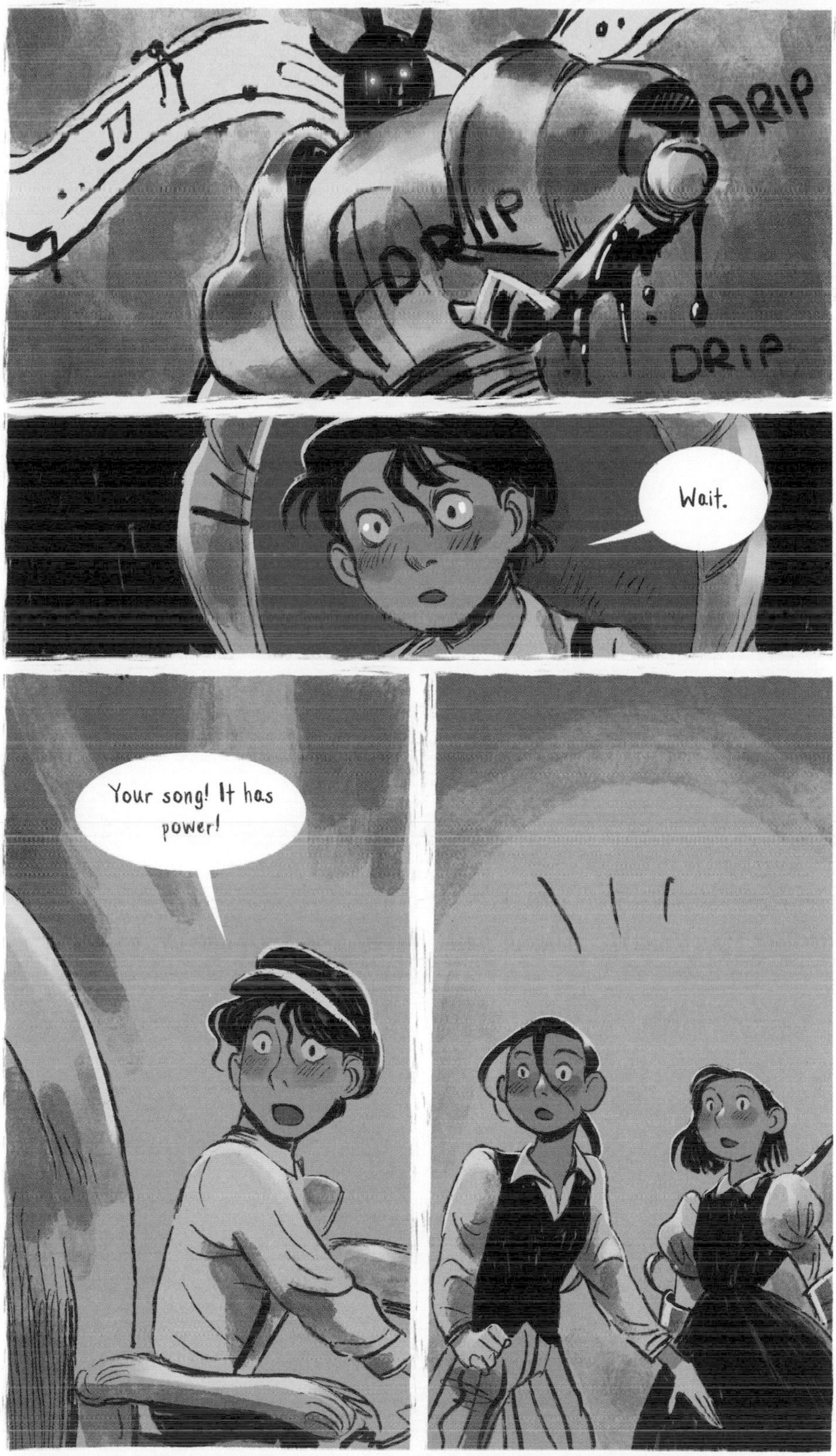
DRIP
DRIP
DRIP
DRIP
Wait.
Your song! It has power!

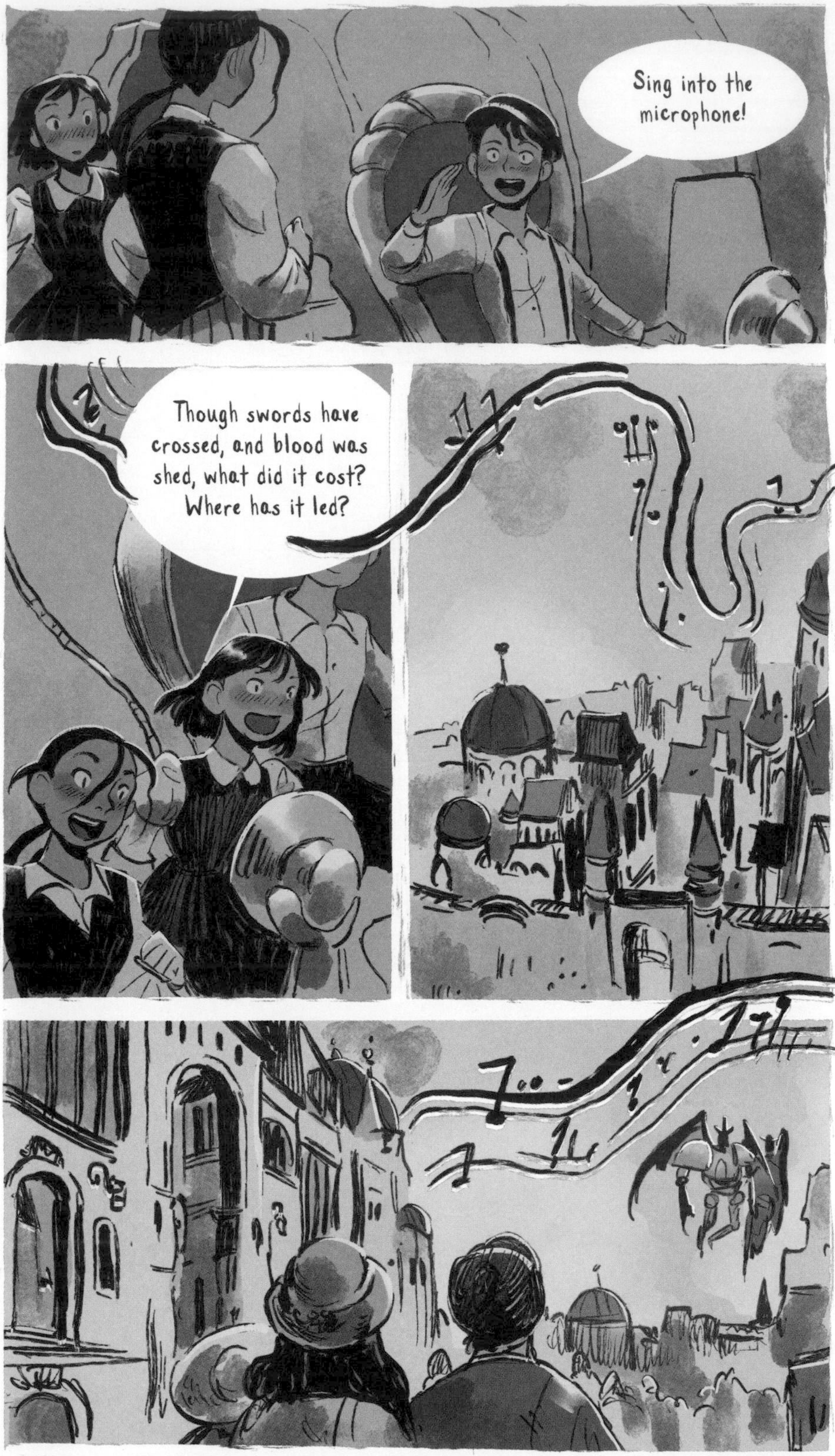
Sing into the microphone!
Though swords have crossed, and blood was shed, what did it cost? Where has it led?

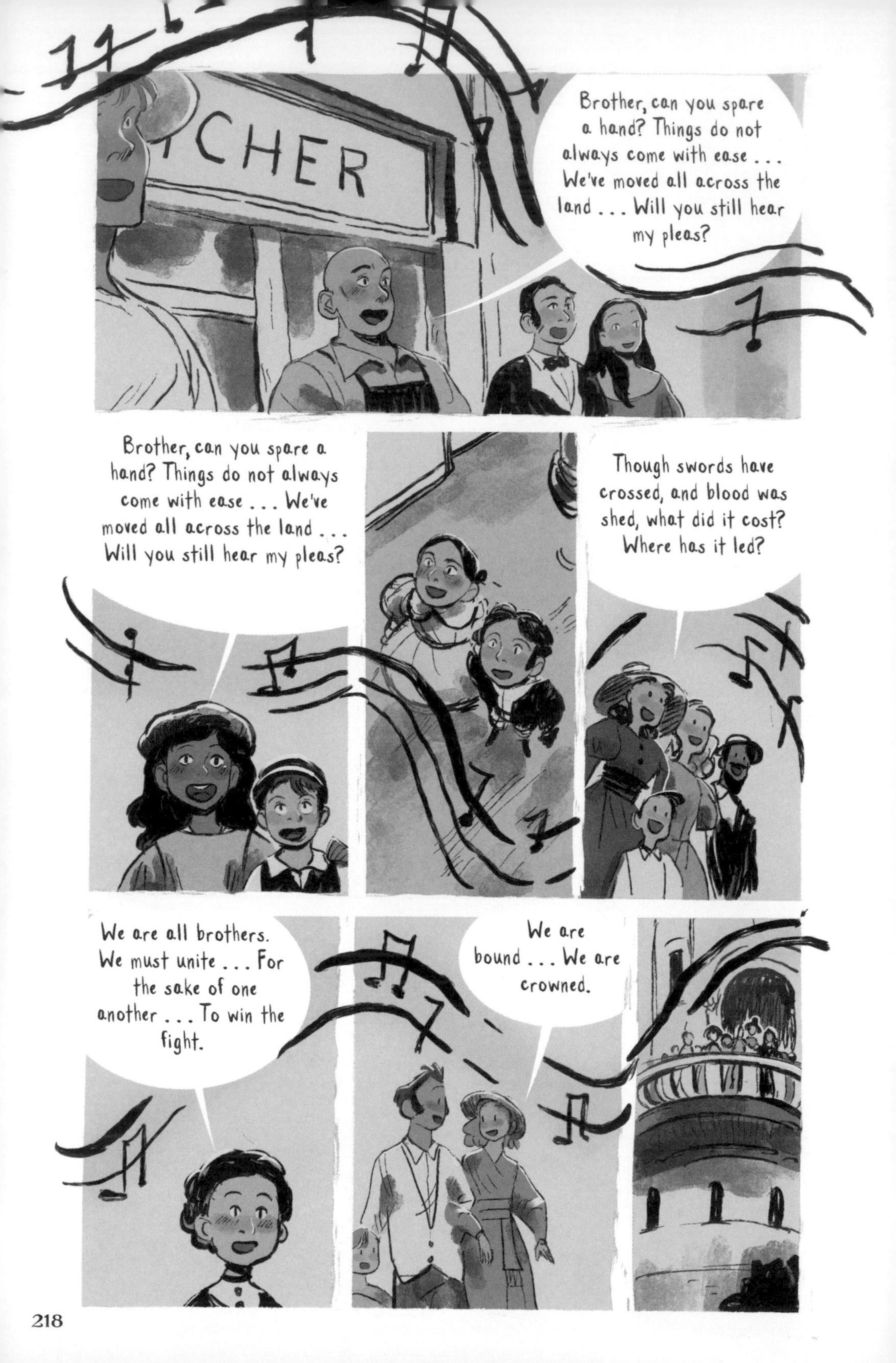
ICHER
Brother, can you spare a hand? Things do not always come with ease . . . We've moved all across the land . . . Will you still hear my pleas?
Brother, can you spare a hand? Things do not always come with ease . . . We've moved all across the land . . . Will you still hear my pleas?
Though swords have crossed, and blood was shed, what did it cost? Where has it led?
We are all brothers. We must unite . . . For the sake of one another . . . To win the fight.
We are bound . . . We are crowned.

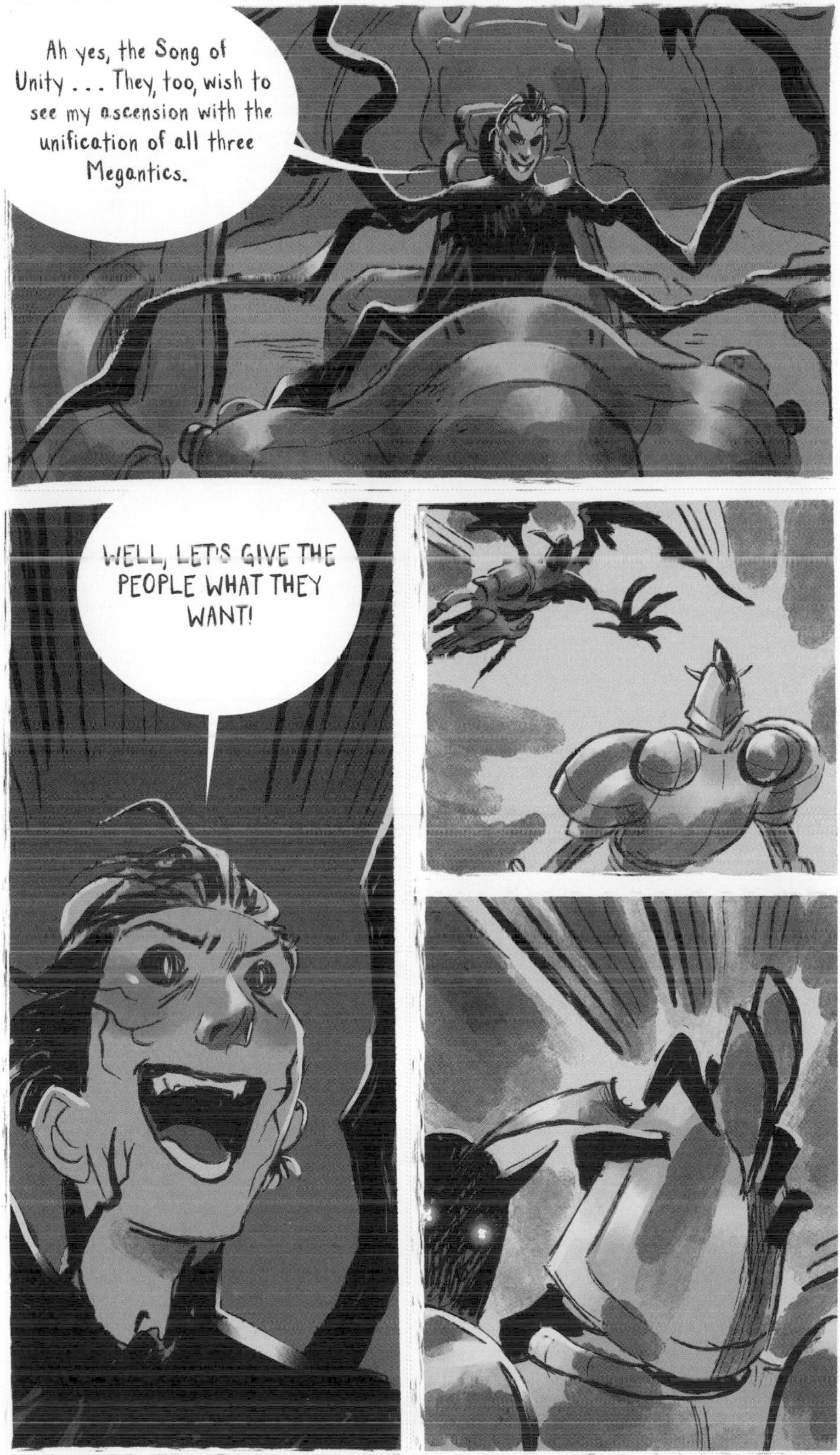
Ah yes, the Song of Unity . . . They, too, wish to see my ascension with the unification of all three Megantics.
WELL, LET'S GIVE THE PEOPLE WHAT THEY WANT!

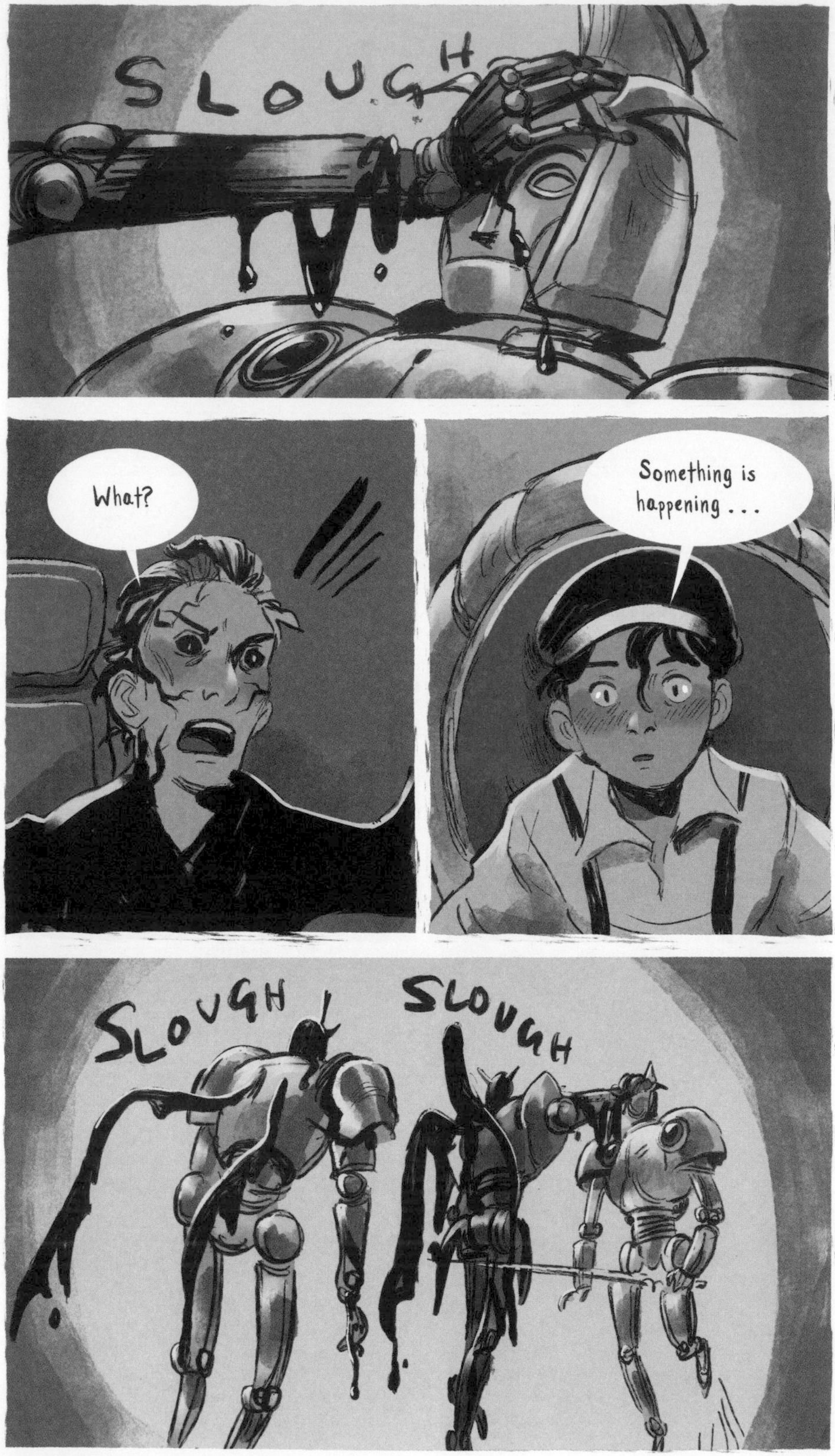
SLOUGH
What?
Something is happening . . .
SLOUGH
SLOUGH

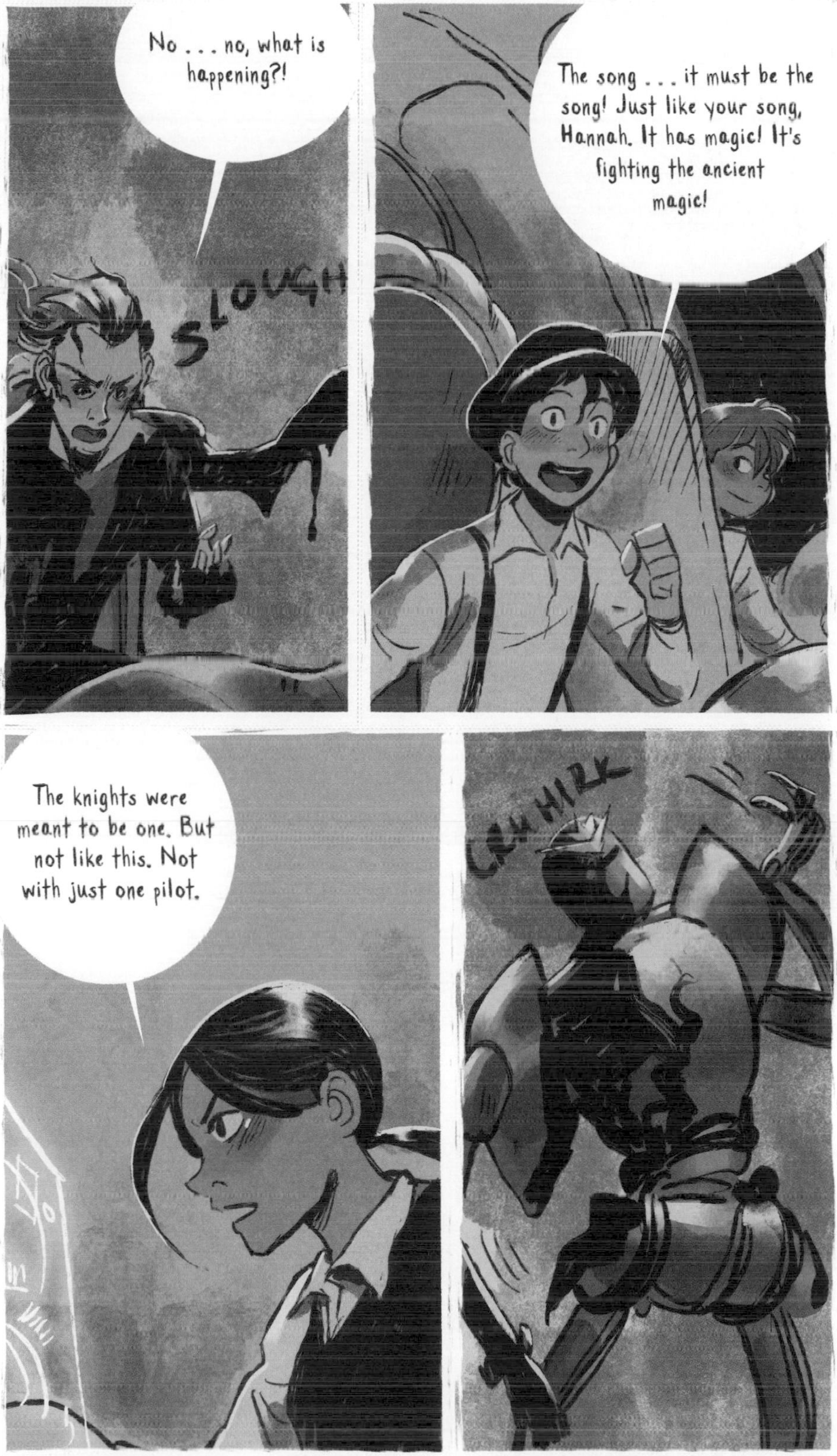
No . . . no, what is happening?!
SLOUGH
The song . . . it must be the song! Just like your song, Hannah. It has magic! It's fighting the ancient magic!
The knights were meant to be one. But not like this. Not with just one pilot.
CRUHIRK

SHOOM

AHHHHHH!

Ever, let's get these guys out of here!

Right!

VWOOM

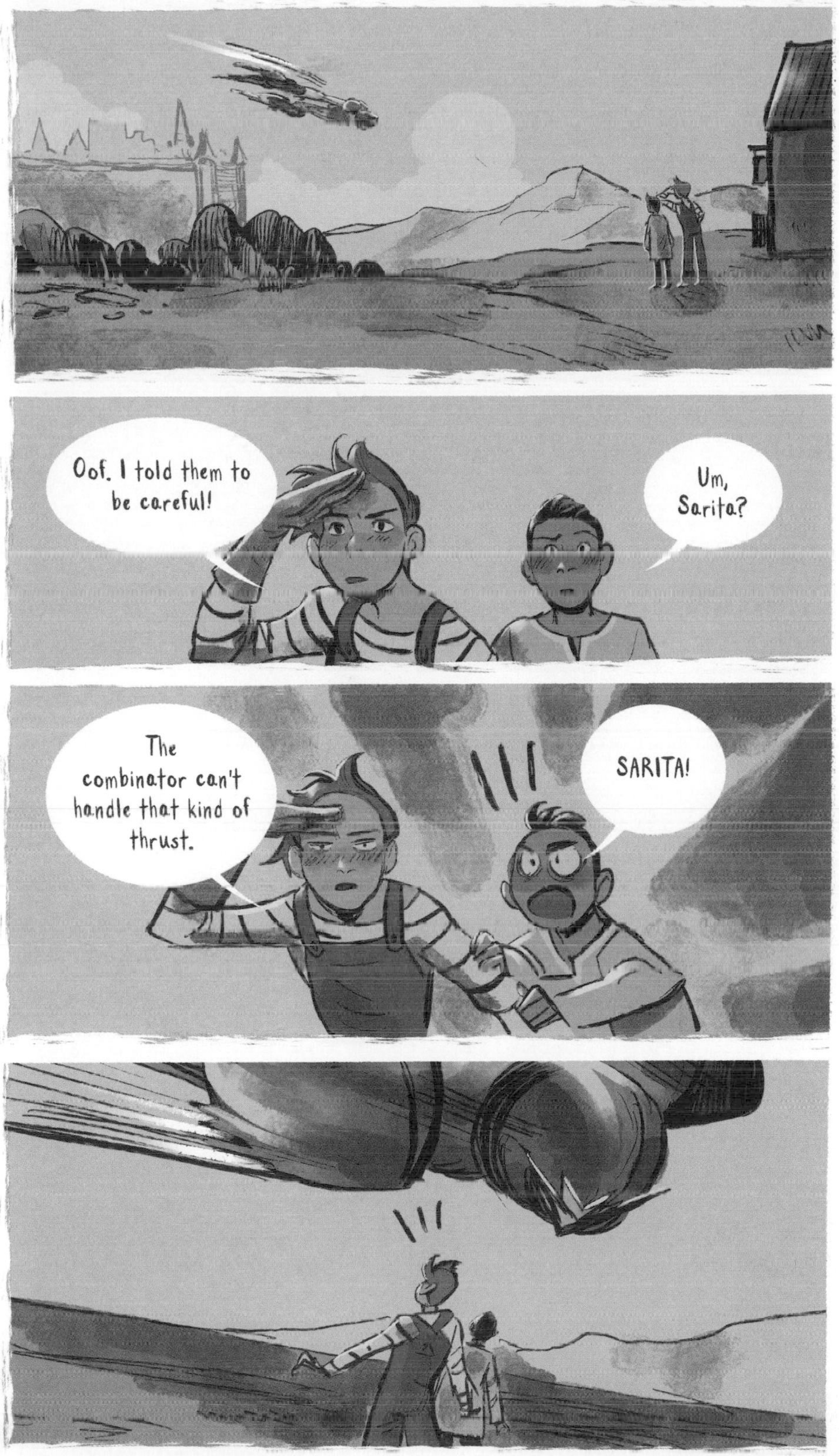
Oof. I told them to be careful!
Um, Sarita?
The combinator can't handle that kind of thrust.
SARITA!

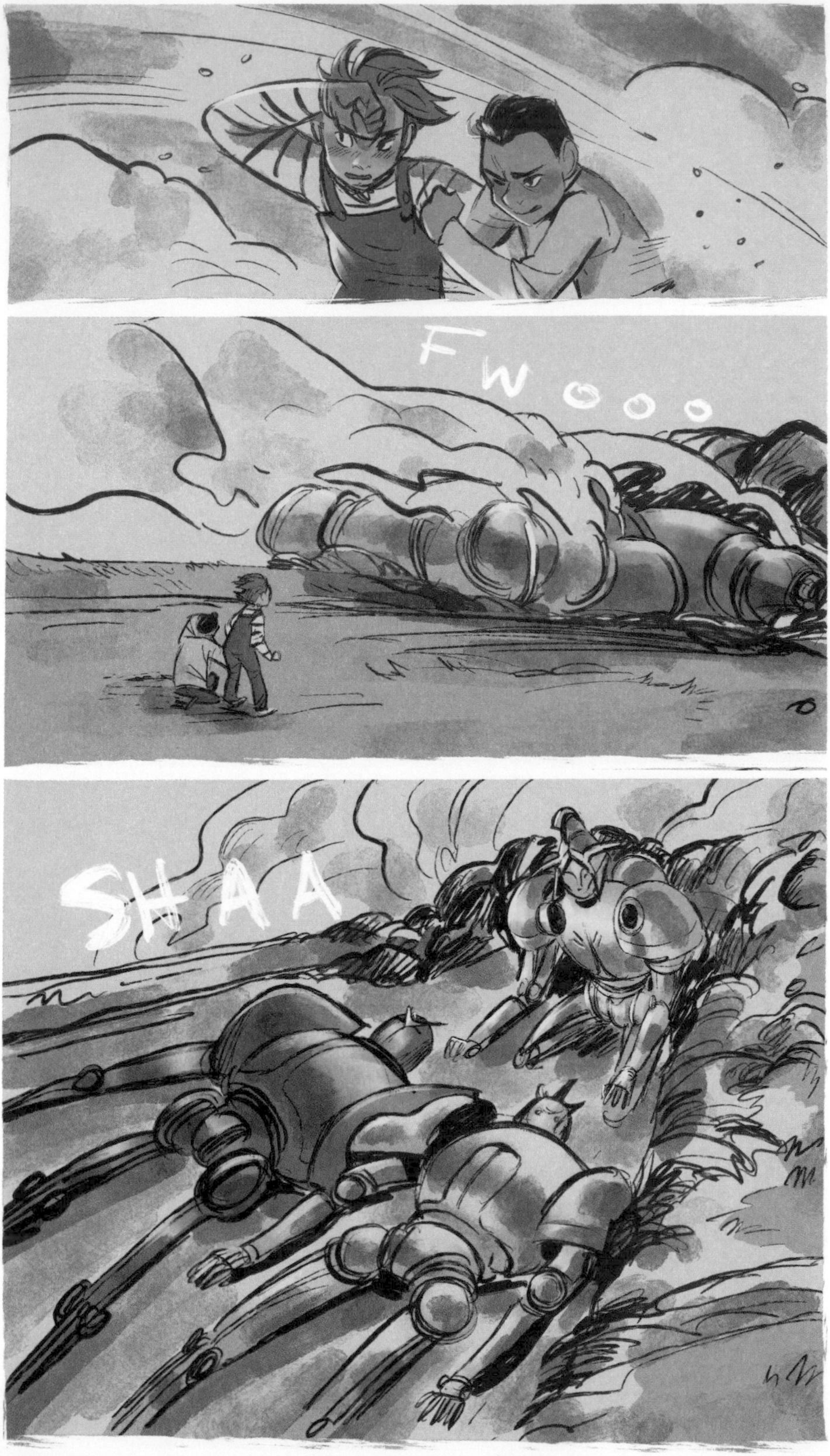
FWOOO
SHAA

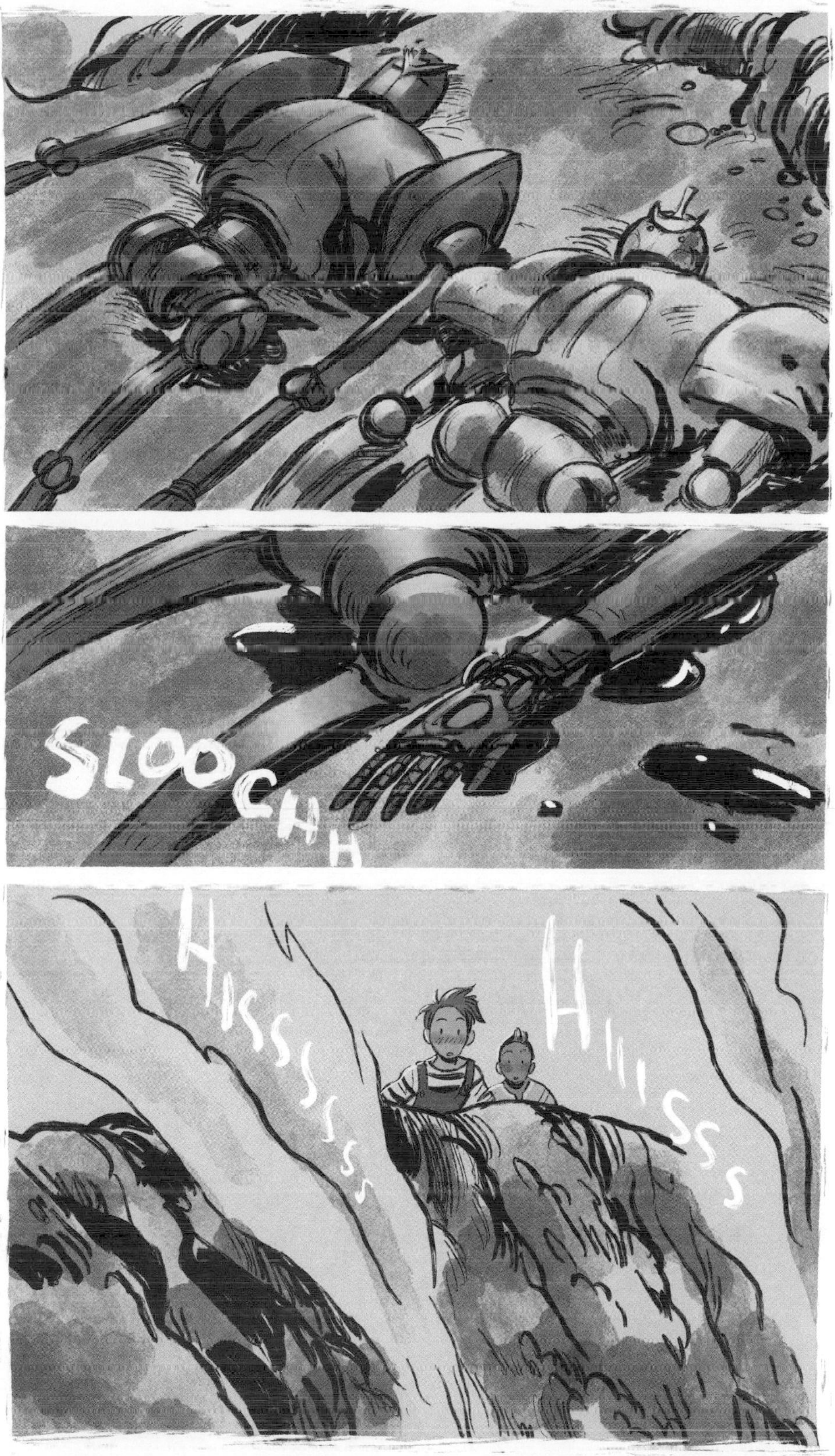
SLOOCHH
HISSSSSS
HIISSSS

The three knights.
Like from the story.
SHOOOP

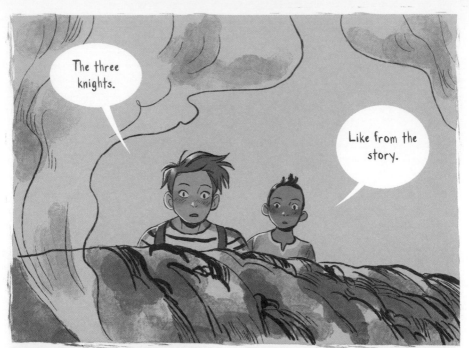

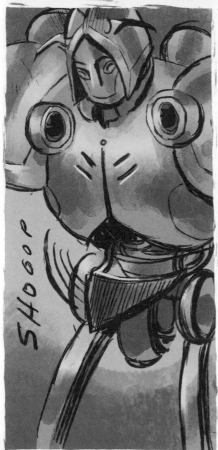

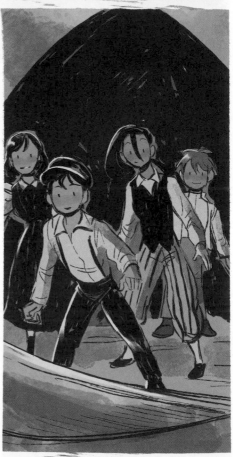

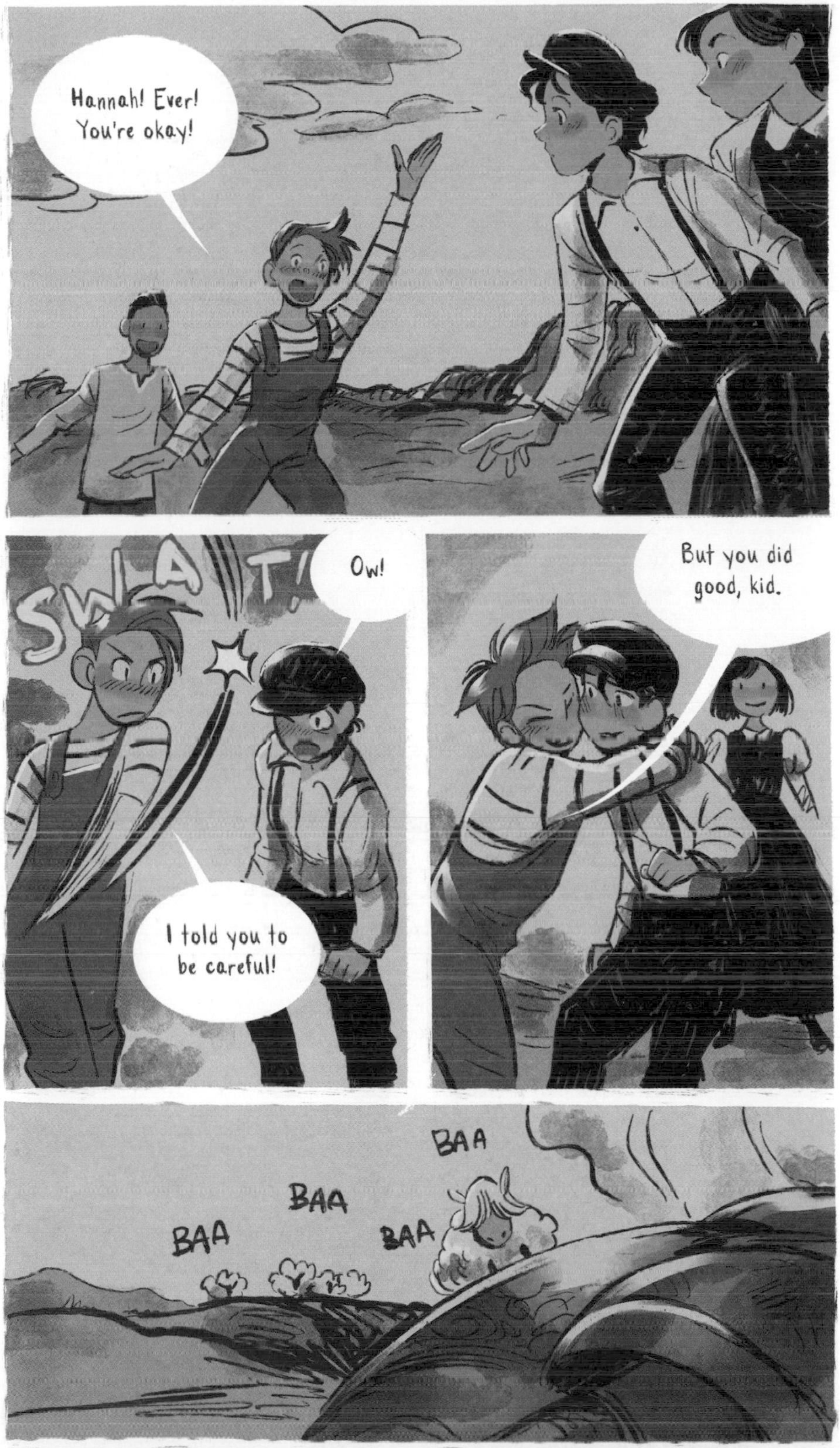
Hannah! Ever! You're okay!
SWAT!
Ow!
I told you to be careful!
But you did good, kid.
BAA
BAA
BAA
BAA

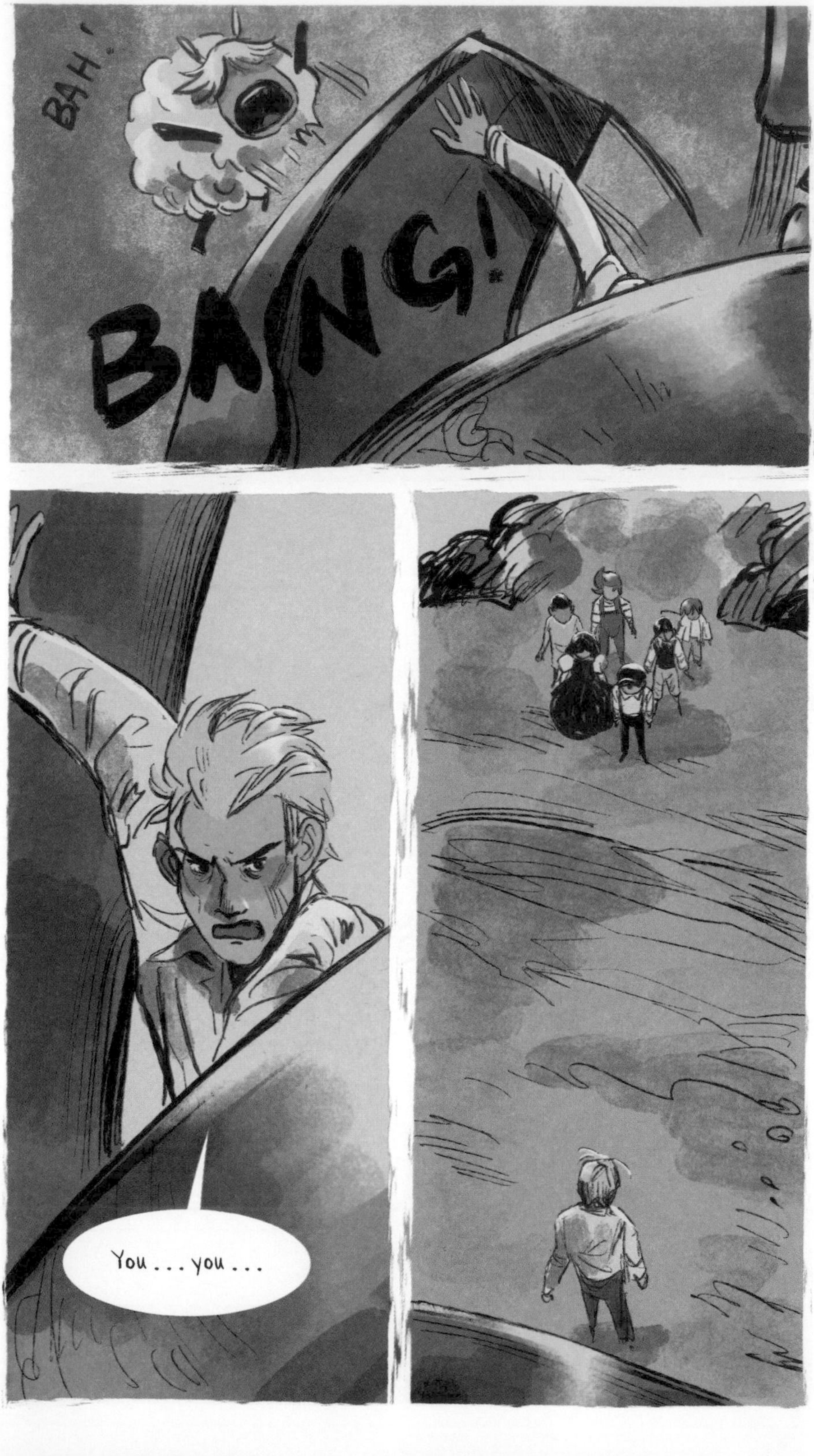
BAH!
BANG!
You . . . you . . .

You lost, Vash.
Not yet.

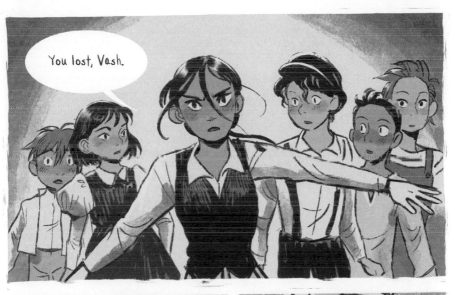

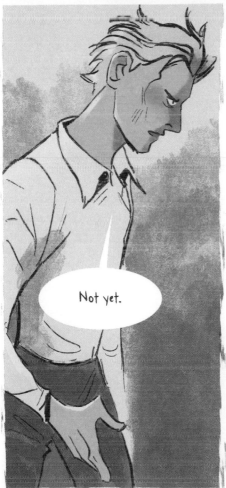

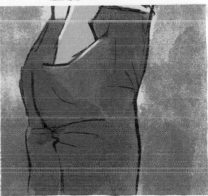

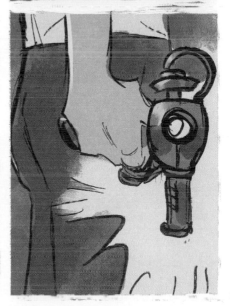

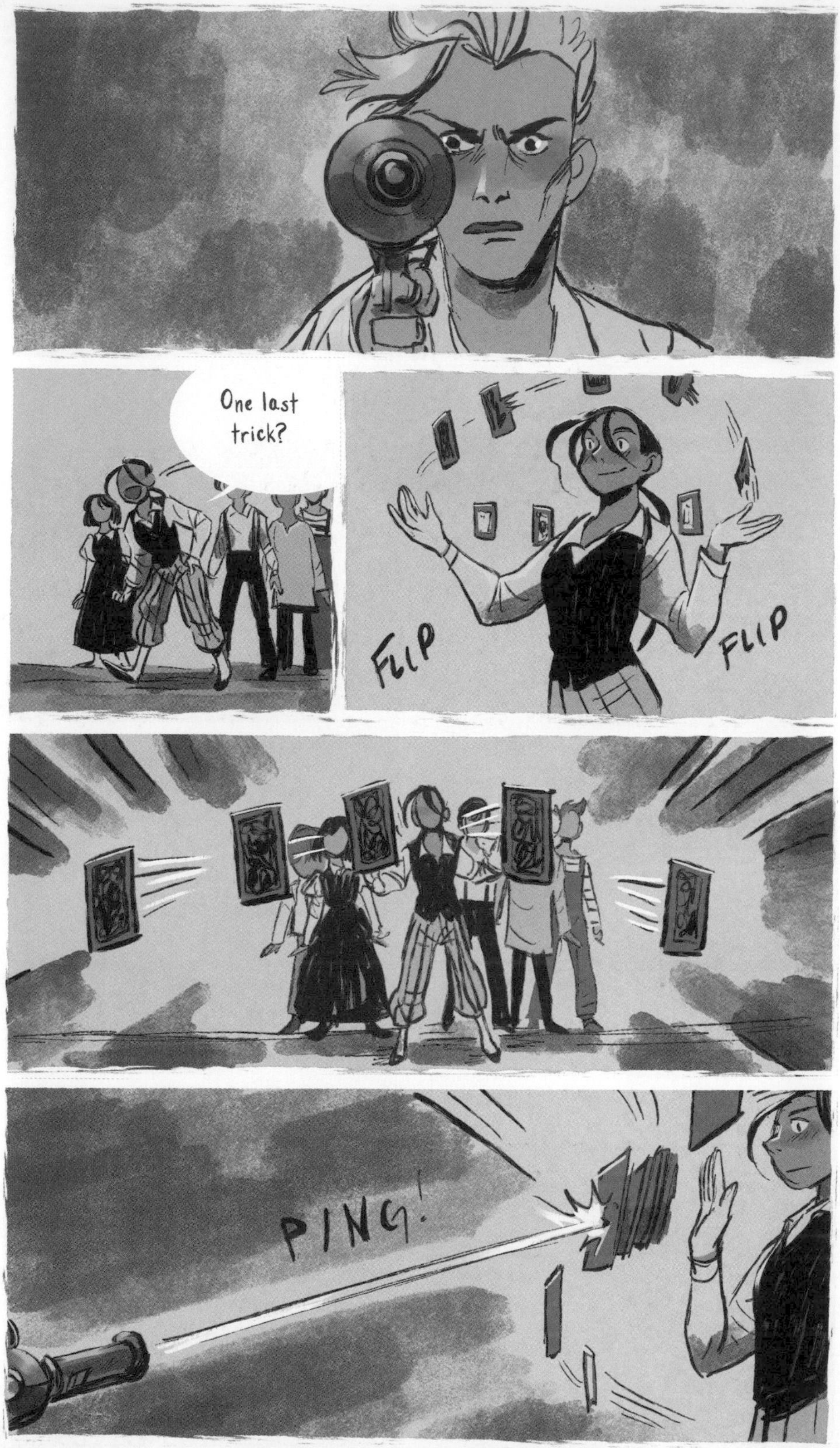
One last trick?
FLIP
FLIP
PING!

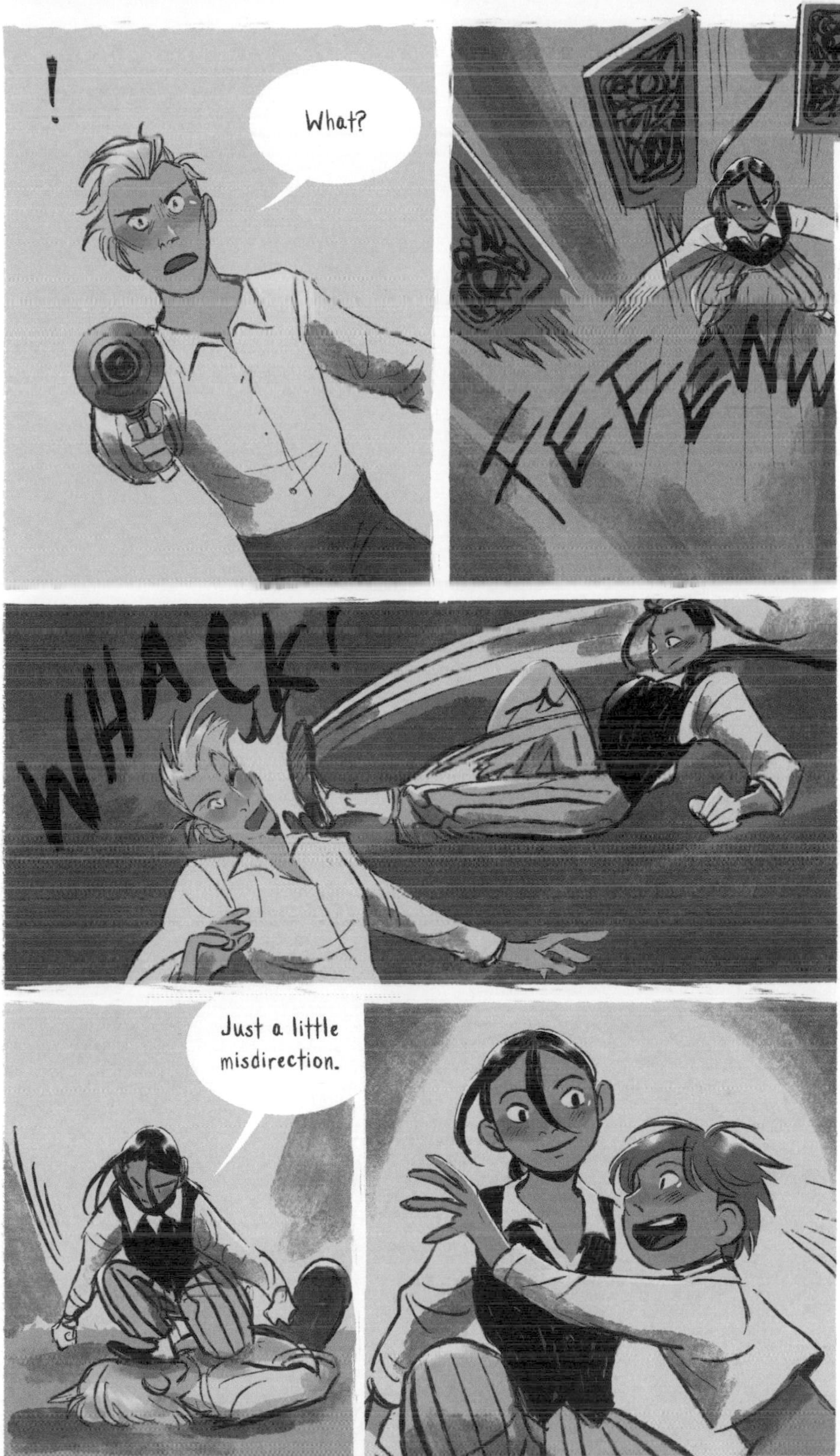
!
What?
FEEEWW
WHACK!
Just a little misdirection.

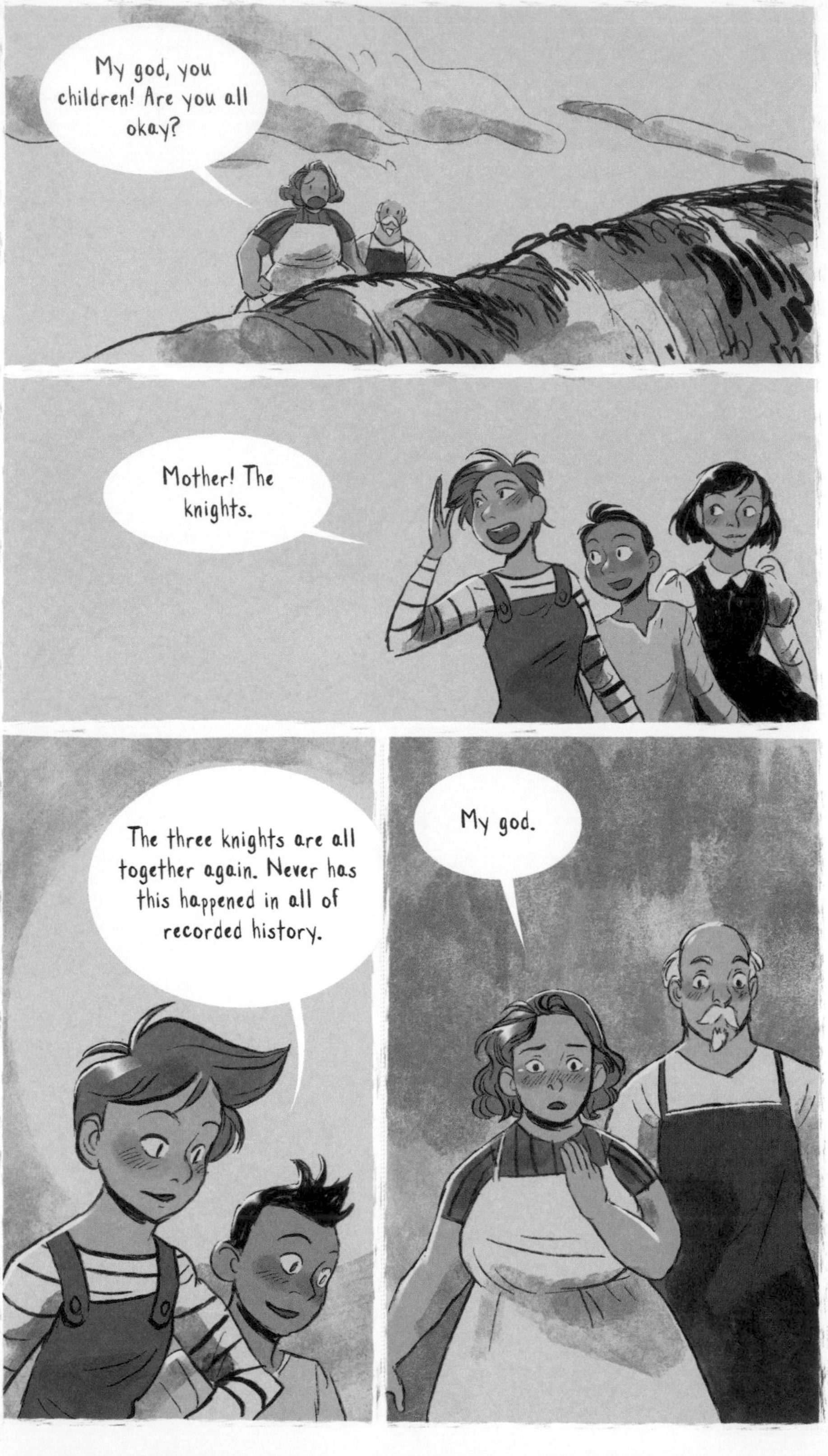
My god, you children! Are you all okay?
Mother! The knights.
The three knights are all together again. Never has this happened in all of recorded history.
My god.

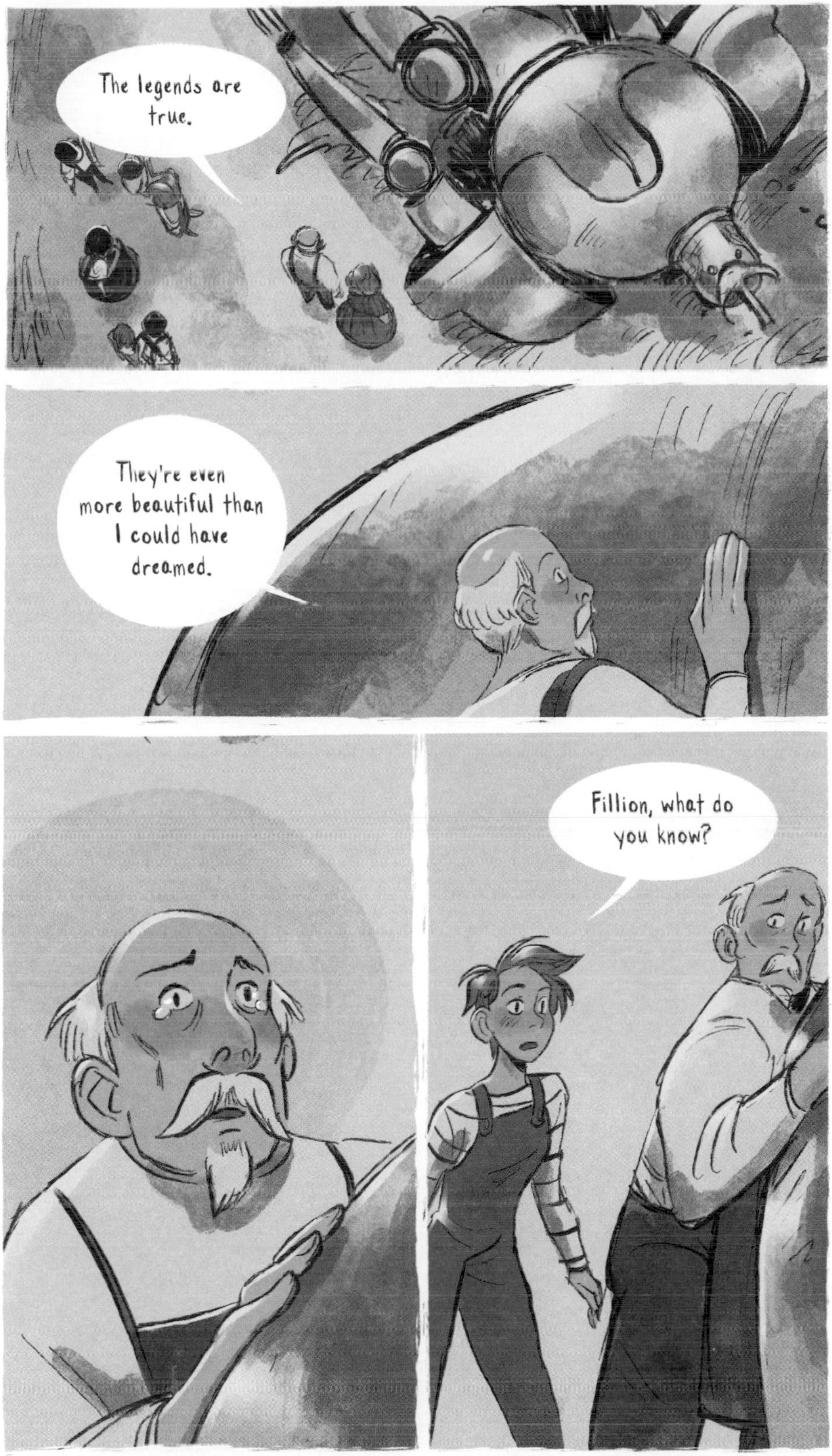
The legends are true.
They're even more beautiful than I could have dreamed.
Fillion, what do you know?

I don't KNOW anything. Nobody has seen the knights for five generations . . . but look here.

The puzzle box in the story, some say it's not a physical object but a riddle.

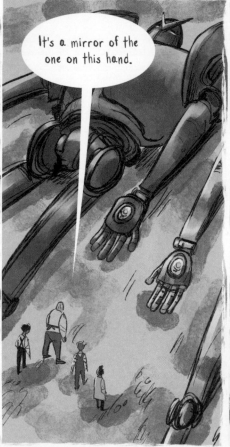

It's a mirror of the one on this hand.

They match! Ever! Can you get the knights to hold hands?

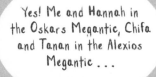

Yes! Me and Hannah in the Oskars Megantic, Chifa and Tanan in the Alexios Megantic . . .

. . . and if you and Ravi can try to operate the Edmonda Megantic, I think we can do it.

POP!

235

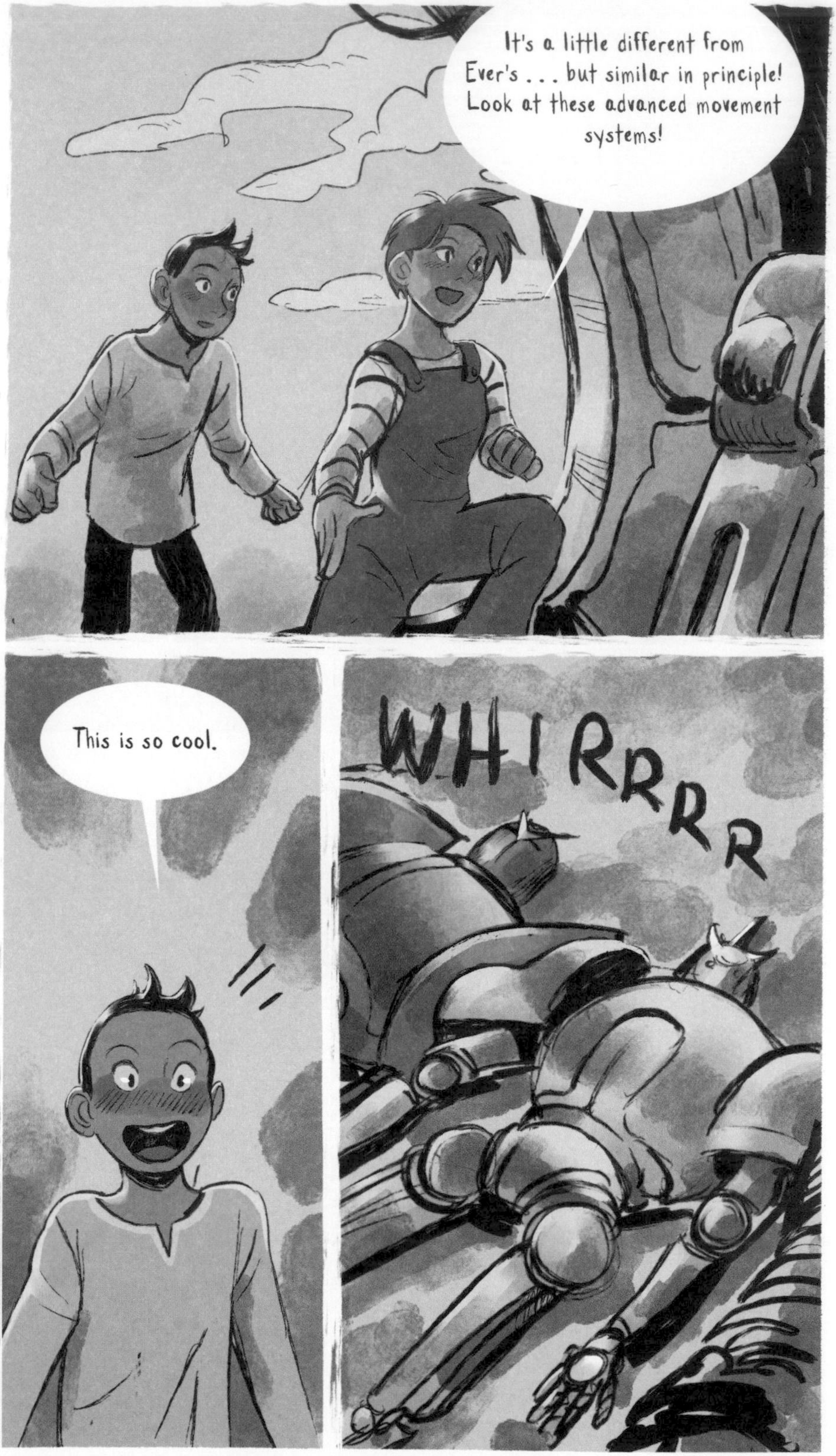
It's a little different from Ever's . . . but similar in principle! Look at these advanced movement systems!
This is so cool.
WHIRRRRR

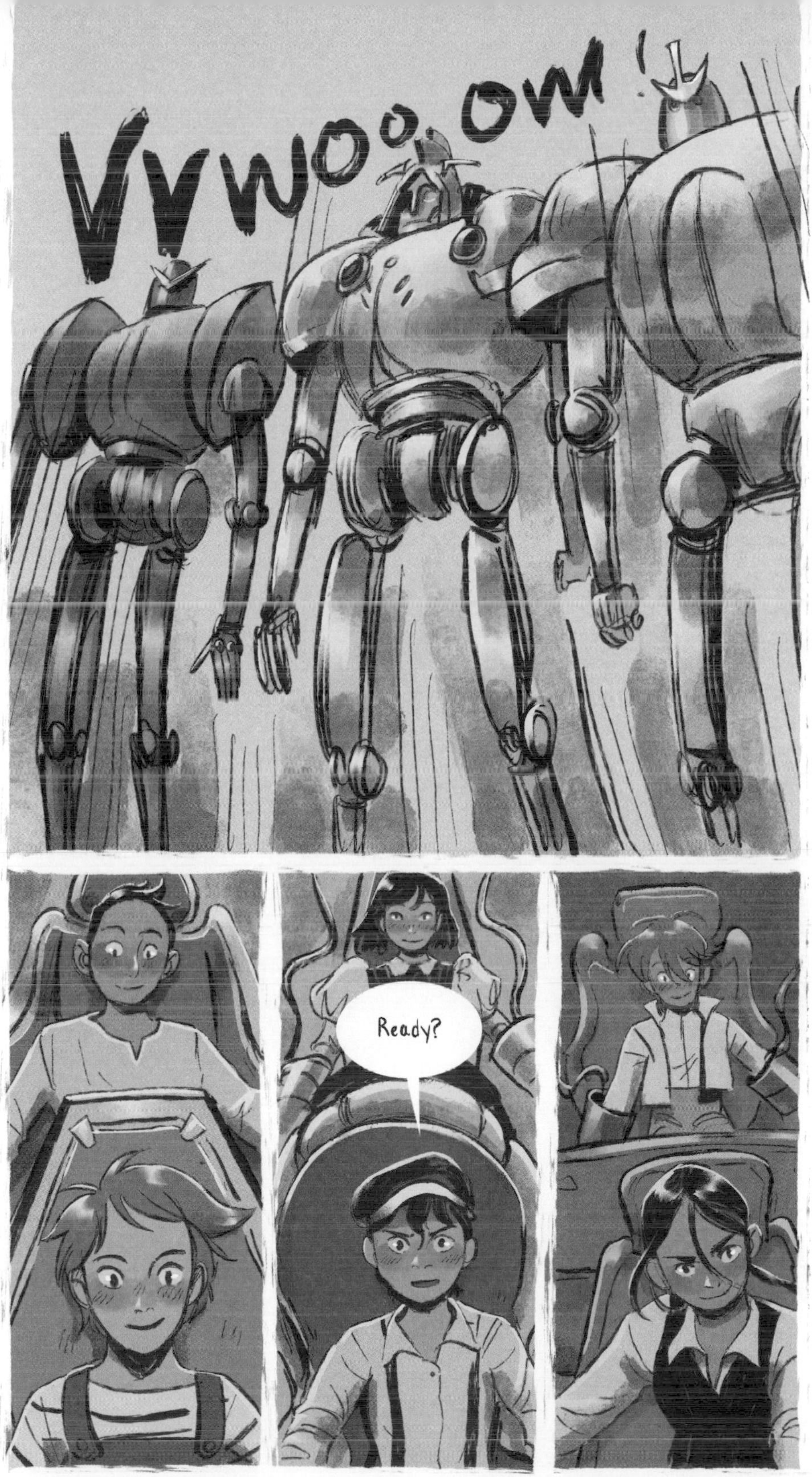
VVWOOOOM!
Ready?

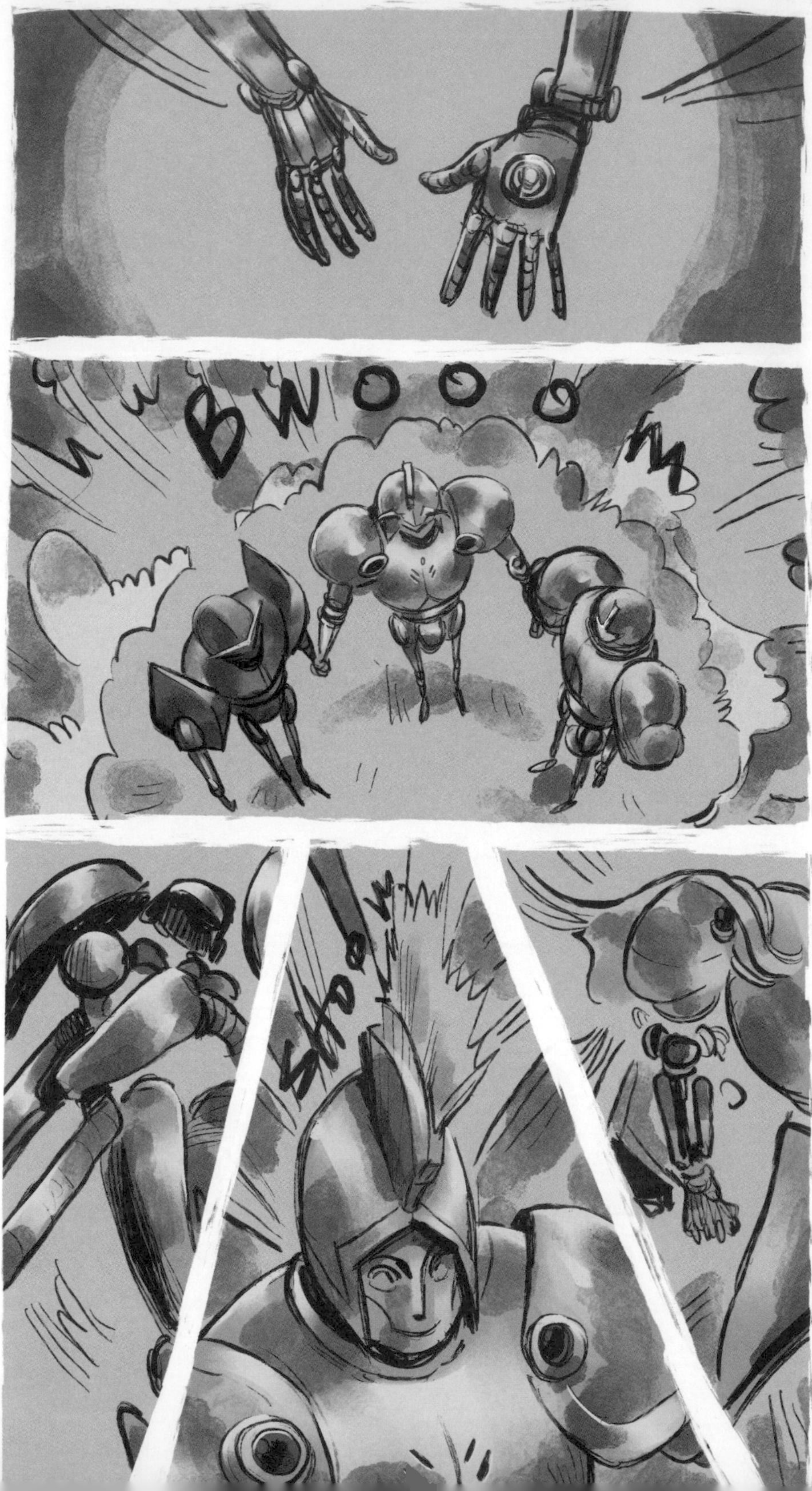
BWOOOOM

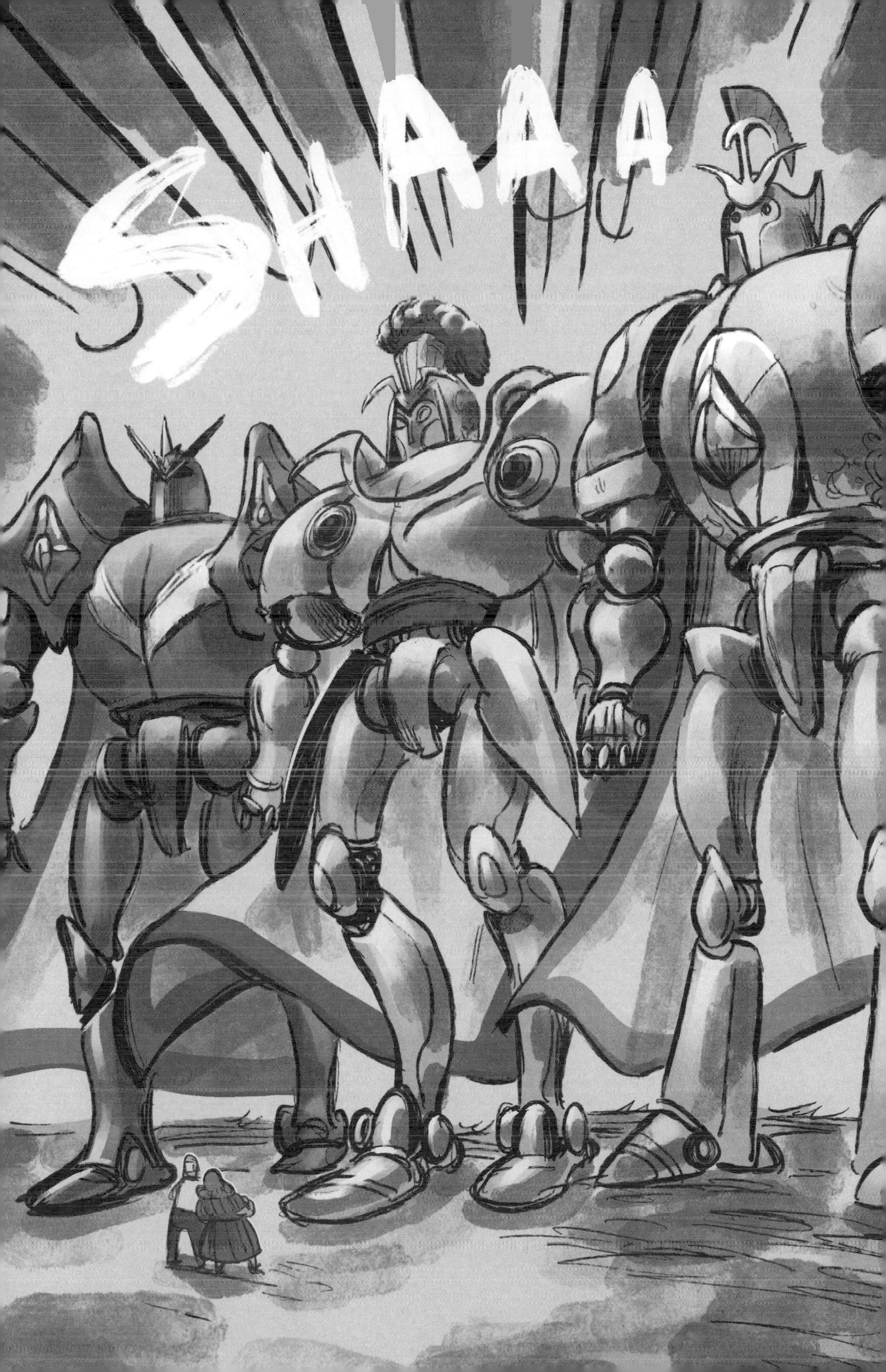
SHAAAA

My god.
The knights, they are reconciled.
The answer to the puzzle box riddle is . . . unity.
STP!
STP!
VWUMM

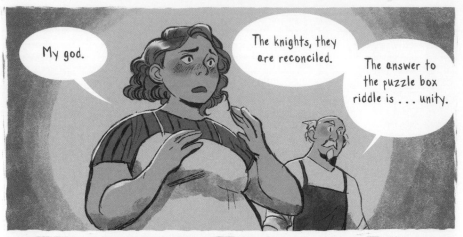

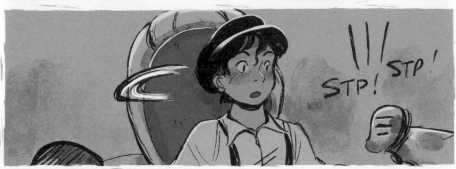

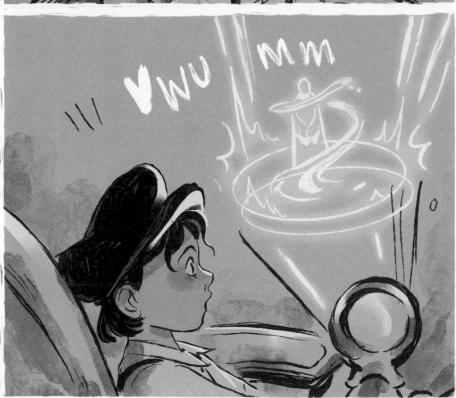

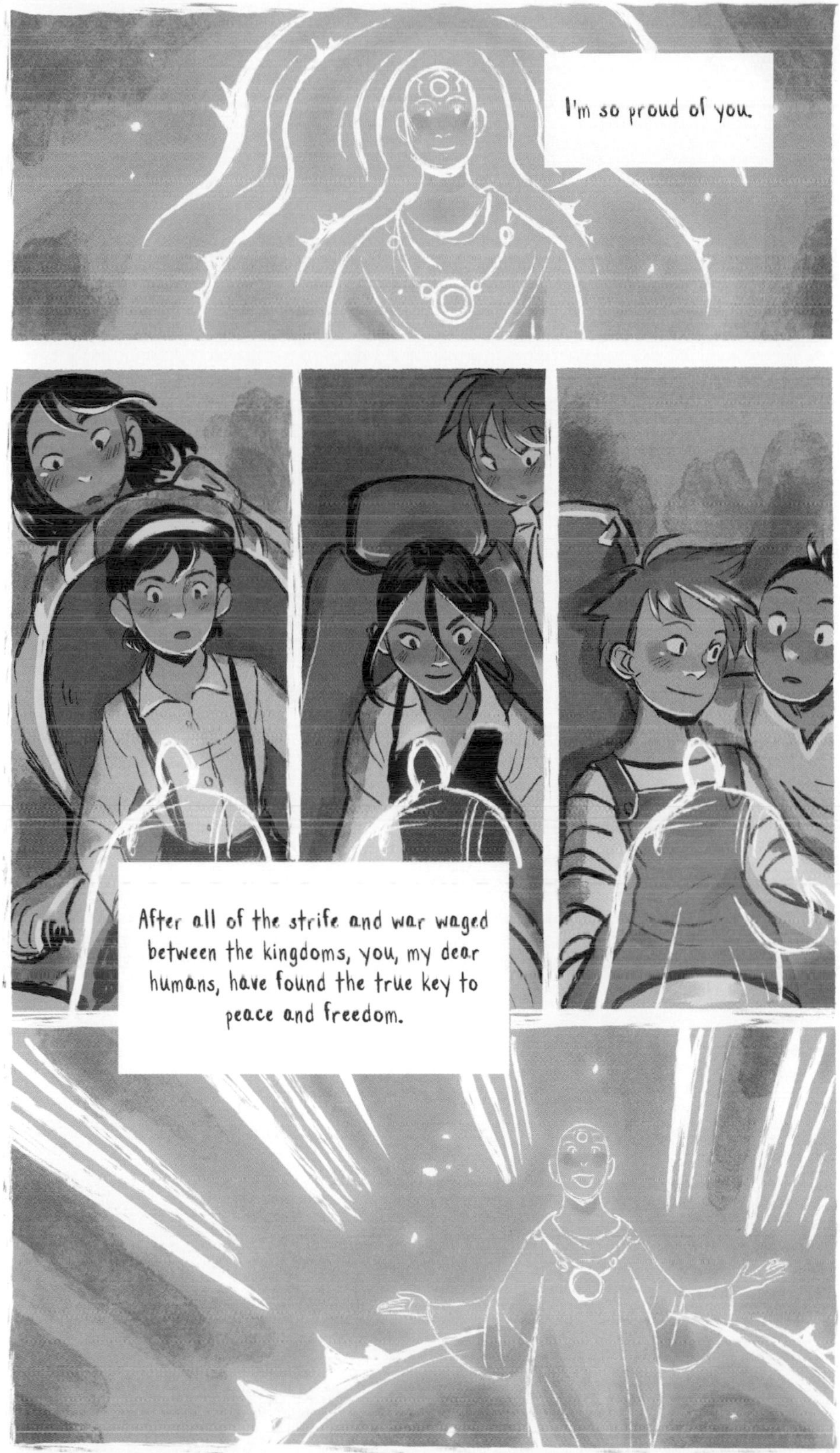
I'm so proud of you.
After all of the strife and war waged between the kingdoms, you, my dear humans, have found the true key to peace and freedom.

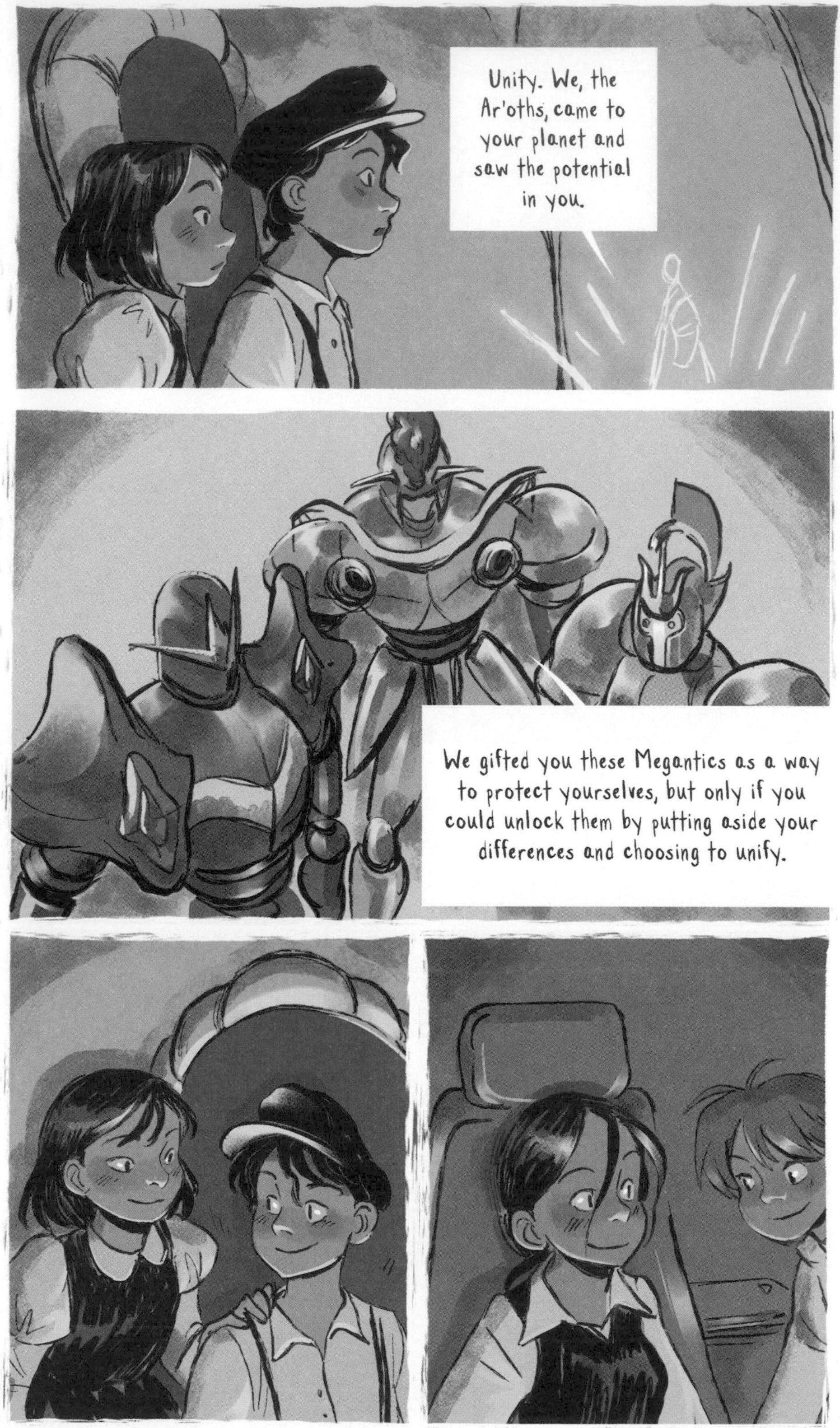
Unity. We, the Ar'oths, came to your planet and saw the potential in you.
We gifted you these Megantics as a way to protect yourselves, but only if you could unlock them by putting aside your differences and choosing to unify.

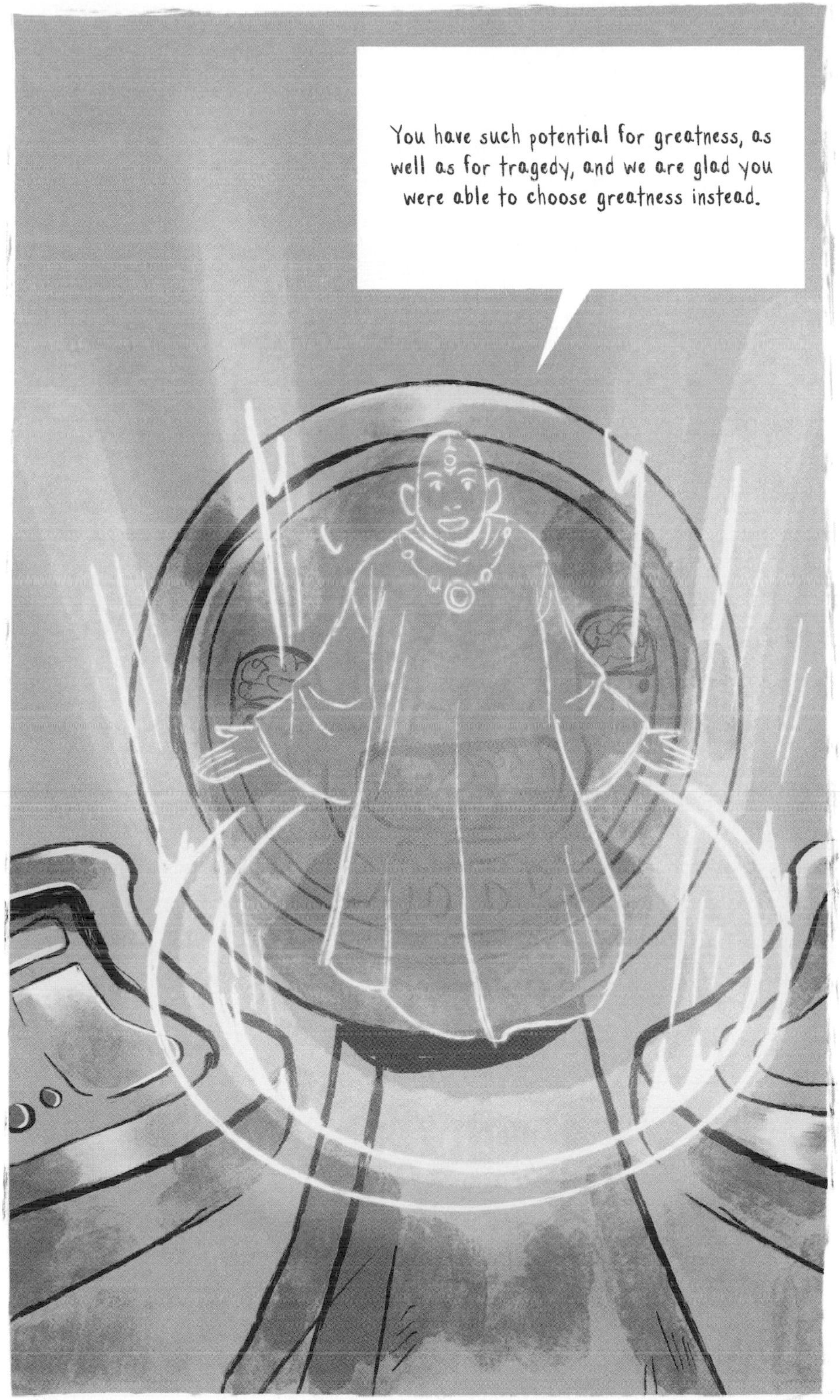
You have such potential for greatness, as well as for tragedy, and we are glad you were able to choose greatness instead.

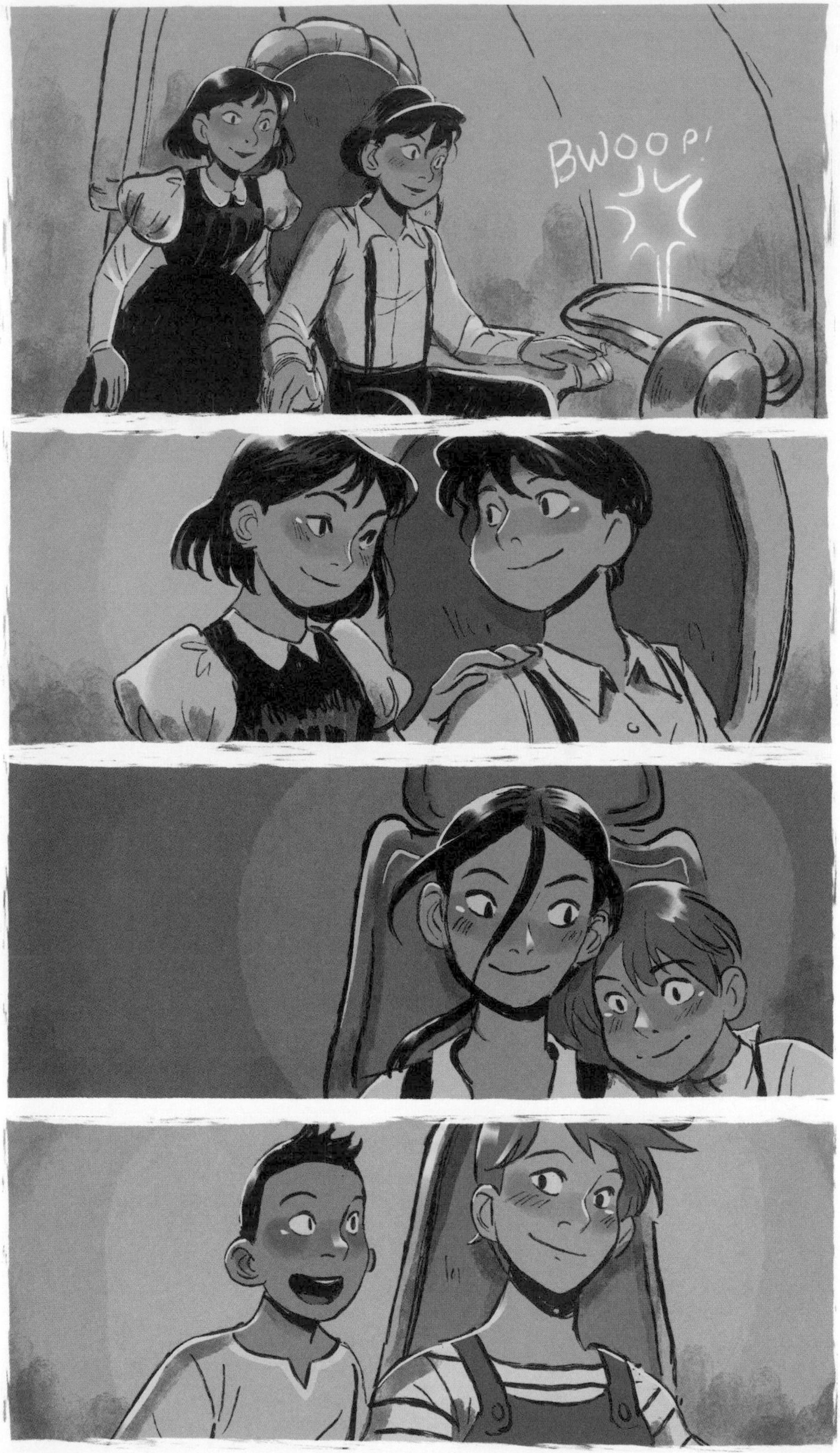
BWOOP!

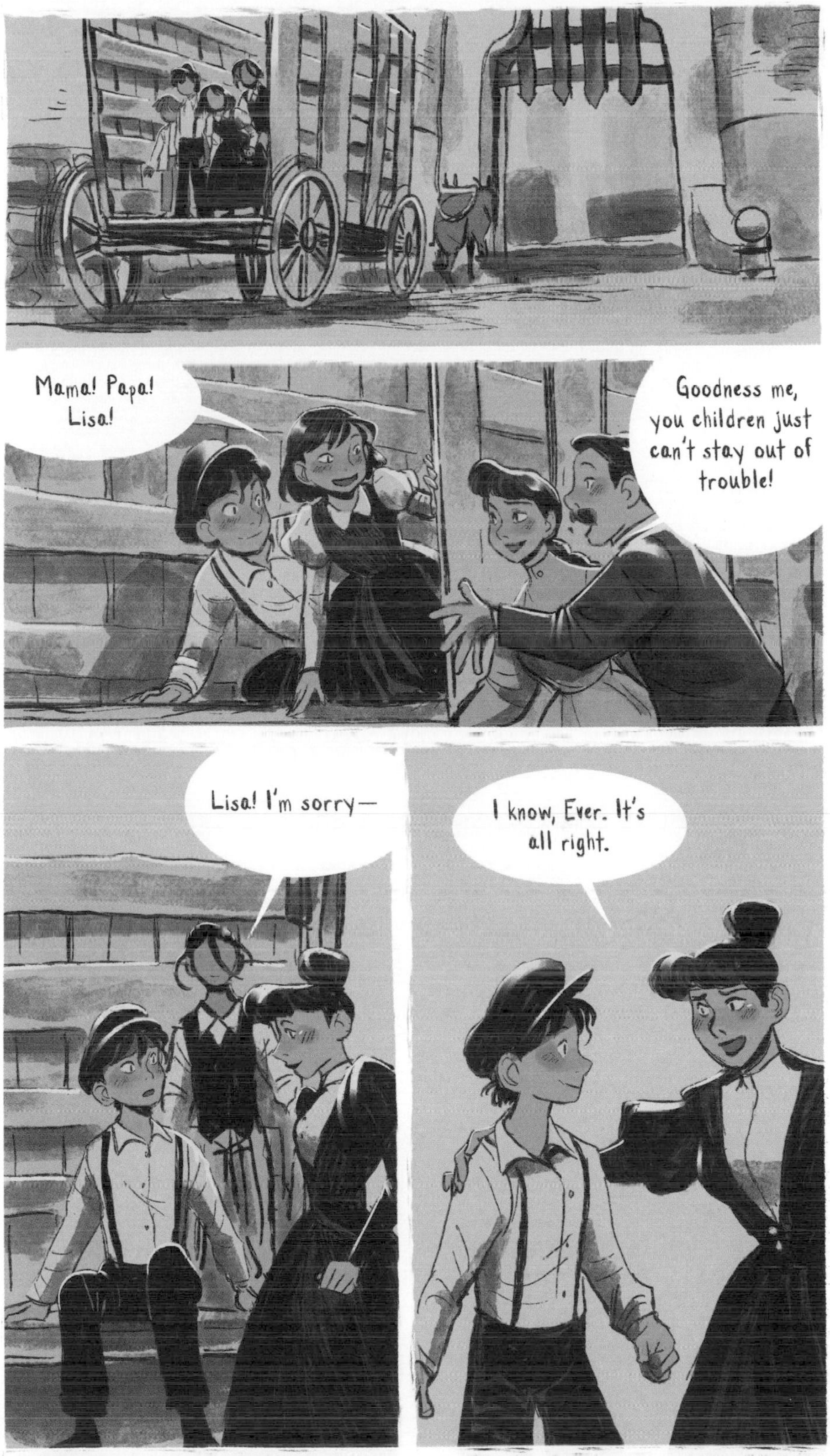
Mama! Papa!
Lisa!
Goodness me, you children just can't stay out of trouble!
Lisa! I'm sorry—
I know, Ever. It's all right.

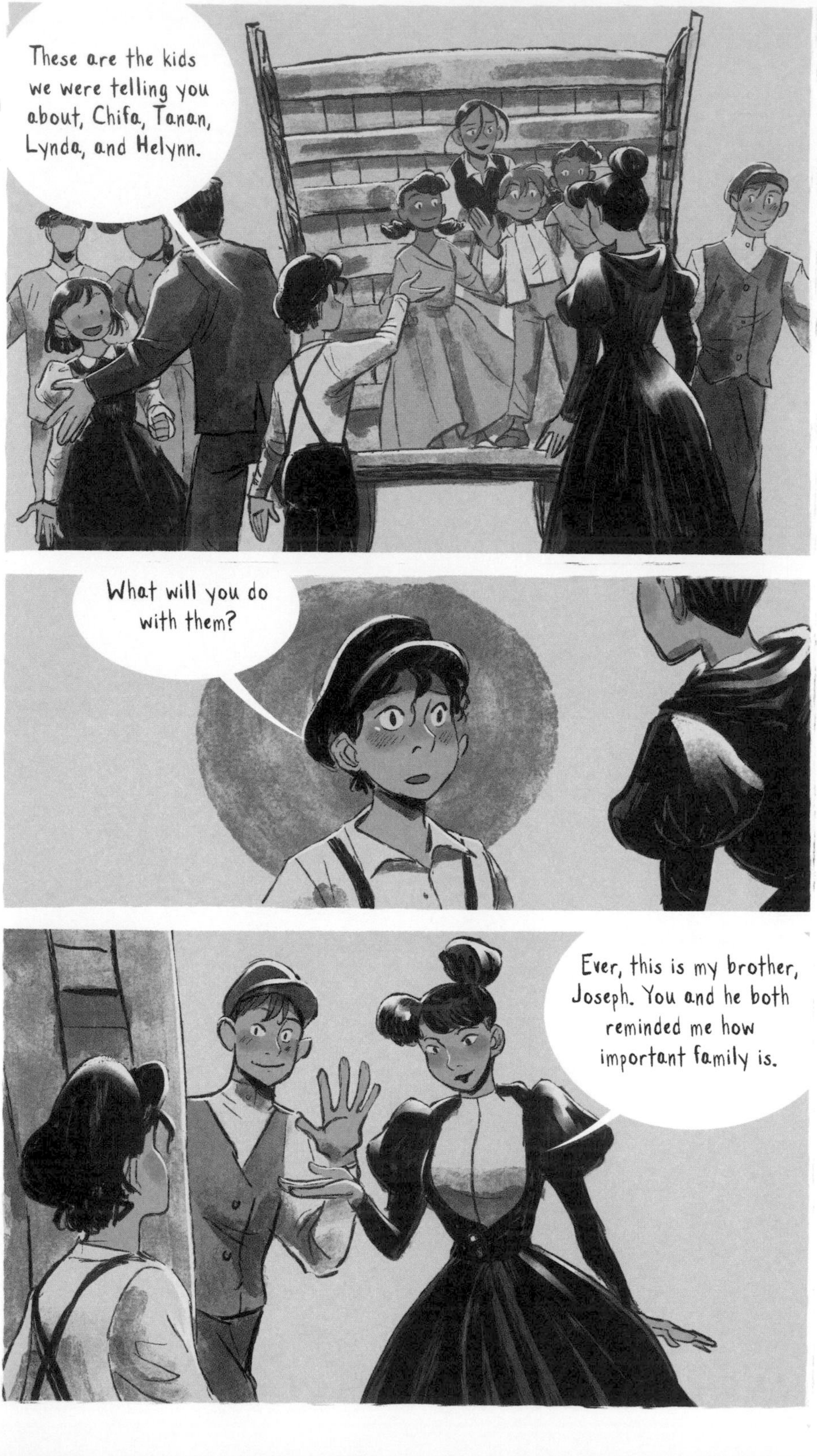
These are the kids we were telling you about, Chifa, Tanan, Lynda, and Helynn.
What will you do with them?
Ever, this is my brother, Joseph. You and he both reminded me how important family is.

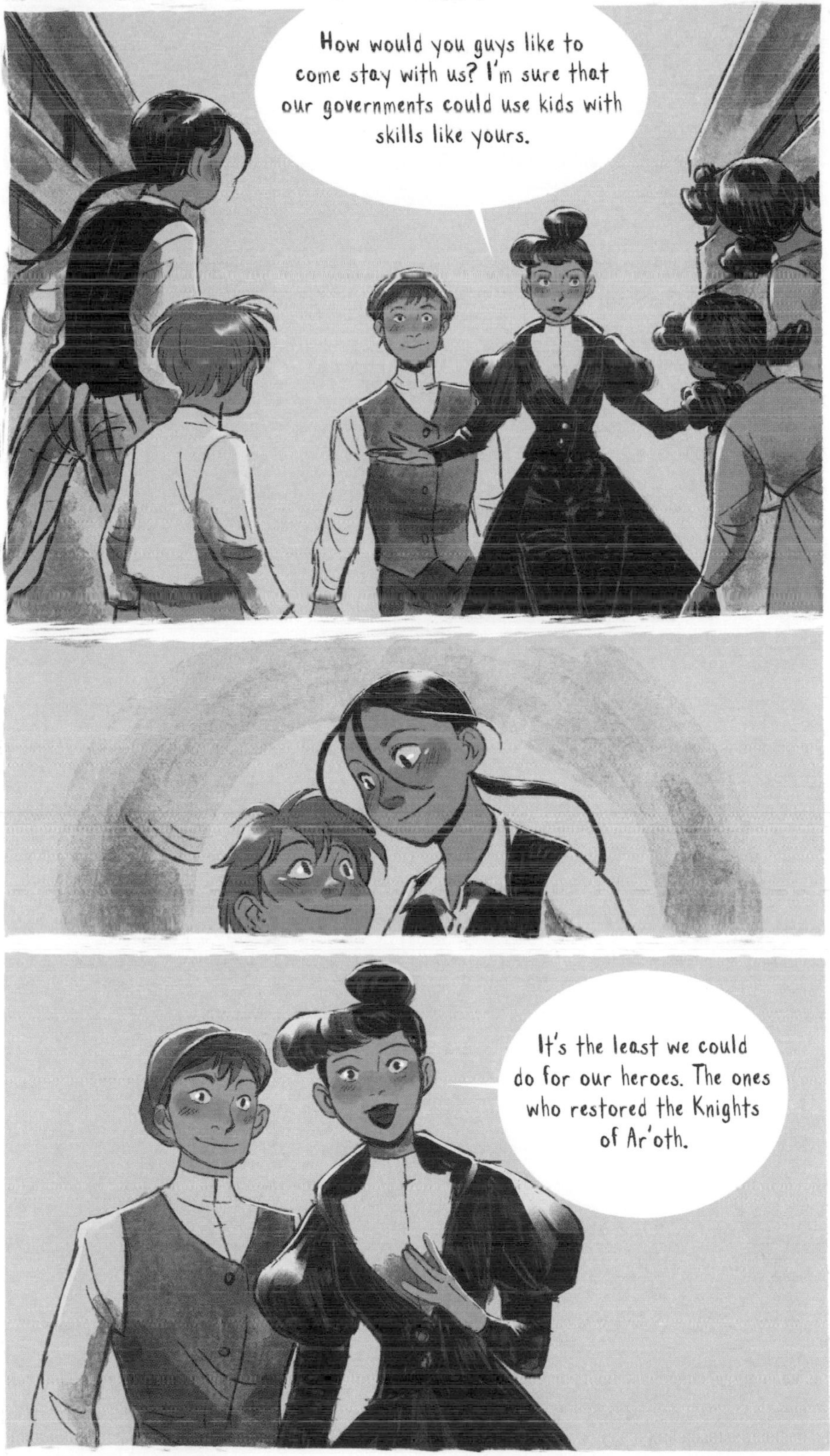
How would you guys like to come stay with us? I'm sure that our governments could use kids with skills like yours.
It's the least we could do for our heroes. The ones who restored the Knights of Ar'oth.

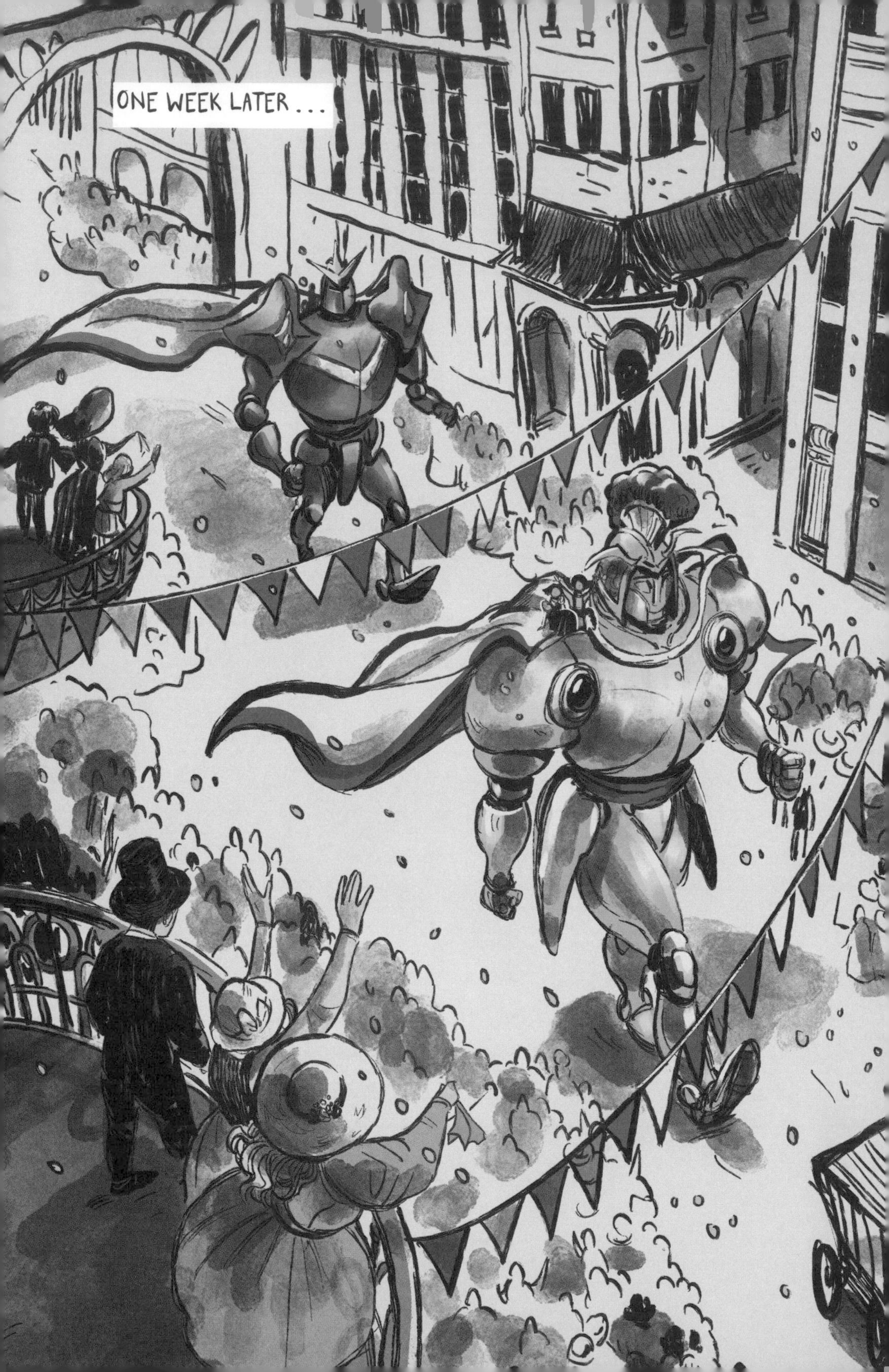
ONE WEEK LATER . . .

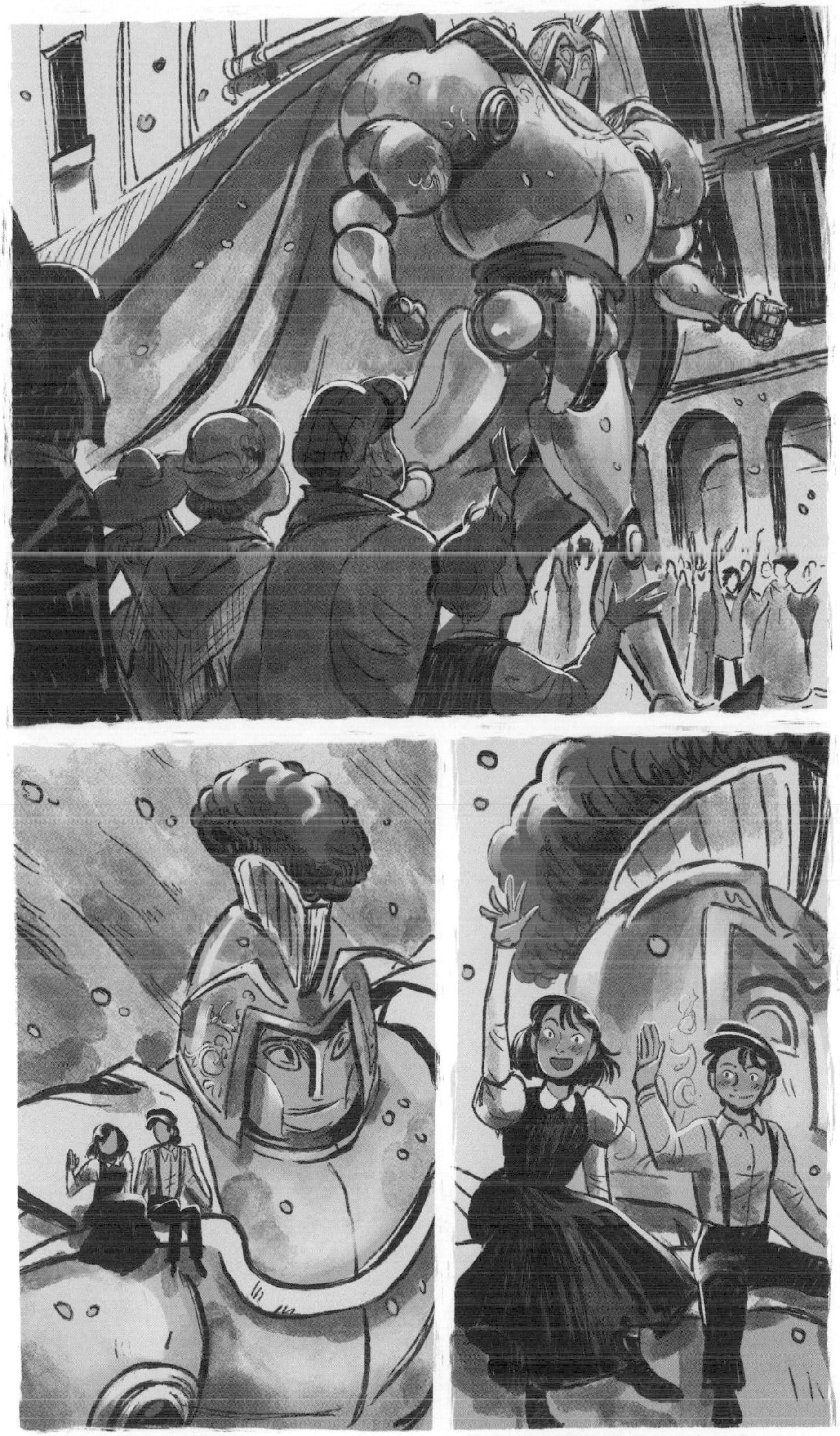

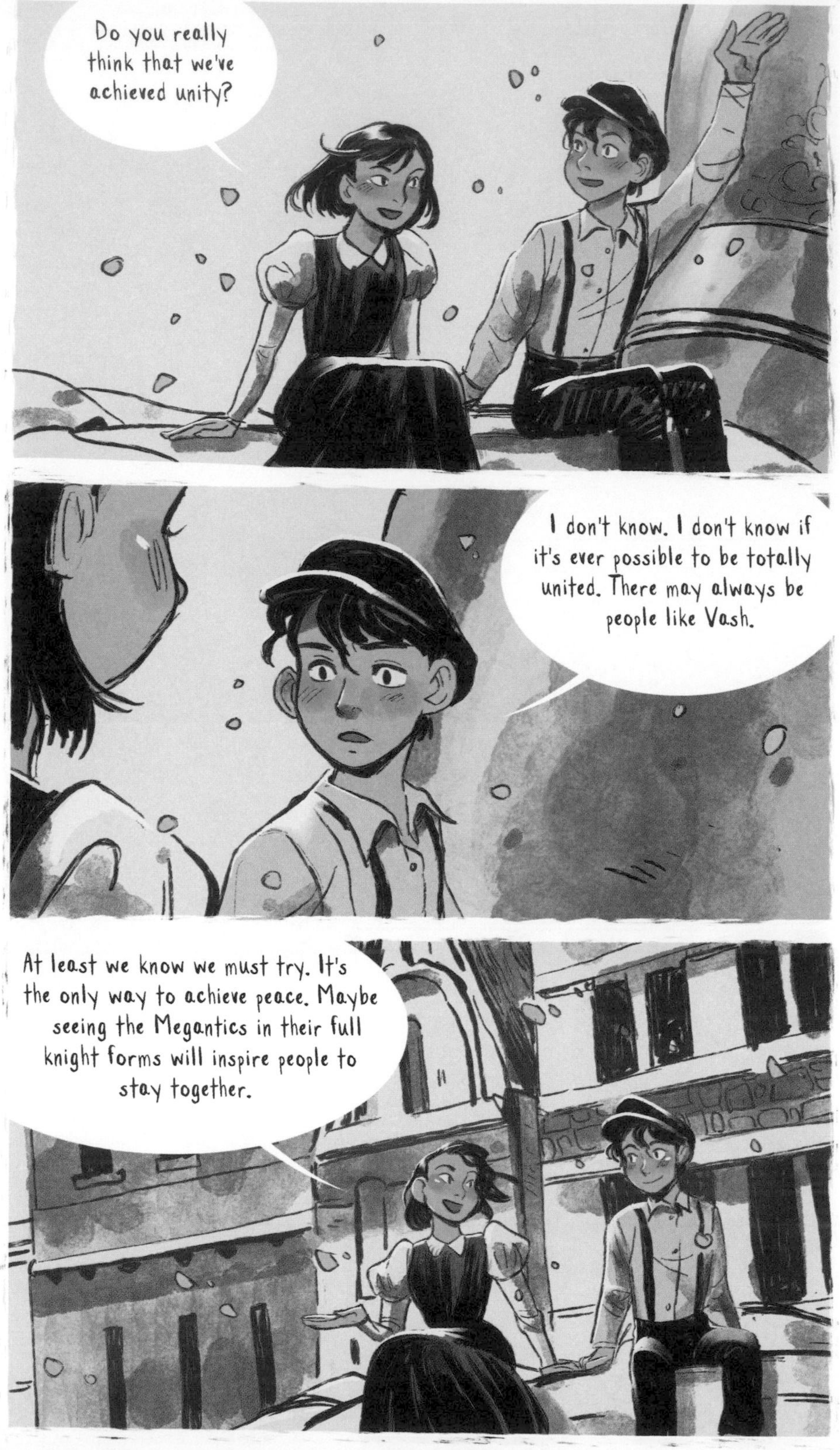
Do you really think that we've achieved unity?
I don't know. I don't know if it's ever possible to be totally united. There may always be people like Vash.
At least we know we must try. It's the only way to achieve peace. Maybe seeing the Megantics in their full knight forms will inspire people to stay together.

People can change. We just have to give them a chance.

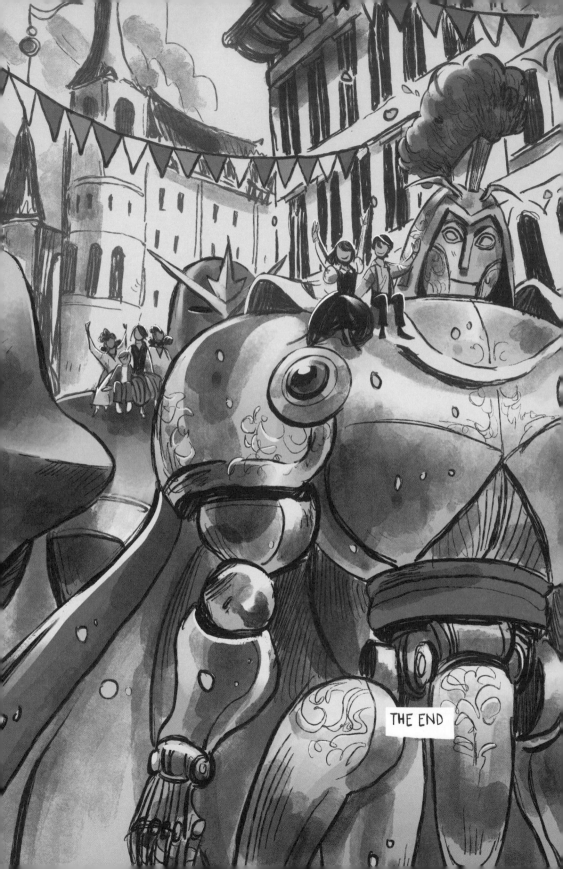

THE END